Alexander Pushkin

Novels, Tales, Journeys

Alexander Pushkin (1799–1837) was a poet, playwright, and novel-ist who achieved literary prominence before he was twenty. His radical politics led to government censorship and periods of ban-ishment from the capital, but he eventually married a popular soci-ety beauty and became a regular part of court life. Notoriously touchy about his honor, he died at age thirty-seven in a duel with his wife's alleged lover.

Together, Richard Pevear and Larissa Volokhonsky have translated works by Tolstoy, Dostoevsky, Chekhov, Gogol, Bulgakov, Les-kov, and Pasternak. They were twice awarded the PEN/Book-of-the-Month Club Translation Prize (for Dostoevsky's *The Brothers Karamazov* and Tolstoy's *Anna Karenina*). They are married and live in France.

T0190541

Novels, Tales, Journeys

Novels

—◆—

Tales

—◆—

Journeys

—◆—

The Complete Prose of Alexander Pushkin

Alexander Pushkin

TRANSLATED BY

RICHARD PEVEAR & LARISSA VOLOKHONSKY

VINTAGE CLASSICS
Vintage Books
A Division of Penguin Random House LLC
New York

FIRST VINTAGE CLASSICS EDITION, OCTOBER 2017

Copyright © 2016 by Richard Pevear and Larissa Volokhonsky
Foreword copyright © 2016 by Richard Pevear

This collection follows the contents and order in volume 5 of the
"Khudozhestvennaya Literatura" edition of Pushkin's works (Moscow, 1975),
omitting a few very brief fragments.

The Library of Congress has cataloged the Knopf edition as follows:
Names: Pushkin, Aleksandr Sergeevich, 1799–1837, author. | Pevear, Richard,
translator. | Volokhonsky, Larissa, translator.
Title: Novels, tales, journeys / by Alexander Pushkin ;
a new translation by Richard Pevear and Larissa Volokhonsky.
Description: New York : Alfred A. Knopf, 2016. |
Includes bibliographical references.
Identifiers: LCCN 2015049350 (print) | LCCN 2016000916 (ebook)
Classification: LCC pg3347.a15 2016 (print) | LCC pg3347 (ebook) |
DDC 891.73/3—dc23
LC record available at http://lccn.loc.gov/2015049350

Vintage Books Trade Paperback ISBN: 978-0-307-94988-2
eBook ISBN: 978-0-307-95963-8

www.vintagebooks.com

Printed in the United States of America

Contents

Introduction

Alexander Pushkin was mortally wounded in a duel on the afternoon of January 27, 1837, at Chernaya Rechka, just outside Petersburg. "It is thus that the figure of Pushkin remains in our memory—with a pistol," Andrei Sinyavsky wrote in *Strolls with Pushkin*.* "Little Pushkin with a big pistol. A civilian, but louder than a soldier. A general. An ace. Pushkin! Crude, but just. The first poet with his own biography—how else would you have him up and die, this first poet, who inscribed himself with blood and powder in the history of art?"

Pushkin was just thirty-seven when he died, but he had already been acknowledged as Russia's greatest poet, a title that has since been defined and redefined but never disputed. In the decade before his death, however, he had also become the true originator of Russian prose. Sinyavsky is right to say that Pushkin lives in Russian memory as more than a writer, more than a poet—as "Pushkin!" In a speech delivered at a commemoration in revolutionary Petrograd in February 1921, the poet Alexander Blok said: "From early childhood our memory keeps the cheerful name: Pushkin. This name, this sound fills many days of our life. The grim names of emperors, generals, inventors of the tools of murder, the tormented and the tormentors of life. And beside them—this light name: Pushkin." Yet his personal presence is in marked contrast with the essential impersonality of Pushkin's art. It is not that he celebrated himself and sang himself: he never did. In a letter to his friend Nikolai Raevsky, written in July 1825, Pushkin criticized Byron (whom he generally admired) for the constant intrusion of his personality: "Byron . . . has parceled out among his characters

---

* Sinyavsky wrote the book as letters to his wife while he was serving a seven-year sentence in a Soviet labor camp, and published it in 1975 under his pseudonym, Abram Tertz, after his release and forced emigration. An English translation by Catharine Theimer Nepomnyashchy and Slava Yastremski was published by Yale University Press in 1994.

such-and-such a trait of his own character; his pride to one, his hate
to another, his melancholy to a third, etc."* And he contrasts Byron's
practice with the multifarious receptivity he had come to admire in
Shakespeare—his "negative capability," as Keats called it. Sinyavsky
intensifies Keats's paradox: "Emptiness is Pushkin's content. Without
it he would not be full, he would not *be*, just as there is no fire without
air, no breathing in without breathing out." Impersonality, openness,
and lightness are the essential qualities of his prose.

Our collection includes Pushkin's few finished and published
works of fiction—*The Tales of the Late Ivan Petrovich Belkin, The Queen
of Spades, Kirdjali, The Captain's Daughter*—each different and all mas-
terpieces. It also includes his experiments in various forms, borrowing
from and parodying well-known European models, consciously trying
out the possibilities of Russian prose. The closest he came to a self-
portrait is perhaps the character of Charsky in the fragmentary *Egyptian Nights;* otherwise he appears in person only in the nonfictional
Journey to Arzrum, where, as D. S. Mirsky wrote, "he reached the limits
of noble and bare terseness."†

Pushkin's family on his father's side belonged to the old military-
feudal aristocracy, the Russian boyars, dating back some six centuries
to the founding of the Grand Duchy of Moscow. He proudly refers
to their "six-hundred-year standing" more than once in his letters.
He was also proud of the rebelliousness of some of his ancestors, one
of whom was executed by Peter the Great for opposing his political
reforms, another of whom (his grandfather) was imprisoned for pro-
testing against the "usurpation" of the throne by the Prussian-born
Catherine the Great. The new gentry that arose in the eighteenth century as a result of Peter's reforms more or less eclipsed the old boyars,
and Pushkin's father was left with relatively modest means.

On his mother's side, Pushkin's ancestors bore the name of Gannibal, from his great-grandfather Ibrahim Gannibal. It was long thought
(by Pushkin among others) that Ibrahim was the son of a minor Ethio-
pian prince, though recently it has been argued that he came from the
sultanate of Logone-Birni in Cameroon. In any case at around the age

* *The Letters of Alexander Pushkin*, edited and translated by J. Thomas Shaw (Madison: University of Wisconsin Press, 1967), p. 237.
† *A History of Russian Literature* (Evanston, IL: Northwestern University Press, 1999), p. 124.

of five he was sent as a hostage or slave to the court of the Ottoman sultan in Istanbul, and a year later was either ransomed or stolen by Sava Vladislavich-Raguzinsky, advisor to the Russian ambassador, and brought to Petersburg, where he was presented to Peter the Great. Peter was very taken with the boy, stood as godfather at his baptism, gave him the patronymic Petrovich from his own name, and had him educated in the best European fashion. Ibrahim rose to the rank of general, was granted nobility, and had a long military and political career in the reigns of Peter and his daughter Elizabeth. While serving in the French army in his youth he adopted the surname Gannibal, or Hannibal, after the great Carthaginian general.

Pushkin prized his African ancestry, and his African ancestor, highly, and when he decided, in 1827, to try his hand at a historical novel along the lines of Walter Scott's immensely popular *Waverley* (published in 1814), he chose the life of Ibrahim as his subject. The result was *The Moor of Peter the Great*. In an article published three years later, he observed: "In our time, by the term novel we mean an historical epoch developed in a fictional narrative."* And indeed, while the two protagonists, Ibrahim and Peter the Great, are fully historical, his portrayal of their interactions is almost entirely invented. We first meet Ibrahim during his military service in the decadent Paris of Philippe d'Orléans's regency (1715–1723), and hear mainly about the complications of his love life, both in France and on his return to Russia. Peter, meanwhile, is busy building his new capital in the north, "a vast factory," as it appears to Ibrahim, and though the emperor is referred to at one point as "the hero of Poltava, the powerful and terrible reformer of Russia," we see him mainly as the "gentle and hospitable host" of his godson. More historical and personal complexity is suggested in later chapters, in Peter's relations with the old boyar aristocrats and with the entrance of Ibrahim's rival Valerian, but Pushkin abandoned the novel just at that point and never went back to the *Waverley* manner.

That was in 1828. A year or two later, one of Pushkin's literary enemies, Faddei Bulgarin (Pushkin liked to call him "Figlyarin," from *figlyar,* "buffoon"), wrote a scurrilous article about a certain unnamed poet whose grandfather was not a Negro prince, as he boasted, but

* *The Critical Prose of Alexander Pushkin,* edited and translated by Carl R. Proffer (Bloomington. Indiana University Press, 1969), p. 80.

had been bought by a sea captain for a bottle of rum. Pushkin replied in a *post scriptum* to his poem "My Genealogy": "That skipper was the glorious skipper / Who started our land moving, / Who forcefully took the helm of our native ship / And set it on a majestic course." Pushkin's awareness of himself as a descendant both of old boyar stock and of the reformer's black godson nourished his meditations on state power in all its contradictions. In the same year that he abandoned his first novel, he wrote the long poem *Poltava*, about Peter's decisive victory in 1709 over the Swedish forces of Charles XII, which led to the emergence of Russia as the predominant nation of northern Europe. The "terrible reformer," grown more ambiguous and demonic in the grim figure of his statue, is also the subject of Pushkin's last long poem, *The Bronze Horseman*, written in 1833. D. S. Mirsky has called it "the greatest work ever penned in Russian verse."*

Pushkin's own confrontation with imperial power had begun many years earlier. After the defeat of Napoleon, Russian troops occupied Paris and camped along the Champs-Élysées. The victorious coalition restored the French monarchy, but the young Russian officers picked up French revolutionary thinking in the process and came home with new notions of political liberty. French culture had been the dominant influence in Russia since the time of Catherine the Great, who reigned from 1762 until her death in 1796. The aristocracy spoke French, which was Pushkin's first language. In 1811, the emperor Alexander I founded a school which he called by the French name of *lycée* (*litsei* in Russian) in the imperial village of Tsarskoe Selo, some eighteen miles south of Petersburg, to give the sons of the aristocracy a European education, after which they were to take up important posts in government service. Pushkin was in the first class of thirty, and his years at the lycée remained central to his life. There he began to write poetry, first in French, then in Russian, and by the age of fourteen he had already seen his work published and praised. On graduating in 1817, he moved to Petersburg, where he held a nominal post in the service, which did not keep him from living a rather wild life, gambling, womanizing, dueling. In Petersburg he also got to know some of the young officers who had come back from Paris. He shared their thoughts and hopes, and in that spirit wrote a number of poems which were not very

---

* D. S. Mirsky, *Pushkin* (New York: E. P. Dutton, 1963), p. 212.

pleasing to the authorities. One of them, the ode "Liberty," written as early as 1817, praises "the exalted son of Gaul" who sang of Liberty and denounced "enthroned vice" with its scourges, irons, and serfdom. Against "lawless Authority" it invokes "the trustworthy shelter of the Law." This, along with some biting epigrams on various government officials, was finally too much even for the rather liberal Alexander. Pushkin was relieved of his post in Petersburg and "exiled" to the south, to serve in Ekaterinoslav, Kishinev, and finally Odessa.

Pushkin was absent from Petersburg from 1820 to 1826. During those years he wrote a great deal of poetry, some of it based on his travels to the Caucasus and the Crimea with General Nikolai Raevsky, a retired hero of the Napoleonic Wars, and his sons Alexander and Nikolai, who became his close friends. He detested life in backward Kishinev, which had been ceded to Russia by the Turks in 1812, managed to get transferred to Odessa, but caused himself trouble there as well, particularly with the beautiful young wife of the governor-general, Prince Mikhail Vorontsov. He wrote a notorious epigram about the governor-general:

> Half milord, half merchant,
> Half wise man, half ignoramus,
> Half scoundrel, but there's hope
> He'll finally become a full one.

The post office routinely opened Pushkin's mail, and in one letter found him sympathizing with the atheistic arguments of a local philosopher (a certain "deaf Englishman"). This was enough to allow Vorontsov to petition for Pushkin's removal from Odessa. By imperial order he was expelled from the service and confined to his mother's small estate at Mikhailovskoe, near Pskov, where he was to be kept under surveillance by his father and the local authorities.

In a way the two years of this "house arrest" were Pushkin's salvation. He was left free to read and to write, and he produced more than he had in the previous four years. Along with many of his finest lyric poems, which went into the collection he was gathering then and published in 1826, he finished his long poem *The Gypsies*, begun in Kishinev, wrote two more long poems, *The Bridegroom* and the comic parody *Count Nulin*, completed three chapters of his novel in verse

Evgeny Onegin, and wrote his first and longest play, the historical tragedy *Boris Godunov*. And he worked on yet another narrative poem, *Cleopatra*, parts of which eventually found their way into the prose/verse fragment *Egyptian Nights*, included in our collection.

In a letter to his brother in November 1824, he describes his typical day: "I write memoirs until dinner; I dine late. After dinner I ride on horseback. In the evening I listen to fairy tales, and thereby I am compensating for the insufficiencies of my accursed upbringing. How charming these fairy tales are!"* The storyteller was his former nanny, the house serf Arina Rodionovna, who at first was his only company on the estate. Pushkin was deeply struck by her tales, kept notes on them, and a few years later turned them into some of his finest poems: *Tsar Saltan*, *The Golden Cockerel*, and *The Dead Princess and the Seven Mighty Men*. He also collected her sayings and expressions, a trove of Russian speech that was part of the compensation for his "accursed upbringing."

But his confinement to Mikhailovskoe saved him in a more literal sense as well. The young officers who had come back from France began to organize a movement for political reform and in 1816 founded a secret society called the Union of Salvation, based in Petersburg with branches in other cities. The Union later divided into the Northern Society in Petersburg and the Southern Society in the Ukraine. Their aims included the abolition of serfdom, the election of a legislative assembly, and the drafting of a constitution limiting the powers of the monarchy. The Southern Society, led by Colonel Pavel Pestel, went further, advocating universal suffrage and the abolition of the monarchy. Both foresaw the inevitability of an armed uprising.

Their chance came in December 1825. The emperor Alexander died suddenly on December 1, at the age of forty-eight, leaving no direct heir. The elder of his two brothers, Constantine, had married a Polish woman and Roman Catholic, and had renounced his right of succession, but only Alexander knew of it. There was uncertainty for several weeks before the younger brother, Nicholas, was prevailed upon to accept the throne. The secret societies decided to take the opportunity of his coronation on December 26 to stage their uprising, earning themselves the name of Decembrists. Some three thousand

---

* *Letters*, pp. 188–189.

soldiers, led by the young officers of the Northern Society, appeared in Senate Square in Petersburg, calling for the formation of a provisional government. A few days later the Southern Society incited a mutiny among the troops in the Ukraine. But the revolts were poorly organized and, after the initial shock, were quickly suppressed. The instigators were arrested; five of them, including Colonel Pestel and the poet Kondraty Ryleev, were executed, and another 120 were sent into permanent exile in Siberia.

Pushkin, like many of his young friends, shared the liberal ideas of the Decembrists. The Raevsky brothers had joined the Southern Society, though they pulled out of it some time before the uprising. He had made the acquaintance of Pestel during his time in Kishinev and had been struck by his forceful personality. Later, as he records in *Journey to Arzrum*, Pushkin ran into many former Decembrists who had been sent to serve in the Caucasus as "punishment" for their radical views. In September 1826, during a private meeting in Moscow, the new emperor asked him where he would have been on December 26. Pushkin replied candidly: "On Senate Square with the rebels."

That conversation took place soon after Nicholas decided to end Pushkin's exile. A messenger brought the news to Mikhailovskoe. Pushkin left the same day and on September 8 arrived in Moscow. The emperor met with him at once and explained his new situation. His work would no longer be subject to official censorship; instead it would be submitted for approval to the emperor himself. Pushkin, charmed by Nicholas's apparent benevolence during their meeting, took that as an honor, not realizing that the real censor would be Count Benckendorf, head of the Third Section, his majesty's new secret police. He soon began to feel the burden of that blessing, but for some time he was reluctant to blame it on Nicholas himself. Nevertheless, it weighed on him for the rest of his life.

In 1827 he was allowed to move to Petersburg. There he lived more or less as he had before his banishment, and was able to enjoy the company of some of his oldest literary friends. In 1829 he met and fell in love with a beautiful young woman of seventeen, Natalya Goncharova. He proposed to her almost at once, but was refused. He also wanted very much to travel abroad, but that, too, was denied him. Suddenly the capital felt stifling to him, and he took off without permission to join the army in the Caucasus, where the Raevskys were serving. This was during one of the Russo-Turkish Wars. He recounts his experiences in *Journey to Arzrum*, published six years later. Some of his finest poems also came from events he encountered along the way.

On his return, Pushkin went to Moscow, where he continued his courtship of Natalya Goncharova. In April 1830 he proposed to her a second time and was accepted. His father, with whom he had always had strained relations, was pleased at this sign of maturity and respectability and settled on him the small estate of Boldino in the region of Nizhny Novgorod, some 385 miles east of Moscow. In late summer, prior to the wedding, Pushkin went to look over the property, intending to stay a few weeks at most, but a cholera epidemic broke out, quarantines closed the roads, and he ended up staying for three months. This period of suspension, the most fruitful in his creative life, came to be known as the "Boldino Autumn." During it he wrote some thirty lyric poems, the last two chapters of *Evgeny Onegin*, the comic narrative poem *The Little House in Kolomna*, and the four superb short plays he referred to as "Little Tragedies": *The Miserly Knight, Mozart and Salieri, The Stone Guest*, and *A Feast in a Time of Plague*. And it was during those months that he also wrote his first finished work of fiction, the five *Tales of the Late Ivan Petrovich Belkin*, with their companion piece, *The History of the Village of Goryukhino*.

The tales are epitomes of Pushkin's fiction. "Inspiration finds the poet," he says in the preface to *Arzrum*, but prose he worked at very consciously. His aim was to make the tales as unpoetic, as purely narrative, as possible. They have no commentary, no psychology, no ideas, no flights of rhetoric or authorial digressions. They are cast as local anecdotes, and are told so simply and artlessly that at first one barely notices the subtlety of their composition, the shifts in time and point of view, the reversals of expectation, the elements of parody, the ambiguity of their resolutions. Pushkin attributed them to the naïve country squire Ivan Petrovich Belkin, who in turn claimed to have collected them from various local sources. Belkin's life is briefly sketched in a prefatory letter from one of his neighbors. Pushkin himself appears only as "the publisher" over the initials A. P.

Belkin seems to have occurred to Pushkin after the tales were written, in connection with their publication. For one thing, the disguise enabled him to elude Benckendorf's censorship. Mirsky suggests that he may also have wanted an alias because the tales were experimental and he was not sure how they would be received. If so, his uncertainty proved justified. "The stories met with no success," Mirsky continues. "When they appeared without Pushkin's name the critics paid no attention to them, and when his authorship was divulged, like good critics, they declared that the stories were not worthy of their author and that they marked a grievous decline in his talent."* Their artistic perfection went unnoticed, as did their originality in the development of Russian fiction.

Once Belkin appeared, however, he took on his own life in Pushkin's imagination, resulting in *The History of the Village of Goryukhino*. It consists of two parts. The first is a superbly comic rendering of Belkin's (and Pushkin's) development as a writer, from his initial poetic ambitions to his eventual decision to "descend into prose," as he puts it himself. The unfinished second part is the history of Goryukhino proper—an equally comic parody of historiography and, behind that, a biting satire on rural life and the evils of serfdom.

Pushkin's own "descent into prose" continued throughout his last years. The unfinished works, fragments, and sketches we have included in this collection show not only the breadth of his literary culture but also his conscious experimentation with different formal possibilities: the society novel; the epistolary novel; a Russian variation on Edward Bulwer-Lytton's best-selling novel *Pelham*, published in 1828; a tale set in Roman times; the blending of prose and poetry in *Egyptian Nights*. There is the finished story *Kirdjali*, a briskly narrated and completely unromantic account of the doings of a Bulgarian bandit during the Greek war of independence in 1821. And in contrast to it there is the unfinished *Roslavlev*, narrated by a woman, saturated with literary references and polemics, portraying the French culture of the Russian aristocracy as it was confronted with Napoleon's invasion in 1812, a social satire which suddenly takes a dark turn just as it breaks off . . . (Tolstoy was to play on some of the same ironies thirty years later in *War and Peace*.) Pushkin wrote *Roslavlev* in response to the historical novel of the same name published in 1831 by Mikhail Zagoskin. Zagoskin's first novel, *Yuri Miloslavsky*, published in 1829, was widely acclaimed and made of him the Russian Walter Scott that Pushkin might have become a year earlier if he had not abandoned *The Moor of Peter the Great*. In his *Roslavlev*, Zagoskin made some obvious allusions

* *Pushkin*, pp. 177–178.

to *Evgeny Onegin*, borrowing certain names from Pushkin's novel in verse and playing variations on the characters' fates. Pushkin's narrator, who is Roslavlev's sister, sets out to correct Zagoskin's factual and sentimental misrepresentations.

Dubrovsky, the longest of Pushkin's unfinished works, is an adventure novel with an honest gentleman robber as hero. As such it is often compared to Scott's *Rob Roy* or the tales of Robin Hood. But its portrayal of rural life in eighteenth-century Russia, the relations of landowners and peasants, the connivance of government officials with the rich, has nothing romantic about it, and the quickness and terseness of its prose is the opposite of Scott's leisurely narration. It is an example of the inclusiveness of Pushkin's manner, by turns comic, parodic, melodramatic, grimly realistic, and warmly human—what John Bayley has nicely termed his "power of polyphonic suggestion."*

Pushkin's two most important works of fiction, *The Queen of Spades* (1834) and *The Captain's Daughter* (1836), form a final artistic contrast—the one tense, minimal in detail, impersonal, plot-driven; the other, his only finished novel, a more leisurely memoir, moved by seeming chance, told in the first person. *The Queen of Spades* is a city story, a Petersburg story; *The Captain's Daughter* takes us back to the provinces and as far as the military outposts in the southern Ural region of Orenburg. The two also contrast sharply in their play on fate and chance, darkness and light.

On the surface *The Queen of Spades* is an elaborate anecdote about the passion for gambling, of which Pushkin had great personal experience. But it goes far beyond mere gambling in its brush with the supernatural, or madness, in the fate of its protagonist, the rootless, ambitious army engineer Hermann. The essential ambiguity of the tale is prefigured in the person of the Comte de Saint-Germain, who appears in a flashback early on. Both a typical eighteenth-century aristocrat and the subject of strange legends and mysterious rumors, he is portrayed with considerable sympathy and humor. The same is true of the three main characters—Hermann, the old countess, and her young ward Lizaveta—whose vulnerable humanity tempers the melodrama of the events they are caught up in. Pushkin wisely leaves the central mys-

---

* Introduction to Alexander Pushkin, *The Collected Stories*, translated by Paul Debreczeny (New York: Alfred A. Knopf, 1999), p. xvi.

tery of the tale unresolved, and it lingers darkly in the reader's mind after the summary conclusion.

"The thought of abandoning trivial and dubious anecdotes for the recounting of true and great events had long stirred my imagination." So wrote Ivan Petrovich Belkin in his preface to *The History of the Village of Goryukhino*, anticipating what would be the final stage in Pushkin's own development as a prose writer. One of the few real benefits Pushkin derived from being under the emperor's personal supervision was permission to work in the state archives, granted him in 1832. He made good use of it. His first impulse was to write a history of Peter the Great, which he began that same year but laid aside almost at once. Instead he took up the more recent events of the Cossack rebellion of 1773–1774, the largest peasant revolt of the eighteenth century, led by Emelyan Pugachev, who claimed to be the emperor Peter III. The result was the masterful two-volume *History of the Pugachev Rebellion*, based on over a thousand pages of notes and transcriptions he took from the archives. In the late summer of 1833, during his work on the *History*, he also traveled to the Orenburg region, where the rebellion broke out, and visited the various towns and fortresses connected with it. All of this research nourished his last and longest work of fiction, *The Captain's Daughter*.

In the novel Pushkin deals with the same historical events as in the history, but in an indirect, incidental, almost happenstance way, as the personal experiences of the young officer Pyotr Andreevich Grinyov. What concerns Pushkin is not historical forces, causes and effects, but the working out of destiny through a series of apparent coincidences. Destiny seems like mere chance, but here, as Sinyavsky writes, chance has a formative function. It reveals "the wittiness of life . . . the good sense behind its riddles and mishaps." It depends, as in Shakespeare, not on ineluctable fate, but on the response of the characters to what befalls them.

Pushkin has space in the novel to develop his characters more fully than in his earlier fiction. They are unusual because they are quite ordinary. Grinyov himself is a naïve, impressionable young man. Grinyov's superior at the fortress, Captain Mironov, his wife, and his daughter Masha are simple and good people, portrayed with fine humor, as is Grinyov's tutor, Savelyich. They show a modest but genuine heroism in the face of catastrophe. Grinyov, too, for all his youthful naïveté and impulsiveness, is both steadfast and intelligent. There is no romantic glamour about any of them. They are masterfully drawn, but with such understatement that we hardly notice how it is done. In *Gravity and Grace*, Simone Weil wrote:

Imaginary evil is romantic, varied; real evil is dreary, monotonous, barren, boring. Imaginary good is boring; real good is always new, marvelous, intoxicating. Hence the "literature of imagination" is either boring or immoral (or a mixture of the two). It can only escape this alternative by passing over somehow, by dint of art, to the side of reality—which genius alone can do.

The characters in *The Captain's Daughter* are on the side of reality. The only exception is Shvabrin, the melodramatic villain of the piece, whose villainy, like Iago's in *Othello*, is never explained.

Reality is not banality, as Pushkin constantly shows us. There is nothing documentary about *The Captain's Daughter*; on the contrary, it has elements of the folktale about it—mysterious appearances, interventions, coincidences. It is composed of two intertwining stories: the love story of Grinyov and Masha, and the story of Grinyov's complex relations with the rebel Pugachev (their private conversations are some of the most extraordinary moments in the book). Grinyov's fate is determined, not by some all-ruling historical inevitability, nor by his personal will, but by two chance meetings: his own with the wayfarer at the beginning, and Masha's with a little white dog and its owner at the end.

"Pushkin is the golden section of Russian literature," wrote Sinyavsky. "Having thrust it forcefully into the future, he himself fell back and now plays in it the role of an eternally flowering past to which it returns to be rejuvenated." Tolstoy gave an example of that rejuvenation in a letter describing the beginning of his work on *Anna Karenina*. His wife, he says, had taken down a volume of Pushkin's prose from the shelf to show to their son and had left it on the table.

The other day, after my work, I picked up this volume of Pushkin and as always (for the seventh time, I think) read it from cover to cover, unable to tear myself away, as if I were reading it for the first time. More than that, it was as if it dispelled all my doubts. Never have I admired Pushkin so much, nor any-one else for that matter. *The Shot, Egyptian Nights, The Captain's Daughter!!!* There was also the fragment, "The guests were ar-riving at the dacha." Despite myself, not knowing where or what it would lead to, I imagined characters and events, which I developed, then naturally modified, and suddenly it all came together so well, so solidly, that it turned into a novel . . .

Reading Pushkin's prose will not make great novelists of us all, but we can certainly share Tolstoy's enthusiasm for the incomparable works, both finished and fragmentary, collected in this book.

RICHARD PEVEAR

The Moor of Peter the Great

By Peter's iron will
Russia was transformed.

YAZYKOV[1]

CHAPTER ONE

I am in Paris:
I have begun to live, not just to breathe.

DMITRIEV, *Diary of a Traveler*[2]

Among the young men sent abroad by Peter the Great to acquire the knowledge necessary for the reformed state was his godson, the moor Ibrahim. He studied at the military school in Paris,[3] graduated as a captain of artillery, distinguished himself in the Spanish war,[4] and returned, gravely wounded, to Paris. The emperor, in the midst of his immense labors, never ceased to ask after his favorite and always received flattering reports of his progress and conduct. Peter was very pleased with him and repeatedly called him back to Russia, but Ibrahim was in no hurry. He excused himself on various pretexts—now his wound, now his wish to improve his knowledge, now his lack of money—and Peter condescended to his requests, begged him to look after his health, thanked him for his zeal for learning, and, though extremely thrifty in his own expenses, did not spare his purse for him, supplementing the money with fatherly advice and cautionary admonishments.

From the evidence of all the historical records, nothing could compare with the unbridled frivolity, madness, and luxury of the French at that time. The last years of the reign of Louis XIV, marked by the strict piety of the court, its pomposity and decorum, had left no traces. The duc d'Orléans, who combined many brilliant qualities with all sorts of vices, did not, unfortunately, possess even a shadow of hypocrisy.[5] The orgies in the Palais-Royale were no secret for Paris; the example was contagious. Just then Law appeared;[6] greed for money combined with the desire for pleasure and distraction; estates disappeared; morality perished; the French laughed and calculated, and the state was falling apart to the playful refrains of satirical vaudevilles.

Meanwhile, society presented a most interesting picture. Education and the need for amusement brought all conditions together. Wealth, courtesy, fame, talent, eccentricity itself—all that gave food for curiosity or promised pleasure was received with equal benevolence. Literature, learning, and philosophy left their quiet studies and appeared in the circle of high society to oblige fashion and guide its opinions. Women reigned, but no longer demanded adoration. Superficial politeness replaced profound respect. The pranks of the duc de Richelieu, the Alcibiades of the new Athens, belong to history and give an idea of the morals of the time.[7]

> Temps fortuné, marqué par la license,
> Où la folie, agitant son grelot,
> D'un pied léger parcourt toute la France,
> Où nul mortel ne daigne être dévot,
> Où l'on fait tout excepté pénitence.*

Ibrahim's arrival, his looks, education, and natural intelligence, attracted general attention in Paris. All the ladies wanted to see *le Nègre du czar* in their salons and tried to be the first to catch him; the regent invited him to his merry evenings more than once; he was present at suppers animated by the youth of Arouet and the old age of Chaulieu, the conversation of Montesquieu and Fontenelle;[8] he did not miss a single ball, nor a single fête, nor a single première, and he gave himself to the general whirl with all the ardor of his youth and race. But it was not only the thought of exchanging these diversions, these brilliant amusements, for the stern simplicity of the Petersburg court that horrified Ibrahim. Other stronger bonds tied him to Paris. The young African was in love.

The countess D., no longer in the first bloom of youth, was still famous for her beauty. At the age of seventeen, on leaving the convent,[9] she was given in marriage to a man she had had no time to fall in love with and who never bothered about it afterwards. Rumor ascribed lovers to her, but, by the lenient code of society, she enjoyed a good reputation, for it was impossible to reproach her with any ludicrous or scandalous adventure. Her house was the most fashionable. The best Parisian society gathered there. Ibrahim was introduced to her by the

---

* Lucky time, bearing the mark of license, / When light-footed madness skips about, / Swinging its little bell, all over France, / When no mortal deigns to be devout, / When they do all except for penitence. —Voltaire, *La Pucelle d'Orléans*, Canto XIII.

young Merville, generally regarded as her latest lover—something he tried to make felt by every means possible.

The countess received Ibrahim courteously, but with no special attention. That flattered him. Ordinarily, the young Negro was looked upon as a wonder, was surrounded, showered with greetings and questions, and this curiosity, though hidden behind an appearance of benevolence, offended his self-esteem. Women's sweet attention, all but the unique goal of our efforts, not only did not gladden his heart, but even filled it with bitterness and indignation. He felt that for them he was some rare sort of animal, a special, alien creature, accidentally transported to a world that had nothing in common with him. He even envied people whom nobody noticed, regarding their insignificance as happiness.

The thought that nature had not created him for mutual passion delivered him from conceit and the claims of self-esteem, lending a rare charm to his relations with women. His conversation was simple and dignified; it pleased the countess D., who was sick of the eternal jokes and refined allusions of French wit. Ibrahim often visited her. She gradually became used to the young Negro's appearance, and even began to find something appealing in that curly head, black amidst the powdered wigs in her drawing room. (Ibrahim had been wounded in the head and wore a bandage instead of a wig.) He was twenty-seven years old; he was tall and trim, and more than one beauty gazed at him with a feeling more flattering than mere curiosity, but the prejudiced Ibrahim either noticed nothing, or saw it as mere coquetry. But when his glance met the glance of the countess, his distrust vanished. Her eyes expressed such sweet good-nature, her manner with him was so simple, so unconstrained, that it was impossible to suspect even a shadow of coquettishness or mockery in her.

Love never entered his head—but it had already become necessary for him to see the countess every day. He sought to meet her everywhere, and meeting with her seemed to him each time like an unexpected favor from heaven. The countess guessed his feelings before he did. Say what you like, but love with no hopes or demands touches a woman's heart more surely than all the calculations of seduction. When Ibrahim was present, the countess followed all his movements, listened to all he said; without him she became pensive and lapsed into her usual absentmindedness . . . Merville first noticed this mutual inclination and congratulated Ibrahim. Nothing so inflames love as an encouraging observation from an outsider. Love is blind and, not trusting itself, hastily seizes upon any support. Merville's words awakened Ibrahim. The possibility of possessing the beloved woman had so far not presented itself to his imagination; hope suddenly lit up his soul; he fell madly in love. In vain did the countess, frightened by the frenzy of his passion, try to oppose to it the admonitions of friendship and the counsels of good sense: she herself was weakening. Imprudent rewards quickly followed one after another. And finally, carried away by the power of the passion she had inspired, fainting under its influence, she gave herself to the enraptured Ibrahim . . .

Nothing is hidden from the eyes of observant society. The countess's new liaison soon became known to all. Some ladies were astonished by her choice; many thought it quite natural. Some laughed, others saw it as an unforgivable imprudence. In the first intoxication of passion, Ibrahim and the countess noticed nothing, but soon men's ambiguous jokes and women's caustic remarks began to reach them. Ibrahim's dignified and cool behavior had hitherto shielded him from such attacks; he endured them impatiently and did not know how to ward them off. The countess, accustomed to the respect of society, could not see herself cool-headedly as the object of gossip and mockery. She complained tearfully to Ibrahim, then bitterly reproached him, then begged him not to intercede for her, lest the useless clamor ruin her completely.

A new circumstance complicated her situation still more. The consequences of imprudent love manifested themselves. Consolations, advice, suggestions—all were exhausted and all were rejected. The countess faced inevitable ruin and awaited it with despair.

As soon as the countess's condition became known, gossip sprang up with new force. Sentimental ladies oh-ed and ah-ed in horror; men bet on whether the countess would give birth to a white child or a black one. There was a downpour of epigrams about her husband, who alone in the whole of Paris knew nothing and suspected nothing.

The fatal moment was approaching. The countess was in a terrible state. Ibrahim came to her daily. He saw how her moral and physical strength were gradually dwindling. Her tears, her terror were renewed every moment. Finally she felt the first pangs. Measures were taken at once. A way was found of removing the count. The doctor came. Two days earlier a poor woman had been persuaded to give up her newborn infant into the hands of others; a confidant was sent for him. Ibrahim was in the boudoir just next to the bedroom where the unfortunate countess lay. Not daring to breathe, he heard her muffled moans, the maid's whispers, and the doctor's orders. She suffered for a long time. Her every moan rent his soul; every spell of silence bathed him in terror . . . Suddenly he heard the weak cry of an infant and, unable to contain his rapture, rushed into the countess's room. A black baby lay on the bed at her feet. Ibrahim approached him. His heart was pounding. He blessed his son with a trembling hand. The countess smiled weakly and held out a weak hand to him . . . but the doctor, fearing emotions too strong for the patient, drew Ibrahim away from her bed. The newborn was put in a covered basket and carried out of the house by a secret stairway. The other infant was brought and its cradle was placed in the new mother's bedroom. Ibrahim left somewhat reassured. The count was expected. He came late, learned of his spouse's happy delivery, and was very pleased. Thus the public, awaiting a scandalous outcry, was deceived in its hopes and was forced to console itself with nothing but wicked gossip.

Everything went back to its usual order. But Ibrahim felt that his fate was bound to change and that sooner or later his liaison would become known to Count D. In that case, whatever happened, the countess's ruin was inevitable. He loved her passionately and was loved in the same way; but the countess was whimsical and light-minded. She was not in love for the first time. Loathing, hatred could replace the tenderest feelings in her heart. Ibrahim already foresaw the moment of her cooling; hitherto he had not known jealousy, but he anticipated it with horror; he imagined that the suffering of separation must be less tormenting, and he already intended to break the unfortunate liaison, leave Paris, and go to Russia, where both Peter and an obscure sense of his own duty had long been calling him.

CHAPTER TWO

No longer strongly moved by beauty,
No longer ravished so by joy,
No longer of such flippant wit,
No longer is all so well with me . . .
Desire for honors now torments me,
I hear glory loudly calling!

DERZHAVIN[10]

Days, months went by, but the amorous Ibrahim could not bring himself to leave the woman he had seduced. The countess grew more attached to him by the hour. Their son was being brought up in a distant province. Society's gossip was dying down, and the lovers began to enjoy greater tranquillity, silently remembering the past storm and trying not to think of the future.

One day Ibrahim attended the levee of the duc d'Orléans. The duke, in passing, stopped and handed him a letter, telling him to read it at his leisure. It was a letter from Peter the Great. The sovereign, guessing the true cause of his absence, wrote to the duke that he had no intention of forcing Ibrahim in any way, that he left it to his goodwill to return to Russia or not, but that in any case he would never abandon his former charge. This letter touched Ibrahim to the bottom of his heart. From that moment on, his fate was decided. The next day he announced to the regent his intention to set out for Russia at once.

"Think what you're doing," the duke said to him. "Russia is not your fatherland. I don't think you'll be seeing your torrid birthplace ever again; but your prolonged stay in France has made you equally alien to the climate and way of life of half-savage Russia. You were not born Peter's subject. Trust me: avail yourself of his generous permission. Remain in France, for which you've already shed your blood, and rest assured that here your merits and gifts will not go without their due reward." Ibrahim sincerely thanked the duke, but remained firm in his intention. "I'm sorry," the regent said to him, "but, anyhow, you're right." He promised him retirement and wrote about it all to the Russian tsar.

Ibrahim quickly made ready for the journey. On the eve of his departure, he spent the evening, as usual, at the countess D's. She knew nothing; Ibrahim did not have the courage to be open with her. The countess was calm and cheerful. She called him over several times and joked about his pensiveness. After supper, everybody left. The countess, her husband, and Ibrahim remained in the drawing room. The unfortunate man would have given anything in the world to be left alone with her, but Count D. seemed so calmly settled by the fireplace that there was no hope of getting him to leave the room. The three were silent. *"Bonne nuit,"** the countess finally said. Ibrahim's heart was wrung and suddenly felt all the horror of separation. He stood motionless. *"Bonne nuit, messieurs,"* the countess repeated. He still did not move . . . Finally his vision darkened, his head began to spin, and he was barely able to leave the room. On coming home, almost in oblivion, he wrote the following letter:

I am going away, dear Léonore, I am leaving you forever. I write to you, because I do not have the strength to explain it to you otherwise.

My happiness could not continue. I enjoyed it in defiance of fate and nature. You were bound to fall out of love with me; the enchantment was bound to disappear. That thought always pursued me, even in moments when I seemed to forget everything, when at your feet I reveled in your passionate self-abandon, your infinite tenderness . . . Light-minded society mercilessly persecutes in reality what it allows in theory: sooner or later its cold mockery would have vanquished you, would have subdued your ardent soul, and you would finally have felt ashamed of your passion . . . What would have become of me then? No! Better to die, better to leave you before that terrible moment . . .

Your peace is dearest of all for me: you could not enjoy it while the eyes of society were turned on us. Remember all that you endured, all the injured self-esteem, all the torments of fear; remember the terrible birth of our son. Think: Should I subject you longer to the same anxieties and dangers? Why

* "Good night."

strive to unite the destiny of so delicate, so beautiful a being with the wretched destiny of a Negro, a pitiful creature, barely worthy to be called human?

Farewell, Léonore, farewell, my dear, my only friend. In abandoning you I am abandoning the first and last joys of my life. I have neither fatherland nor family. I am going to sad Russia, where total solitude will be my comfort. Strict labors, to which I shall give myself henceforth, will, if not stifle, at least deflect the tormenting memories of days of rapture and bliss . . . . Farewell, Léonore—I tear myself from this letter as if from your embrace; farewell, be happy—and think sometimes of the poor Negro, your faithful Ibrahim.

That same night he set out for Russia.

The journey did not seem as terrible to him as he had expected. His imagination triumphed over reality. The further he went from Paris, the more vividly, the more closely he pictured to himself the things he had forsaken forever.

Unawares, he found himself on the Russian border. Autumn was already setting in, but the coaches, despite the bad roads, drove like the wind, and on the seventeenth day of his journey, in the morning, he arrived in Krasnoe Selo, which the high road of that time passed through.

It was another twenty miles to Petersburg. While the horses were being harnessed, Ibrahim went into the post-house. In the corner, a tall man in a green kaftan, with a clay pipe in his mouth, his elbows resting on the table, was reading the Hamburg newspapers. Hearing some-one come in, he raised his head. "Hah, Ibrahim?" he cried, getting up from his bench. "Greetings, godson!" Ibrahim, recognizing Peter, joyfully rushed to him, but stopped out of respect. The sovereign came to him, embraced him, and kissed him on the head. "I was forewarned of your arrival," said Peter, "and came to meet you. I've been waiting for you here since yesterday." Ibrahim found no words to express his gratitude. "Order your carriage to follow us," the sovereign went on, "and you get into mine and come with me." The sovereign's carriage was brought; he got in with Ibrahim, and they galloped off. An hour and a half later they arrived in Petersburg. Ibrahim gazed with curios-ity at the newborn capital that was rising from the swamp at a wave of the autocratic hand. Bare dams, canals without embankments, wooden bridges showed everywhere the recent victory of human will over the resisting elements. The houses seemed hastily built. In the whole town there was nothing magnificent except the Neva, not yet adorned by its granite frame, but already covered with warships and merchant vessels. The sovereign's carriage stopped at the palace known as the Tsaritsyn Garden. At the porch Peter was met by a woman of about thirty-five, beautiful, dressed after the latest Parisian fashion. Peter kissed her on the lips and, taking Ibrahim by the hand, said: "Do you recognize my godson, Katenka? Be kind and gracious to him as before." Catherine turned her dark, piercing eyes to him and benevolently offered him her hand. Two young beauties, tall, slender, fresh as roses, stood behind her and respectfully approached Peter. "Liza," he said to one of them, "do you remember the little Moor who stole my apples for you in Oranienbaum? Here he is: I introduce him to you." The grand duchess laughed and blushed. They went to the dining room. The table had been laid in expectation of the sovereign. Peter and all his family sat down to dine, inviting Ibrahim to join them. During dinner the sovereign talked with him about various subjects, questioned him about the Spanish war, about the internal affairs of France, about the regent, whom he liked, though he disapproved of him in many ways. Ibrahim was distinguished by his precise and observant mind. Peter was very pleased with his replies; he recalled some features of Ibrahim's childhood and recounted them with such mirth and good nature that no one could have suspected in the gentle and hospitable host the hero of Poltava, the powerful and dread reformer of Russia.[11]

After dinner the sovereign, following the Russian custom, went to rest. Ibrahim remained with the empress and the grand duchesses. He tried to satisfy their curiosity, described the Parisian way of life, the local fêtes and capricious fashions. Meanwhile some persons close to the sovereign gathered in the palace. Ibrahim recognized the magnificent Prince Menshikov, who, seeing the Moor talking to Catherine, proudly cast a sidelong glance at him; Prince Yakov Dolgoruky, Peter's tough councillor; the learned Bruce, known among the people as the Russian Faust; the young Raguzinsky, his former schoolmate; and others who came to the sovereign with reports or to receive orders.[12]

After some two hours the sovereign appeared. "Let's see if you still remember your old duties," he said to Ibrahim. "Take the slate and follow me." Peter shut himself in the wood-turning shop and busied himself with state affairs. He worked in turn with Bruce, with Prince

Dolgoruky, with the police chief Devier, and dictated several ukases and resolutions to Ibrahim. Ibrahim could not help marveling at his quick and firm mind, the strength and flexibility of his attention, and the diversity of his activities. Having finished work, Peter took a notebook from his pocket to make sure he had done all he had intended to do that day. Then, as he was leaving the wood-turning shop, he said to Ibrahim: "It's already late; you must be tired: spend the night here, as you used to in the old days. I'll wake you up tomorrow."

Left alone, Ibrahim could barely come to his senses. He was in Petersburg, he had seen again the great man close to whom, not yet knowing his worth, he had spent his childhood. Almost with remorse, he confessed in his heart that the countess D., for the first time since their separation, had not been his only thought all day. He saw that the new mode of life awaiting him, activity and constant occupation, could revive his soul, worn out by passion, idleness, and secret dejection. The thought of being a great man's associate, and joining with him to influence the fate of a great nation, for the first time aroused in him a feeling of noble ambition. In that state of mind he lay down on the camp bed prepared for him, and then the habitual dream transported him to far-off Paris, into the arms of his dear countess.

CHAPTER THREE

> Like clouds in the sky,
> So thoughts change their light shape in us,
> What we love today, tomorrow we despise.
>
> W. KÜCHELBECKER[13]

The next day, as he had promised, Peter woke Ibrahim and congratulated him on becoming lieutenant commander of the artillery company of the Preobrazhensky regiment, of which he himself was the commander. The courtiers surrounded Ibrahim, each trying in his own way to make much of the new favorite. The arrogant Prince Menshikov gave him a friendly handshake. Sheremetev inquired about his Parisian acquaintances, and Golovin invited him to dinner.[14] Others followed this last example, so that Ibrahim received invitations for at least a whole month.

Ibrahim spent his days monotonously but actively—as a result, he knew no boredom. Day by day he grew more attached to the sovereign and better comprehended his lofty soul. To follow a great man's thoughts is a most interesting study. Ibrahim saw Peter in the Senate, disputing with Buturlin[15] and Dolgoruky, analyzing important questions of legislation, in the Admiralty College affirming Russia's naval greatness; saw him in hours of leisure going over the translations of foreign publicists with Feofan, Gavriil Buzhinsky, and Kopievich,[16] or visiting a merchant's mill, an artisan's workshop, a scholar's study. Russia appeared to Ibrahim as a vast factory where only machines moved, where each worker, subject to an established order, was taken up with his task. He considered it likewise his duty to labor at his own machine, and he tried to regret the amusements of Parisian life as little as possible. More difficult for him was distancing himself from another sweet memory: he often thought of the countess D., imagined her righteous indignation, her tears and sorrow . . . but sometimes a terrible thought wrung his heart: the distractions of high society, a new liaison, another happy man—he shuddered; jealousy began to seethe in his African blood, and hot tears were ready to flow down his black face.

One morning Ibrahim was sitting in his study, surrounded by business papers, when he suddenly heard a loud greeting in French. He turned quickly, and the young Korsakov, whom he had left in Paris in the whirl of social life, embraced him with joyful exclamations. "I've just arrived," said Korsakov, "and came running straight to you. All our Parisian friends send you their greetings and regret your absence. The countess D. told me to be sure to call you back, and here is a letter from her." Ibrahim seized it, trembling, and gazed at the familiar handwriting, not daring to believe his eyes. "I'm so glad," Korsakov went on, "that you haven't died of boredom yet in this barbaric Petersburg! What do they do here? How do they keep busy? Who is your tailor? Do you at least have an opera?" Ibrahim answered distractedly that right now the sovereign was probably working at the shipyard. Korsakov laughed. "I see you can't be bothered with me now," he said. "We'll talk our fill another time. I'll go and present myself to the sovereign." With those words, he turned on his heel and ran out of the room.

Ibrahim, left alone, hurriedly unsealed the letter. The countess complained tenderly, reproaching him for falsity and mistrustfulness. "You say," she wrote, "that my peace is the dearest thing in the world for you. Ibrahim! If that were true, could you have subjected me to the state into which the unexpected news of your departure threw me? You feared I might hold you back. Rest assured that, despite my love, I would have been able to sacrifice myself for your well-being and for what you consider your duty." The countess ended the letter with passionate assurances of love and entreated him to write to her at least once in a while, even if there was no longer any hope of their seeing each other again.

Ibrahim reread the letter twenty times, rapturously kissing the priceless lines. He burned with impatience to hear something about the countess, and was about to go to the Admiralty in hopes of finding Korsakov still there, when the door opened and Korsakov himself appeared again. He had already presented himself to the sovereign—and, as was his wont, seemed very pleased with himself. "*Entre nous*,"* he said to Ibrahim, "the sovereign's a very strange man. Imagine, I found him in a sort of canvas vest, on the mast of a new ship, which I was forced to clamber up with my dispatches. I stood on a rope ladder and didn't have room enough to make my bows properly, and was thoroughly embarrassed, which has never happened to me in all my born days. However, the sovereign, having read the papers, looked me up and down and was probably pleasantly impressed by the taste and smartness of my clothes; at least he smiled and invited me to this evening's assembly. But I'm a perfect stranger in Petersburg. During my six years of absence I've completely forgotten the local customs. Please be my mentor, come to fetch me and introduce me."

Ibrahim agreed and hastened to turn the conversation to a subject more interesting for him. "Well, how is the countess D.?"

"The countess? She was, naturally, very upset at first by your departure. Then, naturally, she gradually consoled herself and took a new lover. Do you know whom? The lanky marquis R. Why are you goggling your Moorish eyeballs at me? Or does all this seem strange to you? Don't you know that prolonged grief is contrary to human nature, especially a woman's? Give it some good thought, and I'll go and rest from my journey. Don't forget to come and fetch me."

What feelings filled Ibrahim's soul? Jealousy? Fury? Despair? No,

* "Between us."

but a deep, wringing dejection. He repeated to himself: "I foresaw it, it was bound to happen." Then he opened the countess's letter, read it again, hung his head, and wept bitterly. He wept for a long time. The tears eased his heart. Looking at his watch, he saw that it was time to go. Ibrahim would very gladly have excused himself, but an assembly was an official duty, and the sovereign strictly demanded the presence of his retinue. He got dressed and went to fetch Korsakov.

Korsakov was sitting in his dressing gown reading a French book. "So early?" he said, seeing him. "For pity's sake," Ibrahim replied, "it's half past five; we'll be late; get dressed quickly and let's go." Korsakov sprang up, started ringing with all his might; servants came running; he hurriedly began to dress. The French valet gave him shoes with red heels, light blue velvet trousers, a pink kaftan embroidered with sequins; in the front hall his wig was hastily powdered, it was brought, Korsakov put his close-cropped head into it, called for his sword and gloves, turned around some ten times before the mirror, and announced to Ibrahim that he was ready. Lackeys brought them bearskin coats, and they drove off to the Winter Palace.

Korsakov showered Ibrahim with questions: Who was the first beauty in Petersburg? Who was reputed to be the best dancer? What dance was now in fashion? With great reluctance Ibrahim satisfied his curiosity. Meanwhile they drove up to the palace. Many long sledges, old coaches, and gilded carriages already stood in the field. By the porch thronged coachmen in liveries and moustaches, footmen sparkling with baubles, in plumes and with maces, hussars, pages, clumsy lackeys laden with their masters' fur coats and muffs: a necessary suite according to the notions of the boyars of that time. At the sight of Ibrahim, a general murmur arose among them: "The Moor, the Moor, the tsar's Moor!" He quickly led Korsakov through this motley servantry. A court lackey threw the doors open for them, and they entered the hall. Korsakov was dumbfounded . . . In the big room lit by tallow candles, which shone dimly through the clouds of tobacco smoke, dignitaries with blue ribbons over their shoulders,[17] ambassadors, foreign merchants, officers of the guards in green uniforms, shipwrights in jackets and striped trousers, moved back and forth in a crowd to the incessant sounds of a brass band. Ladies sat along the walls. The young ones glittered with all the magnificence of fashion. Gold and silver glittered on their gowns; their narrow waists rose like stems from puffy farthingales; diamonds glittered on their ears, in their long curls, and around their necks. They turned gaily right and left, waiting for the cavaliers and the start of the dancing. Elderly ladies tried cleverly to combine the new way of dressing with the persecuted old fashion: their bonnets tended towards the little sable hat of the tsaritsa Natalia Kirillovna, and their *robes rondes* and mantillas somehow resembled *sarafan*s and *dushegreika*s.[18] It seemed there was more astonishment than enjoyment in their being present at these newfangled festivities, and they glanced sidelong with vexation at the wives and daughters of the Dutch sea captains, in dimity skirts and red blouses, who sat knitting stockings, laughing and talking among themselves as if they were at home. Korsakov could not collect his wits.

Noticing the new guests, a servant approached them with beer and glasses on a tray. *"Que diable est-ce que tout cela?"** Korsakov asked Ibrahim in a low voice. Ibrahim could not help smiling. The empress and the grand duchesses, radiant in their beauty and finery, strolled among the rows of guests, talking affably with them. The sovereign was in another room. Korsakov, wishing to show himself to him, was barely able to make his way there through the ceaselessly moving crowd. Mostly foreigners were sitting there, solemnly smoking their clay pipes and emptying their clay mugs. On the tables there were bottles of beer and wine, leather tobacco pouches, glasses of punch, and chessboards. At one of these tables Peter was playing draughts with a broad-shouldered English skipper. They zealously saluted each other with volleys of tobacco smoke, and the sovereign was so puzzled by his opponent's unexpected move that he did not notice Korsakov, despite all his turning around him. Just then a fat gentleman with a fat bouquet on his chest came bustling in, vociferously announced that the dancing had begun—and left at once. Many of the guests followed him, including Korsakov.

An unexpected sight struck him. For the whole length of the ball-room, to the strains of the most lugubrious music, ladies and cavaliers stood in two rows facing each other; the cavaliers bowed low, the ladies curtsied still lower, first straight ahead, then to the right, then to the left, then straight ahead again, then to the right, and so on. Korsakov, looking at this fanciful pastime, rolled his eyes and bit his lips. The curtsies and bows went on for about half an hour; finally they stopped, and the fat gentleman with the bouquet announced

* "What the devil is all this?"

that the ceremonial dancing was over and told the musicians to play a minuet. Korsakov was overjoyed and got ready to shine. Among the young ladies there was one he especially liked. She was about sixteen, richly but tastefully dressed, and was sitting next to an elderly man of grave and stern appearance. Korsakov flew over to her and asked her to do him the honor of dancing with him. The young beauty looked at him in perplexity and seemed not to know what to say. The man beside her frowned still more. Korsakov waited for her decision, but the gentleman with the bouquet came up to him, led him to the middle of the room, and said gravely: "My dear sir, you are at fault: first, you approached this young person without making the requisite three bows to her; and second, you took it upon yourself to choose her, while in minuets that right belongs to the lady, not to the cavalier. On account of this, you are to be roundly punished, you must drain *the cup of the great eagle.*" Korsakov grew more and more astonished. In a trice the guests encircled him, loudly demanding the immediate fulfillment of the law. Peter, hearing laughter and shouting, came from the other room, having a great fancy for being personally present at such punishments. The crowd parted before him and he entered the circle where the condemned man stood, with the marshal of the assembly before him holding an enormous cup filled with malmsey. He was vainly trying to persuade the offender to obey the law voluntarily.

"Aha," said Peter, seeing Korsakov, "so you've been caught, brother! Now, monsieur, kindly drink up and don't make faces!" There was nothing to be done. The poor dandy emptied the whole cup without stopping for a breath and handed it back to the marshal. "Listen, Korsakov," Peter said to him, "you've got velvet breeches on such as I don't wear myself, and I'm much richer than you are. That's extravagance. Take care that I don't quarrel with you." Having given ear to this reprimand, Korsakov attempted to step out of the circle, but staggered and nearly fell, to the indescribable delight of the sovereign and the whole merry company. This episode not only did not disrupt the unity and entertainment of the main action, but enlivened it still more. The cavaliers began to bow and scrape, and the ladies to curtsy and tap their heels with great eagerness and no longer keeping the cadence. Korsakov could not share in the general merriment. The lady he had chosen went up to Ibrahim, on orders from her father, Gavrila Afanasyevich, and, lowering her blue eyes, gave him her hand. Ibrahim danced the minuet with her and returned her to her former place; then, having located Korsakov, he led him out of the hall, sat him in his carriage, and took him home. On the way, Korsakov first murmured indistinctly: "Damned assembly! . . . Damned cup of the great eagle! . . ." but soon fell fast asleep, did not feel how he came home, how he was undressed and put to bed. He woke up the next day with a headache and a vague recollection of the scraping, the curtsying, the tobacco smoke, the gentleman with the bouquet, and the cup of the great eagle.

CHAPTER FOUR

> Not quickly did our forebears eat,
> Not quickly did they pass around
> The brimming jugs, the silver cups
> Of foaming beer and ruby wine.
>
> *Ruslan and Ludmila*[19]

I must now acquaint the gracious reader with Gavrila Afanasyevich Rzhevsky. He came of old boyar stock, owned a huge estate, was hospitable, loved falconry; his household staff was numerous. In short, he was a true-born Russian squire, could not bear the German spirit, as he put it, and tried in his everyday life to preserve the customs of the old days that were so dear to him.

His daughter was seventeen years old. She lost her mother while still a child. She was brought up in the old-fashioned way, that is, surrounded by nurses, nannies, girlfriends, and maidservants; she did gold embroidery and could not read or write. Her father, despite his loathing for everything foreign, could not oppose her wish to learn German dances from a captive Swedish officer who lived in their house. This worthy dancing master was fifty years old, his right leg had been shot through at Narva[20] and was therefore not quite up to minuets and courantes, but the left brought off the most difficult *pas** with astonishing skill and ease. His pupil did credit to his efforts. Natalya Gavrilovna was famous for being the best dancer at the assemblies, which was partly the cause of Korsakov's offense, for which he came the next day

* steps

to apologize to Gavrila Afanasyevich; but the adroitness and foppishness of the young dandy did not please the proud boyar, who wittily nicknamed him "the French monkey."

It was a holiday. Gavrila Afanasyevich was expecting several relations and friends. A long table was being laid in the old-fashioned dining room. The guests were arriving with their wives and daughters, freed at last from their domestic reclusion by the ukases of the sovereign and his own example. Natalya Gavrilovna held out to each guest a silver tray covered with little gold goblets, and each one drank his, regretting that the kiss, which in former times accompanied such occasions, was no longer customary. They went to the table. In the first place, next to the host, sat his father-in-law, Prince Boris Alexeevich Lykov, a seventy-year-old boyar; the other guests, according to the seniority of their families and thus commemorating the happy days of the order of precedence,[21] took their seats—the men on one side, the women on the other; at the foot of the table, in their customary places, sat the housekeeper in her old-fashioned coat and headdress; a dwarf, a tiny thirty-year-old woman, prim and wrinkled; and the captive Swede in a worn blue uniform. The table, set with a multitude of dishes, was surrounded by bustling and numerous servants, among whom the butler was distinguished by his stern gaze, fat belly, and majestic immobility. The first minutes of the dinner were given over entirely to the products of our time-honored cuisine; only the clank of plates and busy spoons broke the general silence. Finally, the host, seeing it was time to entertain his guests with pleasant conversation, looked about and asked: "And where is Ekimovna? Call her here." Several servants rushed in different directions, but just then an old woman, made up with white greasepaint and rouge, adorned with flowers and baubles, in a damask *robe ronde*, her neck and shoulders bared, came dancing in humming a tune. Her appearance caused general delight.

"Greetings, Ekimovna," said Prince Lykov. "How are you?"

"Healthy and wealthy, uncle; singing and dancing, and a bit of romancing."

"Where have you been, fool?" asked the host.

"Dressing myself up, uncle, for the dear guests, for the holiday star, by command of the tsar, by the rules of boyars, to make all the world laugh, save the Germany half."

At these words there was a loud burst of laughter, and the fool went to take her place behind the host's chair.

"The fool lies away and, forsooth, she lies her way to the truth," said Tatyana Afanasyevna, the host's older sister, whom he sincerely respected. "Today's fashions really do make all the world laugh. Since even you, my dear sirs, have shaved your beards and put on scanty kaftans, then for women's rags, of course, there's nothing to talk about: but it truly is a pity about the sarafan, young girls' ribbons, and the *povoinik*.²² Just look at today's beauties—you'll laugh and weep: hair sticking up like matted felt, greased, sprinkled with French flour, the waist drawn in so tight it might just snap, the petticoats stretched on hoops: they have to get into a carriage sideways, and bend over going through a door. They can neither stand, nor sit, nor take a breath. Real martyrs, my little doves."

"Ah, my dear Tatyana Afanasyevna," said Kirila Petrovich T., former governor-general of Ryazan, where he had acquired three thousand serfs and a young wife for himself, both not without some shadiness. "I say a wife can dress as she pleases, like a scarecrow, or like a Chinese mandarin, so long as she doesn't order new dresses every month and throw out the old ones unworn. It used to be that a granddaughter got her grandmother's sarafan as a dowry, but these *robes rondes* nowadays—just look—today it's on the lady, tomorrow on a serf girl. What can you do? The ruin of the Russian gentry! A disaster, that's what!" With those words he sighed and looked at his Marya Ilyinichna, who, it seemed, was not at all pleased either with his praise of the old days, or with his censure of the new customs. The other beauties shared her displeasure but said nothing, because modesty was then considered a necessary quality in a young woman.

"And who is to blame?" said Gavrila Afanasyevich, filling his mug with foaming mead. "Isn't it we ourselves? Young wenches play the fool, and we indulge them."

"But what can we do, if it's not up to us?" Kirila Petrovich objected. "A man would be glad to lock his wife away in a tower, but she's called to the assembly with a beating of drums; the husband goes for his whip, the wife for her finery. Ah, these assemblies! The Lord's punishing us for our sins."

Marya Ilyinichna was on pins and needles; her tongue was itching; finally, unable to help herself, she turned to her husband and with a sour little smile asked him what he found so bad about the assemblies.

"What's bad about them," her husband replied heatedly, "is that

ever since they were instituted, husbands have been unable to manage their wives. Wives have forgotten the words of the apostle: 'A
wife should *reverence* her husband.'[23] They busy themselves, not with
housekeeping, but with new clothes; they don't think of how to please
their husbands, but of how to catch the eye of some whippersnapper
of an officer. And is it proper, madam, for a Russian gentlewoman or
young lady to be with tobacco-smoking Germans and the girls who
work for them? Who has ever heard of dancing and talking with young
men until late at night—with relatives it would be another thing, but
this is with foreigners, with strangers."

"I'd say a bit more, but the wolf's at the door," Gavrila Afanasyevich said, frowning. "I must confess—assemblies are not to my liking
either: you have to watch out lest you run into a drunk man, or they
make you drunk just for the fun of it. And also watch out lest some
scapegrace get up to mischief with your daughter. Young men these
days are so spoiled, it's beyond anything. The son of the late Evgraf
Sergeevich Korsakov, for instance, caused such an uproar with Natasha at the last assembly that I turned red all over. The next day I look,
he comes rolling right into our courtyard. Who in God's name is it, I
thought, Prince Alexander Danilovich? Not on your life: it was Ivan
Evgrafovich! The man couldn't stop at the gate and take the trouble
of walking up to the porch—oh, no! He came flying in! Bowed and
scraped! Chattered his head off! . . . The fool Ekimovna imitates him
killingly. Come, fool, do the foreign monkey for us."

The fool Ekimovna snatched the lid from a dish, took it under
her arm like a hat, and started grimacing, bowing, and scraping in all
directions, mumbling "*moosieu . . . mamzelle . . . assemblée . . . pardone.*"
General and prolonged laughter again expressed the guests' pleasure.

"That's Korsakov to a T," said old Prince Lykov, wiping tears of
laughter, when calm was gradually restored. "Why not admit it? He's
neither the first nor the last to come back to Holy Russia from foreign parts as a buffoon. What do our children learn there? To bow and
scrape, to babble in God knows what tongues, to show no respect for
their elders, and to dangle after other men's wives. Of all young men
educated abroad (God forgive me), the tsar's Moor most resembles a
human being."

"Of course," observed Gavrila Afanasyevich, "he's a sober and
decent man, not like that featherbrain . . . Who's that driving into the

yard? Not the foreign monkey again? What are you gawking at, you brutes?" he went on, addressing his servants. "Run and tell him we're not receiving, and that in future—"

"Are you raving, old graybeard?" the fool Ekimovna interrupted. "Or are you blind? That's the sovereign's sledge; the tsar has come."

Gavrila Afanasyevich hastily got up from the table; everybody rushed to the windows and indeed saw the sovereign, who was going up the front steps leaning on his orderly's shoulder. A commotion ensued. The host rushed to meet Peter; the servants scattered in all directions like lunatics; the guests were frightened, some even thought of heading for home as quickly as possible. Suddenly Peter's booming voice was heard in the front hall, everything fell silent, and the tsar entered accompanied by the host, dumbstruck with joy.

"Greetings, ladies and gentlemen!" Peter said with a cheerful look. They all bowed deeply. The tsar's quick glance sought out the host's young daughter in the crowd; he called her to him. Natalya Gavrilovna approached quite boldly, but blushing not only to the ears, but down to the shoulders. "You get prettier by the hour," the sovereign said to her and, as was his custom, kissed her on the head; then, turning to the guests: "Well, so? I've disturbed you. You were having dinner. I beg you to sit down again, and you, Gavrila Afanasyevich, give me some anise vodka."

The host rushed to the majestic butler, snatched the tray out of his hands, filled a little gold goblet himself, and offered it to the sovereign with a bow. Peter, having drunk it, took a bite from a pretzel, and again invited the guests to go on with dinner. They all took their former places, except for the dwarf and the housekeeper, who did not dare to remain at a table honored by the tsar's presence. Peter sat down beside the host and asked for cabbage soup. His orderly served him a wooden spoon set with ivory, and a knife and fork with green bone handles, for Peter never used any utensils but his own. The dinner, noisily animated a moment before with merriment and garrulity, went on in silence and constraint. The host, out of deference and joy, ate nothing; the guests also became decorous and listened with reverence as the sovereign talked with the captive Swede about the campaign of 1701. The fool Ekimovna, whom the sovereign questioned a few times, answered with a sort of timid coldness, which (I note in passing) by no means proved her innate stupidity.

Finally the dinner came to an end. The sovereign stood up, and all the guests after him. "Gavrila Afanasyevich," he said to the host, "I must talk with you alone." And taking him by the arm, he led him to the drawing room and shut the door behind them. The guests remained in the dining room, exchanging whispers about this unexpected visit, and, for fear of being indelicate, soon departed one by one, without thanking the host for his hospitality. His father-in-law, daughter, and sister quietly saw them to the porch and remained in the dining room, waiting for the sovereign to come out.

CHAPTER FIVE

> I shall find a wife for thee,
> Or a miller I'll ne'er be.
>
> ABLESIMOV, FROM THE OPERA *The Miller*[24]

Half an hour later the door opened and Peter came out. Gravely inclining his head in response to the threefold bow of Prince Lykov, Tatyana Afanasyevna, and Natasha, he walked straight to the front hall. The host held his red fleece-lined coat for him, saw him to the sledge, and on the porch thanked him again for the honor bestowed on him. Peter drove off.

Returning to the dining room, Gavrila Afanasyevich seemed very preoccupied. He angrily ordered the servants to clear the table at once, sent Natasha to her room, and, announcing to his sister and father-in-law that he had to talk to them, led them to his bedroom, where he usually rested after dinner. The old prince lay down on the oak bed; Tatyana Afanasyevna sat in an old-fashioned damask armchair, moving a footstool closer; Gavrila Afanasyevich shut all the doors, sat on the bed at Prince Lykov's feet, and in a low voice began the following conversation:

"It was not for nothing that the sovereign visited me today. Can you guess what he was pleased to talk with me about?"

"How can we know, brother dear?" said Tatyana Afanasyevna.

"Can the tsar have appointed you governor-general somewhere?"

asked the father-in-law. "It's none too soon. Or has he offered you an ambassadorship? Why not? Noblemen, and not just scribes, are sent to foreign rulers."

"No," his son-in-law replied, frowning. "I'm a man of the old stamp, our services are no longer required, though an Orthodox Russian nobleman may well be worth all these present-day upstarts, pancake makers, and heathens[25]—but that's another subject."

"What was it, then, that he was pleased to talk with you about for so long?" asked Tatyana Afanasyevna. "You're not in some sort of trouble, are you? Lord, save us and have mercy on us!"

"Trouble or no trouble, I must confess it set me thinking."

"What is it, brother? What's the matter?"

"It's a matter of Natasha: the tsar came to make a match for her."

"Thank God," Tatyana Afanasyevna said, crossing herself. "The girl's of marriageable age, and like matchmaker, like suitor—God grant them love and harmony. It's a great honor. For whom is the tsar asking her hand?"

"Hm," grunted Gavrila Afanasyevich. "For whom? That's just it—for whom."

"For whom, then?" Prince Lykov, who was already beginning to doze off, repeated.

"Guess," said Gavrila Afanasyevich.

"Brother dear," the old woman replied "how can we guess? There are lots of suitors at court: any one of them would be glad to take your Natasha. Is it Dolgoruky?"

"No, not Dolgoruky."

"Well, God help him: he's awfully arrogant. Schein? Troekurov?"

"No, neither of them."

"They're not to my liking either: featherbrains, too full of the German spirit. Well, then, Miloslavsky?"

"No, not him."

"And God help him, too: he's rich but stupid. Who, then? Eletsky? Lvov? No? Can it be Raguzinsky? I give up. Who is the tsar choosing for Natasha?"

"The Moor Ibrahim."

The old woman cried out and clasped her hands. Prince Lykov raised his head from the pillows and repeated in amazement: "The Moor Ibrahim!"

"Brother dear," the old woman said in a tearful voice, "don't ruin your own child, don't deliver Natashenka into the clutches of that black devil."

"But how can I refuse the sovereign," Gavrila Afanasyevich protested, "who promises his favor in return, to me and all our family?"

"What?!" exclaimed the old prince, whom sleep had totally deserted. "To have Natasha, my granddaughter, marry a bought blackamoor?!"

"He's not of common stock," said Gavrila Afanasyevich. "He's the son of a Moorish sultan. Some heathens took him captive and sold him in Constantinople, and our ambassador redeemed him and presented him to the tsar. The Moor's elder brother came to Russia with a rich ransom and—"

"My dearest Gavrila Afanasyevich," the old woman interrupted, "we've all heard the tales of Prince Bova and Eruslan Lazarevich.²⁶ You'd better tell us how you replied to the sovereign's matchmaking."

"I told him that the power was with him, and our bounden duty was to obey him in all things."

Just then a noise came from behind the door. Gavrila Afanasyevich went to open it, but, feeling some resistance, he pushed hard on it, the door opened—and they saw Natasha lying unconscious on the bloodied floor.

Her heart had sunk when the sovereign shut himself in with her father. Some presentiment had whispered to her that it had to do with her, and when Gavrila Afanasyevich sent her away, announcing that he had to speak with her aunt and grandfather, feminine curiosity got the better of her, she tiptoed quietly through the inner rooms to the door of the bedroom, and did not miss a single word of the whole terrible conversation. When she heard her father's last words, the poor girl fainted and, falling, struck her head against the iron-bound chest in which her dowry was kept.

Servants came running; Natasha was picked up, carried to her room, and placed on the bed. After some time she came to, opened her eyes, but recognized neither her father nor her aunt. She broke into a high fever, raved about the tsar's Moor, the wedding—and suddenly cried out in a pitiful and piercing voice: "Valerian, dear Valerian, my life! Save me: they're coming, they're coming!. . ." Tatyana Afanasyevna glanced anxiously at her brother, who turned pale, bit his lips, and silently left the room. He went back to the old prince, who, unable to climb the stairs, had remained below.

"How is Natasha?" he asked.

"Not well," the upset father replied, "worse than I thought: she's delirious and raves about Valerian."

"Who is this Valerian?" the old man asked in alarm. "Can it be that orphan, the son of the *strelets*,[27] who was brought up in your house?"

"That's him," Gavrila Afanasyevich replied. "To my misfortune, his father saved my life during the rebellion, and the devil prompted me to take the cursed wolf cub into my house. When he was enlisted in a regiment two years ago, at his own request, Natasha burst into tears as she said good-bye to him, and he stood as if turned to stone. That seemed suspicious to me, and I told my sister about it. But Natasha has never mentioned him since then, and there has been no news from him. I thought she had forgotten him; but obviously not. That settles it: she'll marry the Moor."

Prince Lykov did not contradict him: it would have been useless. He went home; Tatyana Afanasyevna stayed at Natasha's bedside; Gavrila Afanasyevich sent for the doctor, shut himself up in his room, and everything in his house became quiet and sad.

The unexpected matchmaking surprised Ibrahim at least as much as it did Gavrila Afanasyevich. Here is how it happened. Peter, while doing some work with Ibrahim, said to him:

"I notice, brother, that you're in low spirits. Tell me straight out: what is it that you lack?" Ibrahim assured the sovereign that he was content with his lot and did not wish for anything better.

"Good," said the sovereign. "If you're bored for no reason, then I know what will cheer you up."

When they finished their work, Peter asked Ibrahim: "Did you like that girl you danced the minuet with at the last assembly?"

"She's very sweet, Sire, and she seems to be a modest and kind girl."

"Then I shall make you better acquainted. Would you like to marry her?"

"Me, Sire? . . ."

"Listen, Ibrahim, you're a single man, without kith or kin, a stranger to all except myself. If I should die today, what would happen to you tomorrow, my poor blackamoor? We must get you established while there is still time, find support for you in new connections, unite with the Russian boyars."

"Sire, I am happy to have Your Majesty's protection and favor. God grant that I not outlive my tsar and my benefactor—I wish for nothing else. But if I did have a mind to marry, would the young girl and her relations consent? My appearance . . ."

"Your appearance! What nonsense! Aren't you a fine young fellow? A young girl must obey her parents' will, and we'll see what old Gavrila Rzhevsky says when I myself come as your matchmaker!" With those words the sovereign ordered his sledge made ready and left Ibrahim sunk deep in thought.

"To marry!" thought the African. "Why not? Can I be destined to spend my life in solitude and not know the best pleasures and the most sacred duties of man only because I was born below the fifteenth parallel? I cannot hope to be loved: a childish objection! Can one believe in love? Can it exist in a frivolous feminine heart? Renouncing sweet delusions forever, I have chosen other enticements—more substantial ones. The sovereign is right: I must provide for my future. Marriage to Rzhevsky's daughter will connect me with the proud Russian nobility, and I will stop being a stranger in my new fatherland. I'm not going to demand love from my wife, I'll be content with her fidelity, and I'll win her friendship by constant tenderness, trust, and indulgence."

Ibrahim, as was his habit, was about to go back to work, but his imagination was too distracted. He abandoned his papers and went to stroll along the Neva embankment. Suddenly he heard Peter's voice; he turned and saw the sovereign, who had dismissed the sledge and was following him with a cheerful look. "It's all settled, brother," said Peter, taking him under the arm. "I've made your match. Go to your father-in-law tomorrow; but watch yourself, indulge his boyar arrogance; leave your sledge at the gate; cross the yard on foot; talk to him about his services, about his noble birth, and he'll lose his mind over you. And now," he went on, brandishing his cudgel, "take me to that rogue Danilych; I must have it out with him about his latest pranks."

Ibrahim, having warmly thanked Peter for his fatherly care, brought him to Prince Menshikov's magnificent palace and went back home.

CHAPTER SIX

An icon lamp was quietly burning before the glass-covered stand in which the gold and silver casings of the family icons gleamed. Its tremulous light shone weakly on the curtained bed and the little table set with labeled vials. By the stove a maid sat at a spinning wheel, and the faint noise of her spindle alone broke the silence of the room.

"Who's there?" said a weak voice. The maid stood up at once, went over to the bed, and gently raised the curtain. "Will it be daylight soon?" asked Natalya.

"It's already noon," the maid replied.

"Ah, my God, why is it so dark?"

"The blinds are closed, miss."

"Quick, give me my clothes."

"I can't, miss, the doctor forbade it."

"You mean I'm sick? For how long?"

"It's two weeks now."

"Can it be? It seems like I went to bed only yesterday . . ."

Natasha fell silent; she tried to gather her scattered thoughts. Something had happened to her, but precisely what, she could not remember. The maid went on standing before her, waiting for orders. Just then a muffled noise came from below.

"What's that?" asked the sick girl.

"The masters have finished eating," replied the maid. "They're getting up from the table. Tatyana Afanasyevna will come here shortly."

Natasha seemed glad; she waved her arm weakly. The maid closed the curtain and sat down again at her spinning wheel.

After a few minutes a head in a broad white bonnet with dark ribbons appeared in the doorway, and a question was asked in a low voice: "How is Natasha?"

"Good afternoon, auntie," the sick girl said softly; and Tatyana Afanasyevna hastened to her.

"The young lady has come to," said the maid, carefully drawing up an armchair.

The old woman tearfully kissed the pale, languid face of her niece and sat down beside her. After her a German doctor in a black kaftan and a scholar's wig came in, felt Natasha's pulse, and announced in Latin, and then in Russian, that the danger was past. He called for paper and ink, wrote out a new prescription, and left, and the old woman got up, kissed Natasha again, and went downstairs to Gavrila Afanasyevich with the good news.

In the drawing room, in uniform, sword at his side, hat in his hand, sat the tsar's Moor, talking respectfully with Gavrila Afanasyevich. Korsakov, sprawled on a downy sofa, was listening to them absentmindedly and teasing a venerable borzoi hound. Bored with this occupation, he went to the mirror, the usual recourse of his idleness, and in it saw Tatyana Afanasyevna, who was in the doorway making unnoticed signs to her brother.

"You're wanted, Gavrila Afanasyevich," said Korsakov, turning to him and interrupting Ibrahim's speech. Gavrila Afanasyevich went to his sister at once and closed the door behind him.

"I marvel at your patience," Korsakov said to Ibrahim. "For a whole hour you've been listening to this raving about the antiquity of the Lykov and Rzhevsky families and adding your own moralizing observations to it. If I were you, *j'aurais planté là** the old babbler and all his kin, including Natalya Gavrilovna, who minces around, pretending she's sick, *une petite santé*† . . . Tell me honestly, are you really in love with this little *mijaurée?*‡ Listen, Ibrahim, for once at least take my advice; I'm really more sensible than I seem. Drop this foolish notion. Don't get married. It seems to me that your bride-to-be has no particular inclination for you. All sorts of things happen in this world. For instance: I'm not bad-looking, of course, but I've happened to deceive husbands who, by God, were no worse than me. You yourself . . . Remember our Parisian friend, Count D.? You can't trust in a woman's fidelity; happy the man who looks upon it with indifference! But you! . . . With your ardent, brooding, and suspicious character, with your flattened nose, puffy lips, and that mop of wool, to rush into all the dangers of marriage? . . . ."

"Thank you for the friendly advice," Ibrahim interrupted him coldly, "but you know the proverb: Don't go rocking another man's babies . . ."

"Watch out, Ibrahim," Korsakov replied, laughing, "or you may actually get to demonstrate that proverb afterwards, in the literal sense."

But the conversation in the other room was growing heated.

"You'll be the death of her," the old woman was saying. "She won't bear the sight of him."

"But judge for yourself," the obstinate brother objected. "It's already two weeks that he's been coming as a suitor, and he's yet to see

* "I would have dumped"
† "in poor health"
‡ "pretentious young thing"

the bride-to-be. He'll finally start thinking that her illness is an empty device, and that we're just seeking to delay things so as to get rid of him somehow. And what will the tsar say? He's already sent three times to ask after Natalya's health. Like it or not, I have no intention of quarreling with him."

"Lord God," said Tatyana Afanasyevna, "what will become of the poor girl? At least let me prepare her for such a visit." Gavrila Afanasyevich agreed and went back to the drawing room.

"Thank God," he said to Ibrahim, "the danger is past. Natalya is much better. If I weren't ashamed to leave our dear guest, Ivan Evgrafovich, alone here, I'd take you upstairs to have a look at your bride."

Korsakov congratulated Gavrila Afanasyevich, asked him not to worry, assured him that he had to leave, and ran to the front hall, not allowing the host to see him off.

Meanwhile Tatyana Afanasyevna hastened to prepare the sick girl for the appearance of the dreaded guest. Going into the room, she sat down, breathless, by the bed, took Natasha's hand, but, before she had time to utter a word, the door opened. Natasha asked who was there. The old woman froze and went dumb. Gavrila Afanasyevich drew the curtain aside, looked coldly at the sick girl, and asked how she was. The sick girl wanted to smile at him, but could not. Her father's stern gaze stunned her, and she was seized with anxiety. At that moment it seemed that someone was standing at the head of her bed. She raised her head with effort and suddenly recognized the tsar's Moor. Here she remembered everything, all the horror of the future arose before her. But her exhausted nature suffered no noticeable shock. Natasha lowered her head back on the pillow and closed her eyes . . . Her heart was pounding painfully. Tatyana Afanasyevna made a sign to her brother that the sick girl wanted to sleep, and they all quietly left the bedroom, except for the maid, who sat down again at the spinning wheel.

The unhappy beauty opened her eyes and, seeing no one at her bedside now, beckoned to the maid and sent her for the dwarf. But just then the round little old woman came rolling up to her bed like a ball. Lastochka* (that was the dwarf's name) had followed Gavrila Afanasyevich and Ibrahim upstairs as fast as her stubby legs would carry her and hidden behind the door, faithful to the curiosity natural to the

* Literally "swallow."

fair sex. Seeing her, Natasha sent the maid away, and the dwarf seated herself by the bed on a little bench.

Never had so small a body contained in itself so much mental activity. She meddled in everything, knew everything, busied herself with everything. With her clever and insinuating mind, she had managed to earn the love of her masters and the hatred of the rest of the household, which she ruled despotically. Gavrila Afanasyevich heeded her denunciations, complaints, and petty demands; Tatyana Afanasyevna constantly asked her opinion and followed her advice; and Natasha had a boundless affection for her and confided to her all her thoughts and all the stirrings of her sixteen-year-old heart.

"You know, Lastochka," she said, "my father is giving me away to the Moor."

The dwarf sighed deeply, and her wrinkled face became more wrinkled still.

"Is there no hope?" Natasha went on. "Will my father not take pity on me?"

The dwarf shook her little bonnet.

"Won't my grandfather or my aunt intercede for me?"

"No, my young miss. During your illness, the Moor managed to enchant everybody. The master's lost his mind over him, the prince raves only about him, and Tatyana Afanasyevna says: 'Too bad he's a Moor, otherwise we couldn't dream of a better suitor.'"

"My God, my God!" poor Natasha moaned.

"Don't grieve, my beauty," said the dwarf, kissing her weak hand. "Even if you do marry the Moor, you'll still have your freedom. Nowadays it's not the same as in olden times; husbands don't lock their wives up; they say the Moor's rich; your house will be a full cup, your life will flow like a song . . ."

"Poor Valerian," said Natasha, but so softly that the dwarf could only guess at but not hear the words.

"That's just it," she said, lowering her voice mysteriously. "If you thought less about the strelets's orphan, you wouldn't have raved about him in your fever, and your father wouldn't be angry."

"What?" said Natasha, frightened. "I raved about Valerian, my father heard it, my father's angry!"

"That's just the trouble," said the dwarf. "Now, if you ask him not to marry you to the Moor, he'll think it's because of Valerian. Nothing to be done: submit to the parental will, and what will be will be."

Natasha did not utter a word of objection. The thought that her heart's secret was known to her father had a strong effect on her imagination. One hope remained for her: to die before the hateful marriage took place. This thought comforted her. With a weak and sorrowful heart she submitted to her fate.

CHAPTER SEVEN

To the right of the front hall in Gavrila Afanasyevich's house there was a small room with one little window. In it stood a simple bed covered with a flannelette blanket, and before the bed a small deal table on which a tallow candle burned and a musical score lay open. On the wall hung an old blue uniform and an equally old three-cornered hat; over it a cheap woodcut portraying Charles XII on horseback was fastened to the wall with three nails. The sounds of a flute could be heard in this humble abode. The captive dancing master, its solitary inhabitant, in a nightcap and a nankeen dressing gown, charmed away the boredom of the winter evening by playing old Swedish marches, which reminded him of the merry days of his youth. Having devoted a whole two hours to this exercise, the Swede took the flute apart, put it into the case, and began to undress.

Just then the latch of his door was raised, and a tall, handsome young man in a uniform came into the room.

The astonished Swede stood up before the unexpected guest.

"Don't you recognize me, Gustav Adamych?" said the young visitor in a moved voice. "Don't you remember the little boy to whom you taught the Swedish field manual, with whom you almost set fire to this very room, shooting from a toy cannon?"

Gustav Adamych peered at him intently . . .

"A-a-ah!" he cried at last, embracing him. "Greetinks! Zo it's really you! Zit down, my goot scapegrace, let's talk . . ."

The Tales of the
Late Ivan Petrovich Belkin

Mme Prostakova: So, my dear sir, he has been
a lover of stories since childhood.
Skotinin: Mitrofan takes after me.

FONVIZIN, *The Dunce*[1]

Having undertaken the task of publishing *The Tales of I. P. Belkin*, now offered to the public, we wish to attach to them at least a brief biography of the late author and thus satisfy in part the justifiable curiosity of the lovers of our national literature. To that end we addressed ourselves to Marya Alexeevna Trafilina, the closest relation and heir of Ivan Petrovich Belkin; but, unfortunately, she was unable to provide any information about him, for she was not acquainted with the late man at all. She advised us to refer on this subject to a certain estimable gentleman who had been Ivan Petrovich's friend. We followed her advice, and to our letter received the desired reply that follows. We place it here without any changes or commentary, as a precious memorial of a noble way of thinking and of a touching friendship, and at the same time as a perfectly sufficient biographical notice.

My dear Mr. * * *,

On the 23rd of this month I had the honor of receiving your esteemed letter of the 15th of the same month, in which you express to me your wish to have detailed information about the dates of birth and death, the service, the domestic circumstances, and the occupations and character of the late Ivan Petrovich Belkin, formerly my sincere friend and neighboring landowner. It is a great pleasure for me to fulfill your wish and send to you, my dear sir, all that I am able to remember of his conversation, as well as my own observations.

Ivan Petrovich Belkin was born of honorable and noble parents in 1798, in the village of Goryukhino. His late father, Second-Major Pyotr Ivanovich Belkin, was married to Miss Pelageya Gavrilovna, of the house of Trafilin. He was not a wealthy man, but frugal, and quite clever with regard to management. Their son received his primary education from the village sexton. It was to this estimable man, it seems, that he owed his love of reading and his studies of Russian literature.

In 1815 he entered the service in a regiment of the light infantry (I do not remember the number), in which he remained until 1823. The deaths of his parents, which occurred at almost the same time, forced him to retire and return to the village of Goryukhino, his paternal seat.

Having taken over the running of the estate, Ivan Petrovich, owing to his inexperience and soft-heartedness, soon let the management fall into neglect and relaxed the strict discipline his father had established. He replaced the industrious and efficient village headman, with whom the peasants (as is their wont) were displeased, entrusting the running of the village to his old housekeeper, who had gained his confidence by her art of telling stories. This stupid old woman was never able to distinguish between a twenty-five-rouble note and a fifty-rouble one; the peasants, who were all chummy with her, had no fear of her at all; the headman they chose connived with them and cheated so much that Ivan Petrovich was forced to abolish the corvée and institute a very moderate quitrent; but here, too, the peasants, taking advantage of his weakness, requested a significant exemption for the first year, and after that paid more than two-thirds of the quitrent in nuts, whortleberries, and the like; and here, too, there were arrears.

Having been a friend of Ivan Petrovich's late father, I considered it my duty to offer the son my advice and volunteered more than once to re-establish the former order, which he had neglected. To that end, I called on him one day, asked to see the account books, summoned the swindling headman, and began to examine them in Ivan Petrovich's presence. At first the young master followed me with all possible attention and diligence; but when the accounts showed that the number of peasants had increased in the last two years, while the number of the estate's fowl and livestock had significantly decreased, Ivan Petrovich satisfied himself with this initial information and listened no further to me, and at the very moment when, in my investigation and strict questioning, I threw the swindling headman into the utmost confusion and reduced him to total silence, I was greatly annoyed to hear Ivan Petrovich snoring loudly in his chair. After that I stopped interfering in his management and handed his affairs over (as he himself did) to the management of the Almighty.

Our friendly relations, however, were not in the least disturbed by that; for, sympathizing with his weakness and harmful negligence, common to our young nobility, I sincerely loved Ivan Petrovich; indeed it was impossible not to love such a meek and honest young man. For his part, Ivan Petrovich showed respect for my age and was deeply devoted to me. Right up to the end he saw me almost every day, cherishing my simple conversation, though in habits, in character, in our way of thinking, he and I had almost nothing in common.

Ivan Petrovich led a most frugal life, avoiding any sort of excess; never did I see him tipsy (which in our parts can be regarded as an unheard-of miracle); he had a great inclination for the female sex, but his shyness was truly maidenly.*

Besides the tales you are pleased to mention in your letter, Ivan Petrovich left many manuscripts, some of which are in my possession, some of which the housekeeper has put to various domestic uses. For instance, last winter she sealed all of her cottage windows with the first part of a novel he had left unfinished. The above-mentioned tales seem to have been his first experiments. They are, as Ivan Petrovich used to say, mostly true and heard by him from various persons.† However, the names in them are almost all fictitious, and the names of the towns and villages are all borrowed from our neighborhood, which is why my village is also mentioned somewhere. This occurred not from any ill intention, but solely from a lack of imagination.

In the autumn of 1828, Ivan Petrovich came down with a fit of ague that turned into a high fever, and he died, despite the

---

* There follows an anecdote which we do not include, supposing it to be superfluous; however, we assure the reader that it contains nothing prejudicial to the memory of Ivan Petrovich Belkin. (*The Publisher*)

† In fact, in Mr. Belkin's manuscript, at the head of each story there is written in the author's hand: "Heard by me from such-and-such person" with rank or title and initials. We note them down here for curious readers: "The Stationmaster" was told him by the titular councilor A. G. N., "The Shot" by Lieutenant Colonel I. L. P., "The Coffin-Maker" by the clerk B. V., "The Blizzard" and "The Young Lady Peasant" by Miss K. I. T. (*The Publisher*)

indefatigable efforts of our district doctor, a very skillful man, especially in treating inveterate illnesses such as corns and the like. He died in my arms at thirty years of age and is buried in the church of Goryukhino next to his late parents.

Ivan Petrovich was of medium height, had gray eyes, light brown hair, and a straight nose; his face was fair and lean.

That, my dear sir, is all I can remember concerning the way of life, occupations, character, and appearance of my late neighbor and friend. But in case you are pleased to make some use of this letter of mine, I most humbly beg you to make no mention of my name; for though I have great respect and love for writers, I consider it superfluous and, at my age, improper to join their ranks. With my sincere respects, and so on.

16 November 1830
Village of Nenaradovo

Considering it our duty to respect the will of our author's estimable friend, we express our profound gratitude to him for the information he has provided us and hope that the public will value its sincerity and good nature.

A. P.

THE SHOT

We fought a duel.

BARATYNSKY[1]

I swore I would shoot him by the rules of
dueling (I had not yet taken my shot at him).

An Evening at Bivouac[2]

I

We were stationed in the small town of * * *. Everyone is familiar with
the life of an army officer. In the morning, drill and riding practice;
dinner at the regimental commander's or in a Jewish tavern; in the evening, punch and cards. There was not a single open house in * * *, not
a single marriageable girl; we gathered in one another's rooms, where
there was nothing to be seen but our uniforms.

Only one man belonging to our group was not military. He was
about thirty-five, and for that we considered him an old man. Experience gave him many advantages over us; besides that, his habitual sul-
lenness, tough character, and wicked tongue had a strong influence on
our young minds. Some mysteriousness surrounded his fate; he seemed
Russian, but had a foreign name. He had once served in the hussars,
and even successfully; no one knew what motive had prompted him
to retire and settle in a poor little town, where he lived both poorly
and extravagantly: he always went about on foot, in a shabby black
frock coat, yet he kept open house for all the officers of our regiment.
True, his dinners consisted of two or three dishes prepared by a retired
soldier, but then the champagne flowed in streams. No one knew his
fortune, or his income, and no one dared to ask him about it. He had
some books, mostly military, but also novels. He willingly lent them
out, and never asked for them back; then, too, he never returned a

borrowed book to its owner. His main exercise consisted in shooting pistols. The walls of his room were all riddled with bullet holes like a honeycomb. A fine collection of pistols was the only luxury in the poor clay-and-wattle hovel he lived in. The skill he had achieved was unbelievable, and if he had volunteered to knock a pear off of somebody's cap with a bullet, no one in our regiment would have hesitated to offer him his head. The conversation among us often touched upon duels; Silvio (as I shall call him) never mixed into it. To the question of whether he had ever fought a duel, he replied drily that he had, but did not go into the details, and it was clear that such questions displeased him. We supposed that some unfortunate victim of his terrible skill lay on his conscience. However, it never entered our heads to suspect him of anything like cowardice. There are people whose appearance alone removes such suspicions. An unexpected incident amazed us all.

Once some ten of our officers were having dinner at Silvio's. We drank as usual, that is, a great deal; after dinner we started persuading our host to keep the bank for us. He refused for a long time, for he almost never gambled; finally he ordered the cards brought, poured some fifty gold pieces on the table, and sat down to deal. We gathered around him, and the game began. Silvio had the custom while gambling of maintaining a total silence, never argued and never explained. If a punter happened to miscalculate, he either paid what was owing immediately or noted down the excess. We already knew that and did not keep him from handling it his way; but among us there happened to be a recently transferred officer. While playing, he absentmindedly bent down an extra corner, doubling the stake. Silvio took the chalk and corrected the account as he usually did. The officer, thinking he was mistaken, started to explain. Silvio silently went on dealing. The officer, losing patience, took a brush and erased what he thought had been wrongly written. Silvio took the chalk and wrote it again. The officer, flushed with the wine, the gambling, and his comrades' laughter, considered himself cruelly offended and, snatching a brass candlestick from the table in his fury, hurled it at Silvio, who barely managed to duck the blow. We were disconcerted. Silvio stood up, pale with anger, his eyes flashing, and said: "My dear sir, kindly leave, and thank God that this happened in my house."

We had no doubt of the consequences and considered our new comrade already dead. The officer left, saying he was ready to answer for the offense whenever it suited Mister Banker. The play went on for a few more minutes; but, sensing that our host's mind was not on the game, we stopped one by one and wandered off to our quarters, talking about the soon-to-be vacancy.

The next day, at riding practice, we were already asking if the poor lieutenant was still alive, when the man himself appeared among us. We put the same question to him. He replied that he had not yet had any news from Silvio. That surprised us. We went to Silvio and found him in the yard, planting bullet after bullet into an ace glued to the gate. He received us as usual, without saying a word about yesterday's incident. Three days went by, and the lieutenant was still alive. We asked in astonishment: Can it be that Silvio won't fight? Silvio did not fight. He contented himself with a very flimsy explanation and made peace.

This damaged him greatly in the opinion of the young men. Lack of courage is least excusable of all for young people, who usually see bravery as the height of human virtue and the excuse for all possible vices. However, it was all gradually forgotten, and Silvio regained his former influence.

I alone could no longer be around him. Endowed by nature with a romantic imagination, I was formerly attached most strongly of all to the man, whose life was an enigma and who seemed to me the hero of some mysterious tale. He liked me; at any rate, it was only with me that he abandoned his usual biting mockery and discussed various subjects with simple-heartedness and extraordinary charm. But after that unfortunate evening, the thought that his honor was stained and by his own fault had not been washed clean never left me and prevented me from behaving with him as before; I was ashamed to look at him. Silvio was too intelligent and too experienced not to notice it and not to guess the reason for it. It seemed to pain him; at any rate I noticed a couple of times that he wished to talk with me; but I avoided such occasions, and Silvio gave it up. After that I saw him only in the presence of my comrades, and our former candid conversations ceased.

The distracted inhabitants of capitals have no idea of many impressions well known to the inhabitants of villages or small towns, for instance, waiting for mail day. On Tuesdays and Fridays our regimental office was filled with officers: one was waiting for money, another for a letter, yet another for newspapers. Envelopes were usually opened then and there, news was exchanged, and the office presented a picture of great animation. Silvio had his letters addressed to our regiment, and he was usually to be found there. Once he was handed an envelope that he tore open with an air of the greatest impatience. As he skimmed the letter, his eyes flashed. The officers, each occupied with his own letters, did not notice anything. "Gentlemen," Silvio said to them, "circumstances demand that I absent myself at once; I am leaving tonight; I hope you will not refuse to dine with me for a last time. I shall expect you, too," he went on, turning to me. "Come without fail." With those words, he hurriedly left, and, having agreed to meet at Silvio's, each of us went his own way.

I came to Silvio's at the appointed time and found almost all our regiment there. His belongings were already packed; there were only the bare, bullet-riddled walls. We sat down at the table. The host was in extremely high spirits, and his good cheer soon became general. Corks popped every minute, glasses foamed and fizzed nonstop, and with all possible zeal we wished the departing man a good journey and all the best. It was late at night when we rose from the table. As we were going for our caps, Silvio, saying good-bye to everyone, took me by the arm and stopped me at the very moment I was preparing to leave. "I must talk to you," he said softly. I stayed.

The guests were gone. We two remained alone, sat facing each other, and silently lit our pipes. Silvio was preoccupied; there was no trace left of his convulsive gaiety. A grim pallor, flashing eyes, and the thick smoke coming from his mouth gave him the look of a real devil. Several minutes passed, and Silvio broke the silence.

"You and I may never see each other again," he said to me. "Before we part, I would like to have a talk with you. You might have noticed that I have little respect for other people's opinion of me; but I like you, and I feel it would be painful for me to leave an unjust impression in your mind."

He paused and began to refill his burnt-out pipe; I was silent and lowered my eyes.

"You found it strange," he went on, "that I did not demand satisfaction from that drunken madcap R—. You'll agree that, having the right to choose weapons, his life was in my hands, and mine was almost safe. I could ascribe my restraint to magnanimity alone, but I don't want to lie. If I could have punished R— without any risk to my life, I would not have forgiven him for anything."

I looked at Silvio in amazement. This confession totally disconcerted me. Silvio went on.

"Precisely so: I have no right to risk my life. Six years ago I was slapped in the face, and my enemy is still alive."

My curiosity was greatly aroused.

"You didn't fight with him?" I asked. "Circumstances must have separated you?"

"I did fight with him," Silvio replied, "and here is a souvenir of our duel."

Silvio stood up and took from a box a red cap with a gold tassel and galloon (what the French call a *bonnet de police*). He put it on. There was a bullet hole about two inches above the brow.

"You know," Silvio went on, "that I served in the * * * hussar regiment. My character is familiar to you: I am accustomed to taking first place, but in my youth it was my passion. In our time rowdiness was in fashion: I was the foremost rowdy in the army. We boasted of our drunkenness: I outdrank the famous Burtsov, whose praises were sung by Denis Davydov.[3] Duels went on constantly in our regiment: I was in all of them, either as a second or as a participant. My comrades adored me, and the regimental commanders, who were constantly being replaced, looked upon me as a necessary evil.

"I was quietly (or not so quietly) enjoying my reputation, when a young man from a rich and noble family joined our regiment (I don't want to say his name). Never in all my born days had I met a more fortunate and brilliant fellow! Picture to yourself youth, intelligence, good looks, the wildest gaiety, the most carefree courage, a big name, money that he didn't bother to count and that never came to an end, and imagine the effect he was bound to make among us. My primacy was shaken. Enticed by my reputation, he began to seek my friendship; but I received him coldly, and he drew away from me without any regret. I came to hate him. His successes in the regiment and in the society of women drove me to utter despair. I began to seek a quarrel with him. To my epigrams he responded with epigrams which always seemed to me more unexpected and witty than mine, and which were certainly more amusing: he joked, while I was malicious. Once, finally, at a Polish landowner's ball, seeing him the object of attention of all the ladies, and especially of the hostess, with whom I had a liaison, I spoke some crude banality into his ear. He flared up and slapped me. We rushed for our swords; the ladies all swooned; we were dragged apart, and that same night we went out to fight a duel.

"It was at dawn. I stood at the appointed place with my three seconds. With indescribable impatience, I awaited my opponent. The spring sun rose, and its heat could already be felt. I saw him in the distance. He was coming on foot, his jacket hung on his sword, accompanied by one second. We went to meet him. He approached, holding his cap, which was full of cherries. The seconds measured out twelve paces for us. I was supposed to shoot first: but my spiteful agitation was so strong that I could not count on the steadiness of my hand, and, to give myself time to cool off, I offered him the first shot. My opponent did not accept. We decided to draw lots: the first number went to him, the eternal favorite of fortune. He aimed and shot a hole in my cap. It was my turn. His life was finally in my hands; I looked at him greedily, trying to catch at least a trace of uneasiness. He stood facing my pistol, picking ripe cherries from his cap and spitting out the stones, which landed at my feet. His indifference infuriated me. What's the use of taking his life, I thought, if he doesn't value it at all? A malicious thought flashed through my mind. I lowered the pistol.

"'It seems your mind is not on death now,' I said. 'You're having breakfast. I wouldn't want to hinder you.'

"'You're not hindering me in the least,' he retorted. 'Feel free to shoot. But, anyhow, suit yourself. Your shot remains yours; I'm always ready to be at your service.'

"I turned to my seconds, announced that I had no intention of shooting right then, and with that the duel ended.

"I retired from the army and withdrew to this little town. Since then not a single day has gone by that I have not thought of revenge. Now my hour has come . . ."

Silvio took from his pocket the letter he had received in the morning and gave it to me to read. Someone (apparently his agent) wrote from Moscow that *a certain person* would soon be entering into lawful matrimony with a young and beautiful girl.

"You can guess who that *certain person* is," said Silvio. "I am going to Moscow. We shall see whether he accepts death before his wedding with the same indifference as when he awaited it over the cherries!"

With those words, Silvio stood up, flung his cap on the floor, and started pacing the room like a tiger in its cage. I listened to him without moving: strange, contradictory feelings stirred in me.

A servant came in and announced that the horses were ready. Silvio gripped my hand firmly; we kissed. He got into the cart, where two trunks lay, one with pistols, the other with his belongings. We said good-bye once more, and the horses galloped off.

II

Several years went by, and domestic circumstances forced me to settle in a poor little village of the N— district. Busy with my estate, I never stopped secretly sighing for my former noisy and carefree life. Hardest of all was accustoming myself to spending the autumn and winter evenings in complete solitude. I still managed to drag out the time till dinner, talking with the village headman, riding around the farm works, or visiting the new installations; but as soon as it began to get dark, I simply did not know what to do with myself. The small number of books I found in the bottoms of cupboards and in the storeroom I already knew by heart. The housekeeper Kirilovna had told me all the tales she was able to recall; the village women's songs wearied me. I took to unsweetened liqueurs, but they gave me a headache; and, I confess, I was afraid of turning into a *drunkard from grief*, that is, a most *grievous* drunkard, of which I saw many examples in our district. I had no near neighbors except for two or three *grievous* ones, whose conversation consisted mostly of hiccups and sighs. Solitude was more tolerable.

Three miles away from me there was a rich estate that belonged to Countess B—; but no one lived there except the steward, and the countess had visited her estate only once, in the first year of her marriage, and had stayed no more than a month. However, in the second spring of my reclusion, a rumor went around that the countess and her husband were coming to her estate for the summer. In fact, they arrived at the beginning of June.

The arrival of a rich neighbor marks an important epoch for country dwellers. Landowners and their servants discuss it for two months before and three years after. As for me, I must confess that the news of the arrival of a young and beautiful neighbor had a strong effect on me; I burned with impatience to see her, and so, on the first Sunday after their arrival, I went to the village of * * * after dinner to introduce myself to their excellencies as their nearest neighbor and most humble servant.

A footman led me to the count's study and went to announce me. The vast study was decorated with all possible luxury; the walls were lined with bookcases, with a bronze bust on top of each; above the marble fireplace was a wide mirror; the floor was covered with green felt and overlaid with carpets. Having lost the habit of luxury in my poor corner, and not having seen other people's wealth for a long time, I grew timid and waited for the count with a certain trepidation, the way a provincial petitioner awaits the appearance of a minister. The door opened, and a very handsome man of about thirty-two came in. The count approached me with an air of openness and friendliness; I tried to take heart and was about to introduce myself, but he forestalled me. We sat down. His conversation, free and amiable, soon dispelled my wild shyness; I was already beginning to return to my normal state, when the countess suddenly came in, and I was overcome by a greater confusion than before. She was indeed a beauty. The count introduced me; I wanted to seem free and easy, but the more I tried to assume an air of nonchalance, the more awkward I felt. To give me time to recover and accustom myself to my new acquaintances, they started talking to each other, treating me as a good neighbor and without ceremony. Meanwhile I started pacing up and down, examining the books and paintings. I am not a connoisseur of paintings, but one of them caught my attention. It represented some view of Switzerland; but what struck me in it was not the picture, but the fact that it had been pierced by two bullets in the same spot.

"That's fine shooting," I said, turning to the count.

"Yes," he said, "quite remarkable. Are you a good shot?" he went on.

"Fairly good," I replied, glad that the conversation had finally touched upon a subject close to me. "I wouldn't miss a card at thirty paces—with familiar pistols, of course."

"Really?" said the countess, with a look of great attentiveness. "And you, my love, can you hit a card at thirty paces?"

"Someday we'll give it a try," replied the count. "In my time I wasn't a bad shot; but it's four years now since I've touched a pistol."

"Oh," I remarked, "in that case I'll wager Your Excellency couldn't hit a card even from twenty paces: a pistol calls for daily practice. I know that from experience. I was reckoned one of the best shots in our regiment. Once it happened that I didn't touch a pistol for a whole month: mine were being repaired. And what do you think, Your Excellency? The first time I tried shooting after that, I missed a bottle four times in a row at twenty-five paces. We had a captain, a wit, an amusing fellow; he happened to be there and said to me: 'It's obvious, brother, your hand refuses to raise itself against a bottle.' No, Your Excellency, you mustn't neglect that exercise, or else you'll lose the habit just like that. The best shot I ever happened to meet used to practice at least three times before dinner every day. It was a habit with him, like a glass of vodka."

The count and countess were glad that I had gotten to talking.

"And how did he shoot?" the count asked me.

"Here's how, Your Excellency: he would see a fly land on the wall—you laugh, Countess? By God, it's true. He would see the fly and shout, 'Kuzka, my pistol!' Kuzka brings him a loaded pistol. He goes—bang!—and the fly is squashed into the wall!"

"That's astonishing!" said the count. "And what was his name?"

"Silvio, Your Excellency."

"Silvio!" cried the count, jumping from his seat. "You knew Silvio?"

"What else, Your Excellency? We were friends; he was treated by our regiment as one of our own, a comrade; but it's five years now since I've had any news of him. So that means Your Excellency knew him, too?"

"Knew him, yes, I knew him well. Did he never tell you . . . but no, I suppose not. Did he never tell you about one very strange incident?"

"Does Your Excellency mean the slap in the face he received from some scapegrace at a ball?"

"And did he tell you the name of that scapegrace?"

"No, Your Excellency, he didn't . . . Ah, Your Excellency," I went on, guessing the truth, "forgive me . . . I didn't know . . . Can it have been you?"

"I myself," the count replied, looking extremely upset, "and the bullet-pierced painting is a souvenir of our last meeting—"

"Ah, my dear," said the countess, "for God's sake don't tell about it; I'd be frightened to listen."

"No," the count objected, "I'll tell it all. He knows how I offended his friend; let him learn how Silvio took revenge on me."

The count moved an armchair for me, and with the liveliest curiosity I listened to the following story.

"Five years ago I got married. The first month, the 'honey-moon,'* I spent here in this village. I owe to this house the best moments of my life and one of the most oppressive memories.

---

* In English in the original. *Translator.*

"One evening we went out riding together. My wife's horse started to balk; she got frightened, handed me the reins, and went home on foot. I rode ahead. In the yard I saw a traveling cart; I was told that there was a man sitting in my study who did not want to give his name, but simply said he had business with me. I went into that room and saw in the darkness a man covered with dust and overgrown with beard; he was standing here, by the fireplace. I went up to him, trying to recall his features.

"'Don't you recognize me, Count?' he said in a trembling voice.

"'Silvio!' I cried, and I confess, I felt my hair suddenly stand on end.

"'That's right,' he went on. 'I owe you a shot; I've come to discharge my pistol. Are you ready?'

"The pistol was sticking out of his side pocket. I measured off twelve paces and stood there in the corner, begging him to shoot quickly, before my wife came back. He delayed—he asked for light. Candles were brought. I shut the door, gave orders to let no one in, and again begged him to shoot. He drew his pistol and took aim . . . I counted the seconds . . . I thought of her . . . A terrible minute went by! Silvio lowered his arm.

"'I'm sorry,' he said, 'that the pistol isn't loaded with cherry stones . . . bullets are heavy. I keep thinking that what we're doing is not a duel, but murder: I'm not used to aiming at an unarmed man. Let's start over; we'll draw lots for who shoots first.'

"My head was spinning . . . It seems I did not agree . . . Finally we loaded another pistol; we rolled up two pieces of paper; he put them in the cap I had once shot through; again I drew the first number.

"'You're devilishly lucky, Count,' he said with a grin that I will never forget. I don't understand what happened to me and how he forced me into it . . . but—I shot and hit this painting." (The count pointed his finger at the hole in the painting; his face was burning like fire; the countess was paler than her own handkerchief: I couldn't help crying out.)

"I shot," the count went on, "and, thank God, I missed. Then Silvio—he was truly terrible at that moment—Silvio began to take aim at me. Suddenly the door opened, Masha runs in and throws herself on my neck with a shriek. Her presence gave me back all my courage.

"'My dear,' I said to her, 'don't you see we're joking? How frightened you are! Go, drink a glass of water, and come back to us; I'll introduce you to my old friend and comrade.'

"Masha still did not believe it.

"'Tell me, is my husband speaking the truth?' she said, turning to the dreadful Silvio. 'Is it true that you're both joking?'

"'He's always joking, Countess,' Silvio replied. 'He once slapped me in the face for a joke; for a joke he shot a hole in this cap of mine; for a joke he missed hitting me a moment ago. Now I, too, feel like joking a bit . . .'

"With those words, he was about to take aim at me . . . in front of her! Masha threw herself at his feet.

"'Get up, Masha, shame on you!' I cried in fury. 'And you, sir, will you kindly stop taunting the poor woman? Are you going to shoot, or not?'

"'I won't,' Silvio replied. 'I'm satisfied: I've seen your confusion, your dismay; I made you shoot at me, for me that's enough. You will remember me. I leave you to your conscience.' He was on his way out, but stopped in the doorway, glanced at the painting I had shot through, shot at it almost without aiming, and vanished. My wife lay in a swoon; my servants did not dare stop him and watched him with horror. He went out to the porch, called the coachman, and drove off before I had time to come to my senses."

The count fell silent. It was thus that I learned the end of the story, whose beginning had once struck me so much. I never met its hero again. They say that, during the uprising of Alexander Ypsilanti, Silvio led a detachment of Hetairists and was killed at the battle of Skulyani.[4]

THE BLIZZARD

Over the rough road steeds go racing,
Trampling the deep snow . . .
There to one side is God's church
Standing all alone.

. . . .

Suddenly a blizzard fills the air;
Snow falls thick and heavy;
A black raven, a whistling wing,
Hovers above the sledge;
Its prophetic cry gives voice to sorrow!
The steeds go dashing on
Peering into the darkling distance;
Their manes fly in the wind . . .

ZHUKOVSKY[1]

At the end of the year 1811, a memorable epoch for us all, the good Gavrila Gavrilovich R— was living on his estate of Nenaradovo. He was famous throughout the district for his hospitality and warm-heartedness; neighbors constantly came to him to eat, to drink, to gamble away five kopecks playing Boston with his wife, Praskovya Petrovna, and some to gaze at their daughter, Marya Gavrilovna, a slender, pale, and seventeen-year-old girl. She was considered a rich bride, and many a man intended her for himself or for one of his sons.

Marya Gavrilovna had been brought up on French novels and, consequently, was in love. The object of her choice was a poor army ensign on leave in his village. It goes without saying that the young man was burning with an equal passion and that the parents of his beloved, having noticed their mutual inclination, forbade their daughter even to think of him, and received him worse than a retired assessor.

Our lovers were in correspondence, and each day met alone in the pine wood or by the old chapel. There they swore eternal love to each other, bemoaned their fate, and discussed various possibilities. Corresponding and conversing in this way, they arrived (quite naturally) at the following reasoning: Since we cannot draw a breath without each other, and the will of cruel parents is an obstacle to our happiness, can we not get along without them? Of course, this happy thought first occurred to the young man, and it greatly pleased the romantic imagination of Marya Gavrilovna.

Winter came and put an end to their trysts; but their correspondence became all the livelier. In every letter Vladimir Nikolaevich implored her to entrust herself to him, to get married in secret, to hide away for some time, then to throw themselves at the feet of her parents, who of course would be moved in the end by the heroic constancy and unhappiness of the lovers, and would surely say: "Children, come to our arms!"

Marya Gavrilovna hesitated for a long time; many plans for the elopement were rejected. She finally agreed to one: on the appointed day she would not have supper and would withdraw to her room under the pretext of a headache. Her maid was in on the conspiracy; they would both go out to the garden through the back door, find a sledge ready behind the garden, get into it and drive three miles from Nenaradovo to the village of Zhadrino, straight to the church, where Vladimir would be waiting for them.

On the eve of the decisive day, Marya Gavrilovna did not sleep all night; she packed, bundled up her linen and clothes, wrote a long letter to a certain sentimental girlfriend of hers, another to her parents. She said good-bye to them in the most touching expressions, excused her act by the invincible power of passion, and finished by saying that she would count it as the most blessed moment of her life when she would be allowed to throw herself at the feet of her dearest parents. Having sealed her letter with a Tula seal that bore the image of two flaming hearts with an appropriate inscription,[2] she threw herself on the bed before dawn and dozed off; but here, too, terrible dreams kept waking her up. First it seemed to her that, just as she was getting into the sledge to drive off to her wedding, her father stopped her, dragged her over the snow with agonizing speed, and threw her into a dark, bottomless dungeon . . . and she went flying down headlong with an indescribable sinking of the heart. Then she saw Vladimir lying on the grass, pale, bloody. Dying, he begged her in a piercing voice to make haste and marry him . . . Other shapeless, senseless visions raced before her one after another. At last she got up, paler than usual and with an unfeigned headache. Her father and mother noticed her agitation; their tender concern and ceaseless questions—"What's the matter, Masha? Are you unwell, Masha?"—tore her heart. She tried to calm them, to look cheerful, and could not. Evening came. The thought that this was the last time she would see the day off amidst her family wrung her heart. She was barely alive. She secretly took leave of all the persons, of all the objects around her.

Supper was served; her heart began to pound violently. In a trembling voice she announced that she did not want to eat and started saying goodnight to her father and mother. They kissed her and, as usual, gave her their blessing: she all but wept. Coming to her room, she collapsed on an armchair and dissolved in tears. Her maid urged her to calm down and take heart. Everything was ready. In half an hour Masha was to leave forever her parental home, her room, her quiet maidenly life . . . . Outside there was a blizzard; the wind howled, the shutters shook and rattled; everything seemed to her a threat and an omen of sorrow. Soon the whole house became quiet and fell asleep. Masha wrapped herself in a shawl, put on a warm coat, picked up her box, and went out to the back porch. Behind her the maid carried her two bundles. They went down to the garden. The blizzard had not let up; the wind blew in her face, as if trying to stop the young criminal. She was barely able to reach the end of the garden. The sledge was waiting for them on the road. The chilled horses would not stand still; Vladimir's coachman walked about in front of the shafts, restraining their restiveness. He helped the girl and her maid to seat themselves and stow the bundles and the box, took the reins, and the horses flew off. Having entrusted the young lady to the care of fate and the skill of the coachman Tereshka, let us now turn to our young lover.

Vladimir spent the whole day driving around. In the morning he went to see the Zhadrino priest; he had a hard time persuading him; then he went looking for witnesses among the neighboring landowners. The first one he presented himself to, the retired forty-year-old ensign Dravin, accepted willingly. This adventure, he assured him, was reminiscent of the old days and his hussar pranks. He persuaded Vladimir to stay for dinner and assured him that there would be no trouble finding the other two witnesses. In fact, right after dinner the surveyor Schmidt appeared in his moustaches and spurs, and the son of the police chief, a sixteen-year-old boy who had just joined the uhlans. They not only accepted Vladimir's proposal, but even swore they were ready to sacrifice their lives for him. Vladimir embraced them rapturously and went home to make ready.

By then it had long been dark. He sent his trusty Tereshka to Nenaradovo with his troika and with detailed, thorough instructions, and for himself ordered a small one-horse sledge hitched up, and alone, without a coachman, set out for Zhadrino, where Marya Gavrilovna was to arrive in some two hours. He knew the way—it was at most a twenty-minute drive.

But Vladimir had barely reached the fields outside the village when the wind picked up and such a blizzard set in that he could see nothing. In one minute the road was buried; the surroundings disappeared in a dim, yellowish murk, through which white snowflakes flew; the sky merged with the earth. Vladimir ended up in a field and tried in vain to get back to the road; the horse walked at random and kept going up onto drifts, then sinking down into holes; the sledge kept overturning; Vladimir tried only not to lose the right direction. But it seemed to him that more than half an hour had already gone by, and he had not yet reached the wood of Zhadrino. Ten more minutes went by; the wood was still not in sight. Vladimir drove over a field crossed by deep gullies. The blizzard did not let up, the sky did not clear. His horse began to tire, and he himself was dripping with sweat, even though he was constantly up to his waist in snow.

Finally he saw that he was going the wrong way. Vladimir stopped: he began to think, to recall, to consider, and became convinced that he should have turned to the right. He drove to the right. His horse could barely walk. He had already been traveling for more than an hour. Zhadrino had to be close by. But he drove and drove, and there was no end to the field. It was all snowdrifts and gullies; the sledge kept overturning, he kept righting it. Time passed; Vladimir began to worry greatly.

Finally something showed blackly to one side. Vladimir turned that way. Coming closer, he saw a wood. Thank God, he thought, it's close now. He skirted the wood, hoping to fall at once upon the familiar road or to circle the wood: Zhadrino was just beyond it. Soon he found the road and entered the darkness of the trees, bared by winter. The wind could not rage here; the road was smooth; the horse took heart, and Vladimir felt more calm.

But he drove and drove, and there was no sign of Zhadrino; there was no end to the wood. Vladimir realized with horror that he had ended up in an unfamiliar forest. Despair overcame him. He whipped up the horse; the poor animal went into a canter, but soon became tired and after a quarter of an hour slowed to a walk, despite all the efforts of the unfortunate Vladimir.

The trees gradually began to thin out, and Vladimir emerged from the forest. There was no sign of Zhadrino. It must have been around midnight. Tears poured from his eyes; he drove on at random. The weather quieted down, the clouds scattered, before him lay a plain covered with a white, undulating carpet. The night was quite clear. He saw not far away a little village of four or five houses. Vladimir drove there. At the first hut he jumped out of the sledge, ran to the window, and started to knock. After several minutes a wooden shutter rose and an old man stuck out his gray beard.

"What do you want?"

"Is it far to Zhadrino?"

"Far to Zhadrino?"

"Yes, yes! Is it far?"

"Not so far, maybe seven miles."

At that reply, Vladimir seized himself by the hair and stood motionless, like a man condemned to death.

"So where are you from?" the old man went on. Vladimir had no heart to answer questions.

"Listen, old man," he said, "can you get me horses for Zhadrino?"

"What have we got for horses?" the muzhik replied.

"Might I at least have a guide? I'll pay whatever he likes."

"Wait," said the old man, lowering the shutter, "I'll send you my son. He'll take you there."

Vladimir started to wait. A minute had not passed before he began to knock again. The shutter rose, the beard appeared.

"What do you want?"

"Where is your son?"

"He'll be right out, he's putting his boots on. Maybe you're chilly? Come in and warm up."

"No, thank you, send your son out quickly."

The gate creaked; a lad with a cudgel came out and walked ahead, now showing, now searching for the road, buried under snowdrifts.

"What time is it?" asked Vladimir.

"It'll be dawn soon," the young muzhik replied. Vladimir did not say another word.

The cocks were crowing and it was already light when they reached Zhadrino. The church was locked. Vladimir paid his guide and drove to the priest's house. His troika was not in the yard. What news awaited him!

But let us return to the good Nenaradovo landowners and see what is going on there.

Nothing.

The old folk woke up and came out to the drawing room. Gavrila Gavrilovich in a nightcap and flannelette jacket, Praskovya Petrovna in a quilted dressing gown. The samovar was brought, and Gavrila Gavrilovich sent a girl to find out about Marya Gavrilovna's health and how she had slept. The girl came back, announcing that the young lady had slept badly, but that she was better now and would presently come to the drawing room. Indeed, the door opened, and Marya Gavrilovna came to greet her papa and mama.

"How's your head, Masha?" asked Gavrila Gavrilovich.

"Better, papa," Masha replied.

"You must have had fume poisoning yesterday, Masha," said Praskovya Petrovna.

"Perhaps, mama," said Masha.

The day passed well enough, but during the night Masha fell ill. They sent to town for the doctor. He came towards evening and found the patient delirious. She had a high fever, and for two weeks the poor patient lay on the brink of the grave.

No one in the house knew about the proposed elopement. The letters written the day before were burned; her maid said nothing to anyone, fearing the masters' wrath. The priest, the retired ensign, the moustachioed surveyor, and the little uhlan were discreet, and not without reason. Tereshka the coachman never gave away anything unnecessary, even when drunk. Thus the secret was kept by more than half a dozen conspirators. But Marya Gavrilovna herself gave her secret away in her ceaseless raving. However, her words were so incongruous that her mother, who never left her bedside, could understand from them only that her daughter was mortally in love with Vladimir Nikolaevich and that love was probably the cause of her illness. She consulted with her husband, with some neighbors, and in the end they all unanimously decided that this was clearly Marya Gavrilovna's destiny, that you can't escape the one you're meant for, that poverty is no crime, that you live with a man, not with his money, and so on. Moral sayings are surprisingly useful on occasions when we can think up little to justify ourselves on our own.

Meanwhile the young lady was beginning to recover. Vladimir had not been seen in Gavrila Gavrilovich's house for a long time. He was afraid of meeting the usual reception. They decided to send for him and announce to him an unexpected blessing: their acceptance of the marriage. But what was the amazement of the Nenaradovo landowners when, in response to their invitation, they received a half-crazed letter from him! He announced to them that he would never set foot in their house, and asked them to forget a poor wretch for whom death remained the only hope. Some days later they learned that Vladimir had left for the army. It was 1812.[3]

For a long time they did not dare to inform the convalescent Masha of this. She never mentioned Vladimir. Several months later, finding his name among those distinguished and gravely wounded at Borodino,[4] she swooned, and they feared her delirium might return. But, thank God, the swoon had no consequences.

Another sorrow visited her: Gavrila Gavrilovich passed away, leaving her heiress to the entire estate. But the inheritance was no comfort to her; she sincerely shared the grief of poor Praskovya Petrovna, and swore never to part from her; the two women left Nenaradovo, a place of sorrowful memories, and went to live on their estate at * * *.

There, too, wooers swarmed around the sweet and rich young lady; but she gave no one the slightest hope. Her mother occasionally tried to persuade her to choose a companion; Marya Gavrilovna shook her head and grew pensive. Vladimir was no longer of this world: he had died in Moscow, on the eve of the French entry. His memory seemed sacred to Masha; at any rate she cherished everything that could remind her of him: the books he had once read, his drawings, the music and verses he had copied out for her. The neighbors, learning of all this, marveled at her constancy and waited with curiosity for the hero who would finally triumph over the sorrowing fidelity of this virginal Artemisia.[5]

Meanwhile, the war had ended in glory. Our regiments were returning from abroad. People ran to meet them. For music they played conquered songs: "Vive Henri-Quatre," Tyrolean waltzes, and arias from *Joconde*.[6] Officers who went off on campaign as all but boys came back matured by the air of battle and hung with medals. Soldiers talked mer-

rily among themselves, constantly mixing German and French words
into their speech. An unforgettable time! A time of glory and rapture!
How strongly the Russian heart beat at the word "fatherland"! How
sweet were the tears of reunion! With what unanimity we combined
the feeling of national pride with love for the sovereign! And for him,
what a moment it was!

The women, the Russian women, were incomparable then. Their
usual coldness vanished. Their rapture was truly intoxicating when,
meeting the victors, they shouted: *Hurrah!*

And into the air their bonnets threw.[7]

Who among the officers of that time would not confess that it was to
the Russian woman that he owed his best, his most precious reward? . . .

At that brilliant time Marya Gavrilovna was living with her mother
in * * * province and did not see how the two capitals[8] celebrated the
return of the troops. But in the provincial towns and villages the general rapture was perhaps still stronger. The appearance of an officer in
those places was a real triumph for him, and a lover in a frock coat had
a hard time in his vicinity.

We have already said that, despite her coldness, Marya Gavrilovna
was as surrounded by suitors as before. But they all had to step back
when the wounded hussar colonel Burmin appeared in her castle, with
a St. George in his buttonhole[9] and with an "interesting pallor," as the
local young ladies used to say. He was about twenty-six. He came on
leave to his estate, which was next to Marya Gavrilovna's village. Marya
Gavrilovna singled him out at once. In his presence, her habitual pensiveness brightened up. It could not be said that she flirted with him;
but a poet, observing her behavior, would have said:

Se amor non è, che dunque? . . . [10]

Burmin was indeed a very nice young man. His was just the sort
of mind that women like: a mind decorous, observant, without any
pretensions, and light-heartedly mocking. His conduct with Marya
Gavrilovna was simple and unconstrained; but whatever she said or
did, his soul and his gaze followed her. He seemed to be of a quiet and
modest disposition, but rumor averred that he had once been a ter-

rible scapegrace, though that did him no harm in the eyes of Marya Gavrilovna, who (like all young ladies generally) took pleasure in excusing pranks that betrayed a boldness and fervor of character.

But most of all . . . (more than his tenderness, more than his pleasant conversation, more than his interesting pallor, more than his bandaged arm) most of all it was the young hussar's silence that piqued her curiosity and imagination. She could not help realizing that he liked her very much; probably he, too, with his intelligence and experience, had already been able to notice that she had singled him out: how was it, then, that until now she had not seen him at her feet and had not yet heard his declaration? What held him back? The timidity inseparable from true love, pride, the teasing of a clever philanderer? It was a riddle to her. Having given it a good deal of thought, she decided that timidity was the only cause of it, and proposed to encourage him by greater attentiveness and, depending on the circumstances, even by tenderness. She prepared the most unexpected denouement, and awaited with impatience the moment of a romantic declaration. Mystery, of whatever sort it might be, is always a burden for the feminine heart. Her military operation had the desired effect: at any rate Burmin fell into such pensiveness and his dark eyes rested on Marya Gavrilovna with such fire that the decisive moment seemed to be near. The neighbors spoke of the wedding as of an already settled matter, and the good Praskovya Petrovna rejoiced that her daughter had finally found herself a worthy match.

The old woman was sitting alone in the drawing room one day, laying out a game of *grande patience*,[11] when Burmin came into the room and at once inquired about Marya Gavrilovna.

"She's in the garden," the old woman replied. "Go to her, and I'll wait for you here." Burmin went, and the old woman crossed herself and thought, "Maybe the matter will be settled today!"

Burmin found Marya Gavrilovna by the pond, under a willow tree, with a book in her hand and wearing a white dress, a veritable heroine of a novel. After the initial questions, Marya Gavrilovna deliberately stopped keeping up the conversation, thus intensifying the mutual embarrassment, which could only be dispelled by a sudden and resolute declaration. And so it happened: Burmin, feeling the difficulty of his position, declared that he had long been seeking a chance to open his heart to her, and asked for a moment of attention. Marya Gavrilovna closed the book and lowered her eyes in a sign of consent.

"I love you," said Burmin, "I love you passionately . . ." (Marya Gavrilovna blushed and lowered her head still more.) "I have acted imprudently, giving myself up to the sweet habit, the habit of seeing you and hearing you every day . . ." (Marya Gavrilovna recalled the first letter of St. Preux.[12]) "Now it is already too late to resist my fate; your memory, your dear, incomparable image, will henceforth be the torment and delight of my life; but it still remains for me to fulfill a painful duty, to reveal to you a terrible secret, and to place an insurmountable obstacle between us . . ."

"It has always existed," Marya Gavrilovna interrupted with animation. "I could never have been your wife . . ."

"I know," he replied softly. "I know that you once loved, but death and three years of mourning . . . My good, dear Marya Gavrilovna! Do not try to deprive me of my last consolation: the thought that you could have agreed to make my happiness, if . . . don't speak, for God's sake, don't speak. You torment me. Yes, I know, I feel that you could be mine, but—I am the most wretched of creatures . . . I am married!"

Marya Gavrilovna glanced up at him in astonishment.

"I am married," Burmin went on. "I've been married for four years now, and I don't know who my wife is, or where she is, or whether we are ever to see each other!"

"What are you saying?" Marya Gavrilovna exclaimed. "This is so strange! Go on; I'll tell you afterwards . . . but go on, if you please!"

"At the beginning of 1812," said Burmin, "I was hurrying to Vilno, where our regiment was. Coming to a posting station late one night, I ordered horses to be hitched up quickly, when a terrible blizzard suddenly arose, and the stationmaster and the coachmen advised me to wait. I heeded their advice, but an incomprehensible restlessness came over me; it seemed as if someone was pushing me. Meanwhile the blizzard did not let up. I couldn't help myself, ordered them again to hitch up, and drove off into the storm. The coachman took it into his head to go along the river, which was supposed to shorten our way by two miles. The banks were snowbound; the coachman drove past the place where he should have turned onto the road, and as a result we found ourselves in unknown parts. The storm did not let up. I saw a little light and told the coachman to go there. We came to a village; there was a light in the wooden church. The church was open and several sledges stood inside the fence; people were moving about on the porch.

"'This way! This way!' several voices shouted. I told my coachman to go there. " 'For pity's sake, why are you so late?' somebody said to me. 'The bride has fainted; the priest doesn't know what to do; we were about to go back. Get out quickly.' I silently jumped out of the sledge and went into the church, dimly lit by two or three candles. A girl was sitting on a bench in a dark corner of the church; another was rubbing her temples.

" 'Thank God,' she said, 'you've come at last. You were nearly the death of the young miss.'

"The old priest came to me and asked, 'Shall we begin?'

" 'Begin, begin, father,' I replied distractedly.

"The girl was helped to her feet. Not bad looking, I thought . . . Incomprehensible, unpardonable frivolity . . . I stood beside her at the altar; the priest was in a hurry; the three men and the maid supported the bride and were occupied only with her. We were married.

" 'Kiss now,' they said to us. My wife turned her pale face to me. I was about to kiss her . . . She cried out:

" 'Aie! It's not him, not him!' and fell unconscious.

"The witnesses fixed their frightened eyes on me. I turned, walked out of the church unhindered, threw myself into my kibitka, and shouted: 'Drive!' "

"My God!" cried Marya Gavrilovna. "And you don't know what became of your poor wife?"

"No, I don't," replied Burmin. "I don't know the name of the village where I was married; I don't remember what station I stopped at. I ascribed so little importance to my criminal prank at the time that, having driven away from the church, I fell asleep and woke up the next morning, already three stations away. The servant who was with me then died in the campaign, so that I also have no hope of finding the woman on whom I played such a cruel joke and who is now so cruelly revenged."

"My God, my God!" said Marya Gavrilovna, seizing his hand. "So that was you! And you don't recognize me?"

Burmin went pale . . . and threw himself at her feet . . .

THE COFFIN-MAKER

> Do we not gaze every day on coffins,
> The gray hair of the aging universe?

DERZHAVIN[1]

The last belongings of the coffin-maker Adrian Prokhorov were piled
on the hearse, and for the fourth time the scrawny pair dragged it from
Basmannaya to Nikitskaya Street, where the coffin-maker was moving
with all his household. Having locked up the shop, he nailed to the
gate a notice that the house was for sale or rent, and went on foot to
his new home. Approaching the little yellow house that had so long
captivated his imagination, and that he had finally purchased for a considerable sum, the old coffin-maker felt with surprise that his heart
was not rejoicing. Stepping across the unfamiliar threshold and finding
turmoil in his new dwelling, he sighed for the decrepit hovel, where in
the course of eighteen years everything had been managed in the strict-
est order; he started scolding his two daughters and the maidservant
for being slow, and set about helping them himself. Soon order was
established; the icon stand with its icons, the cupboard with its dishes,
the table, the sofa, and the bed took up their appointed corners in the
back room; the kitchen and the living room were filled with the master's handiwork: coffins of all colors and sizes, as well as cupboards with
mourning hats, mantles, and torches. Over the gate rose a signboard
depicting a stout Cupid with an upside down torch in his hand, with
the inscription: "Plain and painted coffins sold and upholstered here,
old ones also rented out and repaired." The girls went to their room.
Adrian took a turn around his dwelling, sat down by the window, and
ordered the samovar prepared.

The enlightened reader knows that Shakespeare and Walter Scott
both presented their gravediggers as merry and jocular people, in order
to strike our imaginations the more forcefully by this contrast. Out of
respect for the truth we cannot follow their example and are forced
to admit that our coffin-maker's disposition suited his gloomy profes-

62 NOVELS, TALES, JOURNEYS

sion perfectly. Adrian Prokhorov was habitually morose and pensive. He broke his silence only to chide his daughters when he found them gazing idly out the window at passersby, or to ask an exorbitant price for his products from those who had the misfortune (or sometimes the pleasure) of needing them. And so Adrian, sitting by the window and drinking his seventh cup of tea, was immersed in his habitual melancholy reflections. He was thinking about the pouring rain which, a week earlier, had met the funeral of a retired brigadier just at the city gates. Many mantles had shrunk because of it, many hats had been deformed. He foresaw inevitable expenses, for his old stock of funerary vestments had fallen into a pitiful state. He hoped to make up for the loss on the old merchant woman Tryukhina, who had been at death's door for about a year already. But Tryukhina was dying in Razgulyai, and Prokhorov feared that her heirs, despite their promise, would be too lazy to send so far for him and would make a deal with a contractor closer by.

These reflections were unexpectedly interrupted by three Masonic knocks on the door.

"Who's there?" asked the coffin-maker.

The door opened, and a man, who could be recognized at first glance as a German artisan, came into the room and with a cheerful air approached the coffin-maker.

"Forgive me, kind neighbor," he said in that Russian parlance which to this day we cannot hear without laughing, "forgive me for bothering you . . . I wished quickly to make your acquaintance. I am a shoemaker, my name is Gottlieb Schultz, I live across the street from you, in that little house opposite your windows. Tomorrow I am celebrating my silver anniversary, and I ask you and your daughters to dine with me in friendly fashion."

The invitation was favorably received. The coffin-maker asked the shoemaker to sit down and have a cup of tea, and, thanks to Gottlieb Schultz's open disposition, they were soon conversing amicably.

"How goes your trade, my dear sir?" Adrian asked.

"Ehh," replied Schultz, "up and down. I can't complain. Though, of course, my trade's not the same as yours: a living man can do without boots, but a dead man can't live without a coffin."

"The exact truth," observed Adrian. "However, if a living man lacks the wherewithal to buy boots, then, no offense intended, he goes around barefoot; while a beggarly dead man gets his coffin for nothing."

Their talk went on like that for some time; finally the shoemaker got up and took leave of the coffin-maker, renewing his invitation.

The next day, at exactly twelve noon, the coffin-maker and his daughters stepped through the gateway of their newly purchased house and headed for their neighbor's. I am not going to describe Adrian Prokhorov's Russian kaftan, nor the European outfits of Akulina and Darya, departing on this occasion from the custom adopted by present-day novelists. I suppose, however, that it is not superfluous to observe that the two girls put on yellow hats and red shoes, which they used to do only on solemn occasions.

The shoemaker's small apartment was filled with guests, mostly German artisans, their wives and apprentices. Of Russian officials there was only the sentry Yurko, a Finn, who, despite his humble rank, had managed to earn the host's special favor. For twenty-five years he had served faithfully in that capacity, like Pogorelsky's postman. The fire of the year twelve, having destroyed the former capital, also did away with his yellow sentry box.[2] But immediately upon the expulsion of the enemy, a new one appeared in its place, gray with little white columns of the Doric order, and Yurko again started pacing before it "with a poleaxe and in a homespun cuirass."[3] He was acquainted with most of the Germans, who lived near the Nikitsky Gate: some of them occasionally even stayed overnight with Yurko from Sunday to Monday. Adrian at once made his acquaintance, as a person he might chance to have need of sooner or later, and when the guests went to the table, they sat next to each other. Mr. and Mrs. Schultz, together with their daughter, the seventeen-year-old Lottchen, while dining with their guests, passed the plates and helped the cook to serve. The beer flowed. Yurko ate enough for four; Adrian did not lag behind him; his daughters behaved decorously; the German conversation grew louder and louder. Suddenly the host called for attention and, uncorking a resin-sealed bottle, pronounced loudly in Russian:

"To the health of my good Louisa!"

The sparkling wine foamed up. The host tenderly kissed the fresh face of his forty-year-old companion, and the guests noisily drank the health of good Louisa.

"To the health of my dear guests!" proposed the host, uncorking a second bottle—and the guests thanked him, emptying their glasses again. Here toasts began to follow one after the other: they drank the health of each particular guest, drank the health of Moscow and a full dozen small German towns, drank the health of all guilds in general and each in particular, drank the health of masters and apprentices. Adrian drank heartily and became so merry that he offered a sort of jocular toast himself. Suddenly one of the guests, a fat baker, raised his glass and exclaimed:

"To the health of those we work for, *unserer Kundleute!*"*

This proposal, like all the others, was received joyfully and unanimously. The guests began bowing to each other, the tailor to the shoemaker, the shoemaker to the tailor, the baker to them both, all of them to the baker, and so on. Amidst these mutual reverences, Yurko cried out, turning to his neighbor:

"So then, brother? Drink to the health of your dead."

Everybody laughed loudly, but the coffin-maker considered himself offended and frowned. Nobody noticed it, the guests went on drinking, and the bells were already ringing for vespers when they got up from the table.

The guests went home late, and for the most part tipsy. The fat baker and the bookbinder,

Whose face seemed bound in red morocco,[4]

took Yurko under the arms to his sentry box, observing in this case the proverb "One good turn deserves another." The coffin-maker came home drunk and angry.

"What is this, really?" he reasoned aloud. "What makes my trade less honored than others? Is a coffin-maker a hangman's brother? Why do those heathens laugh? Is a coffin-maker a Yuletide mummer? I was going to invite them to the housewarming, throw them a big feast: there'll be none of that! I'll invite the ones I work for: the Orthodox dead."

"What's that, dearie?" said his maidservant, who was just taking off his boots. "What's that drivel? Cross yourself! To invite dead people to a housewarming! It's frightful!"

"By God, I will," Adrian went on, "and tomorrow at that. You are welcome, my benefactors, to come and feast with me tomorrow evening; I'll regale you with what God sends me!" With those words the coffin-maker put himself to bed and was soon snoring away.

* "our clientele"

It was still dark outside when Adrian was awakened. Tryukhina, the merchant's wife, had passed away that same night, and a messenger from her steward came galloping to Adrian with the news. For that the coffin-maker tipped him ten kopecks, quickly got dressed, hired a cab, and drove to Razgulyai. Policemen were already standing by the deceased woman's gate, and merchants were strolling about like crows, sensing a dead body. The deceased woman lay on the table,[5] yellow as wax, but not yet disfigured by corruption. Relations, neighbors, and domestics crowded around her. All the windows were open; candles burned; priests were reciting prayers. Adrian went up to Tryukhina's nephew, a young merchant in a fashionable frock coat, and told him that the coffin, the candles, the shroud, and other funerary accessories would be delivered to him at once all in good order. The heir thanked him distractedly, saying that he was not going to haggle over the price, but would rely on his conscience in everything. The coffin-maker, as was his habit, swore by God that he would not overcharge him; he exchanged significant glances with the steward and got busy. He spent the whole day driving from Razgulyai to the Nikitsky Gate and back; by evening everything was arranged, and he went home on foot, dismissing his cabby. It was a moonlit night. The coffin-maker reached the Nikitsky Gate safely. By the Church of the Ascension our acquaintance Yurko hailed him and, recognizing the coffin-maker, wished him a good night. It was late. The coffin-maker was already nearing his house when it suddenly seemed to him that someone came to his gate, opened it, and disappeared through it.

"What can this mean?" thought Adrian. "Does somebody need me again? Or is it a thief breaking in on me? Or maybe it's lovers coming to my two fools, for all I know!" And the coffin-maker was already thinking of calling his friend Yurko to help him. Just then someone else approached the gate and was about to go in, but seeing the owner come running, he stopped and doffed his cocked hat. His face seemed familiar to Adrian, but in his haste he did not manage to make it out properly.

"You've come to see me," Adrian said breathlessly. "Go in, if you please."

"Don't stand on ceremony, my good man," the other replied hollowly. "Go on ahead; show your guests the way!"

Adrian had no time to stand on ceremony. The door was open, he went up the stairs, and the man followed him. Adrian fancied there were people walking about his rooms. "What the devil is this! . . ." he thought and hurriedly went in . . . Here his legs gave way. The room was filled with dead people. The moonlight coming through the window lit up their yellow and blue faces, sunken mouths, dull, half-closed eyes, and protruding noses . . . With horror Adrian recognized them as people buried by his best efforts, and in the guest who had come in with him, the brigadier whose funeral had taken place under the pouring rain. All of them, men and ladies, surrounded the coffin-maker with bows and greetings, except for one poor man, recently buried for free, who, aware and ashamed of his rags, did not come near, but stood humbly in the corner. The rest were dressed properly: the dead ladies in bonnets with ribbons, the dead officials in uniforms, but with unshaven beards, the merchants in their holiday kaftans.

"You see, Prokhorov," the brigadier said on behalf of the whole honorable company, "we all rose up at your invitation; only the really unfit, who have completely fallen apart, or are nothing but skinless bones, stayed home, but even so there was one who couldn't help himself—he wanted so much to visit you . . ."

Just then a little skeleton pushed through the crowd and approached Adrian. His skull was smiling sweetly at the coffin-maker. Scraps of light green and red broadcloth and threadbare linen hung on him here and there as on a pole, and his leg bones knocked about loosely in his high boots, like pestles in mortars.

"You don't recognize me, Prokhorov," said the skeleton. "Remember the retired sergeant of the guards, Pyotr Petrovich Kurilkin, the one you sold your first coffin to in 1799—a pine one that you passed off for oak?"

With these words the dead man held out a bony embrace to him— but Adrian, summoning all his strength, cried out and pushed him away. Pyotr Petrovich staggered, fell, and broke to pieces. A murmur of indignation arose among the dead people; they all defended the honor of their comrade, came at Adrian with curses and threats, and the poor host, deafened by their cries and nearly crushed, lost his presence of mind, fell himself onto the bones of the retired sergeant of the guards, and passed out.

The sun had long been shining on the bed in which the coffin-maker lay. He finally opened his eyes and saw before him the maid-servant, who was blowing on the coals of the samovar. With horror Adrian recalled all of the previous day's events. Tryukhina, the brigadier, and Sergeant Kurilkin arose vaguely in his imagination. He waited silently for the housekeeper to begin a conversation with him and tell him the consequences of the night's adventures.

"How long you've slept, dear Adrian Prokhorovich," said Aksinya, handing him his dressing gown. "Our neighbor the tailor came to see you, and the local sentry ran by to announce that today is the police chief's name day, but you were asleep, and we didn't want to wake you up."

"Did anyone come to me from the late Tryukhina?"

"Late? Did she die?"

"You fool! Didn't you help me arrange her funeral yesterday?"

"What's got into you, dearie? Have you lost your mind, or has yesterday's drunkenness still not left you? What kind of funeral was there yesterday? You spent the whole day feasting at the German's, came home drunk, flopped into bed, and slept right up till now, when they've already rung for the morning liturgy."

"You don't say!" said the overjoyed coffin-maker.

"Sure enough," the housekeeper replied.

"Well, in that case serve the tea quickly and call my daughters."

THE STATIONMASTER

A collegiate registrator,
A post-station dictator.

PRINCE VYAZEMSKY[1]

Who has not cursed stationmasters, who has not quarreled with them? Who, in a moment of anger, has not demanded the fatal book from them, in order to set down in it his useless complaint about their oppression, rudeness, and negligence? Who does not consider them monsters of the human race, on a par with defunct scriveners or, at the very least, the bandits of Murom?[2] Let us be fair, however, let us try to enter into their situation, and perhaps we will judge them much more leniently. What is a stationmaster? A veritable martyr of the fourteenth class,[3] protected by his rank only from beatings, and that not always (I call my reader's conscience to witness). What are the duties of this dictator, as Prince Vyazemsky jokingly calls him? Is it not real penal servitude? No peace day or night. It is on the stationmaster that the traveler vents all the vexation accumulated during his boring journey. The weather is unbearable, the road bad, the coachman pig-headed, the horses don't pull—and it's the stationmaster's fault. Going into his poor dwelling, the traveler looks upon him as an enemy; it's good if he manages to rid himself of the uninvited guest quickly; but if there happen to be no horses? . . . God, what curses, what threats pour down on his head! In rain and slush he is forced to run around outside; in storm, in midwinter frost, he steps out to the entryway, to rest for at least a moment from the shouting and shoving of an irate wayfarer. A general arrives; the trembling stationmaster gives him the last two troikas, including the one reserved for couriers. The general drives off without even thanking him. Five minutes later—the bell! . . . and a government messenger throws his travel papers on the table in front of him! . . . Let us get a good grasp on all of this, and instead of indignation, our hearts will be filled with sincere compassion. A few more words: in the course of twenty years, I have driven over Russia in all directions; I know almost all the post roads; I am acquainted with several generations of coachmen; rare is the stationmaster I don't know by sight, rare are those I have not dealt with; I hope to publish a curious store of my travel observations before too long; meanwhile I will say only that the stationmasters' estate is presented to general opinion in a most false guise. These much-maligned stationmasters are generally peaceable people, obliging by nature, inclined to be sociable, modest in their claim to honors, and not overly fond of money. From their conversation (so unduly scorned by gentleman travelers) one can learn much that is curious and instructive. As for me, I confess that I would rather talk with them than with some functionary of the sixth class traveling on official business.

It can easily be guessed that I have friends among the honorable estate of the stationmasters. In fact, the memory of one of them is precious to me. Circumstances once brought us together, and it is of him that I now intend to speak with my gentle readers.

In 1816, in the month of May, I happened to pass through—sky province, by a highway since abandoned. I was of low rank, went by post, and had a traveling allowance for two horses. As a result, stationmasters did not stand on ceremony with me, and I often had to fight for what, in my opinion, was mine by right. Being young and hotheaded, I was indignant at the baseness and pusillanimity of a stationmaster, when the latter had the troika prepared for me hitched to the carriage of a high-ranking gentleman. It took me just as long to get used to being passed over by a discriminating flunkey at a governor's dinner. Now I find both the one and the other in the order of things. What, in fact, would happen to us if, instead of the all-convenient rule *Let rank honor rank*, something else were introduced, for instance *Let mind honor mind*. What arguments would arise! And with whom would the waiters begin their serving? But I return to my story.

It was a hot day. Two miles from the * * * posting station it started to sprinkle, and a moment later a downpour soaked me to the skin. On reaching the station, my first concern was to change my clothes quickly, the second was to ask for tea.

"Hey, Dunya," shouted the stationmaster, "prepare the samovar and go for cream!"

At these words, a girl of about fourteen came from behind a partition and ran to the front hall. I was struck by her beauty.

"Is that your daughter?" I asked the stationmaster.

"That she is, sir," he answered with an air of contented pride. "And she's such a smart one, such a quick one, just like her late mother."

Here he began to copy out my travel papers, and I set myself to examining the pictures that adorned his humble but well-kept abode. They illustrated the story of the prodigal son.[4] In the first a venerable old man in a nightcap and dressing gown is seeing off a restless young man, who hastily receives his blessing and a bag of money. In the next the young man's dissipated behavior is portrayed in vivid strokes: he sits at a table surrounded by false friends and shameless women. Further on, the ruined young man, in rags and a cocked hat, is tending swine and sharing their meal; his face shows profound sorrow and repentance. Finally, his return to his father is portrayed: the good old man has run out to meet him in the same nightcap and dressing gown; the prodigal son is on his knees; in the background the cook is killing the fatted calf, and the older son is questioning the servants about the cause of such rejoicing. Under each picture I read the appropriate German verses. All of that is preserved in my memory to this day, along with the pots of impatiens, and the bed with the motley canopy, and other objects that surrounded me at that time. I can see, as if it were now, the host himself, a man of about fifty, hale and hearty, and his long green frock coat with three medals on faded ribbons.

No sooner had I paid my old coachman than Dunya returned with the samovar. The little coquette had noticed at second glance the impression she had made on me; she lowered her big blue eyes; I started to converse with her, she replied without any timidity, like a girl who has seen the world. I offered her father a glass of punch, gave Dunya a cup of tea, and the three of us began talking as if we had known each other for ages.

The horses had long been ready, but I still did not feel like parting from the stationmaster and his daughter. At last I took leave of them; the father wished me a good journey, and the daughter saw me off to the carriage. In the entryway I stopped and asked permission to kiss her. Dunya consented . . . I can count many kisses,

Since I first took up that occupation,

but not one of them left me with so lasting, so pleasant a memory.

Several years passed, and circumstance brought me to that same highway, to those same parts. I remembered the old stationmaster's daughter and rejoiced to think that I would see her again. But, I reflected, maybe the old stationmaster has been replaced; Dunya is probably already married. The thought of the death of the one or the other also flashed in my mind, and I approached the * * * station with sad foreboding.

The horses stopped by the little station house. On entering the room, I immediately recognized the pictures illustrating the story of the prodigal son; the table and the bed stood in their former places; but there were no plants in the windows now, and everything around had a look of decline and neglect. The stationmaster was asleep under a sheepskin coat; my arrival awakened him; he got up ... This was indeed Samson Vyrin; but how he had aged! While he was preparing to copy my travel papers, I kept looking at his gray hair, his deeply wrinkled, long-unshaven face, his bent back—and could not stop marveling at how three or four years could turn a hearty fellow into a feeble old man.

"Do you recognize me?" I asked him. "You and I are old acquaintances."

"Maybe so," he answered gloomily. "It's a big road out there; many travelers have passed my way."

"Is your Dunya well?" I went on. The old man frowned.

"God knows," he answered.

"So she's evidently married?" I said. The old man pretended not to hear my question and went on reading my papers in a whisper. I stopped my questions and asked him to put the kettle on. Curiosity was beginning to stir in me, and I hoped that punch would loosen my old acquaintance's tongue.

I was not mistaken: the old man did not refuse the offered glass. I noticed that rum brightened his gloominess. At the second glass he became talkative; he remembered me, or made as if he did, and I learned a story from him which at the time greatly interested and moved me.

"So you knew my Dunya?" he began. "Well, who didn't? Ah, Dunya, Dunya! What a girl she was! It used to be, whoever passed through, they all praised her, nobody said a bad word about her. Ladies gave her presents, one a little shawl, another a pair of earrings. Gentleman travelers stayed longer on purpose, supposedly to have dinner or supper, but really only so as to go on looking at her. It used to be, however angry a master was, he'd calm down with her there and talk kindly to me. Would you believe it, sir: couriers, government messengers, sat talking to her for half an hour at a time. She ran the household: what to tidy up, what to prepare, she kept it all going. And I, old fool that I am, couldn't admire her enough, couldn't rejoice enough. Didn't I love my Dunya, didn't I cherish my little one; wasn't that the life for her? But no, you can't pray trouble away; what's fated won't pass you by."

Here he began telling me his grief in detail.

Once, three years ago, on a winter evening, when the stationmaster was drawing lines in a new register and his daughter behind the partition was sewing herself a dress, a troika drove up and a traveler in a Circassian hat, a military greatcoat, wrapped in a scarf, came into the room and demanded horses. The horses were all gone. At that news, the traveler raised his voice and his whip; but Dunya, who was used to such scenes, ran out from behind the partition and sweetly addressed him with a question: Wouldn't he like something to eat? Dunya's appearance produced its usual effect. The traveler's anger went away; he agreed to wait for horses and ordered supper. Having taken off the wet, shaggy hat, unwound the scarf, and pulled off the greatcoat, the traveler emerged as a young, trim hussar with a small black moustache. He made himself comfortable at the stationmaster's and began conversing gaily with him and his daughter. Supper was served. Meanwhile horses arrived, and the stationmaster ordered them hitched to the traveler's kibitka at once, without being fed; but, on going back inside, he found the young man lying nearly unconscious on a bench: he felt faint, had a headache, it was impossible to go on . . . What could they do! The stationmaster yielded his bed to him, and it was decided that, if the sick man did not feel better, they would send to S— the next morning for a doctor.

The next day the hussar was worse. His man rode to town for the doctor. Dunya tied a handkerchief moistened with vinegar around his head and sat down by his bed with her sewing. In front of the stationmaster, the sick man groaned and said scarcely a word; however, he drank two cups of coffee and, groaning, ordered dinner for himself. Dunya never left his side. He kept asking to drink, and Dunya offered him a mug of her specially prepared lemonade. The sick man moistened his lips, and each time he handed back the mug, he pressed Dunyushka's hand with his own weak hand in token of gratitude. Towards dinnertime the doctor came. He took the sick man's pulse, talked with him in German, and announced in Russian that all he needed was peace and quiet, and that he could set out on his way in a couple of days. The hussar handed him twenty-five roubles for the visit and invited him for dinner; the doctor accepted; the two ate with great appetite, drank a bottle of wine, and parted very pleased with each other.

Another day went by, and the hussar recovered completely. He was extremely cheerful, joked incessantly now with Dunya, now with the stationmaster, whistled tunes, talked with the travelers, copied their papers into the register, and was so much to the good stationmaster's liking that on the third day he was sorry to part with his amiable guest. It was Sunday; Dunya was about to go to church. The hussar's kibitka was ready. He said good-bye to the stationmaster, rewarded him generously for his bed and board; said good-bye to Dunya as well, and volunteered to take her to the church, which was at the edge of the village. Dunya stood in perplexity . . .

"What are you afraid of?" her father said to her. "His honor's not a wolf, he's not going eat you: ride to church with him."

Dunya got into the kibitka beside the hussar, the servant leaped up onto the box, the coachman whistled, and the horses galloped off.

The poor stationmaster could not understand how on earth he could have allowed his Dunya to go off with the hussar, how such blindness could have come over him, and what had happened then to his reason. Before half an hour went by, his heart began to ache, to ache, and anxiety took such hold of him that he could not bear it and went to church himself. Coming to the church, he saw that people were already leaving, but Dunya was neither within the fence nor on the porch. He hurriedly went into the church: the priest was coming out of the sanctuary; the sexton was putting out the candles; two old women were still praying in one corner; but there was no Dunya in the church. The poor father barely brought himself to ask the sexton if she had been at the service. The sexton replied that she had not. The stationmaster went home more dead than alive. One hope remained for him: Dunya, with the flightiness of youth, might have taken it into her head to go on to the next station, where her godmother lived. In painful agitation he waited for the return of the troika in which he had sent her off. The coachman did not return. Finally, in the evening, he came back alone and drunk, with devastating news: "Dunya went on from that station with the hussar."

The old man could not bear his misfortune; he took at once to that same bed in which the young deceiver had lain the day before. Now, considering all the circumstances, the stationmaster figured out that the illness had been feigned. The poor man came down with a high fever; he was taken to S— and another man temporarily filled his place. He was treated by the same doctor who had visited the young hussar. He assured the stationmaster that the young man had been perfectly well and that even then he had guessed his evil intentions, but had said nothing for fear of his whip. Whether the German was telling the truth, or merely wished to boast of his prescience, he did not comfort his poor patient in the least. Having barely recovered from his illness, the stationmaster obtained a two-month leave from his superior in S— and, telling no one of his intentions, set out on foot after his daughter. From the travel papers he knew that cavalry captain Minsky was going from Smolensk to Petersburg. The coachman who had driven him said that Dunya had wept all the time on the way, though she seemed to be going of her own will.

"Maybe I'll bring my lost sheep home," thought the stationmaster. With that thought in mind, he arrived in Petersburg, stopped in the neighborhood of the Izmailovsky regiment, at the house of a retired corporal whom he had once served with, and began his search. He soon found out that cavalry captain Minsky was in Petersburg and living at the Demut Inn.⁵ The stationmaster decided to go and see him.

Early in the morning he came to the front hall and asked them to inform his honor that an old soldier was asking to see him. The orderly, who was polishing a boot on a boot tree, told him that his master was asleep and that he did not receive anyone before eleven o'clock. The stationmaster went away and came back at the appointed time. Minsky himself came out to him, in a dressing gown and a red skullcap.

"What do you want, brother?" he asked.

The old man's blood began to boil, tears welled up in his eyes, and in a trembling voice all he said was: "Your Honor! . . . Show me this divine mercy! . . ."

Minsky glanced quickly at him, flushed, took him by the hand, led him to his study, and shut the door behind him.

"Your Honor!" the old man went on. "What falls off the cart is lost for good; at least give me back my poor Dunya. You've had your fun with her; don't ruin her for nothing."

"What's done can't be undone," the young man said in the utmost embarrassment. "I'm guilty before you, and I gladly ask your forgiveness; but don't think that I could forsake Dunya: she'll be happy, I give you my word of honor. What do you want her for? She loves me; she's lost the habit of her former situation. Neither you nor she will forget what's happened."

Then, slipping something into the old man's cuff, he opened the door, and the stationmaster, without knowing how, found himself in the street.

For a long time he stood motionless, but finally he noticed a wad of papers behind the cuff of his sleeve. He took them out and unfolded several crumpled five- and ten-rouble banknotes. Tears welled up in his eyes again, tears of indignation! He rolled the papers into a ball, threw them on the ground, stamped on them with his heel, and walked away . . . After going several steps, he stopped, reflected . . . and turned back . . . but the banknotes were no longer there. A well-dressed young man, seeing him, ran over to a cab, quickly got in, and shouted: "Drive! . . ." The stationmaster did not chase after him. He decided to go back home to his station, but first he wanted to see his poor Dunya at least once more. For that he went back to Minsky's a couple of days later; but the orderly told him sternly that the master was not receiving anybody, pushed him out of the front hall with his chest, and slammed the door in his face. The stationmaster stood there, stood there—and then left.

That same day, in the evening, he was walking down Liteiny Street, after having prayers said at the Joy of the Afflicted.[6] Suddenly a smart droshky raced past him, and the stationmaster recognized Minsky. The droshky stopped in front of a three-story house, just by the entrance, and the hussar went running up to the porch. A happy thought flashed in the stationmaster's head. He turned around and coming alongside the coachman, asked:

"Whose horse is that, brother? Is it Minsky's?"

"That's right," replied the coachman. "What's it to you?"

"It's this: your master told me to take a note to his Dunya, but I forget where his Dunya lives."

"Right here, on the second floor. You're late with your note, brother; he's already with her now."

"Never mind," the stationmaster objected with an inexplicable stirring of the heart. "Thanks for telling me, I'll do what I'm supposed to." And with those words he went up the stairs.

The door was locked. He rang and spent several painful seconds waiting. A key jangled, the door opened.

"Does Avdotya Samsonovna live here?" he asked.

"Yes," a young maid replied. "What do you want with her?"
The stationmaster, without replying, went into the room.
"You mustn't, you mustn't!" the maid called after him. "Avdotya
Samsonovna has visitors!"

But the stationmaster did not listen and went on. The first two
rooms were dark, in the third there was light. He went up to the open
door and stopped. In a beautifully decorated room, Minsky sat deep
in thought. Dunya, dressed with all the luxury of fashion, was sitting
on the arm of his chair like a horsewoman on an English saddle. She
looked at Minsky with tenderness, winding his black locks around her
sparkling fingers. Poor stationmaster! Never had his daughter seemed
so beautiful to him; he admired her despite himself.

"Who's there?" she asked, without raising her head. He kept silent.
Receiving no answer, Dunya raised her head . . . and with a cry fell to
the carpet. The frightened Minsky rushed to pick her up, but, suddenly
seeing the old stationmaster in the doorway, he left Dunya and went
over to him, trembling with wrath.

"What do you want?" he said, clenching his teeth. "Why are you
slinking after me everywhere like a robber? Do you want to put a knife
in me? Get out!" And seizing the old man by the collar with his strong
hand, he pushed him out to the stairs.

The old man went back to his quarters. His friend advised him to
lodge a complaint; but the stationmaster reflected, waved his hand, and
decided to give up. Two days later he left Petersburg, went back to his
station, and took up his duties again.

"For three years now," he concluded, "I've lived without Dunya
and without any news of her. God knows whether she's still alive or
not. All sorts of things happen. She's neither the first nor the last to
be seduced by a passing rake, who'll keep a girl and then abandon her.
There's lots of those young fools in Petersburg, in satin and velvet
today, and tomorrow, just look, they're sweeping the streets along with
some drunken riffraff. When you think sometimes that Dunya, too,
may be perishing like that, you can't help sinning by wishing her in her
grave . . ."

Such was the story of my friend, the old stationmaster, a story interrupted more than once by tears, which he picturesquely wiped with the
skirt of his coat, like the zealous Terentyich in Dmitriev's wonderful
ballad.[7] Those tears were provoked in part by the punch, of which he
drained five glasses in the course of his narrative; but, however it was,

they touched my heart strongly. Having parted from him, for a long time I could not forget the old stationmaster, for a long time I thought about poor Dunya . . .

Just recently, passing through the little town of * * *, I remembered about my friend; I learned that the station he had been in charge of had since been abolished. To my question "Is the old stationmaster still alive?"—no one could give me a satisfactory answer. I decided to visit those familiar parts, hired some private horses, and set out for the village of N—.

This happened in the autumn. Grayish clouds covered the sky; a cold wind blew from the harvested fields, carrying off red and yellow leaves from the trees it met on its way. I reached the village at sunset and stopped by the little station house. A fat peasant woman came out to the front hall (where poor Dunya once gave me a kiss), and to my questions replied that the old stationmaster had died about a year before, that a brewer now lived there, and that she was the brewer's wife. I began to regret my useless trip and the seven roubles I had spent for nothing.

"What did he die of?" I asked the brewer's wife.

"Of drink, my good sir," she replied.

"Where was he buried?"

"At the edge of the village, next to his late wife."

"Couldn't someone take me to his grave?"

"Why not? Hey, Vanka! Enough fooling with the cat. Take the mister to the cemetery and show him the stationmaster's grave."

At these words a raggedy boy, redheaded and one-eyed, ran out to me and immediately led me to edge of the village.

"Did you know the deceased?" I asked him on the way.

"How could I not! He taught me to whittle pipes. He used to come from the pot-house (God rest his soul!), and we'd follow after him: 'Grandpa, grandpa! Give us some nuts!' And he'd give us nuts. He used to play with us all the time."

"Do travelers remember him?"

"There's not many travelers nowadays; the assessor drops by sometimes, but he can't be bothered with dead people. There was a lady passed by last summer, and she did ask about the old stationmaster and went to his grave."

"What kind of lady?" I asked with curiosity.

"A beautiful lady," the boy replied. "She rode in a coach-and-six, with three little sirs, and a wet nurse, and a black pug; and when they told her the old stationmaster had died, she wept and said to the children: 'Sit quietly, while I go to the cemetery.' I volunteered to take her there. But the lady said: 'I know the way myself.' And she gave me five silver kopecks—such a kind lady! . . ."

We came to the cemetery, a bare place, no fence around it, studded with wooden crosses, not shaded by a single tree. In all my born days I had never seen such a desolate cemetery.

"Here's the old stationmaster's grave," said the boy, jumping onto a pile of sand in which a black cross with a brass icon was planted.

"And the lady came here?" I asked.

"Yes, she did," replied Vanka, "I watched her from further off. She lay down here and went on lying for a long time. Then the lady went to the village and summoned the priest, gave him money, and drove away, and me she gave five silver kopecks—such a nice lady!"

I, too, gave the boy five kopecks and no longer regretted either the trip or the seven roubles it had cost me.

THE YOUNG LADY PEASANT

You look lovely, Dushenka, in any garments.

BOGDANOVICH[1]

In one of our remote provinces lay the estate of Ivan Petrovich Berestov. He served with the guards in his youth, retired at the beginning of
1797, went to his village, and after that never left it. He married a poor
noblewoman, who died in childbirth while he was out hunting. The
exercise of estate management soon consoled him. He built a house
to his own plan, started a fulling mill, tripled his income, and began to
consider himself the most intelligent man in the whole neighborhood,
in which he was not contradicted by his neighbors, who came to visit
him with their families and dogs. On weekdays he went around in a vel-
veteen jacket, for Sundays he put on a frock coat of homespun broadcloth; he kept the accounts himself and read nothing except the *Senate
Gazette*. He was generally liked, though he was considered proud. The
only one who did not get along with him was Grigory Ivanovich Muromsky, his nearest neighbor. This was a real Russian squire. Having
squandered the greater part of his fortune in Moscow and become a
widower at the same time, he left for the last of his holdings, where
he went on playing pranks, but now of a different sort. He planted an
English garden, into which he poured almost all his remaining income.
His stable-boys were dressed like English jockeys. His daughter had
an English governess. He cultivated his fields following the English
method,

But Russian grain won't grow in foreign fashion,[2]

and, despite a significant reduction of expenses, Grigory Ivanovich's
income did not increase; he found ways to make new debts in the country as well; yet for all that he was considered none too stupid, because
among the landowners of his province he was the first to mortgage
his estate to the Government Trust: a transaction which at that time

seemed extremely complicated and courageous.[3] Of people who disapproved of him, the most severe was Berestov. Hatred of innovation was the distinguishing mark of his character. He could not speak indifferently about his neighbor's anglomania, and constantly found occasions to criticize him. He would show a guest over his domain, and in reply to praise of his management, would say with a sly smile:

"Yes, sir, with me it's not like with my neighbor Grigory Ivanovich! We won't go ruining ourselves English-style! It's enough if we get our fill Russian-style."

These and similar jests, through the diligence of obliging neighbors, were made known to Grigory Ivanovich with additions and explanations. The anglomaniac bore criticism no more patiently than do our journalists. He raged and dubbed his detractor a bear and a provincial.

Such were the relations between these two proprietors when Berestov's son came to his village. He had been educated at * * * University and had intended to enter military service, but his father would not consent to it. The young man felt himself totally unsuited to civil service. Neither would yield to the other, and the young man began meanwhile to live as a squire, letting his moustache grow just in case.

Alexei was indeed a fine fellow. It really would have been a pity if a military uniform were never to hug his slender waist, and if, instead of showing himself off on horseback, he were to spend his youth hunched over office papers. Seeing how he always galloped at the head of the hunt, heedless of the road, the neighbors all agreed that he would never make a worthwhile department chief. The young ladies cast an eye on him, some even fixed an eye on him; but Alexei paid little attention to them, and they supposed that the cause of his insensibility was a love intrigue. Indeed, a copy of the address from one of his letters was passed around: *To Akulina Petrovna Kurochkina, in Moscow, opposite the St. Alexei Monastery, in the house of the coppersmith Savelyev, humbly requesting that you deliver this letter to A. N. R.*

Those of my readers who have never lived in the country cannot imagine how charming these provincial young ladies are! Brought up on fresh air, in the shade of their apple orchards, they draw their knowledge of the world and of life from books. Solitude, freedom, and reading develop early in them feelings and passions unknown to our distracted beauties. For such a young lady the jingle of bells is already an adventure, a trip to the nearest town is considered epoch-making, and the visit of a guest leaves a lasting, sometimes even eternal, memory. Of course, anyone is free to laugh at some of their oddities, but the jests of the superficial observer cannot do away with their essential merits, the main one being "a particularity of character, a uniqueness (*individualité*)," without which, in the opinion of Jean-Paul, there can be no human greatness.[4] In the capitals women may receive a better education; but social habits soon smooth their character away and make their souls as alike as their hats. This is said neither in judgment nor in condemnation,[5] but still *nota nostra manet*,* as an ancient commentator writes.

It is easy to imagine what impression Alexei would make in the circle of our young ladies. He was the first to appear before them looking gloomy and disillusioned, the first to speak to them of lost joys and his faded youth; on top of that, he wore a black ring with the image of a death's head. All this was extremely new in that province. The young ladies lost their minds over him.

But most interested of all in him was the daughter of my anglomaniac, Liza (or Betsy, as Grigory Ivanovich usually called her). The fathers did not call on each other, and she had not yet seen Alexei, while all her young neighbors talked only of him. She was seventeen years old. Dark eyes enlivened her swarthy and very pleasant face. She was an only child and consequently spoiled. Her playfulness and perpetual pranks delighted her father and drove to despair her governess, Miss Jackson, a prim old maid of forty, who whitened her face, blackened her eyebrows, reread *Pamela*[6] twice a year, was paid two thousand roubles for it, and was dying of boredom "in this barbaric Russia."

Liza was looked after by Nastya; she was a bit older, but as flighty as her young mistress. Liza loved her very much, revealed all her secrets to her, thought over all her fancies with her; in short, Nastya was a much more important person in the village of Priluchino than any confidante in a French tragedy.

"Allow me to go visiting today," Nastya said one day as she was dressing the young lady.

"Of course; but where?"

"To Tugilovo, to the Berestovs'. Today is the cook's wife's name day. She came yesterday to invite us to dinner."

"So," said Liza, "the masters quarrel, and the servants entertain each other!"

* Our observation stands. *Translator.*

"What do we care about the masters!" Nastya retorted. "Besides, I'm yours, not your father's. You haven't quarreled with young Berestov yet. Let the old folk fight, if it makes them happy."

"Try to catch a glimpse of Alexei Berestov, Nastya, and tell me just exactly how he looks and what sort of man he is."

Nastya promised, and Liza waited impatiently all day for her return. Nastya appeared in the evening.

"Well, Lizaveta Grigoryevna," she said, coming into the room, "I saw young Berestov: had a good enough look at him; we spent the whole day together."

"How's that? Tell me, tell me everything in order."

"As you please, miss. We went, me, Anisya Egorovna, Nenila, Dunka . . ."

"All right, I know. So then?"

"Please, miss, I'll tell it all in order. So we came just in time for dinner. The room was full of people. There were some from Kolbino, Zakharyevo, the clerk's wife from Khlupino and her daughters . . ."

"Well, what about Berestov?"

"Wait, miss. So we sat down at the table, the clerk's wife at the head, me next to her . . . The daughters pouted, but who cares about them . . ."

"Ah, Nastya, how boring you are with your eternal details!"

"And how impatient you are! Well, so we got up from the table . . . and we'd been sitting there for about three hours, and it was a nice dinner; blancmange for dessert, blue, red, and stripy . . . So we got up from the table and went to the garden to play tag, and it was then that the young master appeared."

"Well, so? Is it true he's so good-looking?"

"Astonishingly good-looking, a handsome man, you might say. Tall, slender, all ruddy-cheeked . . ."

"Really? And I thought he had a pale face. So? How did he seem to you? Sad? Pensive?"

"What? Never in my life have I seen such a wild one. He took a notion to play tag with us."

"To play tag with you! Impossible!"

"Very possible! And he had other notions, too! He'd catch a girl and start kissing her!"

"Say what you like, Nastya, you're lying."

"Say what you like, I'm not lying. I could barely fight him off. He spent the whole day playing with us."

"How is it they say he's in love and doesn't look at anybody."

"I don't know, miss, but he looked at me quite a lot, and at Tanya, the clerk's daughter, too; and at Pasha from Kolbino, and, it's sinful to say it, but there's nobody he left out—such a naughty boy."

"That's amazing! And what do the servants say about him?"

"An excellent master, they say: so kind, so cheerful. The only bad thing is that he's too fond of chasing after the girls. But for me there's no harm in that: he'll settle down in time."

"How I'd love to see him!" Liza said with a sigh.

"What's so tricky about that? Tugilovo isn't far from us, only two miles: take a stroll in that direction, or go on horseback; you're sure to meet him. Every day, early in the morning, he takes his gun and goes hunting."

"No, no good. He might think I was chasing after him. Besides, our fathers have quarreled, so it will be impossible for me to get acquainted with him . . . Ah, Nastya! You know what? I'll dress up like a peasant girl!"

"That's it! Put on a coarse shirt, a sarafan, and set out boldly for Tugilovo. I guarantee you Berestov won't pass you by."

"And I can talk perfectly the local way. Ah, Nastya, dear Nastya! What a fine idea!" And Liza lay down to sleep with the firm intention of carrying out her amusing proposal.

The next day she proceeded to carry out her plan. She sent to the market for coarse linen, simple blue cotton, and copper buttons; cut out a shirt and a sarafan with Nastya's help, had all the maidservants sit down to sew, and by evening everything was ready. Liza tried on the new outfit and confessed before the mirror that she had never yet found herself so pretty. She practiced her role, making low bows as she walked, then wagging her head several times like a china cat, talked in peasant parlance, covered her face with her sleeve when she laughed, and earned Nastya's full approval. One difficulty remained: she tried walking barefoot in the yard, but the grass pricked her tender feet, and she found sand and gravel unbearable. Nastya was of help here, too: she measured Liza's foot, ran out to the fields to the shepherd Trofim, and ordered a pair of bast shoes to that measure. The next day Liza woke up bright and early. The whole house was still asleep. Nastya waited for the shepherd outside the gate. A horn sounded, and the village flock filed past the master's yard. Trofim, walking by Nastya, gave her the motley little bast shoes and received a fifty-kopeck reward from her. Liza quietly dressed herself as a peasant, whispered her instructions to Nastya regarding Miss Jackson, left by the back porch, and ran through the kitchen garden to the fields.

Dawn shone in the east, and the golden ranks of clouds seemed to be awaiting the sun, the way courtiers await the sovereign; the clear sky, the morning freshness, the dew, the breeze, and the birds' singing filled Liza's heart with a childlike gaiety. Fearing to meet someone she knew, she seemed not to walk but to fly. Approaching the wood that stood at the boundary of her father's property, Liza slowed her pace. Here she was to await Alexei. Her heart beat fast, not knowing why itself; but the fear that accompanies our youthful pranks is their chief delight. Liza entered the twilight of the wood. Its muted, rolling murmur greeted the girl. Her gaiety died down. She gradually abandoned herself to a sweet reverie. She was thinking . . . but is it possible to define precisely what a seventeen-year-old girl is thinking, alone, in a wood, at five o'clock on a spring morning? And so, she walked deep in thought down the road, shaded on both sides by tall trees, when suddenly a handsome pointer barked at her. Liza was frightened and cried out. Just then a voice said: "*Tout beau, Sbogar, ici . . .*"*—and a young hunter appeared from behind the bushes.

"Don't be afraid, dear," he said to Liza, "my dog doesn't bite."

Liza had already recovered from her fright and managed to take advantage of the circumstances.

"No, master," she said, pretending to be half frightened, half shy, "I am afraid. See how vicious he is; he may go for me again."

Alexei (the reader has already recognized him) meanwhile gazed intently at the young peasant girl.

"I'll accompany you, if you're afraid," he said to her. "Will you allow me to walk beside you?"

"Who's to stop you?" Liza replied. "Freedom is as freedom does, and the road's for everybody."

"Where are you from?"

"From Priluchino. I'm the blacksmith Vassily's daughter; I'm gath-

* "Stay, Sbogar, here . . ." *Translator.*

ering mushrooms." (Liza was carrying a basket on a string.) "And you, master? From Tugilovo, is it?"

"That's right," Alexei replied, "I'm the young master's valet." Alexei wanted to smooth over their difference. But Liza looked at him and laughed.

"That's a lie," she said. "Don't take me for a fool. I can see you're the master himself."

"Why do you think so?"

"From everything."

"What, though?"

"Can't I tell a master from a servant? You dress different, talk different, and you don't call your dog the way we do."

Alexei liked Liza more and more every moment. Unaccustomed to any formalities in dealing with pretty village girls, he was about to embrace her, but Liza jumped away from him and adopted such a stern and cold look that, while Alexei nearly laughed, he refrained from further attempts.

"If you want us to be friends in the future," she said with dignity, "kindly do not forget yourself."

"Who taught you such great wisdom?" Alexei asked, bursting into laughter. "Was it my acquaintance, Nastenka, your mistress's maid? See by what paths enlightenment spreads!"

Liza felt she had stepped out of her role, and put things right at once.

"And what are you thinking?" she said. "As if I've never set foot in the master's yard? Don't worry, I've heard and seen all kinds of things. Anyhow," she went on, "if I chatter with you, I won't gather any mushrooms. You go this way, master, and I'll go that. Begging your pardon . . ."

Liza was about to leave, but Alexei caught her by the hand.

"What's your name, dear heart?"

"Akulina," Liza replied, trying to free her fingers from Alexei's grip. "Do let me go, sir; it's time I went home."

"Well, Akulina, my friend, I'll be sure to visit your father, the blacksmith Vassily."

"Oh, no," Liza objected quickly, "for Christ's sake, don't go there. If they find out at home that I was chatting with a squire alone in the wood, it'll be bad for me: my father, the blacksmith Vassily, will beat me to death."

"But I want to be sure I'll see you again."

"Well, I'll come here again some time gathering mushrooms."

"When?"

"Oh, tomorrow, say."

"Dear Akulina, I'd kiss you, but I don't dare. So, tomorrow, at the same time, is that right?"

"Yes, yes."

"And you won't deceive me?"

"No, I won't."

"Swear to God?"

"Well, so I swear to you by Saint Friday, I'll come."[7]

The young people parted. Liza emerged from the wood, crossed the fields, stole into the garden, and rushed headlong to the barn, where Nastya was waiting for her. There she changed, absentmindedly answering her impatient confidante's questions, and presented herself in the drawing room. The table was laid, breakfast was ready, and Miss Jackson, already whitened and laced in like a wineglass, was cutting thin slices of bread. Her father praised her for her early walk.

"There's nothing healthier than getting up at dawn," he said.

Here he cited several examples of human longevity, drawn from English magazines, noting that all people who lived to be over a hundred abstained from drink and arose at dawn both winter and summer. Liza did not listen to him. In her thoughts she went over all the circumstances of the morning's meeting, the whole conversation of Akulina and the young hunter, and her conscience began to torment her. In vain did she object to herself that their talk had not gone beyond the limits of propriety, that this prank could not have any consequences—her conscience murmured louder than her reason. The promise she had given for the next day troubled her most of all: she very nearly decided not to keep her solemn oath. But Alexei, having waited for her in vain, might go looking in the village for the daughter of the blacksmith Vassily, the real Akulina, a fat, pockmarked wench, and thus figure out her light-minded prank. This thought frightened Liza, and she decided to go to the wood again the next morning as Akulina.

For his part, Alexei was delighted; all day he thought about his new acquaintance; during the night the image of the swarthy beauty haunted his imagination even in sleep. Dawn had barely broken when he was already dressed. Giving himself no time to load his gun, he went out to the fields with his faithful Sbogar and ran to the place of the promised meeting. Around half an hour passed in unbearable expectation; at last he glimpsed the blue sarafan flashing amidst the bushes, and he rushed to meet dear Akulina. She smiled at his rapturous gratitude; but Alexei at once noticed traces of dismay and uneasiness on her face. He wanted to know the reason for it. Liza confessed that her conduct seemed light-minded to her, that she regretted it, that she had not wanted to break the word she had given this once, but that this meeting would be the last, and she asked him to end their acquaintance, which could not lead them to any good. This was all said, of course, in peasant parlance; but the thoughts and feelings, unusual in a simple girl, struck Alexei. He used all his eloquence to talk Akulina out of her intention; assured her of the innocence of his desires, promised never to give her any cause for regret, to obey her in all things, implored her not to deprive him of one delight: of seeing her alone, if only every other day, or at least twice a week. He spoke the language of true passion and in that moment was indeed in love. Liza listened to him silently.

"Give me your word," she said finally, "that you will never look for me in the village or make inquiries about me. Give me your word that you will not seek any other meetings with me than those I set up myself."

Alexei was about to swear by Saint Friday, but Liza stopped him with a smile.

"I have no need of an oath," she said. "Your promise is enough."

After that they talked amiably, strolling together through the wood, until Liza said to him: "It's time." They parted, and Alexei, left alone, could not understand how it was that in two meetings a simple village girl had managed to gain real power over him. His relations with Akulina had the charm of novelty for him, and though the strange peasant girl's prescriptions seemed burdensome to him, the thought of not keeping his word never even entered his head. The thing was that Alexei, despite the fatal ring, the mysterious correspondence, and the gloomy disillusionment, was a good and ardent lad and had a pure heart, capable of feeling the joys of innocence.

If I were to heed only my own wishes, I would certainly describe in full detail the young people's meetings, their growing inclination for and trust in each other, their occupations, their conversations; but I know that the majority of my readers would not share my pleasure. Such details, generally, are bound to seem cloying, and so I will skip them, saying briefly that, before two months were out, my Alexei loved her to distraction, and Liza, though quieter, was no more indifferent than he was. They were both happy with the present and gave little thought to the future.

The thought of indissoluble bonds flashed through their minds quite often, but they never spoke of it to each other. The reason was clear: Alexei, attached as he was to his dear Akulina, always remembered the distance that existed between him and the poor peasant girl; while Liza knew what hatred existed between their fathers, and dared not hope for a mutual reconciliation. Besides that, her vanity was secretly piqued by the vague, romantic hope of finally seeing the Tugilovo landowner at the feet of the Priluchino blacksmith's daughter. Suddenly a major event nearly altered their mutual relations.

One clear, cold morning (of the sort our Russian autumn is so rich in), Ivan Petrovich Berestov went out for a ride on horseback, taking along, just in case, three brace of borzois, a groom, and several serf boys with clappers. At the same time, Grigory Ivanovich Muromsky, tempted by the fine weather, ordered his bobtailed filly saddled and went trotting around his anglicized domain. Approaching the wood, he saw his neighbor, proudly sitting on his horse, in a Caucasian jacket lined with fox fur, waiting for a hare that the boys were trying to drive out of the bushes by shouting and clapping. If Grigory Ivanovich could have foreseen this encounter, he would certainly have turned aside; but he rode into Berestov quite unexpectedly and suddenly found himself within a pistol shot of him. There was nothing to be done. Muromsky, being an educated European, rode up to his adversary and greeted him politely. Berestov responded with all the diligence of a chained bear bowing to the "ladies and gentlemen" at his leader's command. Just then a hare shot out of the wood and ran across the field. Berestov and his groom shouted at the top of their lungs, loosed the dogs, and galloped after them at top speed. Muromsky's horse, who had never been at a hunt, took fright and bolted. Muromsky, who proclaimed himself an excellent horseman, gave her free rein and was inwardly pleased at the chance to rid himself of his obnoxious interlocutor. But the horse, coming to a gully she had not noticed before, suddenly swerved aside, and Muromsky was unseated. Falling rather heavily onto the frozen ground, he lay there cursing his bobtailed filly, who, as if coming to her senses, stopped at once, as soon as she felt herself riderless. Ivan Petrovich galloped over to him and asked if he was hurt. Meanwhile the groom brought the guilty horse, leading her by the bridle. He helped

Muromsky to climb into the saddle, and Berestov invited him to his house. Muromsky could not refuse, for he felt himself obliged, and thus Berestov returned home in glory, having hunted down a hare and leading his adversary, wounded and almost a prisoner of war.

Over lunch the neighbors fell to talking quite amicably. Muromsky asked Berestov to lend him a droshky, for he confessed that on account of the pain he was in no condition to make it home on horseback. Berestov saw him off to the porch, and Muromsky left, but not before obtaining his word of honor that he would come the very next day (and with Alexei Ivanovich) for a friendly dinner in Priluchino. Thus an ancient and deeply rooted enmity seemed about to end owing to the shying of a bobtailed filly.

Liza ran out to meet Grigory Ivanovich.

"What does this mean, papa?" she said in surprise. "Why are you limping? Where's your horse? Whose droshky is this?"

"You'll never guess, *my dear*,"* Grigory Ivanovich replied, and he told her everything that had happened. Liza could not believe her ears. Giving her no time to recover, Grigory Ivanovich announced that the two Berestovs would dine with them the next day.

"What are you saying!" she cried, turning pale. "The Berestovs, father and son! Dining with us tomorrow! No, papa, say what you like, I won't show myself for anything."

"What, have you lost your mind?" her father retorted. "Since when have you become so bashful, or are you nursing a hereditary hatred for them, like a romantic heroine? Enough, don't play the fool . . ."

"No, papa, not for anything in the world, not for the finest treasure will I appear before the Berestovs."

Grigory Ivanovich shrugged and did not argue any more with her, for he knew that he would get nowhere by contradicting her, and he went to rest from his noteworthy ride.

Lizaveta Grigoryevna went off to her room and sent for Nastya. The two spent a long time discussing the next day's visit. What would Alexei think if he recognized the well-bred young lady as his Akulina? What opinion would he have of her conduct and principles, of her sagacity? On the other hand, Liza wanted very much to see what impression such an unexpected encounter would make on him . . . Suddenly a thought flashed through her mind. She immediately told it to

* In English in the original. *Translator.*

Nastya; they were both pleased with such a godsend and decided to carry it out without fail.

The next day over breakfast Grigory Ivanovich asked his daughter whether she still intended to hide from the Berestovs.

"Papa," Liza replied, "I'll receive them if you like, only on one condition: however I appear before them, whatever I do, you're not to scold me or show any sign of surprise or displeasure."

"Again some sort of pranks!" Grigory Ivanovich said, laughing. "Very well, very well, I agree; do whatever you like, my dark-eyed little mischief." With those words he kissed her on the forehead, and Liza ran off to get ready.

At exactly two o'clock a homemade carriage harnessed to six horses drove into the yard and rolled around the densely green circle of the lawn. Old Berestov went up the steps supported by two of Muromsky's liveried lackeys. Behind him came his son, who arrived on horseback, and together they went into the dining room, where the table was already laid. Muromsky could not have received his neighbors more affably, proposed to show them the garden and the menagerie before dinner, and led them down the path, carefully swept and sprinkled with sand. Old Berestov inwardly begrudged the labor and time wasted on such useless whims, but kept silent out of politeness. His son shared neither the economical landowner's displeasure, nor the vain anglomaniac's raptures; he impatiently awaited the appearance of the host's daughter, of whom he had heard so much, and though his heart, as we know, was already taken, a young beauty always had a right to his imagination.

Returning to the drawing room, the three sat down: the old men recalled former times and stories from their service, while Alexei reflected on the role he would play in the presence of Liza. He decided that in any case cold distraction would be the most suitable of all and prepared himself accordingly. The door opened, he turned his head with such indifference, with such proud nonchalance, that the heart of the most inveterate coquette was bound to shudder. Unfortunately, instead of Liza, old Miss Jackson came in, whitened, tight-laced, with downcast eyes and a little curtsy, and Alexei's splendid military maneuver went for naught. Before he had time to regroup his forces, the door opened again, and this time Liza came in. They all rose. The father was just beginning to introduce the guests, but suddenly stopped and quickly bit his lip . . . Liza, his swarthy Liza, was whitened to the ears, her brows blackened even more than Miss Jackson's; false curls, much lighter than her own hair, were fluffed up like a Louis XIV wig; sleeves *à l'imbécile*[8] stuck out like Madame de Pompadour's farthingale; her waist was laced up like the letter X, and all her mother's diamonds that had not yet been pawned shone on her fingers, neck, and ears. Alexei could not have recognized his Akulina in this ridiculous and glittering young miss. His father went to kiss her hand, and he vexedly followed him; when he touched her white fingers, it seemed to him that they were trembling. At the same time he noticed a little foot, deliberately exposed and shod with all possible coquetry. That reconciled him somewhat to the rest of her attire. As for the white and black greasepaint, it must be confessed that in the simplicity of his heart he did not notice them at first glance, nor did he suspect them later on. Grigory Ivanovich remembered his promise and tried not to show any surprise; but his daughter's mischief seemed so amusing to him that he could barely control himself. The prim Englishwoman was in no mood for laughter. She guessed that the black and white greasepaint had been purloined from her chest of drawers, and a crimson flush of vexation showed through the artificial whiteness of her face. She cast fiery glances at the young prankster, who, putting off all explanations for another time, pretended not to notice them.

They sat down at the table. Alexei went on playing the role of the distracted and pensive one. Liza minced, spoke in singsong through her teeth, and only in French. Her father kept peering at her, not understanding what she was up to, but finding it all quite amusing. The Englishwoman was furious and said nothing. Only Ivan Petrovich felt at home: he ate for two, drank his fill, laughed at his own jokes, and talked and guffawed more and more amiably every moment.

They finally got up from the table; the guests left, and Grigory Ivanovich gave free rein to his laughter and his questions. "What gave you a mind to fool them?" he asked Liza. "And do you know something? White greasepaint really becomes you; I won't enter into the mysteries of feminine toilette, but in your place I'd use white greasepaint; not too much, of course, just a little."

Liza was delighted with the success of her hoax. She embraced her father, promised to think over his advice, and ran to propitiate the annoyed Miss Jackson, who could hardly be persuaded to open her door and listen to her excuses. Liza had been ashamed to show such a swarthy face to strangers; she had not dared to ask . . . she was sure that

good, kind Miss Jackson would forgive her . . . and so on and so forth.
Miss Jackson, now persuaded that Liza had not thought to make fun of
her, calmed down, kissed Liza, and in token of their reconciliation gave
her a little jar of white English greasepaint, which Liza accepted with
expressions of sincere gratitude.

The reader can guess that the next morning Liza was not slow to
make her appearance in the grove of their meetings.

"Did you go to our masters' yesterday, sir?" she asked Alexei at
once. "How did you find the young lady?"

Alexei replied that he had not noticed her.

"A pity," Liza retorted.

"Why is that?" asked Alexei.

"Because I wanted to ask you whether it's true what they say . . ."

"What do they say?"

"Whether it's true, as they say, that I supposedly resemble the
young lady?"

"What nonsense! Next to you, she's a real fright."

"Ah, sir, it's sinful for you to say so; our young lady's so white, so
elegant! As if I could compare with her!"

Alexei swore to her that she was better than all possible white-
skinned young ladies and, to reassure her completely, began to portray
her mistress in such funny strokes that Liza laughed heartily.

"Still and all," she said with a sigh, "though my young lady may be
ridiculous, I'm just an illiterate fool next to her."

"Eh," said Alexei, "there's nothing to grieve over! If you like, I'll
teach you to read and write at once."

"Really," said Liza, "why not give it a try?"

"Very well, my dear, we'll begin right now."

They sat down. Alexei took a pencil and a notebook from his
pocket, and Akulina learned the alphabet with surprising ease. Alexei
could not marvel enough at her quick-wittedness. The next morning
she also wanted to try writing; at first the pencil would not obey her,
but after a few minutes she began to trace letters quite decently.

"What a wonder!" said Alexei. "Our studies go more quickly than
by the Lancaster system."[9]

Indeed, at the third lesson Akulina could already read "Natalya, the
Boyar's Daughter"[10] syllable by syllable, interrupting her reading with
remarks which truly amazed Alexei, and she covered a whole sheet of
paper with aphorisms chosen from the same tale.

A week went by and they began to exchange letters. The post office was set up in a hole in an old oak tree. Nastya secretly performed the duties of postman. There Alexei brought letters written in a round hand, and there, on plain blue paper, he found the scribbles of his beloved. Akulina was evidently growing accustomed to a better turn of style, and her mind was noticeably developing and forming.

Meanwhile the recent acquaintance between Ivan Petrovich Berestov and Grigory Ivanovich Muromsky strengthened more and more and soon turned into friendship, owing to this particular circumstance: the thought often occurred to Muromsky that, at Ivan Petrovich's death, all his property would pass into Alexei Ivanovich's hands; that Alexei Ivanovich would thus become one of the richest landowners in the province; and that there was no reason why he should not marry Liza. Old Berestov, for his part, though he acknowledged a certain extravagance (or English folly, as he put it) in his neighbor, still did not deny that he had many excellent qualities—for instance, a rare resourcefulness: Grigory Ivanovich was closely related to Count Pronsky, a distinguished and powerful man; the count could be very useful to Alexei, and Muromsky (so thought Ivan Petrovich) would probably be glad of the chance to give his daughter away in a profitable manner. The old men thought so much about all this, each to himself, that they finally talked it over together, embraced, promised to work things out properly, and set about it, each for his own part. Muromsky was faced with a difficulty: persuading his Betsy to get more closely acquainted with Alexei, whom she had not seen since that memorable dinner. It seemed they had not liked each other very much; at least Alexei never came back to Priluchino, and Liza went to her room each time Ivan Petrovich honored them with a visit.

"But," thought Grigory Ivanovich, "if Alexei came here every day, Betsy would be bound to fall in love with him. That's in the nature of things. Time puts everything right."

Ivan Petrovich was less worried about the success of his intentions. That same evening he summoned his son to his study, lit his pipe, and, after a brief silence, said:

"Why is it, Alyosha, that you haven't mentioned military service for so long now? Or perhaps the hussar uniform no longer tempts you! . . ."

"No, papa," Alexei replied respectfully. "I see it is not your wish that I join the hussars; it is my duty to obey you."

"Very well," replied Ivan Petrovich, "I see you are an obedient son. That is a comfort to me. Nor do I want to force you; I will not compel you to enter . . . government service . . . at once; but meanwhile I intend to get you married."

"To whom, papa?" asked the amazed Alexei.

"To Lizaveta Grigoryevna Muromsky," replied Ivan Petrovich. "Quite the bride, isn't she?"

"I'm not thinking of marrying yet, papa."

"You're not thinking, so I've thought for you and thought well."

"Say what you like, Liza Muromsky doesn't please me at all."

"She'll please you later. Habit and love go hand in glove."

"I don't feel capable of making her happy."

"Her happiness is not your worry. What? So this is how you respect the parental will? Very well!"

"As you please, I don't want to marry and I won't marry."

"You'll marry, or I'll curse you, and—as God is holy!—I'll sell the estate and squander the money, and you won't get half a kopeck! I'll give you three days to reflect, and meanwhile don't you dare show your face to me."

Alexei knew that once his father got something into his head, in Taras Skotinin's words, even a nail couldn't drive it out;[11] but Alexei took after his papa, and it was just as hard to out-argue him. He went to his room and began to reflect on the limits of parental power, on Lizaveta Grigoryevna, on his father's solemn promise to make a beggar of him, and finally on Akulina. For the first time he saw clearly that he was passionately in love with her; the romantic notion of marrying a peasant girl and living by his own labors came to his head, and the more he thought about this decisive step, the more reasonable he found it. For some time their meetings in the grove had broken off on account of rainy weather. He wrote Akulina a letter in the clearest handwriting and the most frantic style, announced to her the ruin that threatened them, and at the same time offered her his hand. He at once took the letter to the post office, the hole in the tree, and lay down to sleep quite pleased with himself.

The next day Alexei, firm in his intention, went to Muromsky early in the morning to have a frank talk with him. He hoped to arouse his magnanimity and win him over to his side.

"Is Grigory Ivanovich at home?" he asked, stopping his horse before the porch of the Priluchino castle.

"No, he's not," answered the servant. "Grigory Ivanovich went out early this morning."

"How annoying!" thought Alexei. "Then is Lizaveta Grigoryevna at home, at least?"

"Yes, sir."

Alexei jumped off his horse, handed the bridle to the lackey, and went in without being announced.

"All will be decided," he thought, approaching the drawing room. "I'll talk it over with the girl herself."

He went in . . . and was dumbfounded! Liza . . . no, Akulina, dear, swarthy Akulina, not in a sarafan, but in a white morning dress, was sitting by the window and reading his letter. She was so taken up with it that she did not hear him come in. Alexei could not hold back an exclamation of joy. Liza gave a start, raised her head, cried out, and was about to run away. He rushed to hold her back.

"Akulina, Akulina! . . ."

Liza tried to free herself . . .

"*Mais laissez-moi donc, monsieur; mais êtes-vous fou?*"* she kept saying, turning away.

"Akulina! My dear friend, Akulina!" he kept saying, kissing her hands. Miss Jackson, a witness to this scene, did not know what to think. Just then the door opened and Grigory Ivanovich came in.

"Aha!" said Muromsky. "It seems the matter's already quite settled between you . . ."

My readers will spare me the unnecessary duty of describing the denouement.

End of The Tales of I. P. Belkin

---

* "Leave me alone, sir; are you mad?" *Translator.*

The History of the
Village of Goryukhino

———

If God sends me readers, they might be curious to know how it was that I decided to write *The History of the Village of Goryukhino*. For that I must go into a few preliminary details.

I was born of honorable and noble parents in the village of Goryukhino on April 1st in the year 1801, and received my primary education from our sexton. To this estimable man I owe the love of reading and of literary occupations in general that subsequently developed in me. My progress was slow but certain, for at the age of ten I already knew almost all that has remained till now in my memory, which was weak by nature and which, on account of my equally weak health, I was not allowed to burden unnecessarily.

The title of man of letters always seemed most enviable to me. My parents, estimable people, but simple and educated in an old-fashioned way, never read anything, and there were no books in the whole house except for the ABC they bought for me, some almanacs, and the *New Grammar*.[1] Reading the *Grammar* was long the favorite of my exercises. I knew it by heart, and, despite that, I found new, unnoticed beauties in it every day. After General Plemyannikov, under whom my father had once served as adjutant, Kurganov seemed to me the greatest of men. I asked everyone about him, but, unfortunately, no one could satisfy my curiosity, no one had known him personally, and to all my questions they answered only that Kurganov wrote the *New Grammar*, which I already knew very well. The darkness of the unknown surrounded him like some ancient demigod; sometimes I even doubted the truth of his existence. His name seemed invented and the talk about him an empty myth waiting to be investigated by a new Niebuhr.[2] However, he still haunted my imagination, I tried to attach some likeness to this mysterious person, and finally decided that he must resemble the zemstvo assessor Koryuchkin,[3] a little old man with a red nose and flashing eyes.

In the year 1812 I was taken to Moscow and placed in Karl Ivanovich Meyer's boarding school, where I spent no more than three months, for we were disbanded before the enemy entered, and I returned to the country.[4] Once the twelve nations were driven out, they wanted to take me to Moscow again, to see if Karl Ivanovich had returned to his former hearth and home, or, in the contrary case, to place me in another school, but I persuaded my dear mother to keep me in the country, my health preventing me from getting up at seven, as is the custom in all boarding schools. Thus I reached the age of sixteen, remaining with my primary education and playing ball with my playmates, the only science of which I acquired sufficient knowledge during my stay in boarding school.

At that time I enlisted as a cadet in the * * * infantry regiment, in which I remained until this past year of 18—. My term in the regiment left me with few pleasant impressions apart from being promoted to officer and winning 245 roubles at a time when I had only one rouble and sixty kopecks left in my pocket. The death of my beloved parents forced me to resign my commission and return to my paternal seat.

This epoch of my life is so important for me that I intend to enlarge upon it, begging the kindly reader's pardon beforehand if I am making ill use of his indulgent attention.

The day was autumnal and bleak. Having reached the station where I had to turn off to Goryukhino, I hired a private coach and drove down the country road. Though I am of mild temperament by nature, I was so gripped by impatience to see again the places where I had spent my best years that I kept urging my coachman on, now promising him a tip, now threatening him with a beating, and since it was more convenient for me to nudge him in the back than to take out and undo my purse, I confess I struck him two or three times, something that had never happened to me in all my life, for, though I don't know why myself, the coachman's estate has always been especially dear to me. The coachman urged his troika on, but it seemed to me that, as is usual with coachmen, while talking to the horses and waving his whip, he kept tightening the reins. At last I glimpsed the Goryukhino grove, and ten minutes later we drove into the courtyard. My heart was beating hard—I looked around me with indescribable emotion. I had not seen Goryukhino for eight years. The little birches that had been planted by the fence when I was there had grown and were now tall, branchy trees. The courtyard, in former times adorned by three regular flowerbeds with wide, sand-strewn paths between them, had been turned into an unmowed meadow on which a brown cow grazed. My britzka stopped at the front porch. My servant went to open the door, but it was boarded up, though the shutters were open and the house seemed inhabited. A woman came out of the servants' cottage and asked whom I wanted. Learning that the master had arrived, she ran back to the cottage, and soon the domestics surrounded me. I was touched to the bottom of my heart, seeing familiar and unfamiliar faces, and I exchanged friendly kisses with them all: the boys I had played with were grown men, and the girls who used to sit on the floor waiting for errands were married women. The men wept. To the women I said unceremoniously: "How you've aged!" And they replied with feeling: "And how plain you've grown, dear master!" They took me to the back porch, where I met my wet nurse, who embraced me with tears and sobs as a much-enduring Odysseus. They ran to heat up the bathhouse. The cook, who in his current inactivity had grown a beard, offered to prepare dinner for me, or supper—for it was already getting dark. The rooms in which the wet nurse and my late mother's maids had been living were cleared for me at once, and I found myself in my humble ancestral abode and fell asleep in the same room I had been born in twenty-three years earlier.

I spent some three weeks in all sorts of business—dealing with assessors, marshals, and provincial officials of every description. At last I came into my inheritance and took possession of my ancestral seat: I calmed down, but soon the boredom of inactivity began to torment me. I was not yet acquainted with my good and estimable neighbor * * *. Running an estate was an occupation entirely foreign to me. The conversation of my wet nurse, whom I had promoted to housekeeper and steward, consisted of exactly fifteen family anecdotes, very interesting for me, but always recounted in the same way, so that she became for me another *New Grammar*, in which I knew every line on every page. The real, time-honored grammar I found in the pantry, amidst all sorts of junk, in lamentable condition. I brought it into the light and tried to read it, but Kurganov had lost his former charm for me; I read it through once more and never opened it again.

In this extremity the thought came to me: why not try writing something myself? The indulgent reader already knows that I received a skimpy education and had no chance to acquire for myself what had once been neglected, having played with serf boys until I was sixteen, and then moving from province to province, from quarters to quarters, spending time with Jews and sutlers, playing on shabby billiard tables, and marching in the mud.

Besides that, being a writer seemed to me so complicated, so beyond the reach of the uninitiated, that the thought of taking up the pen frightened me at first. Could I dare hope to find myself someday numbered among the writers, when my ardent desire to meet even one of them had never been fulfilled? But this reminds me of an occasion which I intend to tell about as proof of my constant passion for our native literature.

In 1820, while still a cadet, I happened to be in Petersburg on official business. I lived there for a week, and despite the fact that I did not know a single person there, I had an extremely merry time of it: each day I slipped away to the theater, to the gallery of the fourth circle. I learned the names of all the actors and fell passionately in love with * * *, who one Sunday played with great artfulness the role of Amalia in the drama *Misanthropy and Repentance*.[5] In the morning, returning from general headquarters, I usually went to a basement tearoom and read literary magazines over a cup of hot chocolate. Once I was sitting there immersed in a critical article in *The Well-Intentioned;* someone in a pea-green overcoat came over to me and quietly pulled a page of the *Hamburg Gazette* from under my journal.[6] I was so taken up that I did not even raise my eyes. The stranger ordered himself a beefsteak and sat down facing me; I went on reading and paid no attention to him; meanwhile he finished his lunch, angrily scolded the waiter for negligence, drank half a bottle of wine, and left.

Two young men were there having lunch. "Do you know who that was?" one said to the other. "That was B., the writer."

"The writer!" I exclaimed involuntarily and, abandoning the journal half read and the cup half drunk, I rushed to pay and, without waiting for the change, ran out to the street. Looking in all directions, I saw a pea-green overcoat in the distance and set out after it down Nevsky Prospect almost at a run. Having gone a few steps, I suddenly felt I was being stopped—I turned to look, an officer of the guards pointed out to me that I ought not to have shoved him off the sidewalk, but rather to have stopped and stood at attention. After this reprimand I became more careful; to my misfortune I kept meeting officers, I kept stopping, and the writer was getting further ahead of me. Never in my life was my soldier's uniform so burdensome to me, never in my life had epaulettes seemed to me so enviable. By the Anichkin Bridge I finally caught up with the pea-green overcoat.

"Allow me to ask," I said, putting my hand to my brow, "are you Mr. B., whose excellent articles I have had the good fortune to read in *The Zealot for Enlightenment?*"

"No, sir," he replied, "I'm not a writer, I'm a lawyer, but I know B. very well. I met him a quarter of an hour ago at the Police Bridge."

Thus my respect for Russian literature cost me thirty kopecks in forfeited change, an official reprimand, and a near arrest—and all for nothing.

Despite all the objections of my reason, the bold thought of becoming a writer kept running through my head. Finally, unable to resist the pull of nature any longer, I stitched together a thick notebook with the firm intention of filling it with whatever might come along. I investigated and evaluated all kinds of poetry (for I had yet to think about humble prose) and decided to venture upon an epic poem drawn from Russian history. It did not take me long to find a hero. I chose Rurik[7]— and set to work.

I had acquired a certain knack for verses by copying the notebooks that were handed around among our officers—namely: *The Dangerous Neighbor, Critique of the Moscow Boulevard* or *of the Presnya Ponds*, and so on. In spite of that my poem advanced slowly, and I abandoned it at the third verse. I thought that the epic genre was not my genre, and began a tragedy of Rurik. The tragedy didn't get going. I tried turning it into a ballad—but the ballad somehow didn't work out for me either. Finally inspiration dawned on me, I began and successfully finished an inscription for a portrait of Rurik.

Though my inscription was not entirely unworthy of attention, especially as the first production of a young versifier, I nevertheless felt that I was not born to be a poet, and satisfied myself with this first experience. But my creative endeavors so attached me to literary pursuits that I could no longer part with the notebook and the inkpot. I wanted to descend to prose. First off, not wishing to busy myself with doing preliminary research, laying out a plan, putting parts together, and so on, I conceived the idea of writing down separate thoughts, with no connection, with no order, just as they presented themselves to me. Unfortunately, thoughts did not enter my head, and in two whole days all I came up with was the following observation:

A man who does not obey the laws of reason and is used to following the promptings of passion, often errs and subjects himself to later remorse.

A correct thought, of course, but no longer a new one. Abandoning thoughts, I took up stories, but, having no habit of organizing fictional events, I chose some remarkable anecdotes I had heard formerly from various persons, and tried to adorn the truth by lively storytelling, and occasionally also by the flowers of my own imagination. In putting these stories together, I gradually formed my style and grew accustomed to expressing myself correctly, pleasantly, and freely. But my store soon ran out, and again I began to seek a subject for my literary activity.

The thought of abandoning trivial and dubious anecdotes for the recounting of true and great events had long stirred my imagination. To be the judge, observer, and prophet of epochs and nations seemed to me the greatest height a writer could attain. But what sort of history could I write with my pitiful education, where would I not have been preceded by men of great learning and conscientiousness? What genre of history have they not yet exhausted? I might start writing world history—but does the immortal work of the Abbé Millot not exist already? Should I turn to the history of our fatherland? But what can I say after Tatishchev, Boltin, and Golikov?[8] And is it for me to rummage in chronicles and delve into the secret meaning of an obsolete language, when I could not even learn Slavonic numerals? I thought of a less voluminous history, for instance, the history of our provincial capital; but here, too, I faced so many insurmountable obstacles! The trip to the city, visits to the governor and the bishop, requests for admission to the archives and monastery storerooms, and so on. The history of our district town would have been more suitable for me, but it was of no interest either for the philosopher or for the pragmatist, and offered little food for eloquence: the village * * * was renamed a town in the year 17—, and the only remarkable event preserved in its chronicles was a terrible fire that had occurred ten years earlier and had destroyed the marketplace and the government buildings.

An unexpected event resolved my perplexity. A peasant woman who was hanging laundry in the attic found an old basket filled with woodchips, litter, and books. The whole house knew my love of reading. At the very time when I was sitting over my notebook, chewing my pen and thinking of experimenting with country preaching, my housekeeper triumphantly lugged the basket into my room, exclaiming joyfully:

"Books! Books!"

"Books!" I repeated in rapture and rushed to the basket.

In fact, I saw a whole pile of books with green and blue paper covers. It was a collection of old almanacs. This discovery cooled my rapture, but even so I was glad of the unexpected find, even so they were books, and I generously rewarded the laundress's zeal with fifty silver kopecks. Left alone, I started to examine my almanacs, and soon my attention was strongly engaged by them. They made up a continuous sequence of years from 1744 to 1799, that is, exactly fifty-five years. The blue pages usually bound into almanacs were covered with old-fashioned handwriting. Casting a glance at these lines, I saw with amazement that they contained not only observations about the weather and household accounts, but also brief historical notices about the village of Goryukhino. I immediately began sorting through these precious notes and soon found that they presented a complete history of my paternal seat over the course of almost an entire century in the most strict chronological order. On top of that they contained an inexhaustible store of economic, statistical, meteorological, and other learned observations. Since then the study of these notes has occupied me exclusively, for I saw the possibility of extracting from them a well-ordered, interesting, and instructive narrative. After familiarizing myself sufficiently with these precious memorials, I began to search for new sources for the history of the village of Goryukhino. And the abundance of them soon amazed me. Having devoted a whole six months to preliminary research, I finally took up the long-desired work and with God's help completed it this November 3rd of the year 1827.

Now, like a certain historian similar to me, whose name I cannot recall, having finished my arduous task, I set down my pen and with sadness go to my garden to reflect upon what I have accomplished. It seems to me, too, that, having written *The History of Goryukhino*, I am no longer needed in this world, that my duty has been done, and it is time I went to my rest!

⸺

Here I append a list of the sources I have used in compiling *The History of Goryukhino*:

1. The collection of old almanacs. *Fifty-four parts.* The first twenty parts written in an old-fashioned hand with contractions. This chronicle was composed by my great-grandfather, Andrei Stepanovich Belkin. It is distinguished by clarity and brevity of style; for instance: "May 4—Snow. Trishka beaten for rudeness. 6—Brown cow died. Senka beaten for drunkenness. 8—Fair weather. 9—Rain and snow. Trishka beaten on

account of weather. 11—Fair weather. Fresh snowfall. Hunted down three hares . . ." and so on, without any reflections. The remaining thirty-five parts are written in various hands, mostly in what is known as "shopkeeper's style," with or without contractions, are generally prolix, incoherent, and do not follow the rules of orthography. Here and there a woman's hand is noticeable. This portion includes the notes of my grandfather, Ivan Andreevich Belkin, and my grandmother, his spouse, Evpraxia Alexeevna, as well as the notes of the clerk Garbovitsky.

2. The chronicle of the Goryukhino sexton. This curious manuscript I dug up at my priest's, who is married to the chronicler's daughter. The first pages had been torn out by the priest's children and used for so-called kites. One of them fell in the middle of my courtyard. I picked it up and was about to give it back to the children, when I noticed that it was covered with writing. From the first lines I saw that the kite had been made from a chronicle, the rest of which I luckily managed to save. This chronicle, which I acquired for a quarter measure of oats, is distinguished by its profundity and uncommon grandiloquence.

3. Oral tradition. I did not neglect any sources. But I am especially indebted to Agrafena Trifonova, mother of the headman Avdei, and, it was said, the mistress of the clerk Garbovitsky.

4. Census records, with observations by previous headmen (ledgers and expense accounts) concerning the morality and living conditions of the peasants.

The land known as Goryukhino, after the name of its capital, occupies more than 650 acres of the earthly globe. The number of its residents amounts to sixty-three souls. To the north it borders on the villages of Deriukhovo and Perkukhovo,[9] whose inhabitants are poor, scrawny, and undersized, and whose proud proprietors are devoted to the warlike exercise of hare hunting. To the south the river Sivka separates it from the domain of the Karachevo free plowmen, restless neighbors, known for the violent cruelty of their temper. To the west it is surrounded by the flourishing fields of Zakharyino, prospering under the rule of wise and enlightened landowners. To the east it adjoins wild, uninhabited territory, an impassable swamp, where only wild cranberry grows, where the sole sound is the monotonous croaking of frogs, and which superstitious tradition supposes to be the dwelling-place of a certain demon.

NB. This place is in fact known as *Demon's Swamp*. The story goes that a half-witted girl tended a heard of swine not far from this solitary place. She got pregnant and could give no satisfactory explanation of her misadventure. The voice of the people accused the swamp demon; but this tale is not worthy of a historian's attention, and after Niebuhr it would be unpardonable to believe it.

———

From olden times Goryukhino had been famous for its fertility and favorable climate. Rye, oats, barley, and buckwheat thrive in its rich fields. A birch grove and a pine forest provide the inhabitants with timber and windfalls for building and heating their dwellings. There is no lack of nuts, cranberries, whortleberries, and bilberries. Mushrooms spring up in extraordinary numbers; fried with sour cream, they provide pleasant, though unhealthy, nourishment. The pond is full of carp, and in the river Sivka there are pike and burbot.

———

The male inhabitants of Goryukhino are for the most part of average height, of sturdy and manly build, their eyes gray, their hair brown or red. The women are distinguished by their slightly upturned noses, prominent cheekbones, and corpulence. NB. *A buxom wench:* this expression is found frequently in the headman's notes to the census records. The men are well-behaved, hardworking (especially on their own land), brave, pugnacious: many of them go alone against bears and are famous in the neighborhood for fist-fighting; they are all generally inclined to the sensual pleasure of drunkenness. On top of housework, the women share a large part of the men's labors; they yield nothing to them in bravery, and scarcely a one of them stands in fear of the headman. They make up a powerful public guard, tirelessly vigilant in the master's courtyard, and are called "halberdears" (from the old word "halberd"). The chief duty of the halberdears is to bang a stone on a cast-iron plate as often as possible and thereby terrify evildoers. They are as chaste as they are beautiful, responding to audacious attempts both sternly and expressively.

The residents of Goryukhino have long carried on an abundant trade in bast, bast baskets, and bast shoes. It is favored by the river Sivka, which they cross in spring in dugout boats, like the ancient Scandinavians, and at other times of the year on foot, first rolling up their trousers to the knees.

The Goryukhino language is decidedly an offshoot of Slavic, but differs from it as much as Russian does. It is filled with abbreviations and contractions, some letters being quite abolished in it or replaced by others. However, a Russian can easily understand a Goryukhiner and vice versa.

The men were usually married at the age of thirteen to girls of twenty. The wives beat their husbands for the first four or five years. After that the husbands started beating their wives. In this way both sexes had their time of power, and balance was maintained.

The funeral rite took place in the following way. On the day of his death, the deceased was taken to the cemetery, so that the dead man would not uselessly take up space in the cottage. As a result it happened, to the indescribable joy of his family, that a dead man would sneeze or yawn at the very moment he was being carried out of the village in his coffin. Wives would weep over their husbands, wailing and saying: "My bright light, my brave heart! Why have you abandoned me? What will I remember you by?" With the return from the cemetery, a memorial banquet would begin in honor of the deceased, and relations and friends would be drunk for two or three days or even a whole week, depending on their zeal and their fondness for his memory. These ancient rites have survived to this day.

The Goryukhiners' clothing consisted of a shirt worn over the trousers, which is a distinctive token of their Slavic origin. In winter they wore sheepskin coats, but more for the beauty of it than from real need, for they usually slung the coat over one shoulder and threw it off at the least effort calling for movement.

Learning, art, and poetry had been in a rather flourishing state in Goryukhino since ancient times. On top of the priests and lectors, there had always been literate men. The chronicles mention the local scribe Terenty, who lived around 1767, and who was able to write not only with his right hand but also with his left. This extraordinary man became famous in the neighborhood by composing all sorts of letters, petitions, civilian passports, and so on. Having suffered more than once for his art, for his obligingness, and for taking part in various remarkable adventures, he died in extreme old age, just as he was training himself to write with his right foot, for the writing of both of his hands had become too well known. As the reader will see below, he also plays an important role in the history of Goryukhino.

Music was always the favorite art of educated Goryukhiners: balalaikas and bagpipes, to the delight of their sensitive hearts, resound in their dwellings to this day, especially in the ancient public establishment adorned with a fir tree and the image of a double-headed eagle.[10]

Poetry once flourished in ancient Goryukhino. Verses by Arkhip the Bald have been preserved till now in the memory of posterity.

In delicacy they yield nothing to the eclogues of the well-known Virgil; in beauty of imagination they far exceed the idylls of Mr. Sumarokov.[11] And though in dashing style they yield to the latest works of our Muses, they still equal them in whimsicality and wit.

Let us cite as an example this satirical poem:

> Into the master's yard
> The headman Anton sallies,
> Bearing a bunch of tallies.
> The squire then inquires
> Just what these sticks might be.
> Ah, headman Anton, see—
> You've robbed us all around
> You've left us barren ground,
> And the village goes without,
> While your fine wife struts about.

Having thus acquainted my reader with the ethnographic and statistical situation of Goryukhino, and with the manners and customs of its inhabitants, let us now begin the narrative itself.

LEGENDARY TIMES

THE HEADMAN TRIFON

The form of government in Goryukhino has changed several times. It has been by turns under the rule of elders chosen by the community, under stewards appointed by the landowner, and finally under the direct control of the landowners themselves. The advantages and disadvantages of these different forms of government will be expanded upon in the course of my narrative.

The founding of Goryukhino and its initial population are shrouded in the darkness of the unknown. Obscure legends tell us that Goryukhino was once a rich and extensive village, that its inhabitants were all well-to-do, that its quitrent was collected once a year and sent to no one knew whom on several carts. In that time everything was bought cheaply and sold dearly. Stewards did not exist, the headmen offended nobody, the inhabitants worked little and lived in clover, and the shepherds tended the flocks in boots. We should not be seduced by this charming picture. The notion of a golden age is inherent in all people and proves only that they are never pleased with the present and, experience giving them little hope for the future, adorn the irretrievable past with all the flowers of their imagination. Here is what is certain:

The village of Goryukhino from olden times has belonged to the illustrious Belkin family. But my ancestors, owners of many other country seats, gave no attention to this remote land. Goryukhino paid small tribute and was ruled by elders elected by the people of the *veche*, or community assembly.

But with the passage of time the Belkins' ancestral holdings were broken up and went into decline. The impoverished grandchildren of a rich grandfather could not get out of their habit of luxury and demanded the former full income from an estate that by then had diminished tenfold. Threatening orders followed one after another. The headmen read them to the *veche*; the elder oratorized, the peasants became agitated, and the masters, instead of a double quitrent, received cunning excuses and humble complaints written on greasy paper and sealed with a copper coin.

A dark cloud hung over Goryukhino, but nobody even thought about it. In the last year of the rule of Trifon, the last headman elected by the people, on the very day of the church feast, when all the folk noisily surrounded the pleasure establishment (pot-house, in simple parlance) or wandered through the streets embracing each other and loudly singing the songs of Arkhip the Bald, a bast-covered britzka drove into the village, hitched to a pair of barely alive nags; on the box sat a ragged Jew, while a head in a visored cap stuck itself out of the britzka and seemed to gaze curiously at the merrymaking folk. The residents met the vehicle with laughter and crude mockery. (*NB.*

"Rolling the hems of their clothes into tubes, the madmen jeered at the Jewish driver and exclaimed mockingly: 'Jew, Jew, eat the sow's ear! . . .'" *Chronicle of the Goryukhino Sexton.*) But how amazed they were when the britzka stopped in the middle of the village and the new arrival, leaping out of it, in an imperious voice summoned the headman Trifon. This dignitary was in the pleasure establishment, from which two elders respectfully led him under the arms. The stranger, giving him a terrible look, handed him a letter and ordered him to read it immediately. The Goryukhino headmen had the habit of never reading anything themselves. The headman was illiterate. They sent for the village clerk Avdei. He was found not far away, sleeping under a fence in a lane, and was brought to the stranger. But, once brought, either from sudden fright, or from rueful premonition, he seemed to find the clearly written characters of the letter blurred, and he was unable to make them out. The stranger, with terrible oaths, sent the headman Trifon and the clerk Avdei to bed, postponed the reading of the letter until the next day, and went to the office cottage, where the Jew carried his small trunk after him.

The Goryukhiners gazed upon this extraordinary incident in mute amazement, but the britzka, the Jew, and the stranger were soon forgotten. The day ended noisily and merrily, and Goryukhino fell asleep, not foreseeing what awaited it.

With the morning sunrise the residents were awakened by a knocking on the windows and a call to a community assembly. The citizens appeared one after another in the courtyard of the office cottage, which served as a meeting place. Their eyes were bleary and red, their faces swollen; yawning and scratching themselves, they looked at the man in the visored cap and old blue kaftan, standing solemnly on the porch of the office cottage, and tried to recall his features, which they had seen sometime or other. The headman Trifon and the clerk Avdei stood hatless beside him with a look of servility and profound sadness.

"Everybody here?" asked the stranger.

"Is everybody here?" repeated the headman.

"Yes, everybody," replied the citizens.

Then the headman announced that a decree had been received from the master, and he ordered the clerk to read it for all the assembly to hear. Avdei stepped forward and read aloud the following. (*NB.* "This ill-omened decree I copied from the headman Trifon's, who kept it in a coffer together with other mementos of his rule over Goryukhino." I myself could not find this curious letter.)

Trifon Ivanov!

The bearer of this letter, my agent * * *, is going to my native village Goryukhino in order to take upon himself the administration of same. Immediately upon his arrival, gather the muzhiks and announce to them my will; to wit: The orders of my agent * * * are to be obeyed by them, the muzhiks, as my own. All that he demands of them is to be fulfilled unquestioningly; in the contrary case he, * * *, is to treat them with all possible severity. I am forced into this by their shameless disobedience and your knavish connivance, Trifon Ivanov.

(Signed) N. N.

Then, legs spread like the letter X and hands on his hips like a Φ, * * * delivered the following brief and expressive speech:

"Watch out you don't get too smart on me; I know you're spoilt folk, but don't worry, I'll knock the foolishness out of your heads quicker than yesterday's drunkenness."

There was no drunkenness left in anyone's head. As if thunderstruck, the Goryukhiners hung their heads and in terror dispersed to their homes.

THE RULE OF THE STEWARD * * *

* * * took the reins of government and set about implementing his political system. It merits special examination.

Its main foundation was the following axiom: The richer the muzhik, the more spoiled he is; the poorer, the more humble. Consequently, * * * strove for humility on the estate as the main peasant virtue. He demanded a list of the peasants, and divided them into rich and poor. (1) The arrears were distributed among the well-to-do muzhiks and exacted from them with all possible strictness. (2) The slackers and holiday revelers were immediately put to the plow, and if, by his reckoning, their work proved insufficient, he sent them to other peasants as hired hands, for which they paid him a voluntary contribution, while those sent into bondage had the full right to buy themselves out by paying a double quitrent on top of the arrears. Any community obli-

THE HISTORY OF THE VILLAGE OF GORYUKHINO

gations fell to the well-to-do muzhiks. Recruitment was a triumph for the mercenary-minded ruler; one by one the rich muzhiks all bought themselves out, so that the lot finally fell upon the scoundrels or the ruined.* Community assemblies were abolished. He collected quitrent in small installments all year round. On top of that, he took up unexpected collections. The muzhiks, it seems, did not even pay that much more than in former times, but they simply could not earn or save enough money. In three years Goryukhino was totally destitute.

Goryukhino became cheerless, the marketplace was empty, the songs of Arkhip the Bald fell silent. Young children went begging. Half the muzhiks were in the fields, the other half served as hired hands; and the day of the church feast became, in the chronicler's expression, not a day of joy and exultation, but an anniversary of grief and sorrowful remembrance.

---

* "The accursed steward put Anton Timofeev in irons, but old Timofei bought his son out for one hundred roubles; the steward shackled Petrushka Eremeev, and his father bought him out for sixty-eight roubles, and the accursed one wanted to chain up Lyokha Tarasov, but the man fled to the forest, and the steward was greatly distressed and waxed verbally violent, and it was the drunkard Vanka who was taken to town and sent off as a recruit." (From a report by the Goryukhino muzhiks.)

Roslavlev

Reading *Roslavlev*,[1] I was amazed to see that its plot is based on a real event that I know all too well. I was once a friend of the unfortunate woman Mr. Zagoskin chose as the heroine of his story. He has turned public attention anew to the forgotten event, awakened feelings of indignation lulled to sleep by time, and disturbed the peace of the grave. I will defend the shade—and let the reader forgive the weakness of my pen out of respect for the promptings of my heart. I must needs speak a good deal about myself, because my fate was long bound up with the lot of my poor friend.

My coming out was in the winter of 1811. I will not describe my first impressions. It can easily be imagined what the feelings of a sixteen-year-old girl must be in exchanging upstairs rooms and teachers for continuous balls. I gave myself to the whirl of merriment with all the liveliness of my years and as yet without reflection ... A pity: those times were worth observing.

Among the girls who came out together with me, Princess * * * distinguished herself (Mr. Zagoskin has called her Polina; I shall let her keep that name). We quickly became friends, and this was the occasion.

My brother, a lad of twenty-two, belonged to the ranks of the dandies back then; he had been assigned to the Foreign Office and lived in Moscow, dancing and leading a wild life. He fell in love with Polina and entreated me to bring our families closer together. My brother was the idol of our whole family, and with me he did as he liked.

Having become close with Polina to please him, I soon found myself sincerely attached to her. There was much that was strange in her and still more that was attractive. I did not yet understand her, but I already loved her. Imperceptibly I began to look with her eyes and to think with her thoughts.

Polina's father was a worthy man, i.e., he drove a tandem and wore a key and a star, though he was simple and flighty. Her mother, on the other hand, was a staid woman and distinguished by her gravity and common sense.

Polina appeared everywhere; she was surrounded by admirers; they paid court to her—but she was bored, and boredom gave her an air of pride and coldness. That went extraordinarily well with her Grecian face and dark eyebrows. I exulted when my satirical observations brought a smile to that regular and bored face.

Polina read an extraordinary amount, and without any discrimination. She had the key to her father's library. The library consisted for the most part of works by eighteenth-century writers. She knew French literature from Montesquieu to the novels of Crébillon. Rousseau she knew by heart. There was not a single Russian book in the library, except for the works of Sumarokov, which Polina never opened.[2] She told me that it was hard for her to decipher Russian type, and she probably never read anything in Russian, not even the little verses offered her by Moscow poetasters.

Here I shall allow myself a small digression. It is thirty years now, praise God, since they began reproaching poor us for not reading in Russian and for (supposedly) being unable to express ourselves in our native language. (*NB*. The author of *Yuri Miloslavsky* wrongly repeats these banal accusations. We have all read him, and it seems he owes to one of us the translation of his novel into French.) The thing is that we would even be glad to read in Russian; but it seems our literature is no older than Lomonosov[3] and is still extremely limited. Of course, it does present us with several excellent poets, but it is impossible to demand of all readers an exceptional interest in poetry. In prose we have only Karamzin's *History;*[4] the first two or three novels appeared two or three years ago, while in France, England, and Germany books, one more remarkable than the other, follow one after the other. We do not even see translations; and if we do, then, say what you like, I still prefer the originals. Our journals are of interest only to our literati. We are forced to draw everything, news and ideas, from foreign books; thus we also think in foreign languages (all those, at least, who do think and who follow the thoughts of the human race). Our most famous literati have admitted it to me. The eternal complaints of our writers about the neglect to which we relegate Russian books are like the complaints of Russian tradeswomen, who are indignant that we buy our hats at Sichler's and are not content with the products of Kostroma milliners. I return back to my subject.

Memories of high society life are usually weak and insignificant even in historic epochs. However, one traveler's appearance in Moscow left a deep impression on me. That traveler was Mme de Staël.[5] She came in the summer, when most of Moscow's inhabitants had left for the country. Russian hospitality began to bustle; they went out of their

way to entertain the famous foreigner. Naturally, they gave dinners
for her. Gentlemen and ladies gathered to gawk at her and were for
the most part displeased. They saw in her a fat fifty-year-old woman,
whose dress did not suit her age. They did not like her tone, her talk
seemed too long, and her sleeves too short. Polina's father, who had
known Mme de Staël back in Paris, gave a dinner for her, to which he
invited all our Moscow wits. There I saw the author of *Corinne*. She
sat in the place of honor, her elbows leaning on the table, her beautiful fingers rolling and unrolling a little paper tube. She seemed out of
sorts, began to speak several times, but could not go on. Our wits ate
and drank their fill and seemed much more pleased with the prince's
fish soup than with Mme de Staël's conversation. The ladies kept aloof.
The ones and the others only rarely broke the silence, convinced of
the insignificance of their thoughts and intimidated in the presence of
the European celebrity. All through dinner Polina sat as if on pins and
needles. The guests' attention was divided between the sturgeon and
Mme de Staël. They expected a *bon mot* from her any moment; finally
a double entendre escaped her, even quite a bold one. Everyone picked
it up, laughed loudly, a murmur of astonishment arose; the prince was
beside himself with joy. I glanced at Polina. Her face was ablaze, and
tears showed in her eyes. The guests got up from the table completely
reconciled with Mme de Staël: she had made a pun, and they galloped
off to spread it all over the city.

"What's happened to you, *ma chère?*" I asked Polina. "Can it be that
a slightly frivolous joke could embarrass you so much?"

"Ah, my dear," Polina replied, "I am in despair! How insignificant
our high society must have seemed to this extraordinary woman! She
is used to being surrounded by people who understand her, on whom
a brilliant observation, a strong impulse of the heart, an inspired word
are never lost; she is used to fascinating conversations of the highest
cultivation. And here . . . My God! Not a single thought, not a single
remarkable word in a whole three hours! Dull faces, dull solemnity—
that's all! How boring it was for her! How weary she seemed! She saw
what they needed, what these apes of enlightenment could understand,
and she tossed them a pun. And how they fell upon it! I was burning
with shame and ready to weep . . . But let her," Polina went on heatedly, "let her take away the opinion of our society rabble that they
deserve. At least she's seen our good simple folk and understands them.
You heard what she said to that unbearable old buffoon, who, just to

please the foreigner, took it into his head to laugh at Russian beards: 'A people who a hundred years ago stood up for their beards, will today stand up for their heads.' How dear she is! How I love her! How I hate her persecutor!"

I was not the only one to notice Polina's embarrassment. Another pair of keen eyes rested on her at the same moment: the dark eyes of Mme de Staël herself. I don't know what she was thinking, but only that she approached my friend after dinner and got to talking with her. A few days later, Mme de Staël wrote her the following note:

> *Ma chère enfant, je suis toute malade. Il serait bien aimable à vous de venir me ranimer. Tâchez de l'obtenir de mme votre mère et veuillez lui presenter les respects de votre amie* de S.*

This letter is in my keeping. Polina never explained to me her relations with Mme de Staël, for all my curiosity. She was mad about the famous woman, who was as good-natured as she was gifted.

What the passion for malicious talk can reduce one to! Not long ago I told about all this in a certain very decent company.

"Perhaps," it was pointed out to me, "Mme de Staël was none other than Napoleon's spy, and Princess * * * provided her with the information she needed."

"For pity's sake," I said, "Mme de Staël, who was persecuted by Napoleon for ten years; the noble, good Mme de Staël, who barely managed to escape under the protection of the Russian emperor, Mme de Staël, the friend of Chateaubriand and Byron, Mme de Staël— Napoleon's spy! . . ."

"It's quite, quite possible," the sharp-nosed Countess B. objected. "Napoleon was such a sly fox, and Mme de Staël is a subtle thing herself!"

Everyone was talking about the approaching war and, as far as I remember, rather light-mindedly. Imitation of the French tone from the time of Louis XV was in fashion. Love of the fatherland seemed like pedantry. The wits of the day extolled Napoleon with fanatical servility and joked about our reverses. Unfortunately, the defenders of the fatherland were a bit simple-minded; they were mocked rather amus-

---

* My dear child, I am quite sick. It would be very nice of you to come and revive me. Try to get madame your mother's permission and give her the respects of your friend *de S.*

ingly and had no influence. Their patriotism was limited to a severe criticism of the use of the French language at gatherings, of the introduction of foreign words, to menacing outbursts against the Kuznetsky Bridge,[6] and the like. Young people spoke of everything Russian with contempt or indifference and jokingly predicted for Russia the lot of the Confederation of the Rhine.[7] In short, society was rather vile.

Suddenly news of the invasion and the sovereign's appeal shocked us. Moscow was agitated. Count Rastopchin's folk-style leaflets appeared; the people became furious. The society babblers quieted down; the ladies lost courage. The persecutors of the French language and the Kuznetsky Bridge took a firm upper hand in society, and the drawing rooms filled with patriots: one poured the French snuff from his snuffbox and began sniffing Russian; another burned a dozen French brochures; another renounced Lafite and took up foaming mead. Everybody swore off speaking French; everybody shouted about Pozharsky and Minin and started preaching a national war, while preparing for the long drive to their Saratov estates.[8]

Polina could not hide her contempt, just as earlier she had not concealed her indignation. Such a swift about-face and such cowardice put her out of patience. On promenades, at the Presnya Ponds, she deliberately spoke French; at the table, in the presence of servants, she deliberately challenged patriotic boasting, deliberately spoke of the numerical strength of Napoleon's army, of his military genius. Those present turned pale, fearing denunciation, and hastened to reproach her with devotion to the enemy of the fatherland. Polina would smile contemptuously.

"God grant," she would say, "that all Russians love their fatherland as I love it." She astonished me. I had always known Polina to be modest and taciturn, and I could not understand where this boldness came from.

"For pity's sake," I said once, "what makes you mix into what's none of our business? Let the men fight and shout about politics; women don't go to war, and they have no business with Bonaparte."

Her eyes flashed.

"Shame on you," she said. "Don't women have a fatherland? Don't they have fathers, brothers, husbands? Is Russian blood alien to us? Or do you think we're born only to be spun around in the ecossaise at balls and compelled to embroider little dogs on canvas at home? No, I know what effect a woman can have on public opinion or even on the heart of just one man. I don't accept the humiliation we're condemned to. Look at Mme de Staël: Napoleon fought with her as with an enemy force . . . And uncle still dares to mock her fearfulness at the approach of the French army! 'Don't worry, madam: Napoleon is making war on Russia, not on you . . .' Oh, yes! If uncle were caught by the French, he'd be allowed to stroll about the Palais-Royal; but Mme de Staël in such a case would die in a state prison. And Charlotte Corday? And our Marfa Posadnitsa? And Princess Dashkova?[9] How am I inferior to them? Certainly not in boldness of heart and resoluteness."

I listened to Polina with amazement. Never had I suspected such ardor, such ambition in her. Alas! What had her extraordinary inner qualities and courageous loftiness of mind brought her to? It's true what my favorite writer said: *Il n'est de bonheur que dans les voies communes.**

The sovereign's arrival redoubled the general agitation. The ecstasy of patriotism finally took hold of high society. Drawing rooms became debating chambers. Everywhere there was talk of patriotic donations. They repeated the immortal speech of the young Count Mamonov, who donated his entire fortune.[10] After that some mamas observed that the count was no longer such an enviable match, but we all admired him. Polina raved about him.

"What are you going to donate?" she once asked my brother.

"I haven't come into my fortune yet," my scapegrace replied. "All in all, I've got thirty thousand in debts: I donate that on the altar of the fatherland."

Polina became angry.

"For some people," she said, "honor and the fatherland are mere trifles. Their brothers die on the battlefield, and they play the fool in drawing rooms. I don't know if you could find a woman base enough to allow such a buffoon to pretend he's in love with her."

My brother flared up.

"You're too exacting, Princess," he retorted. "You demand that everyone see Mme de Staël in you and speak to you in tirades from *Corinne*. Know that a man may joke with a woman and not joke before the fatherland and its enemies."

With those words, he turned away. I thought they had quarreled

---

* The words are apparently Chateaubriand's. *Pushkin's note.* [The words are a slightly inexact quotation from the end of Chateaubriand's short novel *René* (1802): "There is happiness only along common paths." *Translator.*]

forever, but I was mistaken: Polina liked my brother's impertinence, she forgave him his inappropriate joke for the noble impulse of indignation, and, learning a week later that he had joined Mamonov's regiment, she herself asked me to reconcile them. My brother was in ecstasy. He immediately offered her his hand. She accepted, but put off the wedding until the end of the war. The next day my brother left for the army.

Napoleon was approaching Moscow; our troops were retreating; Moscow was alarmed. Her inhabitants were getting out one after the other. The prince and princess persuaded mother to go with them to their estate in —sky province.

We arrived in * * *, an enormous village fifteen miles from the provincial capital. There were a great many neighbors around us, most of them newly arrived from Moscow. We all got together each day; our country life was just like city life. Letters from the army came almost every day; the old ladies looked for the location of the bivouac on the map and were angry at not finding it. Polina was interested only in politics, read nothing but newspapers and Rastopchin's handbills, and did not open a single book. Surrounded by people whose notions were limited, constantly hearing absurd opinions and ill-founded news, she fell into deep despondency; languor took possession of her soul. She despaired of the salvation of the fatherland, it seemed to her that Russia was quickly approaching its fall, each report redoubled her hopelessness, Count Rastopchin's police announcements put her out of patience. She found their jocular tone the height of indecency, and the measures he had taken an insufferable barbarity. She did not grasp the idea of that time, so great in its horror, the idea whose bold execution saved Russia and freed Europe. She spent hours at a time, her elbows propped on a map of Russia, counting the miles, following the quick movements of the troops. Strange ideas came to her head. Once she declared to me her intention of leaving our village, going to the French camp, making her way to Napoleon, and killing him there with her own hands. I had no difficulty persuading her of the madness of such an undertaking. But the thought of Charlotte Corday stayed with her for a long time.

Her father, as you already know, was a rather light-minded man; all he thought about was living in the country in as much of a Moscow style as possible. He gave dinners, started a *théâtre de société* where he staged French *proverbes*, and tried in every way possible to diversify our pleasures. Several captured officers arrived in town. The prince was glad of the new faces and talked the governor into letting him house them at his place . . .

There were four of them. Three were quite insignificant men, fanatically devoted to Napoleon, unbearably loud-mouthed, though in truth they had paid for their boastfulness with their honorable wounds. But the fourth was an extremely remarkable man.

He was then twenty-six years old. He belonged to a good family. His face was pleasant. His tone was very good. We paid attention to him at once. He accepted our kindnesses with noble modesty. He spoke little, but what he said was well grounded. Polina liked him, because he was the first who could clearly explain military actions and troop movements to her. He calmed her down, explaining that the retreat of the Russian army was not a senseless flight and was as disturbing for the French as it was infuriating for the Russians.

"But you," Polina asked him, "aren't you convinced of your emperor's invincibility?"

Sénicourt (I shall also call him by the name Mr. Zagoskin gave him)—Sénicourt, after a brief pause, replied that in his situation frankness would be awkward. Polina insistently demanded an answer. Sénicourt admitted that the thrust of French troops into the heart of Russia could prove dangerous for them, that it seemed the campaign of 1812 was over, but had produced nothing decisive.

"Over!" Polina objected. "Yet Napoleon still keeps going forward, and we still keep retreating!"

"So much the worse for us," Sénicourt replied, and changed the subject.

Polina, who was sick of both the cowardly prophecies and the foolish boasting of our neighbors, listened eagerly to judgments based on actual knowledge and impartiality. From my brother I received letters which it was impossible to make any sense of. They were filled with jokes, clever and bad, questions about Polina, banal assurances of love, and so on. Polina, reading them, became annoyed and shrugged her shoulders.

"Admit," she said, "that your Alexei is a most empty man. Even in the present circumstances, from the battlefield, he finds a way of writing letters that mean nothing at all. What sort of conversation will he have with me in the course of a quiet family life?"

She was mistaken. The emptiness of my brother's letters proceeded not from his own nonentity, but from a prejudice—a most insulting one for us, however: he supposed that with women one should use language adapted to the weakness of their understanding, and that important subjects do not concern us. Such an opinion would be impolite anywhere, but with us it is also stupid. There is no doubt that Russian women are better educated, read more, and think more than the men, who busy themselves with God knows what.

News spread of the battle of Borodino.[11] Everyone talked about it; each one had his own most accurate information; each one had a list of the dead and wounded. My brother did not write to us. We were extremely alarmed. Finally one of those purveyors of all sorts of stuff came to inform us that he had been taken prisoner, and meanwhile announced in a whisper to Polina that he was dead. Polina was deeply upset. She was not in love with my brother and was often annoyed with him, but at that moment she saw him as a martyr, a hero, and she mourned for him in secret from me. Several times I found her in tears. That did not surprise me; I knew how painfully concerned she was with the fate of our suffering fatherland. I did not suspect that the cause of her grief was something else.

One morning I went for a stroll in the garden; Sénicourt walked beside me; we talked about Polina. I had noticed that he deeply sensed her extraordinary qualities and that her beauty had made a strong impression on him. I laughingly observed that his situation was most romantic. A wounded knight captured by the enemy falls in love with the noble mistress of the castle, touches her heart, and finally wins her hand.

"No," Sénicourt said to me, "the princess sees me as an enemy of Russia and will never agree to leave her fatherland."

Just then Polina appeared at the end of the alleé; we went to meet her. She approached with quick steps. Her pallor struck me.

"Moscow is taken," she said to me, ignoring Sénicourt's bow. My heart was wrung, tears poured down in streams. Sénicourt kept silent, his eyes lowered. "The noble, enlightened French," she went on in a voice trembling with indignation, "celebrated their triumph in a worthy way. They set fire to Moscow. Moscow has been burning for two days now."

"What are you saying?" cried Sénicourt. "It can't be."

"Wait till night," she replied drily. "Maybe you'll see the glow."

"My God! He's done for," said Sénicourt. "Can't you see that the burning of Moscow is the ruin of the whole French army, that Napoleon will have nothing to hold on to anywhere, that he will be forced to retreat quickly through the devastated, deserted land at the approach of winter with a disorderly and discontented army! And you could think that the French dug such a hell for themselves! No, no, the Russians, the Russians set fire to Moscow. What terrible, barbaric magnanimity! Now it's all decided: your fatherland is no longer in danger; but what will happen to us, what will happen to our emperor . . ."

He left us. Polina and I could not collect our wits.

"Can it be," she said, "that Sénicourt is right, that the burning of Moscow is the work of our own hands? If so . . . Oh, I can take pride in the name of the Russian woman! The whole universe will be amazed at so great a sacrifice! Now even our downfall doesn't frighten me, our honor is saved; never again will Europe dare to fight with a people who cut off their own hands and burn their capital."

Her eyes shone, her voice rang. I embraced her, we mingled tears of noble rapture with ardent prayers for our fatherland.

"You don't know?" Polina said to me with an inspired look. "Your brother . . . He's a happy man, he's not a prisoner. Rejoice: he was killed for the salvation of Russia."

I cried out and fell unconscious into her arms . . .

Dubrovsky

Volume One

CHAPTER ONE

Several years ago there lived on one of his estates an old-time Russian squire, Kirila Petrovich Troekurov. His wealth, noble birth, and connections gave him great weight in the provinces where his properties lay. Neighbors were happy to satisfy his slightest whim; provincial officials trembled at his name; Kirila Petrovich received these tokens of servility as a fitting tribute; his house was always full of guests ready to entertain his squirely idleness, to share in his noisy and sometimes wild amusements. No one dared to refuse his invitations or not to appear with due respect on certain days in the village of Pokrovskoe. In his domestic life Kirila Petrovich displayed all the vices of an uncultivated man. Spoiled by all that surrounded him, he was accustomed to giving free rein to all the impulses of his hot temper and all the fancies of his rather limited mind. Despite an extraordinarily strong constitution, he suffered twice a week or so from his gluttony and was in his cups every evening. In one wing of his house lived sixteen maidservants, occupied with handwork suited to their sex. The windows in the wing had wooden bars; the doors were locked, and Kirila Petrovich kept the keys. At appointed hours the young recluses were let out to the garden and strolled under the supervision of two old women. From time to time Kirila Petrovich gave some of them away in marriage, and new ones came to replace them. His treatment of the peasants and house serfs was severe and arbitrary; yet they were devoted to him: they were proud of their master's wealth and renown, and in their turn allowed themselves much in relation to their neighbors, trusting in his powerful protection.

Troekurov's customary occupations consisted of driving around his vast domain, of prolonged banquets, and of pranks invented each day and whose victim was usually some new acquaintance; though old friends did not always manage to evade them, with the sole exception of Andrei Gavrilovich Dubrovsky. This Dubrovsky, a retired lieutenant of the guards, was his nearest neighbor and owned seventy souls.[1]

Troekurov, arrogant in his dealings with people of the highest rank, respected Dubrovsky in spite of his humble condition. They had once been comrades-in-arms, and Troekurov knew from experience the impatience and resoluteness of his character. Circumstances had kept them apart for a long time. Dubrovsky, his fortune in disarray, had been forced to go into retirement and settle on his one remaining estate. On learning that, Kirila Petrovich offered him his protection, but Dubrovsky thanked him and remained poor and independent. After a few years, Troekurov, a retired general-en-chef, came to his estate; they met and were glad of each other. From then on they got together every day, and Kirila Petrovich, who in all his born days had never honored anyone with a visit, would drop in unceremoniously at his old comrade's little house. Being of the same age, born to the same social class, brought up in the same way, they partly resembled each other in both character and inclinations. In certain respects their fates were also the same: both had married for love, both had soon been widowed, both had been left with a child. Dubrovsky's son had been educated in Petersburg, Kirila Petrovich's daughter had grown up under her father's eye, and Troekurov often said to Dubrovsky:

"Listen, brother Andrei Gavrilovich: if your Volodka turns out well, I'll give him Masha; never mind if he's poor as a coot."

Andrei Gavrilovich would usually shake his head and reply:

"No, Kirila Petrovich, my Volodka's no match for Marya Kirilovna. A poor gentleman the likes of him would do better to marry a poor young miss and be the head of the household, than to become the steward of a spoiled wench."

Everybody envied the harmony that reigned between the haughty Troekurov and his poor neighbor, and marveled at the latter's boldness when, at Kirila Petrovich's table, he spoke his opinion straight out, regardless of whether it contradicted the host's opinion or not. Some tried to imitate him and cross the line of proper obedience, but Kirila Petrovich put such a scare into them that they forever lost their taste for such attempts, and Dubrovsky alone remained outside the general law. An unexpected event upset and altered all that.

Once, at the beginning of autumn, Kirila Petrovich was getting ready to go hunting. The previous evening orders had been given to the huntsmen and grooms to be ready by five in the morning. The tent and field kitchen were sent on ahead to the place where Kirila Petrovich was to dine. The host and guests went to the kennels, where more than five hundred hounds and borzoi lived in warmth and plenty, extolling Kirila Petrovich's generosity in their doggy language. Here there was also a clinic for sick dogs, supervised by the staff medic Timoshka, and a section where noble bitches whelped and nursed their pups. Kirila Petrovich was proud of this fine institution and never missed a chance to boast of it to his guests, each of whom was already viewing it for at least the twentieth time. He strutted about the kennels, surrounded by his guests and accompanied by Timoshka and the chief huntsmen, stopped before certain kennels, now inquiring after the health of the sick, now making more or less stern and just observations, now calling over the dogs he knew and speaking amiably with them. The guests considered it their duty to admire Kirila Petrovich's kennels. Dubrovsky alone frowned and kept silent. He was an ardent hunter. His situation allowed him to keep only two hounds and one leash of borzoi; he could not help being slightly envious at the sight of this magnificent institution.

"Why are you frowning, my friend?" Kirila Petrovich asked him. "Don't you like my kennel?"

"No," he replied severely, "the kennel's a marvel; it's unlikely your servants live as well as your dogs do."

One of the huntsmen took offense.

"We don't complain of our life," he said, "thanks to God and the master, but it's true enough that some gentleman wouldn't do badly to exchange his estate for any of these kennels. He'd be warmer and better fed."

Kirila Petrovich laughed loudly at his serf's insolent remark, and the guests burst out laughing after him, though they sensed that the huntsman's joke could refer just as well to them. Dubrovsky turned pale and did not say a word. Just then Kirila Petrovich was brought some newborn puppies in a basket; he busied himself with them, chose two, and ordered the others drowned. Meanwhile Andrei Gavrilovich disappeared, and nobody noticed it.

On returning from the kennels with his guests, Kirila Petrovich sat down to supper, and only then, not seeing Dubrovsky, did he notice his absence. The servants told him that Andrei Gavrilovich had gone home. Troekurov immediately told them to overtake him and bring him back without fail. Never yet had he gone hunting without Dubrovsky, an experienced and fine connoisseur of canine qualities and a faultless arbiter of various hunting disputes. The servant who galloped after

him came back while they were still at the table and reported to his
master that Andrei Gavrilovich refused to listen and would not come
back. Kirila Petrovich, flushed with liqueurs as he usually was, became
angry and sent the same servant a second time to tell Andrei Gavrilovich that if he did not come at once to spend the night at Pokrovskoe,
he, Troekurov, would break with him forever. The servant rode off
again, Kirila Petrovich got up from the table, dismissed his guests, and
went to bed.

The next morning his first question was: Is Andrei Gavrilovich
here? Instead of an answer, he was handed a letter folded into a tri-
angle. Kirila Petrovich told his clerk to read it aloud, and this is what
he heard:

My most gracious sir,

I have no intention of going to Pokrovskoe until you send me
the huntsman Paramoshka with an apology. It will be up to me
whether to punish or pardon him, but I have no intention of
taking jokes from your serfs, nor will I endure them from you,
because I am not a buffoon, but of ancient nobility.
With that I remain your most humble servant,
Andrei Dubrovsky.

By present-day notions of etiquette, this letter would be quite
improper, but it angered Kirila Petrovich not by its odd style and atti-
tude, but only by its substance.

"What?" Troekurov thundered, jumping out of bed barefoot.
"Send him my servants with apologies, it's for him to pardon or punish
them! What on earth is he thinking of? Does he know who he's dealing
with? I'll show him . . . He'll rue the day! He'll learn what it means to
go against Troekurov!"

Kirila Petrovich dressed and rode out to the hunt with his usual
splendor, but the hunt was no success. In the whole day they saw only
one hare, and it got away. Dinner in the field under the tent was no
success either, or at least it was not to the taste of Kirila Petrovich, who
beat the cook, yelled at the guests, and on the way back deliberately
rode with all his hunt across Dubrovsky's fields.

Several days went by and the hostility between the two neighbors
did not subside. Andrei Gavrilovich did not go back to Pokrovskoe,

Kirila Petrovich was bored without him, and his vexation loudly gave vent to itself in the most insulting expressions, which, thanks to the diligence of the local gentlefolk, reached Dubrovsky with additions and corrections. Then a new circumstance destroyed the last hope of reconciliation.

One day Dubrovsky was driving around his small domain. Approaching a birch grove, he heard the blows of an axe and a minute later the crash of a falling tree. He hastened to the grove and came upon some Pokrovskoe muzhiks calmly stealing his wood. Seeing him, they tried to run away. Dubrovsky and his coachman caught two of them, tied them up, and brought them to his place. Three enemy horses were also taken as spoils by the victor. Dubrovsky was extremely angry: before then Troekurov's people, who were well-known robbers, had not dared to do any mischief within the boundaries of his domain, knowing of his friendship with their master. Dubrovsky saw that they were now taking advantage of the rift that had occurred, and decided, against all notions of the rules of war, to teach his prisoners a lesson with the rods they had provided for themselves in his grove, and to set the horses to work, adding them to the manor's herd.

Rumors of this incident reached Kirila Petrovich that same day. He was beside himself and in the first moment of wrath was about to set off with all his house serfs to launch an attack on Kistenevka (so his neighbor's estate was called), utterly lay waste to it, and besiege the landowner himself in his own house. Such feats were nothing unusual for him. But his thoughts soon took a different turn.

Pacing with heavy steps up and down the hall, he happened to glance out the window and saw a troika stop at the gate. A little man in a leather cap and a frieze overcoat got out of the cart and went to the steward in the wing. Troekurov recognized the assessor Shabashkin and had him summoned. A moment later Shabashkin was already standing before Kirila Petrovich, making one bow after another and reverently awaiting his orders.

"Hello, what's-your-name," Troekurov said to him. "Why the visit?"

"I was going to town, Your Excellency," replied Shabashkin, "and stopped at Ivan Demyanovich's to find out if there were any orders from Your Excellency."

"You've come very opportunely, what's-your-name; I have need of you. Drink some vodka and listen."

Such a warm reception pleasantly surprised the assessor. He declined the vodka and started listening to Kirila Petrovich with all possible attention.

"I have a neighbor," said Troekurov, "a petty-landowning boor. I want to take his estate from him. What do you think of that?"

"Your Excellency, if there are any sort of documents or . . ."

"Nonsense, brother, forget about documents. That means law. The whole point is to take the estate from him without any right. Wait a minute, though. That estate used to belong to us; it was bought from a certain Spitsyn, and then sold to Dubrovsky's father. Can't we hang something on that?"

"It's tricky, Your Excellency; the sale was probably done in accordance with the law."

"Think, brother, put your mind to it."

"If, for instance, Your Excellency could in some way or other obtain from your neighbor the record or deed of purchase authorizing his ownership of the estate, then of course . . ."

"I understand, but the trouble is—all his papers got burned up in a fire."

"What, Your Excellency, his papers got burned up?! Could anything be better? In that case you can proceed according to the law, and you will undoubtedly obtain full satisfaction."

"You think so? Well, look sharp, then. I rely on your diligence, and you can be sure of my gratitude."

Shabashkin bowed almost to the ground, left, started busying himself that same day with the projected case, and, thanks to his adroitness, exactly two weeks later Dubrovsky received an invitation from town to provide immediately a proper explanation regarding his ownership of the village of Kistenevka.

Andrei Gavrilovich, astonished by the unexpected request, wrote in reply that same day a rather rude declaration, in which he stated that the village of Kistenevka had become his at the death of his late parent, that he owned it by right of inheritance, that Troekurov had nothing to do with the matter, and that any outside claim to his property was calumny and fraud.

This letter made a rather pleasant impression on the soul of the assessor Shabashkin. He saw, first, that Dubrovsky knew little about legal affairs, and, second, that it would be easy to put such a hot-tempered and imprudent man in a most disadvantageous position.

Andrei Gavrilovich, having considered the assessor's inquiries cool-headedly, saw the necessity of responding in more detail. He wrote a rather sensible paper, but subsequently it turned out to be insufficient. The case dragged on. Convinced that he was in the right, Andrei Gavrilovich worried little about it, had neither the wish nor the means to throw money around, and though he used to be the first to mock the bought conscience of the ink-slinging tribe, the thought of falling victim to calumny never entered his head. For his part, Troekurov cared just as little about the success of the case he had undertaken. Shabashkin bustled about for him, acted in his name, threatened and bribed judges, and interpreted various decrees either straightly or crookedly.

Be that as it may, in the year 18—, on the 9th day of February, Dubrovsky received, through the town police, a summons to appear before the * * * district judge for the hearing of his decision in the affair of the estate contested between him, Lieutenant Dubrovsky, and General-en-chef Troekurov and the signing of his accord or disaccord. That same day Dubrovsky set out for town; on the way Troekurov overtook him. They looked at each other proudly, and Dubrovsky noticed a malicious smile on his adversary's face.

CHAPTER TWO

Having arrived in town, Andrei Gavrilovich stopped with a merchant acquaintance, spent the night there, and the next morning appeared in the office of the district court. No one paid any attention to him. After him came Kirila Petrovich. The clerks rose and put their pens behind their ears. The members of the court received him with expressions of profound obsequiousness, moved a chair for him in a show of respect for his rank, years, and portliness; he sat down by the open door. Andrei Gavrilovich stood leaning against the wall. A profound silence ensued, and the secretary in a ringing voice began to read the decision of the court. We insert it here in full,[2] supposing that everyone will be pleased to see one of the means by which we in Russia can be deprived of an estate, to the ownership of which we have an indisputable right.

In the year 18—, the 27th day of October, the district court examined the case of the wrongful possession by Lieutenant of the Guards Dubrovsky, Andrei Gavrilovich, of an estate belonging to General-en-chef Troekurov, Kirila Petrovich, situated in * * * province in the village of Kistenevka, consisting of * * * male souls and of * * * acres of land with meadows and appurtenances. The case presents the following: on the 9th day of June past, in the year of 18—, the aforesaid General-en-chef Troekurov submitted to this court a petition to the effect that his late father, the collegiate assessor and chevalier Troekurov, Pyotr Efimovich, in the year 17—, on the 14th day of August, while serving as provincial secretary in a local office, did purchase from the gentleman and chancery clerk Spitsyn, Fadei Egorovich, an estate lying in the * * * township, in the aforementioned village of Kistenevka (which village, according to the * * * census, was then called the Kistenevka settlements), consisting, according to the 4th census, of * * * souls of the male sex with all their peasant chattels, the farmstead, with arable and non-arable land, woods, hayfields, fishing in the river, called the Kistenevka, and with all the appurtenances belonging to the estate and the wooden manor house, and, in short, everything without exception that his father, the village constable Spitsyn, Egor Terentyevich, gentleman, had left him as inheritance and that had been in his possession, not excluding a single soul, nor a single square foot of land, for the price of 2,500 roubles, the deed for which was signed on the same day in the * * * court of justice, and on the 26th day of that same August at the district court his father entered into possession and the seizin for it was recorded.—And finally, in the year 17—, the 6th day of September, by the will of God his father died, and meanwhile he, the petitioner, General-en-chef Troekurov, had been in the military service since the year 17—, almost from infancy, and for the most part had been on campaigns abroad, for which reason he could not have information of his father's death, nor likewise of the property left to him. Now, having gone into full retirement from the service and returned to his father's estates, located in * * * and * * * provinces, * * * and * * * districts, in various villages, comprising 3,000 souls in all, he discovers that, of the number of these above-listed estates mentioned in the * * * census, the souls (some * * * souls in that village at the present date * * *), with land and with all appurtenances, is without any title in the possession

of the aforementioned Lieutenant of the Guards Andrei Dubrovsky, for which reason, presenting along with his petition
the original deed of purchase which his father received from
the seller Spitsyn, Troekurov requests that the said estate, removed from the wrongful possession of Dubrovsky, be placed
at the full disposal of its rightful owner, Troekurov. And for the
unlawful appropriation of it, with the profits he gained from its
use, after making a proper inquiry into them, a penalty in accordance with the law be imposed on him, Dubrovsky, to his,
Troekurov's, satisfaction.

The investigation of this petition by the * * * district court
has discovered: that the said present owner of the disputed estate, Lieutenant of the Guards Dubrovsky, gave the local assessor of the nobility the explanation that the estate now in
his possession, the said village of Kistenevka, * * * souls with
land and appurtenances, came to him as an inheritance after
the death of his father, Sub-lieutenant of Artillery Dubrovsky,
Gavrila Evgrafovich, who obtained it through purchase from
the petitioner's father, former provincial secretary, later collegiate assessor Troekurov, through the power of attorney granted by him in the year 17—, on the 30th day of August, notarized in the * * * district court, to the titular councilor Sobolev,
Grigory Vassilyevich, who was to provide him, Dubrovsky's father, with the deed, in which it would be stated that the entire
estate, * * * souls with the land, obtained by him, Troekurov,
through purchase from the clerk Spitsyn, had been sold to his,
Dubrovsky's, father, and the agreed sum, 3,200 roubles, had
been received from the father in full and without return, and it
was requested that the attorney Sobolev provide his father with
the official deed. And meanwhile his father, by the same power
of attorney, having paid the full sum, was to take over this estate purchased by him and manage it as its lawful owner until
the deed was executed, and neither he, the seller Troekurov,
nor anyone else was to intervene henceforth in this estate. But
precisely when and in what office the deed was executed and
given by Sobolev to his father, he, Andrei Dubrovsky, does not
know, for he was in his earliest infancy at the time, and after
his father's death he was unable to find the said deed, and supposes that it may have been burned up, along with other papers

and property, during the fire in their house that took place in
the year of 17—, as is also known to the inhabitants of the village. And that the estate, since the purchase from Troekurov or
the receipt of the power of attorney by Sobolev, that is, since
the year 17—, and from the death of his father until the present day, has been in their, the Dubrovskys', undisputed possession, this has been testified to by the local inhabitants, 52
persons in all, who, being questioned under oath, bore witness
that indeed, as far as they could remember, the said disputed
estate had been in the possession of the aforesaid Messrs Dubrovsky for some 70 years now with no dispute from anyone,
but by precisely what act or deed they do not know. Whether
the previous purchaser of the estate mentioned in this case, the
former provincial secretary Pyotr Troekurov, had owned the
said estate, they do not recall. The house of Messrs Dubrovsky
burned down in a fire that occurred in the village during the
nighttime some 30 years ago, while disinterested persons suppose that the average income of the aforementioned disputed
estate, counting from that time on, could be no less than 2,000
roubles annually.

　　Counter to that, General-en-chef Troekurov, Kirila Petrovich, on January 3rd of this year, addressed this court with a
petition that, although the aforesaid Lieutenant of the Guards
Andrei Dubrovsky did present to the court the power of attorney that his father had issued to the titular councilor Sobolev,
neither the original deed of purchase nor any sufficiently clear
proof of such a deed, in compliance with the general regula-
tions of chapter 19 and the decision handed down in the year
of 1752 on the 29th day of November, was presented. Consequently, the power of attorney itself, owing to the death of its
issuer, his father, by the decision of the year 1818, the * * * day
of May, is now completely null and void. And moreover—

　　it is ordered that disputed estates be returned to their
owners—by deed where there is a deed, and by investigation
where there is no deed.

　　For the which estate, belonging to his father, he has already presented in evidence a deed of purchase, from which
it follows, based on the aforesaid statutes, that it should be
taken from the wrongful possession of the aforementioned

Dubrovsky and given to him by right of inheritance. And since the aforesaid landowners, having in their possession an estate not belonging to them and without any legality, and wrongfully enjoying profits from it not belonging to them, then by calculation, as much as is due by right of . . . should be exacted from the landowner Dubrovsky and be given to him, Troekurov, in satisfaction.—Upon the examination of which case and of extracts from it and from the law in the * * * district court, *it is determined:*

Concerning the aforesaid disputed estate, presently in the possession of Lieutenant of the Guards Dubrovsky, Andrei Gavrilovich, consisting of the village of Kistenevka, with * * * souls of the male sex according to the recent . . . census, with land and appurtenances, the case makes it clear that General-en-chef Troekurov, Kirila Petrovich, has presented the original deed of purchase by his late father, a provincial secretary, later a collegiate assessor, in the year 17—, from the chancery clerk Fadei Spitsyn, gentleman, and moreover this purchaser, Troekurov, as is clear from an addendum to the said deed, was put in possession of it by the * * * district court, which estate was already in his seizin, and though counter to that a power of attorney was presented on the part of Lieutenant of the Guards Andrei Dubrovsky, granted by the deceased purchaser Troekurov to the titular councilor Sobolev for carrying out the purchase in the name of his, Dubrovsky's, father, in such transactions not only the maintaining of a deed to real estate, but even temporary possession is prohibited by decree of . . . , since with the death of the grantor, the power of attorney is rendered completely null and void. Moreover, Dubrovsky for his part has presented no clear evidence of where and when the above-mentioned disputed estate was actually purchased by his power of attorney from the start of proceedings, that is in the year 18—, until the present time. And therefore this court decides: to confirm that the above-mentioned estate, * * * souls, with land and appurtenances, in the condition in which it now finds itself, belongs, in accordance with the deed of purchase presented, to General-en-chef Troekurov; to remove Lieutenant of the Guards Dubrovsky from disposal of it, and to put Mr. Troekurov in proper possession of it, and to require the

* * * court to issue a seizin for it as coming to him by inheritance. Moreover, General-en-chef Troekurov also petitions for the recovery from Lieutenant of the Guards Dubrovsky of the profits appropriated by him through the unlawful possession of his inherited estate. But since the said estate, according to the testimony of the old people, had been in the uncontested possession of Messrs Dubrovsky for some years, and the present investigation has not discovered any previous petitions on the part of Mr. Troekurov of such wrongful possession of the said estate by the Dubrovskys, according to the code—

it is ordered, that if someone sows on another's land, or fences it in and builds on it, and a complaint about wrongful seizure is made, and the truth is found out, then the rightful owner should be given back the land, with the crops, and the fence, and the buildings—

and therefore General-en-chef Troekurov is refused in his claim against Lieutenant of the Guards Dubrovsky, for the estate belonging to him is returned to his possession, with nothing removed from it. But if on entering it he should find that all is not where it should be, General-en-chef Troekurov has leave meanwhile, if he should have clear and legal proof of such a claim, to petition separately in the proper place. Which decision is announced in advance, on a legal basis, by appellate procedure, to the plaintiff as well as to the defendant, who will be summoned to this court for hearing of the decision and signing their accord or disaccord through the police.

Which decision is signed by all those present at the court.

The secretary fell silent, the assessor rose and, with a low bow, turned to Troekurov, inviting him to sign the proffered document, and the triumphant Troekurov, taking the pen from him, signed under the court's *decision* his full accord. It was Dubrovsky's turn. The secretary offered him the paper. But Dubrovsky stood motionless, his head lowered.

The secretary repeated his invitation to sign his full and complete accord or his outright disaccord, if contrary to expectation he felt in all conscience that his cause was just, and intended within the time prescribed by law to make an appeal to the proper quarters. Dubrovsky was silent . . . Suddenly he raised his head, his eyes flashed, he stamped his foot, shoved the secretary away with such force that the man fell down, and, seizing the ink bottle, flung it at the assessor. Everybody was horrified.

"What! You don't respect the church of God! Away, heathenish tribe!" Then, turning to Kirila Petrovich: "It's unheard of, Your Excellency," he went on, "hunters bringing dogs into the church of God! Dogs running all over the church! Just you wait, I'll teach you . . ."

Hearing the noise, the guards rushed in and with difficulty overpowered him. He was taken out and seated in the sledge. Troekurov came out after him, accompanied by the whole court. Dubrovsky's sudden madness had a strong effect on his imagination and poisoned his triumph.

The judges, who had hoped for his gratitude, were not honored with a single pleasant word from him. He left for Pokrovskoe that same day. Meanwhile, Dubrovsky lay in bed; the district doctor, fortunately not a total ignoramus, managed to bleed him and treat him with leeches and Spanish flies. Towards evening the sick man became better and regained consciousness. The next day he was driven to Kistenevka, which now almost did not belong to him.

CHAPTER THREE

Some time passed, but poor Dubrovsky's health was still bad. True, the fits of madness were not renewed, but his forces were noticeably weakened. He forgot his former occupations, rarely left his room, and spent whole days lost in thought. Egorovna, a kindly old woman who had once looked after his son, now became his own nanny. She watched over him as if over a child, reminded him of the times to eat and sleep, fed him, put him to bed. Andrei Gavrilovich quietly obeyed her and aside from her had no relations with anybody. He was in no condition to think about his affairs, to run the estate, and Egorovna saw the necessity of writing about it all to the young Dubrovsky, who served in one of the infantry guards regiments and was in Petersburg at the time. And so, tearing a page from the account book, she dictated a letter to the only literate man in Kistenevka, the cook Khariton, and sent it that same day to the post office in town.

But it is time the reader became acquainted with the real hero of our story.

Vladimir Dubrovsky was educated in the Cadet Corps[3] and graduated as an ensign in the guards. His father spared nothing for his proper
keeping, and the young man received more from home than he should
have expected. Being extravagant and ambitious, he allowed himself
luxurious whims, gambled and got into debt, did not worry about the
future, and foresaw a rich bride for himself sooner or later—the dream
of a poor young man.

One evening, when several officers were sitting around at his place,
sprawled on the sofas and smoking his amber-stemmed pipes, Grisha,
his valet, handed him a letter, the address and seal of which struck the
young man at once. He quickly opened it and read the following:

Dear Master, Vladimir Andreevich –

I, your old nanny, have decided to report to you on your papa's
health! He is very poorly, sometimes rambles in his speech, and
sits all day like a stupid child, but in life and death it is as God
wills. Come to us here, my bright falcon, we will send horses
to Pesochnoe for you. We have heard that the district court
will be coming to us to put us under the authority of Kirila
Petrovich Troekurov, because we are said to belong to him, but
we have been yours time out of mind, and never in our lives
heard such. Maybe, living in Petersburg, you could tell that to
our dear tsar, and he will not let us be offended. I remain your
faithful servant and nanny,
                                        Orina Egorovna Buzyreva.

I send my maternal blessing to Grisha, does he serve you well?
It is the second week we are having rain, and the shepherd
Rodya died around St. Nicholas's day.

Vladimir Dubrovsky reread these rather muddled lines several
times with extraordinary agitation. He had lost his mother in childhood and, barely knowing his father, had been brought to Petersburg
in his eighth year; but for all that he was romantically attached to him
and loved family life all the more, the less he had managed to savor its
quiet joys.

The thought of losing his father wrung his heart painfully, and the
situation of the poor sick man, which he surmised from his nanny's

letter, horrified him. He pictured his father, abandoned in a remote village, in the hands of a stupid old woman and some servants, threatened by some sort of calamity, and fading away without help in the sufferings of body and soul. Vladimir reproached himself for criminal neglect. For a long time he had received no letters from his father and had never thought of inquiring about him, supposing that he was traveling or busy with the estate.

He decided to go to him and even to retire from the service, if his father's ailing condition required his presence. His comrades, noticing his uneasiness, went home. Vladimir, left alone, wrote a request for a leave of absence, lit his pipe, and fell into deep reflection.

That same day he turned in his request, and three days later he was already on the high road.

Vladimir Andreevich was approaching the posting station where he had to turn off for Kistenevka. His heart was full of sad forebodings, he feared he would not find his father alive, he pictured the melancholy way of life awaiting him in the country, the remoteness, the solitude, the poverty, and the bother with things he knew nothing about. On reaching the station, he went to the stationmaster and inquired about hiring horses. The stationmaster asked him where he had to go, and announced that horses sent from Kistenevka had already been awaiting him for three days. Soon the old coachman Anton, who once used to take him around the stables and looked after his little horse, appeared before Vladimir Andreevich. Anton shed a few tears on seeing him, bowed to the ground, said that the old master was still alive, and ran to hitch up the horses. Vladimir Andreevich refused the lunch offered him and hastened to set off. Anton drove him along the country roads, and a conversation started between them.

"Tell me, please, Anton, what's this business between my father and Troekurov?"

"God knows about them, dear Vladimir Andreevich . . . They say the master didn't see eye to eye with Kirila Petrovich, and the man took it to court, though oftener than not he's his own court. It's not a servant's business to sort out the master's will, but, by God, your father shouldn't have gone against Kirila Petrovich. You can't chop down a tree with a penknife."

"So it's clear this Kirila Petrovich does whatever he likes around here?"

"That he does, master: they say he doesn't give a hoot about the assessor, and the police chief just runs errands for him. Squires come and fawn on him, and as the saying goes, where there's a trough, there'll be pigs."

"Is it true that he's taking away our estate?"

"Oh, master, we've heard that, too. The other day the Pokrovskoe sacristan said at a christening at our village headman's: 'Your fun is over; Kirila Petrovich'll take you in hand.' Mikita the blacksmith said to him: 'Enough, Savelyich, don't upset the host, don't trouble the guests. Kirila Petrovich is his own man, and Andrei Gavrilovich is his own man, and we're all God's and the sovereign's; but still, you can't button another man's lip.'"

"Meaning you don't want to be owned by Troekurov?"

"Owned by Troekurov! Lord, save us and deliver us! His own people sometimes have a bad time of it, but once he gets hold of another man's, he won't just skin them, he'll tear them to pieces. No, God grant Andrei Gavrilovich a long life, and if God takes him, we don't want anybody but you, our provider. Don't give us up, and we'll stand by you."

With those words, Anton swung the whip, shook the reins, and his horses broke into a brisk trot.

Touched by the old coachman's devotion, Dubrovsky kept silent and fell again into reflection. More than an hour went by; suddenly Grisha wakened him with the exclamation: "Here's Pokrovskoe!" Dubrovsky raised his head. He was driving along the bank of a wide lake, from which a small river flowed and went meandering among the hills in the distance; on one hill, above the dense greenery of a copse, rose the green roof and belvedere of an immense stone house, on another a five-domed church and an ancient bell tower; peasant cottages were scattered around them, with their wells and kitchen gardens. Dubrovsky recognized these places; he remembered that on that same hill he had played with little Masha Troekurov, who was two years his junior and even then promised to be a beauty. He wanted to ask Anton about her, but some sort of shyness held him back.

Driving up to the manor house, he caught sight of a white dress flashing among the trees in the garden. At that moment Anton whipped up the horses and, obedient to the ambition common to country coachmen and city drivers, raced at top speed over the bridge and past the village. Leaving the village behind, they went up the hill, and Vladimir glimpsed a birch grove and, to the left, in an open space, a small gray house with a red roof. His heart throbbed. Before him he saw Kistenevka and his father's poor home.

Ten minutes later he drove into the courtyard. He looked around him with indescribable emotion. For twelve years he had not seen his birthplace. The birches, which in his time had just been planted along the fence, had grown and were now tall, branchy trees. The courtyard, once adorned with three regular flowerbeds with wide, well-swept paths between them, had been turned into an unmowed meadow on which a hobbled horse grazed. The dogs were beginning to bark, but, recognizing Anton, they stopped and wagged their shaggy tails. Servants poured out of their cottages and surrounded the young master with noisy expressions of joy. He could barely force his way through their zealous crowd and run up the decrepit porch; in the front hall Egorovna met him and tearfully embraced her nursling.

"Hello, hello, nanny," he repeated, pressing the kind old woman to his heart. "What about papa? Where is he? How is he?"

Just then a tall old man, pale and thin, in a dressing gown and a nightcap, came into the room, barely able to move his feet.

"Greetings, Volodka!" he said in a weak voice, and Vladimir warmly embraced his father. Joy produced too great a shock in the sick man, he grew weak, his legs gave way under him, and he would have fallen, if his son had not held him up.

"Why did you get up?" Egorovna said to him. "You can't keep your feet, yet you head off to where people are."

The old man was carried to the bedroom. He kept trying to talk with him, but the thoughts were confused in his head and his words had no connection. He fell silent and lapsed into somnolence. Vladimir was struck by his condition. He settled in his bedroom and asked to be left alone with his father. The servants obeyed, and then they all turned to Grisha and took him to their own quarters, where they regaled him country-style, with all possible hospitality, wearing him out with questions and salutations.

CHAPTER FOUR

The once festive table now bears a coffin.

DERZHAVIN[4]

A few days after his arrival, young Dubrovsky wanted to get down to business, but his father was in no condition to give him the necessary explanations—Andrei Gavrilovich had no attorney. Sorting through his papers, Vladimir found only the first letter from the assessor and the draft of a reply to it; from them he could get no clear idea of the lawsuit and decided to wait for the consequences, trusting in the justice of the cause itself.

Meanwhile, Andrei Gavrilovich's health was getting worse by the hour. Vladimir foresaw his imminent demise and did not leave the old man, who had lapsed into total senility.

Meanwhile, the deadline passed and no appeal was made. Kistenevka belonged to Troekurov. Shabashkin presented himself to him with bows and congratulations and the request that he specify when His Excellency would like to take possession of the newly acquired estate—either in person or through whomever he chose to grant power of attorney. Kirila Petrovich felt embarrassed. He was not mercenary by nature, the desire for revenge had lured him too far, his conscience murmured. He knew what condition his adversary, the old comrade of his youth, was in, and his victory did not gladden his heart. He cast a menacing glance at Shabashkin, seeking some reason to yell at him, but finding no sufficient pretext, said angrily: "Get out, I can't be bothered with you."

Shabashkin, seeing that he was out of sorts, bowed and hastened to withdraw. And Kirila Petrovich, left alone, began to pace up and down, whistling "Thunder of victory resound,"[5] which in him always signified extraordinary mental agitation.

Finally, he ordered a racing droshky hitched up, dressed more warmly (it was already the end of September), and, taking the reins himself, drove out of the yard.

Soon he caught sight of Andrei Gavrilovich's little house, and conflicting feelings filled his soul. Satisfied vengeance and lust of power stifled his more noble feelings to a certain degree, but the latter finally triumphed. He decided to make peace with his old neighbor, to wipe out the traces of their quarrel by giving him back his property. Having unburdened his soul with this good intention, Kirila Petrovich set out at a trot for his neighbor's homestead and drove straight into his yard.

Just then the sick man was sitting at the window in his bedroom. He recognized Kirila Petrovich, and terrible agitation showed on his face: a crimson flush replaced his usual pallor, his eyes flashed, he uttered inarticulate sounds. His son, who was sitting there over the account books, raised his head and was struck by his condition. The sick man was pointing to the yard with an expression of horror and wrath. He hastily gathered the skirts of his dressing gown, preparing to get up from the chair, rose a little . . . and suddenly fell. His son rushed to him. The old man lay without feeling and without breathing, struck by paralysis.

"Quick, quick, send to town for a doctor!" cried Vladimir.

"Kirila Petrovich is asking to see you," said a servant, coming in. Vladimir threw him a terrible glance.

"Tell Kirila Petrovich to get out of here quickly, before I order him driven out . . . Off with you!"

The servant ran joyfully to fulfill his master's order. Egorovna clasped her hands.

"Master dear," she said in a squeaky voice, "it will cost you your head! Kirila Petrovich will eat us up."

"Quiet, nanny," Vladimir said vexedly. "Send Anton to town for a doctor at once."

Egorovna left. There was no one in the front hall; all the servants had run to the yard to look at Kirila Petrovich. She went out to the porch and heard the servant's reply, delivered on behalf of the young master. Kirila Petrovich heard him out sitting in his droshky. His face became darker than night; he smiled contemptuously, glanced menacingly at the servants, and drove slowly around the yard. He looked at the window where Andrei Gavrilovich had been sitting a moment before, but where he no longer was. The nanny stood on the porch, forgetting her master's order. The servants loudly talked over what had happened. Suddenly Vladimir appeared among them and said curtly: "No need for a doctor, father is dead."

A commotion set in. The servants rushed to the old master's room. He lay in the armchair to which Vladimir had moved him; his right

arm hung down to the floor, his head was lowered on his chest, there
was no sign of life in his body, not yet cold, but already disfigured by
death. Egorovna began to wail. The servants surrounded the corpse,
which was left to their care, washed it, dressed it in a uniform made
back in the year 1797, and laid it out on the same table at which they
had served their master for so many years.[6]

CHAPTER FIVE

The funeral took place three days later. The body of the poor old man
lay on the table covered with a shroud and surrounded with candles.
The dining room was filled with servants. They were preparing for the
carrying-out. Vladimir and three servants lifted the coffin. The priest
went ahead; the sexton accompanied him intoning the funeral prayers.
The owner of Kistenevka crossed the threshold of his house for the
last time. The coffin was carried through the grove. The church was
beyond it. The day was clear and cold. Autumn leaves were falling from
the trees.

On coming out of the grove, they saw the Kistenevka wooden
church and the graveyard, shaded by old lindens. There the body of
Vladimir's mother lay at rest; there, beside her grave, a new hole had
been dug the day before.

The church was filled with Kistenevka peasants, who had come to
pay their last respects to their master. Young Dubrovsky stood by the
choir; he did not weep and he did not pray, but his face was terrible.
The mournful rite came to an end. Vladimir went first to take leave
of the body, and after him all the servants. The lid was brought and
nailed to the coffin. The women wailed loudly; the men occasionally
wiped their tears with their fists. Vladimir and the same three servants
carried it to the graveyard, accompanied by the whole village. The
coffin was lowered into the grave, everyone there threw a handful of
earth into it, the hole was filled in, people bowed and went their ways.
Vladimir quickly left, got ahead of everyone, and disappeared into the
Kistenevka grove.

On his behalf, Egorovna invited the priest and the rest of the
church people to a memorial dinner, announcing that the young master
did not intend to be present, and thus Father Anton, his wife Fedotovna,

and the sexton went on foot to the master's house, talking with Egorovna about the dead man's virtues and about what apparently awaited his heir. (Troekurov's visit and the reception he had been shown were already known to the whole neighborhood, and local politicians predicted serious consequences from it.)

"What will be, will be," said the priest's wife, "but it's too bad if Vladimir Andreich is not our master. A fine fellow, I must say."

"But who will be our master if not him?" Egorovna interrupted. "Kirila Petrovich gets worked up for nothing. He's not dealing with the timid sort: no, my young falcon can stand up for himself, and, God willing, his benefactors won't desert him. Kirila Petrovich is mighty arrogant, but I dare say he put his tail between his legs when my Grishka shouted at him: 'Away, you old dog! Clear out of the yard!'"

"Ah, no, Egorovna," said the sexton, "how did Grigory have the pluck to say it? I'd sooner bark at our bishop than look askance at Kirila Petrovich. You see him and you're in fear and trembling, you break into a sweat, and your back just bends, just bends by itself . . ."

"Vanity of vanities," said the priest, "and Kirila Petrovich will have 'Memory Eternal' sung over him,[7] the same as Andrei Gavrilovich did just now, only the funeral will be richer and there'll be more guests invited, but for God it's all the same!"

"Ah, dear father! We, too, wanted to invite the whole neighborhood, but Vladimir Andreich didn't want it. I dare say we've got enough to treat them all, but what could we do? Since there's no people, at least we can feast you, our dear guests."

This agreeable promise and the hope of finding tasty pies quickened the company's steps, and they safely reached the master's house, where the table was already laid and the vodka served.

Meanwhile, Vladimir went ever deeper into the thicket of trees, trying by movement and fatigue to stifle the grief in his soul. He walked without heeding the way; branches kept catching at him and scratching him, his feet kept sinking into the mire—he noticed nothing. He finally reached a small hollow, surrounded by the woods on all sides; a brook meandered silently among the trees, stripped half naked by autumn. Vladimir stopped, sat down on the cold grass, and thoughts, one darker than the other, crowded in his soul . . . He keenly felt his solitude. The future appeared to him covered with menacing clouds. The enmity with Troekurov foreshadowed new misfortunes for him.

His meager inheritance might pass into another's hands—in which case he would face destitution. For a long time he sat motionless in the same place, gazing at the quiet flow of the brook, carrying off a few withered leaves and vividly portraying for him the true likeness of life—such a commonplace likeness. Finally he noticed that it was growing dark; he got up and went in search of the way home, but he still wandered for a long time in the unfamiliar forest, before he hit upon the path that brought him straight to the gates of his house.

On his way Dubrovsky ran into the priest with the rest of the church people. The thought of an unlucky omen came to his head. He automatically turned aside and hid behind a tree. They did not notice him and walked by talking heatedly among themselves.

"Eschew evil, and do good,"[8] the priest was saying to his wife. "There's no need for us to stay here. It's not your trouble, however the matter ends." The wife said something in reply, but Vladimir could not catch it.

Approaching the house, he saw a great many people: peasants and house serfs were crowding in the yard. From a distance Vladimir heard unusual noise and talk. Two troikas stood by the coach house. On the porch several unknown men in uniform seemed to be discussing something.

"What's the meaning of this?" he angrily asked Anton, who came running to meet him. "Who are they, and what do they want?"

"Ah, dear master Vladimir Andreevich," the old man answered breathlessly. "The court has come. They're handing us over to Troekurov, they're taking us from Your Honor! . . ."

Vladimir hung his head; the servants surrounded their unfortunate master.

"You're a father to us," they cried, kissing his hands. "We don't want any other master but you. Order it, sir, and we'll deal with this court. We'll die before we betray you."

Vladimir looked at them and strange feelings stirred him.

"Stand quietly," he said to them, "and I'll have a talk with the officials."

"Talk to them, dear master," they cried to him from the crowd. "Shame the fiends!"

Vladimir went up to the officials. Shabashkin, with a visored cap on his head, stood arms akimbo and proudly looked around him. The police chief, a tall and fat man of about fifty with a red face and a moustache, on seeing Dubrovsky approach, grunted and said in a husky voice:

"So, I repeat to you what I've already said: by decision of the district court, you henceforth belong to Kirila Petrovich Troekurov, whose person is here represented by Mr. Shabashkin. Obey him in everything he orders, and you, women, love and honor him, for he is your great fancier."

At this witticism, the police chief burst out laughing, and Shabashkin and the other members followed suit. Vladimir seethed with indignation.

"Allow me to know the meaning of this," he asked the merry police chief with feigned coolness.

"The meaning of this," the wily official replied, "is that we have come to put Kirila Petrovich Troekurov in possession of the estate and to ask *certain others* to get out while they're still in one piece."

"But it seems you might address yourselves to me, rather than to my peasants, and announce to the landowner that he has been dispossessed . . ."

"And who are you," said Shabashkin with an impudent look. "The former landowner, Andrei Gavrilovich Dubrovsky, is dead by the will of God. You we do not know and do not wish to know."

"Vladimir Andreevich is our young master," said a voice from the crowd.

"Who dared to open his mouth there?" the police chief said menacingly. "What master? What Vladimir Andreevich? Your master is Kirila Petrovich Troekurov, do you hear, you oafs?"

"Nohow," said the same voice.

"This is rebellion!" shouted the police chief. "Hey, headman, come here!"

The headman stepped forward.

"Find out at once who dared to talk back to me. I'll show him!"

The headman turned to the crowd and asked who had spoken, but they all kept silent; soon a murmur sprang up from the back rows, grew louder, and in a moment turned into a terrible uproar. The police chief lowered his voice and tried to reason with them.

"Why stand gaping?" the servants shouted. "Come on, boys, away with them!" And the whole crowd advanced. Shabashkin and the other members hurriedly rushed into the front hall and locked the door behind them.

"Tie 'em up, boys!" the same voice shouted, and the crowd began to press forward . . .

"Stop!" cried Dubrovsky. "You fools! What are you doing? You'll ruin yourselves and me. Go back home and leave me alone. Don't be afraid, the sovereign is merciful, I'll petition him. He won't harm us. We're all his children. But how can he intercede for you, if you start rioting and rampaging?"

The young Dubrovsky's words, his resounding voice and majestic air, produced the desired effect. The people quieted down, dispersed, the yard became deserted. The members sat in the front hall. Finally Shabashkin quietly opened the door, went out to the porch, and with humble bows began to thank Dubrovsky for his merciful intercession. Vladimir listened to him with contempt and made no reply.

"We've decided," the assessor went on, "to spend the night here, with your permission; it's already dark, and your peasants may attack us on the way. Do us a favor, have some straw spread for us in the drawing room; we'll be on our way at dawn."

"Do as you like," Dubrovsky answered him drily. "I'm no longer the master here."

With those words he retired to his father's room and locked the door behind him.

CHAPTER SIX

"So it's all over," he said to himself. "This morning I still had a corner and a crust of bread. Tomorrow I must leave the house where I was born and where my father died to the man who caused his death and my destitution." And his eyes rested fixedly on the portrait of his mother. The painter had portrayed her leaning her elbow on a banister, in a white morning dress, with a red rose in her hair. "And this portrait will be taken by the enemy of my family," thought Vladimir, "and it will be thrown into a storeroom along with some broken chairs, or hung in the front hall, a subject of mockery and rude remarks for his huntsmen, and in her bedroom, the room . . . where father died, he will install his steward or his harem. No! No! I won't let him take the mournful house he's driving me out of!" Vladimir clenched his teeth. Terrible thoughts were forming in his mind. The officials' voices reached him. They were playing the masters, demanding now this, now that, and unpleasantly distracted him amidst his sad reflections. Finally everything grew quiet.

Vladimir opened cupboards and chests and busied himself with sorting out the dead man's papers. They consisted for the most part of household accounts and some business correspondence. Vladimir tore them up without reading them. Among them he came upon a packet with the inscription "Letters from my wife." Deeply moved, Vladimir started on them: they were written during the Turkish campaign[9] and were addressed to the army from Kistenevka. She described her solitary life, her household chores, complained tenderly about their separation, and called him home to the arms of his dear friend. In one of them she expressed her anxiety about little Vladimir's health; in another she rejoiced at his early abilities and predicted a happy and brilliant future for him. Vladimir lost himself in reading and forgot everything else, his soul immersed in the world of family happiness, and he did not notice how the time passed. The wall clock struck eleven. Vladimir put the letters in his pocket, took the candle, and left the study. In the drawing room the officials were asleep on the floor. Empty glasses stood on the table, and the whole room smelled strongly of rum. With disgust Vladimir walked past them to the front hall. The door was locked. Not finding the key, Vladimir went back to the drawing room—the key was lying on the table. Vladimir opened the door and stumbled onto a man crouched in a corner; an axe gleamed in his hand, and, turning to him with the candle, Vladimir recognized the blacksmith Arkhip.

"What are you doing here?" he asked.

"Ah, Vladimir Andreevich, it's you," Arkhip replied in a whisper. "Lord have mercy and save us, it's a good thing you came with a candle!"

Vladimir gazed at him in amazement.

"What are you hiding here for?" he asked the blacksmith.

"I wanted . . . I came . . . it was to see if everybody's at home," Arkhip stammered softly.

"And why the axe?"

"Why the axe? There's no going around nowadays without an axe. These officials are such rascals—next thing you know . . . ."

"You're drunk. Drop the axe and go sleep it off."

"Me drunk? Dear master Vladimir Andreevich, God is my witness, not one drop has passed my lips . . . and who'd have drink on his mind, it's unheard of, scribblers meaning to take us over, scribblers driving our masters out of their own yard . . . Hear 'em snoring, the cursed wretches; get 'em all at once, and there's an end to it."

Dubrovsky frowned.

"Listen, Arkhip," he said, after a brief silence, "what you're doing isn't right. The officials are not to blame. Light a lantern and follow me."

Arkhip took the candle from his master's hand, found a lamp behind the stove, lit it, and they both quietly stepped off the porch and went around the yard. A watchman started banging on a cast-iron bar. Dogs barked.

"Who's on watch?" Dubrovsky asked.

"We are, dear master," a high voice replied. "Vasilisa and Lukerya."

"Go home," Dubrovsky said to them. "You're not needed."

"Knock off," said Arkhip.

"Thank you, our dear provider," the women replied and went home at once.

Dubrovsky walked on. Two men approached him; they called out to him. Dubrovsky recognized the voices of Anton and Grisha.

"Why aren't you asleep?" he asked them.

"As if we could sleep," Anton replied. "Who'd have thought we'd live to see . . ."

"Quiet!" Dubrovsky interrupted. "Where's Egorovna?"

"In the main house, in her attic," Grisha replied.

"Go, bring her here, and get all our people out of the house, so there's not a soul left in it except the officials, and you, Anton, hitch up the wagon."

Grisha left and appeared a minute later with his mother. The old woman had not undressed for the night; apart from the officials, nobody in the house had slept a wink.

"Everybody here?" asked Dubrovsky. "Nobody left in the house?"

"Nobody except the officials," Grisha replied.

"Bring me some hay or straw," said Dubrovsky.

People ran to the stables and came back carrying armfuls of hay.

"Lay it under the porch. Like this. Now, boys, the fire!"

Arkhip opened the lantern; Dubrovsky lit a splinter.

"Wait," he said to Arkhip. "In my haste I think I locked the door to the front hall. Go quick and unlock it."

Arkhip ran to the entryway—the door was unlocked. Arkhip locked it, muttering in a half whisper, "Nohow I'll unlock it!" and went back to Dubrovsky.

Dubrovsky brought the splinter close, the hay caught fire, the flames soared and lit up the whole yard.

"Ah, no!" Egorovna cried pitifully. "Vladimir Andreevich, what are you doing?"

"Quiet!" said Dubrovsky. "And so farewell, children. I'll go where God takes me. Good luck with your new master."

"Our father, our provider," people replied, "we'd rather die than leave you, we'll come with you."

The horses were brought. Dubrovsky got into the wagon along with Grisha and appointed the Kistenevka grove as the meeting place for them all. Anton whipped up the horses, and they drove out of the yard.

The wind picked up. In a moment flames engulfed the whole house. Red smoke whirled above the roof. Glass cracked, rained down, blazing beams began to fall, there were pitiful screams and cries: "We're burning! Help! Help!"

"Nohow," said Arkhip, gazing at the fire with a malicious smile.

"Arkhipushka," Egorovna said to him, "save the fiends. God will reward you."

"Nohow," said the blacksmith.

Just then the officials appeared at the window, trying to break the double frames. But here the roof came crashing down, and the screaming ceased.

Soon all the servants came pouring into the yard. The women, shouting, rushed to save their junk; the children hopped up and down, admiring the fire. Sparks flew like a fiery blizzard; cottages began to burn.

"It's all right now," said Arkhip. "How's that for burning, eh? Bet it looks nice from Pokrovskoe."

Just then a new event caught his attention. A cat went running along the roof of the blazing shed, at a loss where to jump down; it was surrounded on all sides by flames. The poor animal meowed pitifully, calling for help. The boys died with laughter, looking at its despair.

"What're you laughing at, you little devils," the blacksmith said angrily. "You've got no fear of God: God's creature is perishing, and you fools are glad." And leaning a ladder against the already-burning roof, he climbed up for the cat. It understood his intention and with a look of hurried gratitude clung to his sleeve. The half-singed black-smith climbed down with his booty.

"And so farewell, lads," he said to the confused servants. "There's nothing for me to do here. Good luck, and don't hold anything against me."

The blacksmith left. The fire raged for some time. It finally died down, and heaps of flameless embers glowed brightly in the darkness of the night, and around them wandered the burnt-out inhabitants of Kistenevka.

CHAPTER SEVEN

The next day news of the fire spread all over the neighborhood. Every-body explained it with various conjectures and suppositions. Some insisted that Dubrovsky's people had gotten drunk at the funeral and set fire to the house out of carelessness; others accused the officials, who had made too merry at the housewarming; many were convinced that it had burned down of itself with the court officials and all the ser-vants. Some guessed the truth and maintained that Dubrovsky himself, moved by anger and despair, was to blame for the terrible calamity. Troekurov came to the scene of the fire the next day and conducted an investigation himself. It turned out that the police chief, the local court assessor, the lawyer, and the clerk, as well as Vladimir Dubrovsky, the nanny Egorovna, the servant Grigory, the coachman Anton, and the blacksmith Arkhip had disappeared no one knew where. All the servants testified that the officials had burned up when the roof col-lapsed. Their charred bones were unearthed. The women Vasilisa and Lukerya said they had seen Dubrovsky and the blacksmith Arkhip a few minutes before the fire. The blacksmith Arkhip, according to gen-eral testimony, was alive and was probably the main one, if not the only one, to blame for the fire. Dubrovsky, too, was under strong suspicion. Kirila Petrovich sent the governor a detailed account of the whole inci-dent, and a new case was started.

Soon other news gave other food for curiosity and gossip. Robbers had appeared in * * * and spread terror through the whole region. The measures taken against them by the government proved inadequate. Robberies, one more remarkable than the other, followed one after the other. There was no safety either on the roads or in the villages. Several troikas full of robbers drove in broad daylight all over the province, stopped travelers and the post, rode into villages, robbed landowners' houses and committed them to the flames. The chief of the band became known for his intelligence, daring, and a sort of magnanimity. Wonders were told of him; the name of Dubrovsky was on everybody's lips, everybody was sure that he and no one else was the leader of these daring evildoers. One thing was astonishing: Troekurov's estates had been spared; not a single barn had been robbed, not a single cart had been stopped. With his usual arrogance, Troekurov ascribed this exception to the fear he had been able to instill in the whole province, and also to the excellent quality of the police he had established in his villages. At first the neighbors laughed among themselves at Troekurov's haughtiness, and expected every day that the uninvited guests would visit Pokrovskoe, where there was a good haul to be made, but they were finally forced to agree with him and admit that the robbers, too, had an incomprehensible respect for him . . . Troekurov was triumphant, and each time there was news of a new robbery by Dubrovsky, he burst into mockery of the governor, the police chiefs and company commanders from whom Dubrovsky always escaped unharmed.

Meanwhile October 1st came—the day of the church feast in Troekurov's village. But before we set about describing this solemnity and the subsequent events, we ought to acquaint the reader with some persons new to him, or of whom we made only slight mention at the beginning of our story.

CHAPTER EIGHT

The reader has probably guessed that Kirila Petrovich's daughter, of whom we have as yet said only a few words, is the heroine of our story. In the period we are describing, she was seventeen years old and her beauty was in full bloom. Her father loved her to distraction, but treated her with his own special willfulness, now trying to cater to her slightest whims, then frightening her with severe and sometimes cruel treatment. Assured of her affection, he could never gain her confidence. She was used to concealing her feelings and thoughts from him, because she could never know for certain how they would be received. She had no friends and grew up in solitude. The neighbors' wives and daughters rarely visited Kirila Petrovich, whose habitual conversation and amusements called for the camaraderie of men and not the presence of ladies. Rarely did our beauty appear among the guests feasting at Kirila Petrovich's. An enormous library, consisting for the most part of works by eighteenth-century French writers, was put at her disposal. Her father, who never read anything except *The Perfect Cook*, could not guide her in the choice of books, and Masha, having leafed through works of various sorts, quite naturally settled on novels. It was thus that she completed her education, begun previously under the guidance of Mam'selle Mimi, to whom Kirila Petrovich had shown great confidence and benevolence, and whom he had finally been forced to send quietly to another estate, once the consequences of his friendship became too obvious. Mam'selle Mimi left quite a pleasant memory behind her. She was a good girl and never misused the influence she obviously had over Kirila Petrovich, differing in this from other confidantes, who were replaced every minute. Kirila Petrovich himself seemed to have liked her more than the others, and a dark-eyed boy, a scamp of about nine, recalling Mam'selle Mimi's southern features, was brought up in the house and recognized as his son, though many barefoot children, as like him as two drops of water, ran around outside his windows and were considered serfs. For his little Sasha, Kirila Petrovich invited a French tutor from Moscow, who arrived in Pokrovskoe during the events we are now describing.

Kirila Petrovich liked this tutor for his pleasant appearance and simple manners. He presented Kirila Petrovich with his references and a letter from one of Troekurov's relations, with whom he had lived for four years as a tutor. Kirila Petrovich looked through it all and was displeased only by his Frenchman's youth—not that he considered this agreeable drawback incompatible with the patience and experience so necessary to the unfortunate position of tutor, but he had doubts of his own, which he decided at once to explain to him. For that he ordered Masha to be sent to him (Kirila Petrovich did not speak French, and she served as his interpreter).

"Come here, Masha. Tell this moosieu that, so be it, I'll take him;

only provided that he not dare to go chasing after my girls, otherwise
I'll show the son of a dog . . . Translate that for him, Masha."

Masha blushed and, turning to the tutor, told him in French that
her father hoped for his modesty and proper behavior.

The Frenchman bowed and replied that he hoped to earn respect,
even if favor were denied him.

Masha translated his reply word for word.

"All right, all right," said Kirila Petrovich. "He has no need of favor
or respect. His business is to look after Sasha and teach him grammar
and geography. Translate that for him."

Marya softened her father's crude expressions in her translation,
and Kirila Petrovich sent his Frenchman off to the wing, where a room
had been assigned to him.

Masha, having been brought up with aristocratic prejudices, paid
no attention to the young Frenchman. For her a tutor was a sort of
servant or artisan, and servants or artisans did not seem like men to her.
Nor did she notice the impression she had made on M. Desforges, his
confusion, his trembling, his altered voice. After that, for several days
in a row she met him rather often, without paying any greater attention to him. In an unexpected way, she acquired a completely new idea
of him.

Several bear cubs were usually reared in Kirila Petrovich's yard
and constituted one of the Pokrovskoe landowner's chief amusements.
While still young, the cubs would be brought each day to the drawing
room, where Kirila Petrovich would spend hours at a time playing with
them, setting them at cats and puppies. Grown up, they would be put
on chains, in anticipation of real baiting. Now and then they would be
brought before the windows of the master's house and an empty wine
barrel bristling with nails would be rolled up to them. The bear would
sniff it, then touch it lightly, pricking its paws, angrily shove it harder,
and make the pain worse. It would fly into a complete rage, rush at the
barrel with a roar, and stop only when the object of the poor beast's
vain fury was taken away. Or else a team of bears would be hitched to
a wagon, some guests, willingly or unwillingly, would be seated in it,
and they would be sent galloping off God knows where. But to Kirila
Petrovich's mind the best joke was the following.

A hungry bear would be locked in an empty room, tied with a rope
to a ring screwed into the wall. The rope was almost the length of the

whole room, so that only the opposite corner could be safe from the fearsome beast's attack. They would bring someone, usually a novice, to the door of this room, as if inadvertently shove him in with the bear, lock the door, and the unfortunate victim would be left alone with the shaggy hermit. The poor guest, his coattails shredded and himself scratched and bleeding, would soon find the safe corner, but would sometimes be forced to stand for a whole three hours pressed to the wall and watch as the infuriated beast two steps away roared, jumped, reared, and strained, trying to reach him. Such were the noble amusements of the Russian squire! A few days after the tutor's arrival, Troekurov remembered about him and conceived the idea of treating him to the bear room. To that end, summoning him one morning, he led him along the dark corridors; suddenly a side door opened, two servants shoved the Frenchman in and locked the door with a key. Coming to his senses, the tutor saw the tied-up bear; the beast began to snort, sniffing at his guest from a distance, and suddenly, rising on his hind legs, came towards him . . . The Frenchman did not panic, did not run, but waited for the attack. The bear came close; Desforges drew a small pistol from his pocket, put it into the hungry beast's ear, and fired. The bear collapsed. Everyone came running, the door opened, Kirila Petrovich came in, amazed at the outcome of his joke. Kirila Petrovich wanted the whole matter explained at once: who had warned Desforges of the joke prepared for him, or why was there a loaded pistol in his pocket? He sent for Masha. Masha came running and translated her father's questions for the Frenchman.

"I had not heard about the bear," Desforges replied, "but I always carry pistols on me, because I do not intend to put up with offenses for which, owing to my position, I cannot demand satisfaction."

Masha looked at him in amazement and translated his words for Kirila Petrovich. Kirila Petrovich made no reply, ordered the bear taken away and skinned; then, turning to his servants, he said: "There's a fine fellow! He wasn't scared, by God, he wasn't scared!" From that moment on he came to like Desforges and no longer thought of testing him.

But this incident made a still greater impression on Marya Kirilovna. Her imagination was struck: she saw the dead bear, and Desforges calmly standing over him and calmly conversing with her. She saw that courage and proud self-esteem did not belong exclusively to one estate, and from then on she began to show the young tutor a respect which grew more attentive by the hour. Certain relations were established between them. Masha had a beautiful voice and great musical ability. Desforges volunteered to give her lessons. After that it will not be hard for the reader to guess that Masha fell in love with him, though she did not yet admit it to herself.

Volume Two

CHAPTER NINE

On the eve of the feast, the guests began to arrive. Some stayed in the manor house or in the wings, others at the steward's, still others at the priest's, and others again with well-to-do peasants. The stables were filled with carriage horses, the yards and coach houses were cluttered with all sorts of vehicles. At nine o'clock in the morning, the bells rang for the liturgy, and everyone moved towards the new stone church, built by Kirila Petrovich and adorned every year with his offerings. Such a multitude of honorable worshippers gathered that simple peasants could not get into the church and stood on the porch or inside the fence. The liturgy had not started yet; they were waiting for Kirila Petrovich. He drove up in a coach-and-six and solemnly walked to his place accompanied by Marya Kirilovna. The eyes of men and women turned to her; the former marveled at her beauty, the latter attentively examined her dress. The liturgy began, the serf choir sang, Kirila Petrovich himself joined in, prayed, looking neither right nor left, and bowed to the ground with proud humility when the deacon made vociferous mention of "the benefactor of this church."

The liturgy ended. Kirila Petrovich went up first to kiss the cross. Everyone followed after him, then the neighbors approached him deferentially. The ladies surrounded Masha. Kirila Petrovich, coming out of the church, invited them all to dinner, got into his carriage, and went home. They all drove along behind him. The rooms filled with guests. New persons came in every minute and could barely make their way to the host. The ladies sat in a decorous semicircle, dressed in outmoded fashion, in much-worn but expensive outfits, all covered with pearls and diamonds; the men crowded around the caviar and vodka, talking among themselves in a loud hubbub. In the reception room the table was being laid for eighty people. Servants bustled about, arranging bottles and carafes and adjusting tablecloths. Finally the butler announced "Dinner is served"—and Kirila Petrovich went first to take his place at the table; the ladies followed after him and solemnly took their seats, with some observance of seniority; the girls crowded together like a flock of timid little goats and chose seats next to each other. The men placed themselves opposite them. At the end of the table sat the tutor beside little Sasha.

The servants began to serve dishes according to rank, guiding themselves in perplexing cases by Lavaterian guesswork,[10] almost always unerringly. The clatter of dishes and spoons merged with the loud talk of the guests. Kirila Petrovich cheerfully surveyed his table and fully relished the happiness of a hospitable host. Just then a carriage drawn by six horses drove into the yard.

"Who's this?" asked the host.

"Anton Pafnutych," replied several voices.

The door opened and Anton Pafnutych Spitsyn, a fat man of about fifty with a round and pockmarked face adorned by a triple chin, lumbered into the dining room, bowing, smiling, and already preparing to apologize . . .

"A place for him!" shouted Kirila Petrovich. "Welcome, Anton Pafnutych, sit down and tell us what this means: you weren't in church and you're late for dinner. It's not like you: you're very devout and you love to eat."

"Sorry," replied Anton Pafnutych, tying a napkin to the buttonhole of his pea-green kaftan, "sorry, my dear Kirila Petrovich. I set out early, but before I'd gone seven miles, the tire on the front wheel suddenly broke in two—what was I to do? Fortunately, there was a village not far away. By the time we dragged ourselves there, and found the blacksmith, and everything got somehow fixed, three hours had gone by— no help for it. I didn't dare take the short cut through the Kistenevka wood, so I went around . . ."

"Aha!" Kirila Petrovich interrupted. "So you're not one of the brave! What are you afraid of?"

"What do you mean what, my dear Kirila Petrovich? And Dubrovsky? I might just fall into his clutches. He's nobody's fool, he doesn't miss a trick, and as for me, why, he'd skin me twice over."

"Why such distinction, brother?"

"What do you mean why, my dear Kirila Petrovich? Because of the lawsuit against the late Andrei Gavrilovich. Didn't I give evidence, for your good pleasure—that is, in all honesty and fairness—that the Dubrovskys were masters of Kistenevka without any right, but solely by your indulgence? The deceased (God rest his soul) vowed to get even with me in his own way, and the boy might just keep the father's word. So far God has been merciful. Only one of my barns has been looted, but they could get to the house any time now."

"And in the house they'll have a heyday," Kirila Petrovich observed. "I'll bet the little red cashbox is stuffed full . . ."

"Ah, no, my dear Kirila Petrovich. It was full once, but now it's quite empty!"

"Enough nonsense, Anton Pafnutych. We know you. Where do you go spending any money? At home you live like a pig, you don't receive anybody, you fleece your peasants, hoarding is all you know."

"You keep joking, my dear Kirila Petrovich," Anton Pafnutych muttered with a smile, "but, by God, we're completely ruined"—and having swallowed his host's cavalier joke, he bit into a hunk of rich meat pie. Kirila Petrovich dropped him and turned to the new police chief, who was visiting him for the first time and was sitting at the other end of the table next to the tutor.

"And so, Mister Police Chief, will you at least catch Dubrovsky?"

The police chief shrank, bowed, smiled, stammered, and finally managed to say: "We'll try hard, Your Excellency."

"Hm, 'we'll try hard.' They've been trying for a long, long time now, but nothing's come of it. And, indeed, why catch him? Dubrovsky's robberies are blessings for the police chiefs: travels, investigations, supplies, and money in the pocket. Why rid yourself of such a benefactor? Isn't that so, Mister Police Chief?"

"Quite so, Your Excellency," replied the totally embarrassed police chief.

The guests burst out laughing.

"I love the lad for his sincerity," said Kirila Petrovich, "but it's a pity about our late police chief Taras Alexeevich; if they hadn't burned him up, the neighborhood would be much quieter. But what news of Dubrovsky? Where was he last seen?"

"At my house, Kirila Petrovich," squeaked a lady's fat voice. "Last Tuesday he dined at my house . . ."

All eyes turned to Anna Savishna Globova, a rather simple widow, loved by all for her kind and cheerful nature. They all prepared themselves with curiosity to hear her story.

"You should know that three weeks ago I sent my steward to the post office with money for my Vanyusha. I don't spoil my son, and I'm not in a position to spoil him even if I wanted to; however, you yourselves will kindly agree that an officer of the guards needs to keep up a proper appearance, so I share my little income with Vanyusha as far as I can. So I sent him two thousand roubles. Though Dubrovsky came to my mind more than once, still I thought: the town's close by, five miles at most, maybe God will spare us. In the evening my steward comes back, pale, ragged, and on foot—I just gasped: 'What is it? What's happened to you?' He says: 'Anna Savishna, dear, thieves robbed me; they nearly killed me, Dubrovsky himself was there, he wanted to hang me, then had pity and let me go, but he robbed me of everything, took the horse and the cart.' My heart sank. Lord in Heaven, what will happen to my Vanyusha? Nothing to be done: I wrote a letter to my son, told him everything, and sent him my blessing without a penny.

"A week went by, then another—suddenly a carriage drives into my courtyard. Some general asks to see me: I bid him welcome. A man of about thirty-five comes in, dark-haired, moustache, beard, the perfect portrait of Kulnev,[11] introduces himself as a friend and army comrade of my late husband, Ivan Andreevich. He was driving by and couldn't go without visiting his widow, knowing that I lived here. I treated him to whatever God provided, we talked about this and that, and finally about Dubrovsky. I told him of my misfortune. My general frowned. 'That's strange,' he said. 'I've heard that Dubrovsky doesn't attack just anybody, but only the notoriously rich, and even then he splits with them and doesn't clean them out, and nobody accuses him of murder. There must be some hoax here. Have them send for your steward.' The steward was sent for; he appeared; the moment he saw the general, he was simply dumbfounded. 'Tell me now, brother, how Dubrovsky went about robbing you and how he wanted to hang you.' My steward trembled and fell at the general's feet. 'I'm guilty, dear master—it was the devil's work—I lied.' 'In that case,' said the general, 'kindly tell the lady how it all happened, and I'll listen.' The steward couldn't come to his senses. 'Well, so,' the general continued, 'tell us: where did you run into Dubrovsky?' 'By the twin pines, dear master, by the twin pines.' 'And what did he say to you?' 'He asked me whose I was, where I was going, and why.' 'Well, and then?' 'And then he demanded the letter and the money.' 'Well?' 'I gave him the letter and the money.' 'And he? . . . Well, and he?' 'I'm guilty, dear master.' 'Well, so what did he do? . . .' 'He gave me back the money and the letter and said, "Go with God, put it in the post."' 'Well, and you?' 'I'm guilty, dear master.' 'I'll make short work of you, dear boy,' the general said menacingly. 'And you, my lady, have this swindler's trunk searched and hand him over to me. I'll teach him. Know that Dubrovsky was an officer of the guards himself, and he would not want to harm a comrade.' I had an idea who his excellency was, there was nothing for me to discuss with him. The coachman tied the steward to the box of his carriage. The money was found; the general dined with me, then left at once and took the steward with him. My steward was found the next day in the forest, tied to an oak tree and stripped clean."

They all listened silently to Anna Savishna's story, especially the young ladies. Many of them secretly wished Dubrovsky well, seeing him as a romantic hero, especially Marya Kirilovna, an ardent dreamer, imbued with the mysterious horrors of Radcliffe.[12]

"And you suppose, Anna Savishna, that it was Dubrovsky himself?" asked Kirila Petrovich. "You're quite mistaken. I don't know who your visitor was, but it was not Dubrovsky."

"How's that, my dear sir? Not Dubrovsky? Who else takes to the highway, stopping travelers and searching them?"

"I don't know, but it was surely not Dubrovsky. I remember him as a child; I don't know if his hair has turned black; back then he was a curly-headed blond boy; but I know for certain that Dubrovsky is five years older than my Masha, and that means he's not thirty-five, but around twenty-three."

"Exactly right, Your Excellency," the police chief exclaimed. "I have Vladimir Dubrovsky's description in my pocket. It says that he is indeed twenty-three years old."

"Ah!" said Kirila Petrovich, "that's handy: read it to us and we'll listen; it won't be bad for us to know his description; if we chance to lay eyes on him, he won't slip away."

The police chief took a very soiled sheet of paper from his pocket, solemnly unfolded it, and began to read in a singsong voice:

"Description of Vladimir Dubrovsky, based on the testimony of his former household serfs.

"Twenty-three years old. Height: medium; complexion: clear; beard: shaved; eyes: brown; hair: light brown; nose: straight. Distinguishing marks: none found."

"And that's all?" asked Kirila Petrovich.

"That's all," replied the police chief, folding the document.

"Congratulations, Mister Police Chief. What a document! With that description it'll be easy for you to track down Dubrovsky. Who isn't of medium height, who doesn't have light brown hair, a straight nose, and brown eyes! I'll bet you could talk to Dubrovsky himself for three hours straight and not guess whom God has brought you together with. Brainy officials, to say the least!"

The police chief meekly put the document back in his pocket and quietly started on the goose and cabbage. Meanwhile the servants had already gone around several times filling each guest's glass. Several bottles of Gorsky and Tsimliansky wine had been loudly uncorked and graciously received under the name of champagne, faces began to glow, conversations grew more noisy, incoherent, and merry.

"No," Kirila Petrovich continued, "we won't see another police chief like the late Taras Alexeevich! He was no foozler, no slouch. A pity the fine lad got burned up, otherwise not a single one of that whole band would escape him. He'd catch every one of them, and Dubrovsky himself wouldn't give him the slip or buy his way out. Taras Alexeevich would take his money and not let the man go: that was the late man's way. Nothing to be done, it looks like I'll have to intervene in the matter and go against the robbers with my own people. I'll send some twenty men to begin with, so they can clear the thieves' woods; they're not cowardly folk, each of them goes up against a bear single-handed, they won't back away from robbers."

"How's your bear, my dear Kirila Petrovich?" asked Anton Pafnutych, reminded by those words of his shaggy acquaintance and certain jokes he had once been the victim of.

"Misha[13] has bid us farewell," Kirila Petrovich replied. "He died a glorious death at the hands of the enemy. There's his vanquisher." Kirila Petrovich pointed to Desforges. "Venerate the holy image of my Frenchman. He avenged your . . . if I may put it so . . . Remember?"

"How could I not?" Anton Pafnutych said, scratching himself. "I remember very well. So Misha's dead. What a pity, by God, what a pity! He was so amusing! So clever! There's no other bear like him. Why did moosieu kill him?"

With great pleasure, Kirila Petrovich began to tell the story of his Frenchman's exploit, for he had a lucky capacity for glorying in all that surrounded him. The guests listened attentively to the tale of Misha's death and glanced with amazement at Desforges, who, not suspecting that the conversation was about his courage, calmly sat in his place and made moral observations to his frisky charge.

The dinner, which had gone on for about three hours, came to an end; the host placed his napkin on the table; everyone stood up and went to the drawing room, where coffee, cards, and the continuation of the drinking so nicely begun in the dining room awaited them.

CHAPTER TEN

Around seven o'clock in the evening some of the guests wanted to leave, but the host, made merry by the punch, ordered the gates locked and announced that no one would go until the next morning. Soon music rang out, the doors to the reception room were opened, and a ball began. The host and his entourage sat in a corner, drinking glass after glass and admiring the young people's gaiety. The old ladies played cards. Since there were fewer cavaliers than ladies, as everywhere where no uhlan brigade is quartered, all the men capable of dancing were recruited. The tutor distinguished himself among them all, he danced more than any of them, the young ladies all chose him and found him quite adept at waltzing. He made several turns with Marya Kirilovna, and the young ladies took mocking notice of them. Finally, around midnight, the tired host stopped the dancing, ordered supper served, and took himself off to bed.

Kirila Petrovich's absence gave the company more freedom and animation. The cavaliers ventured to sit beside the ladies. The girls laughed and exchanged whispers with their neighbors; the ladies conversed loudly across the table. The men drank, argued, and guffawed—in short, the supper was extremely merry and left many pleasant memories behind it.

Only one person did not share in the general mirth: Anton Pafnutych sat gloomy and silent in his place, ate distractedly, and seemed extremely uneasy. The talk about robbers had stirred his imagination. We shall soon see that he had sufficient reason to fear them.

Anton Pafnutych, in calling upon God to witness that his red cashbox was empty, had not lied and had not sinned: the red cashbox was indeed empty; the money once kept in it had been transferred to a leather pouch, which he wore on his breast under his shirt. Only by this precaution had he calmed his mistrust of everyone and his eternal fear. Being forced to spend the night in a strange house, he was afraid lest they put him in a solitary room, where thieves might easily break in, and looking around for a trustworthy companion, he finally

chose Desforges. His appearance betokened strength, and, more than
that, the courage he had shown in the encounter with the bear, whom
poor Anton Pafnutych could not recall without a shudder, determined
his choice. When they got up from the table, Anton Pafnutych began
circling around the young Frenchman, grunting and coughing, and
finally addressed him with an explanation.

"Ahem, ahem, moosieu, might I not spend the night in your little
nook, because kindly see . . ."

"*Que désire monsieur?*"* asked Desforges, bowing courteously to
him.

"Too bad you still haven't learned Russian, moosieu. Zhe veuh,
mooah, shay voo kooshay,† do you understand?"

"*Monsieur, très volontiers,*" replied Desforges. "*Veuillez donner des
ordres en conséquence.*"‡

Anton Pafnutych, very pleased with his knowledge of French, went
at once to make the arrangements.

The guests started saying good night to each other, and each went
to the room assigned to him. Anton Pafnutych went off to the wing
with the tutor. The night was dark. Desforges lit the way with a lantern, Anton Pafnutych followed him quite cheerfully, every now and
then pressing the secret pouch to his breast to make sure the money
was still there.

They came to the wing, the tutor lit a candle, and they both started
to undress; at the same time, Anton Pafnutych strolled around the
room, examining the locks and windows and shaking his head at the
inauspicious inspection. The door had only one latch, the windows did
not yet have double frames. He tried to complain about it to Desforges,
but his knowledge of French was too limited for such a complicated
explanation; the Frenchman did not understand him, and Anton Pafnutych was forced to abandon his complaints. Their beds stood opposite
each other, they both lay down, and the tutor snuffed out the candle.

"Poorkwa voo snuffay, poorkwa voo snuffay,"§ cried Anton Pafnutych, barely managing to conjugate the verb "to snuff" in the French
way. "I can't *dormir*¶ in the dark."

---

* "What does monsieur wish?"
† I.e., *Je veux, moi, chez vous coucher* ["I want, me, to sleep in your room"].
‡ "Very gladly, monsieur . . . Please give orders to that effect."
§ *Pourquoi vous snuffez, pourquoi vous snuffez?* ["Why do you snuff it, why do you snuff it?"]
¶ sleep

Desforges did not understand his exclamations and wished him good night.

"Cursed heathen," Spitsyn grumbled, wrapping himself in the blanket. "As if he needed to snuff out the candle. The worse for him. I can't sleep without a light. Moosieu, moosieu," he went on, "zhe veuh avek voo parlay."* But the Frenchman did not reply and soon began to snore.

"The beastly Frenchman's snoring away," Anton Pafnutych thought, "and I can't even conceive of sleeping. At any moment thieves might come in the open door or climb through the window, and him, the beast, even gunshots won't wake him up."

"Moosieu, hey, moosieu, devil take you!"

Anton Pafnutych fell silent—fatigue and alcoholic vapors gradually overcame his fearfulness, he began to doze off, and soon deep sleep enveloped him completely.

A strange awakening was in store for him. Through sleep he felt someone gently pulling at his shirt collar. Anton Pafnutych opened his eyes and in the pale light of the autumn morning saw Desforges before him; the Frenchman held a pocket pistol in one hand, and with the other was unfastening the cherished pouch. Anton Pafnutych went numb.

"Kess ke say, moosieu, kess ke say?"† he said in a trembling voice.

"Shh, keep still," the tutor replied in pure Russian, "keep still, or you're lost. I am Dubrovsky."

CHAPTER ELEVEN

Now we ask the reader's permission to explain the latest events in our story by prior circumstances, which we have not yet had time to relate.

At the * * * posting station, in the house of the stationmaster, whom we have already mentioned, a traveler sat in a corner with a humble and patient air, betokening a commoner or a foreigner, that is, someone who has no voice on the post road. His britzka stood in the yard waiting to be greased. In it lay a small suitcase, meager evidence of a

---

* *Monsieur, monsieur . . . je veux avec vous parler* ["Monsieur, monsieur . . . I want with you to talk"].

† *Qu'est-ce que c'est, monsieur, qu'est-ce que c'est?* ["What is this, monsieur, what is this?"]

none-too-substantial fortune. The traveler did not ask for tea or coffee; he kept glancing out the window and whistling, to the great displeasure of the stationmaster's wife, who was sitting behind the partition.

"The Lord God's sent us a whistler," she said in a half whisper. "Just keeps on whistling, blast him, the cursed heathen."

"So what?" said the stationmaster. "Where's the harm in it, let him whistle."

"Where's the harm?" his angry spouse retorted. "Don't you know about the omen?"

"What omen? That whistling drives out money? Ahh, Pakhomovna, with us, whistle or not, there's never any anyway!"

"Send him on his way, Sidorych. Why on earth keep him? Give him horses and let him go to the devil."

"He can wait, Pakhomovna, we've only got three troikas in the stables, the fourth one's resting. Good travelers may turn up in a wink; I don't want to answer for the Frenchman with my neck. There! Hear that? Somebody's galloping up. Oh-ho-ho, quite a clip! A general, maybe?"

A carriage stopped at the porch. A servant jumped off the box, opened the doors, and a moment later a young man in a military great-coat and a white visored cap came into the stationmaster's house. After him the servant brought in a box and set it on the windowsill.

"Horses," the officer said peremptorily.

"This minute," the stationmaster replied. "Your travel papers, please."

"I have no papers. I'm turning off for . . . Don't you recognize me?"

The stationmaster got into a bustle and ran out to hurry the coachmen. The young man started pacing up and down the room, went behind the partition, and quietly asked the stationmaster's wife who the traveler was.

"God knows," the woman replied. "Some Frenchman. He's been waiting five hours for horses and keeps whistling. He's a damned nuisance."

The young man addressed the traveler in French.

"Where might you be going?" he asked him.

"To the next town," the Frenchman replied, "and from there I'll make my way to a certain landowner who has hired me as a tutor sight unseen. I had hoped to get there today, but it seems Mister Stationmaster has judged otherwise. It is difficult to find horses in these parts, Mister Officer."

"And with which of the local landowners have you found employment?" asked the officer.

"With Mr. Troekurov," replied the Frenchman.

"Troekurov? Who is this Troekurov?"

"*Ma foi, mon officier* . . . I've heard little good of him. They say that he is a proud and capricious gentleman, that he is cruel in the treatment of his domestics, that no one can get along with him, that everyone trembles at the sound of his name, that he is unceremonious with tutors (*avec les ouchitels**) and has already whipped two of them to death."

"Good heavens! And you'd venture to be employed by such a monster?"

"What can I do, Mister Officer? He offers me a good salary, three thousand roubles a year and everything provided. Maybe I'll be luckier than the others. I have an old mother, I'll send half the salary for her upkeep, and with the rest of the money I can lay aside a small capital in five years, enough to secure my future independence—and then, *bonsoir*, I'll go to Paris and set up some commercial dealings."

"Does anyone at Troekurov's know you?" he asked.

"No one," replied the tutor. "He invited me from Moscow through one of his friends, whose chef, my compatriot, recommended me. You should know that I was trained to be a pastry chef, not a tutor, but I was told that in your country the title of tutor is much more advantageous . . ."

The officer pondered.

"Listen," he interrupted the Frenchman, "what if, instead of this future, you were offered ten thousand in ready cash, with the provision that you go back to Paris at once?"

The Frenchman looked at the officer in amazement, smiled, and shook his head.

"The horses are ready," said the stationmaster, coming in. The servant confirmed it.

"Right away," said the officer. "Step out for a moment." The stationmaster and the servant left. "I'm not joking," he went on in French.

---

* with the *ouchitels* [Russian for "tutors"]

"I can give you ten thousand. All I need is your absence and your papers." With those words he unlocked the box and took out several wads of banknotes.

The Frenchman goggled his eyes. He did not know what to think.

"My absence . . . my papers," he repeated in amazement. "Here are my papers . . . But you're joking: what do you need my papers for?"

"That's not your business. I'm asking, do you agree or not?"

The Frenchman, still refusing to believe his ears, handed his papers to the young officer, who quickly looked through them.

"Your passport . . . good. A letter of introduction, let's see. Birth certificate, excellent. Well, here's your money, go back home. Good-bye . . ."

The Frenchman stood as if rooted to the spot.

The officer came back.

"I almost forgot the most important thing. Give me your word of honor that all this will remain just between us—your word of honor."

"On my word of honor," said the Frenchman. "But my papers, what am I to do without them?"

"At the first town you come to, declare that you were robbed by Dubrovsky. They'll believe you and give you the necessary papers. Good-bye, and God grant you get to Paris quickly and find your mother in good health."

Dubrovsky left the room, got into the carriage, and galloped off.

The stationmaster was looking out the window, and when the carriage had driven off, he turned to his wife and exclaimed: "Do you know what, Pakhomovna? That was Dubrovsky!"

His wife rushed headlong to the window, but it was too late: Dubrovsky was already far away. She started scolding her husband:

"Have you no fear of God, Sidorych? Why didn't you tell me earlier? I could at least have caught a glimpse of Dubrovsky, but now just sit and wait till he comes this way again! Shame on you, really, shame on you!"

The Frenchman stood as if rooted to the spot. The arrangement with the officer, the money—it all seemed like a dream to him. But the wads of banknotes were there in his pocket and eloquently confirmed the reality of the astonishing incident.

He decided to hire horses for town. The coachman drove at a walk and it was night by the time they dragged their way to town.

Before they reached the town gates, where instead of a sentry there stood a dilapidated sentry box, the Frenchman ordered the driver to stop, got out of the britzka, and continued on foot, explaining by signs to the coachman that he was leaving him the britzka and the suitcase as a tip. The coachman was as amazed at his generosity as the Frenchman himself had been at Dubrovsky's offer. But, concluding that the foreigner had lost his mind, the coachman thanked him with a zealous bow and, deciding it might be best not to drive into the town, headed for a certain pleasure establishment he knew and whose owner was a good acquaintance. There he spent the whole night, and the next morning he set out for home on an empty troika, without the britzka and without the suitcase, his face puffy and his eyes red.

Dubrovsky, having come into possession of the Frenchman's papers, boldly presented himself to Troekurov and, as we have seen, settled in his house. Whatever his secret intentions were (we shall learn of them later), there was nothing reprehensible in his behavior. True, he paid scant attention to little Sasha's education, gave him full freedom to romp about, and was not terribly demanding in his lessons, assigning them only for the sake of form; however, he followed with great diligence the young lady's musical successes and often sat with her at the piano for hours at a time. Everybody loved the young tutor: Kirila Petrovich for his bold agility at hunting; Marya Kirilovna for his boundless zeal and shy attentiveness; Sasha for his indulgence towards his pranks; the domestics for his kindness and for a generosity apparently incompatible with his position. He himself, it seemed, was attached to the whole family and considered himself already a member of it.

About a month went by from his entering into his tutorial position till the memorable feast day, and no one suspected that in the modest young Frenchman was hidden the fearsome robber whose name inspired terror in all the neighboring landowners. During all that time Dubrovsky never absented himself from Pokrovskoe, but the rumors of his robberies did not subside, thanks to the inventive imagination of the village dwellers, though it might also be that his band continued to be active in the absence of their chief.

Spending the night in the same room with a man whom he could consider his personal enemy and one of the chief perpetrators of his misfortune, Dubrovsky could not resist the temptation. He knew of the existence of the pouch and decided to lay hands on it. We saw how he astounded poor Anton Pafnutych by his unexpected transformation from tutor into robber.

At nine o'clock in the morning, the guests who had spent the night in Pokrovskoe gathered one by one in the drawing room, where a samovar was at the boil, beside which Marya Kirilovna sat in a morning dress, and Kirila Petrovich, in a flannel jacket and slippers, was emptying his wide cup, which resembled a barber's basin. The last to appear was Anton Pafnutych; he was so pale and seemed so upset that the sight of him struck everybody, and Kirila Petrovich inquired after his health. Spitsyn made a senseless reply and glanced in terror at the tutor, who sat right there as if nothing had happened. A few minutes later a servant came in and announced that Spitsyn's carriage was ready. Anton Pafnutych hurriedly made his bows and, despite the host's insistence, quickly left the room and drove off at once. No one understood what had happened to him, and Kirila Petrovich decided that he had overeaten. After tea and a farewell breakfast the other guests began to depart, Pokrovskoe was soon deserted, and everything settled into its usual order.

CHAPTER TWELVE

Several days went by and nothing noteworthy happened. The life of Pokrovskoe's inhabitants was monotonous. Kirila Petrovich went out hunting every day; reading, walks, and music lessons occupied Marya Kirilovna, especially music lessons. She was beginning to understand her own heart and acknowledged, with involuntary vexation, that it was not indifferent to the young Frenchman's merits. He, for his part, never went beyond the bounds of respect and strict propriety, and thus set her pride and fearful doubts at ease. With greater and greater trustfulness she gave herself to the captivating habit. She was bored without Desforges, in his presence she was constantly preoccupied with him, wanted to know his opinion about everything, and always agreed with him. Maybe she was not yet in love, but at the first chance obstacle or contrariness of fate, the flame of passion was bound to flare up in her heart.

Once, coming into the reception room where her tutor was waiting for her, Marya Kirilovna was surprised to notice a look of embarrassment on his pale face. She opened the piano, sang a few notes, but Dubrovsky excused himself under the pretext of a headache, broke off the lesson, and, while closing the score, stealthily slipped her a note. Marya Kirilovna, having no time to think better of it, took the note and instantly regretted it, but Dubrovsky was no longer in the room. Marya Kirilovna went to her room, unfolded the note, and read the following:

"Be in the gazebo by the brook at seven o'clock this evening. I must speak with you."

Her curiosity was strongly piqued. She had long been waiting for a confession, wishing for it and fearing it. It would be pleasing for her to hear the confirmation of what she surmised, yet she felt it would be improper for her to listen to such a declaration from a man who by his position could never hope to obtain her hand. She decided to keep the appointment, but was hesitant about one thing: how was she to receive the tutor's confession? With aristocratic indignation? With friendly admonition? With merry jokes, or with silent sympathy? Meanwhile she kept glancing at the clock every minute. It was growing dark, candles were brought. Kirila Petrovich sat down to play Boston with some visiting neighbors. The dining room clock struck a quarter to seven, and Marya Kirilovna quietly went out to the porch, looked all around, and ran to the garden.

The night was dark, the sky covered with clouds, two steps away nothing could be seen, but Marya Kirilovna walked through the darkness by familiar paths and a minute later found herself at the gazebo. There she paused so as to catch her breath and appear before Desforges looking indifferent and unhurried. But Desforges was already standing before her.

"I thank you," he said in a soft and sad voice, "that you did not refuse me in my request. I would be in despair if you had not consented to it."

Marya Kirilovna replied with a prepared phrase:

"I hope that you will not make me repent of my indulgence."

He was silent and seemed to be plucking up his courage.

"Circumstances demand . . . I must leave you," he said at last. "You may soon hear . . . But before we part, I myself must explain to you . . ."

Marya Kirilovna made no reply. In these words she saw a preface to the confession she was expecting.

"I am not what you suppose me to be," he went on, looking down. "I am not the Frenchman Desforges, I am Dubrovsky."

Marya Kirilovna cried out.

"Don't be afraid, for God's sake, you shouldn't be afraid of my name. Yes, I am that unfortunate man whom your father deprived of his crust of bread, drove out of his parental home, and sent to rob on the highways. But you needn't be afraid of me—either for yourself, or for him. It's all over. I've forgiven him. Listen, it was you who saved him. My first bloody exploit was to be done against him. I circled around his house, fixing on where to start the fire, from where to enter his bedroom, how to cut off all ways of escape, and just then you walked past me, like a heavenly vision, and my heart was appeased. I realized that the house you dwelt in was sacred, that not a single being connected to you by ties of blood was subject to my curse. I renounced revenge as folly. For whole days I roamed about the gardens of Pokrovskoe in hopes of seeing your white dress in the distance. I followed you in your imprudent walks, moving stealthily from bush to bush, happy in the thought that I was protecting you, that there was no danger for you where I was secretly present. At last a chance offered itself. I came to live in your house. These three weeks have been days of happiness for me. The memory of them will be the consolation of my sorrowful life . . . Today I received news after which it is impossible for me to stay here any longer. I must part from you today . . . right now . . . But first I had to reveal myself to you, so that you would not curse me, would not despise me. Think now and then of Dubrovsky, know that he was born for a different destiny, that his soul was able to love you, that never . . ."

Here a light whistle was heard, and Dubrovsky fell silent. He seized her hand and pressed it to his burning lips. The whistle was repeated.

"Farewell," said Dubrovsky. "They're calling me; a minute could be my undoing." He walked away, Marya Kirilovna stood motionless, Dubrovsky came back and took her hand again.

"If ever," he said in a tender and touching voice, "if ever misfortune befalls you and you cannot look for help or protection from anyone, in that case will you promise to resort to me, to demand anything from me for your salvation? Do you promise not to reject my devotion?"

Marya Kirilovna was silently weeping. The whistle was heard for a third time.

"You will be my undoing!" cried Dubrovsky. "I won't leave you until you give me an answer. Do you promise or not?"

"I promise," the poor beauty whispered.

Shaken by her meeting with Dubrovsky, Marya Kirilovna came

back from the garden. It seemed to her that all the servants were running around, the house was astir, there were many people in the courtyard, a troika stood by the porch, she heard Kirila Petrovich's voice in
the distance and hurried inside, fearing her absence might have been
noticed. Kirila Petrovich met her in the reception room. The guests
surrounded the police chief, our acquaintance, showering him with
questions. The police chief, dressed for the road, armed from head to
foot, answered them with a mysterious and bustling air.

"Where were you, Masha?" asked Kirila Petrovich. "Did you run
into M. Desforges?"

Masha was barely able to answer in the negative.

"Imagine," Kirila Petrovich went on, "the police chief has come to
arrest him and assures me that he is Dubrovsky himself."

"By all distinguishing marks, Your Excellency," the police chief
said deferentially.

"Eh, brother," Kirila Petrovich interrupted, "you can go you know
where with your distinguishing marks. I won't hand my Frenchman
over to you before I've looked into the matter myself. How can you
believe the word of that coward and liar Anton Pafnutych? He dreamed
up that the tutor wanted to rob him. Why didn't he say a word to me
about it that same morning?"

"The Frenchman intimidated him, Your Excellency," the police
chief replied, "and extracted an oath of silence from him . . ."

"Nonsense!" Kirila Petrovich decided. "I'll get to the bottom of
all this in no time. Where's the tutor?" he asked a servant who had just
come in.

"Nowhere to be found, sir," replied the servant.

"Go and look for him," shouted Troekurov, beginning to have
doubts. "Show me your famous marks," he said to the police chief, who
handed him the paper at once. "Hm, hm, twenty-three years old . . .
That's right, but it doesn't prove anything. What about the tutor?"

"Hasn't been found, sir," was again the answer. Kirila Petrovich
began to worry. Marya Kirilovna was more dead than alive.

"You're pale, Masha," her father observed. "You've been
frightened."

"No, papa," Masha replied, "I have a headache."

"Go to your room, Masha, and don't worry." Masha kissed his hand
and quickly went to her room, where she threw herself on her bed and
sobbed in a fit of hysterics. The maids came running, undressed her,

barely managed to calm her with cold water and all possible spirits, laid her down, and she fell into a slumber.

Meanwhile the Frenchman could not be found. Kirila Petrovich paced up and down the reception room, menacingly whistling "Thunder of victory resound." The guests whispered among themselves, the police chief looked like a fool, the Frenchman was not found. He had probably managed to steal away, having been warned. But by whom and how? That remained a mystery.

It struck eleven and no one even thought of sleeping. Finally Kirila Petrovich said angrily to the police chief:

"Well, so? You're not going to stay here till dawn. My house is not a tavern. It will take more adroitness than you've got to catch Dubrovsky, brother, if that is Dubrovsky. Go back where you came from, and in the future be more efficient. It's time for all of you to go home as well," he went on, addressing his guests. "Order the hitching up, I want to get some sleep."

So ungraciously did Troekurov part from his guests!

CHAPTER THIRTEEN

Some time went by without any notable incidents. But at the beginning of the following summer many changes took place in Kirila Petrovich's family life.

Twenty miles from him lay the rich estate of Prince Vereisky. The prince had been away in foreign parts for a long time, all his property had been managed by a retired major, and there had been no communication between Pokrovskoe and Arbatovo. But at the end of May the prince came back from abroad and went to his village, which he had never seen in his life. Accustomed to distractions, he could not bear solitude, and on the third day after his arrival he set off to have dinner with Troekurov, with whom he had once been acquainted.

The prince was around fifty, but he looked much older. Excesses of all sorts had undermined his health and left their indelible stamp on him. In spite of that, his appearance was pleasant, notable, and the habit of being always in society had lent him a certain amiability, especially with women. He had a constant need of distraction and was constantly bored. Kirila Petrovich was extremely pleased with his visit, taking it as a sign of respect from a man who knew the world; he began, as usual, by treating him to a tour of his establishment and took him to the kennels. But the prince all but choked in the doggy atmosphere and hurriedly left the place, pressing a scented handkerchief to his nose. The old garden with its trimmed lindens, rectangular pond, and regular paths was not to his liking; he preferred English gardens and so-called nature; yet he praised and admired. A servant came to announce that dinner was served. They went to the table. The prince limped, weary from his promenade and already regretting his visit.

But in the reception room they were met by Marya Kirilovna, and the old philanderer was struck by her beauty. Troekurov seated the guest next to her. The prince was revived by her presence, grew merry, and managed several times to attract her attention by his curious stories. After dinner Kirila Petrovich suggested that they go riding, but the prince excused himself, pointing to his velvet boots and joking about his gout; he preferred a promenade in a phaeton, so as not to part from his sweet neighbor. The phaeton was hitched up. The old men and the beauty got in together and drove off. The conversation never lapsed. Marya Kirilovna was listening with pleasure to the flattering and merry compliments of the society man, when Vereisky, suddenly turning to Kirila Petrovich, asked him what was the meaning of that burnt-down building, and did it belong to him? . . . Kirila Petrovich frowned; the memories evoked by the burnt-down manor were unpleasant for him. He replied that the land was now his and that formerly it had belonged to Dubrovsky.

"To Dubrovsky?" Vereisky repeated. "What, to that famous robber?"

"To his father," Troekurov replied, "and the father was a pretty good robber himself."

"What's become of our Rinaldo now?[14] Is he alive? Have they caught him?"

"He's alive and on the loose, and as long as our police connive with thieves, he won't be caught. By the way, Prince, Dubrovsky has paid you a visit in Arbatovo, hasn't he?"

"Yes, last year it seems he did some burning or pillaging . . . It would be curious to become more closely acquainted with this romantic hero, wouldn't it, Marya Kirilovna?"

"Curious, hah!" said Troekurov. "She knows him: he taught her music for a whole three weeks, and took nothing for the lessons, thank God." Here Kirila Petrovich began to tell the story of his French tutor. Marya Kirilovna was on pins and needles. Vereisky listened with great attention, found it all very strange, and changed the subject. On returning, he ordered his carriage brought and, despite Kirila Petrovich's insistent requests that he stay the night, left right after tea. But before that, he begged Kirila Petrovich to come and visit him with Marya Kirilovna, and the proud Troekurov gave his promise, for, taking into consideration the princely rank, the two stars, and the three thousand souls of the family estate, he considered Vereisky to a certain degree his equal.

Two days after this visit, Kirila Petrovich and his daughter went to call on Prince Vereisky. As they approached Arbatovo, he could not help admiring the clean and cheerful peasant cottages and the stone manor house, built after the fashion of English castles. Before the house spread a lush green meadow where Swiss cows grazed, tinkling their bells. A vast park surrounded the house on all sides. The host met his guests at the porch and offered the young beauty his arm. They entered a magnificent reception room, where a table had been laid for three. The prince led his guests to the window, and before them opened a lovely view. The Volga flowed past the windows, with loaded barges floating on it under wind-filled sails, and small fishing boats, so expressively nicknamed "smacks," flitted by. Beyond the river stretched hills and fields, with a few villages animating the landscape. Then they set about examining the gallery of pictures that the prince had bought in foreign parts. The prince explained to Marya Kirilovna their various subjects, the history of the painters, pointed out their merits and shortcomings. He spoke of the pictures not in the conventional language of a pedantic connoisseur, but with feeling and imagination. Marya Kirilovna listened to him with pleasure. They went to the table. Troekurov did full justice to his Amphitryon's wines[15] and to the art of his chef, and Marya Kirilovna did not feel the least embarrassment or constraint conversing with a man she was seeing for the second time in her life. After dinner the host suggested to his guests that they go to the garden. They had coffee in a gazebo on the shore of a wide lake dotted with islands. Suddenly brass music rang out and a six-oared boat moored just by the gazebo. They went out on the lake, around the islands, landed on some of them, on one found a marble statue, on another a secluded grotto, on a third a memorial with a mysterious inscription that aroused Marya Kirilovna's maidenly curiosity, which was not fully satisfied by the prince's courteous reticence. Time passed imperceptibly; it was growing dark. The prince, under the pretext of chilliness and dewfall, hurried them back home. The samovar was waiting for them. He asked Marya Kirilovna to play the hostess in the old bachelor's house. She poured tea, listening to the inexhaustible stories of the amiable chatterer. Suddenly a shot rang out and a rocket lit up the sky. The prince gave Marya Kirilovna her shawl and invited her and Troekurov to the balcony. In the darkness outside the house multicolored fires flashed, spun, soared up like sheaves, palm trees, fountains, showered down like rain, stars, dying out and flaring up again. Marya Kirilovna was happy as a child. Prince Vereisky rejoiced in her delight, and Troekurov was extremely pleased with him, for he took *tous les frais** of the prince as tokens of respect and a desire to oblige him.

The supper was in no way inferior to the dinner. The guests retired to the rooms assigned to them and the next morning parted from the amiable host, promising that they would see each other again soon.

CHAPTER FOURTEEN

Marya Kirilovna sat in her room, embroidering on a tambour by the open window. She did not confuse the silks, as did Konrad's mistress,[16] who, in amorous distraction, embroidered a rose in green silk. Under her needle, the canvas unerringly repeated the original pattern, even though her thoughts did not follow her work but were far away.

Suddenly a hand reached quietly through the window, placed a letter on the tambour, and disappeared before Marya Kirilovna had time to come to her senses. Just then a servant came into her room and summoned her to Kirila Petrovich. She tremblingly hid the letter behind her fichu and hurried to her father's study.

Kirila Petrovich was not alone. Prince Vereisky was sitting with him. At the appearance of Marya Kirilovna, the prince rose and silently bowed to her with an embarrassment unusual for him.

"Come here, Masha," said Kirila Petrovich. "I shall tell you some news, which I hope you will be glad to hear. This is your suitor: the prince has proposed to marry you."

Masha was dumbfounded, a deathly pallor came over her face. She said nothing. The prince went to her, took her hand, and, with appar-

* all the expenses (French)

ent feeling, asked if she would consent to make his happiness. Masha
said nothing.

"She consents, of course, she consents," said Kirila Petrovich. "But
you know, Prince, it's hard for a girl to pronounce that word. So, children, kiss and be happy."

Masha stood motionless, the old prince kissed her hand, and tears
suddenly poured down her pale face. The prince frowned slightly.

"Go, go, go," said Kirila Petrovich, "dry your tears, and come back
a cheerful girl. They all cry at their engagement," he went on, turning
to Vereisky. "It's a custom of theirs . . . Now, Prince, let's talk business,
that is, the dowry."

Marya Kirilovna eagerly availed herself of the permission to leave.
She ran to her room, locked herself in, and gave free rein to her tears,
imagining herself the old prince's wife. He suddenly seemed repulsive
and hateful to her . . . Marriage frightened her like the scaffold, the
grave . . . "No, no," she repeated in despair, "better to die, better to
enter a convent, better to marry Dubrovsky." Here she remembered
about the letter and eagerly hastened to read it, having a presentiment
that it was from him. In fact it was written by him and contained only
the following words:

"This evening at ten o'clock in the same place."

CHAPTER FIFTEEN

The moon shone, the July night was quiet, a breeze arose now and then
and sent a light rustling through the whole garden.

Like a light shadow, the young beauty approached the place of
the appointed meeting. There was nobody to be seen. Suddenly, from
behind the gazebo, Dubrovsky emerged before her.

"I know everything," he said in a soft and sad voice. "Remember
your promise."

"You offer me your protection," Masha replied. "Don't be angry,
but it frightens me. In what way can you be of help to me?"

"I can rid you of the hateful man."

"For God's sake, don't touch him, don't you dare touch him, if you
love me. I don't want to be the cause of some horror . . ."

"I won't touch him, your will is sacred to me. He owes you his life.

Never will villainy be committed in your name. You must be pure even of my crimes. But how am I to save you from your cruel father?"

"There is still hope. I hope to move him by my tears and despair. He's stubborn, but he loves me so."

"Don't have vain hopes: in those tears he'll see only the usual timidity and revulsion common to all young girls when they marry not out of passion, but from sensible convenience. What if he takes it into his head to make you happy despite yourself? What if you're forcibly led to the altar, so that your fate is forever handed over to an old husband's power?"

"Then, then there's no help for it; come for me, I will be your wife."

Dubrovsky trembled and a crimson flush spread over his pale face, which a moment later became still paler than before. For a long time he hung his head and said nothing.

"Gather all your inner forces, beg your father, throw yourself at his feet, picture for him all the horror to come, your youth fading away at the side of a feeble and depraved old man, dare to speak harshly: tell him that if he remains implacable, you . . . you will find a terrible defense . . . Tell him that wealth will not bring you a moment's happiness; that luxury is only a comfort for poverty, and then only for a moment, only from being unaccustomed; don't let up on him, don't be frightened by his wrath or his threats, as long as there's even a shadow of hope, for God's sake, don't let up. But if there's no other way left . . ."

Here Dubrovsky covered his face with his hands, he seemed to be choking. Masha wept . . .

"Oh, my wretched, wretched fate!" he said with a bitter sigh. "I would give my life for you, to see you from afar, to touch your hand would be ecstasy for me. And when the possibility opens for me to press you to my agitated heart and say: 'My angel, let us die!'—wretched man, I must beware of that bliss, I must hold it off with all my strength . . . I dare not fall at your feet, to thank heaven for its incomprehensible, undeserved reward. Oh, how I should hate that man . . . but I feel that there is now no room for hatred in my heart."

He gently put his arms around her slender waist and gently drew her to his heart. She trustingly lowered her head to the young robber's shoulder. Both were silent.

Time flew by.

"I must go," Masha said at last. It was as if Dubrovsky awoke from a trance. He took her hand and placed a ring on her finger.

"If you decide to resort to me," he said, "bring the ring here, put it into the hollow of this oak, and I will know what to do."

Dubrovsky kissed her hand and disappeared into the trees.

CHAPTER SIXTEEN

Prince Vereisky's marriage plans were no longer a secret in the neighborhood. Kirila Petrovich received congratulations, the wedding was in preparation. Masha kept postponing the decisive talk from one day to the next. Meanwhile she treated her elderly suitor coldly and stiffly. The prince was not worried by that. He was not concerned about love, he was satisfied with her tacit consent.

But time was passing. Masha finally decided to act and wrote a letter to Prince Vereisky; she tried to arouse a feeling of magnanimity in his heart, openly admitted that she felt not the slightest attachment to him, begged him to renounce her hand and protect her from parental authority. She handed the letter to Prince Vereisky in secret; he read it when he was alone, and was not moved in the least by his fiancée's candor. On the contrary, he saw the necessity of hastening the wedding, and to that end deemed it proper to show the letter to his future father-in-law.

Kirila Petrovich was furious; the prince barely persuaded him not to let Masha see that he knew about the letter. Kirila Petrovich agreed not to speak to her about it, but decided to waste no time and set the wedding for the very next day. The prince found that quite reasonable, went to his fiancée, told her that the letter had grieved him very much, but that he hoped in time to win her affection, that the thought of losing her was too painful for him, and that he was unable to accept his own death sentence. After which he kissed her hand respectfully and left, not saying a word to her about Kirila Petrovich's decision.

But he had barely had time to drive out of the courtyard before her father came to her and ordered her straight out to be ready for the next day. Marya Kirilovna, already agitated by her talk with Prince Vereisky, dissolved in tears and threw herself at her father's feet.

"Dear papa," she cried in a pitiful voice, "dear papa, don't destroy me, I don't love the prince, I don't want to be his wife . . ."

"What is the meaning of this?" Kirila Petrovich said menacingly. "Up to now you were silent and consenting, but now, when everything's settled, you've taken a notion to be capricious and renounce it. Kindly don't play the fool; that will get you nowhere with me."

"Don't destroy me," poor Masha repeated. "Why do you drive me away and give me to a man I don't love? Are you tired of me? I want to stay with you as before. Dear papa, it will be sad for you without me, and sadder still when you think how unhappy I am, dear papa. Don't force me, I don't want to get married . . ."

Kirila Petrovich was moved, but he concealed his perplexity and, pushing her away, said sternly:

"This is all nonsense, do you hear? I know better than you what's necessary for your happiness. Tears won't help you, your wedding will be the day after tomorrow."

"The day after tomorrow!" cried Masha. "My God! No, no, it's impossible, it will not be. Dear papa, listen, if you're already resolved to destroy me, I'll find a protector, one you've never thought of, you'll see, you'll be horrified at what you've driven me to."

"What? What?" said Troekurov. "So you threaten me, threaten me, you impudent girl! Be it known to you that I shall do something to you that you cannot even imagine. You dare to frighten me with your protector. We'll see who this protector turns out to be."

"Vladimir Dubrovsky," Masha replied in despair.

Kirila Petrovich thought she had gone out of her mind, and stared at her in amazement.

"Very well," he said after a brief silence. "Wait for any deliverer you like, but meanwhile you'll sit in this room, you won't leave it till the wedding itself."

With these words Kirila Petrovich left and locked the door behind him.

The poor girl wept for a long time, imagining all that lay ahead of her, but the stormy talk relieved her soul, and she was now able to reason more calmly about her fate and what she was to do. The main thing for her was to be delivered from the hateful marriage; the fate of a robber's wife seemed to her like paradise compared to the lot being prepared for her. She looked at the ring Dubrovsky had left her. She ardently wished to see him alone and once more talk things over with him at length before the decisive moment. Her intuition told her that in the evening she would find Dubrovsky by the gazebo in the garden; she decided to go and wait for him there as soon as it began to grow dark. It grew dark. Masha made ready, but her door was locked. The maid told her from outside the door that Kirila Petrovich had given orders not to let her out. She was under arrest. Deeply offended, she sat by the window and remained there until late at night without undressing, staring fixedly at the dark sky. At dawn she dozed off, but her light sleep was disturbed by sad visions, and the rays of the rising sun awakened her.

CHAPTER SEVENTEEN

She woke up, and with her first thought all the horror of her situation presented itself to her. She rang, the maid came in, and to her questions replied that Kirila Petrovich had gone to Arbatovo in the evening and come back late, that he had given strict instructions not to let her out of the room and to see that no one talked to her, that, on the other hand, no special preparations for the wedding could be seen, except that the priest had been ordered not to absent himself from the village under any pretext. After this news the maid left Marya Kirilovna and once again locked the door.

Her words infuriated the young captive. Her head was seething, her blood was stirred, she decided to inform Dubrovsky of everything and began to seek some way of sending the ring to the hollow of the secret oak. At that moment a little stone struck her window, the glass made a ping, and Marya Kirilovna looked out and saw little Sasha making mysterious signs to her. She knew his affection for her and was glad to see him. She opened the window.

"Hello, Sasha," she said. "Why are you calling me?"

"I came to find out if you need anything, sister. Papa's angry and has forbidden the whole household to obey you, but tell me and I'll do whatever you like."

"Thank you, my dear Sashenka. Listen: you know the old oak with the hollow that's by the gazebo?"

"I do, sister."

"Then if you love me, run there quickly and put this ring into the hollow, and make sure nobody sees you."

With those words she tossed him the ring and closed the window.

The boy picked up the ring, set off running as fast as he could, and in three minutes reached the secret tree. There he stopped for breath, looked all around, and put the ring into the hollow. Having done his job successfully, he wanted to report at once to Marya Kirilovna, when suddenly a ragged boy, red-haired and squint-eyed, shot from behind the gazebo, dashed to the oak tree, and thrust his hand into the hollow. Sasha rushed at him quicker than a squirrel and caught hold of him with both hands.

"What are you doing here?" he said menacingly.

"None of your business!" the boy replied, trying to free himself.

"Leave that ring alone, you red-haired rat," Sasha shouted, "or I'll teach you what's what."

Instead of an answer, the boy punched him in the face with his fist, but Sasha did not let go and shouted at the top of his voice: "Thieves, thieves, help, help . . ."

The boy tried to break free of him. He was apparently a couple of years older than Sasha and much stronger, but Sasha was more nimble. They struggled for several minutes, and the red-haired boy finally won. He threw Sasha to the ground and took him by the throat.

But just then a strong hand seized his red and bristling hair, and the gardener Stepan lifted him a foot off the ground . . .

"Ah, you red-haired rascal," the gardener said. "How dare you beat the young master . . ."

Sasha had time to jump up and brush himself off.

"You grabbed me under the arms, otherwise you'd never have thrown me down. Give me back the ring and get out of here."

"Nohow," the redhead replied and, suddenly twisting around, freed his bristles from Stepan's hand. Then he broke into a run, but Sasha caught up with him, shoved him in the back, and the boy went sprawling. The gardener seized him again and bound him with his belt.

"Give me the ring!" Sasha shouted.

"Wait, master," said Stepan. "We'll take him to the steward and he'll deal with him."

The gardener led the prisoner to the manor yard, and Sasha went with them, casting worried glances at his torn and grass-stained trousers. Suddenly the three of them found themselves in front of Kirila Petrovich, who was on his way to inspect the stables.

"What's this?" he asked Stepan.

Stepan briefly described the whole incident. Kirila Petrovich listened to him attentively.

"You scapegrace," he said, turning to Sasha. "Why did you have anything to do with him?"

"He stole the ring from the hollow, papa. Tell him to give back the ring."

"What ring, from what hollow?"

"The one Marya Kirilovna . . . the ring she . . ."

Sasha became embarrassed, confused. Kirila Petrovich frowned and said, shaking his head:

"So Marya Kirilovna's mixed up in it. Confess everything, or I'll give you such a birching you won't know who you are."

"By God, papa, I . . . Marya Kirilovna didn't tell me to do anything, papa . . ."

"Stepan, go and cut me a good, fresh birch rod . . ."

"Wait, papa, I'll tell you everything. Today I was running around in the yard, and my sister Marya Kirilovna opened the window, I ran over, and my sister accidentally dropped a ring, and I hid it in the hollow, and . . . and this red-haired boy wanted to steal it."

"She accidentally dropped it, and you wanted to hide it . . . Stepan, fetch the rod."

"Papa, wait, I'll tell you everything. My sister Marya Kirilovna told me to run to the oak and put the ring in the hollow, so I ran and put the ring in it, and this nasty boy . . ."

Kirila Petrovich turned to the nasty boy and asked menacingly: "Whose are you?"

"I'm a household serf of the Dubrovskys," replied the red-haired boy.

Kirila Petrovich's face darkened.

"So it seems you don't recognize me as your master. Fine," he replied. "And what were you doing in my garden?"

"Stealing raspberries," the boy replied with great indifference.

"Aha, servant and master, like priest, like parish. Do my raspberries grow on oak trees?"

The boy made no reply.

"Papa, tell him to give back the ring," said Sasha.

"Quiet, Alexander," replied Kirila Petrovich. "Don't forget, I still intend to settle with you. Go to your room. And you, squint-eye, you seem bright enough. Give me the ring and go home."

The boy opened his fist and showed that he had nothing in his hand.

"If you confess everything to me, I won't thrash you, and I'll give you five kopecks for nuts. If not, I'll do something to you that you'd never expect. Well?"

The boy did not say a word and stood there, hanging his head and giving himself the look of a real little fool.

"Fine," said Kirila Petrovich. "Lock him up somewhere and see that he doesn't escape, or I'll skin the whole household alive."

Stepan took the boy to the dovecote, locked him in, and set the old poultry maid Agafya to keep watch on him.

"Go to town right now for the police chief," said Kirila Petrovich, following the boy with his eyes, "as quick as you can."

"There's no doubt about it. She kept in touch with that cursed Dubrovsky. Can it really be that she called for his help?" thought Kirila Petrovich, pacing the room and angrily whistling "Thunder of victory." "Maybe I've finally found his warm tracks, and he won't get away from us. We must take advantage of the occasion. Hah! A bell. Thank God, it's the police chief."

"Hey! Bring me the boy we caught."

Meanwhile a buggy drove into the yard, and the police chief already known to us came into the room all covered with dust.

"Great news," Kirila Petrovich said to him. "I've caught Dubrovsky."

"Thank God, Your Excellency," the police chief said joyfully. "Where is he?"

"That is, not Dubrovsky, but one of his band. They'll bring him presently. He'll help us to catch their chief. Here he is."

The police chief, who was expecting a fearsome robber, was amazed to see a thirteen-year-old boy of rather weak appearance. He turned to Kirila Petrovich in perplexity and waited for an explanation. Kirila Petrovich began at once to recount the morning's incident, though without mentioning Marya Kirilovna.

The police chief listened to him attentively, glancing every other moment at the little scoundrel, who, pretending to be a fool, seemed to pay no attention to all that was going on around him.

"Allow me to speak with you in private, Your Excellency," the police chief finally said.

Kirila Petrovich took him to another room and locked the door behind him.

Half an hour later they came back to the reception room where the prisoner was waiting for his fate to be decided.

"The master," said the police chief, "wanted to put you in the town jail, have you flogged and then sent to a penal colony, but I interceded for you and persuaded him to forgive you. Untie him."

The boy was untied.

"Thank the master," said the police chief. The boy went up to Kirila Petrovich and kissed his hand.

"Go on home," Kirila Petrovich said to him, "and in the future don't steal raspberries from hollow trees."

The boy went out, cheerfully jumped off the porch, and ran across the fields to Kistenevka without looking back. On reaching the village, he stopped at a dilapidated hut, the first at the edge, and knocked on the window; the window was raised, and an old woman appeared.

"Give me some bread, grandma," said the boy. "I haven't eaten since morning, I'm starved."

"Ah, it's you, Mitya. Where did you disappear to, you little devil?" the old woman replied.

"I'll tell you later, grandma. Give me some bread, for God's sake."

"Come in, then."

"No time, grandma, I still have to run somewhere else. Bread, for Christ's sake, give me bread."

"What a fidget!" the old woman grumbled. "Here's a slice for you." And she handed a slice of dark bread out the window. The boy greedily bit into it and, chewing, instantly headed off again.

It was growing dark. Mitya made his way past the barns and kitchen gardens to the Kistenevka grove. Having reached the two pine trees that stood as front-line sentinels of the grove, he stopped, looked around, gave an abrupt, piercing whistle, and began to listen; he heard a light and prolonged whistle in response; someone came out of the wood and approached him.

CHAPTER EIGHTEEN

Kirila Petrovich paced up and down the reception room, whistling his song more loudly than usual; the whole house was astir, servants ran around, maids bustled, in the shed the coachmen hitched up the carriage, people crowded in the courtyard. In the young mistress's dressing room, before the mirror, a lady, surrounded by maids, was decking out the pale, motionless Marya Kirilovna, whose head bent languidly under the weight of the diamonds. She winced slightly when a careless hand pricked her, but kept silent, vacantly gazing into the mirror.

"Soon now?" Kirila Petrovich's voice was heard at the door.

"One moment!" replied the lady. "Marya Kirilovna, stand up, look at yourself, is it all right?"

Marya Kirilovna stood up and made no reply. The door opened.

"The bride is ready," the lady said to Kirila Petrovich. "Have them put her in the carriage."

"Godspeed," replied Kirila Petrovich and, taking an icon from the table, he said in a moved voice. "Come to me, Masha. I give you my blessing . . ."

The poor girl fell at his feet and sobbed.

"Papa . . . dear papa . . ." she said in tears, and her voice died away. Kirila Petrovich hastened to bless her, she was picked up and all but carried to the carriage. Her proxy mother and one of the maids sat with her. They drove to the church. There the groom was already waiting for them. He came out to meet her and was struck by her pallor and strange look. Together they entered the cold, empty church; the door was locked behind them. The priest came out from the altar and began at once. Marya Kirilovna saw nothing, heard nothing, she thought of only one thing: since morning she had waited for Dubrovsky, hope had not abandoned her for a moment, but when the priest turned to her with the usual questions, she shuddered and her heart sank, but she still tarried, still waited. The priest, getting no answer from her, pronounced the irrevocable words.

The ceremony was over. She felt the cold kiss of her unloved husband, she heard the cheerful congratulations of those present, and still could not believe that her life was forever bound, that Dubrovsky had not come flying to set her free. The prince addressed some tender words to her, she did not understand them, they left the church, the porch was crowded with peasants from Pokrovskoe. Her gaze ran quickly over them and again showed the former insensibility. The newlyweds got into the carriage together and drove to Arbatovo; Kirila Petrovich had already gone on ahead so as to meet the newlyweds there. Alone with his young wife, the prince was not put out in the least by her cold look. He did not bother her with sugary talk and ridiculous raptures; his words were simple and called for no response. In this way they drove some seven miles, the horses sped over the bumps of the country road, and the carriage barely rocked on its English springs.

Suddenly shouts of pursuit rang out, the carriage stopped, a crowd of armed men surrounded it, and a man in a half mask, opening the doors on the young princess's side, said to her:

"You're free, come out."

"What is the meaning of this?" cried the prince. "Who are you? ..."

"It's Dubrovsky," said the princess.

The prince, not losing his presence of mind, drew a traveling pistol from his side pocket and fired at the masked robber. The princess cried out and covered her face with both hands in horror. Dubrovsky was wounded in the shoulder; blood appeared. The prince, not wasting a moment, drew a second pistol, but he was given no time to fire. The doors of the carriage were opened and several strong hands pulled him out and tore the pistol from him. Knives flashed over him.

"Don't touch him!" cried Dubrovsky, and his grim accomplices drew back.

"You are free," Dubrovsky went on, turning to the pale princess.

"No," she replied. "It's too late, I'm married, I'm Prince Vereisky's wife."

"What are you saying?" Dubrovsky cried in despair. "No, you're not his wife, you were forced, you could never have consented ...."

"I did consent, I took the vow," she objected firmly. "The prince is my husband, order him freed and leave me with him. I did not deceive you. I waited for you till the last moment ... But now, I tell you, now it's too late. Let us go."

But Dubrovsky no longer heard her. The pain of the wound and the strong agitation of his soul took his strength away. He collapsed by the wheel, the robbers surrounded him. He managed to say a few words to them, they put him on a horse, two of them supported him, a third took the horse by the bridle, and they all went off, leaving the carriage in the middle of the road, with the servants bound, the horses unhitched, but stealing nothing and shedding not a single drop of blood in revenge for the blood of their leader.

CHAPTER NINETEEN

On a narrow clearing in the middle of a dense forest rose a small earthen fortress, consisting of a rampart and a ditch, behind which were several huts and dugouts.

In the yard a large number of men, in varied dress but all of them armed, which showed them at once to be robbers, were having dinner, sitting hatless around a fraternal cauldron. On the rampart, next to a small cannon, sat a sentry, his legs tucked under; he was putting a patch on a certain part of his clothing, working the needle with a skill that betrayed an experienced tailor, and kept glancing in all directions.

Though a dipper had been passed around several times, a strange silence reigned in the company. The robbers finished their dinner, got up one after another, and said a prayer. Some dispersed to the huts, others went off to the forest or lay down for a nap as Russians usually do.

The sentry finished his work, shook out his rag, admired the patch, stuck the needle in his sleeve, sat down astride the cannon, and began to sing at the top of his voice a melancholy old song:

> Rustle not, leafy mother, forest green,
> Keep me not, a fine lad, from thinking my thoughts.

Just then the door to one of the huts opened and an old woman in a white bonnet, neatly and primly dressed, appeared on the threshold.

"Enough of that, Styopka," she said angrily. "The master's asleep and you're bellowing away; you've got no shame or pity."

"Sorry, Egorovna," Styopka replied. "All right, I won't go on. Let our dear master rest and recover."

The old woman went back in, and Styopka started pacing the rampart.

In the hut the old woman had emerged from, behind a partition, the wounded Dubrovsky lay on a camp bed. Before him on a small table lay his pistols, and a saber hung by his head. The floor and walls of the mud hut were covered with luxurious carpets; in the corner was a lady's silver dressing table and a pier glass. Dubrovsky held an open book in his hand, but his eyes were shut. And the old woman, who kept glancing at him from beyond the partition, could not tell whether he was asleep or merely thinking.

Suddenly Dubrovsky gave a start, the alarm rang in the fortress, and Styopka thrust his head through the window.

"Master Vladimir Andreevich," he cried, "our boys have given the signal: they're tracking us down."

Dubrovsky jumped off the bed, grabbed a pistol, and came out of the hut. The robbers were crowding noisily in the yard; at his appearance a deep silence fell.

"Is everybody here?" asked Dubrovsky.

"Everybody except the lookouts," came the answer.

"To your places!" cried Dubrovsky.

And each robber went to his appointed place. Just then three lookouts came running to the gate. Dubrovsky went to meet them.

"What is it?" he asked.

"Soldiers in the forest," they replied. "They're surrounding us."

Dubrovsky ordered the gates locked and went himself to examine the little cannon. From the forest came the sound of several voices, and they began to approach; the robbers waited in silence. Suddenly three or four soldiers emerged from the forest and at once fell back, firing shots to signal their comrades.

"Prepare to fight," said Dubrovsky.

There was a stir among the robbers, after which everything fell silent again. Then they heard the noise of the approaching detachment, weapons gleamed among the trees, some hundred and fifty soldiers poured out of the forest and, shouting loudly, rushed towards the rampart. Dubrovsky touched off the fuse, the shot was lucky: one man had his head blown off, two more were wounded. There was confusion among the soldiers, but the officer threw himself forward, the soldiers followed him and ran down into the ditch. The robbers fired at them with rifles and pistols, and, with axes in their hands, began to defend the rampart, which the enraged soldiers attacked, leaving twenty wounded comrades in the ditch. Hand-to-hand combat began, the soldiers were already on the rampart, the robbers were beginning to fall back, but Dubrovsky, walking up to the officer, put a pistol to his chest and fired. The officer went crashing on his back. Several soldiers picked him up and quickly carried him into the forest; the rest, left without a leader, stopped. The encouraged robbers took advantage of this moment of bewilderment, overran them and drove them into the ditch. The besiegers fled, the robbers, shouting loudly, rushed after them. The victory was assured. Dubrovsky, trusting in the complete discomfiture of the enemy, stopped his men and shut himself up in the fortress, commanding the wounded to be brought in, doubling the sentries, and ordering that nobody leave.

The latest events attracted the government's attention to Dubrovsky's daring brigandage in earnest. Information was gathered concerning his whereabouts. A company of soldiers was sent to take him dead or alive. They caught several men from his band and learned from them that Dubrovsky was no longer among them. A few days after [the battle]* he had gathered all his companions, announced to them that he intended to leave them forever, and advised them to change their way of life.

"You've grown rich under my leadership, each of you has documents with which you can safely make your way to some remote province and there spend the rest of your lives in honest labor and abundance. But you're all rascals and probably won't want to abandon your trade."

After that speech he left them, taking only * * * with him. No one knew where he had disappeared to. At first the truth of this testimony was doubted: the robbers' devotion to their chief was well known. It was supposed that they were trying to protect him. But subsequent events bore them out: the terrible visits, arsons, and robberies ceased. The roads became clear. From other sources it was learned that Dubrovsky had escaped abroad.

* There is a gap here in the original manuscript. *Translator.*

The Queen of Spades

—

The queen of spades signifies secret malevolence.

THE LATEST FORTUNETELLING BOOK

> In nasty weather
> They would all get together
> And play;
> On the table now fifty
> Or, God help them, twice fifty
> They'd lay,
> And whenever they won,
> They chalked up the sum
> On a slate.
> So in nasty weather
> Quite busy together
> They played.[1]

Once they were playing cards at the horse guard Narumov's. The long winter night passed unnoticed; they sat down to supper towards five in the morning. Those who came out winners ate with great appetite; the others sat absently before their empty plates. But champagne appeared, the conversation grew lively, and they all took part in it.

"How did you do, Surin?" asked the host.

"Lost, as usual. I must confess, I'm unlucky: I play *mirandole*,[2] never get excited, nothing throws me off, and yet I keep losing!"

"And you weren't tempted even once? You never once staked *en route*? . . . I find your firmness astonishing."

"What about Hermann?" said one of the guests, pointing to the young engineer. "He's never held cards in his life, never bent down a single *paroli* in his life, yet he sits with us and watches us play till five in the morning."

"The game interests me greatly," said Hermann, "but I am not in a position to sacrifice the necessary in hopes of acquiring the superfluous."

"Hermann is a German: he's calculating, that's all!" Tomsky observed. "But if there's anyone I don't understand, it's my grand-mother, Countess Anna Fedotovna."

"How? What?" the guests cried.

"I can't comprehend," Tomsky went on, "how it is that my grandmother doesn't punt!"

"What's so surprising," said Narumov, "about an eighty-year-old woman not punting?"

"So you know nothing about her?"

"No, nothing at all!"

"Oh, then listen:

"You should know that sixty years ago my grandmother went to Paris and became all the fashion there. People ran after her, to catch a glimpse of *la Vénus moscovite*; Richelieu[3] dangled after her, and my grandmother assures me that he nearly shot himself on account of her cruelty.

"In those days ladies played faro. Once at court she lost quite a lot on credit to the duc d'Orléans. Having come home, my grandmother, while unsticking the beauty spots from her face and untying her farthingales, announced her loss to my grandfather and ordered him to pay.

"My late grandfather, as far as I remember, was a sort of butler to my grandmother. He was mortally afraid of her; however, on hearing of such a terrible loss, he flew into a rage, fetched an abacus, demonstrated to her that in half a year they had spent half a million, that they had no estates near Paris, as they had near Moscow and Saratov, and flatly refused to pay. Grandmother slapped him in the face and went to bed alone as a token of his disgrace.

"The next day she sent for her husband, hoping that the domestic punishment had had an effect on him, but she found him unshakeable. For the first time in her life she stooped to discussions and explanations with him; she hoped to appeal to his conscience, indulgently pointing out to him that there are debts and debts, and there is a difference between a prince and a coach maker. No use! Grandfather was in rebellion. No, and that's final! Grandmother didn't know what to do.

"She was closely acquainted with a very remarkable man. You've heard of the comte de Saint-Germain, of whom so many wonders are told. You know that he passed himself off as the Wandering Jew, the inventor of the elixir of life and the philosopher's stone, and so on. He was laughed at as a charlatan, and Casanova in his memoirs says he was a spy;[4] however, despite his mysteriousness, Saint-Germain was of very dignified appearance and was very amiable in society. Grandmother still loves him to distraction and gets angry if he is spoken of disrespectfully. Grandmother knew that Saint-Germain could have large sums at his disposal. She decided to resort to him. She wrote him a note and asked him to come to her immediately.

"The old eccentric appeared at once and found her in terrible distress. She described her husband's barbarity in the blackest colors, and said finally that all her hope now rested on his friendship and amiability.

"Saint-Germain reflected.

"'I could oblige you with this sum,' he said, 'but I know you will not be at peace until you have repaid it, and I do not wish to bring new troubles upon you. There is another way: you can win it back.'

"'But, my gentle comte,' grandmother replied, 'I tell you we have no money at all.'

"'Money's not needed here,' Saint-Germain rejoined. 'Kindly listen to me.' Here he revealed to her a secret for which any of us would give a great deal . . ."

The young gamblers redoubled their attention. Tomsky lit his pipe, puffed on it, and went on.

"That same evening grandmother appeared at Versailles, *au jeu de la Reine.** The duc d'Orléans kept the bank; grandmother lightly apologized for not having brought her debt, concocting a little story as an excuse, and began to punt against him. She chose three cards, played them one after the other: all three won straight off and grandmother recovered all her losses."

"Pure chance!" said one of the guests.

"A fairy tale!" observed Hermann.

"Marked cards, maybe?" chimed in a third.

"I don't think so," Tomsky replied imposingly.

"What!" said Narumov. "You have a grandmother who can guess three cards in a row, and you still haven't taken over her cabbalistics from her?"

"The devil she'd tell me!" Tomsky replied. "She had four sons, including my father, all four of them desperate gamblers, and she didn't reveal her secret to a one of them; though it wouldn't have been a bad thing for them, or for me either. But here is what my uncle, Count Ivan Ilyich, told me, and he assured me of it on his honor. The late Chaplitsky, the one who died a pauper after squandering millions, in his youth once lost—to Zorich, as I recall—around three hundred thou-

* at the Queen's gaming table

sand. He was in despair. Grandmother, who was always severe towards young people's follies, somehow took pity on Chaplitsky. She gave him three cards, which he was to play one after the other, and made him swear on his honor that he would never gamble afterwards. Chaplitsky appeared before his vanquisher: they sat down to play. Chaplitsky staked fifty thousand on the first card and won straight off; bent down a *paroli*, a double *paroli*—recovered everything and wound up winning even more . . ."

"But it's time for bed; it's a quarter to six."

Indeed, dawn was breaking. The young men finished their glasses and went their ways.

II

> —*Il paraît que monsieur est décidément pour les suivantes.*
> —*Que voulez-vous, madame? Elles sont plus fraîches.**

SOCIETY CONVERSATION[5]

The old countess * * * was sitting in her dressing room before the mirror. Three maids surrounded her. One held a jar of rouge, another a box of hairpins, the third a tall bonnet with flame-colored ribbons. The countess had not the slightest pretension to a beauty faded long ago, but she preserved all the habits of her youth, held strictly to the fashion of the seventies, and dressed just as slowly and just as painstakingly as sixty years ago. By the window a young lady, her ward, sat over her embroidery.

"Greetings, *grand'maman*," said a young officer, coming in. "*Bonjour, mademoiselle Lise. Grand'maman*, I've come to you with a request."

"What is it, Paul?"

"Allow me to introduce one of my friends to you and to bring him to your ball on Friday."

"Bring him straight to the ball and introduce him to me there. Were you at * * *'s last night?"

---

* It seems that the gentleman decidedly prefers the lady's maids. / What do you want, madam? They're fresher.

"What else! It was very merry. We danced till five in the morning. How pretty Eletskaya was!"

"Come, my dear! What's so pretty about her? Is she anything like her grandmother, Princess Darya Petrovna? . . . By the way, I fancy she's aged a lot, Princess Darya Petrovna?"

"Aged, you say?" Tomsky replied distractedly. "She died seven years ago."

The young lady raised her head and made a sign to the young man. He remembered that they were to conceal from the old countess the deaths of women her age, and he bit his tongue. But the countess heard the news, which was new to her, with great indifference.

"Died!" she said. "And I didn't know! We were made ladies-in-waiting together, and when we were presented, the empress . . ."

And for the hundredth time the countess told her grandson the story.

"Well, Paul," she said afterwards, "now help me up. Lizanka, where's my snuffbox?"

And the countess went behind the screen with her maids to finish her toilette. Tomsky remained with the young lady.

"Who is it you want to introduce?" Lizaveta Ivanovna asked softly.

"Narumov. Do you know him?"

"No! Is he military or civilian?"

"Military."

"An engineer?"

"No, a cavalryman. What made you think he was an engineer?"

The young lady laughed and made no reply.

"Paul!" the countess called out from behind the screen. "Send me some new novel, only, please, not like they write nowadays."

"How do you mean, *grand'maman*?"

"I mean the kind of novel where the hero doesn't strangle his father or mother, and where there are no drowned bodies. I'm terribly afraid of drowned bodies!"

"There are no such novels nowadays. Or maybe you'd like a Russian one?"

"You mean there are Russian novels? . . . Send me one, old boy, please do send me one!"

"Excuse me, *grand'maman*, I'm in a hurry . . . Excuse me, Lizaveta Ivanovna! What made you think Narumov was an engineer?"

And Tomsky left the dressing room.

Lizaveta Ivanovna remained alone: she abandoned her work and started looking out the window. Soon a young officer appeared from around the corner of a house on the other side of the street. A flush came to her cheeks: she picked up her work again and bent her head over the canvas. Just then the countess came out, fully dressed.

"Order the carriage, Lizanka," she said, "and we'll go for a ride."

Lizanka got up from her embroidery and started putting her work away.

"What is it, old girl? Are you deaf or something?" the countess cried. "Tell them to hurry up with the carriage."

"At once!" the young lady replied quietly and ran to the front hall.

A servant came in and handed the countess some books from Count Pavel Alexandrovich.

"Very good! Thank him," said the countess. "Lizanka, Lizanka! Where are you running to?"

"To get dressed."

"There's no rush, old girl. Sit here. Open the first volume; read aloud . . ."

The young lady took the book and read out a few lines.

"Louder!" said the countess. "What's wrong with you, old girl? Lost your voice, or something? . . . Wait: move that footstool towards me . . . closer . . . really!"

Lizaveta Ivanovna read two more pages. The countess yawned.

"Enough of this book," she said. "What nonsense! Send it back to Prince Pavel and tell them to thank him . . . Well, what about the carriage?"

"The carriage is ready," Lizaveta Ivanovna said, looking outside.

"Why aren't you dressed?" said the countess. "I always have to wait for you! It's quite insufferable, old girl!"

Liza ran to her room. Two minutes had not gone by before the countess began to ring with all her might. Three maids came running through one door and the valet through the other.

"Why don't you come when you're called?" said the countess. "Tell Lizaveta Ivanovna I'm waiting for her."

Lizaveta Ivanovna came in wearing a cape and a bonnet.

"At last, old girl!" said the countess. "What an outfit! Why this? . . . Whom do you want to entice? . . . And what's the weather like? Windy, it seems."

THE QUEEN OF SPADES

"Not at all, Your Ladyship! It's quite calm!" replied the valet.

"You always talk at random! Open the window. Just so: wind! And very cold, too! Unhitch the carriage! We're not going, Lizanka: there was no point dressing up."

"And that's my life!" thought Lizaveta Ivanovna.

Indeed, Lizaveta Ivanovna was a most unfortunate creature. Bitter is another's bread, says Dante, and hard it is climbing another's stairs,[6] and who knows the bitterness of dependency if not the poor ward of an aristocratic old woman? Countess * * *, of course, did not have a wicked soul; but she was capricious, as a woman spoiled by high society, stingy, and sunk in cold egoism, like all old people, whose time for love is in the past, and who are strangers to the present. She took part in all the vain bustle of high society, dragged herself to balls, where she sat in a corner, all rouged and dressed in the old fashion, like an ugly but necessary ornament of the ballroom. The arriving guests, as if by an established ritual, approached her with low bows, and afterwards no one paid any attention to her. She received the whole town at her house, observing strict etiquette and not recognizing anyone's face. Her numerous servants, having grown fat and gray in her front hall and maids' quarters, did whatever they liked, outdoing each other in robbing the dying old woman. Lizaveta Ivanovna was the household martyr. She poured tea and was reprimanded for using too much sugar; she read novels aloud and was to blame for all the author's mistakes; she accompanied the countess on her walks and was answerable for the weather and the pavement. She had a fixed salary, which was never paid in full; and meanwhile she was required to dress like everyone else— that is, like the very few. In society she played a most pitiable role. Everyone knew her and no one noticed her; at balls she danced only when there was a lack of *vis-à-vis*,* and ladies took her under the arm each time they had to go to the dressing room to straighten something in their outfits. She was proud, felt her position keenly, and looked about—waiting impatiently for a deliverer; but the young men, calculating in their frivolous vanity, did not deem her worthy of attention, though Lizaveta Ivanovna was a hundred times nicer than the cold and insolent brides they dangled after. So many times, quietly leaving the dull and magnificent drawing room, she went to weep in her

---

* Literally "face-to-face," i.e., partners.

poor room, where stood a folding wallpaper screen, a chest of drawers, a small mirror, and a painted bed, and where a tallow candle burned dimly in a brass candlestick!

Once—this happened two days after the evening described at the start of this story and a week before the scene where we paused—once Lizaveta Ivanovna, sitting by the window over her embroidery, inadvertently glanced out and saw a young engineer standing motionless and with his eyes fixed on her window. She lowered her head and went back to work; five minutes later she glanced again—the young officer was standing in the same place. Not being in the habit of flirting with passing officers, she stopped glancing outside and went on stitching for about two hours without raising her head. Dinner was served. She got up, began to put her embroidery away, and, glancing outside inadvertently, again saw the officer. This seemed rather strange to her. After dinner she went to the window with the feeling of a certain uneasiness, but the officer was no longer there—and she forgot about him . . .

Some two days later, going out with the countess to get into the carriage, she saw him again. He was standing just by the front door, covering his face with his beaver collar: his dark eyes flashed from under his hat. Lizaveta Ivanovna felt frightened, not knowing why herself, and got into the carriage with an inexplicable trembling.

On returning home, she ran to the window—the officer was standing in the former place, his eyes fixed on her: she stepped away, tormented by curiosity and stirred by a feeling that was entirely new to her.

Since then no day went by that the young man did not appear at a certain hour under the windows of their house. Unspoken relations were established between them. Sitting at her place over her work, she felt him approach—raised her head, looked at him longer and longer each day. The young man seemed to be grateful to her for that: with the keen eyes of youth, she saw a quick blush cover his pale cheeks each time their eyes met. After a week she smiled at him . . .

When Tomsky asked permission to introduce his friend to the countess, the poor girl's heart leaped. But learning that Narumov was a horse guard and not an engineer, she regretted that an indiscreet question had given away her secret to the featherbrained Tomsky.

Hermann was the son of a Russified German, who had left him a small capital. Being firmly convinced of the necessity of ensuring his independence, Hermann did not even touch the interest, lived on his pay alone, and did not allow himself the slightest whimsy. However, he was secretive and ambitious, and his comrades rarely had the chance to laugh at his excessive frugality. He was a man of strong passions and fiery imagination, but firmness saved him from the usual errors of youth. Thus, for instance, though he was a gambler at heart, he never touched cards, for he reckoned that in his position he could not afford (as he used to say) *to sacrifice the necessary in hopes of acquiring the superfluous*—and meanwhile he spent whole nights at the card tables and followed with feverish trembling the various turns of the game.

The story of the three cards had a strong effect on his imagination and did not leave his mind the whole night. "What if," he thought the next evening, roaming about Petersburg, "what if the old countess should reveal her secret to me! Or tell me the names of those three sure cards! Why not try my luck? . . . Get introduced to her, curry favor with her—maybe become her lover—but all that takes time— and she's eighty-seven years old—she could die in a week—in two days! . . . And the story itself . . . Can you trust it? . . . No! Calculation, moderation, and diligence: those are my three sure cards, there's what will triple, even septuple my capital, and provide me with peace and independence!"

Reasoning thus, he found himself on one of the main streets of Petersburg, in front of a house of old-style architecture. The street was crammed with vehicles; carriages, one after another, rolled up to the brightly lit entrance. Every other minute the slim foot of a young beauty, or a jingling jackboot, or a striped stocking and diplomatic shoe extended from a carriage. Fur coats and cloaks flashed past the majestic doorman. Hermann stopped.

"Whose house is this?" he asked the sentry at the corner.

"Countess * * *'s," replied the sentry.

Hermann trembled. The amazing story arose again in his imagination. He started pacing around near the house, thinking about its mistress and about her wondrous ability. He returned late to his humble corner; for a long time he could not fall asleep, and when sleep did come over him, he dreamed of cards, a green table, stacks of banknotes, and heaps of gold coins. He played one card after another, resolutely bent down corners, kept on winning, raked in the gold, and put the banknotes in his pocket. Waking up late, he sighed at the loss of his phantasmal riches, again went roaming about the city, and again found himself in front of Countess * * *'s house. Some unknown force seemed to draw him to it. He stopped and began to look at the windows. In one of them he saw a dark-haired little head, bent, probably, over a book or some needlework. The head rose. Hermann saw a fresh face and dark eyes. That moment decided his fate.

III

*Vous m'écrivez, mon ange, des lettres de quatre pages plus vite que je ne puis les lire.**

CORRESPONDENCE

Lizaveta Ivanovna had only just taken off her cape and bonnet when the countess sent for her and again ordered the carriage brought. They went out to take their seats. At the same moment as two lackeys picked up the old woman and put her through the door, Lizaveta Ivanovna saw her engineer just by the wheel; he seized her hand; before she could get over her fear, the young man disappeared: a letter remained in her hand. She hid it in her glove and during the whole ride neither heard nor saw anything. The countess had a habit of constantly asking questions as she drove: "Who was that we just passed?" "What's the name of this bridge?" "What's written on that signboard?" This time Lizaveta Ivanovna answered randomly and inaptly and made the countess angry.

"What's the matter with you, old girl! Are you in a stupor or something? Either you don't hear me or you don't understand? . . . Thank God, I don't mumble and haven't lost my mind yet!"

Lizaveta Ivanovna was not listening to her. On returning home, she ran to her room, took the letter from her glove: it was not sealed. Lizaveta Ivanovna read it. The letter contained a declaration of love: it was tender, respectful, and taken word for word from a German novel. But Lizaveta Ivanovna did not know German and was very pleased with it.

However, the letter she had accepted troubled her greatly. It was the first time she had entered into secret, close relations with a young man. His boldness horrified her. She reproached herself for her impru-

* You write me, my angel, four-page letters more quickly than I can read them.

dent behavior and did not know what to do: to stop sitting by the window and by her inattention cool the young officer's desire for further pursuit? To send his letter back? To reply coldly and resolutely? There was no one to advise her, she had neither friend nor preceptress. Lizaveta Ivanovna decided to reply.

She sat down at her little writing table, took a pen, paper—and fell to thinking. Several times she began her letter—and tore it up: the expression seemed to her now too indulgent, now too severe. At last she managed to write a few lines that left her satisfied. "I am sure," she wrote, "that you have honorable intentions and that you did not wish to insult me by a thoughtless act; but our acquaintance should not begin in such a way. I return your letter to you and hope that in future I will have no reason to complain of undeserved disrespect."

The next day, seeing Hermann coming, Lizaveta Ivanovna got up from her embroidery, went to the reception room, opened a window, and threw the letter out, trusting in the young officer's agility. Hermann ran, picked up the letter, and went into a pastry shop. Tearing off the seal, he found his own letter and Lizaveta Ivanovna's reply. He had expected just that and returned home quite caught up in his intrigue.

Three days after that a sharp-eyed young mam'selle brought Lizaveta Ivanovna a note from a dress shop. Lizaveta Ivanovna opened it with trepidation, anticipating a demand for payment, and suddenly recognized Hermann's handwriting.

"You're mistaken, dearest," she said, "this note isn't for me."

"No, it's precisely for you!" the bold girl answered, not concealing a sly smile. "Kindly read it!"

Lizaveta Ivanovna ran through the note. Hermann demanded a rendezvous.

"It can't be!" said Lizaveta Ivanovna, frightened both by the hastiness of the demand and by the means employed. "This surely wasn't written to me!" And she tore the letter into little pieces.

"If the letter wasn't for you, why did you tear it up?" said the mam'selle. "I would have returned it to the one who sent it."

"Please, dearest," said Lizaveta Ivanovna, flaring up at her remark, "in the future don't bring me any notes! And tell the person who sent you that he ought to be ashamed . . ."

But Hermann would not quiet down. Lizaveta Ivanovna received letters from him each day, by one means or another. They were no longer translations from the German. Hermann wrote them, inspired by passion, and spoke a language that was all his own: in them were expressed both the inflexibility of his desires and the disorder of an unbridled imagination. Lizaveta Ivanovna no longer thought of sending them back: she reveled in them; she started replying to them—and her notes grew longer and tenderer by the hour. Finally, she threw the following letter to him from the window:

> Tonight there is a ball at the * * * Embassy. The countess will be there. We will stay till about two o'clock. This is your chance to see me alone. As soon as the countess goes out, her servants will probably retire; there will be a doorman in the entryway, but he, too, usually goes to his closet. Come at 11:30. Go straight up the stairs. If you meet someone in the front hall, ask if the countess is at home. The answer will be no—and there will be nothing to do. You will have to go away. But you will probably not meet anyone. The maids stay in their quarters, all in one room. From the front hall turn left and go straight on to the countess's bedroom. In the bedroom, behind the screen, you will see two small doors: the right one to the study, where the countess never goes; the left one to a corridor, where there is a narrow winding stairway: it leads to my room.

Hermann trembled like a tiger, waiting for the appointed time. By ten o'clock in the evening he was already standing in front of the countess's house. The weather was awful: wind howled, wet snow fell in big flakes; the streetlamps shone dimly; the streets were deserted. Now and then a cabby dragged by with his scrawny nag, looking for a late customer. Hermann stood in nothing but his frock coat, feeling neither wind nor snow. At last the countess's carriage was brought. Hermann saw how the lackeys carried the bent old woman out under the arms, wrapped in a sable fur coat, and how, after her, her ward flashed by in a light cloak, her head adorned with fresh flowers. The doors slammed. The carriage rolled off heavily over the loose snow. The doorman shut the front door. The windows went dark. Hermann started pacing around by the now deserted house: he went up to a streetlamp, looked at his watch—it was twenty past eleven. He stayed under the streetlamp, his eyes on the hands of the watch, counting the remaining minutes. At exactly half past eleven, Hermann stepped onto the count-

ess's porch and went into the brightly lit entryway. The doorman was
not there. Hermann ran up the stairs, opened the door to the front
hall, and saw a servant sleeping under a lamp in an old, soiled armchair.
Hermann walked past him with a light and firm step. The reception
room and drawing room were dark. The lamp in the front hall shone
faintly on them. Hermann went into the bedroom. Before a stand filled
with old icons flickered a golden lamp. Faded damask armchairs and
sofas with down cushions and worn-off gilding stood in mournful sym-
metry against the walls covered with Chinese silk. On the walls hung
two portraits painted in Paris by Mme Lebrun.[7] One of them portrayed a man of about forty, red-cheeked and portly, in a light green
uniform and with a decoration; the other a young beauty with an aquiline nose, her hair brushed back at the temples, powdered and adorned
with a rose. Every corner was jammed with porcelain shepherdesses,
table clocks made by the famous Leroy, little boxes, bandalores, fans,
and various ladies' knickknacks, invented at the end of the last century
along with Montgolfier's balloon and Mesmer's magnetism.[8] Hermann
went behind the screen. There stood a small iron bed; to the right was
the door leading to the study; to the left the other, to the corridor.
Hermann opened it, saw the narrow winding stairway leading to the
poor ward's room . . . But he came back and went into the dark study.

Time passed slowly. All was quiet. In the drawing room it struck
twelve; in all the rooms one after another the clocks rang twelve—and
all fell silent again. Hermann stood leaning against the cold stove. He
was calm; his heart beat regularly, as in a man who has ventured upon
something dangerous but necessary. The clocks struck one and then
two in the morning—and he heard the distant clatter of a carriage.
An involuntary agitation came over him. The carriage drove up and
stopped. He heard the clatter of the flipped-down steps. There was
bustling in the house. Servants ran, voices rang out, and the house lit
up. Three elderly maids rushed into the bedroom, and the countess,
barely alive, came in and sank into the Voltaire armchair. Hermann
watched through a chink: Lizaveta Ivanovna walked past him. Hermann heard her hurrying steps on the stairs. Something like remorse
of conscience stirred in his heart and died down again. He turned to
stone.

The countess started to undress before the mirror. They unpinned
her bonnet, decorated with roses; took the powdered wig from her gray

and close-cropped head. Pins poured down like rain around her. The yellow gown embroidered with silver fell at her swollen feet. Hermann witnessed the repulsive mysteries of her toilette; finally, the countess was left in a bed jacket and nightcap; in this attire, more suitable to her old age, she seemed less horrible and ugly.

Like all old people generally, the countess suffered from insomnia. Having undressed, she sat down by the window in the Voltaire arm-chair and dismissed her maids. The candles were taken away, the room was again lit only by the icon lamp. The countess sat all yellow, moving her pendulous lips, swaying from side to side. Her dull eyes showed a complete absence of thought; looking at her, one might have thought that the frightful old woman's swaying came not from her will, but from the action of some hidden galvanism.

Suddenly that dead face changed inexplicably. Her lips stopped moving, her eyes came to life: before the countess stood an unknown man.

"Don't be afraid, for God's sake, don't be afraid!" he said in a clear and low voice. "I have no intention of harming you; I've come to beg you for a favor."

The old woman silently looked at him and seemed not to hear him. Hermann thought she might be deaf, and, bending close to her ear, repeated the same words. The old woman was silent as before.

"You can make for the happiness of my life," Hermann continued, "and it won't cost you anything: I know that you can guess three cards in a row . . ."

Hermann stopped. The countess seemed to have understood what was asked of her; it seemed she was seeking words for her reply.

"That was a joke," she said at last. "I swear to you! It was a joke!"

"This is no joking matter," Hermann retorted angrily. "Remember Chaplitsky, whom you helped to win back his losses."

The countess was visibly disconcerted. Her features showed strong emotion, but she soon lapsed into her former insensibility.

"Can you name those three sure cards for me?" Hermann continued.

The countess said nothing; Hermann went on.

"Whom are you keeping your secret for? Your grandchildren? They're rich without that; and besides, they don't know the value of money. Your three cards won't help a squanderer. A man who can't hold on to his paternal inheritance will die a pauper anyway, for all the devil's efforts. I'm not a squanderer; I know the value of money. Your three cards won't be wasted on me. Well? . . ."

He stopped and waited in trembling for her reply. The countess said nothing; Hermann went on his knees.

"If your heart has ever known the feeling of love," he said, "if you remember its raptures, if you smiled even once at the cry of your new-born son, if anything human has ever beaten in your breast, I entreat you by the feelings of a wife, a mistress, a mother—by all that is sacred in life—do not refuse my request! Reveal your secret to me! What good is it to you? . . . Perhaps it's connected with a terrible sin, with the forfeit of eternal bliss, a pact with the devil . . . Think: you're old; you don't have long to live—I'm ready to take your sin upon my soul. Only reveal your secret to me. Think: a man's happiness is in your hands; not only I, but my children, my grandchildren and great-grandchildren, will bless your memory and revere it as sacred . . ."

The old woman did not say a word.

Hermann stood up.

"Old witch!" he said, clenching his teeth. "Then I'll make you answer . . ."

With those words he took a pistol from his pocket.

At the sight of the pistol, the countess showed strong emotion for the second time. She shook her head and raised her hand as if to shield herself from the shot . . . Then she fell backwards and remained motionless.

"Stop being childish," said Hermann, taking her hand. "I ask you for the last time: will you name your three cards for me—yes or no?"

The countess did not reply. Hermann saw that she had died.

IV

7 *Mai* 18—
Homme sans moeurs et sans religion!*

CORRESPONDENCE[9]

Lizaveta Ivanovna, still in her ball gown, sat in her room deep in thought. On coming home she had hastily dismissed the sleepy maid, who had reluctantly offered her services, saying that she would undress herself, and, trembling, had gone into her room, hoping to find Hermann there and wishing not to find him. With the first glance she was convinced of his absence, and she thanked fate for the obstacle that had prevented their rendezvous. She sat down without undressing and began to think back over all the circumstances that had lured her so far in so short a time. Three weeks had not passed since she first saw the young man from the window—and she was already in correspondence with him, and he had managed to obtain a night rendezvous from her! She knew his name only because some of his letters were signed; she had never spoken with him, nor heard his voice, nor heard anything about him . . . until that evening. Strange thing! That same evening, at the ball, Tomsky, pouting at the young princess Polina, who, contrary to her usual habit, was flirting with someone else, had wished to revenge himself by a show of indifference: he had invited Lizaveta Ivanovna and danced an endless mazurka with her. He joked all the while about her partiality for engineer officers, assured her that he knew much more than she might suppose, and some of his jokes were so well aimed that Lizaveta Ivanovna thought several times that her secret was known to him.

"Who told you all that?" she asked, laughing.

"A friend of a person known to you," Tomsky replied, "a very remarkable man!"

"Who is this remarkable man?"

"His name is Hermann."

Lizaveta Ivanovna said nothing, but her hands and feet turned to ice . . .

---

* A man without morals and without religion!

"This Hermann," Tomsky went on, "is a truly romantic character: he has the profile of Napoleon and the soul of Mephistopheles. I think there are at least three evil deeds on his conscience. How pale you've turned! . . ."

"I have a headache . . . What did Hermann—or whatever his name is—tell you? . . ."

"Hermann is very displeased with his friend: he says that in his place he would act quite differently . . . I even suspect that Hermann himself has designs on you; at least he's far from indifferent when he listens to his friend's amorous exclamations."

"But where has he seen me?"

"In church, maybe—or on a promenade! . . . God knows with him! Maybe in your room while you were asleep: he's quite capable of . . ."

Three ladies who came up to them with the question *Oubli ou regret?*[10] interrupted the conversation, which had become agonizingly interesting for Lizaveta Ivanovna.

The lady Tomsky chose was the princess Polina herself. She managed to have a talk with him, making an extra turn with him and twirling an extra time in front of her chair. Going back to his place, Tomsky no longer thought either of Hermann or of Lizaveta Ivanovna. She was intent on renewing their interrupted conversation; but the mazurka ended, and soon afterwards the old countess left.

Tomsky's words were nothing but mazurka banter, but they lodged themselves deeply in the young dreamer's soul. The portrait sketched by Tomsky resembled the picture she had put together herself, and, thanks to the latest novels, this already banal character frightened and captivated her imagination. She sat, her bare arms crossed, bowing her head, still adorned with flowers, over her uncovered bosom . . . Suddenly the door opened and Hermann came in. She trembled . . .

"Where were you?" she asked in a frightened whisper.

"In the old countess's bedroom," Hermann replied. "I've just come from her. The countess is dead."

"My God! . . . What are you saying? . . ."

"And it seems," Hermann went on, "that I'm the cause of her death."

Lizaveta Ivanovna looked at him, and Tomsky's words echoed in her heart: *This man has at least three evil deeds on his soul.* Hermann sat down on the windowsill beside her and told her everything.

Lizaveta Ivanovna listened to him with horror. So those passionate letters, those ardent demands, that bold, tenacious pursuit, all of it was not love! Money—that was what his soul hungered for! It was not she who could appease his desires and make him happy! The poor ward was nothing but the blind assistant of a robber, the murderer of her old benefactress! . . . She wept bitterly in her belated, painful repentance. Hermann looked at her in silence: his heart was torn as well, but neither the poor girl's tears nor the astonishing charm of her grief troubled his hardened soul. He felt no remorse of conscience at the thought of the dead old woman. One thing horrified him: the irretrievable loss of the secret by means of which he had expected to make himself rich.

"You're a monster!" Lizaveta Ivanovna said at last.

"I did not wish her death," Hermann replied. "My pistol wasn't loaded."

They fell silent.

Day was breaking. Lizaveta Ivanovna put out the burnt-down candle: a pale light filled her room. She wiped her tearful eyes and raised them to Hermann: he was sitting on the windowsill, his arms folded, frowning terribly. In that pose he bore an astonishing resemblance to the portrait of Napoleon. The likeness even struck Lizaveta Ivanovna.

"How are you going to get out of the house?" Lizaveta Ivanovna said at last. "I thought of leading you by the secret stairway, but we would have to go past the bedroom, and I'm afraid."

"Tell me how to find this secret stairway; I'll let myself out."

Lizaveta Ivanovna stood up, took a key from the chest of drawers, handed it to Hermann, and gave him detailed instructions. Hermann pressed her cold, unresponsive hand, kissed her bowed head, and left.

He went down the winding stairway and again entered the countess's bedroom. The dead old woman sat turned to stone; her face expressed a deep calm. Hermann stopped in front of her, looked at her for a long time, as if wishing to verify the awful truth; finally he went into the study, felt for the door behind the wall-hanging, and began to descend the dark stairway, troubled by strange feelings. "Maybe by this same stairway," he thought, "sixty years ago, at this same hour, into this same bedroom, in an embroidered kaftan, his hair dressed *à l'oiseau royal,** pressing his cocked hat to his heart, a lucky young fellow stole, who has long since turned to dust in his grave, and today the heart of his aged mistress stopped beating . . ."

---

* in "royal bird fashion" (a men's hairstyle with massive curls over the ears)

At the foot of the stairway Hermann came to a door, unlocked it with the same key, and found himself in a through corridor which brought him out to the street.

V

That night the late baroness von W* * * appeared to me. She was dressed all in white and said to me: "How do you do, mister councilor!"

SWEDENBORG[11]

Three days after the fatal night, at nine o'clock in the morning, Hermann went to the * * * convent, where the funeral service was to be held over the body of the deceased countess. Though he felt no remorse, he still could not completely stifle the voice of conscience, which kept repeating to him: "You're the old woman's murderer." Having little true faith, he had a great many superstitions. He believed that the dead countess could have a harmful influence on his life, and decided to attend her funeral in order to ask her forgiveness.

The church was full. Hermann was barely able to make his way through the crowd of people. The coffin stood on a rich catafalque under a velvet canopy. The deceased woman lay in it, her hands folded on her breast, in a lace cap and a white satin dress. Around her stood her household: servants in black kaftans with armorial ribbons on their shoulders and candles in their hands; relations in deep mourning—children, grandchildren, and great-grandchildren. No one wept; tears would have been *une affectation*. The countess was so old that her death could not surprise anyone, and her relations had long looked upon her as having outlived her time. A young bishop gave a funeral oration. In simple and moving words he presented the peaceful passing of the righteous woman, whose long life had been a quiet, sweet preparation for a Christian ending. "The angel of death found her," said the orator, "vigilant in blessed thoughts and in expectation of the midnight Bridegroom."[12] The service was performed with sorrowful decorum. The relations went first to take leave of the body. Then the numerous guests went up to bow to the one who for so long had participated in their vain amusements. After them came the entire household. And finally the old housekeeper, who was the same age as the deceased. Two young girls led her by the arms. She was unable to bow down to the ground, and was alone in shedding a few tears as she kissed her mistress's cold hand. After her, Hermann decided to approach the coffin. He bowed to the ground and for a few minutes lay on the cold floor strewn with fir branches. He finally got up, pale as the old woman herself, climbed the steps of the catafalque, and bent over . . . At that moment it seemed to him that the dead woman glanced mockingly at him, winking one eye. Hermann, hurriedly stepping away, stumbled and went crashing down on his back. They picked him up. At the same time, Lizaveta Ivanovna was carried out to the porch in a swoon. This episode disturbed the solemnity of the somber ritual for a few minutes. A dull murmur arose among those present, and a lean chamberlain, a close relation of the deceased, whispered in the ear of an Englishman standing next to him that the young officer was her natural son, to which the Englishman replied coldly: "Oh?"

Hermann was extremely upset the whole day. Dining in an out-of-the-way tavern, he, contrary to his custom, drank a great deal, in hopes of stifling his inner agitation. But the wine fired his imagination still more. Returning home, he threw himself on the bed without undressing and fell fast asleep.

When he woke up, it was already night: his room was filled with moonlight. He glanced at the clock: it was a quarter to three. Sleep had left him; he sat on his bed and thought about the old countess's funeral.

Just then someone peeked through his window from outside—and stepped away at once. Hermann paid no attention to it. A moment later he heard the door in his front room being opened. Hermann thought it was his orderly, drunk as usual, coming back from a night out. But he heard unfamiliar steps: someone was walking about, quietly shuffling in slippers. The door opened and a woman in a white dress came in. Hermann took her for his old wet nurse and wondered what could have brought her at such an hour. But the white woman, gliding about, suddenly turned up in front of him—and Hermann recognized the countess!

"I have come to you against my will," she said in a firm voice, "but I have been ordered to fulfill your request. Three, seven, and ace, in that order, will win for you—but on condition that you do not stake on more than one card in twenty-four hours, and after that never play

again for the rest of your life. I forgive you my death, on condition that
you marry my ward Lizaveta Ivanovna . . ."

With those words she quietly turned around, went to the door, and
disappeared, shuffling her slippers. Hermann heard the door in the
front hall slam, and saw someone peek again through his window.

For a long time Hermann could not come to his senses. He went
to the other room. His orderly was asleep on the floor; Hermann was
barely able to wake him up. He was drunk as usual: there was no getting any sense out of him. The door to the front hall was locked. Hermann went back to his room, lit a candle, and wrote down his vision.

VI

> *"Attendez!"*
> "How dare you say *attendez* to me?"
> "Your Excellency, I said *attendez, sir!*"[13]

Two fixed ideas cannot coexist in the moral realm, just as in the physical world two bodies cannot occupy the same place. Three, seven,
ace—soon eclipsed the image of the dead old woman in Hermann's
imagination. Three, seven, ace—never left his head and hovered on
his lips. Seeing a young girl, he said: "How shapely! A real three of
hearts!" When asked, "What time is it?" he said, "Five minutes to the
seven." Every pot-bellied man reminded him of the ace. Three, seven,
ace—pursued him in his sleep, assuming all possible shapes: the three
blossomed before him as a luxuriant grandiflora, the seven looked like
a Gothic gate, the ace like an enormous spider. All his thoughts merged
into one—to make use of the secret that had cost him so dearly. He
began to think about retiring from the army and traveling. He wanted
to force enchanted Fortuna to yield up her treasure in the open gambling houses of Paris. Chance spared him the trouble.

A company of rich gamblers had been formed in Moscow, presided
over by the famous Chekalinsky, who had spent all his life at cards
and had once made millions, taking winnings in promissory notes and
paying losses in ready cash. Long experience had earned him the trust
of his comrades, and his open house, fine chef, affable and cheerful
disposition the respect of the public. He came to Petersburg. Young

men flocked to him, forgetting balls for cards and preferring the temptations of faro to the allurements of philandering. Narumov brought Hermann to him.

They walked through a succession of magnificent rooms, filled with courteous attendants. Several generals and privy councilors were playing whist; young men sat sprawled on the damask sofas, ate ice cream and smoked pipes. In the drawing room, at a long table around which some twenty players crowded, the host sat keeping the bank. He was a man of about sixty, of very dignified appearance; his head was covered with a silvery gray; his full and fresh face was a picture of good nature; his eyes sparkled, enlivened by a perpetual smile. Narumov presented Hermann to him. Chekalinsky shook his hand amicably, asked him not to stand on ceremony, and went back to dealing.

The round lasted a long time. There were more than thirty cards on the table. Chekalinsky paused after each stake to give the players time to make their arrangements, wrote down their losses, courteously listened to their requests, still more courteously unbent the superfluous corner bent down by a distracted hand. At last the round was over. Chekalinsky shuffled the cards and prepared to deal another.

"Allow me to play a card," said Hermann, reaching out his hand from behind a fat gentleman who was there punting. Chekalinsky smiled and bowed silently, as a sign of his obedient consent. Narumov, laughing, congratulated Hermann for breaking his lengthy fast and wished him a lucky start.

"Here goes!" said Hermann, chalking a large sum above his card.

"How much, sir?" the host asked, narrowing his eyes. "Excuse me, sir, I can't make it out."

"Forty-seven thousand," replied Hermann.

At these words all heads turned instantly, and all eyes were fixed on Hermann.

"He's gone mad!" thought Narumov.

"Allow me to point out to you," Chekalinsky said with his invariable smile, "that you are playing a strong game. No one here has ever staked more than two hundred and seventy-five on a *simple*."

"What of it?" Hermann retorted. "Will you cover my card or not?"

Chekalinsky bowed with the same air of humble consent.

"I only wished to inform you," he said, "that, honored by my comrades' trust, I cannot bank otherwise than on ready cash. I'm sure, for my part, that your word is enough, but for the good order of the game and the accounting I beg you to place cash on the card."

Hermann took a bank note from his pocket and handed it to Chekalinsky, who gave it a cursory glance and placed it on Hermann's card.

He began to deal. On the right lay a nine, on the left a three.

"Mine wins!" said Hermann, showing his card.

Whispering arose among the players. Chekalinsky frowned, but the smile at once returned to his face.

"Would you like it now?" asked Chekalinsky.

"If you please."

Chekalinsky drew several bank notes from his pocket and settled up at once. Hermann took his money and left the table. Narumov could not get over it. Hermann drank a glass of lemonade and went home.

The next evening he appeared again at Chekalinsky's. The host was dealing. Hermann went up to the table; the punters made room for him at once. Chekalinsky bowed affably to him.

Hermann waited for the new round, put down a card, placed on it his forty-seven thousand and the previous day's winnings.

Chekalinsky began to deal. A jack fell to the right, a seven to the left. Hermann turned over his seven.

Everyone gasped. Chekalinsky was visibly disconcerted. He counted out ninety-four thousand and handed the money to Hermann. Hermann took it with great coolness and immediately withdrew.

On the following evening Hermann again appeared at the table. Everyone was expecting him. The generals and privy councilors abandoned their whist, so as to see such extraordinary play. The young officers leaped up from the sofas; all the attendants gathered in the drawing room. Everyone surrounded Hermann. The other players did not play their cards, waiting impatiently for the outcome. Hermann stood at the table, preparing to punt alone against the pale but still smiling Chekalinsky. They each unsealed a deck of cards. Chekalinsky shuffled. Hermann drew and put down his card, covering it with a heap of bank notes. It was like a duel. Deep silence reigned all around.

Chekalinsky began to deal, his hands trembling. On the right lay a queen, on the left an ace.

"The ace wins!" said Hermann, and he turned over his card.

"Your queen loses," Chekalinsky said affably.

Hermann shuddered: indeed, instead of an ace, the queen of spades stood before him. He did not believe his eyes, did not understand how he could have drawn the wrong card.

At that moment it seemed to him that the queen of spades winked and grinned. The extraordinary likeness struck him . . .

"The old woman!" he cried in horror.

Chekalinsky drew the bank notes to him. Hermann stood motionless. When he left the table, noisy talk sprang up.

"Beautifully punted!" said the players. Chekalinsky shuffled the cards again: the game went on.

CONCLUSION

Hermann went mad. He sits in the Obukhov Hospital, room 17, does not answer any questions, and mutters with extraordinary rapidity: "Three, seven, ace! Three, seven, queen! . . ."

Lizaveta Ivanovna has married a very amiable young man; he is in government service somewhere and has a decent fortune: he is the son of the old countess's former steward. Lizaveta Ivanovna is bringing up a poor girl from her family.

Tomsky has been promoted to captain and is marrying Princess Polina.

Kirdjali

A Story

Kirdjali was Bulgarian by birth. *Kirdjali* in Turkish means "warrior," "daredevil." I do not know his real name.

Kirdjali, with his banditry, brought terror to the whole of Moldavia. To give some idea of him, I will recount one of his exploits. One night he and the Arnaut* Mikhailaki raided a Bulgarian village together. They set fire to it from both ends and started going from hut to hut. Kirdjali wielded the knife and Mikhailaki carried the booty. They both shouted "Kirdjali! Kirdjali!" The whole village took to its heels.

When Alexander Ypsilanti proclaimed the insurrection[1] and began to recruit his army, Kirdjali brought him several of his old comrades. The real goal of the Hetairists was scarcely known to them, but the war provided an occasion for getting rich at the expense of the Turks, and maybe also of the Moldavians—and that they found clear enough.

Alexander Ypsilanti was personally courageous, but he did not possess the qualities necessary for the role he had assumed so ardently and so imprudently. He was unable to get along with the men he had to lead. They neither respected nor trusted him. After the unfortunate battle in which the flower of Greek youth perished, Iordaki Olymbioti advised him to retire and took his place himself. Ypsilanti galloped off to the Austrian border and from there sent his curses upon the men, whom he called rebels, cowards, and blackguards. Most of these cowards and blackguards perished within the walls of the Seku monastery or on the banks of the Prut, desperately defending themselves against a ten times stronger adversary.

Kirdjali was in the detachment of Georgi Kantakuzin,[2] of whom the same thing might be repeated as was said of Ypsilanti. On the eve of the battle of Skulyani, Kantakuzin asked the Russian authorities for permission to join our border post. The detachment remained without a leader; but Kirdjali, Saphianos, Kantagoni, and the others found no need for a leader.

It seems that no one has described the battle of Skulyani in all its touching truth. Picture to yourself seven hundred men—Arnauts, Albanians, Greeks, Bulgarians, and all sorts of riffraff—with no notion

* Albanian (Turkish)

of the art of war, retreating in the face of fifteen thousand Turkish cavalry. This detachment huddled against the bank of the Prut and set up two small cannon found in the *gospodar*'s* courtyard in Jassy, used for firing salutes during birthday parties. The Turks would have been glad to use grapeshot, but did not dare to without permission from the Russian authorities: the shot was bound to fly over to our bank. The commander of the border post (by now deceased), who had been in military service for forty years, had never in his life heard the whistle of bullets, but this time God granted him the chance. A few whizzed past his ears. The dear old fellow got very angry and sharply scolded the major of the Okhotsky infantry regiment attached to the post. The major, not knowing what to do, went running to the river and shook his finger at the *delibash*,† who were prancing on the opposite bank. The delibash, seeing that, turned and galloped off, and the whole Turkish detachment followed them. The major who shook his finger was called Khorchevsky. I do not know what became of him.

The next day, however, the Turks attacked the Hetairists. Not daring to use either grapeshot or cannonballs, they ventured, contrary to their custom, to use cold steel. It was a stiff battle. They wielded *yatagans*.‡ Lances were noticed for the first time on the Turkish side; these lances were Russian: Nekrasovists[3] were fighting in their ranks. The Hetairists were permitted by our sovereign to cross the Prut and take refuge in our border post. They began to cross. Kantagoni and Saphianos were the last ones left on the Turkish side. Kirdjali, wounded the day before, already lay in the border post. Saphianos was killed. Kantagoni, a very fat man, was wounded in the belly by a lance. He raised his saber with one hand, took hold of the enemy's lance with the other, drove it deeper into himself, and was thus able to reach his killer with the saber and fall together with him.

It was all over. The Turks came out victorious. Moldavia was cleared. Some six hundred Arnauts scattered over Bessarabia; they had no idea how to feed themselves, but were still grateful to Russia for her protection. The life they led was idle, but not dissipated. They were always to be seen in the coffeehouses of half-Turkish Bessarabia, with

* governor's
† cavalrymen of the Turkish army
‡ long, curved Turkish sabers

long chibouks in their mouths, sipping coffee grounds from little cups. Their embroidered jackets and pointed red slippers had already begun to wear out, but they still wore their tasseled caps cocked, and yatagans and pistols still stuck from behind their wide belts. No one complained of them. It was impossible to imagine that these poor, peaceable fellows were the notorious Klephtes[4] of Moldavia, comrades of the terrible Kirdjali, and that he himself was among them.

The pasha in command of Jassy learned of it and, on the basis of peace treaties, demanded that the Russian authorities turn the bandit over.

The police began to investigate. They found out that Kirdjali was indeed in Kishinev. He was caught in the house of a fugitive monk, in the evening, when he was having supper, sitting in the dark with seven comrades.

Kirdjali was put under guard. He did not try to conceal the truth and admitted that he was Kirdjali.

"But," he added, "since I crossed the Prut, I haven't touched even a hair of anyone's property, I haven't harmed the least Gypsy. For the Turks, the Moldavians, the Wallachians, I am, of course, a bandit, but for the Russians I am a guest. When Saphianos, having spent all his grapeshot, came to us in the border post, to take buttons, nails, chains, and yatagan handles from the wounded men for his last shots, I gave him twenty *beshliks** and was left without money. As God is my witness, I, Kirdjali, lived by begging! Why do the Russians now turn me over to my enemies?"

After that, Kirdjali fell silent and calmly began to wait for the deciding of his fate.

He did not wait long. The authorities, not being obliged to look at bandits from their romantic side, and convinced of the justice of the demand, ordered Kirdjali sent to Jassy.

A man of intelligence and heart, then an unknown young official, now occupying an important post,[5] gave me a vivid description of his departure:

At the gates of the jail stood a postal *karutsa* . . . (Perhaps you do not know what a karutsa is. It is a low wicker cart, to which until recently six or eight little nags would be hitched. A Moldavian in moustaches and a lambskin hat rode on one of them, constantly shouting

* Turkish silver coins

and cracking his whip, and his nags went at a rather swift trot. If one of them began to falter, he would unhitch it with terrible curses and abandon it by the roadside, unconcerned for its fate. On his way back he was sure to find it in the same place, calmly grazing on the green steppe. It was not infrequent that a traveler, leaving one station with eight horses, would arrive at the next with a pair. That was fifteen years ago. Nowadays, in Russified Bessarabia, they have adopted the Russian way of harnessing and the Russian cart.)

Such a karutsa stood by the gates of the jail in 1821, on one of the last days of September. Jewesses, their sleeves hanging and their slippers dragging, Arnauts in their ragged and picturesque attire, slender Moldavian women with black-eyed children in their arms, surrounded the karutsa. The men kept silent, the women excitedly awaited something.

The gates opened and several police officers came out; after them two soldiers led out the fettered Kirdjali.

He seemed to be about thirty years old. The features of his swarthy face were regular and stern. He was tall, broad-shouldered, and gave a general impression of extraordinary physical strength. A multicolored turban covered his head at an angle, a broad belt girded his slender waist; a dolman of thick blue broadcloth, the wide folds of a shirt falling to his knees, and beautiful shoes completed his attire. His look was proud and calm.

One of the officers, a red-faced little old man in a faded uniform with three buttons dangling from it, pinched a pair of tin-rimmed spectacles to the purple bump that served him as a nose, unfolded a document, and, with a nasal twang, began to read in Moldavian. From time to time he glanced haughtily at the fettered Kirdjali, to whom the document apparently referred. Kirdjali listened to him attentively. The official finished his reading, folded the document, shouted menacingly at the people, commanded them to make way, and ordered the karutsa brought. Then Kirdjali turned to him and spoke a few words in Moldavian; his voice trembled, his face changed; he wept and fell at the feet of the police officer, clanking his chains. The police officer, frightened, jumped back; the soldiers were about to pick Kirdjali up, but he got up by himself, gathered his shackles, stepped into the karutsa, and shouted "*Haida!*"* A gendarme sat beside him, the Moldavian cracked his whip, and the karutsa rolled off.

* "Let's go!" (Tatar)

"What did Kirdjali say to you?" the young official asked the policeman.

"You see, sir," the policeman replied, laughing, "he begged me to take care of his wife and child, who live in a Bulgarian village not far from Kilia. He's afraid they may suffer *on account of him*. Stupid folk, sir."

The young official's account moved me deeply. I felt sorry for poor Kirdjali. For a long time I knew nothing of his fate. It was several years later that I ran into that young official. We got to talking of past times.

"And what about your friend Kirdjali?" I asked. "Do you know what's become of him?"

"That I do," he replied, and told me the following:

Kirdjali, having been brought to Jassy, was presented to the pasha, who condemned him to be impaled. The execution was put off until some holiday or other. Meanwhile he was locked up in prison.

The prisoner was guarded by seven Turks (simple people and at heart just as much bandits as Kirdjali); they respected him and listened to his wondrous tales with an eagerness common to the whole of the East.

Close relations developed between the guards and the prisoner. One day Kirdjali said to them: "Brothers, my hour is near! No one can escape his fate. Soon I shall part with you. I would like to leave you something to remember me by."

The Turks were all ears.

"Brothers," Kirdjali went on, "three years ago, when the late Mikhailaki and I were bandits, we buried a pot of *galbeni** on the steppe not far from Jassy. It looks like neither of us is going to have that pot. So be it: take it yourselves and divide it up amicably."

The Turks nearly lost their minds. A discussion went on about how to find the secret spot. They thought and thought, and decided that Kirdjali himself should take them there.

Night came. The Turks removed the fetters from the captive's feet, tied his hands with a rope, and set off with him from town to the steppe.

Kirdjali led them, keeping to the same direction, from one burial mound to another. They walked for a long time. Finally, Kirdjali stopped by a wide stone, counted off twenty paces to the south, stamped his foot, and said: "Here."

* Romanian gold coins

The Turks arranged themselves. Four drew their yatagans and began to dig. Three remained on guard. Kirdjali sat down on a stone and watched them work.

"Well, so? Soon now?" he asked. "Have you found it?"

"Not yet," replied the Turks, working so hard that the sweat poured off them.

Kirdjali began to show impatience.

"What people," he said. "You don't even know how to dig. I'd have done it in two minutes. Untie my hands, boys, give me a yatagan."

The Turks pondered and started talking it over.

"Why not?" they decided. "Let's untie his hands and give him a yatagan. Where's the harm? There's one of him and seven of us."

And the Turks untied his hands and gave him a yatagan.

At last Kirdjali was free and armed. What he must have felt! . . . He promptly started digging, the guards were helping him . . . Suddenly he stabbed one of them with his yatagan and, leaving the steel in his chest, snatched two pistols from behind his belt.

The remaining six, seeing Kirdjali armed with two pistols, took to their heels.

Nowadays Kirdjali does his banditry around Jassy. He recently wrote to the gospodar, demanding five thousand *levi** from him and threatening, in case of failure to pay, to set fire to Jassy and get as far as the gospodar himself. The five thousand levi were conveyed to him.

That's Kirdjali!

---

* Bulgarian currency, from the word for lion (*lev*)

Egyptian Nights

CHAPTER ONE

—Quel est cet homme?
—Ha, c'est un bien grand talent, il fait de sa voix tout ce qu'il veut.
—Il devrait bien, madame, s'en faire une culotte.*

Charsky was a native of Petersburg. He was not yet thirty; he was not married; he was not burdened by government service. His late uncle, who had been a vice-governor in better days, had left him a decent inheritance. His life could have been very pleasant; but he had the misfortune to write and publish verses. In the magazines he was called a poet, and in the servants' quarters a penman.

Despite the enormous privileges enjoyed by verse writers (to tell the truth, apart from the right to use the accusative case instead of the genitive, and some other so-called poetic licenses, no special privileges of Russian verse writers are known to us)—be that as it may, despite all their possible privileges, these people are subject to great disadvantages and discomforts. The most bitter, most unbearable ill for a poet is his title and label, with which he is branded and which never wears off. The public look at him as their property; in their opinion, he was born for their *benefit and pleasure*. If he comes back from the country, the first person he meets asks him: "Have you brought us some new little thing?" If he starts thinking about his disorderly affairs, about the illness of someone dear to him, at once a trite smile accompanies a trite exclamation: "You must be composing something!" If he falls in love?—his beauty buys an album[1] in the English shop and is already waiting for an elegy. If he comes to someone he barely knows to discuss important business, the man at once calls his little boy and makes him recite some verses by so-and-so; and the boy treats the poet to a distortion of his own verses. And these are still the flowers of the trade! What about the adversities? Charsky confessed he was so sick of greetings,

---

* "Who is this man?" "Ah, he's a great talent, he makes his voice into whatever he wants." "Then he ought, madam, to make it into a pair of pants." [From the French *Almanach des calembours* (1771). *Translator.*]

requests, albums, and little boys that he had constantly to refrain from some sort of rudeness.

Charsky made every possible effort to rid himself of the intolerable label. He avoided the company of his fellow litterateurs and preferred society people, even the most vapid of them. His conversation was the most banal and never touched on literature. In his dress he always observed the latest fashion with the shyness and superstition of a young Muscovite arriving in Petersburg for the first time in his life. In his study, decorated like a lady's bedroom, there was nothing reminiscent of a writer; no books were scattered over and under the tables; the sofa was not spattered with ink; there was no disorder betraying the presence of the muse and the absence of a broom and brush. Charsky was in despair if one of his society friends found him with pen in hand. It was hard to believe what trifles a man could sink to, one who was, incidentally, endowed with talent and soul. He pretended to be now a passionate fancier of horses, now a desperate gambler, now a refined gastronome; though he was unable to tell a mountain breed from an Arabian, could never remember trumps, and secretly preferred baked potatoes to all possible concoctions of French cuisine. He led a most dissipated life; hung around at all the balls, overate at all the diplomatic dinners, and was as unavoidable at every soirée as Rezanov's ice cream.

And yet he was a poet, and his passion was insuperable: when such *rubbish* (as he called inspiration) came over him, Charsky shut himself up in his study and wrote from morning till late at night. He confessed to his close friends that only then did he know true happiness. The rest of the time he strolled about, posturing and shamming and constantly hearing the famous question: "Have you written some new little thing?"

One morning Charsky felt that blessed state of mind when dreams are clearly outlined before you and you find vivid, unexpected words to embody your visions, when verses lie down easily under your pen and sonorous rhymes rush to meet harmonious thoughts. Charsky's soul was plunged in sweet oblivion . . . and society, and society's opinion, and his own caprices did not exist for him. He was writing verses.

Suddenly the door of his study creaked and a stranger's head appeared. Charsky gave a start and frowned.

"Who's there?" he asked with vexation, cursing his servants to himself for never staying put in the front hall.

The stranger came in.

He was tall, lean, and seemed about thirty years old. The features of his swarthy face were expressive: the pale, high forehead overhung by black locks of hair, the dark, flashing eyes, the aquiline nose, and the thick beard surrounding the sunken, swarthy yellow cheeks, betrayed him as a foreigner. He was wearing a black tailcoat, already discolored at the seams; summer trousers (though outside it was already deep autumn); a false diamond gleamed under a shabby black cravat over his yellowed shirtfront; his rough felt hat seemed to have seen both fair weather and foul. Meeting such a man in the forest, you would have taken him for a robber; in society, for a political conspirator; in the front hall, for a quack peddling elixirs and arsenic.

"What do you want?" Charsky asked him in French.

"*Signor*," the foreigner replied with low bows, "*Lei voglia perdonarmi se . . .*"*

Charsky did not offer him a chair and stood up himself; the conversation went on in Italian.

"I am a Neapolitan artist," said the stranger. "Circumstances have forced me to leave my fatherland. I came to Russia with hopes for my talent."

Charsky thought that the Neapolitan was preparing to give some cello concerts and was selling tickets door to door. He was about to hand him his twenty-five roubles, the sooner to be rid of him, but the stranger added:

"I hope, *signor*, that you will be of friendly assistance to your confrere and introduce me in the houses to which you yourself have access."

It would have been impossible to deliver a more painful blow to Charsky's vanity. He glanced haughtily at the man who called himself his confrere.

"Allow me to ask, who are you and whom do you take me for?" he asked, barely controlling his indignation.

The Neapolitan noticed his vexation.

"*Signor*," he replied, faltering . . . "*ho creduto . . . ho sentito . . . la vostra Eccelenza mi perdonera . . .*"†

"What do you want?" Charsky repeated drily.

"I have heard much about your astonishing talent; I am sure that the local gentry consider it an honor to offer all possible patronage to

* "Sir . . . please forgive me if . . ."
† "Sir . . . I believed . . . I felt . . . Your Excellency must forgive me . . ."

so excellent a poet," replied the Italian, "and I therefore made so bold as to come to you . . ."

"You are mistaken, *signor*," Charsky interrupted him. "The title of poet does not exist among us. Our poets do not enjoy the patronage of the gentry; our poets are gentry themselves, and if our Maecenases (devil take them!) don't know it, so much the worse for them. We have no ragged abbés[2] whom musicians pluck from the street to compose a libretto. Our poets don't go from house to house begging for assistance. However, they were probably joking when they told you I was a great poet. True, I once wrote a few bad epigrams, but, thank God, I have nothing in common with these gentlemen verse writers and do not wish to have."

The poor Italian was confused. He looked around. The paintings, marble statues, bronzes, costly knickknacks set up on Gothic whatnots, struck him. He realized that between the arrogant dandy who stood before him in a tasseled brocade cap, a golden Chinese housecoat, girded with a Turkish shawl, and himself, a poor migrant artist in a shabby cravat and a threadbare tailcoat, there was nothing in common. He muttered several incoherent apologies, bowed, and was about to leave. His pathetic look touched Charsky, who, despite some small flaws of character, had a kind and noble heart. He was ashamed of his irritable vanity.

"Where are you off to?" he asked the Italian. "Wait . . . I had to decline the undeserved title and confess to you that I am not a poet. Now let's talk about your affairs. I'm ready to serve you however I can. You are a musician?"

"No, *Eccelenza*," replied the Italian, "I am a poor improvisator."

"An improvisator!" Charsky cried out, feeling all the cruelty of his treatment. "Why didn't you tell me before that you were an improvisator?" And Charsky pressed his hand with a feeling of sincere regret.

His friendly air encouraged the Italian. He simple-heartedly told about his intentions. His appearance was not deceptive; he needed money; he hoped that in Russia he could somehow straighten out his home situation. Charsky listened to him attentively.

"I hope you will have success," he said to the poor artist. "Society here has never yet heard an improvisator. Curiosity will be aroused. True, the Italian language is not in common use among us, you won't be understood; but that doesn't matter; the main thing is to become the fashion."

"But if no one understands Italian," the improvisator said pensively, "who will come to listen to me?"

"They'll come—don't you worry: some out of curiosity, others to spend an evening somehow, still others to show they understand Italian. I repeat, all you need is to become the fashion; and you will become the fashion, here's my hand on it."

Charsky parted amiably with the improvisator, taking down his address, and that same evening he went about soliciting for him.

CHAPTER TWO

> I am a king, I am a slave, I am a worm, I am God.
>
> DERZHAVIN[3]

The next day Charsky was searching for room number 35 in the dark and dirty corridor of an inn. He stopped at a door and knocked. Yesterday's Italian opened it.

"Victory!" Charsky said to him. "Your affair is in the hat. Princess * * * offers you her reception room; at a rout yesterday I managed to recruit half of Petersburg; print the tickets and announcements. I guarantee you, if not the triumph, at least the gain . . ."

"And that's the main thing!" cried the Italian, expressing his joy with the lively gestures peculiar to his southern race. "I knew you would help me. *Corpo di Bacco!** You're a poet, the same as I am; and, whatever you say, poets are fine lads! How can I show you my gratitude? Wait . . . would you like to hear an improvisation?"

"An improvisation! . . . You mean you can do without the public, without music, without the thunder of applause?"

"Trifles, trifles! Where could I find myself a better public? You're a poet, you'll understand me better than they will, and your quiet approval is dearer to me than a whole storm of applause . . . Sit down somewhere and give me a theme."

Charsky sat down on a suitcase (of the two chairs in the cramped little hovel, one was broken, the other heaped with papers and under-

---

* "Devil take it!" (Literally, "Body of Bacchus!")

wear). The improvisator took a guitar from the table and stood before
Charsky, strumming it with his bony fingers and awaiting his order.

"Here's a theme for you," Charsky said to him: *"The poet himself
chooses the subjects for his songs; the mob has no right to control his inspiration."*

The Italian's eyes flashed, he played several chords, proudly raised
his head, and passionate stanzas, expressive of instantaneous emotion,
flew harmoniously from his lips . . . Here they are, freely passed on by
one of our friends from words preserved in Charsky's memory:

> The poet goes, eyes open wide,
> And yet he sees no one at all;
> Meanwhile, drawing him aside,
> A passing stranger asks, appalled:
> "Tell me: why this aimless wandering?
> No sooner have you scaled the heights
> Than you are bent upon descending
> Into the vale as dark as night.
> The well-formed world you see but vaguely;
> A fruitless ardor wears you out;
> Some paltry matter constantly
> Lures you and beckons you about.
> A genius should strive toward the heavens,
> To the true poet it belongs
> To choose himself the purest leaven
> As matter for inspired songs."
> —Why is it that wind whirls and scatters
> Leaves and dust across the heath,
> While a ship in unmoving waters
> Languishes, longing for its breath?
> Why from the peaks, past lofty towers,
> Does the great eagle, for all his powers,
> Fly down to a withered stump? Ask him.
> Why does young Desdemona trim
> Her love for a blackamoor's delight,
> As the moon loves the dark of night?
> Because law has no hold upon
> Eagle, or wind, or a maiden's heart.
> Such is the poet: like Aquilon
> He takes what he fancies for his part,

Then eagle-like he flies away,
And asking no one, he aspires,
Like Desdemona in her day,
To the idol of his heart's desires.

The Italian fell silent . . . Charsky said nothing, amazed and moved.
"Well, so?" asked the improvisator.

Charsky seized his hand and pressed it hard.

"So?" asked the improvisator. "How was it?"

"Astonishing," the poet replied. "Can it be? Another man's thought barely grazed your hearing and it's already your own, as if you had nurtured it, cherished it, developed it all the while. So neither toil, nor coldness, nor that restlessness that precedes inspiration exist for you? . . . Astonishing, astonishing! . . ."

The improvisator replied:

"Every talent is inexplicable. How is it that a sculptor sees the hidden Jupiter in a block of Carrara marble and brings him to light by smashing his casing with a chisel and hammer? Why does a thought emerge from a poet's head already armed with four rhymes, measured out in regular harmonious feet? So no one except the improvisator himself can understand this quickness of impressions, this close connection between his own inspiration and another's external will—it would be futile for me to try to explain it myself. However . . . we must think about my first night. What do you say? What price should we put on a ticket, so that it's not too hard on the public and I still don't come out the loser? They say Signora Catalani[4] took twenty-five roubles? A decent price . . ."

It was unpleasant for Charsky to fall suddenly from the heights of poetry under a clerk's counter; but he understood worldly necessity very well and entered into the Italian's mercantile calculations. The Italian on this occasion displayed such savage greed, such simple-hearted love of gain, that Charsky found him repulsive and hastened to leave so as not to lose all the feeling of admiration that the brilliant improvisator had aroused in him. The preoccupied Italian did not notice this change and accompanied him through the corridor and down the stairs with deep bows and assurances of eternal gratitude.

CHAPTER THREE

Price of ticket *10* roubles; begins at 7 p.m.

POSTER

Princess * * *'s reception room was placed at the improvisator's disposal. A stage was set up; chairs were arranged in twelve rows. On the appointed day, at seven o'clock in the evening, the lamps were lit; a long-nosed old woman in a gray hat with broken feathers and with rings on all her fingers sat at a little table by the door, selling and taking tickets. Gendarmes stood by the entrance. The public began to gather. Charsky was one of the first to arrive. He was very concerned about the success of the performance and wanted to see the improvisator, to find out whether he was pleased with everything. He found the Italian in a little side room, glancing impatiently at his watch. The Italian was dressed theatrically; he was in black from head to foot; the lace collar of his shirt was open; the strange whiteness of his bare neck contrasted sharply with his thick black beard; locks of hair hung down over his forehead and eyebrows. Charsky disliked all this very much, finding it unpleasant to see a poet dressed like an itinerant mountebank. After a brief conversation, he went back to the reception room, which was filling up more and more.

Soon all the rows of chairs were occupied by glittering ladies; the men stood in a tight frame by the stage, along the walls, and behind the last chairs. Musicians with their music stands occupied both sides of the stage. In the middle a porcelain vase stood on a table. The public was numerous. Everyone impatiently awaited the start; finally, at half past seven, the musicians began to stir, readied their bows, and struck up the overture to *Tancredi*.⁵ Everyone settled down and fell silent; the last sounds of the overture thundered . . . And the improvisator, greeted by deafening applause from all sides, with low bows approached the very edge of the stage.

Charsky waited anxiously for the impression made by the first moment, but he noticed that the costume which had seemed so improper to him did not have the same effect on the public. Charsky himself found nothing ridiculous in him when he saw him on the stage, his pale face brightly lit by a multitude of lamps and candles.

The applause died down; the talking ceased . . . The Italian, expressing himself in poor French, asked the ladies and gentlemen of the audience to set a few themes, writing them down on separate pieces of paper. At this unexpected invitation, they all exchanged silent glances and no one made any reply. The Italian, having waited a little, repeated his request in a timid and humble voice. Charsky was standing just under the stage; he was seized by anxiety; he sensed that things could not go ahead without him and that he would be forced to write down his theme. In fact, several ladies' heads turned to him and began to call his name, first softly, then louder and louder. Hearing Charsky's name, the improvisator sought him with his eyes and, finding him at his feet, handed him a pencil and a scrap of paper with a friendly smile. Charsky found playing a role in this comedy very unpleasant, but there was nothing to do; he took the pencil and paper from the Italian's hand and wrote a few words; the Italian, taking the vase from the table, stepped down from the stage and carried it to Charsky, who dropped his theme into it. His example worked. Two journalists, in their quality as literary men, considered themselves each obliged to write down a theme; the secretary from the Neapolitan embassy and a young man who recently returned from his travels raving about Florence put their rolled-up papers into the urn; finally, an unattractive girl, on her mother's orders, with tears in her eyes, wrote several lines in Italian and, blushing to the ears, handed them to the improvisator, while the ladies silently watched her with barely perceptible smiles. Going back to his stage, the improvisator placed the urn on the table and started taking the papers out one by one, reading each of them aloud:

> *La famiglia dei Cenci*
> *L'ultimo giorno di Pompeia*
> *Cleopatra e i suoi amanti*
> *La primavera veduta da una prigione*
> *Il trionfo di Tasso.**

"What is the esteemed public's wish?" asked the humble Italian. "Will it set me one of the proposed subjects itself, or let it be decided by lot?"

---

* *The Cenci Family / The Last Day of Pompeii / Cleopatra and Her Lovers / Spring Seen from a Prison / The Triumph of Tasso.*

"By lot! . . ." said a voice from the crowd.

"By lot, by lot!" the public repeated.

The improvisator again stepped down from the stage, holding the urn in his hands, and asked:

"Who would like to draw a theme?"

The improvisator passed a pleading glance over the first rows of chairs. Not one of the glittering ladies sitting there budged. The improvisator, unaccustomed to northern indifference, seemed to be suffering . . . Suddenly he noticed to one side a small white-gloved hand held up; he turned briskly and went over to a majestic young beauty who was sitting at the end of the second row. She rose without any embarrassment and with all possible simplicity lowered her aristocratic little hand into the urn and drew out a slip of paper.

"Kindly unfold it and read it," said the improvisator. The beauty unfolded the paper and read aloud:

"*Cleopatra e i suoi amanti.*"

These words were uttered in a low voice, but such silence reigned in the room that everyone heard them. The improvisator bowed low to the beautiful lady with an air of deep gratitude and went back to his stage.

"Ladies and gentlemen," he said, addressing the public, "the lot has set me Cleopatra and her lovers as the subject of my improvisation. I humbly ask the person who chose this theme to clarify his thought for me: what lovers are we speaking of here, *perché la grande regina n'aveva molto . . .*"*

At these words many of the men burst out laughing. The improvisator became slightly embarrassed.

"I wish to know," he went on, "what historical particulars the person who chose this theme was hinting at. I would be very grateful if that person would please explain."

No one was in a hurry to reply. Several ladies turned their gazes on the unattractive girl who had written a theme on her mother's orders. The poor girl noticed this unfavorable attention and became so embarrassed that tears hung from her eyelashes . . . Charsky could not bear it and, turning to the improvisator, said to him in Italian:

"The proposed theme is mine. I had in mind the evidence of Aurelius Victor,[6] who writes that Cleopatra supposedly set death as the price

---

* because the great queen had many of them . . .

of her love, and that admirers were found who were neither frightened nor repulsed by this condition . . . It seems to me, however, that the subject is somewhat difficult . . . won't you choose another? . . ."

But the improvisator already felt the god's approach . . . He gave the musicians a sign to play . . . His face turned terribly pale; he trembled as if in a fever; his eyes flashed with a wondrous fire; he swept back his black hair with his hand, wiped a handkerchief across his high forehead, which was covered with beads of sweat . . . and suddenly made a step forward, crossed his arms on his chest . . . The music stopped . . . The improvisator began.

> The palace shone. A resounding choir
> Sang to the sounds of flute and lyre.
> And with her voice and gaze, the queen
> Enlivened the splendid banquet scene.
> All hearts were straining toward the throne,
> But suddenly came a change of tone:
> Low to her golden cup she brought
> Her wondrous head, now lost in thought.
>
> Sleep seems to fall on the splendid feast,
> Mute is the choir, hushed are the guests.
> But once more she her brow does raise
> And with a serene air she says:
> "In my love you find heaven's bliss?
> But you must pay for such a tryst.
> Hear me well: I can renew
> Equality between us two.
> Who wants to enter passion's deal?
> I offer my sweet love for sale.
> Who among you agrees to pay
> His life for one night of such play?"
>
> She spoke—and horror seized them all
> And anguish held their hearts in thrall.
> With a cold, insolent expression
> She hears them mutter in confusion,
> Scornfully she glances over
> The circle of her would-be lovers . . .

But suddenly one man steps out,
And then two others, from the crowd.
Their tread is firm, their eyes are calm;
She rises and holds out her arm.
The deal is done, and, briefly wed,
Three men are summoned to death's bed.

With the blessing of the priests,
There before the unmoving guests,
One by one three lots are drawn
Out of the dark and fateful urn.
First the brave soldier, Flavius,
Gone gray-haired in Roman service;
He found such high-and-mighty scorn
From a woman's lips could not be borne;
He took the challenge of brief delight
As he had the challenge of fierce fight
In all his days and years of war.
Then Kriton, a young philosopher,
Born in the groves of Epicure,
Kriton, bard and worshipper
Of the Graces, Cyprus, and Amor . . .
The last one, pleasing to eye and heart
As a fresh-blown flower, played no part
In history and his name's unknown.
His cheeks were covered with a first soft down;
His eyes with rapture gleamed, the force
Of inexperienced passion coursed
Through his young heart . . . With tenderness
The proud queen's gaze on him did rest.

"I swear . . . —O mother of all delight,
I'll serve you well and serve them right;
To the couch of passionate temptation,
I go as a simple boughten woman.
Then, mighty Cyprus, hear my word,
And you, kings of the nether world,
O gods of terrible Hades—know
That till the dawn begins to glow

I'll weary with my sensual fires
All of my masters' sweet desires
And sate them with my secret kiss
And wondrous languor—but I swear this:
Just when eternal Aurora spreads
Her purple robe above my bed,
The deadly axe will fall upon
The heads of all my lucky ones."

The Captain's Daughter

—◆—

Look after your honor when it's young.

PROVERB

CHAPTER ONE

A Sergeant of the Guards

> "Tomorrow he could well be a captain of the guards."
> "There's no need for that; let him serve in the ranks."
> "Rightly said! Let him suffer a bit for his thanks."
> . . . .
> And who is his father?
>
> KNYAZHNIN[1]

My father, Andrei Petrovich Grinyov, served under Count Münnich[2] in his youth and retired as a lieutenant colonel in 17—. After that he lived on his estate in Simbirsk province, where he married Miss Avdotya Vasilyevna Yu., the daughter of a poor local gentleman. They had nine children. All my brothers and sisters died in infancy.

While my mother was still pregnant with me, I was already enlisted as a sergeant in the Semyonovsky regiment,[3] through the graces of Prince B., a major of the guards and our close relative. If, against all expectations, my mother had given birth to a girl, my father would have informed the proper authorities of the death of the non-reporting sergeant, and the matter would have ended there. I was considered on leave until I finished my studies. Back then we were not educated as nowadays. At the age of five I was put into the hands of the groom Savelyich, who for his sober behavior was accorded the honor of being my attendant. Under his supervision, by the age of twelve I had learned to read and write in Russian and was a very sound judge of the qualities of the male borzoi. At that time father hired a French tutor for me, Monsieur Beaupré, whom he ordered from Moscow together with a year's supply of wine and olive oil. His arrival greatly displeased Savelyich. "Thank God," he grumbled to himself, "it seems the little one's washed, combed, and fed. Why go spending extra money hiring a moosieu, as if his own people weren't enough!"

In his own country, Beaupré had been a hairdresser, then in Prussia a soldier, then he came to Russia *pour être outchitel*,* not understanding very well the meaning of the word. He was a nice fellow, but flighty and extremely dissipated. His main weakness was a passion for the fair sex; not infrequently he received kicks for his tender advances, which left him groaning for whole days. What's more, he was (to use his own expression) "no enemy of the bottle," that is (in Russian) he liked to take a drop too much. But since in our house wine was only served with dinner, and by the glass at that, the tutor usually being passed over, my Beaupré very quickly accustomed himself to Russian liqueurs and even came to prefer them to the wines of his own country, as incomparably more wholesome for the stomach. We hit it off at once, and though by contract he was supposed to teach me "in French, in German, and all the subjects," he preferred to pick up some Russian chatter from me—and then each of us minded his own business. We lived in perfect harmony. I wished for no other mentor. But fate soon parted us, and here is how it happened.

The laundress Palashka, a fat and pockmarked wench, and the one-eyed milkmaid Akulka decided one day to throw themselves at my mother's feet together, confessing to a criminal weakness and tearfully complaining about the moosieu who had seduced their inexperience. Mother did not take such things lightly and complained to my father. His justice was summary. He sent for the French rascal at once. He was informed that moosieu was giving me a lesson. Father went to my room. Just then Beaupré was lying on the bed sleeping the sleep of the innocent. I was busy with my own things. It should be mentioned that a geographical map had been ordered for me from Moscow. It hung quite uselessly on the wall, and the size and quality of the paper had long been tempting me. I decided to make a kite out of it and, taking advantage of Beaupré's sleep, set to work. Father walked in just as I was attaching a bast tail to the Cape of Good Hope. Seeing my exercises in geography, my father yanked my ear, then ran over to Beaupré, woke him up quite unceremoniously, and began to shower him with reproaches. In his confusion Beaupré tried to get up but could not: the unfortunate Frenchman was dead drunk. Seven ills, one cure. Father picked him up from the bed by the scruff of the neck, pushed him out the door, and drove him off the premises that same day, to the indescribable joy of Savelyich. And that was the end of my education.

* to be an *ouchitel* (the French spelling of the Russian word for tutor)

I lived as a young dunce, chasing pigeons and playing leapfrog with the servants' kids. Meanwhile I turned sixteen. Here my fate changed.

One autumn day mother was cooking honey preserve in the drawing room, while I, licking my lips, kept my eyes on the boiling scum. Father sat by the window reading the Court Almanac, which he received every year. This book always had a strong effect on him: he could never read it without special concern, and this reading always caused an extraordinary stirring of the bile in him. Mother, who knew all his ways and displays by heart, always tried to tuck the wretched book as far away as possible, and thus the Court Almanac sometimes did not catch his eye for whole months. But then, when he chanced to find it, for whole hours he would not let it out of his hands. And so, father was reading the Court Almanac, shrugging from time to time and repeating under his breath: "Lieutenant general! . . . He was a sergeant in my company! . . . A chevalier of both Russian orders! . . . Was it so long ago that we . . ." Finally, father flung the almanac onto the sofa and sank into a brooding that boded no good.

Suddenly he turned to mother: "Avdotya Vasilyevna, how old is Petrusha?"

"He's going on seventeen," mother replied. "Petrusha was born the same year that aunt Nastasya Gerasimovna went one-eyed, and when . . ."

"Good," father interrupted. "It's time he was in the service. Enough of him running around the maids' rooms and climbing the dovecotes."

The thought of soon parting with me so struck my mother that she dropped her spoon into the pot and tears poured down her face. On the other hand, it is hard to describe my delight. The thought of the service merged in me with thoughts of freedom and the pleasures of Petersburg life. I pictured myself as an officer of the guards, which, in my opinion, was the height of human happiness.

Father did not like either to change his intentions or to postpone their execution. The day of my departure was appointed. On the eve, father announced that he intended to send with me a letter to my future superior, and he asked for pen and paper.

"Don't forget, Andrei Petrovich," mother said, "to pay my respects to Prince B. as well; tell him I hope he won't deprive Petrusha of his favors."

"What nonsense!" father replied, frowning. "Why on earth should I write to Prince B.?"

"But you just said you were going to write to Petrusha's superior."

"Well, what of it?"

"Petrusha's commander is Prince B. Petrusha is enlisted in the Semyonovsky regiment."

"Enlisted! What do I care if he's enlisted? Petrusha's not going to Petersburg. What will he learn, serving in Petersburg? To squander and philander? No, let him serve in the army, pull his load, get a whiff of powder, and be a soldier, not a wastrel. Enlisted in the guards! Where's his passport?⁴ Give it here."

Mother found my passport, which she kept in a box along with my baptismal gown, and held it out to father with a trembling hand. Father read it attentively, placed it in front of him on the table, and began his letter.

Curiosity tormented me: where was I being sent, if not to Petersburg? I did not take my eyes off father's quill, which moved quite slowly. He finally finished, sealed the letter in the same envelope with the passport, took off his spectacles, and, beckoning to me, said: "Here's a letter to Andrei Karlovich R., my old comrade and friend. You're going to Orenburg⁵ to serve under him."

And so all my bright hopes were dashed! Instead of a gay Petersburg life, garrison boredom awaited me in remote and godforsaken parts. Army service, which I had thought of a moment before with such rapture, now seemed to me like a dire misfortune. But there was no point in arguing. The next morning a traveling kibitka was brought to the porch; a trunk, a cellaret with tea things, and bundles of rolls and pies—the last tokens of a pampered home life—were put into it. My parents blessed me. Father said to me:

"Good-bye, Pyotr. Serve faithfully the one you are sworn to serve; obey your commanders; don't curry favor with them; don't thrust yourself into service; don't excuse yourself from service; and remember the proverb: 'Look after your clothes when they're new, and your honor when it's young.'" Mother tearfully bade me to look after my health, and Savelyich to watch over her little one. They put a hareskin coat on me, and a fox fur over it. I got into the kibitka with Savelyich and set off, drowning myself in tears.

That same night I arrived in Simbirsk, where I was to spend a day buying necessary things, a task that had been entrusted to Savelyich. I put up at an inn. The next morning Savelyich headed off to the shops.

Bored with looking out the window at the muddy alley, I went rambling about all the rooms. Going into the billiard room, I saw a tall gentleman of about thirty-five, with long black moustaches, in a dressing gown, with a cue in his hand and a pipe in his teeth. He was playing with the marker, who drank a glass of vodka when he won, and had to crawl on all fours under the table when he lost. I started watching their game. The longer it went on, the more frequent became the promenades on all fours, until the marker finally just stayed under the table. The gentleman pronounced several strong phrases over him by way of a funeral oration and offered to play a round with me. Not knowing how to play, I declined. That evidently seemed strange to him. He gave me a pitying look; nevertheless we got to talking. I learned that his name was Ivan Ivanovich Zurin, that he was a captain in the * * * hussar regiment, that he was in Simbirsk to take recruits and was staying at the inn. Zurin invited me to share a meal with him, soldier fashion, of whatever there was. I eagerly accepted. We sat down at the table. Zurin drank a lot and also treated me, saying that I needed to get used to the service; he told me army jokes that had me nearly rolling with laughter, and we got up from the table as fast friends. Here he volunteered to teach me to play billiards.

"That," he said, "is necessary for a fellow serviceman. On campaign, for instance, you come to some little place—what are you going to do with yourself? You can't beat Jews all the time. Willy-nilly you go to the inn and play billiards; and for that you have to know how to play!"

I was fully convinced and set about learning with great diligence. Zurin loudly cheered me on, marveled at my quick progress, and, after a few lessons, suggested that we play for money, only half-kopecks, not for gain, but just so as not to play for nothing, which was, as he put it, the nastiest of habits. I accepted that, too, and Zurin ordered punch and persuaded me to try it, repeating that I needed to get used to the service; and what was the service without punch! I obeyed him. Meanwhile our game went on. The more often I sipped from my glass, the more valiant I became. The balls kept flying over the cushion on me; I got excited, scolded the marker, who scored God knows how, increased my stakes time after time—in short, behaved like a boy broken free. Meanwhile the time passed imperceptibly. Zurin glanced at his watch, put down his cue, and announced that I had lost a hundred roubles.

That threw me off a little. My money was with Savelyich. I started to apologize. Zurin interrupted me:

"For pity's sake! Kindly don't trouble yourself. I can wait, and meantime we'll go to Arinushka's."

What was I to do? I ended the day in dissipation, just as I had begun it. We had supper at Arinushka's. Zurin kept filling my glass, repeating that I had to get used to the service. When I got up from the table, I could barely keep my feet; at midnight Zurin took me back to the inn.

Savelyich met us on the porch. He gasped, seeing indisputable signs of my zeal for the service.

"What's happened to you, master?" he asked in a rueful voice. "Where did you get so loaded? Ah, lordy me, you've never been in such a bad way!"

"Shut up, you old geezer!" I replied haltingly. "You must be drunk. Go to sleep . . . and put me to bed."

The next day I woke up with a headache, vaguely recalling the events of the day before. My reflections were interrupted by Savelyich, who came in with a cup of tea.

"It's too early, Pyotr Andreevich," he said to me, shaking his head, "you've started carousing too early. Who are you taking after? It seems neither your father nor your grandfather was a drunkard, not to mention your mother: in all her born days she's never touched anything but kvass. And whose fault is it all? That cursed moosieu. Time and again he'd go running to Antipyevna: *'Madame, zhe voo pree, vodkyoo.'** There's a *zhe voo pree* for you! No denying it: he taught you well, the son of a dog. And they just had to go and hire a heathen for a tutor, as if the master didn't have people of his own!"

I was ashamed. I turned away and said: "Get out, Savelyich; I don't want any tea." But there was no stopping Savelyich once he started to sermonize.

"So you see, Pyotr Andreevich, where carousing gets you. Your little head is heavy, and you don't want to eat. A drinking man is good for nothing . . . Have some pickling brine with honey, or best of all a half glass of liqueur for the hair of the dog. What do you say?"

Just then a boy came in and handed me a note from I. I. Zurin. I opened it and read the following lines:

---

* 'Madame, please, some vodka.' (Russified French)

My dear Pyotr Andreevich,

Please send me with my boy the hundred roubles you lost to me yesterday. I am in urgent need of money.

At your service,
Ivan Zurin

There was nothing to be done. I assumed an air of indifference and, turning to Savelyich, who was "the keeper of my money, of my linen and my affairs,"[6] ordered him to give the boy a hundred roubles.

"What? Why?" asked the astonished Savelyich.

"I owe it to him," I replied with all possible coolness.

"Owe it!" retorted Savelyich, whose astonishment was growing by the minute. "When was it, sir, that you managed to get into debt to him? Something's not right here. Like it or not, sir, I won't hand over the money."

I thought that if in this decisive moment I did not argue down the stubborn old man, it would be hard for me to free myself from his tutelage later on, and, glancing haughtily at him, I said:

"I am your master, and you are my servant. The money is mine. I lost it gambling because I felt like it. I advise you not to be too clever and to do as you're told."

Savelyich was so shocked by my words that he clasped his hands and stood dumbstruck.

"What are you standing there for!" I shouted angrily.

Savelyich wept.

"Dearest Pyotr Andreevich," he uttered in a trembling voice, "don't make me die of grief. Light of my life! Listen to me, an old man: write to this robber that you were joking, that we don't even have that kind of money. A hundred roubles! Merciful God! Tell him your parents strictly forbade you to gamble, except for nuts . . ."

"Enough babble," I interrupted sternly. "Bring me the money or I'll chuck you out."

Savelyich looked at me with deep sorrow and went to fetch my debt. I pitied the poor old man; but I wanted to break free and prove that I was no longer a child. The money was delivered to Zurin. Savelyich hastened to take me away from the accursed inn. He appeared with the news that the horses were ready. With an uneasy conscience and silent remorse I drove out of Simbirsk without saying good-bye to my teacher or thinking I would ever see him again.

CHAPTER TWO

The Guide

Land of mine, dear land of mine,
Land unknown to me!
Not on my own did I come to thee,
Nor was it my good steed that brought me.
What brought me, fine lad that I am,
Was youthful swiftness, youthful boldness,
And tavern drunkenness.

AN OLD SONG

My reflections on the way were not very pleasant. My loss, by the value back then, was not inconsiderable. Deep in my heart I knew that my behavior at the Simbirsk inn had been stupid, and I felt myself guilty before Savelyich. It all tormented me. The old man sat sullenly on the box, his back turned to me, and said nothing, but only groaned now and then. I certainly wanted to make peace with him, but did not know where to begin. Finally I said to him:

"Now, now, Savelyich! Enough, let's make peace, it was my fault; I see myself that it was my fault. I got up to some mischief yesterday, and I wrongfully offended you. I promise to behave more sensibly in the future and to listen to you. Don't be angry; let's make peace."

"Eh, dearest Pyotr Andreevich!" he replied with a deep sigh. "It's my own self I'm angry at; it's my fault all around. How could I have left you alone at the inn! But there it is! The devil put it into my head to go and see the sexton's wife; she's my cousin. So there: go to your cousin, wind up in prison. It's as bad as that! . . . How can I show my face to the masters? What'll they say when they find out the little one drinks and gambles?"

To comfort poor Savelyich, I gave him my word that in the future

I would not dispose of a single kopeck without his consent. He gradually calmed down, though he still grumbled now and then, shaking his head: "A hundred roubles! It's no laughing matter!"

I was drawing near to my destination. Around me stretched a dismal wasteland crosscut by hills and ravines. Everything was covered with snow. The sun was setting. Our kibitka drove along the narrow road, or, rather, track, left by peasant sledges. Suddenly the driver started looking to one side, and finally, taking off his cap, turned around to me and said:

"Master, won't you order me to turn back?"

"Why?"

"The weather's uncertain: the wind's picking up a little—see how it's sweeping off the fresh snow?"

"What's the harm in that?"

"And do you see that there?" (The driver pointed to the east with his whip.)

"I see nothing but the white steppe and the clear sky."

"No, there—over there: that little cloud."

I did in fact see a white cloud on the edge of the horizon, which I took at first for a distant hill. The driver explained to me that the little cloud heralded a storm.

I had heard about the blizzards in those parts and knew that they could bury whole trains of sledges. Savelyich, agreeing with the driver, advised me to turn back. But the wind did not seem strong to me; I hoped to reach the next posting station in good time and told them to speed it up.

The driver went into a gallop; but he kept glancing to the east. The horses raced swiftly. The wind meanwhile was growing stronger by the minute. The little cloud turned into a white storm-cloud, which rose heavily, grew, and gradually covered the sky. Fine snow began to fall—and suddenly thick flakes came pouring down. The wind howled; a blizzard set in. In one moment the dark sky blended with the sea of snow. Everything vanished.

"Well, master," shouted the driver, "bad luck: it's a snowstorm."

I peeked out of the kibitka: everything was dark and whirling. The wind howled with such fierce expressiveness that it seemed animate; Savelyich and I were covered with snow; the horses slowed to a walk—and soon stopped.

"Why don't you go on?" I asked the driver impatiently.

"Why go on?" he replied, climbing down from the box. "We don't know where we've got to as it is: there's no road, and darkness all around."

I started to scold him. Savelyich interceded for him.

"Why on earth didn't you listen to him?" he said crossly. "You should have gone back to the inn, drunk your tea, slept till morning, the storm would have died down, we would have gone on. What's the hurry? It's not as if there's a wedding!"

Savelyich was right. There was nothing to be done. The snow just poured down. A drift was piling up around the kibitka. The horses stood hanging their heads and shuddering occasionally. The driver walked around and, having nothing to do, kept adjusting the harness. Savelyich grumbled; I looked in all directions, hoping to see at least some sign of a dwelling or a road, but could make out nothing except the hazy whirl of the blizzard . . . Suddenly I saw something black.

"Hey, driver!" I shouted. "Look: what's that blackness over there?"

The driver strained his eyes.

"God knows, master," he said, climbing back into his seat. "Could be a wagon, could be a tree, but it seems like it's moving. Must be either a wolf or a man."

I ordered him to drive towards the unknown object, which at once started to move towards us. Two minutes later we came up to a man.

"Hey, my good man!" the driver called to him. "Tell us, do you know where the road is?"

"The road's right here; I'm standing on a firm strip of it," the way-farer said. "But what use is that?"

"Listen, good fellow," I said to him, "are you familiar with these parts? Can you lead me to a night's lodgings?"

"I know these parts," the wayfarer replied. "By God, I've roamed and ridden all over them. But you see what the weather's like: you're sure to lose your way. Better stay here and wait it out, Maybe the storm will die down and the sky will clear: then we'll find our way by the stars."

His coolheadedness encouraged me. I had already resolved to entrust myself to God's will and spend the night in the middle of the steppe, when the wayfarer suddenly climbed nimbly up to the box and said to the driver:

"Well, by God, there's a house nearby; turn right and drive on."

"Why should I go to the right?" the driver asked with displeasure.

"Where do you see a road? Oh, yes, yes, of course: why spare another man's horse?"

The driver seemed right to me.

"In fact," I said, "what makes you think there's a house nearby?"

"Because the wind blew from there," said the wayfarer, "and I smelled smoke. We must be close to a village."

His shrewdness and keen sense of smell amazed me. I told the driver to go there. The horses stepped heavily through the deep snow. The kibitka moved slowly, now driving up a drift, now sinking into a gully, and tilting now to one side, now to the other. It was like a ship sailing on a stormy sea. Savelyich groaned and kept lurching into me. I lowered the matting, wrapped myself in my fur coat, and dozed off, lulled by the singing of the storm and the rocking of the slowly moving kibitka.

I had a dream, which I can never forget and in which to this day I see something prophetic, when I weigh it against the strange circumstances of my life. The reader will forgive me, for he probably knows from his own experience how natural it is for a man to give himself up to superstition, despite all possible scorn for such prejudices.

I was in that state of mind and feeling when reality, yielding to reverie, merges with it in the vague visions of first sleep. It seemed to me that the storm was still raging and we were still wandering in the snowy desert . . . Suddenly I saw gates and drove into the courtyard of our estate. My first thought was fear that father might be angry at my involuntary return under the parental roof and would consider it deliberate disobedience. In apprehension I jumped out of the kibitka, and I see mother coming to meet me on the porch with a look of profound grief. "Quiet," she says to me, "father is ill and dying, and he wishes to bid you farewell." Stricken with fear, I follow her to the bedroom. I see that the room is faintly lit; by the bed stand people with sorrowful faces. I quietly approach the bed; mother lifts the curtain and says: "Andrei Petrovich, Petrusha is here; he came back, having learned of your illness; give him your blessing." I knelt down and turned my eyes to the sick man. What's this? . . . Instead of my father, I see a muzhik with a black beard lying in the bed and looking merrily at me. In bewilderment I turn to mother, I say to her: "What does this mean? This isn't father. Why on earth should I ask a blessing from a muzhik?" "Never mind, Petrusha," mother replied. "He is your proxy father; kiss his hand and let him bless you . . ." I did not consent. Then the muzhik leaped up from the bed, snatched an axe from behind his back, and started swinging it in all directions. I wanted to flee . . . and could not; the room became filled with dead bodies; I stumbled over bodies and slipped in pools of blood . . . The frightful muzhik called to me affectionately, saying: "Don't be afeared, come, I'll give you my blessing . . ." Terror and bewilderment seized me . . . And just then I woke up. The horses had stopped; Savelyich was pulling me by the arm, saying: "Get out, master: we've arrived."

"Arrived where?" I asked, rubbing my eyes.

"At a coaching inn. The Lord helped us, we ran right into the fence. Get out, master, go quickly and warm up."

I got out of the kibitka. The storm was still going on, though with less force. It was pitch-dark. The innkeeper met us at the gate, holding a lantern under the skirt of his coat, and led me to a room, small but quite clean; it was lit by a pine splint. On the wall hung a rifle and a tall Cossack hat.

The innkeeper, a Yaik Cossack,[7] seemed to be about sixty, still hale and hearty. Savelyich followed me in, carrying the cellaret, called for fire so as to prepare tea, which had never before seemed so necessary to me. The innkeeper went to see to it.

"And where is our guide?" I asked Savelyich.

"Here, Your Honor," answered a voice from above. I looked up at the sleeping shelf above the stove[8] and saw a black beard and two flashing eyes.

"What, brother, chilled through?"

"How could I not be, in nothing but a flimsy coat! There was a sheepskin, but, why hide my sins, I pawned it yesterday in the pothouse: it didn't seem all that cold."

Just then the innkeeper came in with a boiling samovar. I offered our guide a cup of tea; the muzhik climbed down from the shelf. His appearance struck me as remarkable: he was about forty, of average height, lean and broad-shouldered. His black beard had streaks of gray; his lively big eyes darted about. His face had a rather pleasant but sly expression. His hair was trimmed in a bowl cut. He wore a ragged coat and Tatar balloon trousers. I handed him a cup of tea; he tried it and winced.

"Your Honor, do me a favor—tell them to bring me a glass of vodka; tea's not a Cossack drink."

I willingly carried out his wish. The innkeeper took a bottle and a glass from the sideboard, went up to him, and, looking him in the face, said: "Aha, so you're in our parts again! What wind blows you here?"

My guide winked meaningfully and answered with a saying: "To the garden I flew; pecked hempseed and rue; granny threw a stone— but missed. And what about your folk?"

"Our folk!" the innkeeper replied, continuing the allegorical conversation. "They were about to ring for vespers. 'No, don't,' the priest's wife whispers. The priest has gone away; the devils in the churchyard play."

"Quiet, uncle," my vagabond retorted. "If there's rain, there'll be mushrooms; and if there's mushrooms, there'll be a basket. But for now," here he winked again, "hide your axe behind your back: the forester's around. Your Honor! To your health!" With those words he took the glass, crossed himself, and drank it at one gulp. Then he bowed to me and went back to the shelf.

I could understand nothing of this thieves' talk then; but later I realized that it had to do with the affairs of the Yaik army, just pacified after the revolt of 1772.[9] Savelyich listened with an air of great displeasure. He kept glancing suspiciously now at the innkeeper, now at the guide. The coaching inn, or *umyet*, as it is called locally, was set apart, in the steppe, far from any village, and very much resembled a robbers' den. But there was nothing to be done. It was impossible to think of continuing on our way. Savelyich's anxiety amused me greatly. Meanwhile I settled down to spend the night and lay on a bench. Savelyich decided to install himself on the stove; the innkeeper lay on the floor. Soon the whole cottage was snoring, and I fell into a dead sleep.

Waking up rather late the next morning, I saw that the storm had abated. The sun was shining. Snow lay in a dazzling mantle over the boundless steppe. The horses were harnessed. I paid the innkeeper, who took such a moderate payment that even Savelyich did not argue with him and start bargaining as he usually did, and the previous day's suspicions were completely erased from his mind. I summoned our guide, thanked him for his help, and told Savelyich to tip him fifty kopecks. Savelyich frowned.

"Tip him fifty kopecks!" he said. "What for? Because you were so good as to bring him to the inn? Say what you like, sir: we have no extra half-roubles. If we tip everybody, we'll go hungry ourselves soon enough."

I could not argue with Savelyich. The money, by my promise, was entirely at his disposal. I was annoyed, however, that I could not thank a man who had saved me, if not from disaster, at least from a very unpleasant situation.

"Very well," I said coolly, "if you don't want to give him fifty kopecks, find him something from my clothes. He's dressed too lightly. Give him my hareskin coat."

"Mercy me, dearest Pyotr Andreich!" said Savelyich. "Why give him your hareskin coat? The dog will drink it up at the first pot-house."

"It's no care of yours, old fellow," said my vagabond, "whether I drink it up or not. His Honor is granting me a coat off his back: that's your master's will, and your serf business is to obey, not to argue."

"You've got no fear of God, you robber!" Savelyich replied in an angry voice. "You see the little one still can't reason, and you're glad to fleece him on account of his simplicity. What do you need the master's coat for? It won't even fit on your cursed shoulders."

"I beg you not to be too clever," I said to my tutor. "Bring the coat here right now."

"Lord God!" my Savelyich groaned. "The hareskin coat's nearly brand-new! And it's for anybody but this beggarly drunkard!"

Nevertheless, the hareskin coat appeared. The muzhik tried it on at once. Indeed, the coat, which I had already outgrown, was a bit tight on him. Nevertheless, he contrived to get into it, bursting it at the seams. Savelyich almost howled when he heard the threads rip. The vagabond was extremely pleased with my gift. He took me to the kibitka and said with a low bow: "Thank you, Your Honor! May the Lord reward you for your kindness. I'll never forget your good turn." He went his way, and I headed further on, paying no attention to Savelyich's annoyance, and soon forgot about the previous day's blizzard, my guide, and my hareskin coat.

On arriving in Orenburg, I went straight to the general. I saw a man, tall but already bent with age. His long hair was completely white. His old, faded uniform recalled the warrior from the time of Anna Ioannovna,[10] and his speech strongly smacked of German pronunciation. I handed him father's letter. Seeing his name, he gave me a quick glance.

"My Gott," he said, "it dossn't seem so long since Andrei Petrofich vas your age, and now see vat a fine young man he's got for himzelf. Ach, time, time!"

He unsealed the letter and began to read it in a low voice, making his own observations:

"'My dear sir, Andrei Karlovich, I hope that Your Excellency . . .' Vat are dese ceremonies? Pah, he should be ashamed! Off course, discipline iss before efferyting, but iss diss the vay to write to an old kamrad? . . . 'Your Excellency hass not forgotten . . .' Hm . . . 'and . . . when . . . de late field marshal Mün . . . campaign . . . and also . . . Karolinka . . .' Aha, *Bruder*! So he still remembers our old pranks? 'Now about business . . . to you my scapegrace' . . . Hm . . . 'keep him in hedgehog mittens' . . . Vat are dese 'hedgehog mittens'? Muss be a Russian saying . . . Vass iss diss 'keep him in hedgehog mittens'?" he repeated, turning to me.

"It means," I replied, looking as innocent as I could, "to treat gently, not too strictly, allow greater freedom—keep in hedgehog mittens."

"Hm, I see . . . 'and allow him no freedom' . . . no, 'hedgehog mittens' muss mean something else . . . 'Vit this . . . his passport' . . . Vere iss it? Ah, here it iss . . . 'report to the Semyonovsky' . . . Goot, goot: it vill all be done . . . 'Allow me, ignoring rank, to embrace you and . . . old comrade and friend'—ah! dere it iss . . . and so on and so forth . . . Well, my dear fellow," he said, having read the letter and set my passport aside, "it will all be done: you'll be transferred to the * * * regiment as an officer, and, so that you lose no time, you'll go tomorrow to the Belogorsk fortress, where you will be under the command of Captain Mironov, a good and honorable man. You'll be in real army service, and learn discipline. There's nothing for you to do in Orenburg: dissipation is harmful for a young man. And today you are welcome to dine with me."

"Worse and worse," I thought to myself. "What use was it being a sergeant of the guards in my mother's womb! Where did it get me? To the * * * regiment and a godforsaken fortress on the edge of the Kirghiz-Kaissak steppe! . . ."

I had dinner with Andrei Karlovich, the third man being his old adjutant. Strict German economy reigned at his table, and I think the fear of occasionally seeing an extra guest at his bachelor meals was partly the cause of my hasty removal to the garrison. The next day I took leave of the general and headed for my destination.

CHAPTER THREE

The Fortress

> So the fortress is our home,
> Bread and water we live by;
> And when our fierce foes do come
> To snatch a piece of our good pie,
> We prepare a merry feast
> Of grapeshot for our welcome guests.

SOLDIERS' SONG

Old-fashioned folk, my dear sir.

The Dunce[11]

The Belogorsk fortress was twenty-five miles from Orenburg. The road went along the steep bank of the Yaik. The river was not yet frozen over, and its leaden waves showed a dreary black between the monotonous banks covered with white snow. Beyond them stretched the Kirghiz steppe. I sank into reflections, for the most part sad. Garrison life held little attraction for me. I tried to imagine Captain Mironov, my future superior, and pictured him as a stern, cross old man, who knew nothing except his service, and ready to put me under arrest on bread and water for any trifle. Meanwhile it was getting dark. We were driving rather quickly.

"Is it far to the fortress?" I asked the driver.

"Not far," he replied. "There, you can already see it."

I looked all around, expecting to see formidable bastions, towers, and ramparts; but I saw nothing except a little village surrounded by a stockade. On one side stood three or four haystacks, half covered with snow; on the other, a lopsided windmill with its bast sails hanging lazily.

"Where is the fortress?" I asked in surprise.

"Here," the driver replied, pointing to the little village, and with those words we drove into it. By the gate I saw an old cast-iron cannon; the streets were narrow and crooked, the cottages low and mostly thatch-roofed. I ordered the driver to go to the commandant's, and a moment later the kibitka drew up in front of a little wooden house, built on a rise near a church, also wooden.

No one came out to meet me. I went into the front hall and opened the door to the anteroom. An old veteran was sitting on a table, sewing a blue patch on the elbow of a green uniform. I told him to announce me.

"Go on in, my dear man," the veteran replied. "Our people are at home."

I entered a clean little room, decorated in the old-fashioned way. In one corner stood a china cupboard; on the wall hung an officer's diploma under glass and in a frame; around it were proudly displayed some woodblock prints depicting the taking of Küstrin and Ochakov,[12] as well as the choosing of a bride and the burial of a cat. By the window sat an old woman in a quilted vest and with a kerchief on her head. She was unwinding yarn, which a one-eyed old man in an officer's uniform was holding on his outstretched arms.

"What can I do for you, my dear man?" she asked, going on with her work.

I replied that I had come to serve and was reporting for duty to the captain, addressing these last words to the one-eyed old man, whom I took for the commandant; but the lady of the house interrupted my prepared speech.

"Ivan Kuzmich is not at home," she said. "He's gone to visit Father Gerasim. But it makes no difference, my dear, I am his missis. Come right in. Sit down, dear."

She called the serving girl and told her to summon the sergeant. The old man kept glancing at me curiously with his solitary eye.

"Dare I ask," he said, "in what regiment you were pleased to serve?"

I satisfied his curiosity.

"And dare I ask," he continued, "why you were pleased to transfer from the guards to the garrison?"

I replied that such was the will of my superiors.

"I suspect it was for behavior unbecoming to a guards officer," the indefatigable questioner continued.

"Enough nonsense," the captain's wife said to him. "You can see the young man's tired from the journey; he can't be bothered with you . . . Hold your arms straight . . . And you, my dear," she continued, turning to me, "don't grieve that they've bundled you off to our backwater.

You're not the first, and you're not the last. Habit and love go hand in glove. Shvabrin, Alexei Ivanych, was transferred to us nearly five years ago for killing a man. God knows what devil got into him. You see, he went outside town with a certain lieutenant, and they took swords, and then up and started poking them at each other; and Alexei Ivanych stabbed the lieutenant to death, and that in front of two witnesses! What can you do? The devil knows no master."

Just then the sergeant came in, a strapping young Cossack.

"Maximych!" the captain's wife said to him. "Find quarters for the good officer—of the cleaner sort."

"Yes, ma'am, Vasilisa Egorovna," replied the sergeant. "Why not put his honor up with Ivan Polezhaev?"

"No good, Maximych," said the captain's wife. "It's crowded at Polezhaev's; besides, he's a friend and mindful that we're his superiors. Take the good officer . . . What's your name, my dear? Pyotr Andreich? . . . Take Pyotr Andreich to Semyon Kuzov's. The rascal let his horse get into my kitchen garden. Well, so, Maximych, is everything all right?"

"Yes, thank God, everything's quiet," replied the Cossack, "only Corporal Prokhorov had a fight in the bathhouse with Ustinya Negulina over a basin of hot water."

"Ivan Ignatyich!" the captain's wife said to the one-eyed old man. "Sort it out between Prokhorov and Ustinya, who's right and who's wrong. And punish both of them. Well, Maximych, off you go, and God be with you. Pyotr Andreich, Maximych will take you to your quarters."

I bowed and left. The sergeant brought me to the cottage, which stood on a high riverbank at the very edge of the fortress. One half of the cottage was occupied by Semyon Kuzov's family, the other was allotted to me. It consisted of one rather tidy room divided in two by a partition. Savelyich started putting things in order; I started looking out the narrow window. Before me stretched the dismal steppe. To one side stood several huts; several chickens were wandering in the street. An old woman, standing on the porch with a tub, was calling her pigs, who answered with friendly grunts. And such was the place where I was condemned to spend my youth! Anguish came over me; I left the window and went to bed without supper, despite the admonitions of Savelyich, who kept repeating in distress: "God Almighty! He doesn't want to eat anything! What will the mistress say if the little one's taken ill?"

The next morning, just as I was beginning to dress, the door opened and a young officer came in, a short man with a swarthy and singularly unattractive, but extremely animated, face.

"Excuse me," he said in French, "for coming without ceremony to make your acquaintance. Yesterday I learned of your arrival; the wish to see a human face at last took such hold of me that I couldn't help myself. You'll understand when you've lived here a little while."

I guessed that this was the officer discharged from the guards for fighting a duel. We became acquainted at once. Shvabrin was far from stupid. His conversation was witty and entertaining. He described for me with great merriment the commandant's family, their society, and the place that fate had brought me to. I was laughing wholeheartedly, when that same veteran who had been mending the uniform in the commandant's anteroom came in and told me that Vasilisa Egorovna invited me to dine with them. Shvabrin volunteered to go with me.

As we approached the commandant's house, we saw on a little square some twenty old veterans with long queues and three-cornered hats. They were lined up at attention. Before them stood the commandant, a tall and vigorous old man in a nightcap and a nankeen dressing gown. Seeing us, he came over and said a few kind words to me, and then went back to giving orders. We were going to stop and watch the drill; but he asked us to go to Vasilisa Egorovna, promising to follow us. "And here," he added, "there's nothing for you to watch."

Vasilisa Egorovna received us simply and cordially and treated me as if she had known me for ages. The veteran and Palashka were setting the table.

"Why is my Ivan Kuzmich drilling so long today?" said the commandant's wife. "Palashka, call the master to dinner. And where is Masha?"

Just then a girl of about eighteen came in, round-faced, rosy-cheeked, with light brown hair combed smoothly behind her ears, which were burning red. At first glance I did not like her very much. I looked at her with prejudice: Shvabrin had described Masha, the captain's daughter, as a perfect little fool. Marya Ivanovna sat down in the corner and began to sew. Meanwhile cabbage soup was served. Vasilisa Egorovna, not seeing her husband, sent Palashka for him a second time.

"Tell the master: the guests are waiting, the soup's getting cold;

thank God, the drilling won't run away; he'll have time to shout his fill."

The captain soon appeared, accompanied by the one-eyed old man. "What's this, my dearest?" his wife said to him. "The food's long been served and there's no sign of you."

"See here, Vasilisa Egorovna," Ivan Kuzmich replied, "I've been busy with my duties, drilling my good soldiers."

"Enough now!" retorted the captain's wife. "They only call it drill: your soldiers never learn, and you don't know the first thing about it. Sit at home and pray to God—that would be better. Dear guests, please come to the table."

We sat down to dinner. Vasilisa Egorovna did not stop talking for a moment and showered me with questions: who were my parents, were they still living, where did they live, and what was their situation? On hearing that my father owned three hundred peasant souls, she said:

"Fancy that! So there are rich people in the world! And all we have for souls, my dear, is the wench Palashka; but, thank God, we get by. There's just one trouble: Masha. The girl's of marrying age, but what dowry has she got? A besom, a brush, and three kopecks in cash (God forgive me!) to go to the bathhouse. It's fine if a good man turns up; otherwise she'll sit there a maiden bride forevermore."

I glanced at Marya Ivanovna. She blushed all over, and tears even fell on her plate. I felt sorry for her, and I hastened to change the conversation.

"I've heard," I said, rather beside the point, "that the Bashkirs[13] are preparing to attack your fortress."

"From whom, my dear boy, were you pleased to hear that?" asked Ivan Kuzmich.

"They told me so in Orenburg," I replied.

"Fiddlesticks!" said the commandant. "We've heard nothing for a long time. The Bashkirs are frightened folk, and the Kirghiz have also been taught a good lesson. They're not likely to go poking at us; and if they do, I'll put such a scare into them, they'll stay quiet for ten years."

"And you're not afraid," I went on, turning to the captain's wife, "to stay in a fortress exposed to such dangers?"

"Habit, my dear," she replied. "It's some twenty years ago that we were transferred here from the regiment, and, Lord help me, how afraid I was of those accursed heathens! The moment I saw their lynx hats and heard their shrieks, believe me, dear, my heart would stop dead! But now I'm so used to it that, if they come and tell us the villains are roaming around the fortress, I don't even flinch."

"Vasilisa Egorovna is a most courageous lady," Shvabrin observed solemnly. "Ivan Kuzmich can testify to that."

"Yes, see here," said Ivan Kuzmich, "the woman doesn't scare easily."

"And Marya Ivanovna?" I asked. "Is she as brave as you are?"

"Masha, brave?" her mother replied. "No, Masha's a coward. To this day she can't bear the sound of shooting: just trembles all over. And two years ago, when Ivan Kuzmich took it into his head to fire off our cannon on my name day, my little dove nearly departed this life from fright. We haven't fired the cursed cannon again since."

We got up from the table. The captain and his wife went off to sleep; and I went to Shvabrin's, where I spent the whole evening.

CHAPTER FOUR

The Duel

> Very well, stand straight and true,
> And watch me as I run you through.
>
> KNYAZHNIN[14]

Several weeks went by, and my life in the Belogorsk fortress became not only tolerable for me, but even agreeable. In the commandant's house I was received as one of their own. The husband and wife were most honorable people. Ivan Kuzmich, who had risen from the ranks to become an officer, was a simple, uneducated man, but most honest and good. His wife ruled him, which agreed with his easygoing nature. Vasilisa Egorovna looked upon matters of the service as her household chores, and ran the fortress as she did her own little house. Marya Ivanovna soon stopped being shy with me. We became acquainted. I found her to be a reasonable and sensitive girl. Imperceptibly, I became attached to this good family, even to Ivan Ignatyich, the one-eyed garrison lieutenant, for whom Shvabrin invented inadmissible relations with Vasilisa Egorovna, which did not have a shadow of plausibility; but Shvabrin was not worried about that.

I was made an officer. The service was no burden to me. In the God-protected fortress there were no reviews, nor drills, nor watches. The commandant, on his own initiative, occasionally drilled his soldiers; but he still could not get all of them to tell right from left, though many of them, to avoid making a mistake, made the sign of the cross over themselves before each turn. Shvabrin had several French books. I began to read, and an interest in literature awakened in me. In the mornings I read, practiced translation, and sometimes also wrote verses. I almost always dined at the commandant's, where I usually spent the rest of the day, and where in the evening Father Gerasim would sometimes come with his wife, Akulina Pamfilovna, the foremost talebearer of the neighborhood. A. I. Shvabrin, naturally, I saw every day; but his conversation became less and less agreeable to me. His habitual jokes about the commandant's family displeased me very much, especially his caustic remarks about Marya Ivanovna. There was no other society in the fortress, but I wished for no other.

In spite of the predictions, the Bashkirs did not revolt. Calm reigned around our fortress. But the peace was disrupted by sudden internecine strife.

I have already said that I occupied myself with literature. My attempts, for that time, were fairly good, and several years later Alexander Petrovich Sumarokov[15] praised them highly. Once I succeeded in writing a little song that pleased me. It is a known thing that writers, under the pretext of seeking advice, occasionally look for a benevolent listener. So, having copied out my song, I took it to Shvabrin, who alone in the whole fortress could appreciate a verse writer's production. After a brief preamble, I took my notebook out of my pocket and read him the following little verses:

Amorous thoughts in me destroying,
I strive of her beauty to be free,
And, oh, sweet Masha, thee avoiding,
Freedom at last I hope to see!

But the eyes that me have captured
Are before me all the time,

And my spirit they have raptured,
Ruining my peace of mind.

Thou, of my misfortune learning,
Take pity, Masha, upon me,
Who in this cruel trap am turning,
Being imprisoned here by thee.

"How do you find it?" I asked Shvabrin, expecting the praise that was certainly due me. But, to my great vexation, Shvabrin, usually indulgent, resolutely informed me that my song was no good.

"Why so?" I asked, concealing my vexation.

"Because," he replied, "such verses are worthy of my tutor, Vasily Kirilych Tredyakovsky,[16] and remind me very much of his love couplets."

Here he took my notebook from me and mercilessly began to analyze each line and each word, jeering at me in the most caustic manner. I could not bear it, tore my notebook from his hands, and said I would never again show him my writings. Shvabrin laughed at that threat as well.

"We'll see if you keep your word," he said. "A poet has need of a listener, just as Ivan Kuzmich has need of a dram of vodka before dinner. And who is this Masha to whom you declare your tender passion and amorous tribulation? Might it not be Marya Ivanovna?"

"It's none of your business," I replied, frowning, "whoever this Masha might be. I ask neither for your opinions nor for your conjectures."

"Oho! A touchy poet and a discreet lover!" Shvabrin went on, annoying me more and more all the time. "But listen to some friendly advice: if you want to succeed, I advise you to do it otherwise than by little songs."

"What is the meaning of that, sir? Kindly explain yourself."

"Gladly. It means that if you want Masha Mironov to meet you after dark, then instead of tender verses, give her a pair of earrings."

My blood boiled.

"And why do you have such an opinion of her?" I asked, barely controlling my indignation.

"Because," he replied with an infernal grin, "I know her ways and habits from experience."

"You're lying, scoundrel!" I cried in fury. "You're lying most shamelessly!"

Shvabrin's countenance changed.

"That you will not get away with," he said, gripping my arm. "You will give me satisfaction."

"Very well; whenever you like!" I replied joyfully. At that moment I was ready to tear him to pieces.

I went at once to Ivan Ignatyich and found him with a needle in his hand: on orders from the commandant's wife, he was stringing mushrooms to be dried for winter.

"Ah, Pyotr Andreich!" he said, seeing me. "Welcome! What good fortune brings you here? And on what business, may I ask?"

I explained to him in a few words that I had quarreled with Alexei Ivanych, and asked him, Ivan Ignatyich, to be my second. Ivan Ignatyich listened to me attentively, goggling his only eye at me.

"You're pleased to be saying," he said to me, "that you want to skewer Alexei Ivanyich and wish me to be a witness to it? Is that it, may I ask?"

"Exactly."

"For pity's sake, Pyotr Andreich! What are you getting into! You and Alexei Ivanych have quarreled? It's no big thing! Bad words don't stick. He called you names, and you swore at him; he punches you in the nose, you box him on the ear two, three times—and you go your own ways; and we'll get you to make peace. Or else what: is it a good thing to skewer your neighbor, may I ask? And good enough if you skewer him: God help Alexei Ivanych; I'm no great fancier of him myself. But what if he puts a hole in you? How will that be? Who'll be the fool then, may I ask?"

The sensible lieutenant's reasoning did not make me waver. I clung to my intention.

"As you like," said Ivan Ignatyich, "do what you've a mind to. But why should I be a witness to it? What on earth for? Men fight, so what else is new, may I ask? Good God, I went to war with the Swedes and the Turks: I've seen it all."

I tried to explain to him the duties of a second, but Ivan Ignatyich simply could not understand me.

"Have it your way," he said. "If I'm to get mixed up in this business, I'd better go to Ivan Kuzmich and dutifully inform him that there's some evildoing afoot in the fortress, contrary to official interest: might it be the commandant's goodwill to take suitable measures . . ."

I became frightened and started begging Ivan Ignatyich to say nothing to the commandant. I barely managed to persuade him. He gave me his word, and I decided to let it go at that.

I spent the evening, as was my habit, at the commandant's. I tried to seem cheerful and indifferent, so as not to arouse any suspicions and avoid importunate questions; but I confess, I did not have the composure of which those in my position almost always boast. That evening I was disposed to tenderness and affection. I liked Marya Ivanovna more than usual. The thought that I might be seeing her for the last time endowed her, in my eyes, with something touching. Shvabrin, too, showed up. I drew him aside and informed him of my conversation with Ivan Ignatyich.

"What do we need seconds for?" he said to me drily. "We'll do without them."

We arranged to fight behind the haystacks near the fortress, and to meet there by seven the next morning. We seemed to be conversing so amicably that Ivan Ignatyich, in his joy, almost blurted everything out.

"None too soon," he said to me, looking pleased. "Better a bad peace than a good quarrel; the less honor, the more health."

"What, what, Ivan Ignatyich?" asked the commandant's wife, who was in the corner telling fortunes with cards. "I didn't quite hear."

Ivan Ignatyich, seeing signs of displeasure in me and remembering his promise, became confused and did not know how to reply. Shvabrin rushed to his aid.

"Ivan Ignatyich," he said, "approves of our peacemaking."

"And who did you quarrel with, my dear?"

"I had a rather big argument with Pyotr Andreich."

"Over what?"

"Over a mere trifle: over a little song, Vasilisa Egorovna."

"What a thing to quarrel over! A little song! . . . How did it happen?"

"Like this: Pyotr Andreich recently composed a song and today he sang it for me, and I struck up my favorite:

O Captain's daughter, hark,
Don't go wand'ring after dark . . .

It turned into a disagreement. Pyotr Andreich was angry at first, but then he decided that everybody's free to sing what he likes. And the matter ended there."

Shvabrin's shamelessness nearly threw me into a rage; but nobody except myself understood his crude insinuations; at least nobody paid attention to them. From songs the conversation turned to poets, and the commandant observed that they were all dissipated people and hardened drunkards, and advised me in friendly fashion to give up verse writing as an occupation contrary to the service and leading to no good.

Shvabrin's presence was unbearable to me. I quickly took leave of the commandant and his family; on coming home I examined my sword, tried the point, and went to bed, having asked Savelyich to wake me up after six.

The next day at the appointed time I was already standing behind the haystacks waiting for my adversary. He soon appeared.

"They may catch us at it," he said to me. "We'll have to hurry up." We took off our uniform coats, remaining in our waistcoats, and drew our swords. Just then Ivan Ignatyich and five veterans suddenly appeared from behind the haystacks. He summoned us to the commandant. We grudgingly obeyed; the soldiers surrounded us, and we headed for the fortress, following Ivan Ignatyich, who led us in triumph, striding along with extraordinary solemnity.

We went into the commandant's house. Ivan Ignatyich opened the door, announcing triumphantly:

"I've brought them!"

We were met by Vasilisa Egorovna.

"Ah, my dears! What's this? How? Why? Bringing murder into our fortress? Ivan Kuzmich, arrest them at once! Pyotr Andreich! Alexei Ivanych! Give your swords here, give them here, give them here. Palashka, take these swords to the storeroom. Pyotr Andreich! I didn't expect this from you! Aren't you ashamed? Alexei Ivanych is another thing: he was dismissed from the guards for killing a man, and he doesn't believe in the Lord God—but you? Are you going the same way?"

Ivan Kuzmich agreed completely with his wife and kept repeating: "See here, Vasilisa Egorovna's right. Duels are formally forbidden by the articles of war."[17]

Meanwhile Palashka took our swords from us and carried them to the storeroom. I could not help laughing. Shvabrin preserved his solemnity.

"With all due respect," he said to her coolly, "I cannot help but observe that you need not trouble yourself, subjecting us to your judgment. Leave it to Ivan Kuzmich: it is his business."

"Ah, my dear," the commandant's wife retorted, "aren't husband and wife one spirit and one flesh?[18] Ivan Kuzmich! What are you gawking at? Separate them at once in different corners on bread and water till their foolishness goes away; and let Father Gerasim put a penance on them, so that they ask forgiveness of God and repent before men."

Ivan Kuzmich could not decide what to do. Marya Ivanovna was extremely pale. The storm gradually subsided: the commandant's wife calmed down and made us kiss each other. Palashka brought us our swords. We left the commandant's apparently reconciled. Ivan Ignatyich accompanied us.

"Weren't you ashamed," I said to him angrily, "to inform on us to the commandant after you promised me you wouldn't?"

"As God is holy, I didn't say a word to Ivan Kuzmich," he replied. "Vasilisa Egorovna wormed it all out of me. And she gave all the orders without the commandant's knowledge. Anyhow, thank God it's all ended like this." With those words he headed for home, and Shvabrin and I were left alone.

"We can't end things like that," I said to him.

"Of course not," Shvabrin replied. "You'll answer me for your impudence with your blood. But they'll probably keep an eye on us. We'll have to pretend for a few days. Good-bye!" And we parted as if nothing had happened.

On returning to the commandant's, I sat down, as usual, near Marya Ivanovna. Ivan Kuzmich was not at home; Vasilisa Egorovna was busy around the house. We talked in low voices. Marya Ivanovna chided me tenderly for the worry my quarrel with Shvabrin had caused them all.

"My heart just sank," she said, "when they said you were going to fight with swords. How strange men are! For one little word, which they'd surely forget about in a week, they're ready to cut each other up and sacrifice not only their lives but their consciences, and the well-being of those who . . . But I'm sure it wasn't you who started the quarrel. Surely Alexei Ivanych is to blame."

"And why do you think so, Marya Ivanovna?"

"It's just . . . he's such a scoffer! I don't like Alexei Ivanyich. He really disgusts me; but it's strange: I wouldn't want him to dislike me for anything. That would worry me dreadfully."

"And what do you think, Marya Ivanovna? Does he like you or not?"

Marya Ivanovna hesitated and blushed.

"It seems to me . . ." she said. "I think he does."

"Why does it seem so to you?"

"Because he asked to marry me."

"To marry you! He asked to marry you? When was that?"

"Last year. About two months before your arrival."

"And you didn't accept him?"

"As you can see. Alexei Ivanych is, of course, an intelligent man, and from a good family, and he has means; but when I think that I'd have to kiss him before the altar in front of everybody . . . Not for anything! Not for all the blessings in the world!"

Marya Ivanovna's words opened my eyes and explained many things to me. I understood the persistent maligning with which Shvabrin pursued her. He had probably noticed our mutual inclination and was trying to draw us away from each other. The words that had given rise to our quarrel seemed still more vile to me, now that I saw them, not as coarse and indecent mockery, but as deliberate slander. The wish to punish the insolent maligner grew still stronger in me, and I started waiting impatiently for a convenient occasion.

I did not have to wait long. The next day, as I sat over an elegy and gnawed my pen while waiting for a rhyme, Shvabrin knocked at my window. I set down the pen, took up my sword, and went out to him.

"Why put it off?" said Shvabrin. "We're not being watched. Let's go down to the river. Nobody will interfere with us there."

We set off in silence. Having gone down the steep path, we stopped by the river and drew our swords. Shvabrin was more skillful than I, but I was stronger and bolder, and Monsieur Beaupré, who had once been a soldier, had given me several lessons in fencing, which I made use of. Shvabrin had not expected to find me such a dangerous opponent. For a long time we could not do each other any harm; finally, noticing that Shvabrin was weakening, I stepped up my attack and almost drove him into the river. Suddenly I heard my name uttered loudly. I turned and saw Savelyich running to me down the hillside path . . . At that same moment I felt a sharp stab in my chest under the right shoulder; I fell down and lost consciousness.

CHAPTER FIVE

Love

> Ah, you, maiden, pretty maiden,
> Don't go marrying so young.
> Ask your father, ask your mother,
> Father, mother, and all your kin;
> Store up, maiden, wit and wisdom,
> Wit and wisdom your dowry be.
>
> FOLK SONG

> If you find a better one, you'll forget me,
> If you find a worse one, you'll remember me.
>
> DITTO

On coming to, I could not collect my senses for a while and did not understand what had happened to me. I was lying on a bed in an unfamiliar room, and felt a great weakness. Before me stood Savelyich with a candle in his hand. Someone was carefully unwinding the bandages that bound my chest and shoulder. My thoughts gradually cleared. I remembered my duel and realized that I had been wounded. Just then the door creaked.

"Well? How is he?" whispered a voice that made me tremble.

"Still in the same condition," Savelyich answered with a sigh, "still unconscious, for the fifth day now."

I wanted to turn, but could not.

"Where am I? Who's here?" I said with effort.

Marya Ivanovna came up to my bed and bent over me.

"Well? How are you feeling?" she said.

"Thank God," I replied in a weak voice. "Is it you, Marya Ivanovna? Tell me . . ." I had no strength to go on and fell silent. Savelyich gasped. Joy showed on his face.

"He's come around! He's come around!" he repeated. "Thank the Lord! Well, dearest Pyotr Andreich, how you frightened me! Just fancy—five days!"

Marya Ivanovna interrupted him.

"Don't talk to him much, Savelyich," she said. "He's still weak."

She went out and quietly closed the door. My thoughts were in turmoil. So I was in the commandant's house, Marya Ivanovna had come to me. I wanted to ask Savelyich some questions, but the old man shook his head and stopped his ears. I closed my eyes in vexation and soon sank into sleep.

On waking up, I called Savelyich and instead of him saw Marya Ivanovna standing there; her angelic voice greeted me. I cannot express the sweet feeling that came over me at that moment. I seized her hand and clung to it, pouring out tears of tenderness. Masha did not pull it away . . . and suddenly her lips touched my cheek, and I felt their ardent and fresh kiss. Fire ran through me.

"Dear, good Marya Ivanovna," I said to her, "be my wife, consent to make my happiness."

She came to her senses.

"For God's sake, calm down," she said, taking her hand from me. "You're still in danger: the wound may open. Look after yourself, if only for my sake." With those words she went out, leaving me in drunken ecstasy. Happiness resurrected me. She'll be mine! She loves me! This thought filled the whole of my being.

After that I grew better by the hour. I was treated by the regimental barber, for there was no other doctor in the fortress, and, thank God, he did not get too clever. Youth and nature speeded my recovery. The commandant's whole family took care of me. Marya Ivanovna never left my side. Naturally, at the first good opportunity I took up my interrupted declaration, and Marya Ivanovna listened to me more patiently. Without any affectation, she confessed to me her heartfelt inclination and said that her parents would of course be glad of her happiness.

"But think well," she added. "Will there be no obstacle on your parents' side?"

I fell to thinking. Of my mother's fondness I had no doubt, but,

knowing my father's character and way of thinking, I sensed that my
love would not move him very much and that he would regard it as
a young man's caprice. I confessed it frankly to Marya Ivanovna and
resolved, nevertheless, to write to my father as eloquently as I could,
asking for their parental blessing. I showed the letter to Marya Ivanovna, who found it so persuasive and moving that she had no doubts
of its success and yielded to the feelings of her tender heart with all the
trustfulness of youth and love.

I made peace with Shvabrin in the first days of my recovery. Ivan
Kuzmich, reprimanding me for the duel, said:

"Ah, Pyotr Andreich, I ought to put you under arrest, but you've
already been punished as it is. And I've got Alexei Ivanych sitting in the
granary under guard, and Vasilisa Egorovna has locked up his sword.
Let him think it over and repent."

I felt too happy to go storing up hostile feelings in my heart. I
began to intercede for Shvabrin, and the kind commandant, with
his wife's approval, decided to release him. Shvabrin came to me; he
expressed profound regret for what had happened between us, admitted that he was roundly to blame, and begged me to forget the past.
Not being rancorous by nature, I sincerely forgave him both for our
quarrel and for the wound I had received from him. In his slander I
saw the vexation of hurt pride and rejected love, and I magnanimously
excused my unlucky rival.

I soon recovered and was able to move back to my own quarters.
I waited impatiently for the reply to my letter, not daring to hope and
trying to stifle my sad presentiments. I had not yet talked with Vasilisa Egorovna and her husband; but my proposal would be no surprise
to them. Neither I nor Marya Ivanovna tried to conceal our feelings
from them, and we were certain beforehand of their consent.

Finally one morning Savelyich came into my room holding a letter in his hand. I seized it, trembling. The address was written in my
father's hand. That prepared me for something important, for my
mother usually wrote me letters, and he would add a few lines at the
end. I did not open the envelope for some time and kept rereading the
solemn inscription: "To my son Pyotr Andreevich Grinyov, Belogorsk
Fortress, Orenburg Province." I tried to guess from the handwriting
the state of mind in which the letter had been written; finally I ventured to unseal it, and saw from the first lines that the whole thing had
gone to the devil. The contents of the letter were as follows:

My son Pyotr,

The letter, in which you ask for our parental blessing and consent to your marriage with Miss Marya Ivanovna Mironov, we
received on the 15th of this month, and not only do I have
no intention of giving you my blessing or my consent, but I
am also going to get after you and teach you a proper lesson
for your mischief, little boy that you are, despite your officer's
rank: for you have proven that you are still unworthy to bear
the sword, which was bestowed on you to defend your fatherland and not for duels with such madcaps as yourself. I shall
write at once to Andrei Karlovich, asking him to transfer you
from the Belogorsk fortress to somewhere further away, where
you will be cured of your folly. Your mother, having learned of
your duel and of your wound, fell ill with grief and now lies in
bed. What will become of you? I pray to God that you mend
your ways, though I dare not hope for His great mercy.

Your father, A. G.

The reading of this letter aroused various feelings in me. The cruel
expressions, on which my father did not stint, insulted me deeply. The
disdain with which he referred to Marya Ivanovna seemed to me as
unseemly as it was unjust. The thought of my being transferred from
the Belogorsk fortress horrified me, but what upset me most of all was
the news of my mother's illness. I was indignant with Savelyich, having no doubt that my duel became known to my parents through him.
Pacing up and down my narrow room, I stopped before him and said,
glaring at him menacingly:

"I see you don't find it enough that, thanks to you, I was wounded
and for a whole month was on the brink of the grave: you also want to
kill my mother."

Savelyich was thunderstruck.

"Mercy, sir," he said, all but weeping, "what's this you're pleased
to be saying? I'm the cause of your being wounded! God knows, I was
running to shield you with my breast from Alexei Ivanych's sword! My
cursed old age prevented me. And what have I done to your mother?"

"What have you done?" I replied. "Who asked you to inform on
me? Have you been attached to me as a spy?"

"Me? Inform on you?" Savelyich replied in tears. "Lord God in heaven! Kindly read what the master writes to me: you'll see how I informed on you." Here he took a letter from his pocket, and I read the following:

> Shame on you, you old dog, that, despite my strict orders, you did not inform me about my son Pyotr Andrevich and that strangers have had to tell me about his mischief. Is this how you fulfill your duties and your master's will? I'll send you to herd swine, you old dog, for concealing the truth and covering up for the young man. With the receipt of this, I order you to write back to me immediately about the state of his health now, of which they write to me that it has improved, as well as the exact place of the wound and whether he has been properly treated.

It was obvious that Savelyich was in the right before me and that I had wrongfully offended him with my reproaches and suspicions. I asked his forgiveness, but the old man was inconsolable.

"So I've lived to see this," he repeated. "So this is how the masters reward me for my services! I'm an old dog and a swineherd, and I'm also the cause of your wound? No, my dear Pyotr Andreich! It's not me, it's that cursed moosieu who's to blame for it all: he taught you to go poking with iron skewers and stamping your feet, as if by poking and stamping you could protect yourself from a wicked man. What need was there to hire a moosieu and throw good money away?"

But who, then, had taken the trouble to inform my father of my behavior? The general? But he did not seem overly concerned with me; and Ivan Kuzmich had not considered it necessary to report my duel. I was torn by conjectures. My suspicions rested on Shvabrin. He alone would profit by the denunciation, the consequence of which could be my removal from the fortress and my break with the commandant's family. I went to tell all this to Marya Ivanovna. She met me on the porch.

"What's happened to you?" she said on seeing me. "You're so pale!"

"It's all over!" I replied and handed her my father's letter.

She went pale in her turn. Having read it, she gave me back the letter with a trembling hand and said in a trembling voice:

"Clearly, it's not my fate . . . Your parents don't want me in their family. The Lord's will be done in everything! God knows what we need better than we do. There's nothing to be done, Pyotr Andreich. May you at least be happy . . ."

"This will not be!" I cried, seizing her by the hand. "You love me; I'm ready for anything. Let's go and throw ourselves at your parents' feet. They're simple people, not hard-hearted and proud . . . They'll give us their blessing; we'll get married . . . and then, in time, I'm sure we'll win my father over; mother will be for us; he'll forgive me . . ."

"No, Pyotr Andreich," Masha replied, "I won't marry you without your parents' blessing. Without their blessing there will be no happiness for you. Let us submit to God's will. If you find the one who is meant for you, if you come to love another—God be with you, Pyotr Andreich; and you will both be in my . . ."

Here she began to weep and left me. I wanted to follow her inside, but felt that I was in no condition to control myself and went home.

I was sitting plunged in deep thought when Savelyich suddenly interrupted my reflections.

"Here, sir," he said, handing me a sheet of paper covered with writing. "See whether I'm an informer on my master and am trying to make trouble between father and son."

I took the paper from him: it was Savelyich's reply to the letter he had received. Here it is word for word:

Gracious master and father, Andrei Petrovich!

I have received your gracious letter, in which you are pleased to be angry with me, your bondsman, for the shame of my not fulfilling my master's orders; but I, not an old dog, but your faithful servant, do obey my master's orders and have always served you zealously and have lived to be gray-haired. I did not write you anything about Pyotr Andreich's wound, so as not to frighten you needlessly, and I hear that the mistress, our mother, Avdotya Vasilievna, has taken to her bed from fright even so, and I will pray to God for her health. And Pyotr Andreich was wounded under the right shoulder, in the chest just under the bone, two inches deep, and he lay in the commandant's bed, where we brought him from the riverbank, and he was treated by the local barber, Stepan Paramonov; and now, thank God, Pyotr Andreich is well, and there is nothing to write about him except good things. The superiors, I hear, are pleased with him, and Vasilisa Egorovna treats him like her own son. And the boy should not be reproached for such a mishap: a horse has four legs, and still he stumbles. And you were pleased to write that you would send me to herd swine, and so be it by your lordly will. With my servile respects,

> Your faithful serf,
> Arkhip Savelyevich

I could not help smiling several times, reading the good old man's letter. I was in no condition to write a reply to my father; and Savelyich's letter seemed enough to reassure my mother.

From then on my situation changed. Marya Ivanovna hardly spoke to me and tried in every way to avoid me. The commandant's house became hateful to me. I gradually accustomed myself to sitting at home alone. At first Vasilisa Egorovna chided me for that; but, seeing my persistence, she left me in peace. I saw Ivan Kuzmich only when the service called for it. I met Shvabrin rarely and reluctantly, the more so as I noticed in him a concealed animosity towards me, which confirmed me in my suspicions. My life became unbearable to me. I fell into a dark brooding, nourished by loneliness and inactivity. My love flared up in solitude and became more and more hard to bear. I lost the appetite for reading and literature. My spirits sank. I was afraid I would either go mad or throw myself into dissipation. Unexpected events, which were to have a significant influence on my whole life, suddenly gave my soul a strong and salutary shock.

CHAPTER SIX

The Pugachev Rebellion

> You young striplings, listen well
> To what we oldsters have to tell.
>
> A SONG

Before I set out to describe the strange events I was witness to, I must say a few words about the situation in which the province of Orenburg found itself at the end of 1773.

This vast and rich province was inhabited by a multitude of half-savage peoples, who had only recently recognized the sovereignty of the Russian emperors. Their constant insurrections, unfamiliarity with law and civic life, light-mindedness and cruelty, demanded constant surveillance on the part of the government to keep them in obedience. Fortresses had been built in places considered suitable, and were occupied for the most part by Cossacks, longtime inhabitants of the banks of the Yaik. But the Yaik Cossacks themselves, whose duty it was to safeguard the peace and security of the region, had for some time been troublesome and dangerous subjects for the government. In 1772 there was an insurrection in their main town. It was caused by the strict measures taken by Major General Traubenberg[19] to reduce the army to proper obedience. The result was the barbarous murder of Traubenberg, a high-handed change of regime, and, finally, the putting down of the rebellion by cannon fire and severe punishments.

This happened a short time before my arrival at the Belogorsk fortress. Everything was already quiet, or seemed so; the authorities trusted all too easily in the sham repentance of the cunning rebels, who nursed their malice in secret and awaited a good opportunity for renewed upheavals.

I return to my story.

One evening (it was at the beginning of October 1773) I was sitting at home alone, listening to the howling of the autumn wind and looking through the window at the clouds racing past the moon. They came to summon me on behalf of the commandant. I went at once. At the commandant's I found Shvabrin, Ivan Ignatyich, and the Cossack sergeant. Neither Vasilisa Egorovna nor Marya Ivanovna was in the room. The commandant greeted me with a preoccupied air. He shut the door, had us all sit down—except for the sergeant, who stood by the door—took a paper from his pocket, and said to us: "Gentlemen officers, important news! Listen to what the general writes."

Then he put on his spectacles and read the following:

To Captain Mironov, commandant of the Belogorsk fortress.

Confidential.

I hereby inform you that the fugitive Don Cossack and schismatic Emelyan Pugachev, having committed the unpardonable impudence of taking upon himself the name of the late emperor Peter III,[20] has gathered a band of villains, stirred up an insurrection in the villages of the Yaik region, and already taken and ravaged several fortresses, carrying out robberies and murders everywhere. As a result, Captain, upon receipt of this, you are immediately to take appropriate measures for repulsing the said villain and impostor, and, if possible, for his total annihilation, in case he moves against the fortress entrusted to your care.

"Take appropriate measures," said the commandant, removing his spectacles and folding the paper. "That's easy enough to say. The villain seems to be strong; and we have all of a hundred and thirty men, not counting the Cossacks, who are none too trusty—no offense intended, Maximych." (The sergeant grinned.) "However, there's nothing to be done, gentlemen! Do your duty, set up sentries and a night watch; in case of attack, lock the gate and muster your men. You, Maximych, keep a sharp eye on your Cossacks. Inspect the cannon and clean it well. And, above all, keep the whole thing secret, so that nobody in the fortress learns of it ahead of time."

Having given these orders, Ivan Kuzmich dismissed us. I went out together with Shvabrin, discussing what we had just heard.

"How do you think it will end?" I asked him.

"God knows," he replied. "We'll find out. For the time being I don't see it as anything important. But if . . ."

Here he became thoughtful and started absentmindedly whistling a French air.

In spite of all our precautions, news of Pugachev's appearance spread through the fortress. Ivan Kuzmich had great respect for his wife, but not for anything in the world would he have revealed to her a secret entrusted to him by the service. On receiving the general's letter, he had contrived to send Vasilisa Egorovna away, telling her that Father Gerasim had received some remarkable news from Orenburg, which he was keeping in great secrecy. Vasilisa Egorovna immediately wanted to go and visit the priest's wife, and, on Ivan Kuzmich's advice, took Masha along with her, so that she would not be bored alone.

Ivan Kuzmich, left in full control, at once sent for us and locked Palashka in the storeroom, so that she could not overhear us.

Vasilisa Egorovna came home, having failed to find out anything from the priest's wife, and learned that during her absence Ivan Kuzmich had held a meeting and that Palashka had been locked up. She realized that her husband had tricked her and accosted him with questions. But Ivan Kuzmich was prepared for the attack. He was not put out in the least and cheerfully answered his inquisitive consort:

"You know, dearest, our womenfolk took it into their heads to heat their stoves with straw; and since that could lead to disaster, I gave strict orders that in future our womenfolk heat their stoves, not with straw, but with brushwood and fallen branches."

"And why did you have to lock up Palashka?" asked his wife. "Why was the poor girl left sitting in the storeroom till we came back?"

Ivan Kuzmich was not prepared for such a question; he became muddled and muttered something quite incoherent. Vasilisa Egorovna saw her husband's perfidy; but knowing that she would get nothing out of him, she broke off her questions and started talking about pickled cucumbers, which Akulina Pamfilovna prepared in a totally unusual way. Vasilisa Egorovna could not sleep all night and simply could not figure out what was in her husband's head that she was not allowed to know.

The next day, coming back from church, she saw Ivan Ignatyich pulling out of the cannon rags, gravel, wood chips, knucklebones, and all sorts of trash that the children had stuffed into it.

"What might these military preparations mean?" the commandant's wife thought. "Are they expecting an attack from the Kirghiz? Can it be that Ivan Kuzmich would conceal such trifles from me?"

She called Ivan Ignatyich with the firm intention of wheedling out of him the secret that tormented her feminine curiosity.

Vasilisa Egorovna made several observations to him concerning household matters, like a judge who begins an investigation with unrelated questions, so as to put the defendant off guard. Then, after a few moments' silence, she sighed deeply and said, shaking her head: "Lord God! Such news! What will come of it?"

"Eh, dear lady!" Ivan Ignatyich replied. "God is merciful, we've got enough soldiers, plenty of powder, and I've cleaned the cannon. Maybe we'll fend off Pugachev. If God doesn't forget us, the pigs won't get us."

"And what sort of man is this Pugachev?" asked the commandant's wife.

Here Ivan Ignatyich realized that he had made a gaffe and bit his tongue. But it was too late. Vasilisa Egorovna forced him to confess everything, giving him her word that she would not tell anybody.

Vasilisa Egorovna kept her promise and did not say a word to anybody, except for the priest's wife, and then only because her cow grazed on the steppe and could be seized by the villains.

Soon everybody was talking about Pugachev. The rumors varied. The commandant sent the Cossack sergeant out, charging him to thoroughly reconnoiter the surrounding villages and fortresses. The sergeant came back in two days and reported that on the steppe, about forty miles from the fortress, he had seen many lights, and he had heard from the Bashkirs that an unknown force was coming. However, he could not say anything definite, because he had been afraid to go on further.

In the fortress an unusual agitation could be noticed among the Cossacks; they clustered everywhere in little groups, talked softly among themselves, and dispersed on seeing a dragoon or a garrison soldier. Spies were sent among them. Yulai, a baptized Kalmyk, brought important intelligence to the commandant. The sergeant's information, according to Yulai, was false: on his return, the cunning Cossack told his comrades that he had gone to the rebels, had presented himself to their leader in person, who had allowed him to kiss his hand and talked at length with him. The commandant immediately put the sergeant under guard and appointed Yulai in his place. The Cossacks received this news with obvious displeasure. They murmured loudly, and Ivan Ignatyich, who carried out the commandant's order, with his own ears heard them say: "You're going to get it, you garrison rat!" The commandant intended to question his prisoner that same day; but the sergeant escaped from the guard, probably with the help of his accomplices.

A new circumstance increased the commandant's anxiety. A Bashkir was seized with inflammatory leaflets. On this occasion the commandant again intended to gather his officers and for that again wanted to send Vasilisa Egorovna away on some plausible pretext. But since Ivan Kuzmich was a most straightforward and truthful man, he found no other way than the same one he had already employed.

"See here, Vasilisa Egorovna," he said, clearing his throat, "they say Father Gerasim has received from town . . ."

"Enough nonsense, Ivan Kuzmich," his wife interrupted. "So you want to call a meeting and talk about Emelyan Pugachev without me; but this time you won't pull it off!"

Ivan Kuzmich goggled his eyes.

"Well, dearest," he said, "since you know everything, you might as well stay; we'll talk with you here."

"That's the way, my dear," she replied. "You're no good at trickery. Send for the officers."

We gathered again. Ivan Kuzmich, in the presence of his wife, read to us Pugachev's proclamation, written by some semiliterate Cossack. The brigand announced his intention to go at once against our fortress; he invited the Cossacks and the soldiers to join his band, and exhorted the commanders to put up no resistance, threatening them with execution otherwise. The proclamation was written in crude but forceful language and was bound to make a dangerous impression on the minds of simple people.

"What a fraud!" exclaimed the commandant's wife. "How dare he make us such offers! To go out to him and lay our banners at his feet! Ah, the son of a dog! Doesn't he know we've already been forty years in the service and, thank God, seen it all? Can such commanders be found as would listen to the brigand?"

"Seems like there shouldn't be," Ivan Kuzmich replied. "Yet they say the villain has already taken many fortresses."

"He must be really strong, then," observed Shvabrin.

"We'll soon see just how strong he is," said the commandant. "Vasilisa Egorovna, give me the key to the shed. Ivan Ignatyich, bring that Bashkir and tell Yulai to fetch us a whip."

"Wait, Ivan Kuzmich," said his wife, getting up. "Let me take Masha away somewhere; she'll hear the screams and get frightened. And, to tell the truth, I'm no lover of interrogations either. Good-bye and good luck."

In the old days torture was so ingrained in legal procedure that the beneficial decree that abolished it long remained without any effect.[21] The thinking was that a criminal's own confession was necessary for his full conviction—an idea not only without foundation, but totally contrary to juridical common sense: for if a criminal's denial is not accepted as proof of his innocence, still less should his confession be proof of his guilt. Even now I sometimes hear old judges regretting the abolition of this barbaric custom. But in our day nobody doubted the necessity of torture, neither the judges, nor the accused. And so, the commandant's order neither surprised nor alarmed any of us. Ivan Ignatyich went for the Bashkir, who sat locked in Vasilisa Egorovna's shed, and a few minutes later the prisoner was led into the front hall. The commandant ordered that he be brought before him.

The Bashkir stepped across the threshold with difficulty (he was in clogs) and, taking off his tall hat, stopped by the door. I looked at him and shuddered. Never will I forget this man. He looked to be over seventy. He had no nose or ears. His head was shaved; instead of a beard several gray hairs stuck out; he was short, skinny, and bent; but his narrow eyes still flashed fire.

"Aha!" said the commandant, recognizing by his terrible marks one of the rebels punished in 1741.[22] "It's clear you're an old wolf—you've visited our traps. Must be this isn't your first rebellion, since your nob's been planed so smooth. Come closer; tell us, who sent you?"

The old Bashkir said nothing and looked at the commandant with a totally vacant air.

"Why are you silent?" Ivan Kuzmich went on. "Or maybe you don't have a lick of Russian? Yulai, ask him in your language who sent him to our fortress."

Yulai repeated Ivan Kuzmich's question in Tatar. But the Bashkir looked at him with the same expression and answered not a word.

"*Yakshi*,"* said the commandant, "you'll speak to me yet. Hey, lads! Take off his stupid stripy robe and hemstitch his back. Look to it, Yulai: give it to him good!"

Two veterans began to undress the Bashkir. The poor man's face showed anxiety. He looked all around like a little animal caught by children. But when one of the veterans took his arms, put them around his neck, and raised the old man onto his shoulders, while Yulai took

* "Very well." (Tatar)

the whip and swung it—then the Bashkir moaned in a weak, pleading voice, and, wagging his head, opened his mouth, in which, instead of a tongue, a short stump twitched.

When I recall that this happened in my lifetime and that I have now lived to see the mild reign of the emperor Alexander,[23] I cannot help marveling at the rapid success of enlightenment and the spread of the principles of humanity. Young man, if my notes find themselves in your hands, remember that the best and most lasting changes are those that proceed from the improvement of morals, without any violent upheavals.

We were all shocked.

"Well," said the commandant, "it's clear we won't get any sense out of him. Yulai, take the Bashkir back to the shed. And we, gentlemen, still have a thing or two to talk over."

We had begun to discuss our situation, when Vasilisa Egorovna suddenly came in, breathless and looking extremely alarmed.

"What's happened to you?" asked the astonished commandant.

"Big trouble, my dears!" Vasilisa Egorovna replied. "The Nizhneozerny fortress was taken this morning. Father Gerasim's hired man just came back from there. He saw it taken. The commandant and all the officers were hanged. All the soldiers were taken prisoner. Before you notice, the villains will be here."

The unexpected news shocked me greatly. I knew the commandant of the Nizhneozerny fortress, a quiet and modest young man: some two months earlier he had been passing by from Orenburg with his young wife and put up at Ivan Kuzmich's. The Nizhneozerny was about sixteen miles from our fortress. At any moment we, too, could expect Pugachev to attack. I vividly pictured Marya Ivanovna's lot, and my heart sank.

"Listen, Ivan Kuzmich!" I said to the commandant. "Our duty is to defend the fortress to our last breath; that goes without saying. But we must think of the safety of the women. Send them to Orenburg, if the road is still open, or to some safer, more distant fortress that the villains won't reach."

Ivan Kuzmich turned to his wife and said:

"See here, dearest. In fact, why don't we send you farther away, until we've dealt with the rebels?"

"Ehh, trifles!" said the commandant's wife. "Where is there a fortress that hasn't seen bullets flying? What's unsafe about Belogorsk?

Thank God, it's twenty-two years we've lived in it. We've seen the Bashkirs and the Kirghiz; chances are we'll outsit Pugachev, too!"

"Well, dearest," Ivan Kuzmich rejoined, "you're welcome to stay, since you trust in our fortress. But what are we to do with Masha? It's fine if we sit it out or succor comes; but what if the villains take the fortress?"

"Well, then . . ." Here Vasilisa Egorovna hesitated and fell silent, looking extremely worried.

"No, Vasilisa Egorovna," the commandant went on, noticing that his words had had an effect on her, perhaps for the first time in his life. "It won't do for Masha to stay here. Let's send her to Orenburg, to her godmother: they have troops and cannon aplenty, and the walls are stone. And I'd advise you to go there with her; never mind that you're an old woman, just consider what would happen to you if they were to take the fortress by assault."

"Very well," said his wife, "so be it, we'll send Masha off. But don't dream of asking me to go: I won't. Nothing will make me part from you in my old age and seek a solitary grave in strange parts somewhere. Together we've lived, and together we'll die."

"That's it, then," said the commandant. "Well, there's no point in tarrying. Go, prepare Masha for the journey. Tomorrow at dawn we'll send her off, and we'll give her an escort, though we have no men to spare. But where is Masha?"

"At Akulina Pamfilovna's," his wife replied. "She felt faint when she heard that the Nizhneozerny fortress had been taken; I'm afraid she may fall ill. Lord God, that we've lived to see this!"

Vasilisa Egorovna went to busy herself with her daughter's departure. The conversation at the commandant's went on; but I no longer entered into it and was not listening. Marya Ivanovna appeared at supper pale and tear-stained. We finished supper in silence and got up from the table sooner than usual; taking leave of the whole family, we went to our homes. But I deliberately forgot my sword and went back for it; I had a feeling I would find Marya Ivanovna alone. Indeed, she met me at the door and handed me my sword.

"Good-bye, Pyotr Andreich!" she said to me in tears. "They're sending me to Orenburg. May you live and be happy; perhaps the Lord will grant us to see each other again; but if not . . ."

Here she burst into sobs. I embraced her.

"Farewell, my angel," I said, "farewell, my dear one, my heart's desire! Whatever happens to me, trust that my last thought and last prayer will be about you!"

Masha sobbed, clinging to my breast. I kissed her ardently and hurried out of the room.

CHAPTER SEVEN

The Assault

Head of mine, dear head of mine,
This my dear long-serving head,
It has served, dear head of mine,
Exactly three and thirty years.
Ah, it has earned, this head of mine,
Naught of profit, naught of joy,
Naught of any kindly word
And naught of any higher rank;
All it has earned, this head of mine,
Is two lofty wooden posts,
A crossbar made of maple wood,
And a simple silken noose.

FOLK SONG

That night I did not sleep, nor did I undress. I intended to go at dawn to the fortress gate, from which Marya Ivanovna was to leave, and there say good-bye to her for the last time. I felt a great change in myself: the agitation of my soul was much less burdensome for me than the dejection I had been sunk in still recently. The sadness of separation mingled in me with vague but sweet hopes, the impatient expectation of danger, and a sense of noble ambition. The night passed imperceptibly. I was about to leave my house when the door opened and a corporal appeared with the report that the Cossacks had left the fortress during the night, taking Yulai with them by force, and that unknown men were riding around the fortress. The thought that Marya Ivanovna would not have time to leave horrified me; I quickly gave the corporal a few instructions and rushed at once to the commandant.

Dawn was breaking. I was flying down the street when I heard my name called. I stopped.

"Where are you going?" asked Ivan Ignatyich, catching up with me. "Ivan Kuzmich is on the rampart and sent me for you. Pugach has come."

"Has Marya Ivanovna left?" I asked with a trembling heart.

"She didn't have time," Ivan Ignatyich replied. "The road to Orenburg has been cut; the fortress is surrounded. Things are bad, Pyotr Andreich!"

We went up to the rampart, an elevation formed by nature and fortified by a palisade. All the inhabitants of the fortress were already crowding there. The garrison stood under arms. The cannon had been moved there the day before. The commandant paced up and down in front of his scanty ranks. The proximity of danger inspired the old warrior with an extraordinary animation. On the steppe, no great distance from the fortress, some twenty horsemen were riding about. They seemed to be Cossacks, but there were also Bashkirs among them, easily recognizable by their lynx hats and their quivers. The commandant made the round of his troops, saying to his soldiers:

"Well, lads, let's stand today for our mother empress and prove to the whole world that we are brave men faithful to our oath!"

The soldiers loudly voiced their zeal. Shvabrin stood next to me and gazed intently at the enemy. The people riding about on the steppe, noticing movement in the fortress, gathered into a little knot and started talking among themselves. The commandant ordered Ivan Ignatyich to point the cannon at them and put the match to it himself. The cannonball went whizzing over them without doing any damage. The riders, dispersing, galloped out of sight at once, and the steppe was left empty.

Then Vasilisa Egorovna appeared on the rampart, and with her Masha, who did not want to stay behind.

"Well, so?" said the commandant's wife. "How's the battle going? Where's the enemy?"

"The enemy's not far off," replied Ivan Kuzmich. "God grant all will be well. What, Masha, are you scared?"

"No, papa," replied Marya Ivanovna. "It's scarier at home alone."

Then she glanced at me and tried to smile. I involuntarily gripped the hilt of my sword, remembering that the day before I had received it from her hands, as if for the protection of my beloved. My heart glowed. I imagined myself as her knight. I longed to prove myself worthy of her trust, and waited impatiently for the decisive moment.

Just then new groups of horsemen appeared from over the rise half a mile from the fortress, and soon the steppe was strewn with a multitude of people, armed with lances and bows. Among them, on a white horse, rode a man in a red kaftan, with a drawn sword in his hand: this was Pugachev himself. He stopped; the men surrounded him, and, apparently at his command, four men separated from them and galloped at top speed right up to the fortress. We recognized them as our traitors. One of them held a sheet of paper under his hat; another had Yulai's head stuck on his lance, which he shook off and threw over the paling to our side. The poor Kalmyk's head landed at the commandant's feet. The traitors shouted: "Don't shoot; come out to the sovereign. The sovereign's here!"

"I'll give it to you!" cried Ivan Kuzmich. "Fire, lads!"

Our soldiers loosed a volley. The Cossack holding the letter reeled and fell off his horse; the others galloped back. I looked at Marya Ivanovna. Shocked by the sight of Yulai's bloody head, deafened by the volley, she seemed to be in a daze. The commandant summoned the corporal and ordered him to take the piece of paper from the dead Cossack's hand. The corporal went out to the field and came back leading the dead man's horse by the bridle. He handed the commandant the letter. Ivan Kuzmich read it to himself and then tore it into little pieces. Meanwhile the rebels were evidently preparing for action. Soon bullets began to whistle past our ears and several arrows stuck into the ground and the palings near us.

"Vasilisa Egorovna!" said the commandant. "Women have no business here. Take Masha away. Look: the girl's more dead than alive."

Vasilisa Egorovna, grown quiet under the bullets, glanced at the steppe, on which great movement could be seen; then she turned to her husband and said to him:

"Ivan Kuzmich, life and death are as God wills: bless Masha. Masha, go to your father."

Masha, pale and trembling, went to Ivan Kuzmich, knelt, and bowed to the ground before him. The old commandant crossed her three times; then he raised her up, kissed her, and said in an altered voice:

"Well, Masha, be happy. Pray to God: he won't abandon you. If a good man comes along, God grant you love and harmony. Live as Vasilisa Egorovna and I have lived. So, farewell, Masha. Vasilisa Egorovna, take her away quickly."

Masha threw herself on his neck and burst into sobs.

"Let's us, too, kiss each other," the commandant's wife said, weeping. "Farewell, my Ivan Kuzmich. Forgive me if I've vexed you in any way!"

"Farewell, farewell, my dearest!" said the commandant, embracing his old woman. "Enough, now! Go, go home; and if you have time, put Masha in a peasant dress."

The commandant's wife and daughter went away. I followed Marya Ivanovna with my eyes; she looked back and nodded to me. Then Ivan Kuzmich turned to us, and fixed all his attention on the enemy. The rebels were gathering around their leader and suddenly began to dismount.

"Stand firm now," said the commandant. "There'll be an assault. . . ."

Just then a terrible shrieking and shouting rang out; the rebels were rushing towards the fortress. Our cannon was loaded with grapeshot. The commandant let them get as close as possible and suddenly fired again. The grapeshot struck right in the middle of their crowd. The rebels shied away on either side and fell back. Their leader was left alone out in front . . . He brandished his sword and seemed to be heatedly exhorting them . . . The shouting and shrieking, which had ceased for a moment, revived again at once.

"Now, lads," said the commandant, "open the gates, beat the drum. Forward, lads! Into the attack, follow me!"

The commandant, Ivan Ignatyich, and I instantly found ourselves outside the rampart; but the frightened soldiers did not budge.

"Why are you standing there, children?" Ivan Kuzmich shouted. "If we die, we die: it comes with the job!"

Just then the rebels overran us and burst into the fortress. The drumbeat stopped; the garrison dropped their guns; I was knocked off my feet, but I got up and entered the fortress along with the rebels. The commandant, wounded in the head, stood in a little knot of the villains, who were demanding the keys from him. I was just rushing to his aid when several stalwart Cossacks seized me and bound me with belts, repeating all the while: "Ah, you're going to get it for disobeying the sovereign!" They dragged us down the street; people were coming out of the houses with bread and salt.[24] Church bells rang. Suddenly someone in the crowd shouted that the sovereign was in the square, waiting for the prisoners and receiving oaths of allegiance. People thronged towards the square; we, too, were driven there.

Pugachev was sitting in an armchair on the porch of the commandant's house. He was wearing a red Cossack kaftan trimmed with galloons. A tall sable hat with gold tassels was pulled down to his flashing eyes. His face seemed familiar to me. Cossack chiefs surrounded him. Father Gerasim, pale and trembling, stood by the porch with a cross in his hands and seemed to be silently pleading with him for the soon-to-be victims. A gallows was being hastily set up on the square. When we came closer, the Bashkirs drove the people aside, and we were introduced to Pugachev. The bells stopped ringing; a deep silence ensued.

"Which is the commandant?" asked the impostor. Our sergeant stepped out of the crowd and pointed to Ivan Kuzmich. Pugachev looked menacingly at the old man and said to him:

"How dared you oppose me, your sovereign?"

The commandant, growing faint from his wound, gathered his last strength and replied in a firm voice:

"You are not my sovereign, you are a thief and an impostor, see here!"

Pugachev frowned darkly and waved a white handkerchief. Several Cossacks picked up the old captain and dragged him to the gallows. The mutilated Bashkir whom we had questioned the day before turned up sitting astride the crossbar. He held a rope in his hand, and a moment later I saw poor Ivan Kuzmich hoisted into the air. Then Ivan Ignatyich was brought before Pugachev.

"Swear allegiance," Pugachev said to him, "to the sovereign Pyotr Feodorovich!"[25]

"You're not our sovereign," Ivan Ignatyich answered, repeating his captain's words. "You, uncle, are a thief and an impostor!"

Pugachev waved his handkerchief again, and the good lieutenant hung beside his old superior.

It was my turn. I looked boldly at Pugachev, preparing to repeat the response of my noble-hearted comrades. Then, to my indescribable amazement, I saw Shvabrin among the rebel chiefs, his hair in a bowl cut and wearing a Cossack kaftan. He went up to Pugachev and said a few words in his ear.

"Hang him!" said Pugachev, without even glancing at me.

They threw the noose around my neck. I began to recite a prayer to myself, offering God sincere repentance for all my transgressions and asking for the salvation of all who were near to my heart. They dragged me under the gallows.

"Don't be afraid, don't be afraid," repeated my undoers, perhaps truly wishing to hearten me. Suddenly I heard a shout:

"Stop, you fiends, wait! . . ."

The executioners stopped. I looked: Savelyich was lying at Pugachev's feet.

"Dear father!" my poor tutor was saying. "What is the death of my master's child to you? Let him go; you'll get a ransom for him; and as an example and so as to put fear into people, have them hang my old self instead."

Pugachev gave a sign, and they unbound me at once and let me go.

"Our father pardons you," they said to me.

I cannot say that I was glad at that moment of my deliverance, though I also cannot say I regretted it. My feelings were too blurred. They brought me to the impostor again and made me go on my knees before him. Pugachev offered me his sinewy hand.

"Kiss his hand, kiss his hand!" said those around me. But I would have preferred the most cruel punishment to such base humiliation.

"Dearest Pyotr Andreich!" Savelyich whispered, standing behind me and prodding me. "Don't be stubborn! What is it to you? Spit on it and kiss the vill— . . . pfui! . . . kiss his hand."

I did not stir. Pugachev lowered his hand, saying with a little smirk:

"Seems his honor's stupefied with joy. Stand him up!"

They stood me up and set me free. I started watching the continuation of the gruesome comedy.

The inhabitants began to swear allegiance. They went up one after the other, kissed the crucifix, and then bowed to the impostor. The garrison soldiers stood there, too. The company tailor, armed with his dull scissors, cut off their queues. They shook themselves and went up to kiss the hand of Pugachev, who declared them pardoned and received them into his band. All this took about three hours. Finally Pugachev got up from his chair and came down from the porch, accompanied by his chiefs. A white horse adorned with rich harness was brought to him. Two Cossacks took him under the arms and seated him on the saddle. He told Father Gerasim that he would dine with him. Just then I heard a woman's shout. Several of the brigands dragged Vasilisa Egorovna out to the porch, disheveled and stripped naked. One of them had already managed to dress himself in her warm vest. Others were carrying featherbeds, trunks, tea sets, linen, and all sorts of chattels.

"My dear ones!" the poor old woman cried. "Let me go in peace. Kind people, take me to Ivan Kuzmich."

Suddenly she glanced at the gallows and recognized her husband.

"Villains!" she cried in frenzy. "What have you done to him? Light of my life, Ivan Kuzmich, my brave soldier! Neither Prussian bayonets nor Turkish bullets could touch you; you laid down your life not in fair combat, but undone by a runaway convict!"

"Silence the old witch!" said Pugachev.

Here a young Cossack struck her on the head with his sword, and she fell dead on the steps of the porch. Pugachev rode off; the people rushed after him.

CHAPTER EIGHT

An Uninvited Guest

> An uninvited guest is worse than a Tatar.
>
> PROVERB

The square was deserted. I went on standing in the same place and could not put my thoughts in order, confused as they were by such terrible impressions.

Uncertainty about the fate of Marya Ivanovna tormented me most of all. Where was she? What had happened to her? Had she had time to hide? Was her refuge safe? . . . Filled with anxious thoughts, I entered the commandant's house . . . It was devastated; the chairs, tables, trunks were all broken; the dishes were all smashed; everything was pulled apart. I ran up the little stairway that led to the upper chamber and for the first time in my life entered Marya Ivanovna's room. I saw her bed ransacked by the brigands; the wardrobe was broken and pillaged; a lamp still flickered before the empty icon stand. The little mirror on the wall between the windows was also intact . . . Where was the mistress of this humble maiden's cell? A terrible thought flashed through my mind: I pictured her in the hands of the brigands . . . My heart was wrung . . . I wept bitter, bitter tears and loudly uttered the name of my beloved . . . Just then I heard a slight rustle and Palasha appeared from behind the wardrobe, pale and trembling.

"Ah, Pyotr Andreich!" she said, clasping her hands. "What a day! What horrors! . . ."

"And Marya Ivanovna?" I asked impatiently. "What of Marya Ivanovna?"

"The young miss is alive," Palasha replied. "She's in hiding at Akulina Pamfilovna's."

"At the priest's!" I cried in horror. "My God! Pugachev's there! . . ."

I rushed out of the room, instantly found myself in the street, and ran headlong to the priest's house, seeing and feeling nothing. There was shouting, guffawing, and singing there . . . Pugachev was feasting with his comrades. Palasha came running after me. I sent her to call Akulina Pamfilovna out quietly. A moment later the priest's wife came out to me in the front hall with an empty bottle in her hand.

"For God's sake, where is Marya Ivanovna?" I asked with indescribable anxiety.

"She's lying in my bed, the little dove, there, behind the partition," the priest's wife replied. "Well, Pyotr Andreich, misfortune nearly befell us, but, thank God, it all turned out well: the villain had just sat down to dinner when the poor thing came to and moaned! . . . I nearly fainted away. He heard it: 'Who's that groaning there, old woman?' I bowed low to the thief: 'My niece, Your Majesty. She was taken ill; it's two weeks now she's been lying there.' 'Is your niece young?' 'Yes, Your Majesty.' 'Show me your niece, old woman.' My heart just sank, but there was nothing to be done. 'If you please, sir; only the girl can't get up and come to your honor.' 'Never mind, old woman, I'll go and look myself.' And he did, the fiend, he went behind the partition; and what do you think! He pulled the curtain aside, stared with his hawk's eyes!— and that's all . . . God spared us! Would you believe, right then my husband and I were ready for a martyr's death. Luckily, my little dove didn't recognize him. Lord God, what high days we've lived to see! I must say! Poor Ivan Kuzmich, who'd have imagined! . . . And Vasilisa Egorovna? And Ivan Ignatyich? What harm did he do? ... How is it you were spared? And what about this Shvabrin, Alexei Ivanyich? Got himself a bowl haircut and now he sits here feasting with them! A nimble one, I must say! And when I mentioned the sick niece, would you believe, he shot me a glance like the stab of a knife; didn't give me away, though, thanks be for that."

Just then we heard drunken shouts from the guests and the voice of Father Gerasim. The guests were demanding vodka, the host was calling for his wife. She got into a flurry.

"Go home, Pyotr Andreich," she said. "I can't stay with you now, the villains are carousing. It'll be bad if you fall into their drunken hands. Good-bye, Pyotr Andreich. What will be, will be; maybe God won't forsake us."

The priest's wife left. Somewhat reassured, I went back to my quarters. Walking past the square, I saw several Bashkirs crowding around the gallows and pulling the boots off the hanged men; I barely controlled a burst of indignation, sensing the uselessness of interference. The brigands ran all over the fortress, looting the officers' houses. The shouts of the drunken rebels could be heard everywhere. I reached home. Savelyich met me on the threshold.

"Thank God!" he cried on seeing me. "I was thinking the villains had got hold of you again. Well, my dear Pyotr Andreich, would you believe it? The rascals have robbed us of everything: clothes, linen, belongings, crockery—they left us nothing. But so what! Thank God they let you go alive! Did you recognize their leader, sir?"

"No, I didn't. Who is he?"

"What, my dearest? Have you forgotten that drunkard who wheedled the coat out of you at the inn? A hareskin coat, quite a new one; and the brute burst all the seams as he pulled it on!"

I was amazed. In fact, the resemblance between Pugachev and my guide was striking. I realized that he and Pugachev were one and the same person, and understood then the reason for the mercy he had shown me. I could only marvel at the strange chain of events: a child's coat given to a vagabond delivered me from the noose, and a drunkard roaming the wayside inns besieged fortresses and shook the state!

"Wouldn't you care to eat?" asked Savelyich, unchanged in his habits. "We've got nothing at home. I'll go rustle something up and prepare it for you."

Left alone, I became lost in ruminations. What was I to do? To remain in the fortress subject to the villain, or to follow his band, was unbecoming to an officer. Duty demanded that I go where my service could still be useful to the fatherland in the present difficult circumstances ... But love strongly advised me to stay by Marya Ivanovna and be her defender and protector. Though I foresaw a swift and sure change of circumstances, I still could not help but tremble, picturing the danger of her situation.

My ruminations were interrupted by the arrival of one of the Cossacks, who came running to announce that "the great sovereign summons you to him."

"Where is he?" I asked, preparing to obey.

"In the commandant's house," replied the Cossack. "After dinner, our good father went to the bathhouse, and now he's resting. Well, Your Honor, by all tokens, he's a distinguished person: at dinner he was pleased to eat two roasted suckling pigs, and he made the steam in the bath so hot that even Taras Kurochkin couldn't stand it, gave his whisk to Fomka Bikbaev, and barely revived under cold water. I tell you true: all his ways are so grand ... And they say in the bathhouse he showed the signs that he's a tsar on his chest: on one side a double-headed eagle as big as a five-kopeck piece, and on the other his own person."

I did not deem it necessary to dispute the Cossack's opinion and went with him to the commandant's house, imagining beforehand my meeting with Pugachev and trying to foresee how it would end. The reader may easily imagine that I was not entirely coolheaded.

It was getting dark when I came to the commandant's house. The gallows with its victims loomed black and dreadful. The body of the poor commandant's wife still lay at the foot of the porch, by which two Cossacks stood guard. The Cossack who brought me went to announce my arrival and, coming back at once, led me to the same room where, the day before, I had so tenderly bid farewell to Marya Ivanovna.

An extraordinary picture presented itself to me: at the table, covered with a tablecloth and set with bottles and glasses, Pugachev and some ten Cossack chiefs sat, wearing hats and bright-colored shirts, flushed with vodka, their mugs red and their eyes gleaming. Neither Shvabrin nor our sergeant, the newly recruited traitors, was among them.

"Ah, Your Honor!" said Pugachev on seeing me. "Welcome! Sit

yourself down, be my guest." His companions made room. I silently sat down at the edge of the table. My neighbor, a young Cossack, slender and handsome, poured me a glass of plain vodka, which I did not touch. I started examining the company with curiosity. Pugachev sat at the head, leaning his elbow on the table and propping his black beard with his broad fist. His features, regular and quite pleasant, did not betray any ferocity. He often turned to a man of about fifty, referring to him now as Count, now as Timofeich, and sometimes calling him "uncle." They all treated one another as comrades and showed no special preference for their leader. The conversation was about the morning's assault, the success of the rebellion, and future actions. Each man boasted, offered his opinions, and freely disputed with Pugachev. And it was at this strange military council that it was decided to march on Orenburg: a bold action, and one which was nearly crowned with calamitous success! The campaign was announced for the next day.

"Well, brothers," said Pugachev, "before we go to bed let's strike up my favorite song. Chumakov,[26] begin!"

In a high voice, my neighbor struck up a melancholy barge hauler's song, and they all joined in the chorus:

> Rustle not, leafy mother, forest green,
> Keep me not, a fine lad, from thinking my thoughts.
> Tomorrow, fine lad, I must go to be questioned
> Before the dread judge, the great tsar himself.
> And here is what the sovereign tsar will ask me:
> "Tell me, tell me, my stout peasant lad,
> With whom did you steal, with whom did you rob,
> And how many comrades went by your side?"
> "I will tell you, trusty Orthodox tsar,
> In all truth I will tell you, and in all verity,
> I had four comrades by my side:
> My first comrade was the pitch-dark night,
> My second comrade a knife of damask steel,
> For my third comrade I had my good steed,
> My fourth comrade was a taut-strung bow,
> And tempered steel arrows were my messengers."
> Then up speaks the trusty Orthodox tsar:
> "Praise to you, my stout peasant lad,
> That you know how to steal and how to reply!

For that, my stout fellow, I grant to you
A lofty mansion in the midst of the fields—
A pair of straight posts and a sturdy crossbeam."

It is impossible to describe the effect that this simple folk song about the gallows, sung by men destined for the gallows, had on me. Their stern faces, harmonious voices, the melancholy expression they gave to words that were expressive even without that—all of it shook me with a sort of poetic dread.

The guests drank one more glass, got up from the table, and took leave of Pugachev. I was going to follow them, but Pugachev said to me:

"Sit down; I want to talk to you."

We remained face-to-face.

Our mutual silence continued for several minutes. Pugachev looked at me intently, occasionally narrowing his left eye with an extraordinary expression of slyness and mockery. Finally he burst out laughing, and with such unfeigned gaiety that, looking at him, I, too, began to laugh, not knowing why myself.

"Well, Your Honor?" he said to me. "So you turned coward, admit it, when my lads put the rope around your neck? I bet your blood ran cold . . . And you'd be swinging from the crossbeam if it wasn't for your servant. I recognized the old geezer at once. Well, did it occur to you, Your Honor, that the man who led you to that inn was the great sovereign himself?" (Here he assumed an imposing and mysterious air.) "Your guilt before me is big," he went on, "but I had mercy on you for your goodness, because you did me a service when I was forced to hide from my foes. And you'll see more yet! I'll show you still more favor, when I come to rule my kingdom! Do you promise to serve me with zeal?"

The rascal's question and his brazenness seemed so amusing that I could not help smiling.

"What are you smiling at?" he asked me, frowning. "Or don't you believe I'm the great sovereign? Tell me straight."

I was perplexed. To acknowledge the vagabond as sovereign was impossible: it seemed inexcusably fainthearted to me. To call him a humbug to his face was to expose myself to destruction; and what I had been ready for under the gallows in the eyes of all the people and in the first heat of indignation, now seemed to me useless bravado. I hesitated. Pugachev grimly awaited my reply. Finally (and even now I remember this moment with self-satisfaction) the sense of duty won out in me over human weakness. I replied to Pugachev:

"Listen, I'll tell you the whole truth. Just consider, can I acknowledge you as my sovereign? You're a sensible man: you'd see yourself that I was being devious."

"Who am I then, to your mind?"

"God knows; but whoever you are, you're playing a dangerous game."

Pugachev gave me a quick glance.

"So you don't believe that I'm the sovereign Pyotr Fyodorovich?" he said. "Well, all right. But doesn't fortune favor the bold? Didn't Grishka Otrepev[27] reign in the old days? Think what you like of me, but stay by me. What do you care one way or the other? As I say, so I am. Serve me faithfully and truly, and I'll make you a field marshal and a prince. What do you think?"

"No," I replied firmly. "I was born a nobleman; I swore allegiance to our sovereign empress: I cannot serve you. If you really wish me well, let me go to Orenburg."

Pugachev reflected.

"And if I do," he said, "will you promise at least not to fight against me?"

"How can I promise you that?" I replied. "You know yourself that it's not up to me: if they order me to go against you, I'll go—there's nothing to be done. You're a commander now yourself; you demand obedience from your men. How would it look if I refused to serve when my service was needed? My life is in your hands: if you let me go, thank you; if you hang me, God be your judge; but I've told you the truth."

My frankness struck Pugachev.

"So be it," he said, slapping me on the shoulder. "If it's hanging, it's hanging; if it's pardon, it's pardon. Go where the wind blows you and do whatever you like. Tomorrow come and say good-bye to me, and now go to bed—I'm nodding off myself."

I left Pugachev and went out to the street. The night was calm and cold. The moon and stars shone brightly, illuminating the square and the gallows. In the fortress all was still and dark. Only in the pot-house was there light and one could hear the shouts of the belated revelers. I looked at the priest's house. The shutters and gates were closed. It seemed that all was quiet inside.

I came to my quarters and found Savelyich grief-stricken over my absence. The news of my freedom delighted him beyond words.

"Glory be to God!" he said, crossing himself. "At first light we'll leave the fortress and go wherever our feet take us. I've prepared you a little something; eat, dearest, and sleep till morning as in Christ's bosom."

I followed his advice and, having eaten supper with great appetite, fell asleep on the bare floor, mentally and physically exhausted.

CHAPTER NINE

Parting

> Sweet was the meeting of two hearts,
> Thine and mine, my lovely girl;
> Sad, how sad it is to part,
> As sad as parting with my soul.
>
> KHERASKOV[28]

Early in the morning I was awakened by the drumroll. I went to the place of assembly. There Pugachev's crowds were already lining up by the gallows, where yesterday's victims were still hanging. The Cossacks were on horseback, the soldiers under arms. Banners were flying. Several cannon, among which I recognized ours, were set up on mobile gun-carriages. All the inhabitants were there awaiting the impostor. By the porch of the commandant's house, a Cossack was holding a fine white Kirghiz horse by the bridle. I searched with my eyes for the body of the commandant's wife. It had been carried slightly to one side and covered with a bast mat. Finally Pugachev came out. The people took their hats off. Pugachev stopped on the porch and greeted them all. One of the chiefs gave him a sack of copper coins, and he started casting them around by the handful. With shouts, the people rushed to pick them up, and the matter did not end without serious injury.

Pugachev was surrounded by his chief confederates. Among them stood Shvabrin. Our eyes met; in mine he could read contempt, and he turned away with an expression of genuine malice and feigned mockery. Pugachev, seeing me in the crowd, nodded his head to me and called me to him.

"Listen," he said to me. "Go to Orenburg at once and tell the governor and all the generals from me to expect me there in a week. Advise them to meet me with childlike love and obedience; otherwise they will not escape a cruel death. Good journey, Your Honor!"

Then he turned to the people and said, pointing at Shvabrin:

"Here, dear children, is your new commander: obey him in all things; he is answerable to me for you and for the fortress."

I heard these words with horror: Shvabrin was made commander of the fortress; Marya Ivanovna remained in his power! My God, what would happen to her! Pugachev went down the steps. The horse was brought to him. He leaped nimbly into the saddle, without waiting for the Cossacks who wanted to help him up.

Just then I saw my Savelyich step out of the crowd, approach Pugachev, and hand him a sheet of paper. I could not imagine what it could be about.

"What is this?" Pugachev asked imposingly.

"Read it and you'll kindly see," replied Savelyich.

Pugachev took the paper and studied it for a long time with a significant air.

"What's this queer handwriting?" he said finally. "Our princely eyes can make nothing of it. Where is my head secretary?"

A young fellow in a corporal's uniform swiftly ran up to Pugachev.

"Read it aloud," said the impostor, handing him the paper. I was very curious to know what my tutor had decided to write to Pugachev about. The head secretary loudly began to recite the following:

"Two dressing gowns, one calico and the other of striped silk: six roubles."

"What does that mean?" said Pugachev, frowning.

"Order him to read further," Savelyich replied calmly.

The head secretary went on:

"A uniform jacket of fine green broadcloth: seven roubles.

"White broadcloth britches: five roubles.

"Twelve shirts of Dutch linen with cuffs: ten roubles.

"A cellaret with a tea service: two roubles fifty . . ."

"What's this blather?" Pugachev interrupted. "What have I got to do with cellarets and britches with cuffs?"

Savelyich cleared his throat and began to explain:

"This, my dear man, if you please, is a list of my master's possessions stolen by the villains . . ."

"What villains?" Pugachev asked menacingly.

"Sorry, it just slipped out," Savelyich replied. "Villains or not, your boys ransacked the place and took everything. Don't be angry: a horse has four legs and still he stumbles. Tell him to finish reading."

"Finish reading," said Pugachev. The secretary went on:

"A chintz blanket, another of taffeta lined with cotton: four roubles.

"A crimson ratteen coat lined with fox fur: forty roubles.

"Also the hareskin coat given to Your Grace at the inn: fifteen roubles."

"What's this now?" Pugachev shouted, flashing his fiery eyes.

I confess I was afraid for my poor tutor. He was about to launch into his explanations again, but Pugachev interrupted him:

"How dare you get at me with such nonsense?" he cried, snatching the paper from the secretary's hand and flinging it in Savelyich's face. "Stupid old man! You've been robbed: too bad! You old geezer, you ought to pray to God eternally for me and my boys: you and your master could be hanging here with the disobedient ones . . . A hareskin coat! I'll give you a hareskin coat! You know what, I'll skin you alive and have coats made out of your hide!"

"As you please," replied Savelyich, "but I'm a dependent man and must answer for my master's property."

Pugachev was obviously in a fit of magnanimity. He turned away and rode off without another word. Shvabrin and the Cossack chiefs followed him. The band left the fortress in orderly fashion. The people went to accompany Pugachev. I remained alone on the square with Savelyich. My tutor was holding his inventory and studying it with a look of deep regret.

Seeing I was on good terms with Pugachev, he had thought to make use of it, but this wise intention had not succeeded. I was about to chide him for his misplaced zeal, but could not help laughing.

"Laugh, sir," said Savelyich, "laugh; but when we have to set up your whole household again, we'll see how funny it is."

I hurried to the priest's house to see Marya Ivanovna. The priest's wife met me with sad news. During the night Marya Ivanovna had come down with a high fever. She lay unconscious and in delirium. The priest's wife led me to her room. I quietly approached her bed. The change in her face shocked me. The sick girl did not recognize me. I stood by her for a long time, listening neither to Father Gerasim nor to his good wife, who seemed to be comforting me. Dark thoughts troubled me. The plight of the poor, defenseless orphan, left among malicious rebels, as well as my own powerlessness, horrified me. Shvabrin, Shvabrin most of all, tormented my imagination. Invested with power by the impostor, put in command of the fortress, where the unfortunate girl, the innocent object of his hatred, remained, he could resolve on anything. What was I to do? How could I help her? How deliver her from the villain's hands? One means was left me: I decided to go at once to Orenburg, to hasten the deliverance of the Belogorsk fortress and contribute to it as much as possible. I took leave of the priest and Akulina Pamfilovna, ardently entrusting to them the one whom I already considered my wife. I took the poor girl's hand and kissed it, wetting it with my tears.

"Good-bye," the priest's wife said to me, "good-bye, Pyotr Andreich. Maybe we'll see each other in better times. Don't forget us and write to us often. Apart from you, poor Marya Ivanovna now has neither comfort nor protection."

Coming out to the square, I stopped for a moment, looked at the gallows, bowed to it, left the fortress, and went down the Orenburg road, accompanied by Savelyich, who never left my side.

I walked along, caught up in my reflections, when I suddenly heard the hoofbeats of a horse behind me. I turned to look; I saw a Cossack galloping from the fortress, holding a Bashkir horse by the bridle and gesturing to me from afar. I stopped and soon recognized our sergeant. Galloping up, he got off his horse and said, handing me the bridle of the other:

"Your Honor! Our father grants you a horse and the fur coat off his back" (a sheepskin coat was tied to the saddle). "And," the sergeant added, faltering, "he also grants you . . . fifty kopecks . . . only I lost them on the way. Have the goodness to forgive me."

Savelyich looked at him suspiciously and growled:

"Lost them on the way! And what's that jingling under your shirt? Shame on you!"

"What's jingling under my shirt?" the sergeant retorted, not embarrassed in the least. "God help you, good old man! It's the bridle, not the fifty kopecks."

"All right," I said, interrupting the argument. "Give my thanks to the one who sent you; as for the lost fifty kopecks, try to pick them up on the way back and treat yourself to some vodka."

"Many thanks, Your Honor," he replied, turning his horse around. "I'll forever pray to God for you."

With those words he galloped back, holding one hand to his shirt front, and in a moment he was out of sight.

I put the coat on and mounted up, seating Savelyich behind me.

"So you see, sir," said the old man, "it was not in vain that I gave the rascal my petition: the thief felt ashamed, though the lanky Bashkir nag and the sheepskin coat aren't worth a half of what the rascals stole from us and what you gave him yourself; still, it's something—a clump of fur from a vicious dog."

CHAPTER TEN

The Siege of the Town

> Invading fields and hills around,
> From high up, like an eagle, he surveyed the town.
> Behind the camp he built a wooden gun-cart and installed
> His thunderbolts within it, and by night came to the wall.
>
> KHERASKOV[29]

As we approached Orenburg, we saw a crowd of convicts with shaved heads, their faces disfigured by the executioner's pincers. They were working around the fortifications under the surveillance of the garrison veterans. Some were removing cartloads of the litter that filled the moat; others were digging the earth with spades; on the rampart masons were toting bricks and repairing the town wall. At the gate the sentries stopped us and demanded our passports. As soon as the sergeant heard that I was coming from the Belogorsk fortress, he led me straight to the general's house.

I found him in the garden. He was looking over the apple trees, bared by the breath of autumn, and, with the help of an old gardener, was carefully wrapping them in warm straw. His face was the picture of calm, health, and good nature. He was glad to see me and started questioning me about the terrible events I had witnessed. I told him everything. The old man listened to me attentively, and meanwhile kept cutting back the dead branches.

"Poor Mironov!" he said, when I finished my sad story. "I'm sorry for him: he was a good officer. And Madam Mironov was a kind lady and such an expert at pickling mushrooms! But what about Masha, the captain's daughter?"

I replied that she remained in the fortress, in the care of the priest's wife.

"Aie, aie, aie!" the general observed. "That's bad, very bad. There is no relying on the bandits' discipline. What will happen to the poor girl?"

I replied that the Belogorsk fortress was not far away and that his excellency would probably not be slow in sending an army to free its poor inhabitants. The general shook his head with a doubtful air.

"We'll see, we'll see," he said. "We still have time to discuss that. Allow me to invite you for a cup of tea: there will be a council of war today at my place. You can give us reliable information about this worthless Pugachev and his troops. In the meantime go and get some rest."

I went to the quarters assigned to me, where Savelyich was already settling in, and began to wait impatiently for the appointed time. The reader will easily imagine that I did not fail to show up at a council that was to have such influence upon my fate. At the appointed hour I was already at the general's.

I found there one of the town officials, the director of customs, as I recall, a fat and ruddy-cheeked old man in a brocade kaftan. He started questioning me about the fate of Ivan Kuzmich, whom he called a family friend, and often interrupted my speech with additional questions and moralizing observations, which, if they did not show him to be a man well-versed in the military art, at least revealed his keen wit and innate intelligence. Meanwhile all the other invitees gathered. Among them, apart from the general himself, there was not a single military man. When they had all been seated and served a cup of tea, the general explained, very clearly and extensively, how things stood.

"Now, gentlemen," he went on, "we must decide how to act against the rebels: *offensively* or *defensively*. Each of these methods has its advantages and its disadvantages. Offensive action offers greater hopes for the speedy destruction of the enemy; defensive action is more trustworthy and safe . . . And so, let us put it to a vote in lawful order, that is, beginning with the lowest in rank. Mr. Lieutenant!" he went on, turning to me. "Kindly give us your opinion."

I rose and, first briefly describing Pugachev and his band, stated positively that there was no way the impostor could stand up against regular arms.

My opinion was met by the officials with obvious disapproval. They saw in it the recklessness and boldness of a young man. Murmuring arose, and I clearly heard the word "greenhorn" uttered by someone in a low voice. The general turned to me and said with a smile:

"Mr. Lieutenant, the first votes at military councils are usually given in favor of offensive action; that is in the order of things. We will now continue with the voting. Mr. Collegiate Councilor,[30] tell us your opinion!"

The little old man in the brocade kaftan hastily finished his third cup of tea, liberally laced with rum, and answered the general:

"I think, Your Excellency, that we should act neither offensively nor defensively."

"How's that, Mr. Collegiate Councilor?" the amazed general rejoined. "Tactics offer no other way: either offensive action or defensive . . ."

"Your Excellency, act corruptively."

"Heh-heh-heh! Your opinion is quite sensible. Tactics allow for corruptive actions, and we will make use of your advice. We could promise . . . maybe seventy roubles for the worthless fellow's head . . . or even a hundred . . . from a special fund . . ."

"And then," the director of customs interrupted, "I'm a Kirghiz sheep and no collegiate councilor if these thieves don't give up their leader to us, bound hand and foot in irons."

"We'll think about it and discuss it further," the general replied. "However, we ought in any case to take military measures as well. Gentlemen, give us your votes in due order."

All the opinions turned out to be opposed to mine. All the officials spoke of the unreliability of the troops, of the uncertainty of success, of prudence and the like. They all thought it more sensible to stay under cover of the cannon, behind strong stone walls, than to try the fortune of arms in the open field. Finally the general, having listened to all the opinions, knocked the ashes from his pipe and delivered the following speech:

"My dear sirs! I must declare to you that I, for my part, agree completely with the opinion of Mr. Lieutenant: for that opinion is based on all the rules of sound tactics, which almost always prefer the offensive actions to the defensive actions."

Here he paused and began to fill his pipe. My vanity was triumphant. I cast a proud glance at the officials, who exchanged whispers among themselves with an air of displeasure and uneasiness.

"But, my dear sirs," he went on, letting out, along with a deep sigh, a dense stream of tobacco smoke, "I dare not take upon myself so great a responsibility, when it comes to the safety of the provinces entrusted to me by her imperial majesty, my most sovereign lady. And so I agree with the majority of voices, which have decided that it is most sensible and safe to await the siege within the town, and to repel the enemy's assaults by force of artillery and (if it proves possible) by sorties."

The officials in their turn glanced mockingly at me. The council broke up. I could not help regretting the weakness of the venerable soldier, who, contrary to his own conviction, decided to follow the opinions of uninformed and inexperienced people.

Several days after this illustrious council, we learned that Pugachev, faithful to his promise, was approaching Orenburg. I saw the rebel army from the height of the town wall. It seemed to me that their number had increased tenfold since the time of the last assault, of which I had been a witness. They had artillery with them, taken by Pugachev from the small fortresses he had already subjugated. Recalling the council's decision, I foresaw a long confinement within the walls of Orenburg and all but wept with vexation.

I will not describe the Orenburg siege, which belongs to history and not to family memoirs. I will say briefly that, owing to the imprudence of the local authorities, this siege was disastrous for the inhabitants, who suffered hunger and all possible distress. It can easily be imagined that life in Orenburg was utterly unbearable. Everyone waited dejectedly for their fate to be decided; everyone groaned about the high prices, which indeed were terrible. The inhabitants got used to cannonballs flying into their courtyards; even Pugachev's assaults no longer attracted general curiosity. I was dying of boredom. Time was passing. I received no letters from the Belogorsk fortress. All the roads were cut off. Separation from Marya Ivanovna became intolerable for me. Ignorance of her fate tormented me. My only diversion consisted in mounted sorties. Thanks to Pugachev, I had a good horse, with which I shared my scanty food and on which I rode out of town daily to exchange fire with Pugachev's horsemen. In these skirmishes the odds were usually on the side of the villains, who were well fed, well drunk, and well mounted. The scrawny town cavalry could not overcome them. Occasionally our hungry infantry also took the field; but the deep snow prevented it from acting successfully against the scattered horsemen. The artillery thundered futilely from the high rampart, and in the field it got mired down and was unable to move because the horses were exhausted. Such was the mode of our military action! And this was what the Orenburg officials called prudence and good sense!

Once, when we somehow managed to break up and drive back a rather dense crowd, I ran into a Cossack who had lagged behind his comrades; I was about to strike him with my Turkish saber when he suddenly took off his hat and shouted:

"Hello, Pyotr Andreich! How's God treating you?"

I looked and recognized our sergeant. I was inexpressibly glad to see him.

"Hello, Maximych," I said to him. "Have you been away from the Belogorsk fortress for long?"

"Not long, dear Pyotr Andreich; I went back just yesterday. I've got a little letter for you."

"Where is it?" I cried, flushing all over.

"With me," replied Maximych, putting his hand under his shirt. "I promised Palasha I'd deliver it to you somehow." Here he handed me a folded piece of paper and galloped off at once. I unfolded it and with trembling read the following lines:

It pleased God to deprive me suddenly of my father and mother: I have no family or protectors on earth. I turn to you, knowing that you always wished me well and that you are ready to help any person. I pray to God that this letter somehow reaches you! Maximych has promised to deliver it. Also Palasha has heard from Maximych that he frequently sees you from a distance on sorties, and that you show no regard for yourself at all and do not think of those who pray to God for you in tears. I was sick for a long time; and when I got well, Alexei Ivanovich, who is in command here in place of my late father, forced Father Gerasim to hand me over to him for fear of Pugachev. I live in our house under guard. Alexei Ivanovich is forcing me to marry him. He says he saved my life, because he concealed Akulina Pamfilovna's deception in telling the villains I was her niece. For me it would be easier to die than to become the wife of a man like Alexei Ivanovich. He treats me with great cruelty and threatens that if I don't change my mind and consent, he'll take me to the villains' camp and it will be the same for me as it was for Lizaveta Kharlova.[31] I begged Alexei Ivanovich to let me think it over. He agreed to wait three more days. If I don't marry him in three days, there will be no mercy. Dearest Pyotr Andreevich, you are the only protector I have! Intercede for a poor girl! Persuade the general and all the commanders to send us help quickly, and come yourself, if you can. I remain obediently yours,

The poor orphan, Marya Mironova.

After reading this letter, I nearly lost my mind. I started back to town, mercilessly spurring on my poor horse. As I rode I kept thinking over one way or another to rescue the poor girl and could not come up with anything. Galloping into town, I went straight to the general's and burst into his room.

The general was pacing up and down, smoking his meerschaum pipe. Seeing me, he stopped. My look probably struck him; he inquired solicitously about the cause of my hasty arrival.

"Your Excellency," I said to him, "I come to you as to my own father; for God's sake don't deny me my request: it's a matter of the happiness of my whole life."

"What is it, dear boy?" asked the astonished old man. "What can I do for you? Tell me."

"Your Excellency, order me to take a company of soldiers and some fifty Cossacks and let me clear out the Belogorsk fortress."

The general looked at me intently, probably thinking I had lost my mind (in which he was not far wrong).

"How's that? Clear out the Belogorsk fortress?" he said finally.

"I guarantee success," I replied vehemently. "Just let me go."

"No, young man," he said, shaking his head. "At such a great distance the enemy will easily cut you off from communications with the main strategic point and obtain a complete victory over you. The suppression of communications . . ."

I got frightened, seeing him going off into military explanations, and hastened to interrupt him.

"Captain Mironov's daughter," I said to him, "has written me a letter: she asks for help; Shvabrin is forcing her to marry him."

"Really? Oh, that Shvabrin is a great *Schelm*,* and if I get hold of him, I'll order him court-martialed within twenty-four hours, and we'll shoot him on the parapet of the fortress! But meanwhile we must take patience . . ."

"Take patience!" I shouted, beside myself. "And meanwhile he'll marry Marya Ivanovna! . . ."

"Oh!" objected the general. "That's not so bad: it's better for her to be Shvabrin's wife for a while: he can protect her now; and once we've shot him, then, God willing, she'll find some little suitors for herself. Pretty widows don't stay old maids for long—that is, I mean to say, a pretty widow will find herself a husband sooner than a maiden."

"I'd sooner agree to die," I said in a fury, "than yield her up to Shvabrin!"

"Oh, ho, ho, ho!" the old man said. "Now I see: you're obviously in love with Marya Ivanovna. Oh, that's a different matter! Poor fellow! But all the same I can't give you a company of soldiers and fifty Cossacks. Such an expedition would be unreasonable; I cannot take responsibility for it."

I hung my head; despair overcame me. Suddenly a thought flashed through my mind: what it was, the reader will see in the next chapter, as old-fashioned novelists say.

* rogue (German)

CHAPTER ELEVEN

The Rebel Camp

The lion, though fierce by nature, was not hungry then.
"Pray tell me why this sudden visit to my den?"
He gently asked.

A. SUMAROKOV[32]

I left the general and hastened to my quarters. Savelyich met me with his usual admonitions.

"What makes you so eager, sir, to deal with these drunken brigands? Is it fit for a gentleman? Luck is fickle: you may perish for nothing. It would be one thing if it was against the Turks or the Swedes, but it's sinful even to say who they are."

I interrupted him with a question: How much money did I have all told?

"Enough for you," he replied with a pleased look. "Much as the rascals rummaged around, I still managed to hide it." And with those words he pulled from his pocket a long knitted purse full of silver coins.

"Well, Savelyich," I said to him, "give me half of it now, and take the rest yourself. I'm going to the Belogorsk fortress."

"Dearest Pyotr Andreich!" my good tutor said in a trembling voice. "Fear God: how can you take to the road in such times, when there's no getting anywhere on account of the rogues? Have pity on your parents at least, if you have none on yourself. Where are you going? Why? Wait a little: the army will come, they'll catch all the rascals; then go where the wind blows you."

But my decision was firmly taken.

"It's too late to discuss it," I replied to the old man. "I must go, I can't not go. Don't grieve, Savelyich: God is merciful; maybe we'll see each other again! Look, just don't be ashamed and don't scrimp. Buy whatever you may need, even at triple the price. I'm giving you this money. If I'm not back in three days . . ."

"What are you saying, sir?" Savelyich interrupted me. "As if I'd let you go alone! Don't even dream of asking! If you're determined to go, I'll follow after you even on foot, but I won't abandon you. As if I'd stay sitting behind a stone wall without you! Do you think I've lost my mind? As you please, sir, I won't stay here without you."

I knew there was no point in arguing with Savelyich, and I allowed him to prepare for the journey. Half an hour later I mounted my fine horse, and Savelyich a skinny and lame nag given him by one of the inhabitants, who lacked the means to go on feeding it. We rode up to the town gates; the sentries let us through; we rode out of Orenburg.

Darkness was falling. My way led past the village of Berda, Pugachev's camp. The straight road was covered with snow; but horse tracks could be seen all over the steppe, renewed daily. I rode at a long trot. Savelyich was barely able to follow my pace and kept shouting to me:

"Slow down, sir, for God's sake, slow down! My cursed nag can't keep up with your long-legged demon. Where are you hurrying to? A feast would be one thing, but this is more likely under the axe, for all I know . . . Pyotr Andreich . . . dearest Pyotr Andreich! . . . Don't do us in! . . . Lord God, the master's child will perish!"

Soon the lights of Berda began to glimmer. We approached the ravines, the natural fortifications of the village. Savelyich did not lag behind me, nor did he break off his pitiful entreaties. I was hoping to skirt the village successfully, when suddenly I saw right in front of me in the dark some five muzhiks armed with cudgels: this was the advance guard of Pugachev's camp. They called to us. Not knowing the password, I wanted to ride past them in silence; but they immediately surrounded me, and one of them seized my horse by the bridle. I drew my sword and struck the muzhik on the head; his hat saved him, but he staggered and let go of the bridle. The others panicked and fled; I took advantage of the moment, spurred my horse, and galloped on.

The darkness of the approaching night could have saved me from any danger, but suddenly, looking back, I saw that Savelyich was not with me. The poor old man on his lame horse had not escaped the brigands. What was I to do? After waiting a few minutes for him and making sure that he had been detained, I turned my horse around and went to rescue him.

Approaching the ravine, I heard noise, shouting, and the voice of my Savelyich in the distance. I speeded up and soon was back among the muzhik guards who had stopped me a few minutes earlier. Savelyich was among them. They had dragged the old man off his nag and were preparing to bind him. My arrival heartened them. They fell upon me with shouts and instantly dragged me off my horse. One of them, apparently the chief, told us that he would now take us to the sovereign.

"And it's as our dear father wills," he added, "whether we hang you now or wait till daybreak."

I did not resist; Savelyich followed my example, and the guards led us away in triumph.

We crossed the ravine and entered the village. Lights were burning in all the cottages. Noise and shouts rang out everywhere. In the street I met many people; but in the dark no one noticed us or recognized me as an Orenburg officer. We were brought straight to a cottage that stood at the corner of an intersection. By the gate stood several wine casks and two cannons.

"Here's the palace," said one of the muzhiks. "We'll announce you at once."

He went into the cottage. I glanced at Savelyich; the old man was crossing himself, silently reciting a prayer. I waited for a long time; finally the muzhik came back and said to me:

"Go in: our dear father orders the officer to be admitted."

I went into the cottage—or palace, as the muzhiks called it. It was lit by two tallow candles, and the walls were pasted over with gold paper; however, the benches, the table, the wash pot on a cord, the towel on a nail, the oven fork in the corner, and the wide hearth covered with pots—all of it was as in any ordinary cottage. Pugachev was sitting under the icons[33] in a red kaftan and a tall hat, his arms imposingly akimbo. Around him stood several of his chief comrades, with an air of feigned obsequiousness. It was clear that the news of the arrival of an officer from Orenburg had aroused strong curiosity in the rebels, and they had prepared to meet me with ceremony. Pugachev recognized me at first glance. His pretended importance suddenly vanished.

"Ah, Your Honor!" he said with animation. "How are you doing? What brings you here?"

I told him that I was going about my own business and that his people had stopped me.

"On what sort of business?" he asked.

I did not know how to reply. Pugachev, supposing that I did not want to explain myself in front of witnesses, turned to his comrades and ordered them to leave. They all obeyed except for two, who did not budge.

"Talk freely in front of them," said Pugachev. "I don't hide anything from them."

I cast a sidelong glance at the impostor's confidants. One of them, a frail and bent old man with a gray little beard, had nothing remarkable about him, except for a blue ribbon worn over the shoulder of his gray peasant coat.[34] But I will never forget his comrade. He was tall, burly, and broad-shouldered, and looked to be about forty-five. A thick red beard, flashing gray eyes, a nose without nostrils, and reddish spots on his forehead and cheeks gave his broad, pockmarked face an indescribable expression. He was wearing a red shirt, a Kirghiz robe, and Cossack balloon trousers. The first (as I learned later) was the fugitive Corporal Beloborodov; the second—Afanasy Sokolov (nicknamed Khlopusha), an exiled convict, who had escaped three times from the Siberian mines. Despite the feelings that troubled me exclusively, the company in which I so unexpectedly found myself greatly aroused my imagination. But Pugachev brought me back to myself by his question:

"Speak: On what sort of business did you leave Orenburg?"

A strange thought occurred to me: it seemed to me that Providence, which had brought me to Pugachev a second time, was giving me the chance to carry out my intention. I decided to take advantage of it and, having no time to think over what I decided, I answered Pugachev's question:

"I was going to the Belogorsk fortress to rescue an orphan who is being mistreated there."

Pugachev's eyes flashed.

"Who of my people dares to mistreat an orphan?" he cried. "Though he be sly as a fox, he won't escape my justice. Speak: Who is the guilty one?"

"Shvabrin," I replied. "He's holding captive the girl you saw sick at the priest's wife's and wants to force her to marry him."

"I'll teach Shvabrin," Pugachev said menacingly. "He'll learn from me what it means to do as he likes and mistreat people. I'll hang him."

"Allow me to put in a word," said Khlopusha in a hoarse voice. "You were in a hurry to appoint Shvabrin commandant of the fortress, and now you're in a hurry to hang him. You've already offended the Cossacks by setting up a nobleman as their superior; don't frighten the nobility now by executing them at the first bit of slander."

"There's no cause to pity them or approve of them," said the little old man with the blue ribbon. "Nothing's wrong with executing Shvabrin; but it wouldn't be bad to give Mister Officer here a proper questioning as to why he was pleased to come calling. If he doesn't recognize you as the sovereign, he needn't look to you for your justice, and if he does, why has he sat there in Orenburg with your enemies up to now? Why don't you order him taken to the guardhouse and have them start a little fire there: something tells me his honor's been sent to us by the Orenburg commanders."

I found the old villain's logic quite persuasive. Chills came over me at the thought of whose hands I was in. Pugachev noticed my confusion.

"Eh, Your Honor?" he said, winking at me. "My field marshal seems to be talking sense. What do you think?"

Pugachev's mockery restored my courage. I replied calmly that I was in his power and he was free to do whatever he liked with me.

"Fine," said Pugachev. "Now tell me, what shape is your town in?"

"Thank God," I replied, "everything's quite well."

"Quite well?" Pugachev repeated. "But people are dying of hunger!"

The impostor was telling the truth; but, being duty-bound, I began to assure him that these were all empty rumors and there was enough of all sorts of supplies in Orenburg.

"You see," the little old man broke in, "he lies to you right in your face. All the fugitives testify as one that there's starvation and pestilence in Orenburg, that they eat carrion and are happy to have that; and his honor assures us there's plenty of everything. If you want to hang Shvabrin, hang this fine fellow from the same gallows, so there's no bad feelings."

The cursed old man's words seemed to make Pugachev hesitate. Luckily, Khlopusha began to contradict his comrade.

"Enough, Naumych," he said to him. "With you it's all strangling and stabbing. What kind of mighty man are you? By the look of it, you can barely keep body and soul together. You're staring into the grave yourself, and you destroy others. Isn't there enough blood on your conscience?"

"And what sort of saint are you?" Beloborodov retorted. "Where did you suddenly get this pity?"

"Of course," replied Khlopusha, "I'm sinful, too, and this right arm" (here he clenched his bony fist and, pushing up his sleeve, bared his shaggy arm), "and this right arm is guilty of shedding Christian blood. But I killed my enemy, not my guest; at open crossroads and in the dark forest, not at home, sitting warm and cozy; with a bludgeon and an axe, not with womanish slander."

The old man turned away and muttered the words: "Torn nostrils! . . ."

"What's that you're whispering, you old geezer?" cried Khlopusha. "I'll show you torn nostrils; just wait, your time will come; God grant, you'll get a taste of the pincers yourself . . . And meanwhile watch out or I'll tear your little beard off!"

"Gentlemen yennerals!" Pugachev intoned solemnly. "Enough of your quarreling. There's nothing wrong if all the Orenburg dogs jerk their legs under the same crossbeam; it is wrong if our own start snapping at each other. Make peace now."

Khlopusha and Beloborodov did not say a word and looked darkly at each other. I saw it was necessary to change the conversation, which could have ended very unprofitably for me, and, turning to Pugachev, I told him with a cheerful air:

"Ah! I almost forgot to thank you for the horse and the coat. Without you I wouldn't have made it to the town and would have frozen on the way."

My ruse worked. Pugachev cheered up.

"One good turn deserves another," he said, winking and narrowing his eyes. "Tell me now, what have you got to do with the girl Shvabrin's mistreating? Not the darling of a young lad's heart, is she?"

"She's my bride-to-be," I replied to Pugachev, seeing the weather change for the better and finding no need to conceal the truth.

"Your bride-to-be!" cried Pugachev. "Why didn't you say so before? We'll get you married and feast at your wedding!" Then, turning to Beloborodov: "Listen, Field Marshal! His honor and I are old friends; let's sit down and have supper; morning's wiser than evening. Tomorrow we'll see what we'll do with him."

I would have been glad to decline the proposed honor, but there was no help for it. Two young Cossack women, the daughters of the cottage's owner, covered the table with a white tablecloth, brought some bread, fish soup, and several bottles of vodka and beer, and for the second time I found myself sharing a meal with Pugachev and his frightful comrades.

The orgy of which I was an involuntary witness lasted till late in the night. Finally drunkenness began to get the better of the company. Pugachev dozed off where he sat; his comrades stood up and gave me a sign to leave him. I went out together with them. On Khlopusha's orders, a Cossack led me to the guardhouse, where I found Savelyich and where we were locked up together. My tutor was so amazed at the sight of all that was going on that he did not ask me any questions. He lay down in the dark and sighed and groaned for a long time; finally he started snoring, and I gave myself up to reflections that did not allow me to doze off for a single moment all night.

In the morning Pugachev sent for me. I went to him. By his gate stood a kibitka hitched to a troika of Tatar horses. People crowded the street. In the entryway I ran into Pugachev: he was dressed for the road, in a fur coat and a Kirghiz hat. Yesterday's companions surrounded him, assuming an air of obsequiousness that sharply contradicted everything I had witnessed the evening before. Pugachev greeted me cheerfully and ordered me to get into the kibitka with him.

We took our seats.

"To the Belogorsk fortress!" Pugachev said to the broad-shouldered Tatar, who drove the troika standing up. My heart beat fast. The horses started, the bell jingled, the kibitka flew off . . .

"Stop! Stop!" called out a voice all too familiar to me, and I saw Savelyich running towards us. Pugachev gave the order to stop. "Dearest Pyotr Andreich!" my tutor shouted. "Don't abandon me in my old age among these rasc—"

"Ah, the old geezer!" Pugachev said to him. "So God's brought us together again. Well, get up on the box."

"Thank you, good sir, thank you, dear father!" Savelyich said, seating himself. "God grant you prosper a hundred years for minding and comforting an old man like me. I'll pray to God for you all my days, and won't even mention the hareskin coat."

This hareskin coat could finally have made Pugachev downright angry. Luckily, the impostor either did not hear or ignored the awkward hint. The horses galloped off; people in the street stopped and bowed low. Pugachev nodded his head to both sides. A moment later we were outside the village and racing down a smooth road.

It can easily be imagined what I was feeling at that moment. In a few hours I was going to see the one whom I had already considered lost for me. I pictured the moment of our reunion . . . I also thought about the man who had my destiny in his hands and who by a strange concurrence of circumstances was mysteriously connected with me. I recalled the impulsive cruelty, the bloodthirsty habits, of the one who had volunteered to deliver my beloved! Pugachev did not know she was Captain Mironov's daughter; the malicious Shvabrin might reveal everything to him; Pugachev might find out the truth in some other way . . . Then what would become of Marya Ivanovna? Chills came over me, and my hair stood on end . . .

Suddenly Pugachev interrupted my reflections, turning to me with a question:

"What might you be thinking about, Your Honor?"

"How can I not be thinking?" I replied. "I'm an officer and a gentleman; just yesterday I was fighting against you, and today I'm riding with you in the same kibitka, and the happiness of my whole life depends on you."

"What, then?" asked Pugachev. "Are you afraid?"

I replied that, having been spared by him once already, I hoped not only for his mercy, but even for his help.

"And you're right, by God, you're right!" said the impostor. "You saw that my boys looked askance at you; and today, too, the old man insisted that you're a spy and that you should be tortured and hanged; but I didn't agree," he added, lowering his voice, so that Savelyich and the Tatar could not hear him, "remembering the glass of vodka and the hareskin coat. You see, I'm not as bloodthirsty as your fellows say I am."

I recalled the taking of the Belogorsk fortress; but I did not consider it necessary to contradict him and said nothing in reply.

"What do they say about me in Orenburg?" Pugachev asked after some silence.

"They say it's pretty hard dealing with you; there's no denying you've made yourself felt."

The impostor's face expressed satisfied vanity.

"Yes!" he said with a cheerful air. "At fighting I'm as good as they come. Do your people in Orenburg know about the battle of Yuzeevo?[35] Forty yennerals killed, four armies taken captive. What do you think: could the king of Prussia vie with me?"

I found the brigand's boasting amusing.

"What do you think yourself?" I said to him. "Could you handle Frederick?"[36]

"Fyodor Fyodorovich? Why not? I've handled your yennerals all right, and they beat him. So far my arms have been lucky. Wait and see, there'll be more still, when I march on Moscow."

"So you suppose you'll march on Moscow?"

The impostor thought a little and said in a low voice:

"God knows. My street's narrow; I've got little freedom. My boys play it too smart. They're thieves. I have to keep my ears pricked up; at the first setback they'll save their necks with my head."

"So there!" I said to Pugachev. "Wouldn't it be better for you to break with them yourself, in good time, and throw yourself on the empress's mercy?"

Pugachev smiled bitterly.

"No," he replied, "it's too late for me to repent. There will be no pardon for me. I'll keep on as I started. Who knows? Maybe I'll bring it off! After all, Grishka Otrepev did reign over Moscow."

"And do you know how he ended? They threw him out the window, slaughtered him, burned him, loaded a cannon with his ashes, and fired it off!"

"Listen," said Pugachev with a sort of wild inspiration. "I'll tell you a tale that I heard as a child from an old Kalmyk woman. Once an eagle asked a raven: 'Tell me, raven-bird, why do you live three hundred years in the wide world, and I all in all only thirty-three?' 'Because, my dear friend,' the raven answered him, 'you drink living blood, while I feed on dead meat.' The eagle thought: 'Let's us try feeding on the same.' Good. So the eagle and the raven flew off. They saw a dead horse; they flew down and alighted. The raven started pecking and praising. The eagle pecked once, pecked twice, waved his wing, and said to the raven: 'No, brother raven, rather than feed on carrion for three hundred years, it's better to drink living blood once, and then take what God sends!' How's that for a Kalmyk tale?"

"Ingenious," I replied. "But to live by murder and robbery for me means to peck at dead meat."

Pugachev looked at me in surprise and made no reply. We both fell silent, each immersed in his own reflections. The Tatar struck up a mournful song; Savelyich, dozing, swayed on the box. The kibitka flew down the smooth winter road . . . Suddenly I saw a hamlet on the steep bank of the Yaik, with a palisade and a belfry—and a quarter of an hour later we drove into the Belogorsk fortress.

CHAPTER TWELVE

The Orphan

> Our pretty little apple tree
> Has no branches and no crown;
> Our pretty little princess-bride
> Has no father and no mother.
> There is nobody to dress her,
> There is nobody to bless her.
>
> WEDDING SONG

The kibitka drove up to the porch of the commandant's house. The people recognized Pugachev's harness bell and ran thronging after him. Shvabrin met the impostor on the porch. He was dressed as a Cossack and had let his beard grow. The traitor helped Pugachev out of the kibitka, expressing his joy and zeal in abject phrases. Seeing me, he was perplexed, but quickly recovered and gave me his hand, saying:

"So you're one of us? None too soon!"

I turned away from him and made no reply.

My heart was wrung when we found ourselves in the long-familiar room, where the late commandant's diploma still hung on the wall as a sorrowful epitaph of past times. Pugachev sat down on the same sofa on which Ivan Kuzmich used to doze, lulled by the grumbling of his spouse. Shvabrin himself served him vodka. Pugachev drank off the glass and said to him, pointing at me:

"Offer some to his honor."

Shvabrin came up to me with his tray; but I turned away from him for the second time. He seemed not himself. With his usual sharpness he had, of course, realized that Pugachev was displeased with him. He was afraid of him and kept glancing at me suspiciously. Pugachev inquired about the condition of the fortress, the rumors about the enemy army, and so on, and suddenly asked him unexpectedly:

"Tell me, brother, who is this girl you're keeping here under guard? Show her to me."

Shvabrin turned deathly pale.

"My sovereign," he said in a trembling voice, "my sovereign, she's not under guard . . . She's ill . . . lying in her room."

"Take me to her," said the impostor, standing up. It was impossible to get out of it. Shvabrin led Pugachev to Marya Ivanovna's room. I followed them.

Shvabrin stopped on the stairs.

"My sovereign!" he said. "It is in your power to ask anything you like from me; but do not allow a stranger to enter my wife's bedroom."

I shuddered.

"So you're married!" I said to Shvabrin, ready to tear him to pieces.

"Quiet!" Pugachev interrupted. "This is my business. And you," he went on, turning to Shvabrin, "stop being clever and making difficulties: wife or not, I'll take anyone I want to her. Follow me, Your Honor."

At the door of the bedroom Shvabrin stopped again and said in a faltering voice:

"My sovereign, I warn you that she's delirious and has been raving these past three days."

"Open up!" said Pugachev.

Shvabrin started searching in his pockets and said he had not taken the key with him. Pugachev shoved the door with his foot; the latch tore loose; the door opened and we went in.

I looked and my heart sank. On the floor, in a ragged peasant dress, sat Marya Ivanovna, pale, thin, with disheveled hair. Before her stood a jug of water covered with a hunk of bread. Seeing me, she gave a start and cried out. What I felt then—I don't remember.

Pugachev looked at Shvabrin and said with a wry grin:

"A nice sick ward you've got here!" Then, going to Marya Ivanovna: "Tell me, dear heart, what is your husband punishing you for? What wrong have you done him?"

"My husband!" she repeated. "He is not my husband. I will never be his wife! I'd rather die, and I will die, if nobody saves me."

Pugachev cast a terrible glance at Shvabrin.

"So you dared to deceive me!" he said to him. "Do you know, wastrel, what you deserve for that?"

Shvabrin fell on his knees . . . At that moment contempt stifled all feelings of hatred and wrath in me. I looked with loathing at a nobleman lying at the feet of a fugitive Cossack. Pugachev softened.

"I'll pardon you this time," he said to Shvabrin, "but know that if you make another slip, I'll also remember this one."

Then he turned to Marya Ivanovna and said to her gently:

"Go, fair maiden; I grant you freedom. I am the sovereign."

Marya Ivanovna glanced quickly at him and realized that before her was her parents' murderer. She covered her face with both hands and fainted. I rushed to her, but just then my old acquaintance Palasha quite boldly thrust herself into the room and started looking after her young mistress. Pugachev left the bedroom, and the three of us went down to the drawing room.

"So, Your Honor?" Pugachev said, laughing. "We've rescued the fair maiden! What do you think, shall we send for the priest and have him marry off his niece? If you like, I'll be the bride's proxy father and Shvabrin the best man; we'll feast, we'll revel—and send the rest to the devil!"

What I feared was what happened. Hearing Pugachev's suggestion, Shvabrin lost all control.

"My sovereign!" he cried in a frenzy. "I'm guilty, I lied to you; but Grinyov has also deceived you. This girl is not the local priest's niece: she's the daughter of Ivan Mironov, who was executed when the fortress was taken."

Pugachev fixed his fiery eyes on me.

"What's this now?" he asked, bewildered.

"Shvabrin is telling the truth," I replied firmly.

"You didn't tell me that," remarked Pugachev, whose face darkened.

"Judge for yourself," I replied. "Was it possible to announce in front of your people that Mironov's daughter was alive? They'd have chewed her to pieces. Nothing could have saved her!"

"True enough," said Pugachev, laughing. "My drunkards wouldn't have spared the poor girl. The priest's good wife did well to deceive them."

"Listen," I said, seeing his good humor. "I don't know what to call you, and I don't want to know . . . But, as God is my witness, I would gladly repay you with my life for what you've done for me. Only don't demand what goes against my honor and my Christian conscience. You are my benefactor. Finish as you began: let me and the poor orphan go wherever God leads us. And wherever you may be and whatever may happen to you, we will pray to God every day for the salvation of your sinful soul . . ."

It seemed that Pugachev's rude soul was touched.

"Be it as you say!" he said. "If it's hanging, it's hanging; if it's mercy, it's mercy: that's my custom. Take your beauty; go wherever you want with her, and God grant you love and harmony."

Here he turned to Shvabrin and ordered him to issue me a pass for all the outposts and fortresses subject to him. Shvabrin, totally crushed, stood as if dumbstruck. Pugachev went to inspect the fortress. Shvabrin went with him; but I stayed behind on the pretext of preparing for departure.

I ran to Masha's room. The door was locked. I knocked.

"Who's there?" asked Palasha. I gave my name. Marya Ivanovna's dear little voice came from behind the door.

"Wait, Pyotr Andreich. I'm changing. Go to Akulina Pamfilovna's: I'll be there in a minute."

I obeyed and went to Father Gerasim's house. He and his wife came running out to meet me. Savelyich had already forewarned them.

"Greetings, Pyotr Andreich," said the priest's wife. "So God has granted that we meet again. How are you? We've talked about you every day. And Marya Ivanovna, my little dove, what she's gone through without you! . . . But tell me, my dear, how is it you get along with this Pugachev? How is it he hasn't done you in? Well, thanks to the villain for that at least."

"Enough, old woman," Father Gerasim interrupted. "Don't blurt out everything in your head. There is no salvation in much talk. Dearest Pyotr Andreich, come in and be welcome. We haven't seen you for a long, long time."

His wife started offering me whatever they had to eat. Meanwhile she talked nonstop. She told me how Shvabrin had forced them to hand over Marya Ivanovna to him; how Marya Ivanovna had wept and had not wanted to part from them; how Marya Ivanovna had always kept in touch with them through Palashka (a pert young girl, who even made the sergeant dance to her tune); how she had advised Marya Ivanovna to write me a letter, and so on. And I in turn briefly told her my story. The priest and his wife crossed themselves on hearing that Pugachev knew of their deception.

"The power of the Cross be with us!" said Akulina Pamfilovna. "God grant that the cloud passes over. Ah, that Alexei Ivanych, really: what a fine goose he is!"

At that same moment the door opened, and Marya Ivanovna came in with a smile on her pale face. She had abandoned her peasant clothes and was dressed as before, simply and nicely.

I seized her hand and for a long time could not utter a word. Our hearts were so full we could not speak. Our hosts sensed that we had no need of them and left us. We remained alone. All else was forgotten. We talked and could not have enough of talking. Marya Ivanovna told me everything that had happened to her since the fortress was taken; she described all the horror of her situation, all the ordeals the vile Shvabrin had put her through. We also recalled the former happy time . . . We both wept . . . Finally I began to explain my proposals to her. To remain in a fortress subject to Pugachev and commanded by Shvabrin was impossible. There was no thinking of Orenburg, which was suffering all the adversities of the siege. She did not have a single relation in the world. I proposed that she go to my parents' estate. At first she hesitated: she knew that my father was ill-disposed towards her and she was frightened. I reassured her. I knew that my father would count it as happiness and make it his duty to receive the daughter of a distinguished soldier who had died for the fatherland.

"Dear Marya Ivanovna!" I said finally. "I consider you my wife. Wondrous circumstances have united us indissolubly: nothing in the world can separate us."

Marya Ivanovna listened to me simply, without affected shyness, without contrived reservations. She felt that her fate was united with mine. But she repeated that she would not marry me otherwise than with my parents' consent. I did not contradict her. We kissed warmly, sincerely—and thus everything was decided between us.

An hour later the sergeant brought me a pass, signed with Pugachev's scrawl, and told me he wished to see me. I found him ready to set out. I cannot express what I felt, parting with this terrible man, a monster, a villain for everyone but me alone. Why not tell the truth? At that moment strong compassion drew me to him. I ardently wished to snatch him away from the midst of the villains whose chief he was, and to save his head while there was still time. Shvabrin and the people crowding around us prevented me from saying all that filled my heart.

We parted friends. Pugachev, seeing Akulina Pamfilovna in the crowd, shook his finger at her and winked significantly; then he got into the kibitka, gave orders to drive to Berda, and as the horses started, stuck his head out of the kibitka once more and called to me:

"Farewell, Your Honor! Maybe we'll see each other again sometime."

And indeed we did see each other again, but in what circumstances! . . .

Pugachev was gone. I gazed for a long time at the white steppe over which his troika was racing. The people dispersed. Shvabrin disappeared. I returned to the priest's house. Everything was ready for our departure; I did not want to tarry any longer. Our belongings were all packed in the commandant's old wagon. The drivers hitched up the horses in an instant. Marya Ivanovna went to take leave of the graves of her parents, who had been buried behind the church. I wanted to accompany her, but she begged me to let her go alone. After a few minutes she came back, silently pouring out gentle tears. The wagon was ready. Father Gerasim and his wife came out to the porch. The three of us got into the kibitka: Marya Ivanovna, Palasha, and I. Savelyich climbed up on the box.

"Farewell, Marya Ivanovna, my little dove! Farewell, Pyotr Andreich, our bright falcon!" said the priest's kindly wife. "Have a good journey, and God grant you both happiness!"

We drove off. I saw Shvabrin standing at the window of the commandant's house. Dark malice was written on his face. I had no wish to triumph over a crushed enemy and turned my eyes the other way. At last we drove through the fortress gates and left the Belogorsk fortress forever.

CHAPTER THIRTEEN

The Arrest

"Do not be angry, sir: my duty doth compel
That at this very hour I lock you in a cell."
"As you please, I'm ready; but ere you take me out
I hope I may explain what this is all about."

KNYAZHNIN[37]

United so unexpectedly with the dear girl about whom I had been so painfully worried that same morning, I did not believe my own self and wondered whether all that had happened to me was not an empty dream. Marya Ivanovna gazed pensively now at me, now at the road, and, it seemed, had not yet managed to recover and come to her senses. We were silent. Our hearts were too weary. In some imperceptible way, after about two hours we found ourselves in the neighboring fortress, also subject to Pugachev. Here we changed horses. By the speed with which they were harnessed, by the bustling servility of the bewhiskered Cossack Pugachev had installed as commandant, I saw that, owing to the garrulousness of the driver who had brought us, I was taken for a court favorite.

We drove on. It was getting dark. We were nearing a little town, where, according to the bearded commandant, there was a strong detachment on its way to join the impostor. We were stopped by the sentries. To the question "Who goes there?" the driver answered in a loud voice: "A friend of the sovereign and his little missis." Suddenly a crowd of hussars surrounded us with terrible curses.

"Get out, you friend of the devil!" a moustached sergeant said to me. "You're going to get it hot now, you and your little missis!"

I got out of the kibitka and demanded that they take me to their commander. Seeing an officer, the soldiers stopped cursing. The sergeant took me to the major. Savelyich came along behind me, muttering to himself:

"There's a friend of the sovereign for you! Out of the frying pan into the fire . . . Lord God! where will it all end?"

The kibitka followed us at a walking pace.

In five minutes we came to a little house, brightly lit. The sergeant left me with the sentry and went to announce me. He came back at once and told me that his honor had no time to receive me, and that he ordered me to be taken to jail, and my little missis to himself.

"What's the meaning of this?" I cried in fury. "Is he out of his mind?"

"It's not for me to know, Your Honor," the sergeant replied. "It's just that his high honor ordered that Your Honor be taken to jail and her honor be taken to his high honor, Your Honor!"

I dashed up to the porch. The sentries did not think of holding me back, and I ran straight into the room, where some six hussar officers were playing faro. The major was keeping the bank. What was my amazement when, glancing at him, I recognized Ivan Ivanovich Zurin, who once upon a time had beaten me at billiards in the Simbirsk inn!

"Can it be?" I cried. "Ivan Ivanych! Is it you?"

"Well, well, well, Pyotr Andreich! What wind blows you here? Where from? Greetings, brother. Want to stake on a card?"

"Thanks. Better tell them to show me to some quarters."

"What quarters? Stay with me."

"I can't: I'm not alone."

"Well, bring your comrade here, too."

"I'm not with a comrade; I'm . . . with a lady."

"A lady! Where did you pick her up? Ho-ho, brother!" (With those words Zurin whistled so expressively that they all burst out laughing, and I became completely embarrassed.)

"Well," Zurin continued, "so be it. You'll have your quarters. A pity, though . . . We could have feasted a bit like the old days . . . Hey, boy! Why don't they bring Pugachev's lady friend? Or is she holding back? Tell her not to be afraid, the master's a fine gentleman, he won't do her any harm—and give her a good shove."

"What do you mean?" I said to Zurin. "What Pugachev's lady friend? She's the daughter of the late Captain Mironov. I rescued her from captivity, and I'm now accompanying her to my father's estate, where I will leave her."

"How's that? So you're the one they just reported to me? Good Lord, what does it mean?"

"I'll tell you everything later. But now, for God's sake, reassure the poor girl; your hussars have frightened her badly."

Zurin saw to it at once. He went out himself to apologize to Marya Ivanovna for the unintentional misunderstanding and ordered the sergeant to take her to the best quarters in town. I spent the night at his place.

We had supper, and when the two of us were left alone, I told him my adventures. Zurin listened to me with great attention. When I finished, he shook his head and said:

"That's all very good, brother; just one thing isn't good: why the devil do you want to get married? As an honest officer, I don't want to deceive you: believe me, marriage is folly. I mean, why go bothering with a wife and fussing with little kids? Ah, spit on it. Listen to me: unhitch yourself from the captain's daughter. I've cleared the road to Simbirsk and it's safe. Send her to your parents tomorrow on her own; and you stay with my detachment. There's no need for you to go back to Orenburg. If you wind up in the hands of the rebels again, it's unlikely you'll shake them off a second time. This way your amorous folly will go away by itself, and all will be well."

Although I did not entirely agree with him, nevertheless I felt that the duty of honor demanded my presence in the empress's army. I decided to follow Zurin's advice: to send Marya Ivanovna to the estate and stay in his detachment.

Savelyich came to help me undress; I told him that the next day he should be ready to travel with Marya Ivanovna. He began to protest.

"What do you mean, sir? How can I abandon you? Who will take care of you? What will your parents say?"

Knowing my tutor's stubbornness, I decided to persuade him by means of gentleness and sincerity.

"My dear friend Arkhip Savelyich!" I said to him. "Don't refuse me, be my benefactor; I'll have no need of a servant here, and I won't be at peace if Marya Ivanovna travels without you. Serving her, you serve me, because, as soon as circumstances permit, I'm firmly resolved to marry her."

Here Savelyich clasped his hands with a look of indescribable amazement.

"Marry!" he repeated. "The little one wants to marry! And what will your father say, and what will your mother think?"

"They'll agree, they're sure to agree," I replied, "once they get to know Marya Ivanovna. I'm also relying on you. My father and mother trust you: you'll intercede for us, won't you?"

The old man was touched.

"Ah, my dearest Pyotr Andreich!" he replied. "Though it's a bit early for you to think of marrying, still Marya Ivanovna is such a good young lady that it would be a sin to miss the chance. Let it be your way! I'll go with the little angel, and faithfully tell your parents that such a bride even needs no dowry."

I thanked Savelyich and went off to sleep in the same room with Zurin. Flushed and excited, I chattered away. At first Zurin talked to me willingly; but his words gradually became fewer and less coherent; finally, instead of an answer to some question, he snored and whistled. I fell silent and soon followed his example.

The next morning I went to see Marya Ivanovna. I informed her of my proposals. She acknowledged that they were sensible and agreed with me at once. Zurin's detachment was to leave town that same day.

There could be no tarrying. I took leave of Marya Ivanovna there and then, having entrusted her to Savelyich and given her a letter to my parents. Marya Ivanovna wept.

"Farewell, Pyotr Andreich!" she said in a low voice. "God alone knows if we'll see each other again; but I'll never forget you; till the grave you alone will remain in my heart."

I could make no reply. We were surrounded by people. I did not want to abandon myself in front of them to the feelings that stirred in me. She finally left. I returned to Zurin sad and silent. He wanted to cheer me up; I hoped to be diverted: we spent the day noisily and wildly, and in the evening set out on the march.

That was at the end of February. Winter, which had hampered military operations, would soon be over, and our generals were preparing for concerted action. Pugachev was still encamped near Orenburg. Meanwhile our detachments were joining forces and approaching the villain's nest from all sides. The rebellious villages, at the sight of our troops, turned submissive; the bands of brigands fled from us everywhere, and everything betokened a swift and successful end.

Prince Golitsyn[38] soon crushed Pugachev near the Tatishchevo fortress, scattered his hordes, liberated Orenburg, and, it seemed, delivered the final and decisive blow to the rebellion. At that time Zurin was dispatched against a band of mutinous Bashkirs, who scattered before we even saw them. Spring besieged us in a little Tatar village. The rivers overflowed and the roads became impassable. In our inaction we comforted ourselves with the thought of the imminent cessation of the tedious and petty war with brigands and savages.

But Pugachev had not been caught. He showed up in Siberian mills, gathered new bands there, and again began his villainies. Rumors of his successes spread once more. We learned of the devastation of Siberian fortresses. Soon the army commanders, who were counting on the despicable rebel's weakness, were aroused from their carefree slumber by news of the taking of Kazan and the impostor's march on Moscow. Zurin received orders to cross the Volga.*

I will not describe our campaign and the end of the war. I will say briefly that the calamity was extreme. We passed through villages devastated by the rebels and unwillingly took from the poor inhabitants

---

* The "omitted chapter" (see pp. 347–357), rejected by Pushkin and preserved only in rough draft, would have gone here. *Translator.*

what little they had managed to save. Order broke down everywhere: the landowners hid in the forests. Bands of brigands spread their villainies everywhere; the commanders of separate detachments punished and pardoned arbitrarily; the condition of the whole vast region where the conflagration raged was terrible . . . God keep us from ever seeing a Russian rebellion—senseless and merciless!

Pugachev fled, pursued by Ivan Ivanovich Mikhelson.[39] Soon we learned of his total defeat. Zurin finally received news of the impostor's capture, and along with it the order to halt. The war was over. I could finally go to my parents! The thought of embracing them, of seeing Marya Ivanovna, from whom I had had no news, filled me with rapture. I leaped about like a child. Zurin laughed and said, shrugging his shoulders:

"No, you won't end well! You'll get married—and perish for nothing!"

But meanwhile a strange feeling poisoned my joy: the thought of the villain drenched in the blood of so many innocent victims, and of the execution that awaited him, troubled me against my will. "Emelya, Emelya!" I thought with vexation. "Why didn't you run onto a bayonet or catch a load of grapeshot? You couldn't have come up with anything better." What could I do? The thought of him was inseparable in me from the thought of the mercy he granted me in one of the moments when he was most terrible, and of the deliverance of my bride-to-be from the hands of the vile Shvabrin.

Zurin gave me a leave of absence. In a few days I was to find myself again in the bosom of my family, to see again my Marya Ivanovna . . . Suddenly an unexpected storm broke over me.

On the day appointed for my departure, at the very moment I was preparing to set off, Zurin came into my cottage with an extremely worried look, holding a paper in his hand. Something stabbed my heart. I became frightened, without knowing of what. He sent my orderly away and told me he had some business with me.

"What is it?" I asked uneasily.

"A small unpleasantness," he replied, handing me the paper. "Read what I just received."

I started to read: it was a secret order to all detachment commanders to arrest me wherever I might be found and send me at once under guard to Kazan, to the Investigation Commission set up for the Pugachev affair.

The paper nearly dropped from my hands.

"Nothing to be done!" said Zurin. "My duty is to obey orders. Rumors of your friendly travels with Pugachev have probably somehow reached the authorities. I hope the affair won't have any consequences and that you'll vindicate yourself before the commission. Don't lose heart, just get on your way."

My conscience was clear; I was not afraid of the tribunal; but the thought of putting off the moment of sweet reunion, maybe for several more months, appalled me. The wagon was ready. Zurin bade me a friendly farewell. I was put into the wagon. Two hussars with drawn swords got in with me, and I drove off down the high road.

CHAPTER FOURTEEN

The Tribunal

Worldly rumor—
Sea waves' murmur.

PROVERB

I was certain that my whole fault lay in my unauthorized absence from Orenburg. I could easily justify myself: sorties not only had never been forbidden, but had even been strongly encouraged. I could be accused of excessive fervor, but not of disobedience. But my friendly relations with Pugachev could be proved by many witnesses and would have to seem at the very least highly suspicious. For the whole journey I reflected on the interrogations awaiting me, thought over my responses, and decided to tell the whole truth before the tribunal, considering this means of justifying myself to be the most simple and at the same time the most reliable.

I arrived in devastated and burnt-down Kazan. In the streets, instead of houses, lay heaps of embers, and sooty walls stuck up without roofs or windows. Such were the traces left by Pugachev! They brought me to the fortress, left whole in the midst of the fire-ravaged town. The hussars handed me over to a guards officer. He ordered a blacksmith sent for. Shackles were put on my legs and riveted tightly. Then they took me to the prison and left me alone in a narrow and dark cell, with nothing but bare walls and a little window barred by an iron grille.

Such a beginning boded no good for me. However, I lost neither courage nor hope. I resorted to the consolation of all the afflicted and, tasting for the first time the sweetness of prayer poured forth from a pure but tormented heart, fell peacefully asleep, not caring what might happen to me.

The next day the prison guard woke me up with the announcement that I was summoned before the commission. Two soldiers led me across the yard to the commandant's house, stopped in the front hall, and let me go inside alone.

I entered a rather big room. At a table covered with papers sat two men: an elderly general of stern and cold appearance, and a young captain of the guards, about twenty-eight years old, very pleasant in appearance, free and easy in manner. By the window at a special table sat a secretary with a pen behind his ear, bending over his paper, ready to take down my testimony. The interrogation began. They asked me my name and rank. The general inquired whether I was the son of Andrei Petrovich Grinyov. And to my reply retorted sternly:

"A pity such an estimable man should have such an unworthy son!"

I calmly replied that, whatever the accusations hanging over me, I hoped to dispel them by a frank explanation of the truth. He did not like my assurance.

"You're a sharp one, brother," he said to me, frowning, "but we've seen sharper!"

Then the young man asked me by what chance and at what time I had entered Pugachev's service, and on what assignments I had been employed by him.

I replied with indignation that, as an officer and a gentleman, I could not enter into any service with Pugachev or accept any assignments from him.

"How is it, then," my interrogator rejoined, "that the gentleman and officer was the only one spared by the impostor, while all his comrades were villainously put to death? How is it that this same officer and gentleman feasts amicably with the rebels, and accepts from the chief villain gifts of a fur coat, a horse, and fifty kopecks? How did such a strange friendship come about and what was it based on, if not on treason or at least on vile and criminal cowardice?"

I was deeply offended by the guards officer's words and hotly began to justify myself. I told how my acquaintance with Pugachev began on the steppe, during a snowstorm; how, when the Belogorsk fortress was taken, he recognized me and spared me. I said that, in fact, I was not ashamed to have taken the coat and the horse from the impostor; but that I had defended the Belogorsk fortress from the villain to the final limit. Finally I referred to my general, who could testify to my zeal during the calamitous siege of Orenburg.

The stern old man took an opened letter from the table and began to read it aloud:

To Your Excellency's inquiry concerning Lieutenant Grinyov, alleged to be involved in the present commotion and to have entered into relations with the villain impermissible in the service and contrary to his sworn duty, I have the honor to explain that the said Lieutenant Grinyov served in Orenburg from the beginning of October of last year, 1773, until the 24th of February of the present year, on which day he left town and thereafter has not presented himself under my command. But it has been heard from deserters that he was in Pugachev's camp, and together with him drove to the Belogorsk fortress, where he used to serve; as concerns his behavior, I can . . .

Here he broke off his reading and said to me severely:

"What will you say now to justify yourself?"

I was going to go on as I had begun and explain my connection with Marya Ivanovna as frankly as all the rest. But I suddenly felt an insurmountable repugnance. It occurred to me that if I named her, the commission would call on her to testify; and the thought of mixing her name with the vile denunciations of villains and of her being brought in person to confront them—this terrible thought shocked me so much that I faltered and became confused.

My judges, who, it seemed, were beginning to listen to my responses with some benevolence, again became prejudiced against me, seeing my embarrassment. The officer of the guards requested that I be confronted with the main informer. The general ordered "yesterday's vil-

lain" to be called. I turned briskly to the door, waiting for my accuser
to appear. A few minutes later chains clanked, the door opened, and in
came—Shvabrin. I was amazed at the change in him. He was terribly
thin and pale. His hair, jet-black still recently, had turned completely
gray; his long beard was disheveled. He repeated his accusations in a
weak but resolute voice. According to him, I had been sent to Orenburg
by Pugachev as a spy; I had ridden out on skirmishes every day in order
to transmit news in writing about all that was going on in the town;
then I had openly gone over to the impostor, had driven with him from
fortress to fortress, trying in all ways to ruin my comrade-traitors, so as
to take their places and profit from the rewards bestowed by the impostor. I heard him out silently and was pleased with one thing: the vile
villain did not utter Marya Ivanovna's name, either because his vanity
suffered at the thought of the one who had scornfully rejected him, or
because hidden in his heart was a spark of the same feeling that had
also made me keep silent—however it was, the name of the Belogorsk
commandant's daughter was not uttered in the presence of the commission. I became still more firm in my resolve, and when the judges
asked how I could refute Shvabrin's testimony, I replied that I stuck to
my first explanation and could say nothing more to justify myself. The
general ordered us taken away. We went out together. I glanced calmly
at Shvabrin, but did not say a word to him. He grinned maliciously at
me and, picking up his chains, went ahead of me and quickened his
pace. I was taken back to prison and was not summoned for any further
questioning.

I was not a witness to everything of which it now remains for me
to inform the reader; but I have so often heard stories about it that the
smallest details are engraved in my memory, and it seems to me as if I
had been invisibly present.

Marya Ivanovna was received by my parents with that sincere cordiality which distinguished people of the old days. They saw it as a
blessing from God that they had the chance to shelter and show kindness to the poor orphan. Soon they became sincerely attached to her,
because it was impossible to know her and not love her. My love no
longer seemed an empty whim to my father; and my mother wished
only that her Petrusha should marry the captain's dear daughter.

The rumor of my arrest shocked my whole family. Marya Ivanovna
had told my parents so simply about my strange acquaintance with

Pugachev that it not only had not troubled them, but had often even made them laugh wholeheartedly. My father did not want to believe that I could have been involved in a vile rebellion, the aim of which was the overthrow of the throne and the extermination of the nobility. He closely questioned Savelyich. My tutor did not conceal that his master had visited Emelka Pugachev and that the villain had, in fact, received him well; but he swore that he had not heard of any treason. The old folks calmed down and started waiting impatiently for favorable news. Marya Ivanovna was deeply troubled, but said nothing, for she was endowed in the highest degree with modesty and prudence.

Several weeks went by . . . Suddenly my father received a letter from Petersburg, from our relation, Prince B. The prince wrote to him about me. After the usual preliminaries, he informed him that the suspicions concerning my participation in the rebels' schemes had turned out, unfortunately, to be all too substantial, that exemplary punishment should have been meted out to me, but that the empress, out of respect for my father's merits and his advanced age, decided to show mercy to his criminal son and, sparing him an ignominious execution, ordered him only to be sent to a remote corner of Siberia in perpetual exile.

This unexpected blow nearly killed my father. He lost his habitual firmness, and his grief (usually mute) poured out in bitter lamentations. "What!" he repeated, beside himself. "My son took part in Pugachev's schemes! Good God, that I should live to see it! The empress spares him execution! Does that make it easier for me? Execution is nothing frightening: a forebear of mine died on the scaffold defending something his conscience held sacred; my father suffered along with Volynsky and Khrushchev.[40] But for a nobleman to betray his oath, to join with brigands, murderers, runaway slaves! . . . Shame and disgrace on our name! . . ."

Frightened by his despair, mother did not dare to weep in his presence, and tried to restore his good spirits, talking about the inaccuracy of rumors, the shakiness of people's opinions. My father was inconsolable.

Marya Ivanovna was the most tormented of all. Being certain that I could justify myself if only I wanted to, she guessed the truth and considered herself the cause of my misfortune. She concealed her tears and suffering from everyone, and meanwhile kept thinking of ways to save me.

One evening my father was sitting on the sofa, turning the pages of the Court Almanac; but his thoughts were far away, and the reading did not have its usual effect on him. He was whistling an old marching tune. Mother was silently knitting a woolen vest, and tears occasionally dropped on her work. Suddenly Marya Ivanovna, who was sitting there over her own work, announced that necessity forced her to go to Petersburg and that she asked them to provide her with the means for going. Mother was very upset.

"What is there for you in Petersburg?" she said. "Can it be, Marya Ivanovna, that you, too, want to abandon us?"

Marya Ivanovna replied that her whole future fate depended on this journey, that she was going to seek protection and help from powerful people, as the daughter of a man who had suffered for his loyalty.

My father hung his head: every word that reminded him of his son's supposed crime weighed heavily on him and seemed like a stinging reproach.

"Go, my dear!" he said with a sigh. "We don't want to be an obstacle to your happiness. God grant you a good man for a husband, not a dishonored traitor."

He got up and walked out of the room.

Marya Ivanovna, left alone with my mother, partly explained her intentions. Mother embraced her in tears and prayed to God for a favorable outcome of her plan. They fitted Marya Ivanovna out, and a few days later she set off with faithful Palasha and faithful Savelyich, who, forcibly separated from me, comforted himself with the thought that he was at least serving my bride-to-be.

Marya Ivanovna arrived safely in Sofia, and, learning at the posting station that the court was just then in Tsarskoe Selo, decided to stop there.[41] She was given a corner behind a partition. The stationmaster's wife at once fell to talking with her, told her she was the niece of a court stoker, and initiated her into all the mysteries of court life. She told her at what hour the empress usually awoke, had coffee, went for a stroll; what courtiers attended her then; what she had been pleased to say yesterday at the table, whom she had received in the evening—in short, Anna Vlasyevna's conversation was worth several pages of historical memoirs and would have been of great value to posterity. Marya Ivanovna listened to her attentively. They went out to the gardens. Anna Vlasyevna told her the story of each alley and each little bridge, and, having had a good walk, they returned to the station very pleased with each other.

Early the next morning Marya Ivanovna woke up, dressed, and quietly went out to the gardens. The morning was beautiful, the sun lit up the tops of the lindens, already turned yellow under the cool breath of autumn. The wide lake shone motionlessly. The just-awakened swans glided majestically from under the bushes overshadowing the bank. Marya Ivanovna walked by a beautiful meadow where a monument had just been set up in honor of Count Pyotr Alexandrovich Rumyantsev's recent victories.[42] Suddenly a little white dog of English breed barked and ran towards her. Marya Ivanovna was frightened and stopped. At that same moment she heard a pleasant woman's voice:

"Don't be afraid, she doesn't bite."

And Marya Ivanovna saw a lady sitting on a bench opposite the monument. Marya Ivanovna sat down at the other end of the bench. The lady looked at her intently; Marya Ivanovna, for her part, casting several sidelong glances, managed to examine her from head to foot. She was wearing a white morning dress, a nightcap, and a jacket. She seemed about forty. Her face, plump and red-cheeked, expressed dignity and calm, and her light-blue eyes and slight smile had an ineffable charm. The lady was the first to break the silence.

"You're probably not from here?" she said.

"That's right, ma'am: I came from the provinces only yesterday."

"You came with your family?"

"No, ma'am. I came alone."

"Alone! But you're still so young."

"I have no father or mother."

"You're here, of course, on some kind of business?"

"Yes, ma'am. I've come to submit a petition to the empress."

"You're an orphan: you probably want to complain of injustice and offense?"

"No, ma'am. I've come to ask for mercy, not for justice."

"Who are you, if I may ask?"

"I am Captain Mironov's daughter."

"Captain Mironov! The one who was commandant of one of the Orenburg fortresses?"

"Yes, ma'am."

The lady seemed to be moved.

"Forgive me," she said in a still gentler voice, "if I'm interfering in your affairs; but I am received at court; tell me what your petition is about, and maybe I'll be able to help you."

Marya Ivanovna rose and respectfully thanked her. Everything about the unknown lady spontaneously attracted her heart and inspired trust. Marya Ivanovna took a folded paper from her pocket and gave it to her unknown protectress, who started reading it to herself.

At first she read with an attentive and benevolent air; but suddenly her countenance changed—and Marya Ivanovna, who was following all her movements with her eyes, was frightened by the severe expression of this face, which a moment before had been so pleasant and calm.

"You're petitioning for Grinyov?" the lady said with a cold look. "The empress cannot forgive him. He joined the impostor not out of ignorance and gullibility, but as an immoral and pernicious scoundrel."

"Oh, that's not true!" cried Marya Ivanovna.

"How, not true!" the lady retorted, flushing all over.

"Not true, by God, not true! I know everything, I'll tell you everything. He underwent all that befell him only for my sake. And if he did not justify himself before the judges, it was only because he didn't want to entangle me in it." Here she ardently recounted everything that is already known to my reader.

The lady heard her out attentively.

"Where are you staying?" she asked then; and, hearing that it was at Anna Vlasyevna's, she added with a smile: "Ah, I know! Good-bye; don't tell anyone about our meeting. I hope you will not have to wait long for an answer to your letter."

With those words she stood up and went off into a covered alley, and Marya Ivanovna returned to Anna Vlasyevna filled with joyful hope.

Her hostess chided her for the early autumnal promenade, harmful, so she said, for a young girl's health. She brought the samovar and, over a cup of tea, was just starting on her endless stories about the court, when a court carriage suddenly pulled up to the porch and an imperial footman came in and announced that her majesty was pleased to invite Miss Mironov to call on her.

Anna Vlasyevna was amazed and flustered.

"Good Lord!" she cried. "The empress is summoning you to the court. How on earth did she find out about you? How, my dear girl, are you going to present yourself to the empress? I suppose you don't even know how to walk at court . . . Shouldn't I come with you? At least I could warn you about certain things. And how are you going to go in your traveling clothes? Shouldn't we send to the midwife for her yellow robe ronde?"

The imperial footman said that the empress wished to have Marya Ivanovna come alone and dressed just as she was. There was nothing to be done: Marya Ivanovna got into the carriage and set off for the palace accompanied by the instructions and blessings of Anna Vlasyevna.

Marya Ivanovna had a presentiment that our fate was to be decided; her heart now pounded, now sank. A few minutes later the carriage drew up to the palace. Marya Ivanovna tremblingly climbed the stairs. The doors were flung open before her. She walked through a long row of magnificent empty rooms; the imperial footman showed her the way. Finally, coming to a closed door, he said that she would presently be announced, and left her there alone.

The thought of seeing the empress face-to-face so terrified her that she could barely keep her feet. A minute later the door opened and she entered the empress's dressing room.

The empress was sitting at her toilette table. Several courtiers surrounded her, and they deferentially made way for Marya Ivanovna. The empress turned to her kindly, and Marya Ivanovna recognized her as the lady she had talked with so candidly a few minutes earlier. The empress told her to come closer and said with a smile:

"I'm glad that I can keep my word to you and grant your petition. Your affair is settled. I am convinced of the innocence of your betrothed. Here is a letter which you yourself will be so good as to deliver to your future father-in-law."

Marya Ivanovna took the letter with a trembling hand and, weeping, fell at the feet of the empress, who raised her up and kissed her. The empress talked more with her.

"I know you're not rich," she said, "but I am in debt to Captain Mironov's daughter. Don't worry about your future. I take it upon myself to see you established."

Having shown the poor orphan such kindness, the empress let her go. Marya Ivanovna drove off in the same court carriage. Anna Vlasyevna, who was impatiently awaiting her return, showered her with questions, which Marya Ivanovna answered absently. Though Anna Vlasyevna was displeased by such obliviousness, she ascribed it to provincial timidity and magnanimously forgave it. That same day, Marya

Ivanovna, not at all curious to have a look at Petersburg, went back to the country ...

———•———

The notes of Pyotr Andreevich Grinyov end here. From family tradition it is known that he was released from prison at the end of 1774, by imperial order; that he was present at the execution of Pugachev, who recognized him in the crowd and nodded to him with his head, which a moment later was shown, dead and bloodied, to the people. Soon afterwards Pyotr Andreevich married Marya Ivanovna. Their descendants still prosper in Simbirsk province. Twenty miles from * * * there is a village belonging to ten landowners. In one wing of the manor house a letter in the hand of Catherine II is displayed under glass and in a frame. It was written to Pyotr Andreevich's father and contains the vindication of his son and praise of the mind and heart of Captain Mironov's daughter. Pyotr Andreevich Grinyov's manuscript was furnished us by one of his grandsons, who learned that we were occupied with a work related to the time described by his grandfather. We have decided, with the family's permission, to publish it separately, having found a suitable epigraph for each chapter and allowed ourselves to change some proper names.

The Publisher

19 OCT. 1836

THE OMITTED CHAPTER*

We were approaching the banks of the Volga; our regiment entered the village of * * * and stayed there for the night. The headman told me that all the villages on the opposite bank were in rebellion, that bands of Pugachev's people were roaming everywhere. The news greatly alarmed me. We were supposed to cross the next morning. I was seized

* This chapter was not included in the final version of *The Captain's Daughter*; it was preserved in a rough draft with the title "The Omitted Chapter." It would have formed a continuation or extension of chapter 13. In it Grinyov is called Bulanin and Zurin is called Grinyov, but we have kept the names as they are in the rest of the novel. *Translator.*

with impatience. My father's estate was on the other side, twenty miles away. I asked if a ferryman could be found. All the peasants were fishermen; there were many boats. I went to Zurin and told him of my intention.

"Watch out," he said to me. "It's dangerous to go alone. Wait till morning. We'll go across first and bring fifty hussars to visit your parents just in case."

I insisted on my way. A boat was ready. I got into it with two oarsmen. They pushed off and plied their oars.

The sky was clear. The moon shone. The weather was calm. The Volga flowed smoothly and quietly. The boat, gently rocking, glided swiftly over the dark waves. I immersed myself in the dreams of my imagination. About half an hour went by. We had already reached the middle of the river . . . Suddenly the oarsmen began whispering to each other.

"What is it?" I asked, coming to myself.

"God only knows," replied the oarsmen, looking off to one side. My eyes turned in the same direction, and in the darkness I saw something floating down the Volga. The unknown object was coming closer. I told the oarsmen to stop and wait for it. The moon went behind a cloud. The floating phantom became still more vague. It was already close to me, and I could not yet make it out.

"What could it be?" the oarsmen said. "A sail, a mast, or maybe not . . ."

Suddenly the moon came from behind the cloud and lit up a terrible sight. Floating towards us was a gallows mounted on a raft, with three bodies hanging from the crossbar. I was overcome with morbid curiosity. I wanted to look into the faces of the hanged men.

On my order the oarsmen caught the raft with a boathook, and my boat nudged against the floating gallows. I jumped out and found myself between the terrible posts. The bright moon lit up the disfigured faces of the unfortunate men. One of them was an old Chuvash, another a Russian peasant, a strong and robust lad of about twenty. But, glancing at the third, I was deeply shocked and could not help crying out pitifully: it was Vanka, my poor Vanka, who in his foolishness had joined Pugachev. Above them a black board had been nailed, on which was written in large white letters: "Thieves and Rebels." The oarsmen looked on indifferently and waited for me, keeping hold of the raft with the boathook. I got back into the boat. The raft floated on down the

river. For a long time the gallows loomed black in the darkness. Finally
it disappeared, and my boat moored on the high and steep bank . . . .

I paid the oarsmen generously. One of them took me to the headman of the village near the landing. I went into the cottage with him.
The headman, hearing that I was requesting horses, received me quite
rudely, but my guide quietly said a few words to him, and his severity
turned at once into a hurried obligingness. In one minute a troika was
ready, I got into the cart and ordered myself taken to our village.

I galloped along the high road past sleeping villages. I was afraid of
one thing: being stopped on the road. If my night meeting on the Volga
had proved the presence of rebels, it had proved at the same time a
strong government counteraction. Just in case, I had in my pocket both
the pass given to me by Pugachev and the order of Colonel Zurin. But
I met no one, and by morning I caught sight of the river and the pine
grove beyond which lay our village. The driver whipped up the horses,
and a quarter of an hour later I drove into * * *.

The manor house was at the other end of the village. The horses
raced along at full speed. Suddenly, in the middle of the village, the
driver began to rein them in.

"What's the matter?" I asked impatiently.

"A barrier," the driver replied, barely able to stop his furious horses.
Indeed, I saw a spiked bar and a sentry with a club. The muzhik came
up to me and, taking off his hat, asked for my passport.

"What's the meaning of this?" I asked him. "What's this bar doing
here? Who are you guarding?"

"You see, good sir, we're rebelling," he replied, scratching himself.

"And where are your masters?" I asked with a sinking heart . . . .

"Our masters?" repeated the muzhik. "Our masters are in the
granary."

"What? In the granary?"

"You see, Andryushka, the bailiff, put them in fetters and wants to
take them to our father-sovereign."

"Good God! Raise the barrier, you fool. What are you gaping at?"

The sentry lingered. I leaped from the cart, gave him a clout (sorry)
on the ear, and raised the bar myself. My muzhik stared at me in stupid
perplexity. I got back into the cart and ordered the driver to gallop to
the manor house. The granary was in the yard. At the door stood two
muzhiks, also with clubs. The cart stopped right in front of them. I
jumped out and rushed straight at them.

"Open the doors!" I said to them. My look probably terrified them. In any case, they both ran away, dropping their clubs. I tried to smash the padlock and to break down the doors, but the doors were of oak and the enormous padlock was indestructible. At that moment a stalwart young muzhik came out of the servants' cottage and, with an arrogant air, asked me how I dared to make a row.

"Where's Andryushka the bailiff?" I shouted. "Call him to me."

"I myself am Andrei Afanasyevich, and not any Andryushka," he replied, his arms proudly akimbo. "What do you want?"

Instead of an answer, I seized him by the collar and, dragging him to the granary doors, ordered him to open them. The bailiff tried to protest, but a "fatherly" punishment worked on him as well. He took out a key and opened the granary. I threw myself across the threshold and in a dark corner, dimly lit by a narrow slot cut in the ceiling, saw my mother and father. Their hands were bound and their feet were in fetters. I rushed to embrace them and could not utter a single word. They both stared at me with amazement—three years of army life had changed me so much that they could not recognize me. My mother gasped and burst into tears.

Suddenly I heard a dear, familiar voice.

"Pyotr Andreich! It's you!" I was dumbfounded . . . looked around and in another corner saw Marya Ivanovna, also bound.

My father looked at me in silence, not daring to believe his own eyes. Joy shone on his face. I hurriedly cut the knots of their ropes with my sword.

"Greetings, greetings, Petrusha," my father said, pressing me to his heart. "Thank God, we've been waiting . . ."

"Petrusha, my dearest," my mother said. "So the Lord has brought you to us! Are you well?"

I was hurrying to bring them out of their imprisonment—but, going to the door, I found it locked again.

"Andryushka," I shouted, "open up!"

"Nohow," the bailiff answered through the door. "Sit yourself down there. We'll teach you to make a row and drag state officials around by the collar!"

I started looking over the granary to see if there was some way of getting out.

"Don't bother," my father said to me. "I'm not the sort of landowner whose barns have holes for thieves to go in and out."

My mother, overjoyed for a moment by my appearance, fell into despair, seeing that I, too, was to share in the doom of the whole family. But I was more at peace, since I was with them and with Marya Ivanovna. I had a sword and two pistols with me; I could still withstand a siege. Zurin was supposed to make it by evening, in time to rescue us. I told all that to my parents and managed to calm my mother down. They gave themselves fully to the joy of our reunion.

"Well, Pyotr," my father said to me, "you got up to plenty of mischief, and I was thoroughly angry with you. But there's no point in dwelling on the past. I hope you've mended your ways now and are done with foolery. I know you served as befits an honorable officer. Thank you. That's a comfort to my old age. If I owe you my deliverance, life will be doubly agreeable to me."

In tears I kissed his hand and looked at Marya Ivanovna, who was so overjoyed by my presence that she seemed perfectly happy and calm.

Towards noon we heard extraordinary noise and shouting.

"What does this mean?" said my father. "Can your colonel have made it in such good time?"

"Impossible," I replied. "He won't be here before evening."

The noise grew louder. The alarm bell rang. Mounted men were galloping around the yard. At that moment the gray head of Savelyich thrust itself into the narrow slot cut in the wall, and my poor tutor said in a pitiful voice:

"Andrei Petrovich, Avdotya Vasilyevna, my dear Pyotr Andreich, dearest Marya Ivanovna—trouble! The brigands have entered the village. And do you know, Pyotr Andreich, who's brought them? Shvabrin, Alexei Ivanych, deuce take him!"

Hearing the hateful name, Marya Ivanovna clasped her hands and stood motionless.

"Listen," I said to Savelyich, "send someone on horseback to the * * * ferry, to meet the hussar regiment and give their colonel word of our danger."

"Who can I send, sir? All the boys are rebelling, and the horses have all been taken! Oh, Lord! They're already in the yard. They're heading for the granary."

Just then we heard several voices outside the door. I silently made a sign to my mother and Marya Ivanovna to retreat into a corner, drew my sword, and leaned against the wall right next to the door. My father took the pistols, cocked them both, and stood beside me. The padlock clacked, the door opened, and the bailiff's head appeared. I struck it with my sword and he fell, blocking the entrance. At the same moment my father fired a pistol through the doorway. The crowd besieging us ran off cursing. I dragged the wounded man across the threshold and bolted the door from inside. The yard was full of armed men. Among them I recognized Shvabrin.

"Don't be afraid," I said to the women. "There's hope. And you, father, don't shoot again. Let's save the last shot."

Mother silently prayed to God; Marya Ivanovna stood beside her, waiting with angelic calm for our fate to be decided. Outside the door we heard threats, abuse, and curses. I stood in my place, ready to cut down the first daredevil to come in. Suddenly the villains fell silent. I heard the voice of Shvabrin calling me by name.

"I'm here. What do you want?"

"Surrender, Grinyov, it's useless to resist. Have pity on your old ones. Obstinacy won't save you. I'm going to get you all!"

"Just try it, traitor!"

"I won't risk my neck for nothing, or waste my people's lives. I'll order them to set the granary on fire, and then we'll see what you do, Don Quixote of Belogorsk. It's dinnertime now. Sit there for a while and think things over at your leisure. Good-bye, Marya Ivanovna, I won't apologize to you: you're probably not bored there in the dark with your knight."

Shvabrin went away and left a guard by the granary. We were silent. Each of us was thinking to himself, not daring to share his thoughts with the others. I imagined all that the resentful Shvabrin was capable of inflicting on us. I cared little about myself. Shall I confess it? Even my parents' lot did not horrify me so much as the fate of Marya Ivanovna. I knew that my mother was adored by the peasants and the house serfs; that my father, for all his strictness, was also loved, for he was a fair man and knew the true needs of the people subject to him. Their rebellion was a delusion, a momentary drunkenness, not the expression of their indignation. Here mercy was likely. But Marya Ivanovna? What lot had the depraved and shameless man prepared for her? I did not dare to dwell on that horrible thought, and prepared myself, God forgive me, sooner to kill her than to see her a second time in the hands of the cruel enemy.

About another hour went by. There was drunken singing in the village. Our guards were envious and, vexed with us, swore and taunted us with torture and death. We awaited the sequel to Shvabrin's threats. Finally there came a big commotion in the yard, and again we heard Shvabrin's voice:

"So, have you made up your mind? Do you voluntarily surrender to me?"

No one answered him. Having waited a little, Shvabrin ordered straw brought. After a few minutes, a burst of fire lit up the dark granary, and smoke began to make its way through the chink under the door. Then Marya Ivanovna came to me and, taking me by the hand, said softly:

"Enough, Pyotr Andreich! Don't destroy yourself and your parents on account of me. Let me out. Shvabrin will listen to me."

"Not for anything," I cried hotly. "Do you know what awaits you?"

"I won't survive dishonor," she replied calmly. "But maybe I'll save my deliverer and the family that so magnanimously sheltered a poor orphan. Farewell, Andrei Petrovich. Farewell, Avdotya Vasilyevna. You were more than benefactors to me. Give me your blessing. Farewell and forgive me, Pyotr Andreich. Be assured that . . . that . . ." Here she burst into tears and buried her face in her hands . . . I was like a madman. My mother wept.

"Enough nonsense, Marya Ivanovna," said my father. "Who is going to let you go to these brigands alone? Sit here and be quiet. If we're to die, we'll die together. Listen, what are they saying now?"

"Do you surrender?" Shvabrin shouted. "See? In five minutes you'll be roasted."

"We don't surrender, villain!" my father answered him in a firm voice.

His face, covered with wrinkles, was animated by astonishing courage, his eyes flashed menacingly under his gray eyebrows. And, turning to me, he said:

"Now's the time!"

He opened the door. Flames burst in and shot up the beams caulked with dry moss. My father fired his pistol and stepped across the blazing threshold, shouting: "Everyone, follow me!" I seized my mother and Marya Ivanovna by the hands and quickly led them outside. By the threshold lay Shvabrin, shot down by my father's decrepit hand; the crowd of brigands, who fled before our unexpected sortie, at once took courage and began to surround us. I still managed to deal several blows, but a well-thrown brick struck me full in the chest. I fell down and lost consciousness for a moment. On coming to, I saw Shvabrin sitting on the bloody grass, and before him our whole family. I was supported under the arms. The crowd of peasants, Cossacks, and Bashkirs stood around us. Shvabrin was terribly pale. He pressed one hand to his wounded side. His face expressed suffering and spite. He slowly raised his head, looked at me, and pronounced in a weak and indistinct voice:

"Hang him . . . hang all of them . . . except her . . ."

The crowd of villains surrounded us at once and, shouting, dragged us to the gates. But suddenly they abandoned us and scattered; through the gates rode Zurin and behind him his entire squadron with drawn swords.

———————

The rebels scurried off in all directions; the hussars pursued them, cut them down and took them prisoner. Zurin jumped off his horse, bowed to my mother and father, and firmly shook my hand.

"Looks like I made it just in time," he said to us. "Ah! Here's your bride-to-be."

Marya Ivanovna blushed to the ears. My father came up to him and thanked him with a calm, though moved, air. My mother embraced him, calling him an angel of deliverance.

"We bid you welcome," my father said to him and led him to our house.

Going past Shvabrin, Zurin stopped.

"Who is this?" he asked, looking at the wounded man.

"That is the leader himself, the head of the band," my father answered with a certain pride, revealing the old warrior in him. "God helped my decrepit hand to punish the young villain and revenge my son's blood."

"It's Shvabrin," I said to Zurin.

"Shvabrin! Very glad! Hussars! Take him! And tell our doctor to bandage his wound and cherish him like the apple of his eye. Shvabrin absolutely must be brought before the Kazan secret commission. He's one of the chief criminals, and his testimony is sure to be important."

Shvabrin gave him a languishing look. His face showed nothing but physical pain. The hussars carried him away on a cape.

We went into the house. I trembled as I looked around, recalling my young years. Nothing in the house had changed, everything was in the same place. Shvabrin had not allowed it to be looted, preserving in his very abasement an instinctive aversion to dishonorable greed. The servants came to the front hall. They had not taken part in the rebellion and rejoiced wholeheartedly in our deliverance. Savelyich was triumphant. It should be known that during the alarm caused by the brigands' attack, he ran to the stable where Shvabrin's horse was, saddled it, led it out quietly, and, thanks to the tumult, galloped off unnoticed to the crossing. He met the regiment, which was already resting on this side of the Volga. Zurin, learning of our danger from him, ordered his men to saddle up, commanded them forward, forward at a gallop—and, thank God, arrived in time.

Zurin insisted that the bailiff's head be exposed on a pole by the tavern for several hours.

The hussars came back from their pursuit, having taken several prisoners. They were locked up in the same granary in which we had withstood the memorable siege.

We went off to our separate rooms. My old parents needed rest. Not having slept all night, I threw myself on the bed and fell fast asleep. Zurin went to give his orders.

In the evening we gathered in the drawing room around the samovar, cheerfully talking about the past danger. Marya Ivanovna poured tea, I sat beside her and was occupied with her exclusively. My parents seemed to look favorably on the tenderness of our relations. That evening lives in my memory to this day. I was happy, perfectly happy, and how many such moments are there in a poor human life?

The next day my father was informed that the peasants had come to the courtyard to confess their wrong. My father went out to the porch to meet them. When he appeared, the muzhiks knelt down.

"Well, you fools," he said to them, "what put it into your heads to rebel?"

"We were wrong, master," they replied with one voice.

"So you were wrong. You get up to mischief, and you're not glad of it yourselves. I forgive you out of joy that God has let me see my son Pyotr Andreich. Well, all right: a repentant head isn't put to the sword. You were wrong! Of course you were wrong! God has sent us fair weather, it's time to get the hay in; and you, foolish people, what did you do for a whole three days? Headman! Send every man of them to the haymaking; and see to it, you red-haired rogue, that all the hay is in stacks for me by St. Elijah's day.¹ Off with you!"

The muzhiks bowed and went to their labor as if nothing had happened.

Shvabrin's wound turned out not to be mortal. He was sent to Kazan under convoy. I saw from the window how they laid him in a cart. Our eyes met, he lowered his head, and I quickly stepped away from the window. I was afraid to seem as if I were triumphing over my unfortunate and humiliated enemy.

Zurin had to move further on. I decided to follow him, despite my wish to spend a few more days amidst my family. On the eve of the march I came to my parents and, following the custom of the time, bowed at their feet, asking their blessing for my marriage to Marya Ivanovna. The old people raised me up and with joyful tears gave their consent. I brought Marya Ivanovna to them, pale and trembling. They blessed us . . . What I felt then I am not going to describe. Whoever has been in my situation will understand me without that; whoever has not, I can only pity and advise, while there is still time, to fall in love and receive the blessing of his parents.

The next day the regiment made ready. Zurin took leave of our family. We were all certain that military action would soon be over; I hoped to be a husband within a month. Marya Ivanovna, saying good-bye to me, kissed me in front of everyone. I mounted up. Savelyich again followed me—and the regiment left.

For a long time I looked back at the country house I was again abandoning. A dark foreboding troubled me. Someone was whispering to me that my misfortunes were not all behind me. My heart sensed a new storm.

I will not describe our march and the end of the war with Pugachev. We passed through villages devastated by Pugachev, and of necessity took from the poor inhabitants what the brigands had left them.

They did not know whom to obey. Order broke down everywhere. Landowners hid in the forests. Bands of brigands spread their villainies everywhere. The commanders of separate detachments, sent in pursuit of Pugachev, who was then fleeing towards Astrakhan, arbitrarily punished the guilty and the guiltless . . . The condition of the whole region where the conflagration raged was terrible. God keep us from ever seeing a Russian rebellion—senseless and merciless. Those among us who plot impossible revolutions are either young and do not know our people, or are hard-hearted men, for whom another man's head is worth little, and their own but little more.

Pugachev fled, pursued by Iv. Iv. Mikhelson. Soon we learned of his total defeat. Zurin finally received from his general the news of the impostor's capture, and with it the order to halt. I could finally go home. I was in raptures; but a strange feeling clouded my joy.

Journey to Arzrum

During the Campaign of 1829

PREFACE

Not long ago there came into my hands a book published in Paris last year (1834) under the title *Voyages en Orient entrepris par ordre du Gouvernement Français.*[*][1] The author, giving his own description of the campaign of 1829, ends his reflections with the following words:

> *Un poète distingué par son imagination a trouvé dans tant de hauts faits dont il a été témoin non le sujet d'un poème, mais celui d'une satyre.*[†]

Of poets who took part in the Turkish campaign, I knew only A. S. Khomyakov and A. N. Muravyov. Both were in the army of Count Dibich.[2] At that time the former wrote some fine lyric poems; the latter was thinking over his journey to the holy places, which was to produce such a strong impression. But I had not read any satire on the Arzrum campaign.

I could never have thought that the matter here concerned myself, if in that same book I had not found my own name among the names of generals of the Detached Caucasus Corps.[3] *Parmis les chefs qui la commandaient (l'armée du Prince Paskewitch) on distinguait le Général Mouravieff . . . le Prince Géorgian Tsitsevaze . . . le Prince Arménien Beboutof . . . le Prince Potemkine, le Général Raiewsky, et enfin—M-r Pouchkine . . . qui avait quitté la capitale pour chanter les exploits de ses compatriotes.*[‡][4]

I confess: the lines of the French traveler, despite the flattering epithets, vexed me far more than the abuse of Russian journals. To "seek inspiration" has always seemed to me a ridiculous and absurd fancy: inspiration cannot be sought out; it must find the poet. For me, to go to war in order to sing future exploits would have been, on the one hand,

---

* "Travels to the East undertaken by order of the French Government."

† A poet distinguished by his imagination found in the many lofty deeds he witnessed the subject, not of a poem, but of a satire.

‡ Among the leaders who commanded it (the army of Prince Paskevich) one singled out General Muraviev . . . the Georgian Prince Chavchavadze . . . the Armenian Prince Bebutov . . . Prince Potemkin, General Raevsky, and finally—Mr. Pushkin . . . who had left the capital in order to sing the exploits of his compatriots.

too vain, and on the other, too indecent. I do not meddle in military judgments. That is not my business. It may be that the bold march over Sagan-loo, a maneuver by which Count Paskevich cut the *seraskir* off from Osman Pasha,[5] the defeat of two enemy corps in one day's time, the quick march to Arzrum—it may be that all this, crowned with complete success, fully deserves to be made a laughingstock by military men (such as, for instance, Mr. Merchant Consul Fontanier, author of the *Travels to the East*), but I would be ashamed to write satires on the illustrious commander who graciously received me under the shade of his tent and who, in the midst of his great cares, found time to give me his flattering attention. A man who has no need of being patronized by the powerful values their cordiality and hospitality, because he has nothing else to ask of them. Unlike trifling criticism or literary abuse, an accusation of ingratitude should not go without objection. That is why I have decided to publish this preface and to bring out my travel notes as *all* that I have written about the campaign of 1829.[6]

A. PUSHKIN

CHAPTER ONE

The Steppes. A Kalmyk kibitka. The Caucasian hot springs. The Georgian military highway. Vladikavkaz. An Ossetian funeral. The Terek. The Darial gorge. Crossing the snowy mountains. The first glimpse of Georgia. Aqueducts. Khozrev-Mirza. The mayor of Dusheti.

. . . From Moscow I went to Kaluga, Belev, and Orel, and thus added an extra hundred and thirty miles; on the other hand I met Ermolov.[7] He lives in Orel, his country estate being close by. I came to him at eight o'clock in the morning and did not find him at home. My driver told me that Ermolov did not visit anyone except his father, a simple, pious old man, that the only people he did not receive were town officials, and that anyone else had free access to him. An hour later I came to him again. Ermolov received me with his usual courtesy. At first glance I did not find in him the least resemblance to his portraits, painted usually in profile. A round face, fiery gray eyes, bushy gray hair. A tiger's head on a herculean torso. His smile is unpleasant, because it is unnatural. But when he falls to thinking and frowns, he becomes superb and strikingly resembles the poetical portrait painted by Dawe.[8] He was wearing a green Circassian jacket. On the walls of his study hung sabers and daggers, souvenirs of his rule over the Caucasus. He appears to bear his inaction with impatience. Several times he began talking about Paskevich, and always sarcastically; talking of the ease of his victories, he compared him to the son of Nun, before whom walls fell down at the sounding of trumpets, and called the count of Erevan the count of Jericho.[9] "Let him run into a pasha who is not intelligent, not skillful, but merely stubborn—for instance, the pasha who ruled in Shumla," said Ermolov, "and Paskevich is done for." I passed on to Ermolov the words of Count Tolstoy,[10] that Paskevich had acted so well during the Persian campaign that the only thing left for an intelligent man was to act worse, in order to be distinguished from him. Ermolov laughed, but did not agree. "Men and expenses could have been spared," he said. I think he is writing or wants to write his memoirs. He is not pleased with Karamzin's *History;*[11] he wishes that an ardent pen would portray the transition of the Russian nation from insignificance to glory and power. He spoke of Prince Kurbsky's writings *con amore*.[12] The Germans took a beating. "Some fifty years hence," he said, "people will think there was an auxiliary Prussian or Austrian army in our campaign, commanded by this or that German general." I stayed with him for about two hours. He was vexed that he had not remembered my full name. He apologized by means of compliments. The conversation turned several times to literature. Of Griboedov's verse he says that reading it makes his jaws ache.[13] Of government and politics there was not a word.

My route lay through Kursk and Kharkov, but I turned off onto the direct road to Tiflis, sacrificing a good dinner in a Kursk inn (no trifling thing in our travels) and not curious to visit Kharkov University, which could not match a meal in Kursk.

The roads as far as Elets are terrible. My carriage sank several times into mud worthy of the mud of Odessa. Sometimes I managed to make no more than thirty miles in a day. Finally I saw the steppes of Voronezh and rolled on freely over the green plain. In Novocherkassk I found Count Pushkin, who was also going to Tiflis, and we agreed to travel together.[14]

The transition from Europe to Asia is felt more and more by the hour: forests disappear, hills smooth out, grass becomes thicker and shows more vegetative force; birds unknown in our forests appear; eagles sit like sentinels on the mounds that mark the high road and gaze proudly at the travelers; over the fertile pastures

> Indomitable mares
> Proudly stray in herds.[15]

Kalmyks settle around the station huts. Near their kibitkas graze their ugly, shaggy horses, known to you from the fine drawings of Orlovsky.[16]

The other day I visited a Kalmyk kibitka (crisscross wattle, covered with white felt). The whole family was preparing to have lunch. In the center a cauldron was boiling, and the smoke went out through an opening in the top of the kibitka. A young Kalmyk girl, not bad-looking at all, was sewing and smoking a pipe. I sat down beside her. "What's your name?"—"* * *"—"How old are you?"—"Ten and eight."—"What are you sewing?"—"Pant."—"For whom?"—"For self." She handed me her pipe and started on lunch. In the cauldron tea was boiling with mutton fat and salt. She offered me her dipper. I did not want to refuse and took a sip, trying to hold my breath. I do not think any other national cuisine could produce anything more vile. I asked for something to follow it up. They gave me a piece of dried mare's meat; I was glad enough of that. Kalmyk coquetry scared me; I hastily got out of the kibitka and rode away from the Circe of the steppe.

In Stavropol I saw clouds on the edge of the sky that had struck my eyes exactly nine years earlier. They were still the same, still in the same place. These were the snowy peaks of the Caucasian mountain range.

From Georgievsk I went to see Hot Springs.[17] There I found great changes: in my time the baths were in huts hastily slapped together. The springs, most of them in their primitive state, spurted, steamed, and poured down the mountain in all directions, leaving white or reddish traces behind them. We scooped up the seething water with a dipper made of bark, or with the bottom of a broken bottle. Now magnificent baths and houses have been built. A boulevard lined with lindens follows around the slope of Mashuk. Everywhere there are clean paths, green benches, regular flowerbeds, bridges, pavilions. The sources have been fitted out and lined with stone; police notices are tacked to the walls of the baths; everywhere there is order, cleanliness, prettiness . . .

I confess: The Caucasian springs now offer more conveniences; but I regretted their former wild state; I regretted the steep, stony paths, the bushes, and the unfenced precipices over which I once clambered. With sadness I left the springs and made my way back to Georgievsk. Night soon fell. The clear sky was strewn with millions of stars. I rode along the bank of the Podkumok. A. Raevsky[18] used to sit there with me, listening to the melody of the waters. The outline of majestic Beshtau grew blacker and blacker in the distance, surrounded by its vassal mountains, and finally disappeared in the darkness . . .

The next day we went further on and arrived in Ekaterinograd, formerly the seat of the governor-general.

In Ekaterinograd the Georgian military highway begins; the post road ends. You hire horses to Vladikavkaz. You are provided with a convoy of Cossacks, foot soldiers, and one cannon. Mail is sent twice a week and travelers join it: this is known as an "occasion." We did not have long to wait. The mail came the next day, and the morning after, at nine o'clock, we were ready to be on our way. At the assembly place a whole caravan gathered, consisting of somewhere around five hundred people. There was a drum roll. We set off. At the head went the cannon, surrounded by foot soldiers. After it stretched carriages, britzkas, kibitkas for the soldiers' wives, who traveled from one fortress to another; behind them creaked a train of two-wheeled arbas.* Alongside them ran herds of horses and oxen. Next to them galloped Nogai guides in burkas and with lassoes. All this pleased me very much at first, but I soon became bored. The cannon went at a walk, the match smoked and the soldiers lit their pipes from it. The slowness of our march (on the first day we made only ten miles), the insufferable heat, the shortage of supplies, the uncomfortable night stops, and finally the constant creaking of the Nogai arbas drove me out of all patience. The Tatars take pride in this creaking, saying that they drive around like honest people who have no need to hide. This time I would have found it more pleasant to travel in less respectable company. The road is rather monotonous: a plain; hills off to the sides. At the edge of the sky—the peaks of the Caucasus, getting higher and higher each day. Fortresses sufficient for these parts, with moats that any of us could have jumped across in the old days without a running start, with rusty cannon that have not been fired since the time of Count Gudovich,[19] with dilapidated ramparts where a garrison of chickens and geese wanders about. Within the fortress several hovels, where you can obtain with difficulty a dozen eggs and some sour milk.

The first noteworthy place is the fortress of Minaret. Approaching it, our caravan went along a lovely valley, between burial mounds overgrown with lindens and plane trees. These are the graves of several thousands who died from the plague. Gay with flowers sprung from the infected ashes. To the right shone the snowy Caucasus; ahead loomed an enormous tree-clad mountain; beyond it lay the fortress. Around it can be seen the traces of a devastated aul called Tatartub, which was once the main village in Great Kabarda. A slight, solitary minaret testifies to the existence of the vanished settlement. It rises slenderly amidst the heaps of stones on the bank of a dried-up stream. The inner stairway had not yet collapsed. I climbed up it to the platform, from which

---

* See the glossary of Caucasian terms on p. 402.

the mullah's voice is no longer heard. There I found several unknown names scratched into the bricks by fame-loving travelers.

Our road became picturesque. Mountains towered above us. Barely visible flocks crawled over their heights, looking like insects. We also made out a shepherd, maybe a Russian, taken prisoner once and grown old in captivity. We came upon more burial mounds, more ruins. Two or three tombstones stood on the side of the road. There, by Circassian custom, their horsemen are buried. A Tatar inscription, the image of a saber, a tribal emblem cut into the stone, are left to predatory grandsons in memory of a predatory ancestor.

The Circassians hate us. We have forced them out of their open grazing lands; their auls have been devastated, whole tribes have been wiped out. They withdraw further and further into the mountains and from there carry out their raids. The friendship of the *peaceful* Circassians[20] is unreliable; they are always ready to help their violent fellow tribesmen. The spirit of their wild chivalry has noticeably declined. They rarely attack an equal number of Cossacks, never the foot soldiers, and they run away at the sight of a cannon. But they never miss a chance to attack a weaker troop or a defenseless man. The country roundabout is full of rumors of their villainies. There is almost no way to subdue them, so long as they are not disarmed, as the Crimean Tatars were, which is very hard to accomplish on account of the hereditary feuds and blood vengeance that reign among them. Dagger and saber are parts of their body, and a baby begins to wield them sooner than he can prattle. Among them killing is a simple body movement. They keep prisoners in hope of ransom, but they treat them with terrible inhumanity, force them to work beyond their strength, feed them raw dough, beat them whenever they like, and have them guarded by their young boys, who at one word have the right to cut them up with their children's sabers. A peaceful Circassian who had shot at a soldier was recently captured. He justified it by the fact that his rifle had stayed loaded for too long. What to do with such people? It is to be hoped, however, that if we acquire the region east of the Black Sea, cutting the Circassians off from their trade with Turkey, that will force them to become friendlier to us. The influence of luxury could contribute to their taming: the samovar would be an important innovation. There is a means that is stronger, more moral, more consistent with the enlightenment of our age: the preaching of the Gospel. The Circassians embraced the Mohammedan faith very recently. They were carried away by the active fanaticism of the apostles of the Koran, the most notable of whom was Mansur, an extraordinary man, who for a long time stirred up the Caucasus against Russian dominion, was finally seized by our forces, and died in the Solovki monastery.[21] The Caucasus awaits Christian missionaries. But it is easier for our idleness to pour out dead printed letters instead of the living word and to send mute books to people who are illiterate.

We reached Vladikavkaz, the former Kapkai, the threshold of the mountains. It is surrounded by Ossetian auls. I visited one of them and found myself at a funeral. People crowded around a saklia. In the yard stood an arba hitched to two oxen. Relatives and friends of the deceased arrived from all directions and with loud weeping went into the saklia, beating their foreheads with their fists. The women stood quietly. The dead man was carried out on a burka

> . . . like a warrior taking his rest
> With his martial cloak around him.[22]

They placed him on the arba. One of the guests took the deceased's rifle, blew the powder off the pan, and placed it next to the body. The oxen set out. The guests followed. The body was to be buried in the mountains, some twenty miles from the aul. Unfortunately, nobody could explain these rites to me.

The Ossetes are the poorest tribe of the peoples inhabiting the Caucasus; their women are beautiful and, one hears, very well-disposed to travelers. At the gates of the fortress I met the wife and daughter of an imprisoned Ossete. They were bringing him dinner. Both seemed calm and bold; nevertheless, at my approach they both lowered their heads and covered themselves with their tattered chadras. In the fortress I saw Circassian amanats, frisky and handsome boys. They constantly play pranks and escape from the fortress. They are kept in pitiful conditions. They go around in rags, half naked and abominably filthy. On some I saw wooden fetters. The amanats, once they are set free, probably do not miss their stay in Vladikavkaz.

The cannon left us. We went on with the foot soldiers and the Cossacks. The Caucasus took us into its sanctuary. We heard a muted noise and saw the Terek pouring out in various directions. We rode along its left bank. Its noisy waves turn the wheels of the low Ossetian mills, which look like dog kennels. The deeper we penetrated into the mountains, the narrower the gorge became. The constrained Terek throws its muddy waves with a roar over the rocks that bar its way. The gorge meanders along its course. The stone feet of the mountains are polished by its waves. I went on foot and stopped every other minute, struck by the gloomy enchantment of nature. The weather was bleak; clouds stretched heavily along the black peaks. Count Pushkin and Stjernvall, looking at the Terek, recalled Imatra and preferred "the thundering river of the North."[23] But I had nothing with which to compare the spectacle before me.

Before we reached Lars, I lagged behind the convoy, unable to tear my eyes from the enormous cliffs between which the Terek gushes with indescribable fury. Suddenly a soldier comes running towards me, shouting from far off: "Don't stop, Your Honor, they'll kill you!" This warning, unaccustomed as I was, seemed extremely odd to me. The thing was that Ossetian bandits, safe in this narrow spot, shoot at travelers across the Terek. On the eve of our march they made such an attack on General Bekovich,[24] who galloped through their gunfire. Visible on a cliff are the ruins of some citadel: they are stuck all over with the saklias of peaceful Ossetes, as with swallows' nests.

We stopped for the night in Lars. Here we found a French traveler, who frightened us about the road ahead. He advised us to abandon the carriages in Kobi and continue on horseback. With him for the first time we drank Kakheti wine from a stinking wineskin, reminiscent of the feasting in the Iliad:

And in goatskins wine, our great delight![25]

Here I found a soiled copy of *The Prisoner of the Caucasus*,[26] and, I confess, I reread it with great pleasure. It is all weak, youthful, incomplete; but much of it is aptly divined and expressed.

The next morning we went on our way. Turkish prisoners were working on the road. They complained about the food they were given. They could never get used to Russian black bread. That reminded me of the words of my friend Sheremetev on his return from Paris: "Life in Paris is bad, brother: nothing to eat; no black bread for the asking!"

Five miles from Lars is the Darial outpost. The gorge bears the same name. The cliffs on both sides stand like parallel walls. Here it is so narrow, so narrow, one traveler writes, that you not only see but seem to feel the closeness.[27] A scrap of sky like a ribbon shows blue over your head. Rivulets, falling down from the mountainous heights in small and splashing streams, reminded me of Rembrandt's strange painting, *The Rape of Ganymede*.[28] Besides that, the gorge is lighted perfectly in his taste. In some places the Terek washes right at the foot of the cliffs, and stones are piled along the road in the guise of a dam. Not far from the outpost, a little bridge is boldly thrown across the river. You stand on it as if on a mill. The little bridge shakes all over, and the Terek rumbles like the wheels that turn the millstone. Across from Darial on a steep cliff you can see the ruins of a fortress. Legend has it that a certain Queen Daria hid there, giving her name to the gorge: a tall tale. "Darial" in old Persian means "gate." By Pliny's testimony, the Caucasian Gate, which he mistakenly calls Caspian, was here.[29] The gorge had a real gate across it, a wooden one, bound with iron. Under it, writes Pliny, flows the river Diriodoris. Here a fortress was erected to hold off the raids of the wild tribes, and so on. See the journey of Count J. Potocki, whose learned researches are as entertaining as his Spanish novels.[30]

From Darial we set out for Kazbek. We saw the *Trinity Gate* (an arch formed in the cliff by an explosion of powder)—a road used to pass under it, but now the Terek, which often changes its bed, flows there.

Not far from the settlement of Kazbek, we crossed the *Furious Gully*, a ravine which, during heavy rains, turns into a raging torrent. This time it was perfectly dry and roared in name only.

The village of Kazbek is located at the foot of Mount Kazbek and belongs to Prince Kazbek. The prince, a man of about forty-five, is taller than the fugelman of the Preobrazhensky regiment.[31] We found him in the dukhan (the Georgian word for eateries, which are much poorer and no cleaner than Russian ones). In the doorway lay a fat-bellied burdyuk (an oxhide wineskin), spreading its four legs. The giant was sipping chikhir from it, and he asked me several questions, which I answered with a deference suited to his title and size. We parted great friends.

Impressions soon grow dull. Barely twenty-four hours went by, and already the roaring of the Terek and its shapeless waterfalls, already the cliffs and precipices, ceased to draw my attention. I was possessed only by impatience to reach Tiflis. I rode past Kazbek as indifferently as I once sailed past Chatyrdag. It is also true that the rainy and foggy weather prevented me from seeing its snowy heap, which, in a poet's expression, "props up the heavenly vault."[32]

A Persian prince was expected. At some distance from Kazbek several carriages came towards us and obstructed the narrow road. While the vehicles worked past each other, the convoy officer told us that he was accompanying a Persian court poet and, at my wish, introduced me to Fazil Khan.[33] With the help of an interpreter, I started on a grandiloquent oriental greeting; how ashamed I was when Fazil Khan responded to my inappropriate whimsicality with the simple, intelligent courtesy of a decent man! He hoped to see me in Petersburg; he was sorry that our acquaintance would be of short duration, and so on. Embarrassed, I was forced to abandon my pompously jocular tone and descend to ordinary European phrases. This is a lesson for our Russian love of mockery. In the future, I will not judge a man by his lambskin papakha* and painted nails.

The Kobi outpost is located right at the foot of the Mountain of the Cross, which we now had to go over. We spent the night there and started thinking about how to perform this dread exploit: should we abandon our carriages and mount Cossack horses or send for Ossetian oxen? Just in case, I wrote an official request on behalf of our whole caravan to Mr. Chilyaev, who was in command of these parts, and we went to sleep in expectation of the carts.

The next day around noon we heard noise, shouting, and saw an extraordinary spectacle: eighteen pair of skinny, puny oxen, prodded by a crowd of half-naked Ossetes, were dragging with great difficulty the light Viennese carriage of my friend O. This spectacle at once dispelled all my doubts. I decided to send my heavy Petersburg carriage back to Vladikavkaz and ride on horseback to Tiflis. Count Pushkin did not want to follow my example. He preferred to hitch his britzka, laden with all sorts of supplies, to the whole herd of oxen and cross the snowy ridge in triumph. We parted and I went further on with Colonel Ogarev, who was inspecting the local roads.

The road went through an avalanche that had occurred at the end of June, 1827. These things usually happen every seven years. An enormous block fell down, burying the gorge for a mile, and damming up the Terek. Sentries, standing downstream, heard a terrible noise and saw that the river was quickly getting shallow and in a quarter of an

* So Persian caps are called. *Author.*

hour was completely still and drained. The Terek ate its way through the avalanche only two hours later. Oh, how terrifying it was!

We climbed steeply higher and higher. Our horses sank into the loose snow, under which streams gurgled. I looked at the road with amazement and did not understand how it was possible to travel on wheels.

Just then I heard a muted rumble. "That's an avalanche," said Mr. Ogarev. I turned and saw to one side a heap of snow crumbling and slowly sliding down the steep slope. Small avalanches are not uncommon here. Last year a Russian driver was going over the Mountain of the Cross; there was an avalanche: a frightful block of snow fell on his vehicle, swallowed cart, horse, and muzhik, tumbled across the road and down into the abyss with its booty. We reached the very top of the mountain. A granite cross had been set up there, an old monument, restored by Ermolov.

Here travelers usually get out of their carriages and go on foot. Recently some foreign consul came here: he was so shaky that he asked to be blindfolded; he was led under the arms, and when they took off his blindfold, he sank to his knees and thanked God, and so on, which greatly amazed the guides.

The instantaneous transition from the formidable Caucasus to winsome Georgia is ravishing. The air of the south suddenly begins to waft over the traveler. From the height of Mount Gut the Kaishaur valley opens out, with its inhabited cliffs, its gardens, its bright Aragva, meandering like a silver ribbon—and all this in miniature, at the bottom of a two-mile-deep chasm, along which goes a dangerous road.

We were descending into the valley. A young crescent moon appeared in the clear sky. The evening air was gentle and warm. I spent the night on the bank of the Aragva, in the house of Mr. Chilyaev. The next day I parted from my amiable host and went further on.

Here Georgia begins. Bright valleys watered by the merry Aragva replaced the gloomy gorges and the formidable Terek. Instead of bare cliffs I saw around me green mountains and fruit trees. Aqueducts demonstrated the presence of civilization. One of them struck me with a perfect optical illusion: the water seemed to be flowing uphill.

In Paisanaur I stopped to change horses. There I met a Russian officer who was accompanying the Persian prince. Soon I heard the sound of little bells, and a whole line of katars (mules), tied to one another and loaded in the Asian manner, stretched out along the road. I went on foot, without waiting for horses; and half a mile from Ananur, at a turn of the road, I met Khozrev-Mirza.[34] His vehicles were standing there. He looked out of his carriage and nodded to me. A few hours after our meeting the prince was attacked by mountaineers. Hearing the whistle of bullets, Khozrev jumped out of his carriage, mounted a horse, and galloped off. The Russians who were with him marveled at his courage. The thing was that the young Asiatic, unaccustomed to a carriage, saw it as more of a trap than a shelter.

I reached Ananur, not feeling any fatigue. My horses had not come yet. I was told that it was no more than seven miles to the town of Dusheti, and I again set out on foot. But I did not know that the road went uphill. Those seven miles were worth a good fifteen.

Evening fell; I walked on, going higher and higher. It was impossible to lose my way; but in some places the clayey mud produced by the springs reached my knees. I was completely exhausted. It grew darker. I heard howling and barking and rejoiced, fancying that the town was near. I was mistaken: the barking came from the dogs of the Georgian shepherds, and the howling from jackals, common animals in those parts. I cursed my impatience, but there was nothing to be done. At last I saw lights, and around midnight I found myself near houses overshaded by trees. The first man I met volunteered to take me to the mayor and for that demanded an abaz from me.

My appearance at the mayor's, an old Georgian officer, caused a great stir. I requested, first of all, a room where I could undress; second, a glass of wine; third, an abaz for my guide. The mayor did not know how to receive me, and kept glancing at me in perplexity. Seeing he was in no hurry to fulfill my requests, I began to undress in front of him, apologizing de la liberté grande.* Fortunately, in my pocket I found my papers, proving that I was a peaceful traveler and not a Rinaldo Rinaldini.[35] The blessed charter had an immediate effect: I was given a room, a glass of wine was brought, and an abaz was given to my guide, along with a fatherly reprimand for his money-grubbing, insulting to Georgian hospitality. I threw myself on the sofa, hoping after my exploit to sleep a hero's sleep: nothing of the sort. Fleas, far more dangerous than jackals, fell upon me and gave me no rest all night. In the morning my man came to me and said that Count Pushkin had safely crossed the snowy mountains with his oxen and arrived in Dusheti. So

* for the great liberty

much for my hurry! Count Pushkin and Stjernvall called on me and suggested that we go on our way together again. I left Dusheti with the pleasant thought that I would spend the night in Tiflis.

The road was pleasant and picturesque as well, though we rarely saw any signs of population. Several miles from Gartsiskal we crossed the Kura on an ancient bridge, a monument of the Roman campaigns, and at a long trot, at times even a gallop, rode to Tiflis, where we arrived without noticing it and found it was past ten o'clock in the evening.

CHAPTER TWO

Tiflis. The public baths. Noseless Hassan. Georgian ways.
Songs. Kakheti wine. Causes of heat. High prices. Description
of the city. Leaving Tiflis. The Georgian night. The sight of
Armenia. Double distance. An Armenian village. Gergeri.
Griboedov. Bezobdal. A mineral spring. A storm in the
mountains. Night in Gyumri. Ararat. The border. Turkish
hospitality. Kars. An Armenian family. Leaving Kars. Count
Paskevich's camp.

I stayed at an inn, and the next day headed for the famous Tiflis baths. The city seemed populous to me. The Asiatic buildings and the market reminded me of Kishinev.[36] Donkeys with panniers ran along the narrow and crooked streets; arbas harnessed to oxen blocked the way. Armenians, Georgians, Circassians, Persians thronged in the irregular square; among them young Russian officials rode on Karabakh stallions. At the entrance to the baths sat the owner, an old Persian. He opened the door for me, I entered a spacious room, and what did I see? More than fifty women, young and old, half-dressed and completely undressed, sat and stood undressing and dressing at benches placed along the walls. I stopped. "Go on, go on," the owner said to me. "Today is Tuesday: women's day. Never mind, there's no harm." "Of course there's no harm," I replied. "On the contrary." The appearance of men did not make any impression. They went on laughing and talking among themselves. Not one of them hastened to cover herself with her chadra; not one of them stopped undressing. It seemed I had entered invisibly. Many of them were indeed beautiful and justified the imagination of T. Moore:

> . . . a lovely Georgian maid,
> With all the bloom, the freshen'd glow
> Of her own country maiden's looks,
> When warm they rise from Teflis' brooks.
>
> LALLA ROOKH[37]

But I know nothing more repulsive than Georgian old women: they are witches.

The Persian led me to the baths: the hot iron-sulfur spring spilled into a deep basin carved in the rock. Never in my life have I met, either in Russia or in Turkey, with anything more luxurious than the Tiflis baths. I will describe them in detail.

The owner left me in the charge of a Tatar bath attendant. I must inform you that he had no nose, but that did not prevent him from being a master of his trade. Hassan (that was the name of the nose-less Tatar) began by laying me down on the warm stone floor; after which he started wringing my arms and legs, pulling the joints, beating me hard with his fists; I felt not the slightest pain, but an astonishing relief. (Asiatic bath attendants sometimes become ecstatic, jump onto your shoulders, slide their feet over your thighs, do a squatting dance on your back, è sempre bene.*) After that he rubbed me for a long time with a woolen mitten and, dousing me liberally with warm water, began to wash me with a soapy linen pouch. The feeling is ineffable: hot soap pours all over you like air! NB: the woolen mitten and linen pouch should definitely be adopted in Russian baths: connoisseurs will be grateful for such an innovation.

After the pouch, Hassan let me get into the bath; and with that the ceremony was over.

I hoped to find Raevsky in Tiflis, but learning that his regiment was already on the march, I decided to ask Count Paskevich's permission to come to the army.

I spent around two weeks in Tiflis and became acquainted with the local society. Sankovsky, publisher of the Tiflis Gazette, told me

---

* it is always good (Italian)

many curious things about the local area, about Prince Tsitsianov, A. P. Ermolov, and so on.[38] Sankovsky loves Georgia and foresees a brilliant future for her.

Georgia put herself under Russian protection in 1783, which did not prevent the famed Aga Mohammed from taking and destroying Tiflis and carrying off 20,000 of its inhabitants as prisoners (1795).[39] Georgia came under the scepter of the emperor Alexander in 1802. The Georgians are a martial people. They have proved their courage under our banners. Their mental abilities could do with greater cultivation. They are generally of cheerful and sociable character. On holidays the men drink and carouse in the streets. The dark-eyed boys sing, leap, and turn somersaults; the women dance the lezghinka.

The voice of Georgian songs is pleasant. One of them was translated for me word for word; it seems to have been composed recently; there is some oriental nonsense in it, which has its poetic virtue. Here it is:

Soul, recently born in paradise! Soul, created for my happiness!
From you, immortal one, I look for life.

From you, blossoming spring, two-week-old moon, from you, my
guardian angel, from you I look for life.

Your face shines and your smile gladdens. I do not want to possess
the world; I want your gaze. From you I look for life.

Mountain rose, fresh with dew! Chosen favorite of nature! Quiet,
hidden treasure! From you I look for life.

Georgians drink—not as we do, and with amazing fortitude. Their wines do not travel and quickly go bad, but in place they are excellent. Kakheti and Karabakh wines are worth some burgundies. Wine is kept in *maran*s, enormous jars, buried in the ground. They are opened with solemn rituals. Recently a Russian dragoon, having secretly unearthed such a jar, fell into it and drowned in Kakheti wine, like unfortunate Clarence in a barrel of Malaga.[40]

Tiflis is situated on the banks of the Kura, in a valley surrounded by stony mountains. They shield it on all sides from the winds, and, turned burning hot by the sun, do not so much heat as boil the motionless air. That is the cause of the unbearable heat that reigns in Tiflis, even though the city is situated only at just under forty-one degrees latitude. Its very name (*Tbilis-kalar*) means "Hot City."[41]

The greater part of the city is built in the Asiatic way: low houses, flat roofs. In the northern part houses of European architecture rise, and around them regular squares are beginning to form. The market is divided into several rows; the shops are filled with Turkish and Persian goods, rather cheap, if you take into account the universally high prices. Tiflis weapons are highly valued everywhere in the East. Count Samoilov and V., reputed to be mighty men here, used to try out their new swords by cutting a sheep in two or chopping off a bull's head at one stroke.[42]

Armenians make up the main part of the population of Tiflis: in 1825 there were as many as 2,500 families. During the present wars their number has increased still more. Georgian families amount to 1,500. Russians do not consider themselves local residents. The military, bound by duty, live in Georgia because they have been ordered to. Young titular councilors come here in pursuit of the much-desired rank of assessor.[43] Both the former and the latter look upon Georgia as exile.

The Tiflis climate is said to be unhealthy. The local fevers are terrible; they are treated with mercury, the use of which is harmless because of the heat. Doctors feed it to their patients quite shamelessly. General Sipyagin died, they say, because his personal physician, who came with him from Petersburg, was frightened of the dose suggested by the local doctors and did not give it to the sick man.[44] The local fevers resemble those of the Crimea and Moldavia and are treated in the same way.

The inhabitants drink the water of the Kura, cloudy but pleasant. The water of all the springs and wells has a strong taste of sulfur. However, wine here is in such general use that a lack of water would go unnoticed.

I was astonished by the low value of money in Tiflis. Having taken a cab through two streets and let it go after half an hour, I had to pay the cabbie two silver roubles. I thought at first that he wanted to profit from a visitor's ignorance; but I was told that that was indeed the price. Everything else is correspondingly expensive.

We went to the German colony and had dinner there. We drank the beer they make, of a very unpleasant taste, and paid very dearly for a very bad meal. In my inn the food was just as expensive and bad. General Strekalov, a well-known gastronome, once invited me to dinner;

unfortunately, the dishes were served according to rank and there were English officers with general's epaulettes at the table.[45] The servants bypassed me so assiduously that I got up from the table hungry. Devil take the Tiflis gastronome!

I waited impatiently for my fate to be decided. At last I received a note from Raevsky. He wrote that I should make haste to Kars, because in a few days the troops were to go further on. I left the next day.

I went on horseback, changing horses at the Cossack outposts. The earth around me was scorched by the heat. From a distance the Georgian villages looked to me like beautiful gardens, but, on riding up to them, I saw a few poor saklias overshaded by dusty poplars. The sun went down, but the air was still stifling:

> Torrid nights!
> Foreign stars! . . .

The moon shone; all was still; only the trot of my horse rang out in the night's silence. I rode for a long time without meeting any signs of habitation. At last I saw a solitary saklia. I started knocking at the door. The owner came out. I asked for water, first in Russian, then in Tatar. He did not understand me. Amazing nonchalance! Twenty miles from Tiflis and on the road to Persia and Turkey, he did not know a word of Russian or of Tatar.

Having spent the night at a Cossack outpost, I headed further on at dawn. The road went through mountains and forests. I met some traveling Tatars; there were several women among them. They were on horseback, wrapped in chadras; all you could see were their eyes and heels.

I started going up Bezobdal, the mountain that separates Georgia from ancient Armenia. A wide road, overshaded by trees, winds around the mountain. On the summit of Bezobdal I rode through a small gorge, apparently called the Wolf Gate, and found myself on the natural border of Georgia. Before me were new mountains, a new horizon; below me spread fertile green wheatfields. I looked back once more at scorched Georgia and started down the gently sloping mountain to the fresh plains of Armenia. With indescribable pleasure I noticed that the heat suddenly became less intense: the climate was different.

My man with the pack horses lagged behind me. I rode alone in the blossoming desert surrounded by distant mountains. I absentmindedly rode past the post where I was meant to change horses. More than six hours went by, and I began to wonder about the distance I had gone. I saw heaps of stones to one side that looked like saklias, and headed for them. In fact, I came to an Armenian village. Several women in motley rags were sitting on the flat roof of an underground saklia. I expressed myself somehow or other. One of them went down into the saklia and brought up some cheese and milk. After resting for a few minutes, I went on and saw on a high bank opposite me the citadel of Gergeri. Three streams rushed with noise and foam down the high bank. I crossed the river. Two oxen hitched to an arba were going up the steep road. Several Georgians were accompanying it. "Where are you from?" I asked them. "Tehran." "What are you carrying?" "Griboed." It was the body of the slain Griboedov, which they were accompanying to Tiflis.[46]

I never thought I would meet our Griboedov again! I parted with him last year in Petersburg, before he left for Persia. He was sad and had strange premonitions. I began to reassure him; he said to me: *"Vous ne connaissez pas ces gens-là; vous verrez qu'il faudra jouer des couteaux."** He supposed the cause of the bloodshed would be the death of the shah and the internecine war among his seventy sons. But the elderly shah is still alive, and Griboedov's prophetic words came true. He died under Persian daggers, a victim of ignorance and treachery. His disfigured corpse, which for three days was the plaything of the Tehran mob, was recognized only by the hand once pierced by a pistol bullet.

I made the acquaintance of Griboedov in 1817. His melancholy character, his embittered mind, his good-nature, his very weaknesses and vices, inevitable companions of humanity—everything in him was extraordinarily attractive. Born with an ambition equal to his gifts, he was caught for a long time in a web of petty needs and obscurity. His abilities as a statesman remained unemployed; his talent as a poet went unrecognized; even his cold and brilliant courage remained under suspicion for some time. A few friends knew his worth and saw a distrustful smile, that stupid, insufferable smile, when they happened to speak of him as an extraordinary man. People believe only in fame and do not understand that there might be among them some Napoleon, who has never commanded a single company of chasseurs, or another Descartes, who has not published a single line in the *Moscow Telegraph*.

---

* "You don't know those people; you'll see it will come to playing with knives."

However, our respect for fame may well come from vanity: our own voice, too, goes into the making of fame.

Griboedov's life was darkened by certain clouds: the consequence of ardent passions and powerful circumstances. He felt the necessity of settling accounts once and for all with his youth and making a sharp turn in his life. He said good-bye to Petersburg and idle dissipation, and went to Georgia, where he spent eight years in solitary, unremitting work. His return to Moscow in 1824 was a turnabout in his fate and the beginning of continuous successes. His comedy in manuscript, *Woe from Wit*, had an indescribable effect and suddenly placed him in the rank of our foremost poets. A short time after that his perfect knowledge of the region where a war was starting opened up a new career for him; he was appointed ambassador. On coming to Georgia, he married the woman he loved . . . I know of nothing more enviable than the last years of his stormy life. His death itself, overtaking him in the midst of courageous, unequal combat, had nothing terrible, nothing agonizing for Griboedov. It was instantaneous and beautiful.

What a pity that Griboedov did not leave us his memoirs! Writing his biography should be a task for his friends; but among us remarkable people disappear without leaving a trace behind. We are lazy and incurious . . .

In Gergeri I met Buturlin, who, like me, was going to the army.[47] Buturlin traveled with every possible gratification. I had dinner with him as if we were in Petersburg. We decided to travel together; but the demon of impatience took possession of me again. My man asked me for permission to rest. I set out alone, even without a guide. There was only one road, and it was perfectly safe.

Having crossed the mountain and descended into a valley overshaded by trees, I saw a mineral spring flowing across the road. Here I met an Armenian priest who was going to Akhaltsikhe from Erevan. "What's new in Erevan?" I asked him. "In Erevan there's plague," he replied, "and what about Akhaltsikhe?" "In Akhaltsikhe there's plague," I replied. Having exchanged this pleasant news, we parted.

I rode amidst fertile wheatfields and blossoming meadows. The harvest swayed, waiting for the sickle. I admired the beautiful land, the fruitfulness of which was proverbial in the East. By evening I arrived in Pernike. Here was a Cossack outpost. The sergeant predicted a storm and advised me to stay the night, but I wanted to reach Gyumri without fail that same day.

I was to cross some not very high mountains, the natural border of the Kars pashalik. The sky was covered with dark clouds; I hoped that the wind, which was growing stronger every minute, would scatter them. But rain began to sprinkle and kept getting heavier and steadier. It is eighteen miles from Pernike to Gyumri. I tightened the belt of my burka, drew a bashlik over my visored cap, and entrusted myself to Providence.

More than two hours went by. The rain would not let up. Water poured in streams from my now sodden burka and rain-soaked bashlik. Finally a cold stream began to penetrate behind my tie, and soon the rain had soaked me to the skin. The night was dark; a Cossack rode ahead showing me the way. We started up the mountains. Meanwhile the rain stopped and the clouds scattered. It was about six miles to Gyumri. The wind, blowing freely, was so strong that in a quarter of an hour it dried me out completely. I had no hope of avoiding a fever. Finally I reached Gyumri at around midnight. The Cossack led me straight to the outpost. We stopped by a tent, which I hurriedly entered. There I found twelve Cossacks sleeping side by side. Room was made for me; I collapsed on my burka, insensible from fatigue. That day I had ridden fifty miles. I fell into a dead sleep.

The Cossacks awakened me at dawn. My first thought was: have I come down with a fever? But, thank God, I felt hale and hearty; there was no trace, not only of illness, but even of fatigue. I came out of the tent into the fresh morning air. The sun was rising. Against the clear sky stood a white, snowy, two-headed mountain. "What mountain is that?" I asked, stretching, and heard the answer: "It's Ararat." How strong is the effect of sounds! I gazed greedily at the biblical mountain, saw the ark, moored to its top in hopes of renewal and life—and the raven and the dove flying off, symbols of punishment and reconciliation . . .

My horse was ready. I set out with a guide. The morning was beautiful. The sun was shining. We rode across a wide meadow, over thick green grass, washed with dew and the drops of yesterday's rain. Before us sparkled a river, which we would have to ford. "Here is the Arpachai," the Cossack said to me. The Arpachai! Our border! That was worth Ararat. I galloped to the river with an indescribable feeling. I had never yet seen a foreign land. For me there was something mysterious in a border; since childhood travel had been my favorite dream. Later I led a nomadic life for a long time, wandering now in the south, now in the north, but I had never yet escaped the limits of boundless Russia.

I joyfully rode into the cherished river, and my good horse carried me to the Turkish bank. But that bank had already been conquered: I was still in Russia.

I still had fifty miles to go to reach Kars. I hoped to see our camp by evening. I did not stop anywhere. Halfway there, in an Armenian village, built in the mountains on the bank of a little river, I ate, instead of dinner, a cursed *churek*, Armenian flatbread, baked half with ashes, which the Turkish prisoners in the Darial gorge missed so much. I would have paid dearly for a slice of Russian black bread, which they found so disgusting. I was accompanied by a young Turk, a terrible chatterbox. He babbled in Turkish all the way, caring less whether I understood him or not. I strained my attention and tried to guess what he meant. He seemed to be scolding the Russians, and, as he was used to seeing them all in uniform, took me by my clothes for a foreigner. We met a Russian officer going the opposite way. He was coming from our camp and told me that the Russian army had already marched out of Kars. I cannot describe my despair: the thought that I would have to go back to Tiflis, exhausting myself for nothing in deserted Armenia, simply killed me. The officer went on his way; the Turk again began his monologue; but I was past listening to him. I changed from an amble to a long trot and by evening came to a Turkish village located thirteen miles from Kars.

Having leaped off my horse, I was about to enter the first saklia, but the owner appeared in the doorway and pushed me away with curses. I responded to his greeting with my whip. The Turk started shouting; people gathered. My guide apparently intervened for me. They showed me to the caravansarai; I went into a big saklia that resembled a cattle shed; there was no room in it to spread my burka. I requested a horse. The Turkish headman came. To all his incomprehensible talk I made one reply: *verbana at* (give me a horse). The Turks would not consent. Finally it occurred to me to show them some money (which is what I should have done in the first place). A horse was brought at once, and I was given a guide.

I rode through a wide valley surrounded by mountains. Soon I saw Kars, showing white against one of them. My Turk pointed it out to me, repeating "Kars! Kars!" and sent his horse into a gallop; I followed him, suffering from anxiety: my fate would be decided in Kars. There I would find out where our camp was and whether it would still be possible to catch up with the army. Meanwhile the sky clouded over and it rained again; but I no longer cared about that.

We rode into Kars. Riding up to the gate in the wall, I heard a Russian drum: they were beating retreat. A sentry took my pass and went to the commandant. I stood in the rain for about half an hour. Finally they let me in. I told my guide to take me straight to the baths. We rode along the steep and winding streets. The horses slid on the bad Turkish pavement. We stopped in front of a house of rather poor appearance. This was the baths. The Turk dismounted and started knocking on the door. No one answered. Rain poured down on me. Finally a young Armenian came out of a neighboring house and, having talked with my Turk, invited me in, speaking rather good Russian. He led me up a narrow stairway to the second part of the house. In a room furnished with low couches and threadbare carpets sat an old woman, his mother. She came up to me and kissed my hand. Her son told her to start a fire and prepare dinner for me. I took off my burka and sat down by the fire. My host's younger brother, a boy of about seventeen, came in. Both brothers had been in Tiflis and lived there for several months at a time. They told me that our troops had left the day before and that our camp was seventeen miles from Kars. That set me completely at ease. Soon the old woman had prepared me some lamb with onion, which I thought the height of culinary art. We all lay down to sleep in the same room; I sprawled in front of the dying fire and fell asleep in the pleasant hope of seeing Count Paskevich's camp the next day.

In the morning I went to look at the town. The younger of my hosts volunteered to be my cicerone. Examining the fortifications and the citadel, built on an inaccessible cliff, I could not understand how we could have taken Kars. My Armenian explained to me as well as he could the military actions that he himself had witnessed. Noticing an inclination for war in him, I proposed that he go to the army with me. He accepted at once. I sent him for horses. He came back together with an officer, who demanded a written order from me. Judging by the Asiatic features of his face, I did not deem it necessary to rummage among my papers and took from my pocket the first scrap I chanced upon. The officer, having gravely studied it, at once gave instructions that horses be brought to his honor in accordance with the order and gave me back my paper: it was a poem to a Kalmyk girl that I had scribbled in one of the Cossack way stations.[48] Half an hour later I rode out of Kars, and Artemy (the name of my Armenian) was already riding beside me on a Turkish stallion, a supple Kurdish javelin in his hand, a dagger behind his belt, and raving about Turks and battles.

I rode over land sown everywhere with grain; I could see villages around, but they were empty: the inhabitants had fled. The road was excellent and paved in marshy places—stone bridges had been built across the streams. The land was rising noticeably—the advance hills of the Sagan-loo ridge, the ancient Tauris, were beginning to appear. Some two hours went by; I rode up a gentle slope and suddenly saw our camp, pitched on the bank of the Kars-chai; a few minutes later I was already in Raevsky's tent.

CHAPTER THREE

Crossing over Sagan-loo. A skirmish. Camp life. Yazidis.
Battle with the seraskir of Arzrum. A blown-up saklia.

I arrived just in time. That same day (June 13) the army received the order to move forward. Having dinner at Raevsky's, I listened to the young generals discussing the maneuver prescribed for them. General Burtsov[49] was dispatched to the left down the Arzrum high road, straight toward the Turkish camp, while the rest of the army was to move to the right side around the enemy.

The troops set out between four and five. I rode with the Nizhegorodsky dragoon regiment, conversing with Raevsky, whom I had not seen for several years. Night fell; we stopped in the valley where the whole army had made a halt. Here I had the honor of being introduced to Count Paskevich.

I found the count in quarters before a campfire, surrounded by his staff. He was cheerful and received me amicably. A stranger to the military art, I did not suspect that the fate of the campaign was being decided at that moment. Here I saw our Volkhovsky,[50] covered with dust from head to foot, overgrown with beard, exhausted with cares. He found time, however, to talk with me as an old schoolmate. Here I also saw Mikhail Pushchin,[51] who had been wounded the year before. He is loved and respected as a fine comrade and a brave soldier. Many of my old friends surrounded me. How changed they were! How quickly time passes!

Eheu, fugaces, Postume, Postume
labuntur anni . . . *

I went back to Raevsky and spent the night in his tent. In the middle of the night I was awakened by terrible shouting: you might have thought the enemy had made a surprise attack. Raevsky sent to find out the cause of the alarm: several Tatar horses, torn loose from their tethers, were running around the camp, and the Muslims (as the Tatars who serve in our army are called) were trying to catch them.

At dawn the army moved forward. We rode up to the tree-clad mountains. We went down into a gorge. The dragoons talked among themselves: "Watch out, brother, steady now: you'll catch some case shot." In fact, the location was favorable for an ambush; but the Turks, sidetracked by General Burtsov's maneuver, did not take advantage of it. We passed safely through the dangerous gorge and stopped on the heights of Sagan-loo, seven miles from the enemy camp.

The nature around us was dreary. The air was cold, the mountains covered with mournful pines. Snow lay in the glens.

. . . nec Armeniis in oris,
amice Valgi, stat glacies iners
menses per omnis . . . †

We barely had time to rest and have dinner when we heard gunfire. Raevsky sent for information. The report was that the Turks had started a skirmish on our advance picket lines. I went with Semichev[52] to have a look at a picture that was new to me. We met a wounded Cossack: he sat swaying in the saddle, pale and bloody. Two Cossacks were supporting him. "Are there many Turks?" asked Semichev. "A whole swiny swarm, Your Honor," replied one of them. Having passed through the

---

* Alas, Postumus, Postumus, the fleeting / years slip by . . . (Horace, *Odes*, II, 14).
† . . . nor in Armenia, / friend Valgius, does the ice stay inert / for months on end . . . (Horace, *Odes*, II, 9).

gorge, we suddenly saw on the slope of the mountain opposite no less than two hundred Cossacks, formed into a single line, and above them about five hundred Turks. The Cossacks were slowly retreating; the Turks were driving ahead with great boldness, taking aim at twenty paces, firing, galloping back. Their high turbans, handsome dolmans, and brightly caparisoned horses were in sharp contrast with the blue uniforms and simple harness of the Cossacks. Some fifteen of our soldiers had already been wounded. Lieutenant Colonel Basov sent for reinforcements. Just then he himself was wounded in the leg. The Cossacks were in confusion. But Basov mounted up again and remained in command. The reinforcements came quickly. Noticing it, the Turks disappeared at once, leaving on the mountainside a naked Cossack corpse, decapitated and truncated. The Turks send cut-off heads to Constantinople, and the hands they dip in blood and put the prints on their banners. The shooting died down. Eagles, the companions of armies, hovered over the mountain, seeking their prey from on high. Just then a group of generals and officers appeared: Count Paskevich arrived and went up the mountain behind which the Turks had vanished. They were reinforced by four thousand cavalry concealed in the hollow and the ravines. From the top of the mountain the view of the Turkish camp opened out, separated from us by ravines and elevations. We came back late. Going through our camp, I saw our wounded, five of whom died that same night and the next day. In the evening I visited young Osten-Sacken,[53] wounded that day in another battle.

I liked camp life very much. A cannon shot roused us at dawn. Sleeping in a tent was remarkably healthy. At dinner we washed down Asiatic shashlik with English beer and champagne chilled in the snows of Taurida. Our company was diverse. In General Raevsky's tent the beks of the Muslim regiments gathered; the conversation was conducted through an interpreter. In our army there were both people of our Transcaucasian territories and inhabitants of recently conquered areas. Among them I looked with curiosity at the Yazidis, reputed in the East to be devil worshippers.[54] About three hundred families live at the foot of Ararat. They have recognized the rule of the Russian sovereign. Their chief, a tall, ugly man in a red cape and a black hat, occasionally came with his respects to General Raevsky, commander of all the cavalry. I tried to find out from the Yazidi the truth about their beliefs. To my questions he replied that the rumor of the Yazidis supposedly worshipping Satan was an empty fable; that they believe in one God; that, true, by their law it was considered improper and ignoble to curse the devil, for he is now unhappy, but that in time he may be forgiven, for it is impossible to set limits to Allah's mercy. This explanation set me at ease. I was very glad for the Yazidis that they did not worship Satan; and their errors now seemed to me much more forgivable.

My man appeared in the camp three days later. He came with the baggage train, which in full view of the enemy had safely joined the army. NB: During the whole campaign not one arba of our numerous train was captured by the enemy. The orderliness with which the train followed the troops was indeed amazing.

On the morning of June 17 we again heard shooting and two hours later we saw a Karabakh regiment returning with eight Turkish banners: Colonel Frideriks[55] had had a run-in with the enemy, who lodged themselves behind heaps of stone, had forced them out and driven them away; Osman Pasha, commander of the cavalry, had barely managed to escape.

On June 18 the camp moved to another site. On the 19th, the cannon had no sooner roused us than everything in the camp started moving. The generals went to their posts. Regiments formed up; officers went and stood by their platoons. I remained alone, not knowing which way to go and letting my horse take me wherever God willed. I met General Burtsov, who invited me to the left flank. "What is the left flank?" I thought and rode on. I caught sight of General Muravyov, who was positioning cannon. Soon the Turkish delibash appeared and circled around in the valley, exchanging fire with our Cossacks. Meanwhile a dense throng of their infantry was moving along the hollow. General Muravyov gave orders to fire. The case shot struck the very center of their throng. The Turks swarmed to one side and hid behind a rise. I saw Count Paskevich surrounded by his staff. The Turks were flanking our troops, separated from them by a deep ravine. The count sent Pushchin to reconnoiter the ravine. Pushchin galloped off. The Turks took him for a raider and fired a volley at him. Everybody laughed. The count ordered cannon brought up and fired. The enemy scattered over the mountain and into the hollow. On the left flank, where Burtsov had invited me, things were getting hot. In front of us (opposite the center) the Turkish cavalry galloped. Against them the count sent General Raevsky, who ordered his Nizhegorodsky regiment into the attack. The Turks disappeared. Our Tatars surrounded the wounded and promptly stripped them, leaving them naked in the middle of the field. General Raevsky stopped at the edge of the ravine. Two squadrons, separated from the regiment, had gotten carried away in their pursuit; they were rescued by Colonel Simonich.

The battle died down. Before our eyes the Turks began digging in the ground and lugging stones, fortifying themselves in their usual way. They were left in peace. We dismounted and began to dine on whatever God sent us. Just then several prisoners were brought to the count. One of them was badly wounded. They were questioned. At around six o'clock the troops again received orders to go against the enemy. The Turks began to stir behind their rubble-work, met us with cannon fire, and soon beat a retreat. Our cavalry was in the advance; we began to descend into the ravine; the earth broke loose and crumbled under the horses' hooves. My horse might have fallen down at any moment, and then the Combined Uhlan regiment would have ridden over me. But God brought me through. No sooner did we come out onto the wide road that goes through the mountains than our entire cavalry broke into full gallop. The Turks fled; the Cossacks lashed at the cannon abandoned on the road with their whips and raced past. The Turks plunged into the ravines on both sides of the road; they were no longer shooting; at least not a single bullet whizzed past my ears. First in the pursuit were our Tatar regiments, whose horses are notable for their speed and strength. My horse, taking the bit in his teeth, did not lag behind them; it was all I could do to hold him back. We stopped before the corpse of a young Turk lying across the road. He seemed to be about eighteen years old; his pale, girlish face was not disfigured. His turban lay in the dust; the back of his shaven head had been pierced by a bullet. I rode at a walk; soon Raevsky caught up with me. He wrote a report to Count Paskevich in pencil on a scrap of paper about the total defeat of the enemy and rode on. I followed him at a distance. Night fell. My tired horse lagged behind and stumbled at every step. Count Paskevich gave orders not to call off the pursuit and took command of it himself. I was overtaken by our cavalry detachments; I saw Colonel Polyakov, commander of the Cossack artillery, which had played an important role that day, and together with him arrived at the abandoned village where Count Paskevich had stopped, having called off the pursuit on account of nightfall.

We found the count on the roof of an underground saklia, in front of a fire. Prisoners were brought to him. He questioned them. Almost all the commanders were there as well. The Cossacks held their horses by the reins. The fire cast its light on a picture worthy of Salvator Rosa;[56] a river murmured in the darkness. Just then it was reported to the count that powder stores had been hidden in the village and there was danger of an explosion. The count left the saklia with all his retinue. We rode to our camp, which by now was twenty miles from the place where we had spent the night. The road was full of cavalry detachments. We had only just reached the place when the sky was lit up as if by a meteor and we heard a muffled explosion. The saklia we had left fifteen minutes earlier was blown up into the air: there had been stores of powder in it. The hurtling stones crushed several Cossacks.

That was all I managed to see at that time. In the evening I learned that in this battle we had crushed the seraskir of Arzrum, who was going to join Hakki Pasha with 30,000 troops.[57] The seraskir fled to Arzrum; his troops, flung over Sagan-loo, were dispersed, his artillery taken, and only Hakki Pasha was left on our hands. Count Paskevich gave him no time to prepare himself.

CHAPTER FOUR

The battle with Hakki Pasha. The death of a Tatar bek. A hermaphrodite. The captive pasha. Araks. Shepherd's Bridge. Hassan-Kalé. A hot spring. The march to Arzrum. Negotiations. The taking of Arzrum. Turkish prisoners. A dervish.

The next day before five o'clock the camp woke up and received orders to move on. Coming out of my tent, I met Count Paskevich, who got up before everybody else. He saw me. "*Êtes-vous fatigué de la journée d'hier?*"– "*Mais un peu, m. le Comte.*"—"*J'en suis fâché pour vous, car nous allons faire encore une marche pour joindre le Pacha, et puis il faudra poursuivre l'ennemi encore une trentaine de verstes.*"*

We set out and by eight o'clock we came to an elevation from which the camp of Hakki Pasha could be seen as on the palm of your hand.

---

* "Are you tired from yesterday?"—"Just a little, monsieur le Comte."—"That upsets me, because we're going to make another march to catch up with the pasha, and then we'll have to pursue the enemy another thirty versts [twenty miles]."

The Turks opened fire harmlessly from all their batteries. Meanwhile great commotion could be seen in their camp. Fatigue and the morning heat made many of us dismount and lie down on the fresh grass. I wound the reins around my hand and fell into a sweet sleep, while awaiting orders to go forward. A quarter of an hour later I was awakened. Everything was in movement. On one side, columns marched towards the Turkish camp; on the other, the cavalry was preparing to pursue the enemy. I was following the Nizhegorodsky regiment, but my horse limped. I lagged behind. The Uhlan regiment raced past me. Then Volkhovsky galloped by with three cannon. I found myself alone in the wooded mountains. I ran across a dragoon who told me that the woods were full of the enemy. I went back. I met General Muravyov with his infantry regiment. He detached a company to the woods to clear them. Drawing near a hollow, I saw an extraordinary picture. Under a tree lay one of our Tatar beks, mortally wounded. Beside him a boy, his favorite, was sobbing. A mullah, kneeling, was reciting prayers. The dying bek was extremely calm and looked steadily at his young friend. In the hollow some five hundred prisoners were gathered. Several wounded Turks made signs for me to approach, probably taking me for a doctor and seeking help that I could not give them. A Turk emerged from the woods, pressing a bloody rag to his wound. Some soldiers went up to him, intending to finish him off, perhaps out of charity. That aroused my indignation; I interceded for the poor Turk, and with difficulty brought him, exhausted and losing blood, to a group of his comrades. With them was Colonel Anrep.[58] He was amicably smoking their pipes, though there were rumors that the plague had broken out in the Turkish camp. The prisoners sat calmly talking among themselves. They were almost all young men. Having rested, we moved on. There were bodies lying everywhere along the road. After some ten miles I found the Nizhegorodsky regiment, which had paused on the bank of a stream among the rocks. The pursuit went on for several more hours. Towards evening we came to a valley surrounded by a dense forest, and I could finally sleep as long as I liked, having ridden over fifty miles that day.

The next day the troops pursuing the enemy received orders to return to the camp. There we learned that among the prisoners there was a hermaphrodite. At my request, Raevsky ordered him brought. I saw a tall, rather fat muzhik with the face of an old, pug-nosed Finnish woman. We examined him in the presence of a doctor. *Erat vir, mam-*

mosus ut femina, habebat t. non evolutos, p. que parvum et puerilem. Quae-rebamus, sit ne exsectus?– Deus, respondit, castravit me.* On the testimony of travelers, this illness, known to Hippocrates, is frequently met with among the nomadic Tatars and the Turks. *Hoss* is the Turkish name for these alleged hermaphrodites.

Our troops were stationed in the Turkish camp taken the day before. Count Paskevich's tent stood near the green pavilion of Hakki Pasha, taken prisoner by our Cossacks. I went to him and found him surrounded by our officers. He was sitting cross-legged and smoking a pipe. He looked to be about forty. Dignity and profound calm showed on his handsome face. When he surrendered himself, he asked to be given a cup of coffee and to be spared questions.

We were stationed in a valley. The snowy and wooded mountains of Sagan-loo were already behind us. We moved forward, no longer meeting the enemy anywhere. The settlements were empty. The surrounding country was dismal. We saw the Araks flowing swiftly between its stony banks. Ten miles from Hassan-Kalé there was a bridge, beautifully and boldly built on seven unequal arches. Legend ascribes its construction to a shepherd who had grown rich, and had died a hermit on a hilltop, where to this day they show his grave, overshaded by two solitary pines. Neighboring settlers come there to venerate it. The bridge is called Chaban-Kepri (Shepherd's Bridge). The road to Tebriz crosses over it.

I visited the dark ruins of a caravansarai a few paces from the bridge. I found no one there except for a sick donkey, probably abandoned by the fleeing villagers.

On the morning of June 24 we marched to Hassan-Kalé, the ancient fortress, taken the day before by Prince Bekovich. It was ten miles from our night camp. The long marches had tired me. I hoped to get some rest; but it turned out otherwise.

Before the departure of our cavalry, some Armenians who lived in the mountains appeared in our camp, asking to be protected against the Turks, who had driven off their cattle three days earlier. Colonel Anrep, before grasping very well what they wanted, imagined that there was a Turkish detachment in the mountains, and with one squadron of the Uhlan regiment went galloping off in that direction, inform-

* He was a man with a woman's breasts, had undeveloped t[esticles], a puny and boyish p[enis]. We inquired, had he been emasculated?—God, he replied, castrated me.

ing Raevsky that there were three thousand Turks in the mountains. Raevsky set out after him, to reinforce him in case of danger. I considered myself attached to the Nizhegorodsky regiment and in great vexation galloped off to deliver the Armenians. Having gone some fifteen miles, we rode into a village and saw several stray Uhlans with bared swords hurriedly pursuing a few chickens. Here one villager explained to Raevsky that it was a matter of three thousand oxen driven off by the Turks three days earlier and which could be overtaken quite easily in a couple of days. Raevsky ordered the Uhlans to quit pursuing the chickens and sent orders to Colonel Anrep to turn around. We rode back and, emerging from the mountains, arrived at Hassan-Kalé. Thus we made a thirty-mile detour to save the lives of a few Armenian chickens, which I did not find at all amusing.

Hassan-Kalé is considered the key to Arzrum. The town is built at the foot of a cliff crowned by a citadel. In it there were about a hundred Armenian families. Our camp stood on a wide plain spread out in front of the citadel. Here I visited a round stone edifice inside of which was a hot iron-sulfur spring.

The round pool was about twenty feet in diameter. I swam across it twice and, suddenly feeling dizzy and nauseous, barely had strength enough to get out onto the stone edge of the spring. These waters are famous in the East, but, having no proper doctors, the inhabitants use them haphazardly and probably without great success.

Under the walls of Hassan-Kalé flows the little river Murts; its banks are full of ferrous springs which well up from under the stones and feed into the river. They do not have as pleasant a taste as the Caucasian *narzan*, and they smack of copper.

On June 25, the birthday of the sovereign emperor, the regiments attended a prayer service in our camp, under the walls of the citadel. During dinner at Count Paskevich's, when we drank the health of the emperor, the count announced the march to Arzrum. At five o'clock in the afternoon the troops were already setting out.

On June 26 we stopped in the mountains three miles from Arzrum. These mountains are called Ak-Dag (the white mountains); they are of chalk. Their caustic white dust stung our eyes; their mournful look inspired sadness. The nearness of Arzrum and the certainty of the campaign's end comforted us.

In the evening Count Paskevich rode out to survey the terrain. The Turkish horsemen, who had been circling about in front of our pickets all day, began to shoot at him. The count brandished his whip at them several times, not stopping his conversation with General Muravyov. Their shots went unanswered.

Meanwhile there was great confusion in Arzrum. The seraskir, who had fled to the city after his defeat, spread the rumor that the Russians had been completely crushed. Following him, the released prisoners delivered Count Paskevich's appeal to the citizens. The fugitives exposed the seraskir in his lie. Soon news came of the rapid approach of the Russians. The people started talking about surrender. The seraskir and his army were considering defense. Riots ensued. Several Franks[59] were killed by an angry mob.

Deputies from the people and from the seraskir came to our camp (the morning of the 26th); the day was spent in negotiations; at five o'clock in the afternoon the deputies went back to Arzrum and with them went General Bekovich, who had a good knowledge of Asiatic languages and customs.

The next morning our troops moved forward. On the eastern side of Arzrum, on the height of Top-Dag, was a Turkish battery. The regiments went towards it, responding to the Turkish fire with drumbeats and music. The Turks fled, and Top-Dag was taken. I arrived there with the poet Yuzefovich.[60] At the abandoned battery we found Count Paskevich and his whole retinue. From the top of the mountain the view opened onto Arzrum in a hollow, with its citadel, minarets, green roofs stuck one on top of the other. The count was on horseback. Before him on the ground sat the Turkish deputies, who had come with the keys of the city. But in Arzrum agitation could be seen. Suddenly, on the city wall, fire flashed, smoke puffed, and cannonballs came flying at Top-Dag. Several of them flew over Count Paskevich's head. *"Voyez les Turcs,"* he said to me, *"on ne peut jamais se fier à eux."** Just then Prince Bekovich, who had been negotiating in Arzrum since the previous day, came galloping to Top-Dag. He announced that the seraskir and the people had long since agreed to surrender, but that several disobedient Arnauts,[61] under the leadership of Topcha Pasha, had taken over the city batteries and started a rebellion. The generals approached the count, asking permission to silence the Turkish batteries. The Arzrum dignitaries, sitting under the fire of their own cannon, seconded their request. The count did not reply for some time; finally he gave orders,

* "Just look at the Turks . . . you can never trust them." (French)

saying: "Enough of their tomfoolery." Cannon were brought at once, started firing, and the enemy fire gradually subsided. Our regiments entered Arzrum, and on June 27, the anniversary of the battle of Poltava,[62] at six o'clock in the evening the Russian flag unfurled over the citadel of Arzrum.

Raevsky set out for the city—I went with him; we rode into the city, which presented an amazing picture. The Turks from their flat roofs looked at us sullenly. Armenians thronged noisily in the narrow streets. Their little boys ran in front of our horses, crossing themselves and repeating: "Christiyan! Christiyan! . . ." We approached the fortress, where our artillery was entering; with extreme astonishment I met my Artemy here, riding about town in spite of the strict order that no one should absent himself from the camp without special permission.

The streets of the city are narrow and crooked. The houses are rather tall. Multitudes of people—the shops were closed. Having spent some two hours in the city, I went back to the camp: the seraskir and the four captured pashas were already there. One of the pashas, a lean old man, a terrible bustler, was talking animatedly with our generals. Seeing me in a tailcoat, he asked who I was. Pushchin gave me the title of poet. The pasha crossed his arms on his chest and bowed to me, saying through an interpreter: "Blessed is the hour when we meet a poet. The poet is brother to the dervish. He has neither fatherland nor earthly goods; and while we poor men concern ourselves with glory, with power, with treasures, he stands equal with the rulers of the earth and they bow to him."

The pasha's oriental greeting was very much to our liking. I went to have a look at the seraskir. At the entrance to his tent I met his favorite page, a dark-eyed boy of about fourteen, in rich Arnaut dress. The seraskir, a gray-haired old man of the most ordinary appearance, sat in deep dejection. Around him was a crowd of our officers. On coming out of his tent, I saw a young man, half-naked, in a sheepskin hat, with a club in his hand and a wineskin on his shoulder. He was shouting at the top of his lungs. They told me that this was my brother, the dervish, who had come to greet the victors. We had trouble driving him away.

CHAPTER FIVE

Arzrum. Asiatic luxury. The climate. A cemetery. Satirical
verses. The palace of the seraskir. A Turkish pasha's harem.
The plague. The death of Burtsov. Leaving Arzrum. The
return trip. A Russian journal.

Arzrum (incorrectly called Arzerum, Erzrum, Erzron) was founded
around the year 415, in the time of Theodosius the Second,[63] and was
called Theodosiopolis. No historical memories are connected with his
name. I knew only this about it, that here, by the testimony of Hajji-
Baba, a Persian ambassador, in satisfaction for some offense, was presented with calf's ears instead of human ones.[64]

Arzrum is considered the main city of Asiatic Turkey. Its inhabitants are reckoned at 100,000, but the number seems greatly exagger-
ated. Its houses are of stone, the roofs are covered with turf, which
gives the city a very odd appearance if you look at it from above.

The main overland trade between Europe and the East is carried
on through Arzrum. But few goods are on sale there; they are not displayed, something Tournefort also observed, who writes that in Arzrum a sick man may die from the impossibility of obtaining a spoonful
of rhubarb, while whole sacks of it are to be found in the city.[65]

I know of no expression more meaningless than the words "Asiatic luxury." This saying probably originated in the time of the Crusades, when poor knights, having left the bare walls and oaken chairs
of their castles, saw for the first time red couches, multicolored rugs,
and daggers with flashy gems on their hilts. Nowadays we might say
"Asiatic poverty," "Asiatic swinishness," and so on, but luxury is, of
course, proper to Europe. In Arzrum you cannot buy for any amount
of money what can be found in a grocer's shop in any little country
town of Pskov province.

The Arzrum climate is harsh. The city is built in a hollow that is
over 7,000 feet above sea level. The surrounding mountains are covered
with snow for a great part of the year. The land is treeless but fertile.
It is irrigated by many springs and crisscrossed everywhere with aqueducts. Arzrum is famous for its water. The Euphrates flows two miles
from the city. But there are a great many fountains everywhere. Beside
each of them hangs a tin dipper on a chain, and the good Muslims
drink and cannot praise it enough. Timber is supplied from Sagan-loo.

In the Arzrum arsenal we found a great many old weapons, helmets, cuirasses, swords, rusting there probably since the time of Godfrey.[66] The mosques are low and dark. Outside the city there is a cemetery. The tombstones usually consist of posts adorned with stone turbans. The tombs of two or three pashas are distinguished by a greater fancifulness, but there is nothing refined about them: no taste, no thought . . . One traveler writes that of all Asiatic cities, in Arzrum alone did he find a clock tower, and it was broken.

The innovations undertaken by the sultan have not yet penetrated to Arzrum. The troops still wear their picturesque eastern garb. Between Arzrum and Constantinople there is rivalry, as there is between Kazan and Moscow. Here is the beginning of a satirical poem composed by the janissary Amin-Oglu.[67]

> Stambul is praised now by the giaours,
> But tomorrow with an iron heel,
> Like a sleeping snake, they'll crush it,
> And off they'll ride—and leave it so.
> Stambul dozes in the face of trouble.
>
> Stambul has renounced the prophet;
> There the truth of the ancient East
> By the cunning West is clouded.
> Stambul for the sweets of vice
> Betrays both sabre and devotion.
> Stambul forgets the battle's sweat
> And drinks wine at the hour of prayer.
>
> There has died the faith's pure fire,
> In graveyards there the women walk,
> They send old crones out to the crossroads
> And to the harems bring back men,
> While the bribed eunuch lies there sleeping.
>
> Not so is Arzrum in the mountains,
> Our Arzrum of the many roads;
> We sleep not in shameful luxury,
> We dip no disobedient cup
> In the wine of depravity, noise, and fire.

> We fast: and from the streams of sober
> Holy water we quench our thirst;
> In multitudes both swift and dauntless
> Our horsemen into battle fly;
> Our harems are inaccessible,
> Our eunuchs incorrupt and stern,
> And our women sit there peacefully.

I lived in the seraskir's palace, in the rooms where the harem used to be. For a whole day I wandered through countless passages, from room to room, from roof to roof, from stairway to stairway. The palace seemed to have been looted; the seraskir, intending to flee, took with him all that he could. The couches were stripped, the rugs removed. When I strolled around the town, the Turks beckoned to me and showed me their tongues. (They take every Frank for a doctor.) I was tired of it and ready to pay them back in kind. My evenings I spent with the intelligent and amiable Sukhorukov; the similarity of our pursuits brought us together. He told me of his literary intentions, his historical research, once embarked upon with such zeal and success. The limited nature of his wishes and expectations is truly touching. It will be a pity if they are not realized.[68]

The seraskir's palace was a picture of perpetual animation: where the sullen pasha had silently smoked amidst his wives and dishonorable boys, his vanquisher received reports of his generals' victories, gave out pashaliks, discussed new novels. The pasha of Mush came to Count Paskevich to ask for his nephew's post. Walking through the palace, the imposing Turk stopped in one of the rooms, uttered a few words with animation, and then fell to brooding: in that very room his father had been beheaded at the command of the seraskir. There you have real Eastern impressions! The famous Bey-bulat, the terror of the Caucasus,[69] came to Arzrum with the headmen of two Circassian villages that had revolted during the last wars. They dined with Count Paskevich. Bey-bulat is a man of about thirty-five, short and broad-shouldered. He does not speak Russian, or pretends not to. I was glad of his arrival in Arzrum: he had already been my guarantee of a safe passage through the mountains and Kabarda.

Osman Pasha, taken prisoner in Arzrum and sent to Tiflis together with the seraskir, asked Count Paskevich for the safekeeping of the harem he was leaving in Arzrum. During the first few days this was forgotten. One day at dinner, talking about the calm of the Muslim town, occupied by 10,000 troops and in which not one of the inhabitants had made a single complaint about soldierly violence, the count remembered Osman Pasha's harem and told Mr. Abramovich[70] to go to the pasha's house and ask his wives if they were content and there had been no offense against them. I asked leave to accompany Mr. A. We set out. Mr. A. took along as an interpreter a Russian officer who had a curious story. At the age of eighteen he had been taken prisoner by the Persians. They had castrated him, and for more than twenty years he had served as a eunuch in the harem of one of the shah's sons. He told of his misfortune and his life in Persia with touching simpleheartedness. With respect to physiology, his testimony was precious.

We came to Osman Pasha's house; we were shown into an open room, decorated very properly, even with taste—verses from the Koran were written on the stained-glass windows. One of them seemed to me very ingenious for a Muslim harem: "It befits you to bind and to loose." We were treated to coffee in little cups mounted in silver. An old man with a venerable white beard, Osman Pasha's father, came on behalf of the wives to thank Count Paskevich—but Mr. A. said flatly that he had been sent to the wives of Osman Pasha and wished to see them, so as to ascertain from them personally that in the absence of their spouse they were content with everything. The Persian prisoner had barely managed to translate all that, when the old man clucked his tongue in a sign of indignation and declared that he could not possibly agree to our request, and that if the pasha, on his return, found out that other men had seen his wives, he would order that he, the old man, and all the servants of the harem have their heads cut off. The servants, among whom there was not a single eunuch, confirmed the old man's words, but Mr. A. stood firm. "You are afraid of your pasha," he said to them, "and I of my seraskir, and I dare not disobey his orders." There was nothing to be done. They led us through a garden, where two meager fountains spurted. We approached a small stone building. The old man stood between us and the door, opened it warily, not letting go of the latch, and we saw a woman covered from head to yellow slippers in a white chadra. Our interpreter repeated the question for her: we heard the mumbling of a seventy-year-old woman. Mr. A. cut her off: "This is the pasha's mother," he said, "and I've been sent to the wives; bring out one of them." Everyone was amazed at the giaour's shrewdness: the old woman left and a moment later came back with a woman covered in the same way she was—from under the cover came a young, pleasant little voice. She thanked the count for his attentiveness to the poor widows and praised the way the Russians treated them. Mr. A. artfully managed to engage her in further conversation. Meanwhile, gazing around me, I suddenly saw a round window right over the door and in this round window five or six round heads with dark, curious eyes. I was about to tell Mr. A. of my discovery, but the heads began to wag, to wink, and several little fingers made warning signs to me, letting me know that I should keep quiet. I obeyed and did not share my find. They all had pleasant faces, but there was not a single beauty; the one who was talking by the door with Mr. A. was probably the ruler of the harem, the treasury of hearts, the rose of love—so at least I imagined.

Finally Mr. A. ended his questioning. The door closed. The faces in the window disappeared. We looked over the garden and the house and went back very pleased with our embassy.

And so I saw a harem: it is a rare European who manages that. There you have the basis for an oriental novel.

The war seemed to be over. I was preparing for the return journey. On July 14, I went to the public baths and was not glad to be alive. I cursed the dirty sheets, the bad service, and so on. How can you compare the baths of Arzrum with those of Tiflis!

On returning to the palace, I learned from Konovnitsyn,[71] who was standing guard, that plague had broken out in Arzrum. I immediately pictured the horrors of quarantine, and that same day I decided to leave the army. The thought of being in the presence of the plague is very disagreeable if you are not used to it. Wishing to erase this impression, I went for a stroll in the bazaar. Stopping in front of an armorer's shop, I began to examine a dagger, when someone tapped me on the shoulder. I turned: behind me stood a frightful beggar. He was pale as death; tears flowed from his red, festering eyes. The thought of the plague again flashed in my imagination. I pushed the beggar away with a feeling of indescribable revulsion and returned home very displeased with my stroll.

Curiosity, however, got the upper hand; the next day I went with the army doctor to the camp where the plague victims were. I did not dismount and took the precaution of standing upwind. A sick man was brought out to us from a tent: he was very pale and staggered as if drunk. Another sick man lay unconscious. Having looked over the plague victim and promised the unfortunate man a speedy recovery, I turned my attention to the two Turks who had led him out under the arms, undressed him, probed him, as if the plague were no more than a cold. I confess, I was ashamed of my European timidity in the presence of such indifference and hastened back to the city.

On July 19, having come to say good-bye to Count Paskevich, I found him in great distress. The sad news had come that General Burtsov had been killed at Bayburt. It was a pity about brave Burtsov, but the incident could also be fatal for our whole small-numbered army, finding itself deep in a foreign land and surrounded by hostile peoples, ready to rebel at the rumor of the first setback. And so the war started again! The count suggested that I be a witness to further undertakings. But I was hurrying to Russia . . . The count gave me a Turkish sabre as a souvenir. I keep it as a reminder of my travels in the wake of the brilliant hero through the conquered wastes of Armenia. On that same day I left Arzrum.

I went back to Tiflis by the road already familiar to me. Places still recently animated by the presence of an army of 15,000 men were silent and sad. I crossed over Sagan-loo and could scarcely recognize the place where our camp stood. In Gyumri I endured a three-day quarantine. Again I saw Bezobdal and left the high plains of cold Armenia for torrid Georgia. I arrived in Tiflis on the first of August. There I stayed for several days in amiable and merry company. Several evenings were spent in the gardens to the sounds of Georgian music and songs. I went on. My crossing of the mountains was remarkable for me in that I was caught in a storm at night near Kobi. In the morning, going past Kazbek, I saw a marvelous sight: ragged white clouds stretched across the peak of the mountain, and the solitary monastery, lit by the rays of the sun, seemed to be floating in the air, borne up by the clouds. The Furious Gully also showed itself to me in all its grandeur: the ravine, filled with rainwater, surpassed the raging Terek itself, roaring menacingly just beside it. The banks were torn to pieces; enormous rocks were dislodged and blocked the stream. A multitude of Ossetes were working on the road. I crossed over safely. Finally I rode out of the narrow gorge into the expanse of the wide plains of Great Kabarda. In Vladikavkaz I found Dorokhov[72] and Pushchin. They were on their way to the waters to treat the wounds they had received in the present campaigns. On Pushchin's table I found Russian magazines. The first article I happened upon was a review of one of my works. In it I and my verses were denounced in all possible ways. I started reading it aloud. Pushchin interrupted me, demanding that I read with greater mimetic art. It should be noted that the review was decked out with the usual whimsies of our critics: it was a conversation between a sexton, a prosphora baker, and a proofreader, the Mr. Commonsense of this little comedy. I found Pushchin's request so amusing that the vexations produced in me by the reading of the article vanished completely, and we burst into wholehearted laughter.

Such was my first greeting in my dear fatherland.

Glossary of Caucasian Terms

abaz: a silver coin minted by the Russians for use in Georgia

amanat: hostage or hostages, used in the Caucasus for diplomatic purposes

arba: a two- or four-wheeled horse-drawn cart

aul: village

bashlik: a pointed hood with long flaps for tying around the neck

bek: alternate spelling of bey, "chieftain"

burdyuk: a Caucasian wineskin

chadra: a long garment with a headcover or veil

chikhir: young wine

delibash: Turkish cavalrymen

dolman: a long, loose Turkish robe, open in front

pashalik: the territory governed by a Turkish pasha, a high military/ political officer

saklia: a flat-roofed Caucasian mountain dwelling, most often of one room

seraskir: a Turkish army commander

FRAGMENTS AND SKETCHES

The Guests Were Arriving at the Dacha

The guests were arriving at * * *'s dacha. The reception room was filling with ladies and gentlemen, all coming at the same time from the theater, where a new Italian opera had been performed. Order was gradually established. The ladies seated themselves on the sofas. Around them formed a circle of men. Games of whist were set up. Several young men remained standing; and an inspection of Parisian lithographs took the place of general conversation.

Two men sat on the balcony. One of them, a traveling Spaniard, seemed to take a keen delight in the loveliness of the northern night. He gazed admiringly at the clear, pale sky, the majestic Neva illumined by an ineffable light, and the neighboring dachas silhouetted in the transparent twilight.

"How beautiful your northern night is," he said finally, "and how shall I help missing its loveliness even under the sky of my own fatherland?"

"One of our poets," the other answered him, "compared it to a flaxen-haired Russian beauty.[1] I must admit that a swarthy, dark-eyed Italian or Spanish woman, full of vivacity and southern voluptuousness, captivates my imagination more. However, the ancient argument between *la brune et la blonde* has yet to be resolved. By the way, do you know how a certain foreign lady explained to me the strictness and purity of Petersburg morals? She claimed that for amorous adventures our winter nights are too cold and our summer nights too bright."

The Spaniard smiled.

"So it's all thanks to the influence of the climate," he said. "Petersburg is the promised land of beauty, amiability, and irreproachability."

"Beauty is a matter of taste," the Russian answered, "but there's no point in talking about our amiability. It's not fashionable; no one even thinks of it. The women are afraid of being taken for coquettes, the men of losing their dignity. They all strive to be nonentities with taste and decorum. As for purity of morals, so as not to take advantage of a foreigner's trustfulness, I shall tell you . . ."

And the conversation took a most satirical turn.

Just then the door to the reception room opened, and Volskaya came in. She was in the first bloom of youth. Her regular features, her big dark eyes, the vivacity of her movements, the very strangeness of her dress—all could not help but attract attention. The men greeted her with a sort of jocular affability, the ladies with noticeable ill will; but Volskaya noticed nothing; responding obliquely to commonplace questions, she glanced around distractedly; her face, changeable as a cloud, showed vexation; she sat down beside the imposing Princess G. and *se mit à bouder*,* as they say.

Suddenly she gave a start and turned to the balcony. Restlessness came over her. She rose, walked past the chairs and tables, stopped for a moment behind the chair of old General R., made no reply to his subtle compliment, and suddenly slipped out to the balcony.

The Spaniard and the Russian rose. She went up to them and with embarrassment said a few words in Russian. The Spaniard, supposing himself superfluous, left her and went back inside.

The imposing Princess G. followed Volskaya with her eyes and said in a low voice to her neighbor:

"I have never seen the like."

"She's terribly flighty," he replied.

"Flighty? And then some. Her behavior is unforgivable. She can disrespect herself as much as she likes, but society does not deserve such scorn from her. Minsky might let her know that."

"*Il n'en fera rien, trop heureux de pouvoir la compromettre.*† Meanwhile, I'll wager their conversation is quite innocent."

"I'm sure of it . . . Since when are you so benevolent?"

"I confess, I've taken an interest in that young woman's fate. There's a lot of good in her, and much less bad than people think. But passions will be the ruin of her."

"Passions! That's a big word! What are these passions? Are you imagining that she has an ardent heart, a romantic head? She's sim-

---

* began to sulk
† "He'll do nothing of the sort, he's too happy being able to compromise her."

ply ill-bred . . . What is this lithograph? A portrait of Hussein Pasha?[2] Show it to me."

The guests were leaving; not one lady was left in the reception room. Only the hostess stood with obvious displeasure by the table at which two diplomats were finishing a last game of *écarté*.[3] Volskaya suddenly noticed the dawn and hastily left the balcony, where she had spent nearly a whole three hours alone with Minsky. The hostess said good-bye to her coldly, and deliberately did not bestow even a glance on Minsky. At the entrance several guests were waiting for their carriages. Minsky helped Volskaya into hers.

"Seems it's your turn," a young officer said to him.

"Not at all," he replied. "She's taken. I'm simply her confidant, or whatever. But I love her with all my heart—she's killingly funny."

Zinaida Volskaya lost her mother when she was five years old. Her father, a busy and distracted man, handed her over to a French governess, hired all sorts of teachers, and after that no longer bothered with her. At fourteen she was beautiful and wrote love letters to her dancing master. The father learned of it, fired the dancing master, and brought her out in society, considering her education finished. Zinaida's coming out caused a great stir. Volsky, a rich young man accustomed to subjecting his feelings to the opinions of others, fell madly in love with her, because the emperor, having met her on the English Embankment,[4] spent a whole hour talking with her. He proposed. Her father was glad of the chance to get the fashionable bride off his hands. Zinaida was burning with impatience to marry, so as to see the whole town in her house. Besides which Volsky was not repugnant to her, and so her fate was decided.

Her candor, unexpected pranks, childish frivolity, made a pleasant impression at first, and society was even grateful to the one who kept disrupting the solemn monotony of the aristocratic circle. They laughed at her antics, recounted her strange escapades. But years passed, and Zinaida's soul was still fourteen years old. Murmuring began. They found that Volskaya had no sense of the decorum proper to her sex. Women began to distance themselves from her, while the men drew closer. Zinaida thought that she was not the loser, and was comforted.

Rumor began to ascribe lovers to her. Scandal, even without proof,

leaves almost eternal traces. In the social code, plausibility equals prob-
ability, and to be the object of slander humiliates us in our own eyes.
Volskaya, in tears of indignation, resolved to rebel against the power of
unjust society. A chance soon presented itself.

Among the young men of her surroundings Zinaida singled out
Minsky. Evidently a certain similarity of character and circumstances
of life was bound to bring them together. In his early youth Minsky's
wantonness of behavior had earned him the censure of society, which
punished him with slander. Minsky had abandoned society, feigning
indifference. For a time passions stifled in his heart the pangs of amour-
propre; but, tamed by experience, he appeared again on the social scene
and now brought to it, not the ardor of his imprudent youth, but the
indulgence and seemliness of egoism. He did not like society, but he
did not scorn it, for he knew the necessity of its approval. With all that,
while respecting it in general, he did not spare it in its particulars, and
was ready to offer up each of its members in sacrifice to his rancorous
amour-propre. He liked Volskaya because she dared to openly despise
the conventions he hated. He set her on with encouragements and
advice, made himself her confidant, and soon became necessary to her.
B. occupied her imagination for some time.

"He's too insignificant for you," Minsky said to her. "All his intelligence is picked up from *Les Liaisons dangereuses*, just as all his military
theory is stolen from Jomini.[5] Get to know him intimately, and you'll
despise his ponderous immorality, just as military men despise his banal
pronouncements."

"I'd like to fall in love with R.," Zinaida said to him.

"What nonsense!" he replied. "Why on earth would you have anything to do with a man who dyes his hair and rapturously repeats every
five minutes: '*Quand j'étais à Florence . . .*'* They say his insufferable
wife is in love with him; leave them alone: they're made for each other."

"And Baron W.?"

"He's a little girl in uniform; what is there in him . . . but you
know what? Fall in love with L. He'll occupy your imagination: he's as
remarkably intelligent as he is remarkably ugly, *et puis c'est un homme à
grands sentiments;*† he'll be jealous and passionate, he'll torment you and
make you laugh—what more do you want?"

* 'When I was in Florence . . .'
† "and then he's a man of great feelings"

However, Volskaya did not listen to him. Minsky divined her heart; his amour-propre was touched; not supposing that frivolity could be combined with strong passions, he foresaw a liaison without serious consequences, one more woman on the list of his flighty mistresses, and reflected cold-bloodedly on his victory. Most likely, if he could have imagined the storms awaiting him, he would have renounced his triumph, for a man of society easily sacrifices his pleasures and even his vanity to laziness and respectability.

II

Minsky was still lying in bed when a letter was brought to him. He opened it with a yawn, shrugged his shoulders, unfolded two pages covered all over with a woman's minute handwriting. The letter began thus:

> I was unable to speak out to you everything I have in my heart; in your presence I did not find the thoughts that now pursue me so keenly. Your sophisms do not lull my suspicions, but force me to keep silent; that proves your constant superiority to me, but is not enough for happiness, for the ease of my heart . . .

Volskaya reproached him for coldness, mistrust, and so on, complained, pleaded, herself not knowing for what; poured out tender, affectionate assurances—and set up an evening rendezvous with him in her theater box. Minsky answered her in a couple of words, excusing himself with boring, necessary errands, and promising to be in the theater without fail.

III

"You are so open and indulgent," said the Spaniard, "that I venture to ask you to solve a problem for me: I have wandered all over the world, have been presented at all the European courts, have visited high society everywhere, but nowhere have I felt myself so constrained, so awkward, as in your accursed aristocratic circle. Each time I enter Princess

V.'s reception room, and see these mute, motionless mummies, reminding me of Egyptian cemeteries, a sort of chill runs through me. Among them there is not a single moral authority, not a single name that fame has repeated to me—what is it that makes me timid?"

"Ill will," the Russian replied. "It is a trait of our character. Among the people it is expressed by mockery, in high circles by inattention and coldness. Besides, our ladies are very superficially educated, and nothing European occupies their thoughts. Of the men there is even no point in talking. Politics and literature do not exist for them. Wit has long been in disgrace as a sign of frivolity. What have they got to talk about? Themselves? No, they're much too well bred. What remains for them is some sort of domestic, petty, private conversation, comprehensible only to the few—the chosen. And a man who does not belong to that small flock is received as an outsider—and not only a foreigner, but their own as well."

"Forgive me my questions," said the Spaniard, "but I will hardly find satisfactory answers another time, and I hasten to take advantage of you. You have mentioned your aristocracy: what is the Russian aristocracy? Studying your laws, I see that hereditary aristocracy, based on the indivisibility of property, does not exist in Russia. It seems that civic equality exists among your nobility and access to it is not limited in any way. What, then, is your so-called aristocracy based on—can it be on ancient lineage alone?"

The Russian laughed.

"You are mistaken," he replied. "The ancient Russian nobility, owing to the reasons you have mentioned, fell into obscurity and has formed a sort of third estate. Our aristocratic mob, to which I also belong, considers Rurik and Monomakh its ancestors.[6] I say, for instance," the Russian went on with an air of self-satisfied nonchalance, "that the roots of my nobility are lost in remote antiquity, the names of my forebears are on every page of our history. But if I ever thought of calling myself an aristocrat, many people would probably laugh. But our real aristocrats would have a hard time even naming their grandfathers. Their ancient lineages go back to Peter and Elizabeth.[7] Orderlies, choirboys, Ukrainians—those are their family founders. I don't say it in reproach: merit is always merit, and the benefit of the state calls for its elevation. Only it is funny to see in the worthless grandsons of pastry chefs, orderlies, choirboys, and sextons the haughtiness of the duc de Montmorency, the first baron of Christendom, or Clermont-

Tonnerre.[8] We're so matter-of-fact that we go on our knees before the luck, the success of the moment, and . . . but the charm of antiquity, gratitude towards the past, and respect for moral merits do not exist for us. Karamzin recently told us our history.[9] But we hardly paid attention. We're proud, not of our ancestral glory, but of some uncle's rank or the balls given by our cousin. Note that disrespect for one's forebears is the first sign of savagery and immorality."

A Novel in Letters

I. LIZA TO SASHA

You were surprised, of course, dear Sashenka, by my unexpected departure for the country. I hasten to explain it all candidly. The dependency of my position has always been a burden to me. Of course, Avdotya Andreevna brought me up on an equal footing with her niece. But all the same I was a ward in her house, and you cannot imagine how many petty trials are bound up with that title. I had to bear with many things, to give way in many things, to overlook many things, while my amour-propre assiduously noticed the slightest tinge of negligence. My very equality with the princess was a burden to me. When we appeared at a ball, dressed identically, I was annoyed to see no pearls around her neck. I sensed that she did not wear them only so as not to differ from me, and that very attentiveness offended me. Can it be, I thought, that people suspect me of envy or any other such childish weakness? Men's behavior with me, however courteous it might be, constantly wounded my amour-propre. Coolness or affability, it all seemed like disrespect to me. In short, I was a most unhappy creature, and my heart, naturally tender, was becoming more hardened by the hour. Have you noticed that all girls who live as wards, distant relations, *demoiselles de compagnie*,* and the like, are usually either basely subservient or unbearably whimsical? The latter I respect and forgive from the bottom of my heart.

Exactly three weeks ago I received a letter from my poor grandmother. She complained of her solitude and invited me to her country estate. I decided to make use of this opportunity. I barely managed to get Avdotya Andreevna's permission to go, and had to promise to come back to Petersburg in the winter, but I have no intention of keeping my word. Grandmother was extremely glad to see me; she never expected me. Her tears moved me beyond words. I've come to love her with all

* ladies' companions

my heart. She once belonged to high society and has kept much of the amiability of that time.

Now I am living *at home*, I am the mistress, and you would not believe what a true delight it is for me. I got used to country life at once, and the absence of luxury is not strange to me in the least. Our estate is very nice. An old house on a hill, a garden, a lake, pine woods around—it's all a bit dreary in autumn and winter, but in spring and summer it must seem an earthly paradise. We have few neighbors, and I have not yet seen any of them. Solitude actually pleases me, as in the elegies of your Lamartine.[1]

Write to me, my angel, your letters will be a great comfort to me. How are your balls, how are our mutual acquaintances? Though I have made myself a recluse, I have not renounced the vanity of the world altogether—news of it will interest me.

The Village of Pavlovskoe

2. SASHA'S REPLY

Dear Liza,

Imagine my amazement when I learned of your departure for the country. Seeing Princess Olga alone, I thought you were unwell, and did not want to believe her words. The next day I received your letter. I congratulate you, my angel, on your new way of life. I'm glad you like it. Your complaints about your former position moved me to tears, but seemed much too bitter to me. How can you compare yourself with wards and *demoiselles de compagnie*? Everybody knows that Olga's father owed everything to yours and that their friendship was as sacred as the closest family ties. You seemed pleased with your lot. I never supposed there was so much touchiness in you. Confess: Is there not some other, secret reason for your hasty departure? I suspect . . . but you are playing modest with me, and I'm afraid to anger you in absentia with my guesses.

What can I tell you about Petersburg? We're still at our dacha, but almost everyone has already gone. The balls will begin in some two weeks. The weather is fine. I walk a great deal. The other day we had guests for dinner—one of them asked whether I had any news of you. He said that your absence at the balls is noticeable, like a broken string in a piano—and I agree with him completely. I keep hoping that this fit of misanthropy will not last long. Come back, my angel; otherwise I will have no one to share my innocent observations with this winter, and no one to whom I can pass on the epigrams of my heart. Good-bye, my dear—think it over, and think better of it.

Krestovsky Island[2]

3. LIZA TO SASHA

Your letter has comforted me greatly. It reminded me so vividly of Petersburg, it was as if I could hear you! How ridiculous your eternal suppositions are! You suspect some deep, secret feelings in me, some unhappy love—is it not so? Rest assured, my dear, you're mistaken: I resemble a heroine only in that I live in the deep countryside and pour tea like Clarissa Harlowe.[3]

You say you will have no one to whom you can pass on your satiri-cal observations this winter—but what about our correspondence? Write to me everything you notice; I repeat to you that I have not renounced society altogether, that everything concerning it interests me. In proof of that I ask you to write about who it is that finds my absence so noticeable. Is it not our amiable babbler Alexei R.? I'm sure I've guessed right . . . My ears were ever at his service, and that was just what he needed.

I've made the acquaintance of the * * * family. The father is a ban-terer and the soul of hospitality; the mother is a fat, merry woman, a great lover of whist; the daughter—a slender, melancholy girl of about seventeen, brought up on novels and fresh air. She spends all day in the garden or in the fields with a book in her hands, surrounded by yard dogs, talks in singsong about the weather, and with great feeling treats you to preserves. I have discovered that she has a whole bookcase full of old novels. I intend to read them all, and have started with Rich-ardson. One must live in the country to have the possibility of reading the much-praised *Clarissa*. I began, God help me, with the translator's preface and, finding assurance in it that, while the first six parts were a bit boring, the last six would fully reward the reader's patience, I bravely set about it. I read one volume, a second, a third—finally got as far as the sixth—boring, much too much. Well, I thought, now I'll be rewarded for my pains. What then? I read about the death of Clarissa, the death of Lovelace, and that was it. Each volume consisted of two parts, and I had not noticed the transition from the six boring ones to the six interesting ones.

Reading Richardson gave me an occasion to reflect. What a terrible difference between the ideals of grandmothers and of granddaughters! What do Lovelace and Adolphe have in common?[4] Yet the role of women does not change. Except for a few ceremonious curtsies, Clarissa is exactly like the heroine of the latest novels. Perhaps it is because the ways of pleasing, in a man, depend on fashion, on momentary opinion . . . while in women they are based on feeling and nature, which are eternal.

You see: I chatter away with you as usual. Don't you be skimpy in these postal conversations. Write to me as often as you can and as much as you can: you cannot imagine what it means to wait for mail day in the country. Waiting for a ball cannot compare with it.

4. SASHA'S REPLY

You are mistaken, dear Liza. To humble your amour-propre, I announce that R. does not notice your absence at all. He has attached himself to Lady Pelham, a newly arrived Englishwoman, and never leaves her side. To his conversation she responds with a look of innocent amazement and a little "Oho!" . . . and he is in raptures. Know, then, that it is your constant *admirateur* Vladimir * * * who has asked me about you and who regrets your absence with all his heart. Are you pleased? I think you are very pleased, and, as is my wont, I venture to assume that you guessed it even without me. Joking aside, * * * is very taken with you. If I were you, I would lead him a long way. After all, he's an excellent suitor . . . Why not marry him? You would live on the English Embankment,[5] have soirées on Saturdays, and stop by my place every morning. Enough foolishness, my angel; come back to us and marry * * *.

Two days ago there was a ball at the K.'s. No end of people. We danced until five in the morning. K. V. was dressed very simply; a white little crêpe dress, not even any trimmings, and on her head and neck half a million's worth of diamonds: that's all! Z., as is her wont, was dressed killingly. Where does she get her outfits? Her dress had, not flowers, but some sort of dried mushrooms sewn on it. Was it you, my angel, who sent them to her from the country? Vladimir * * * did not dance. He is going on leave. The S.s came (probably the first), sat all night without dancing, and left last. The older one seemed to be wearing rouge—about time . . . The ball was very successful. The men were displeased with the supper, but then they always have to be displeased with something. I had a merry time, even though I danced the *cotillon* with the insufferable diplomat St., who added to his natural stupidity an absentmindedness he imported from Madrid.

I thank you, dear heart, for your report on Richardson. Now I have some idea of him. With my impatience, there is no hope of my ever reading him; I even find superfluous pages in Walter Scott.

By the way, I think the romance between Elena N. and Count L. is ending—at any rate he's so downcast and she's so puffed up that the wedding has probably been decided on. Farewell, my lovely; are you pleased with my babble for today?

5. LIZA TO SASHA

No, my dear matchmaker, I have no thought of leaving the country and coming to you for my wedding. I frankly confess that I liked Vladimir * * *, but I never contemplated marrying him. He is an aristocrat, and I am a humble democrat. I hasten to explain and point out proudly, like a true heroine of a novel, that by birth I belong to the oldest Russian nobility, and that my knight is the grandson of a bearded merchant millionaire. But you know what our aristocracy means. Be that as it may, * * * is a man of the world; he might like me, but he would never sacrifice a rich bride and a profitable alliance for my sake. If I am ever to marry, I will choose some local forty-year-old landowner. He will busy himself with his sugar works, I with the household—and I will be happy without dancing at Count K.'s ball and having Saturdays at my place on the English Embankment.

It's winter here: in the country *c'est un événement.** It changes your way of life completely. Solitary walks cease, little bells jingle, hunters go out with their dogs—everything becomes brighter, more cheerful with the first snow. I never expected it. Winter in the country frightened me. But everything in the world has its good side.

* that is an event

I've become more closely acquainted with Mashenka * * * and have come to love her; there is much in her that is good, much that is original. I learned by chance that * * * is their close relative. Mashenka hasn't seen him for seven years, but she admires him. He spent one summer with them, and Mashenka constantly recounts all the details of his life then. Reading her novels, I find his observations in the margins, written faintly in pencil; one can see he was a child then. He was struck by thoughts and feelings that he would certainly laugh at now; at any rate one can see a fresh, sensitive soul. I do a great deal of reading. You cannot imagine how strange it is to read in 1829 a novel written in 1775. It's as if we suddenly step out of our drawing room into an old-fashioned hall, the walls covered in damask, sit down on fluffy satin-upholstered armchairs, see strange dresses around us, yet the faces are familiar, and we recognize in them our uncles, our grandmothers, but grown young. For the most part these novels have no other virtue. The action is entertaining, the plot well entangled—but Bellecourt speaks askew, and Charlotte replies awry.[6] An intelligent person could take the ready plot, the ready characters, straighten out the style and the absurdities, fill in what is left unsaid, and come up with an excellent, original novel. Tell that to my ungrateful R. from me. Enough of his wasting his intelligence in conversations with Englishwomen! Let him take an old canvas and embroider a new pattern on it, and present to us, in a small frame, a picture of the society and people he knows so well.

Masha knows Russian literature well—in general, people are more interested in it here than in Petersburg. Here they receive magazines, take a lively part in their squabbles, believe alternately in both sides, get angry if their favorite writer is criticized. Now I understand why Vyazemsky and Pushkin are so fond of provincial young ladies.[7] They are their true public. I was glancing at some magazines and started with the critiques in the *Herald of Europe*,[8] but I found their platitudes and servility repulsive—it's funny to see how a seminarian pompously denounces works as immoral and improper, when we have all read them, we—the St. Petersburg touch-me-nots! . . .

6. LIZA TO SASHA

My dear! it is impossible for me to pretend any longer, I need the help and advice of a friend. The one I ran away from, whom I fear like misfortune, * * *, is here. What am I to do? My head is spinning, I'm at a loss, for God's sake decide what I'm to do. I'll tell you all . . .

You noticed last winter that he never left my side. He didn't call on us, but we saw each other everywhere. In vain I armed myself with coldness, even with an air of disdain—in no way could I get rid of him. At balls he eternally found himself a place beside me, at promenades he eternally ran into us, in the theater his lorgnette was aimed at our box.

At first this flattered my amour-propre. Maybe I allowed him to notice it all too well. At any rate, appropriating new rights for himself, he spoke to me all the time about his feelings, now being jealous, now complaining . . . With horror I thought: where is all this leading? And with despair I recognized his power over my soul. I left Petersburg, thinking to cut off the evil at the very beginning. My resoluteness, my assurance that I had fulfilled my duty, was easing my heart, I was beginning to think about him with more indifference, with less sadness. Suddenly I see him.

I see him: yesterday was * * *'s name day. I came for dinner, I go into the drawing room, I find a crowd of guests, uhlan uniforms, ladies surround me, I exchange kisses with them all. Noticing no one, I sit down next to the hostess, I look: * * * is there in front of me. I was dumbfounded . . . He said a few words to me with a look of such tender, sincere joy that I had no strength to conceal either my perplexity or my pleasure.

We went to the table. He sat across from me; I did not dare to look up at him, but I noticed that all eyes were fixed on him. He was silent and distracted. At another time I would have been very interested in the general wish to attract the attention of the visiting officer of the guards, the nervousness of the young ladies, the awkwardness of the men, their laughter at their own jokes, and with it all the polite coldness and total inattention of the guest. After dinner he came up to me. Feeling that I had to say something, I asked rather inappropriately whether he had come to our parts on business. "I've come on a business upon which the happiness of my life depends," he replied in a low voice and stepped away at once. He sat down to play Boston with three old women (including my grandmother), and I went upstairs to Mashenka's room, where I lay till evening on the pretext of a headache. In fact, I was worse than unwell. Mashenka never left my side. She is in raptures over * * *. He will spend a month or more with them. She will be with him all day long. I guess she's in love with him—God grant that he, too, falls in love. She's slender and strange—just what men ask for.

What am I to do, my dear? Here it won't be possible for me to escape his pursuit. He has already managed to charm my grandmother. He'll call on us—again there will be declarations, complaints, vows— *and to what end?* He'll obtain my love, my declaration—then reflect on the disadvantages of the marriage, leave under some pretext, abandon me—and I . . . What a terrible future! For God's sake, give me your hand: I'm drowning.

7. SASHA'S REPLY

How much better it is to relieve your heart with a full confession! None too soon, my angel! What was the point of not admitting to me what I had long known: * * * and you are in love—what's wrong with that? All the best to you. You have a gift for looking at things from God knows what side. You're asking for trouble—beware of bringing it upon yourself. Why shouldn't you marry * * *? Where are the insuperable obstacles? He's rich and you're poor—a trifle! He's rich enough for two—what more do you want? He's an aristocrat; but aren't you also an aristocrat by name, by upbringing?

Not long ago there was an argument about ladies of high society. I learned that R. once declared himself on the side of the aristocracy because they are better shod. So, then, isn't it obvious that you are an aristocrat from head to foot?

Forgive me, my angel, but your heartfelt letter made me laugh. * * * came to the country to see you. How terrible! You're perishing; you ask my advice. Can it be you've turned into a provincial heroine? My advice is: Get married as quickly as possible in your wooden church and come back to us, so that you can appear as Fornarina in the *tableaux vivants* that are being organized at the S.'s.[9] Joking aside, your knight's deed has moved me. Of course, in the old days, for the sake of a favorable glance, a lover would go to fight for three years in Palestine; but in our day, for a man to go three hundred miles from Petersburg to see the mistress of his heart truly means a lot. * * * deserves a reward.

8. VLADIMIR * * * TO HIS FRIEND

Do me a favor, spread the rumor that I'm on my deathbed, I intend to overstay and want to observe all possible proprieties. It's already two weeks that I've been living in the country, and I don't notice how the time flies. I'm resting from Petersburg life, which I'm terribly sick of. Not to love the country is forgivable in a young girl just released from her convent cage, or to an eighteen-year-old kammerjunker. Petersburg is the front hall, Moscow is the maids' quarters, but the country is our study. A decent man passes of necessity through the front hall and rarely glances into the maids' quarters, but sits down in his study. That's how I'll end up. I'll retire, get married, and go off to my Saratov estate. Being a landowner is the same as being in the service. Managing three thousand souls, whose well-being depends entirely on us, is more important than commanding a platoon or copying diplomatic dispatches . . .

The neglect in which we leave our peasants is unforgivable. The more rights we have over them, the more responsibilities we have towards them. We leave them to the mercy of a swindling steward, who oppresses them and robs us. We run through our future earnings in debts, ruin ourselves; old age finds us in need and worry.

There lies the cause of the rapid decline of our nobility: the grandfather was rich, the son is in need, the grandson goes begging. Ancient families fall into insignificance; new ones arise and by the third generation vanish again. Fortunes merge, and no family knows its ancestors. What does such political materialism lead to? I don't know. But it is time to block its path.

I never could behold without sorrow the humiliation of our historic families; no one among us values them, starting with those who belong to them. But then what pride of memory can you expect from people who inscribe on a monument: To Citizen Minin and Prince Pozharsky? Which Prince Pozharsky? What is this Citizen Minin? There was a high-ranking boyar, Prince Dmitri Mikhailovich Pozharsky, and there was a tradesman Kozma Minich Sukhoruky, elected representative by the whole state.[10] But the fatherland forgot even the actual names of its deliverers. The past does not exist for us. A pathetic people!

An aristocracy of functionaries will not replace the hereditary aristocracy. The family memories of the nobility should be the historical memories of the people. But what family memories do the children of a collegiate assessor have?[11]

In speaking in favor of the aristocracy, I am not posing as an English lord; my origin, though I am not ashamed of it, does not give me any right to that. But I agree with La Bruyère: *Affecter le mépris de la naissance est un ridicule dans le parvenu et une lâcheté dans le gentilhomme.**[12]

I have thought all this over, living on someone else's estate, looking at the way petty landowners run things. These gentlemen are not in the service and run their little estates themselves, but I must say, God grant that they go to ruin, like our kind. What savagery! For them the times of Fonvizin have not yet passed! The Prostakovs and Skotinins still flourish among them![13]

That, however, does not apply to my relative, whose guest I am. He is a very kind man, his wife is a very kind woman, his daughter is a very kind girl. You see, I've become very kind. In fact, since I've been in the country, I've become utterly benevolent and tolerant—the effect of my patriarchal life and of Liza * * *'s presence. I was downright bored without her. I came to persuade her to go back to Petersburg. Our first meeting was splendid. It was my aunt's name day. All the neighbors gathered. Liza turned up, too—and could hardly believe her eyes when she saw me. She couldn't help thinking I had come there only for her sake. At any rate I tried to make her feel that. Here my success went beyond my expectations (which means a lot). The old ladies are enraptured with me, the younger ladies simply swarm around me—"And that's because they're patriots."[14] The men are utterly displeased with my *fatuité indolente*,† which is still a novelty here. They are all the more furious because I am extremely courteous and decorous, and they cannot understand precisely what my insolence consists in, though they do feel that I am insolent. Good-bye. What are our friends up to? *Servitor di tutti quanti.*‡ Write to me at the village of * * *.

---

* To affect a scorn of birth is ridiculous in a parvenu and baseness in a gentleman.
† idle foppishness
‡ Humble servant of them all.

9. THE FRIEND'S REPLY

I have carried out your commission. Yesterday in the theater I announced that you have come down with a nervous fever and probably are no longer of this world—so enjoy your life while you have not yet resurrected.

Your moral reflections on the management of estates make me glad for you. So much the better is

> *Un homme sans peur et sans reproche,*
> *Qui n'est ni roi, ni duc, ni comte aussi.**[15]

The position of Russian landowner is, in my opinion, most enviable. Ranks are a necessity in Russia, if only at posting stations, where you cannot obtain horses without them.

Having set out upon a serious discussion, I quite forgot that you cannot be bothered with that now—you are busy with your Liza. Why on earth do you pose as M. Faublas and eternally mess about with women?[16] It's not worthy of you. In this respect you are behind the times and are straying towards the *ci-devant*† hoarse-voiced guardsman of 1807.[17] For the moment it's only a shortcoming, but soon you will be more ridiculous than General G. Wouldn't it be better to accustom yourself ahead of time to the strictness of maturity and voluntarily renounce your fading youth? I know that I am preaching in vain, but such is my role.

Your friends all send their greetings and greatly regret your untimely end—among others your former lady friend, who has come back from Rome in love with the pope. How like her that is and how it should delight you! Won't you come back and be a rival *cum servus servorum dei*?‡ That would be just like you. I'll expect you any day now.

---

* A man without fear or reproach, / Who is neither king, nor duke, nor count.
† former
‡ with the servant of the servants of God [i.e., the pope]

IO. VLADIMIR TO HIS FRIEND

Your reprimands are totally unjust. It is not I but you who are behind the times—by a whole decade. Your speculative and serious reasoning belongs to 1818. At that time strict rules and political economy were fashionable. We attended balls without taking our swords off, it was improper for us to dance, and we had no time to be interested in the ladies. I have the honor of informing you that all that has now changed. The French quadrille has replaced Adam Smith;[18] everyone chases skirts and amuses himself as he can. I follow the spirit of the times; but you are fixed, you are *ci-devant, un homme stéréotype*.* What makes you sit alone, glued to the little bench of the opposition? I hope that Z. will set you on the right path: I entrust you to her Vatican coquetry. As for me, I've given myself completely to the patriarchal life: I go to bed at ten o'clock in the evening, ride out hunting over fresh snow with the local landowners, play Boston for kopecks with the old ladies and get angry when I lose. I see Liza every day—and fall more in love with her by the hour. There is much that is captivating in her. This quiet, noble harmony of behavior, the charm of Petersburg high society, and at the same time something alive, indulgent, of good old stock (as her grandmother says), nothing sharp or rigid in her judgments, she does not shrink from new impressions like a child from rhubarb. She listens and understands—a rare quality in our women. I have often been surprised at the dullness of wit or impurity of imagination in ladies who are otherwise quite amiable. They often take the most refined joke, the most poetic greeting, either as an insolent epigram or as an indecent platitude. In such cases, the cold air they assume is so devastatingly repulsive that the most ardent love cannot stand up to it.

I experienced that with Elena * * *, whom I loved to distraction. I said something tender to her; she took it as rudeness and complained of me to one of her lady friends. That totally disenchanted me. Besides Liza, I have Mashenka * * * for entertainment. She's nice. These girls who grow up under the apple trees and amidst haystacks, educated by their nannies and nature, are far nicer than our monotonous beauties, who hold their mothers' opinions before marriage, and their husbands' after.

* a stereotypical man

Good-bye, my friend. What's new in society? Announce to everybody that I, too, have finally broken into poetry. The other day I composed an inscription for Princess Olga's portrait (for which Liza chided me very sweetly):

Stupid as truth, boring as perfection.

Or maybe better:

Boring as truth, stupid as perfection.

They both have a resemblance to thought. Ask V. to come up with the first line and henceforth consider me a poet.

At the Corner of a Little Square

CHAPTER ONE

Votre coeur est l'éponge imbibée de fiel et de vinaigre.

*Correspondance inédite**

At the corner of a little square, in front of a small wooden house, stood a carriage—a rare occurrence in that remote part of the city. The driver lay asleep on the box, and the postillion was having a snowball fight with some servant boys.

In a room decorated with taste and luxury, on a sofa, dressed with great refinement, propped on pillows, lay a pale lady, no longer young, but still beautiful. Before the fireplace sat a young man of about twenty-six, leafing through the pages of an English novel.

The pale lady did not take from him her dark and sunken eyes, ringed with an unhealthy blue. Night was falling, the fire was dying down; the young man went on with his reading. Finally she said:

"What's the matter with you, Valerian? You're angry today."

"Yes, I am," he replied, without raising his eyes from the book.

"With whom?"

"With Prince Goretsky. He's giving a ball tonight, and I'm not invited."

"And do you want so much to be at his ball?"

"Not in the least. Devil take him and his ball. But if he invites the whole town, he ought to invite me as well."

"Which Goretsky is it? Not Prince Yakov?"

"Not at all. Prince Yakov died long ago. It's his brother, Prince Grigory, a notorious brute."

"Who is he married to?"

---

* "Your heart is a sponge soaked in bile and vinegar." Unpublished correspondence.

"The daughter of that chorister . . . what's his name?"

"I haven't gone out for so long that I've quite lost touch with your high society. So you value very much the attention of Prince Grigory, the notorious scoundrel, and the good graces of his wife, a chorister's daughter?"

"But of course," the young man replied hotly, flinging his book on the table. "I'm a man of society and do not want to be scorned by society aristocrats. I am not concerned either with their genealogies or with their morals."

"Who are you calling aristocrats?"

"Those to whom Countess Fuflygina offers her hand."

"And who is this Countess Fuflygina?"

"An insolent fool."

"And the scorn of people you despise can upset you so much?!" said the lady, after some silence. "Confess, there's some other reason here."

"So: again suspicions! again jealousy! By God, this is insufferable." With those words he stood up and took his hat.

"You're leaving already?" the lady said anxiously. "Don't you want to dine here?"

"No, I gave my word."

"Dine with me," she went on in a gentle and timid voice. "I've ordered champagne."

"What for? Am I some Moscow card player? Can't I do without champagne?"

"But the last time you found my wine bad, you were angry that women are poor judges in that. I can't please you."

"I'm not asking you to please me."

She made no reply. The young man immediately regretted the rudeness of these last words. He went to her, took her hand, and said tenderly:

"Zinaida, forgive me: I'm not myself today; I'm angry with everybody and for everything. At such moments I ought to stay home . . . Forgive me; don't be angry."

"I'm not angry, Valerian; but it pains me to see that for some time now you've been quite changed. You come to see me as if out of duty, not by your heart's prompting. You're bored with me. You keep silent, don't know how to occupy yourself, fumble with books, find fault with me, so as to quarrel with me and leave . . . I'm not reproaching you: our hearts are not in our power, but I . . . ."

Valerian was no longer listening. He was pulling at the glove he had long since put on and kept glancing impatiently outside. She fell silent with an air of restrained vexation. He pressed her hand, said a few meaningless words, and ran out of the room, the way a frisky schoolboy runs out of class. Zinaida went to the window; she watched the carriage brought for him, watched him get into it and drive off. She stood for a long time in the same place, leaning her hot brow against the icy windowpane. Finally she said aloud, "No, he doesn't love me!"—rang for the maid, told her to light the lamp, and sat down at her little writing desk.

CHAPTER TWO

Vous écrivez vos lettres de 4 pages plus vite que je ne puis les lire.

* * * soon became convinced of his wife's infidelity. He found this extremely upsetting. He did not know what course to take: to pretend he had noticed nothing seemed stupid to him; to laugh at such a commonplace misfortune—contemptible; to get downright angry—too sensational; to complain with an air of deeply offended feeling—too ridiculous. Fortunately, his wife came to his aid.

Having fallen in love with Volodsky, she felt an aversion for her husband proper only to women and which only they can understand. One day she went into his study, shut the door behind her, and announced that she loved Volodsky, that she did not want to deceive her husband and dishonor him in secret, and that she had resolved to divorce him. * * * was alarmed by such openness and precipitousness. She gave him no time to recover, moved that same day from the English Embankment to Kolomna, and in a short note made it all known to Volodsky, who was not expecting anything of the sort . . .

He was in despair. He had never thought of binding himself with such ties. He disliked boredom, feared any obligation, and above all valued his egotistical independence. But that was all over. Zinaida was left on his hands. He pretended to be grateful and prepared himself for the bother of a liaison, as for the performance of a duty or the boring obligation of checking his butler's monthly accounts . . .

* "You write your four-page letters more quickly than I can read them."

Notes of a Young Man

On May 4, 1825, I was promoted to officer, on the 6th I received orders to go to the regiment in the small town of Vasilkov, on the 9th I left Petersburg.

Was it not just recently that I was a cadet; just recently that they woke me up at six in the morning; just recently that I pored over my German lesson amid the eternal noise of the corps? Now I'm an ensign, have 475 roubles in my wallet, do what I like, and gallop on post horses to the small town of Vasilkov, where I'll sleep till eight and never speak a single word of German.

In my ears still echo the noise and shouts of frolicking cadets and the monotonous hum of assiduous students repeating vocables—*le bluet, le bluet*, cornflower, *amarante*, amaranth, *amarante, amarante* . . . Now the rumble of the cart and the jingle of the bell alone break the surrounding silence . . . I still cannot get used to this quiet.

At the thought of my freedom, of the pleasures of the way and the adventures awaiting me, a feeling of unutterable joy filled my soul to the point of ecstasy. But I gradually calmed down and began to observe the movement of the front wheels, making mathematical calculations. In some insensible way this pastime wearied me, and the journey no longer seemed as agreeable as at first.

On arriving at the posting station, I gave the one-eyed stationmaster my travel papers and demanded horses quickly. But to my indescribable displeasure I heard that there were no horses. I glanced into the posting register: a traveling sixth-class functionary with attendants had taken twelve horses from the town of * * * to Petersburg; General B.'s wife had taken eight; two troikas had gone off with the mail; our fellow ensign had taken the remaining two. At the station stood one courier troika, and the stationmaster could not give it to me. If perchance a courier or government messenger should come galloping up and find no horses, what would he be in for then, big trouble— he could lose his job, go begging. I tried to buy his conscience, but he stood firm and resolutely rejected my twenty kopecks. No help for it! I yielded to necessity.

"Would you like some tea or coffee?" asked the stationmaster. I thanked him and busied myself with examining the pictures that adorned his humble abode. In them was depicted the story of the prodigal son.[1] In the first picture a venerable old man in a nightcap and dressing gown is sending off a restless young man, who hurriedly receives his blessing and a bag of money. In the second the depraved young man's bad behavior is portrayed in vivid strokes; he sits at a table, surrounded by false friends and shameless women. Next the young wastrel, in a French kaftan and cocked hat, is herding swine and shares their meal with them. His face portrays deep sadness and repentance; he remembers his father's house, where the *least servant*, etc. Finally his return to his father is represented. The good old man in the same nightcap and dressing gown runs out to meet him. The prodigal son is on his knees, in the distance a cook kills the fatted calf, and the older brother vexedly questions the servants about the cause of such rejoicing. German verses are printed under the pictures. I read them with pleasure and copied them down, so as to translate them at leisure.

The rest of the pictures have no frames and are tacked to the wall. They portray the burial of a cat, the dispute between a red nose and a heavy frost, and the like—and, in moral as well as artistic terms, are not worth an educated man's attention.

I sat by the window. No view at all. A close-packed row of uniform cottages leaning against each other. Here and there two or three apple trees, two or three rowan trees, surrounded with a flimsy fence, the unhitched cart with my trunk and cellaret.

A hot day. The coachmen have gone off somewhere. In the street golden-haired, dirty children are playing knucklebones. An old woman sits sorrowfully in front of a cottage facing me. Now and then a cock crows. Dogs lie in the sun or wander around, tongues lolling and tails hanging, and pigs run oinking from under the gate and rush off for no apparent reason.

What boredom! I go for a stroll in the fields. A dilapidated well. Beside it a shallow puddle. In it some yellow ducklings frolic, supervised by a stupid duck, like spoiled children with a French governess.

I go down the high road—to the right skimpy winter rye, to the left bushes and swamp. Flat space around. All you meet are striped mileposts. In the sky a slow sun, here and there a cloud. What boredom! I turn back, having gone two miles and ascertained that it is another fifteen to the next station.

On returning, I tried to get my coachman to talk, but he, as if avoiding any proper conversation, responded to all my questions only with "There's no knowing, Your Honor," "God knows," "But then, too . . ."

I sat by the window again and asked the fat housemaid, who ran past me every other minute, now to the back door, now to the pantry, if there was anything to read. She brought me several books. I was glad and eagerly threw myself into examining them. But I cooled off at once, seeing a well-worn ABC and an arithmetic book published for use in peasant schools. The stationmaster's son, a rowdy boy of about nine, studied in them, as she said, all the tsar's sciences, tearing out the pages as he learned them, for which, by the law of natural retribution, his hair had been pulled . . .

My Fate Is Decided. I Am Getting Married . . .

(From the French)

My fate is decided. I am getting married . . .

She whom I have loved for a whole two years, who has been the first my eyes sought out everywhere, to meet whom seemed like bliss to me—my God—she's . . . nearly mine.

Waiting for the decisive answer was the most painful feeling of my life. Waiting for the last card to be dealt, the pangs of conscience, sleep before a duel—all that means nothing in comparison to it.

The thing was that I was not afraid of refusal alone. One of my friends used to say "I don't understand how one can propose, if one knows for certain there will be no refusal."

To marry! It's easy to say—most people see marriage as shawls bought on credit, a new carriage, and a pink dressing gown.

Others—as a dowry and a settled life . . .

Still others marry just so, because everybody marries—because they're thirty years old. Ask them what marriage is, and in reply they'll repeat to you a banal saying.

I marry, i.e., I sacrifice independence, my carefree, whimsical independence, my luxurious habits, aimless travels, solitude, inconstancy.

I'm ready to double a life which is incomplete even without that. I never bothered about happiness, I could do without it. Now I need enough for two, and where am I to get it?

So long as I'm not married, what is meant by my responsibilities? I have a sick uncle whom I hardly ever see. If I call on him—he's very glad; if I don't—he excuses me: "My scapegrace is young, he can do without me." I don't correspond with anybody, I pay my bills every month. In the morning I get up whenever I like, I receive whomever I like, if I decide to go for a promenade—they saddle my smart, quiet Jenny, I ride along the lanes, look into the windows of low little houses: here a family is sitting around the samovar, there a servant is sweeping the rooms, further on a girl is having a piano lesson, beside her a hired musician. She turns her absentminded face to me, the teacher scolds her, I slowly ride on . . . I come home—sort through books, papers, put my toilet table in order, dress casually if I'm going visiting, with all possible care if I'm dining in a restaurant, where I read either a new novel or some journals; if Walter Scott and Cooper haven't written anything, and there is no criminal trial in the papers, then I order a bottle of champagne on ice, watch the glass turn frosty, drink slowly, happy that the dinner costs me seventeen roubles and that I can allow myself such a caprice. I go to the theater, search the boxes for some remarkable apparel, dark eyes; communication is established between us, I'm occupied till the final curtain. I spend the evening either in a noisy gathering, where the whole city crowds, where I see everyone and everything, and no one notices me, or in a choice and amiable circle, where I talk about myself and they listen to me. I go home late; I fall asleep reading a good book. The next day I again go for a ride along the lanes, past the house where the girl was playing the piano. She is repeating yesterday's lesson. She glances at me as at an old acquaintance and laughs.—Such is my bachelor life . . .

If I'm refused, I think, I'll go abroad—and I already picture myself on a pyroscaphe. They bustle around me, say good-bye, carry trunks, look at their watches. The pyroscaphe sets off: fresh sea air blows in my face; I gaze for a long time at the retreating shore—"My native land, adieu."[1] Beside me a young woman begins to feel sick; this gives her pale face an expression of languid tenderness . . . She asks me for water. Thank God, I'll be occupied till Kronstadt . . .

Just then they bring me a note: the reply to my letter. My fiancée's father affectionately invites me to visit . . . There's no doubt, my proposal has been accepted. Nadenka, my angel, is mine! . . . All sorrowful doubts vanish before this paradisal thought. I rush to the carriage and gallop off; here is the house; I go into the front hall; I can already see from the hurried reception of the servants that I am a fiancé. I'm embarrassed: these people know my heart; they speak of my love in their lackey language! . . .

The father and mother were sitting in the drawing room. The former greeted me with open arms. He took a handkerchief from his pocket, wanted to start weeping but couldn't, and decided to blow his nose. The mother's eyes were red. They sent for Nadenka; she came in, pale, awkward. The father stepped out and came back with the icons of St. Nicholas the Wonderworker and the Kazan Mother of God. They blessed us. Nadenka gave me her cold, unresponding hand. The mother started talking about a dowry, the father about an estate in Saratov province—I am a fiancé.

And so this is no longer the secret of two hearts. It is today's news for the household, tomorrow's for the public square.

Thus a poem, thought up in solitude on moonlit summer nights, is then put on sale in a bookstore and criticized in the journals by fools.

———

Everyone is glad of my happiness, everyone congratulates me, everyone now loves me. They all offer me their services: one his house, another a loan of money, yet another a Bukhara shawl merchant he knows. Someone is worried about my future numerous family and offers me twelve pairs of gloves with the portrait of Mlle Sontag.[2]

The young men begin to be formal with me: they respect me now as an enemy. The ladies praise my choice to my face, but behind my back they pity my bride: "Poor thing! She's so young, so innocent, and he's so flighty, so immoral . . ."

I confess, this is beginning to weary me. I like the custom of some ancient people: the groom secretly abducts his bride. The next day he already presents her to the town gossips as his wife. Among us family happiness is prepared for with printed announcements, gifts known to the whole town, formal letters, visits—in short, by all sorts of temptations . . .

A Romance at the Caucasian Waters

On one of the first days of April 181– there was great turmoil in the house of Katerina Petrovna Tomskaya. The doors were all thrown open; the reception room and the front hall were cluttered with trunks and suitcases; the drawers of all the chests were pulled out; the servants kept running up and down the stairs, the maids fussed and argued; the mistress of the house, a lady of about forty-five, sat in her bedroom, going over the account books brought by the fat steward, who stood before her, hands behind his back and right leg thrust forward. Katerina Petrovna made it look as if she were intimately acquainted with the secrets of management, but her questions and observations betrayed her seignorial ignorance and occasionally provoked a barely perceptible smile on the majestic face of the steward, who nevertheless, with great indulgence, entered in detail into all the explanations she demanded. Just then a servant announced that Paraskovya Ivanovna Povodova had arrived. Katerina Petrovna was glad of the chance to break off her consultation, asked her in, and dismissed the steward.

"Good gracious, dearie," the old lady said, coming in, "you're getting ready to travel! Where on earth are you going?"

"To the Caucasus, my dear Paraskovya Ivanovna."

"To the Caucasus! So Moscow told the truth for once in its life, and I didn't believe it. To the Caucasus! It's so terribly far away. Why do you want to drag yourself God knows where, for God knows what?"

"What can I do? The doctors told me that my Masha needs mineral waters, and hot baths are necessary for my health. I've been suffering for a year and a half already; maybe the Caucasus will help me."

"God grant it. And are you going soon?"

"Some four days from now; at the most, the very most, I may linger for a week; everything's ready. Yesterday they brought me a new traveling carriage, and what a carriage! A toy, a joy to look at—little drawers everywhere, and what does it not have: a bed, a toilet table, a cellaret, a medicine chest, a kitchen, a set of dishes. Do you want to have a look?"

"Gladly, dearie."

And the two ladies went out to the porch. The coachmen pulled the traveling coach out of the shed. Katerina Petrovna told them to open the door, got into the carriage, turned over all the cushions, pulled out all the drawers, showed all the secrets, all the conveniences, raised all the shutters, all the mirrors, turned all the bags inside out—in short, for a sick woman she proved very active and agile. Having admired the equipage, the two ladies returned to the drawing room, where they fell to talking again about the forthcoming journey, the return, the plans for the coming winter:

"I hope to be back by October without fail," said Katerina Petrovna. "I'll have soirées twice a week, and I hope, my dear, that you will transfer your Boston[1] to me."

Just then a girl of about eighteen, slender, tall, with a pale, beautiful face and fiery dark eyes, quietly came into the room, went up to kiss Katerina Petrovna's hand, and curtsied to Povodova.

"Did you sleep well, Masha?" asked Katerina Petrovna.

"Very well, mama; I only just got up. You're surprised at my laziness, Paraskovya Ivanovna? What can I do? For an invalid it's forgivable."

"Sleep, dearie, sleep to your heart's content," Povodova replied, "and be sure to come back from the Caucasus ruddy-cheeked, healthy, and, God willing—married."

"What do you mean, married?" Katerina Petrovna objected, laughing. "Who is she going to marry in the Caucasus? Some Circassian prince? . . ."

"A Circassian! God forbid! They're like Turks and Bukharans[2]—heathens. They'll shave her head and lock her up."

"Let God just send us health," Katerina Petrovna said with a sigh, "and suitors won't stay away. Thank God, Masha's still young, there's a dowry. And if a good man falls in love, he'll take her even without a dowry."

"But all the same it's better with a dowry, dearie," Paraskovya Ivanovna said, standing up. "Well, let's say good-bye, Katerina Petrovna, I won't see you till September. It's a long way to drag myself to you, from Basmannaya to the Arbat[3]—and I won't invite you, I know you have no time now. Good-bye to you, too, my beauty; don't forget my advice."

The ladies took leave of each other, and Paraskovya Ivanovna left.

A Russian Pelham

CHAPTER ONE

My memories begin from the most tender age, and here is a scene that is vividly preserved in my imagination.[1]

Nanny brings me to a big room, dimly lit by a candle under a shade. On a bed under green curtains lies a woman all in white: my father takes me in his arms. She kisses me and weeps. My father sobs loudly, I get frightened and cry out. Nanny takes me away, saying, "Mama wants to go bye-bye." I also remember great turmoil, a lot of guests, servants running from room to room. The sun shines through all the windows, and I'm very cheerful. A monk with a golden cross on his chest blesses me; a long red coffin is carried through the door. That is all that my mother's funeral left in my heart. She was a woman of extraordinary mind and heart, as I learned later from the stories of people who knew how priceless she was.

Here my memories become confused. I cannot give a clear account of myself before I reached my eighth year. But first I must talk about my family.

My father was awarded the rank of sergeant while my grandmother was still pregnant with him. He was educated at home until he was eighteen. His tutor, Monsieur Décor, was a simple and kind old man, who had a very good knowledge of French orthography. It is not known whether my father had any other instructors, but, apart from French orthography, my father had no thorough knowledge of anything. He married against his parents' will a girl who was several years older than he, retired that same year and went to Moscow. Old Savelyich, his valet, told me that the first years of their marriage were happy. My mother managed to reconcile her husband with his family, in which she came to be loved. But my father's frivolous and inconstant character did not allow her to enjoy peace and happiness. He entered into a liaison with a woman known in society for her beauty and her amorous adventures. For him she divorced her husband, who yielded her to my father for ten thousand roubles and afterwards used to dine with us quite frequently. My mother knew it all, and kept silent. Inner suffering ruined her health. She took to her bed and never left it again.

My father owned five thousand souls. Consequently, he was one of those gentlemen whom the late Count Sheremetev called petty landowners, wondering in all honesty how they were able to live![2]— The thing was that my father lived no worse than Count Sheremetev, though he was exactly twenty times poorer. Muscovites still remember his dinners, his private theater, and his horn music. Two years after my mother's death, Anna Petrovna Virlatskaya, the cause of that death, moved into his house. She was, as they say, a fine figure of a woman, though no longer in the first bloom of youth. They brought me a boy in a red jacket with cuffs and told me he was my little brother. I gazed at him all eyes. Mishenka scraped to the right, scraped to the left, and wanted to play with my toy gun; I tore it from his hands, Mishenka began to cry, and my father stood me in the corner and gave my little brother my gun.

Such a beginning did not bode well for me. And indeed my sojourn under the paternal roof left nothing pleasant in my memory. My father loved me, of course, but he did not bother himself about me at all and abandoned me to the care of French tutors, who were constantly being hired and fired. My first tutor turned out to be a drunkard; the second, who was no fool and not lacking in knowledge, had such a violent temper that he nearly killed me with a log because I spilled ink on his waistcoat; the third, who spent a whole year with us, was mad, and the household only realized it when he came to complain to Anna Petrovna that Mishenka and I had incited all the bedbugs in the house to give him no peace and that moreover a little devil had taken to nesting in his nightcap. Other Frenchmen could not get along with Anna Petrovna, who gave them no wine at dinner or horses on Sunday; moreover she paid them very irregularly. I was to blame: Anna Petrovna decided that none of my tutors could manage such an insufferable boy. However, it was also true that there was not one of them that I had not turned into a household laughingstock within two weeks of their entering into their duties. I remember with particular satisfaction Monsieur Groget, a respectable fifty-year-old Genevan, whom I persuaded that Anna Petrovna was in love with him. You should have seen his chaste horror, with a certain admixture of sly coquetry, when Anna Petrovna, glancing sidelong at him at the table, would say in a half whisper: "What a glutton!"

I was frisky, lazy, and hot-tempered, but sentimental and ambitious, and one could get anything from me by kindness; unfortunately, everybody meddled in my education, but nobody knew the right way of dealing with me. I laughed at the teachers and pulled tricks; with Anna Petrovna I fought tooth for tooth; with Mishenka I had incessant quarrels and scuffles. With my father things often went as far as stormy exchanges, which ended with tears on both sides. Finally Anna Petrovna persuaded him to send me to one of the German universities . . . I was then fifteen.

CHAPTER TWO

My university life left me with pleasant memories, which, if you look into them, refer to insignificant, and sometimes unpleasant, events; but youth is a great sorcerer: I would pay dearly to sit again over a mug of beer in a cloud of tobacco smoke, with a cudgel in my hand and a greasy velvet cap on my head. I would pay dearly for my room, eternally filled with people, and God knows what people; for our Latin songs, student duels, and quarrels with the philistines![3]

The freedom of university studies was of greater benefit to me than lessons at home, but in general the only things I learned properly were fencing and making punch. I received money from home at irregular intervals. That accustomed me to debts and insouciance. Three years went by, and I received an order from my father in Petersburg to leave the university and enter government service in Russia. A few words about disordered circumstances, extra expenses, a change of life seemed odd to me, but I did not pay much attention to them. On my departure I gave a farewell banquet, at which I swore to be eternally faithful to friendship and to mankind and never to take the job of censor, and the next day, with a headache and heartburn, I set out on my way.

We Were Spending the Evening at the Dacha

We were spending the evening at the dacha of Princess D.

The conversation somehow touched upon Mme de Staël.[1] Baron D., in poor French, told very poorly a well-known joke: her question to Bonaparte about whom he considered the foremost woman in the world, and his amusing reply: "The one who has had the most children" (*"Celle qui a fait le plus d'enfants"*).

"What a fine epigram!" one of the guests observed.

"And it serves her right!" one lady said. "How could she fish so clumsily for a compliment?"

"But it seems to me," said Sorokhtin, who was dozing in a Gambs armchair,[2] "it seems to me that Mme de Staël was no more thinking of madrigals than Napoleon was of epigrams. She asked the question out of simple curiosity, quite understandably; and Napoleon literally expressed his own personal opinion. But you don't believe in the artlessness of genius."

The guests began to argue, and Sorokhtin dozed off again.

"Really, though," said the hostess, "whom do you consider the foremost woman in the world?"

"Careful, now: you're fishing for a compliment . . ."

"No, joking aside . . ."

Here a discussion set in: some named Mme de Staël, others the Maid of Orleans, still others Elizabeth, the queen of England, Mme de Maintenon, Mme Roland, and so on . . .[3]

A young man standing by the fireplace (because in Petersburg a fireplace is never superfluous) mixed into the conversation for the first time.

"For me," he said, "the most astonishing woman is Cleopatra."

"Cleopatra?" said the guests. "Yes, of course . . . Why, though?"

"There is a feature in her life which is so engraved in my imagination that I can hardly glance at any woman without thinking at once of Cleopatra."

"What is this feature?" asked the hostess. "Tell us."

"I can't; it's a tricky thing to tell."

"Why so? Is it indecent?"

"Yes, like almost everything that vividly portrays the terrible morals of antiquity."

"Ah, tell us, tell us!"

"Ah, no, don't tell us," interrupted Volskaya, a divorced woman, primly lowering her fiery eyes.

"Enough," cried the hostess with impatience. "*Qui est-ce donc que l'on trompe ici?** Yesterday we saw *Antony*, and I have *La Physiologie du mariage* lying there on the mantelpiece.[4] Indecent! Find something else to frighten us with! Stop addling our brains, Alexei Ivanych! You're not a journalist. Tell us simply what you know about Cleopatra . . . though . . . keep it decent, if you can . . ."

Everybody laughed.

"By God," said the young man, "I feel timid: I've become as bashful as our censorship. Well, so be it . . . . You should know that among Latin historians there was a certain Aurelius Victor, whom you've probably never heard of."

"Aurelius Victor?" interrupted Vershnev, who once studied with the Jesuits. "Aurelius Victor was a fourth-century writer. His works have been ascribed to Cornelius Nepos and even to Suetonius.[5] He wrote the book *De Viris Illustribus*—about the famous men of the city of Rome, I know . . ."

"Exactly," Alexei Ivanych went on. "His little book is quite worthless, but in it is found the story of Cleopatra that struck me so much. And, remarkably enough, in that passage the dry and dull Aurelius Victor equals Tacitus in power of expression: '*Haec tantae libidinis fuit ut saepe prostiterit; tanta pulchritudinis ut multi noctem illius morte emerint . . .*'"[†]

"Wonderful!" exclaimed Vershnev. "It reminds me of Sallust—remember? '*Tantae . . .*'"[6]

"What is this, gentlemen?" asked the hostess. "Now you're so good as to talk in Latin! How pleasant for us! Tell me, what is the meaning of your Latin phrase?"

"The point is that Cleopatra sold her beauty and that many bought a night with her at the price of their lives . . ."

* "Who is being fooled here?"
† 'She had so much lust that she often sold herself; so much beauty that many bought a night with her at the price of death.'

"How terrible!" said the ladies. "What do you find astonishing about it?"

"You ask what? It seems to me that Cleopatra was no banal coquette and did not value herself cheaply. I suggested to * * * that he make a poem out of it; he did begin one, but dropped it."

"And he did well."

"What did he want to draw from it? What was the main idea here—do you remember?"

"He begins with the description of a banquet in the gardens of the Egyptian queen."

Dark, sultry night envelops the African sky; Alexandria has fallen asleep; its squares are quiet, its houses dark. The distant Pharos burns solitarily in its vast harbor, like a lamp at the head of a sleeping beauty's bed.

Bright and noisy are the halls of the Ptolemies' palace: Cleopatra is receiving her friends; the table is surrounded by ivory couches; three hundred youths serve the guests, three hundred maidens bring them amphorae filled with Greek wines; three hundred black eunuchs silently oversee them.

The porphyry colonnade open to the south and to the north awaits the wafting of Eurus; but the air is still; the flaming tongues of lamps burn motionlessly; the smoke of incense rises straight up in a motionless stream; the sea, like a mirror, lies motionless at the pink steps of the semicircular porch. The gilded claws and granite tails of the guardian sphinxes are reflected in it . . . only the sounds of cithara and flute stir the lights, the air, and the sea.

Suddenly the queen fell to thinking and sadly hung her wondrous head; the bright banquet was darkened by her sadness, as the sun is darkened by a cloud.

What makes her sad?

> Why does sorrow weigh her down?
> What lacks ancient Egypt's crown?
> In her resplendent capital,
> Protected by a crowd of thralls,
> Peacefully her power she wields.
> The earthly gods to her do yield,
> Filled with wonders are her halls.
> Let Africa's scorching noon befall,
> Let the cool shade of night descend,
> At every hour on her attend
> Luxury and art to gratify
> Her drowsy senses, and to her fly
> From all lands, over all the seas,
> Offerings of rich finery,
> Which she keeps changing in delight:
> Now she shines with rubies bright,
> Now chooses, like the women of Tyre,
> A purple chiton for attire,
> Now on the flood of hoary Nile,
> Shaded by a splendid sail,
> On her golden-decked trireme
> She floats like Cypris in a dream.
> Hourly before her eyes
> Banquet after banquet flies,
> And who in his soul can guess aright
> All the mysteries of her nights? . . .
>
> In vain! Her heart in languor moans,
> She longs for pleasures yet unknown –
> Exhausted, surfeited is she,
> Ill with insensibility . . .

Cleopatra awakens from her pensiveness.

The feast dies down as in a daze,
But she again her head does raise,
Fire is in her haughty eyes,
And with a sudden smile she cries:
"You find my love a blissful force?
Pay heed, then, to the terms I set,
And luck perhaps will still be yours.
All inequality I can forget.
I challenge you: who will say aye?
My nights I offer for a fee:
Say, which of you agrees to buy
At the price of life one night with me?"

"This subject should be given to the marquise George Sand,[7] as shameless a woman as your Cleopatra. She would rework your Egyptian anecdote for present-day morals."

"Impossible. It would have no verisimilitude. This anecdote is perfectly antique. Such an exchange is as unfeasible now as building pyramids."

"Why unfeasible? Can it be that among present-day women not one can be found who would wish to test in reality the truth of what is repeated to her every moment—that her love is dearer to them than life?"

"Let's say it would be interesting to find out. But how can this scientific testing be organized? Cleopatra had every possibility of making her debtors pay. But we? We certainly can't write such terms down on official paper and have it notarized in the civil court."

"In that case we could rely on *word of honor*."

"How so?"

"The woman can take her lover's word of honor that he'll shoot himself the next day."

"And the next day he goes abroad, and she's left a fool."

"Yes, if he agrees to remain forever dishonored in the eyes of the woman he loves. And are the terms themselves really so harsh? Is life such a treasure that one is sorry to buy happiness at the cost of it? Judge for yourself: the first prankster to come along, whom I despise, says something about me that cannot harm me in any way, and I offer my head to his bullet—I have no right to deny this satisfaction to the first bully who comes along and decides to test my sang-froid. Am I going to play the coward when it comes to my own bliss? What is life, if it's poisoned by dejection and empty desires! And what good is it, if its pleasures are exhausted?"

"Are you really capable of entering into such a contract?"

At that moment Volskaya, who had been sitting silently all the while with lowered eyes, quickly shot a glance at Alexei Ivanych.

"I'm not speaking about myself. But a man who is truly in love will of course not hesitate for a single moment . . ."

"What? Even for a woman who doesn't love you? (And one who would agree to your terms surely doesn't love you.) The thought alone of such brutality must destroy the wildest passion . . ."

"No, I would see in her acceptance only a fervid imagination. As for requited love . . . I don't demand that of her: if I love, whose business is it? . . ."

"Stop it—God knows what you're saying. So this is what you didn't want to tell about—"

———

The young countess K., a chubby, homely thing, tried to give an important expression to her nose, which resembled an onion stuck onto a turnip, and said:

"Even nowadays there are women who value themselves more highly . . ."

Her husband, a Polish count, who had married her for her money (mistakenly, they say), lowered his eyes and drank off his cup of tea.

"What do you mean by that, Countess?" asked the young man, barely holding back a smile . . .

"I mean," the countess K. replied, "that a woman who respects herself, who respects . . ." Here she became confused; Vershnev came to her aid.

"You think that a woman who respects herself does not desire the death of a sinner[8]—isn't it so?"

The conversation changed course.

Alexei Ivanych sat down beside Volskaya, bent over as if studying her embroidery, and said to her in a half whisper: "What do you think of Cleopatra's terms?"

Volskaya said nothing. Alexei Ivanych repeated his question.

"What can I tell you? Nowadays, too, some women value themselves highly. But nineteenth-century men are too coldblooded, too reasonable, to agree to such terms."

"Do you think," Alexei Ivanych said in a suddenly altered voice, "do you think that in our time, in Petersburg, here, a woman can be found who would have enough pride, enough inner strength, to lay down Cleopatra's terms to her lover? . . ."

"I think so; I'm even certain."

"You're not deceiving me? Just think: that would be too cruel, more cruel than the terms themselves . . ."

Volskaya looked at him with fiery, piercing eyes and in a firm voice said: "No."

Alexei Ivanych stood up and disappeared at once.

A Story from Roman Life

Caesar was traveling, Titus Petronius[1] and I were following him at a distance. After sunset slaves put up a tent, placed couches; we lay down to feast and converse merrily; at dawn we set out again and fell sweetly asleep each on his own lectica, weary from the heat and the night's pleasures.

We reached Cumae and were already thinking of going further, when a messenger came to us from Nero. He brought Petronius an order from Caesar to return to Rome and there await the deciding of his fate following a hateful denunciation.

We were horror-stricken. Petronius alone listened indifferently to his sentence, dismissed the messenger with a gift, and announced to us his intention to stay in Cumae. He sent his favorite slave to choose and rent a house for him and awaited his return in a cypress grove dedicated to the Eumenides.[2]

We surrounded him uneasily. Flavius Aurelius asked if he meant to stay long in Cumae and whether he was not afraid of irritating Nero by his disobedience.

"I not only do not mean to disobey him," Petronius replied with a smile, "but I even intend to forestall his wishes. But you, my friends, I advise to return. On a clear day a traveler rests in the shade of an oak tree, but during a thunderstorm he prudently distances himself from it, fearing bolts of lightning."

We all expressed a wish to stay with him, and Petronius affectionately thanked us. The servant came back and led us to the house he had chosen. It was on the edge of town. It was managed by an old freedman, in the absence of the owner, who had left Italy long ago. Under his supervision, several slaves kept the rooms and gardens clean. In the wide entryway we found statues of the nine muses; by the door stood two centaurs.

Petronius paused on the marble threshold and read the greeting inscribed on it: *Welcome!* A sad smile appeared on his face. The old steward led him to the library, where we examined several scrolls and then went on to the master's bedroom. It was simply decorated. There were only two family statues in it. One portrayed a matron sitting in a chair, the other a girl playing with a ball. A small lamp stood on a night table by the bed. Here Petronius stayed to rest and dismissed us, inviting us to gather there in the evening.

———

I could not fall asleep; sorrow filled my soul. I saw in Petronius not only a generous benefactor, but also a friend, sincerely attached to me. I respected his vast mind; I loved his beautiful soul. From his conversation I drew a knowledge of the world and of men, which were known to me more from the speculations of the divine Plato than from my own experience. His judgments were usually quick and correct. Indifference toward everything saved him from partiality, and sincerity in regard to himself made him perspicacious. Life could not offer him anything new; he had tasted all pleasures; his senses slumbered, dulled by habit, but his mind kept an astonishing freshness. He liked the play of ideas, as he did the harmony of words. He listened eagerly to philosophical discussions and wrote verses no worse than Catullus.

I went out to the garden and for a long time walked along its winding paths, shaded by old trees. I sat down on a bench in the shadow of a spreading poplar, beside which stood the statue of a young satyr fashioning a reed pipe. Wishing to drive my sad thoughts away somehow, I took out a writing tablet and translated one of the odes of Anacreon, which I have kept in memory of that sad day:

> Gray they've grown, thin they've grown,
> My locks, the honor of my head,
> The teeth have weakened in my gums,
> The fire of my eyes grows dim.
> Not many days are left to me
> Of this sweet life to be seen off,
> The Parcae keep a strict account,
> Tartarus awaits my shade—
> Dreadful the cold of the nether vault,
> The way in is open to us all,
> But there is no coming out of it . . .
> All go down—and lie forgot.[3]

———

The sun was sinking towards the west; I went to Petronius. I found him in the library. He was pacing about; with him was his personal doctor, Septimius. Seeing me, Petronius stopped and recited facetiously:

> Proud steeds are known
> By the brand they bear,
> The arrogant Parthian
> By his tall headpiece,
> Happy lovers I know
> By looking in their eyes.[4]

"You've guessed right," I replied to Petronius and gave him my tablets. He read my verses. A cloud of pensiveness passed over his face and dispersed at once.

"When I read such poems," he said, "I'm always curious to know how those who were so struck by the thought of death died themselves. Anacreon assures us that Tartarus terrifies him, but I don't believe him—just as I don't believe the cowardice of Horace. Do you know his ode?

> Which of the gods restored to me
> The one with whom I first campaigned
> And shared the horror of mortal combat,
> When we were led by desperate Brutus
> In the pursuit of phantom freedom?
> With whom I'd forget the alarms of war
> In a tent over a cup of wine,
> And my locks, entwined with ivy,
> I would anoint with Syrian myrrh?
>
> Remember the hour of dreadful battle,
> When I, a trembling quiritis,
> Fled and shamefully dropped my shield,
> Making vows and saying prayers?
> How frightened I was! How fast I fled!
> But Hermes suddenly covered me
> In a cloud and whirled me far away
> And saved me from a certain death.[5]

"The cunning poet wanted to make Augustus and Maecenas laugh at his cowardice so as not to remind them of the brother-in-arms of Cassius and Brutus. Say what you like, I find more sincerity in his exclamation:

Sweet and seemly it is to die for your country."[6]

Maria Schoning

April 25, W.

Dear Maria,

What has become of you? It is more than four months now that I have not received a single line from you. Are you in good health? If I had not been constantly occupied, I would have come to visit you, but you know: twelve miles is no joke. Without me the household would come to a stop; Fritz understands nothing about it—a real child. Maybe you have gotten married? No, surely you would have remembered your friend and given me the joyful news of your happiness. In your last letter you wrote that your poor father was still ailing; I hope that the spring has helped him and that he is better now. About myself I can say, thank God, that I am healthy and happy. The work goes so-so, but I still do not know how to set prices or bargain. And it is time I learned. Fritz is quite well, but for some time now his wooden leg has been bothering him. He walks little, and in bad weather he moans and groans. However, he is as cheerful as ever, still likes his glass of wine, and still has not finished telling me about his campaigns. The children are growing and getting pretty. Frank is becoming quite a fellow. Imagine, dear Maria, he is already chasing after girls—isn't that something?—and he is not even three years old. And what a rowdy! Fritz cannot stop admiring him and spoils him terribly; instead of calming the child down, he eggs him on and rejoices at all his pranks. Mina is much more composed; true, she is a year older. I am beginning to teach her to read. She catches on very quickly, and it seems she will be pretty. But what are good looks? Let her be kind and reasonable—then most likely she will be happy.

P.S. I am sending you a shawl as a present; put it on next Sunday, dear Maria, when you go to church. It was a gift from Fritz; but red goes better with your dark hair than with my blonde. Men do not understand these things. Blue and red are all the same to them. Forgive, dear Maria, my babbling away with you. Answer me quickly. Give my sincere respects to your father. Write me about his health. I will never forget that I spent three years under his roof, and he treated me, a poor orphan, not as a hired servant, but as a daughter. Our pastor's wife advises him to use red pimpinella instead of tea, a very ordinary flower—I've found its Latin name—any apothecary will show it to you.

MARIA SCHONING TO ANNA HARLIN

April 28

I received your letter last Friday (read it only today). My poor father passed away that same day, at six o'clock in the morning; the funeral was yesterday.

I never imagined that death was so near. All the time recently he was feeling much better, and Dr. Költz had hopes for his full recovery. On Monday he even strolled in our little garden and went as far as the well without getting out of breath. Returning to his room, he felt slightly feverish; I put him to bed and ran to Dr. Költz. He was not at home. Returning to my father, I found him fallen asleep. I thought that sleep might calm him completely. Dr. Költz came in the evening. He examined the sick man and was displeased with his condition. He prescribed him a new medicine. During the night father woke up and asked to eat; I gave him soup; he swallowed one spoonful and did not want any more. He fell asleep again. The next day he had spasms. Dr. Költz never left his side. By evening the pain subsided, but he became so restless that he could not stay in one position for five minutes at a time. I had to keep turning him from one side to the other . . . Towards morning he quieted down and lay asleep for two hours or so. Dr. Költz left, telling me that he would be back in a couple of hours. Suddenly my father raised himself a little and called me. I came to him and asked what he wanted. He said to me: "Maria, why is it so dark? Open the blinds." I became frightened and said to him: "Father, don't you see . . . the blinds are open." He started feeling around him, seized my hand, and said: "Maria! Maria, I'm very ill . . . I'm dying . . . let me bless you . . . quickly!" I threw myself on my knees and put his hand on my head. He said: "Lord, reward her; Lord, I entrust her to you." He fell silent, his hand suddenly felt heavy. I thought he had fallen asleep again, and for several minutes I did not dare to move. Suddenly Dr. Költz came in, removed his hand from my head, and said to me: "Let him be now, go to your room." I looked: father lay pale and motionless. It was all over.

The good Dr. Költz did not leave our house for a whole two days and arranged everything, because I was not up to it. During the last days I was the only one looking after the sick man, there was no one to relieve me. I remembered you often and bitterly regretted that you were not with us . . .

Yesterday I got out of bed and was following the coffin; but I suddenly felt ill. I knelt down, so as to take leave of him from a distance. Frau Rothberg said: "What an actress!" Just imagine, dear Anya, those words gave me back my strength. I followed the coffin with astonishing ease. In the church it seemed extremely bright to me, and everything around me swayed. I did not weep. I felt suffocated, and kept wanting to laugh.

He was carried to the cemetery behind St. Jacob's church, and in my presence was lowered into the grave. I suddenly wanted to dig it up then, because I had not finished taking leave of him. But many people were still walking about the cemetery, and I was afraid that Frau Rothberg would say again: "What an actress!"

How cruel not to allow a daughter to take leave of her dead father as she wishes . . .

On returning home, I found some strangers, who told me it was necessary to seal all of my late father's possessions and papers. They left me my little room, after taking everything out of it except the bed and one chair. Tomorrow is Sunday. I shall not wear your shawl, but I thank you very much for it. I send my regards to your husband, and kiss Frank and Mina. Good-bye.

I write standing at the window, and have borrowed an inkstand from the neighbors.

MARIA SCHONING TO ANNA HARLIN

Dear Anna,

Yesterday an official came to me and announced that all of my late father's possessions must be put up for auction for the benefit of the town treasury, because he had not been assessed for his true worth and the inventory of his possessions showed he was much richer than had been thought. I understand none of it. Lately we had been spending a great deal on medicines. I have only 23 thalers left for expenses—I showed them to the officials, who said, however, that I could keep the money, because the law had no claim to it.

Our house will be sold next week; and I do not know what to do with myself. I went to the herr burgomeister. He received me well, but to my appeals replied that he could do nothing for me. I do not know where to find employment. If you need a maidservant, write to me; you know that I can help you with the housework and the handwork, and besides that I will look after the children and Fritz, if he falls ill. I have learned how to care for the sick. Please write if you have need of me. And do not be embarrassed. I am sure that this will not change our relations in the least and that you will remain for me the same kind and indulgent friend.

—

Old Schoning's little house was full of people. They crowded around the table, which was presided over by the auctioneer. He shouted: "Flannelette waistcoat with brass buttons . . . * * * thalers. Going once, going twice . . . —No higher bidder?—Flannelette waistcoat * * * thalers—sold." The waistcoat went to the hands of its new owner.

The buyers inspected with disparagement and curiosity the objects put up for auction. Frau Rothberg examined the dirty underwear, which had not been washed after Schoning's death; she fingered it, shook it out, repeating, "Trash, rags, tatters," and raised her bids by pennies. The tavern owner Hirtz bought two silver spoons, a half-dozen napkins, and two china cups. The bed on which Schoning had died was bought by Karolina Schmidt, a heavily rouged girl with a modest and humble air.

Maria, pale as a ghost, stood there, silently watching the plundering of her poor chattels. She held * * * thalers in her hand, prepared to buy something, and did not have the courage to outbid the other buyers. People were leaving, carrying off their acquisitions. Two little portraits in fly-specked and once-gilt frames remained unsold. One portrayed Schoning as a young man in a red kaftan. The other Christina, his wife, with a little dog in her arms. Both portraits were painted boldly and brightly. Hirtz wanted to buy them as well, to hang in the corner room of his tavern, because its walls were too bare. The portraits had been appraised at * * * thalers. Hirtz took out his purse. At that moment Maria overcame her timidity and in a trembling voice raised the price. Hirtz cast a scornful glance at her and began to bargain. The price gradually went up to * * * thalers. Maria finally bid * * * thalers. Hirtz gave up, and the portraits remained with her. She handed over the money, put what was left in her pocket, took the portraits, and left the house without waiting for the end of the auction.

When Maria stepped outside with a portrait in each hand, she stopped in perplexity: where was she to go? . . .

A young man in gold-rimmed spectacles came up to her and very politely offered to carry the portraits wherever she liked . . .

"I'm very grateful to you . . . I really don't know." And Maria wondered where she could take the portraits, when she herself had no place to go.

The young man waited a few seconds, then went on his way, and Maria decided to take the portraits to Dr. Költz.

Notes

THE MOOR OF PETER THE GREAT (1827–1828)

1. **Yazykov:** The poet Nikolai Mikhailovich Yazykov (1803–1846) was an acquaintance of Pushkin's. The epigraph is from his historical tale in verse *Ala*, published in 1826. "Peter" is the tsar and later emperor Peter I, known as Peter the Great (1672–1725), who carried out major political, social, and ecclesiastical reforms in Russia, mainly following European examples.

2. **Dmitriev:** Ivan Ivanovich Dmitriev (1760–1837), poet and statesman, was minister of justice under the emperor Alexander I (reigned 1801–1825).

3. **the military school in Paris:** Pushkin's error: the École militaire de Paris was founded only in 1750, thirty years after Ibrahim's service. Ibrahim attended the school of artillery in La Fère in Picardy.

4. **the Spanish war:** The War of the Spanish Succession (1701–1714) pitted England, the Dutch Republic, and Austria against the France of Louis XIV and ended with the Treaty of Utrecht. Conflict broke out anew in 1718, when England and France joined in war against Spain, leading to the defeat of Spain in 1720.

5. **The duc d'Orléans:** Philippe d'Orléans (1674–1723) was the nephew of Louis XIV and regent of the kingdom of France during the minority of Louis XV.

6. **Law:** John Law (1671–1729), Scottish economist, moved to France, where the duc d'Orléans, during his regency, made him general controller of finance. His monetary theories, put into practice, caused enormous speculation quickly followed by panic and total collapse. Law fled Paris in 1728.

7. **the duc de Richelieu . . . Alcibiades:** Armand de Vignerot du Plessis (1696–1788), marshal of France, grand-nephew of Cardinal Richelieu, was a notorious womanizer. Alcibiades (ca. 450–404 BC), of the distinguished Athenian family of the Alcmaeonids, was an orator, politician, and general during the Peloponnesian Wars, in which he changed allegiances several times.

8. **Arouet . . . Chaulieu . . . Montesquieu . . . Fontenelle:** François-Marie

Arouet (1694–1778) wrote under the pen name of Voltaire; Guillaume Am-
frye de Chaulieu (1639–1720) was a poet and wit, prominent in French high
society; Charles-Louis de Secondat, Baron Montesquieu (1689–1755), lawyer,
writer, and philosopher, was one of the major figures of the French Enlightenment, as was Bernard le Bovier de Fontenelle (1657–1757), a member of the
French Academy, who wrote on a wide variety of subjects.

9. **on leaving the convent:** i.e., on leaving school; aristocratic girls were sent
to convents to be educated, as there were no secular girls' schools in Russia
before the mid-nineteenth century.

10. **Derzhavin:** Gavrila Romanovich Derzhavin (1743–1816) was one of the
greatest poets of the generation preceding Pushkin's. The epigraph is from his
ode "On the Death of Prince Meshchersky" (1779).

11. **Poltava:** The battle of Poltava, fought on July 8, 1709, was a major victory of
the forces of Peter the Great over the invading army of Charles XII of Sweden,
during the Great Northern War (1700–1721).

12. **Menshikov ... Dolgoruky ... Bruce ... Raguzinsky:** Prince Alexander
Danilovich Menshikov (1673–1729) was a close associate and friend of Peter
the Great; of humble origin, he rose to great eminence but died in disgrace
and exile. Prince Yakov Fyodorovich Dolgoruky (1639–1720), of old Russian
nobility, was also close to Peter; his ancestor, Yury Dolgoruky, was considered the founder of Moscow in the twelfth century. Count Yakov Vilimovich
Bruce (1669–1735), born James Daniel Bruce, of the Scottish clan Bruce, commanded the artillery at Poltava. A learned man and an author, he was rumored
among the people to be an alchemist and magician. Young Raguzinsky is
probably the son of Count Sava Lukich Vladislavich-Raguzinsky (1669–1738),
a Serbian count and merchant who served Peter on important diplomatic
missions.

13. **Küchelbecker:** The poet Vilhelm Karlovich Küchelbecker (1797–1846) was
a schoolmate and friend of Pushkin. The lines are from his anti-tyrannical
tragedy *The Argives* (1822–1825).

14. **Preobrazhensky regiment ... Sheremetev ... Golovin:** The Preobrazhensky regiment, founded by Peter the Great, became and remained one of the
elite regiments of the Russian army; it was formally disbanded in 1917. Count
Boris Petrovich Sheremetev (1652–1719) was made field marshal during the
Great Northern War and was the first Russian to receive the new title of count
in 1706. Ivan Mikhailovich Golovin (1672–1737) was admiral of the Russian
fleet.

15. **Buturlin:** Alexander Borisovich Buturlin (1694–1767), of old Russian nobility,
became Peter's court chamberlain.

16. **Feofan ... Buzhinsky ... Kopievich:** Bishop Feofan Prokopovich (1681–
1736), archbishop and statesman, guided Peter the Great in his reform of the
Orthodox Church. Gavriil Buzhinsky (1680–1731) was a learned monk, abbot,

and translator. Ilya Fyodorovich Kopievich was a translator and publisher of Russian books in Amsterdam; in fact, he died in 1708, some years before Ibrahim's return to Russia.

17. **blue ribbons over their shoulders:** The Order of St. Andrew, the highest order of chivalry in Russia, established by Peter the Great in 1698, was worn on a light blue ribbon over the right shoulder.

18. *sarafans* **and** *dushegreikas:* The *sarafan* is a traditional woman's outer garment, sleeveless, trapezoidal, with long skirts, worn over a shirt; a *dushegreika* (literally "soul-warmer") is a waist-length jacket worn over the sarafan.

19. *Ruslan and Ludmila:* A narrative poem by the young Pushkin in six cantos with epilogue, based on Russian folktales, published in 1820.

20. **Narva:** The Russians fought two battles against the Swedish at the city of Narva, in Estonia; they lost the first in 1700 but won the second in 1704.

21. **the order of precedence:** An order of preeminence, for instance in seating people at the table, based on aristocratic rank and seniority, set down in the "books of the nobility" and which the tsar himself could not overrule. It was abolished by Peter the Great in 1682.

22. *povoinik:* A married woman's headdress, which completely concealed the hair. Peter's reforms included the "Europeanizing" of clothing and such other details as the introduction of shaving the beard for men.

23. **'A wife should *reverence* her husband':** See St. Paul's Epistle to the Ephesians, 5:33.

24. **Ablesimov . . .** *The Miller:* Alexander Onisimovich Ablesimov (1742–1783), librettist, poet, and journalist, wrote the libretto for the opera *The Miller— Wizard, Trickster, and Matchmaker*, to music by Mikhail Sokolovsky (1756–1795).

25. **pancake makers, and heathens:** Prince Menshikov (see note 12 above) was said to have sold little pies *(pirozhki)* in the street when he was young; "heathens" *(basurmani* in Russian, a corruption of *musulmani)* refers to the non-Orthodox foreigners (Germans in particular) that Peter was bringing into his service.

26. **Prince Bova . . . Eruslan Lazarevich:** Two legendary heroes of European folklore, whose adventures were recounted in widely popular tales published in the seventeenth century with woodblock illustrations.

27. *strelets:* A *strelets* (literally "shooter"; plural *streltsi)* was a member of a special guards unit, originally formed by Ivan the Terrible in the sixteenth century to serve under the tsar's direct command in opposition to the feudal boyars.

THE TALES OF THE LATE IVAN PETROVICH BELKIN (1830)

1. **Fonvizin,** *The Dunce:* Denis Ivanovich Fonvizin (1744–1792) wrote two satirical comedies that became the first classics of the Russian theater. The sec-

ond, *The Dunce* (or *The Minor*—the Russian title, *Nedorosl'*, can mean both), considered his masterpiece, was produced in 1782. Mitrofan is the dunce.

"The Shot"

1. **Baratynsky:** Evgeny Abramovich Baratynsky (1800–1844) was one of the major poets of Pushkin's time; the epigraph is from his poem "The Ball" (1828).
2. *An Evening at Bivouac:* A story by Alexander Alexandrovich Bestuzhev (1797–1837), who wrote under the name of Marlinsky. It was published in 1823.
3. **Denis Davydov:** Denis Vasilyevich Davydov (1784–1839), poet and soldier, much admired by Pushkin, wrote what was known as "hussar poetry," celebrating womanizing, drinking, and friendship. He distinguished himself during the Napoleonic Wars and was the model for the character Denisov in Tolstoy's *War and Peace*. Alexander Petrovich Burtsov (d. 1813) was a hussar officer known for his swordsmanship and carousing. Davydov wrote three poems about him.
4. **Ypsilanti . . . Hetairists . . . Skulyani:** The Greek prince Alexander Ypsilanti (1792–1828) served in Russia as an officer of the imperial cavalry during the Napoleonic Wars and then became leader of the Hetairists (*Filiki Hetairia*, "Society of Friends"), a secret society that instigated the Greek war of independence from the Ottoman Empire in 1821. They were defeated at the battle of Skulyani, in Bessarabia, on June 17, 1821.

"The Blizzard"

1. **Zhukovsky:** Vasily Andreevich Zhukovsky (1783–1852), poet, translator, and tutor to the imperial family, was an older friend and mentor of Pushkin. The epigraph is from his ballad "Svetlana" (1813).
2. **Tula:** A city some 120 miles south of Moscow, known since the twelfth century for its metalwork—samovars, cutlery, firearms, seals—and also for its gingerbread and accordions.
3. **1812:** On June 24, 1812, Napoleon ordered the Grande Armée to cross the River Nemen and the French invasion of Russia began.
4. **Borodino:** The town of Borodino, seventy miles west of Moscow, was the scene of a bloody and indecisive battle between the French and Russian armies, the costliest in the Napoleonic Wars, fought on September 7, 1812. It was the last offensive action of the French.
5. **Artemisia:** Artemisia II of Caria (d. 350 BC) became ruler of Caria at the death of her husband, Mausolus, in commemoration of whom she built the splendid Mausoleum in Halicarnassus, one of the seven wonders of the ancient world. Her grief made her an example of pure marital devotion for later artists and writers.

6. **"Vive Henri-Quatre"** ... *Joconde:* The song "Vive Henri-Quatre" ("Long Live Henry IV") dates back to the time of the king himself (1553–1610); it gained new popularity in the comedy *The Hunting Party of Henri IV* (1770), by the French playwright Charles Collé (1709–1783), and is sung by French prisoners towards the end of *War and Peace. Joconde* (1814) is a comic opera by the French-Maltese composer Nicolas (Nicolò) Isouard (1773–1818).

7. **"And into the air their bonnets threw":** A line from the comedy *Woe from Wit* (1825), the first true masterpiece of Russian theater, by Alexander Sergeevich Griboedov (1795–1829), poet, playwright, and diplomat.

8. **the two capitals:** A customary way of referring to the old capital, Moscow, and the new capital, St. Petersburg, founded by Peter the Great in 1703.

9. **a St. George in his buttonhole:** The Order of St. George is the highest military order in Russia, established by Catherine the Great in 1769.

10. *Se amor non è* ... : The opening words of sonnet 132 from the *Canzoniere* of Francesco Petrarca (1304–1374); the full line is *S'amor non è, che dunque e quel ch'io sento?* ("If it is not love, what then is it that I feel?").

11. *grande patience:* A form of solitaire.

12. **St. Preux:** The middle-class private tutor who falls in love with his aristocratic pupil, Julie, in the epistolary novel *Julie, ou la nouvelle Héloïse* (1761), by Jean-Jacques Rousseau (1712–1778).

"The Coffin-Maker"

1. **Derzhavin:** See note 10 to *The Moor of Peter the Great.* The epigraph is from his poem "The Waterfall" (1794), in memory of Prince Grigory Alexandrovich Potemkin (1739–1791), general and favorite of Catherine the Great.

2. **Pogorelsky's postman ... the former capital:** The reference is to a story from the collection *The Double, or My Evenings in Little Russia* (1828), by Anton Pogorelsky, pseudonym of Count Alexei Alexeevich Perovsky (1787–1836). The "former capital" is Moscow (see note 8 to "The Blizzard"); the city was burned down during the Napoleonic Wars.

3. **"with a poleaxe ... cuirass":** The quotation is from the tale in verse "The Female Fool Pakhomovna," by Alexander Izmailov (1779–1831).

4. **whose face seemed bound in red morocco:** A slightly altered quotation from the comedy *The Braggart* (1786), by Yakov Borisovich Knyazhnin (1742–1791). Knyazhnin was a famous playwright during the reign of Catherine the Great, the son-in-law and successor to Sumarokov (see note 11 to *The History of the Village of Goryukhino*).

5. **The deceased woman lay on the table:** It was customary for a dead person to be laid in state on a table until the coffin was brought.

"The Stationmaster"

1. **Prince Vyazemsky:** Pyotr Andreevich Vyazemsky (1792–1878), one of Pushkin's closest friends, was himself a poet and writer. The epigraph is a slightly
altered quotation from his poem "The Post-Station."

2. **the bandits of Murom:** The dense forest near the old town of Murom, on
the Oka River southeast of Moscow, was notorious for harboring bandits. The
town was also the home of the most famous hero of medieval Russian epic
poetry, Ilya Muromets.

3. **the fourteenth class:** Collegiate registrar, mentioned in the epigraph, was the
lowest of the fourteen ranks of the Russian imperial civil service established by
Peter the Great.

4. **the prodigal son:** Jesus's parable of the prodigal son, from the Gospel of Luke
(15:11–32), forms an ironic backdrop to Pushkin's story.

5. **the Demut Inn:** A small inn on the Moika Embankment in Petersburg,
founded by Philipp-Jakob Demut of Strasbourg, very popular with Pushkin
and the writers of his circle.

6. **the Joy of the Afflicted:** A church built in Petersburg between 1817 and
1820, named for the wonder-working icon of the Mother of God Joy of the
Afflicted, the original of which is in the Church of the Transfiguration in Moscow.

7. **Dmitriev's wonderful ballad:** See note 2 to *The Moor of Peter the Great*. In
Dmitriev's ballad "The Caricature" (1791), a conscripted soldier returns from
years of service and learns from his servant Terentyich that his wife has run off
to join a band of thieves.

"The Young Lady Peasant"

1. **Bogdanovich:** The poet Ippolit Fyodorovich Bogdanovich (1744–1803) was
born of old Ukrainian aristocracy. His long comic poem *Dushenka* (1783),
from which Pushkin quotes here, was modeled on La Fontaine's *Psyche* ("Dushenka" in Russian).

2. **But Russian grain won't grow in foreign fashion:** A line from the first of
the *Satires* by Prince Alexander Alexandrovich Shakhovskoy (1777–1846), a
prolific poet and playwright who remained neoclassical in the age of the ro-
mantics.

3. **mortgage . . . courageous:** Mortgaging one's estate to the government was a
newly instituted way of raising cash, which eventually left many landowners or
their heirs deeply in debt or bankrupt.

4. **Jean-Paul:** Pen name of the prolific German writer Johann Paul Friedrich
Richter (1763–1825). Pushkin was reading him in a French translation: *Pensées
de Jean-Paul extraites de tous ces ouvrages* ("Thoughts of Jean-Paul drawn from
all his works"), a selection published in Paris in 1829.

5. **neither in judgment nor in condemnation:** Words echoing the Orthodox

prayer before communion: "May the communion of Thy most holy mysteries be neither to my judgment nor to my condemnation, O Lord, but to the healing of soul and body."

6. *Pamela:* That is, the English epistolary novel *Pamela, or Virtue Rewarded* (1740), by Samuel Richardson (1689–1761), which was a bestseller in its day.

7. **Saint Friday:** The third-century Greek martyr and saint Paraskeva was named by her parents after Holy Friday (*paraskevi* in Greek). The Russians added the Slavonic version of her name, Pyatnitsa, calling her Paraskeva-Pyatnitsa, and often dropped the first part: hence Svyataya Pyatnitsa, or "Saint Friday," which sounds comical in Russian.

8. **sleeves *à l'imbécile*:** Very ample sleeves with small lead weights added near the elbows to make them hang down.

9. **the Lancaster system:** Joseph Lancaster (1778–1838) invented a system of mutual instruction, having more advanced pupils pass on what they had already learned to younger pupils. The system was widely used in the nineteenth century.

10. **"Natalya, the Boyar's Daughter":** A sentimental historical tale by the poet, writer, and historian Nikolai Mikhailovich Karamzin (1766–1826), who was much admired by Pushkin.

11. **Taras Skotinin:** A character in Fonvizin's *The Dunce* (see note 1 to *The Tales of the Late Ivan Petrovich Belkin*).

THE HISTORY OF THE VILLAGE OF GORYUKHINO (1830)

1. **the *New Grammar*:** The *New Grammar*, published in 1769 by Nikolai Gavrilovich Kurganov (1725–1796), professor of mathematics and navigation at Moscow University, had great influence on later Russian writers, Pushkin among them. Pyotr Grigorievich Plemyannikov (d. 1775) served as general under the empress Elizabeth I (1709–1762), the daughter of Peter the Great.

2. **a new Niebuhr:** Barthold Georg Niebuhr (1776–1831), German historian, was one of the founders of modern historiography.

3. **zemstvo:** The name, derived from *zemlya* (land, earth), for the local organization of peasants in a village or group of villages. It acquired a new official meaning after the reforms of Alexander II in 1864.

4. **the year 1812:** See note 3 to "The Blizzard." "The twelve nations" in the next sentence refers to the alliance that formed the army of Napoleon.

5. *Misanthropy and Repentance:* A play by the German playwright and author August von Kotzebue (1761–1819), who also worked for the Department of Foreign Affairs in Russia and served for a time as Russian consul to Germany. His plays were popular among Russian audiences.

6. *The Well-Intentioned* ... the *Hamburg Gazette: The Well-Intentioned* and *The Zealot for Enlightenment* mentioned later were popular Petersburg journals

of the early nineteenth century. The *Hamburg Gazette*, one of the oldest German newspapers, was in its time the most widely read paper in the world.

7. **Rurik:** Rurik, the ninth-century Swedish Varangian chieftain, invaded Russia, settled near Novgorod, and founded the first dynasty of Russian tsars, who ruled until the seventeenth century.

8. **Millot . . . Tatishchev, Boltin, and Golikov:** The abbé Claude-François-Xavier Millot (1726–1785) was a Jesuit and a historian, author of a number of works, including *Elements of General History Ancient and Modern* (1772–1783). Vasily Nikitich Tatishchev (1686–1750), Ivan Nikitich Boltin (1735–1792), and Ivan Ivanovich Golikov (1735–1801) wrote on various aspects of Russian history. Catherine the Great acquired Boltin's papers after his death and made a gift of them to the Pushkin family.

9. **Deriukhovo and Perkukhovo:** The names are comical in a rather crude way, suggestive of ear-pulling and throat-clearing. Goryukhino itself is formed from the word *gorye* (woe, grief).

10. **a double-headed eagle:** Taverns were licensed by the state and were required to display the state symbol, the double-headed eagle.

11. **Mr. Sumarokov:** Alexander Petrovich Sumarokov (1717–1777), poet and playwright, is considered the first professional man of letters in Russia.

ROSLAVLEV (1831)

1. *Roslavlev: Roslavlev, or the Russians in 1812*, the second novel of Mikhail Nikolaevich Zagoskin (1789–1852), was published in 1831. His first novel, *Yuri Miloslavsky*, published in 1829, became the first Russian bestseller. His work was modeled on the novels of Walter Scott.

2. **Montesquieu . . . Crébillon . . . Rousseau . . . Sumarokov:** For Montesquieu see note 8 to *The Moor of Peter the Great*. Claude Prosper Jolyot de Crébillon (1707–1777), son of a famous playwright and member of the French Academy, was himself a novelist, songwriter, and bon vivant. Rousseau is . . . Rousseau (see note 12 to "The Blizzard"). For Sumarokov, see note 11 to *The History of the Village of Goryukhino*.

3. **Lomonosov:** Mikhail Vasilyevich Lomonosov (1711–1765) wrote on a wide range of subjects—scientific, literary, historical, philological. He was also a poet and was influential in the formation of the Russian literary language.

4. **Karamzin's *History*:** See note 10 to "The Young Lady Peasant." Karamzin's twelve-volume *History of the Russian State* (1816–1826) was the foundational work of Russian historiography.

5. **Mme de Staël:** Anne Louise Germaine de Staël-Holstein (1766–1817), the daughter of Jacques Necker (1732–1804), minister of finance under Louis XVI, is known to literature simply as Mme de Staël. An important writer and

a woman of society, she was an outspoken opponent of Napoleon, who exiled her from Paris several times. *Corinne* (1807), her most famous novel, is based on her travels in Italy during one of those exiles.

6. **Kuznetsky Bridge:** Kuznetsky Bridge is in fact a street in Moscow, which was known at that time for its fashionable shops run by foreigners, most often Frenchmen.

7. **the Confederation of the Rhine:** A confederation of German states formed by Napoleon after his victory at Austerlitz in 1805. It lasted until Napoleon's defeat at Leipzig in 1813.

8. **the sovereign's appeal ... Rastopchin's folk-style leaflets ... Pozharsky and Minin:** The appeal of Alexander I for the defense of Moscow was published in August 1812. Count Fyodor Vasilyevich Rastopchin (1763–1826), military governor of Moscow at the time, ordered the distribution of one-page fliers with woodcut images calling for resistance. In 1612, Prince Dmitri Pozharsky and the merchant Kuzma Minin gathered a volunteer army and drove out the invading forces of the Polish-Lithuanian Commonwealth, ending what is known as the Time of Troubles.

9. **Charlotte Corday ... Marfa Posadnitsa ... Princess Dashkova:** Charlotte Corday (1768–1793) assassinated Jean-Paul Marat (1743–1793), leader of the radical Jacobin faction during the Reign of Terror, for which she was guillotined. Marfa Posadnitsa, the wife of the mayor (*posadnik*) of Novgorod, is the heroine of the last work of fiction by Nikolai Karamzin (see note 4 above); she was involved in the unsuccessful defense of republican Novgorod against monarchical Moscow in 1478. Princess Ekaterina Romanovna Vorontsova-Dashkova (1743–1810) was a close friend of Catherine the Great and by her own account played a central part in the coup d'état of 1762 that brought Catherine to the imperial throne.

10. **Count Mamonov ... entire fortune:** Count Matvey Alexandrovich Dmitriev-Mamonov (1790–1863) was one of the richest landowners in Russia. At the beginning of the war against Napoleon he made a speech to members of the Moscow nobility pledging to give his entire income to the struggle, and he went on to raise a mounted Cossack regiment at his own expense.

11. **Borodino:** See note 4 to "The Blizzard."

DUBROVSKY (1832–1833)

1. **seventy souls:** That is, seventy male serfs—an extremely modest number for a Russian landowner; Count Mamonov, for instance, owned 15,000.

2. **We insert it here in full:** What follows is Pushkin's transcription of an actual court decision of the time; the only change he made was the substitution of the names of his characters for the names of the actual participants.

3. **the Cadet Corps:** An elite school in Petersburg for aristocratic boys, founded by the empress Anna Ioannovna in 1731. Its graduates had favored status for advancement in military or civil careers.

4. **Derzhavin:** See note 10 to *The Moor of Peter the Great.* The line here also comes from the ode "On the Death of Prince Meshchersky" (1779).

5. **"Thunder of victory resound":** The opening words of Derzhavin's choral ode, set to music by Osip Kozlovsky (1757–1831), written for the celebration given by Potemkin (see note 1 to "The Coffin-Maker") on the taking of Izmail in 1791.

6. **laid it out on the same table:** See note 5 to "The Coffin-Maker."

7. **"Vanity of vanities . . . 'Memory Eternal' ":** "Vanity of vanities" comes from the opening of Ecclesiastes (1:2). "Memory Eternal" is the prayer of supplication sung at the end of the Orthodox funeral service.

8. **"Eschew evil and do good":** Words from Psalm 37:27, quoted in the first epistle of Peter (3:11).

9. **the Turkish campaign:** That is, the Russo-Turkish War of 1787–1791.

10. **Lavaterian guesswork:** Johann Kaspar Lavater (1741–1801) was a Swiss poet, philosopher, and theologian, remembered mainly for his book *Physiognomical Fragments* (1775–1778), detailing the analysis of personal character based on facial and bodily features.

11. **Kulnev:** General Yakov Petrovich Kulnev (1763–1812), one of the most popular and colorful figures of the Napoleonic Wars, was killed pursuing the French at the battle of Klyastitsy. His lithographic portrait was widely distributed after his death.

12. **Radcliffe:** The English novelist Ann Radcliffe (1764–1823) perfected what came to be known as the Gothic novel, full of terror and the supernatural. Her most famous work, *The Mysteries of Udolpho* (1794), was very popular in Russia.

13. **Misha:** Misha, the diminutive of Mikhail, is the name traditionally given to bears in Russia.

14. **Rinaldo:** Hero of the popular novel *Rinaldo Rinaldini, the Robber Chief* (1797), by the German author Christian August Vulpius (1762–1827), author of numerous romantic tales and libretti and brother-in-law of Goethe.

15. **Amphitryon's wines:** Amphitryon was a legendary prince of Tiryns, in the Peloponnese. The Roman playwright Plautus (ca. 254–184 BC) made him the hero of a burlesque comedy, which in turn inspired Molière's *Amphitryon* (1668). His name came to stand for a generous host.

16. **Konrad's mistress:** Konrad Wallenrod is the eponymous hero of a narrative poem by the great Polish poet Adam Mickiewicz (1798–1855), who was much admired by Pushkin.

THE QUEEN OF SPADES (1834)

1. The verses of the epigraph to chapter 1 are by Pushkin himself, who partially quotes them in a letter of September 1, 1828, to Vyazemsky (see note 1 to "The Stationmaster"). It has also been said that Pushkin, who was a passionate gambler himself, first wrote them on his sleeve in chalk while playing at Prince Golitsyn's.

2. *mirandole:* A term in the card game of faro, meaning to play only one card at a time and not double your bets. Faro *(pharaon)* is a simple French gambling game in which a banker plays individually against any number of players and winning depends on the matching of cards. To stake *en routé* is to bet repeatedly on the same lucky card. *Paroli* means to double bets on the same card, indicated by bending down the corners of the card. To punt is to place a bet against the bank.

3. **Richelieu:** See note 7 to *The Moor of Peter the Great.*

4. **the comte de Saint-Germain ... Casanova:** The comte de Saint-Germain (ca. 1712–1784) was a prominent figure in European society, a wealthy and well-educated man and an accomplished musician, who claimed to be the son of Francis II Rakóczi, Prince of Transylvania. Various myths arose about him, to do with his interest in mysticism and alchemy, his membership in secret societies, his being the Wandering Jew, a prophet, and an "Ascended Master." Giacomo Girolamo Casanova (1725–1798), born in Venice, was also a notable figure in society, a libertine and womanizer, a friend of royalty and also of Voltaire, Goethe, and Mozart. He is remembered mainly for his autobiography, *Histoire de ma vie* ("The Story of My Life"), written in French—a vivid description of the mores of eighteenth-century Europe and of his own in particular.

5. **Pushkin's friend Denis Davydov (see note 3 to "The Shot") wrote to him about this epigraph:** "Good heavens, what a devilish memory! God knows, I once told you my reply to M. A. Naryshkina about *les suivantes qui sont plus fraîches*, and you set it down word for word as an epigraph to a chapter of *The Queen of Spades.*"

6. **Bitter ... Dante ... stairs:** A paraphrase of *Paradiso* XVII:58–60: *Tu proverai sì come sa di sale / lo pane d'altrui, e come è duro calle / lo scendere e 'l salir per altrui scale* ("You will taste how salty / is another's bread, and how hard a path it is / going down and up another's stairs").

7. **two portraits ... Mme Lebrun:** Elisabeth Vigée-Lebrun (1755–1842) was one of the finest portrait painters of her time. Her successful career in Paris was interrupted in 1789 by the French Revolution, after which she lived abroad until 1802, spending the years from 1795 to 1801 in Russia.

8. **Leroy ... Montgolfier ... Mesmer:** Julien Leroy (1686–1759) was a famous

Parisian clockmaker; in 1739 he was named Royal Clockmaker to Louis XV. The Montgolfier brothers, Joseph-Michel (1740–1810) and Jacques-Etienne (1745–1799), invented the hot-air balloon, which made its first flight in 1783. Franz Mesmer (1734–1815), a German doctor, proposed a theory of the transfer of energy between the animate and the inanimate, which he called "animal magnetism" and which later became known as "mesmerism."

9. *Homme sans moeurs et sans religion!:* The phrase, which was much in the air during the Enlightenment, has been attributed to Diderot and to Voltaire. In the dialogue *Des devoirs de l'Homme et du Prince* ("On the Duties of Man and Prince"), by Jaques Vernet (1698–1789), professor of theology and history in Geneva, Socrates speaks of *"un homme sans religion et sans moeurs."*

10. *Oubli ou regret:* "Forget or regret." A game that allowed ladies to choose a partner at a ball. They would secretly take the name of *oubli* or *regret*, approach the man, and pose the question. He would choose at random and then take the next dance with the lady who bore the name.

11. **Swedenborg:** Emanuel Swedenborg (1688–1772) was a Swedish scientist and inventor who later became a mystic and visionary reformer of Christianity. The epigraph, as is often the case with Pushkin, is a playful stylization.

12. **the midnight Bridegroom:** See Matthew 25:1–13, Christ's parable of the wise and foolish virgins. Pushkin suggests an ironic parallel between the Bridegroom and Hermann.

13. *"Attendez!":* "Wait!" in French. In the original, Pushkin uses the Russified French word *Atandé*, used in faro when a player wants to change his stake before the betting is closed. In the epigraph, the aristocratic banker takes offense at the tone of it.

KIRDJALI (1834)

1. **Ypsilanti . . . insurrection:** See note 4 to "The Shot."

2. **Georgi Kantakuzin:** A Greek prince, one of the notable participants in the Greek uprising. Pushkin met him when he was serving in Kishinev during the early 1820s. Kishinev, now the capital of Moldova, had recently been annexed by Russia from Turkey.

3. **Nekrasovists:** A group of Don Cossacks, led by Ignat Nekrasov (d. 1737). They were Old Believers, condemned as heretics by the Russian Orthodox Church, and fled Russia in 1708.

4. **Klephtes:** Greek for "bandits." The name was given to Greek mountaineers who preserved their independence after the Turkish conquest of the Byzantine empire in the fifteenth century.

5. **A man . . . important post:** Mikhail Ivanovich Leks (1793–1856), whom Pushkin had served under in Kishinev, was by then the director of the chancellery of the Ministry of Interior in Petersburg.

EGYPTIAN NIGHTS (1835)

1. **an album:** A whole culture developed around the personal albums kept by upper-class Russian girls, in which they would ask friends and new acquaintances to write verses or personal messages.

2. **ragged abbés:** *Abbé*, or "abbot," was a title of lower-ranking clergymen in France. Abbés were appointed by the king and received a small income without necessarily serving in an abbey. They sometimes took to writing (see note 8 to *The History of the Village of Goryukhino*). The Abbé Prévost, author of *Manon Lescaut* (1731), is perhaps the most well-known example.

3. **Derzhavin:** See note 10 to *The Moor of Peter the Great*. The line is from Derzhavin's famous ode "God" (1784).

4. **Signora Catalani:** Angelica Catalani (1780–1849) was one of the greatest sopranos in the history of opera, renowned for her three-octave range. She sang in Petersburg in 1820.

5. **Tancredi:** An opera by Gioachino Rossini (1792–1868), based on Voltaire's tragedy *Tancrède* (1760).

6. **Aurelius Victor:** Sextus Aurelius Victor (ca. 320–390 AD), a Roman statesman and historian, wrote a short history of the Roman Empire.

THE CAPTAIN'S DAUGHTER (1836)

1. **Knyazhnin:** See note 4 to "The Coffin-Maker." The quotation is from his comedy *The Braggart* (1786).

2. **Count Münnich:** Burkhard Christoph von Münnich (1683–1767), a German-born military officer and engineer, came to Russia in 1721, was taken into the Russian army by Peter the Great, and rose to become a field marshal and count. He played a major role in Russian military and political affairs under several monarchs.

3. **the Semyonovsky regiment:** Founded in 1683 by Peter the Great, it was one of the two oldest and most distinguished guards regiments in Russia.

4. **passport:** Russians were required to carry an "internal passport" when they traveled within Russia.

5. **Orenburg:** A city in the southern Ural region, over nine hundred miles east of Moscow. It was founded in 1743 as a frontier outpost, bordering on the territory of the nomadic Kazakhs.

6. **"the keeper . . . my affairs":** A quotation from the poem "Epistle to my Servants Shumilov, Vanka, and Petrushka" (1769), by Denis Fonvizin (see note 1 to *The Tales of the Late Ivan Petrovich Belkin*).

7. **a Yaik Cossack:** Yaik was the old name of the Ural River. The Cossacks of the Yaik and the Don served as frontier guards for Russia, in exchange for certain freedoms. After their support for Pugachev's rebellion, Yaik Cos-

sacks lost those privileges and, like the river itself, were renamed Ural Cossacks.

8. **above the stove:** Russian stoves were large and elaborate structures, used for cooking, laundry, bathing, and sleeping, as well as for heating.

9. **the revolt of 1772:** In 1772, just prior to Pugachev's rebellion, there was a revolt of the Yaik Cossacks over forced conscription and low pay, which led to the killing of the Russian military commander of the Orenburg region, the harsh Major General Mikhail Mikhailovich Traubenberg (1719–1772).

10. **the time of Anna Ioannovna:** Anna Ioannovna (1693–1740) was the daughter of Peter the Great's physically and mentally handicapped brother Ivan V, who ruled jointly with Peter until his death in 1696. In 1730 she became empress of Russia.

11. **The Dunce:** See note 1 to *The Tales of the Late Ivan Petrovich Belkin.*

12. **Küstrin and Ochakov:** The Turkish fortress of Ochakov fell to the Russians in 1737, during the Austro-Russian-Turkish War; the Prussian fortress of Küstrin was besieged by the Russians in 1758, during the Seven Years' War, but not actually taken.

13. **Bashkirs:** A Turkic people who inhabited territory to the north of Orenburg on both sides of the Urals. They fought the Russians over the building of the fortress in Orenburg and later supported Pugachev's rebellion.

14. **Knyazhnin:** See note 4 to "The Coffin-Maker." The quotation is from his comedy *The Odd Birds* (1790).

15. **Sumarokov:** See note 11 to *The History of the Village of Goryukhino.*

16. **Tredyakovsky:** Vasily Kirillovich Tredyakovsky (1703–1769), poet, translator, and critic, was of common origin, studied at the Sorbonne, and returned to Petersburg to promote classical notions of versification. Posterity has generally accepted Shvabrin's opinion of his poetry.

17. **"Duels are formally forbidden . . .":** Dueling became so common in the upper ranks of the Russian military that in 1715 Peter the Great formally forbade the practice on pain of death for both duelists.

18. **one spirit and one flesh:** In the Orthodox marriage service, the priest asks of God: "Unite them in one mind; wed them into one flesh." The notion that man and wife are one flesh is repeated in many texts, starting with Genesis 2:22–24.

19. **Major General Traubenberg:** See note 9 above.

20. **the late emperor Peter III:** Peter III (1728–1762), the only child of the eldest daughter of Peter the Great, ruled for only six months before he was assassinated in a conspiracy said to have been headed by his wife, a German princess who went on to become Catherine the Great. After his death, a number of false pretenders appeared claiming to be Peter III, among them Emelyan Pugachev.

21. **torture . . . abolished:** Torture was regulated by law in Russia from the 1740s on; in the 1760s Catherine the Great issued orders against the use of torture, but that did not eliminate it; it was formally abolished in 1801 by a decree of Alexander I.

22. **1741:** Date of the end of the first revolt of the Bashkirs against the building of the Orenburg fortress.

23. **the mild reign of the emperor Alexander:** Alexander I (1777–1825), the grandson of Catherine the Great, reigned from 1801 to 1825. He began in a rather liberal spirit, but became more conservative after the Napoleonic Wars.

24. **bread and salt:** By Russian custom, in the formal reception of honored visitors, an offering of bread and salt would be presented to them on a special embroidered towel.

25. **the sovereign Pyotr Fyodorovich:** That is, Peter III (see note 20 above).

26. **Chumakov:** Fyodor Fedotovich Chumakov (1729–1786), a Yaik Cossack, was Pugachev's commander of artillery. In 1775, however, he seized Pugachev and turned him over to the Russians on the promise of his own pardon and a payment of 100,000 roubles. Pushkin drew the details of this passage from archival records and the accounts of witnesses. The song that follows (two lines of which were quoted in *Dubrovsky*) appears in a collection of Russian folk songs published in 1780.

27. **Grishka Otrepev:** Grigory (Grisha, Grishka) Otrepev, the first of the so-called "False Dmitrys," was a defrocked monk who claimed to be Dmitry Ivanovich, son of Ivan the Terrible and heir to the Russian throne. The real tsarevich Dmitry was murdered in 1591 at the age of nine. Otrepev succeeded in becoming tsar during the Time of Troubles and reigned for ten months (1605–1606).

28. **Kheraskov:** Mikhail Matveevich Kheraskov (1733–1807) came to prominence as a poet during the reign of Catherine the Great. The quotation is from his poem entitled, like the chapter, "Parting."

29. The epigraph is from Kheraskov's *Rossiad* (1771–1779), the first epic poem in Russian to be modeled on Homer and Virgil. The "he" referred to is Ivan the Terrible.

30. **Mr. Collegiate Councilor:** In the Russian table of fourteen civil, military, and court ranks, established by Peter the Great in 1722, collegiate councilor was sixth, the civil equivalent of colonel.

31. **Lizaveta Kharlova:** Daughter and wife of fortress commanders in the Orenburg region. Her father, mother, and husband were captured by Pugachev and brutally murdered; she herself was forced to become Pugachev's concubine, but was later killed by Cossack chiefs.

32. **A. Sumarokov:** See note 11 to *The History of the Village of Goryukhino.* The lines are in fact a pastiche by Pushkin himself.

33. **sitting under the icons:** Icons (images of Christ, the Mother of God, and the saints) are traditionally hung in the far right-hand corner of a room, considered the place of honor.

34. **a blue ribbon . . . gray peasant coat:** See note 17 to *The Moor of Peter the Great.* The Order of St. Andrew accords strangely with a peasant coat.

35. **the battle of Yuzeevo:** Yuzeevo, a village some eighty miles northwest of Orenburg, where on November 8, 1773, Pugachev defeated Russian forces sent to relieve the fortress.

36. **Frederick:** That is, Frederick II (1712–1786), king of Prussia, whose military, political, and cultural achievements won him the title of "the Great." Pugachev, in Russian peasant fashion, fits him out with a Russian name and patronymic.

37. **Knyazhnin:** See note 4 to "The Coffin-Maker." The lines are Pushkin's invention.

38. **Prince Golitsyn:** In August 1774, Russian relief troops under General Pyotr Mikhailovich Golitsyn defeated Pugachev's forces at the town of Tatishchevo.

39. **Ivan Ivanovich Mikhelson:** Mikhelson (1740–1807) was one of the most prominent commanders in the Russian army. While still a lieutenant colonel, he successfully broke Pugachev's siege of Kazan and pursued the enemy to a final defeat against great odds at the battle of Tsaritsyn.

40. **Volynsky and Khrushchev:** Artemy Petrovich Volynsky (1689–1740) was a minister under the cruel and arbitrary empress Anna Ioannovna (see note 10 above). He and his friend and assistant Andrei Fyodorovich Khrushchev (1691–1740) were accused of plotting to replace Anna with Elizabeth, the daughter of Peter the Great, and were executed.

41. **Tsarskoe Selo:** Literally "the Tsar's Village," located fifteen miles south of Petersburg. Originally an estate given by Peter the Great to his wife in 1708, it developed over time into a favorite country residence of the imperial family and the nobility and eventually into a town. Sofia, a neighboring town, merged with Tsarskoe Selo in 1808. Pushkin was in the first graduating class of the lycée at Tsarskoe Selo, founded by Alexander I in 1811. In 1937 the town was renamed Pushkin, in honor of the centenary of his death.

42. **Rumyantsev's recent victories:** Count Pyotr Alexandrovich Rumyantsev (1725–1796) was a brilliant Russian general and later field marshal, involved mainly in the Russo-Turkish wars. His victories during the Russo-Turkish War of 1768–1774 forced the sultan Abdul Hamid I to sue for peace in 1774.

"The Omitted Chapter"

1. **St. Elijah's day:** The Old Testament prophet Elijah (Elias) is commemorated as a saint in both the Catholic and the Orthodox Churches. His day is July 20 by the Julian calendar (still followed by the Russian Orthodox Church), August 2 by the Gregorian calendar.

JOURNEY TO ARZRUM (1836)

1. **Voyages en Orient ...:** The author of the *Voyages* was Victor Fontanier (1796–1857), who was sent as a naturalist attached to the French embassy in Constantinople to explore the regions of the Black Sea and the Ottoman Empire (1822–1829). His book was published between 1829 and 1834.

2. **Khomyakov ... Muravyov ... Count Dibich:** Alexei Stepanovich Khomyakov (1804–1860), poet, philosopher, and co-founder of the Slavophile movement, was one of the most influential Russian thinkers of his time and later. The poet Andrei Nikolaevich Muravyov (1806–1874) published an account of his journey to the Holy Land in 1834. The German-born Count Ivan Ivanovich Dibich, or Diebitsch (1785–1831), became a Russian field marshal and commanded the imperial forces during the Russo-Turkish War of 1828–1829.

3. **Detached Caucasus Corps:** A corps of some 40,000 men, under General Paskevich (see following note), sent to fight the Turks on the Caucasian front of the war, to draw them away from the other front in the Balkan peninsula. The corps included a number of former Decembrists, a group of liberal-minded officers and soldiers who had been arrested after staging an uprising on December 26, 1825, in favor of constitutional reforms. Pushkin had been a close friend of some of the Decembrists and sympathized with their cause.

4. **Paskewitch ... Mouravieff ... Tsitsevaze ... Beboutof ... Potemkine ... Raiewsky:** Pushkin is clearly amused by these French renderings of Russian names, as Byron was in *Don Juan*. Ivan Fyodorovich Paskevich (1782–1856) shared command of the Russian forces with Dibich and headed the army after Dibich's death in 1831. He was a field marshal and in reward for his successes was granted the titles of Count of Erevan and Prince of Warsaw. Nikolai Nikolaevich Muravyov (1794–1866) was chief of staff of the Caucasus Corps under Paskevich. The Georgian prince Alexander Garsevanovich Chavchavadze (1786–1846) was a poet and a general in the Russian army. Vasily Osipovich Bebutov (1791–1858), of Georgian-Armenian nobility, served in the Russian army from 1809 and distinguished himself during the Russo-Turkish wars. Prince Potemkin (see note 1 to "The Coffin-Maker") had nothing to do with the Caucasus Corps. Nikolai Nikolaevich Raevsky (1771–1829) was an important general during the Napoleonic Wars. Pushkin met him in the Caucasus in 1821 and they became good friends; his sons were members of the Southern Society, which helped to plan the Decembrist uprising; they pulled out of the Society before the uprising took place, but were nevertheless "punished" by being sent to serve in the Caucasus.

5. **Osman Pasha:** Osman Pasha ("pasha" being an honorary title) was the governor of Arzrum.

6. **the campaign of 1829:** Paskevich's campaign on the Caucasian front, which ended in September 1829 with the defeat of the Turkish army and the Treaty

of Adrianople. It is the background subject of Pushkin's *Journey to Arzrum*, in addition to which, despite his disclaimer, he also wrote a number of poems based on his experiences during the campaign.

7. **Ermolov:** Alexei Petrovich Ermolov (1777–1861) began his military career in the Preobrazhensky regiment (see note 14 to *The Moor of Peter the Great*), advanced rapidly during the Napoleonic Wars, became chief of staff of the First Western Army in 1812 and then chief of staff of the entire army in the same year. After the defeat of the French, he was made commander in chief of the Caucasus. But his stubborn temperament brought him into conflict with his superiors, and in 1827 Nicholas I abruptly replaced him with Paskevich. He spent the last thirty years of his life on his estate near Orel.

8. **Dawe:** The British painter George Dawe (1781–1829) moved to Petersburg in 1819, where he was commissioned to paint 329 portraits of Russian generals who participated in the Napoleonic Wars, to be hung in the military gallery of the Winter Palace.

9. **the count of Jericho:** For Paskevich see note 4 above. Ermolov plays on the similarity of the Russian words *Erevansky* ("of Erevan") and *Erikhonsky* ("of Jericho").

10. **Count Tolstoy:** Count Fyodor Ivanovich Tolstoy (1782–1846), known as "Tolstoy the American" because he had spent time in the Aleutian Islands during a two-year cruise around the world (1803–1805). He was a high-society bon vivant, duelist, gambler, and at various times Pushkin's friend and enemy.

11. **Karamzin's *History*:** See note 4 to *Roslavlev*.

12. **Prince Kurbsky:** Prince Andrei Mikhailovich Kurbsky (1528–1583) was a close friend and advisor to Ivan the Terrible, but then became his enemy and defected to Lithuania. He is best remembered for his bitter and erudite exchange of letters with the tsar; he also wrote a *History of the Grand Prince of Moscow* on the life of Ivan the Terrible.

13. **Griboedov:** See note 7 to "The Blizzard."

14. **Count Pushkin:** That is, Count Vladimir Alexeevich Musin-Pushkin (1798–1854), a distant relation of Pushkin's. He had been involved in the Decembrist uprising, but was punished only by demotion.

15. **Indomitable mares . . . :** The quotation is from the poem "Peter the Great in Ostrogozhsk" (1823), by the young poet and officer Kondraty Fyodorovich Ryleev (1795–1826), one of the five Decembrists who were hanged for inciting the rebellion.

16. **Orlovsky:** Alexander Osipovich Orlovsky (1777–1832) was a Russian artist of Polish origin. He was most noted for his lively drawings, for which he was invited to Petersburg by Grand Duke Konstantin Pavlovich, brother of the emperors Alexander I and Nicholas I. Pushkin greatly admired his work.

17. **Hot Springs:** Also known as the Caucasian Mineral Waters, now the town of

Pyatigorsk. Pushkin had visited the place some years earlier (see the fragment "A Romance at the Caucasian Waters").

18. **A. Raevsky:** Alexander Nikolaevich Raevsky (1795–1868), the eldest son of General Nikolai Raevsky (see note 4 above), was a close friend of Pushkin's and the model for his poem "The Demon" (1823).

19. **Count Gudovich:** Field Marshal Ivan Vasilyevich Gudovich (1741–1820) took part in the Russo-Turkish wars of 1768–1774, 1787–1791, and 1806–1812, in which his many victories gained him great distinction.

20. **the *peaceful* Circassians:** The Circassians, the last native people of the Caucasus to be subdued by the Russians (only in 1868), had been largely driven out of their territories in what amounted to a genocide. Those who remained were "peaceful" in name only.

21. **Mansur . . . Solovki monastery:** "Mansur" means "the victorious one." His name was Ushurma. His birthdate is variously given as 1732, 1750, and 1760; he died in 1794. A Chechen sheikh and imam, he led a revolt against the Russian invasion of the Caucasus, was finally defeated in 1791, and was imprisoned for life in the Schlüsselburg Fortress near Petersburg. Some say he died in the monastery of Solovki, in the north of Russia.

22. **. . . like a warrior . . . around him:** Pushkin quotes in English from the poem "The Burial of John Moore" (1817), by the Irish poet and clergyman Charles Wolfe (1791–1823), which was much admired by Byron.

23. **Stjernvall . . . North:** The Finnish baron Carl Emil Knut Stjernvall-Walleen (1806–1890) was the brother-in-law of Count Musin-Pushkin (see note 14 above). The quotation is from Derzhavin's poem "The Waterfall" (see note 10 to *The Moor of Peter the Great* and note 1 to "The Coffin-Maker").

24. **General Bekovich:** Fyodor Alexandrovich Bekovich-Cherkassky (1790–1835), a prince of Kabardian origin, served as a Russian general in the Caucasus.

25. **And in goatskins . . . delight:** A line from Book III of the *Iliad*.

26. ***The Prisoner of the Caucasus:*** An early "Byronic" narrative poem by Pushkin, published in 1822.

27. **one traveler writes:** The traveler was Nikolai Alexandrovich Nefedev (1800–1860), whose book *Notes During a Trip to the Caucasus and Georgia in 1827* was published under the initials N. N. in 1829.

28. ***The Rape of Ganymede:*** Rembrandt's painting (1635) from the Dresden Gallery shows a great eagle flying off with a grimacing little boy who is peeing between his legs as he is carried aloft. Pushkin would have known the painting from engravings, which were very popular at the time.

29. **Pliny's testimony:** The Roman historian Pliny the Elder (AD 23/24–79) discusses the names of mountain passes in Book V, chapter 27, of his *Natural History in XXXVII Books*.

30. **Count J. Potocki . . . Spanish novels:** The Polish count and military engi-

neer Jan Potocki (1761–1815) wrote books on his travels to Astrakhan and the Caucasus, as well as to Turkey, Egypt, and Morocco, but his fame rests on his "Spanish" novel *The Manuscript Found in Saragossa* (1814), written in French.

31. **Prince Kazbek ... fugelman ... Preobrazhensky regiment:** Prince Kazbek is probably Gabriel Chopikashvili-Kazbegi, of the ruling family of the mountainous Kazbegi region in northeast Georgia, who remained loyal to Russia when the people of the region rebelled in the early nineteenth century. A fugelman (from the German *flügelmann,* "flank man" or "wing man") was a well-trained soldier who was placed in front of a company at drill as a model for the others. For the Preobrazhensky regiment, see note 14 to *The Moor of Peter the Great.*

32. **"holds up the heavenly vault":** A slightly altered quotation from the poem "A Half-Soldier" (1826), by Denis Davydov (see note 3 to "The Shot").

33. **Fazil Khan:** Fazil Khan Sheyda (1784–1852), a Persian court poet and diplomat, was accompanying a diplomatic mission to Petersburg in 1829 when Pushkin met him. See following note.

34. **Khozrev-Mirza:** The young prince Khozrev-Mirza (1812–1878), grandson of the shah of Persia, led a mission to Petersburg to apologize for the destruction of the Russian ministry in Tehran and the murder of its minister plenipotentiary, the poet Alexander Griboedov (see note 7 to "The Blizzard").

35. **Rinaldo Rinaldini:** See note 14 to *Dubrovsky.*

36. **Kishinev:** See note 2 to *Kirdjali.* The town had been under Ottoman rule since the sixteenth century.

37. **Lalla Rookh:** Pushkin quotes in English from the long poem *Lalla Rookh: An Oriental Romance* (1817), by the Irish poet Thomas Moore (1779–1852).

38. **Sankovsky ... Tsitsianov ... :** Pavel Stepanovich Sankovsky (1798–1832) edited the *Tiflis Gazette,* the first Russian-language newspaper in the Caucasus. He met Pushkin on his way to Arzrum and became his great admirer. The Georgian prince Pavel Dmitrievich Tsitsianov (1754–1806), the hot-headed Russian military commander of Georgia, was killed in action at the siege of Baku.

39. **Aga Mohammed:** Aga Mohammed (1742–1797) was shah of Persia from 1789 until his murder in 1797. He succeeded in reuniting the territories of the Caucasus that had broken away during the previous centuries, and was known for the unusual cruelty of his actions, especially in the taking of Tiflis. It was he who moved the Persian capital to Tehran.

40. **poor Clarence ... Malaga:** Raphael Holinshed (1529–1580), in his *Chronicles of England, Scotland and Ireland* (1577), writes that the Duke of Clarence, the elder brother of Richard III, "was cast into the Tower, and therewith adjudged for a traitor, and privily drowned in a butt of malmsey." Shakespeare included this detail in Richard III (act 1, scene 4), which Pushkin read in French translation. Malmsey was a kind of Madeira, not Malaga.

41. *Tbilis-kalar* . . . **"Hot City":** Pushkin's error: the city was known as "Tbilis-kalak," *kalak* being Georgian for "city." The same error appears in *A Geographical and Statistical Description of Georgia and the Caucasus,* by the German author Ioann-Anton Guldenstedt (1745–1781), published in Russian translation in 1809, which Pushkin probably used.

42. **Count Samoilov:** Nikolai Andreevich Samoilov (1800–1842), an officer in the Preobrazhensky regiment, was the cousin of the younger Raevskys (see note 4 above).

43. **titular councilors . . . assessor:** In the ascending order of the Russian table of ranks (see note 3 to "The Stationmaster"), titular councilor was ninth, equivalent to captain, and collegiate assessor was eighth, equivalent to major. In his story "The Nose" (1836), Pushkin's young friend Nikolai Gogol (1809–1852) speaks of "collegiate assessors who are made in the Caucasus," meaning made quickly.

44. **General Sipyagin:** Nikolai Martyanovich Sipyagin (1785–1828) was the military governor of Tiflis before his sudden death.

45. **General Strekalov:** Stepan Stepanovich Strekalov (1782–1856), who took over as military governor of Tiflis in 1828, arranged with the authorities to keep Pushkin under surveillance while he was in the city.

46. **the slain Griboedov:** See note 7 to "The Blizzard" and note 34 above. The Georgian drivers' distortion of the name, "Griboed," means "Mushroom-eater." They of course had no idea who Griboedov was.

47. **Buturlin:** Nikolai Alexandrovich Buturlin (1801–1867), aide-de-camp to the Russian minister of war, Alexander Ivanovich Chernyshev (1786–1857), was sent to keep an eye on former Decembrists in the Caucasus, including Pushkin and Raevsky, and delivered a detailed report on them when he returned to Petersburg in 1829.

48. **a poem to a Kalmyk girl . . . :** Verses Pushkin jotted down on the occasion of his meeting with the "Circe of the steppe" described early in chapter 1:

The Kalmyk Girl

Farewell, my dear Kalmyk girl!
Thwarting all my plans,
Drawn on by my laudable habit,
I almost followed your kibitka
Off into the steppe.
Your eyes, of course, are narrow,
Your nose flat, your brow wide,
You do not babble in French,
Your legs are not squeezed into silk,
You do not crumble your bread

> English-style by the samovar,
> You do not admire Saint-Mars,
> Give little value to Shakespeare,
> Do not fall into reverie,
> Since there's not a thought in your head,
> You do not sing: *Ma dov'é,*
> Do not leap in the galop at dances.
> Who cares? For a whole half-hour,
> While they were hitching my horses,
> My mind and heart were taken
> With your gaze and your savage beauty.
> Friends, is it not all one
> For your idle soul to be lost
> In a splendid hall, the dress circle,
> Or in a nomadic kibitka?

49. **General Burtsov:** Ivan Grigorievich Burtsov (1794–1829) took part in the Napoleonic Wars and was then involved in the early stages of the Decembrist movement, but withdrew before the uprising. Imprisoned for six months all the same, he was then transferred to the Caucasus, where he served with distinction in the wars with the Persians and the Turks and was killed in action. Pushkin had made Burtsov's acquaintance years earlier, while he was still at the lycée in Tsarskoe Selo (see note 41 to *The Captain's Daughter*).

50. **our Volkhovsky:** Vladimir Dmitrievich Volkhovsky (1798–1841), Pushkin's fellow student at the lycée, joined the Decembrists and as a result was sent in 1826 to serve on Paskevich's staff in the Caucasus.

51. **Mikhail Pushchin:** Mikhail Ivanovich Pushchin (1800–1869), brother of one of Pushkin's closest friends at the lycée, and like his brother a Decembrist, was broken to the ranks in 1826 and sent to serve in the Caucasus. By the time of their meeting in Tiflis, he had been made an officer again and served with the army engineers.

52. **Semichev:** Nikolai Nikolaevich Semichev (1792–1830), also a Decembrist. After six months in prison, he was sent to the Caucasus as a captain in the Nizhegorodsky grenadier regiment. At one point, when Pushkin recklessly threw himself into combat, General Raevsky sent Semichev to drag him away from the front line.

53. **young Osten-Sacken:** A captain of the Nizhegorodsky grenadiers, the younger brother of Dmitry Erofeevich Osten-Sacken (1789–1881), who at that time was chief of staff of the Detached Caucasus Corps under Paskevich. The Osten-Sackens were a distinguished Baltic German family.

54. **Yazidis . . . devil worshippers:** The Yazidis are Kurdish-speaking people settled from ancient times in what is now northern Iraq. Their monotheistic

religion has ties to Zoroastrianism; its somewhat Manichaean vision of good and evil has led other monotheists to persecute them wrongly as "devil worshippers."

55. **Colonel Frideriks . . . General Muravyov . . . Colonel Simonich:** Colonel B. A. Frideriks (1797–1874), mentioned earlier, commanded the Erevan Light Cavalry Regiment. General Nikolai Nikolaevich Muravyov (1794–1866) was Raevsky's immediate superior, and, like Raevsky and Osten-Sacken, sympathized with the Decembrists serving in the Caucasus, which displeased Paskevich, who eventually had them all dismissed from the army. Count Ivan Osipovich Simonich (1792–1851), from Dalmatia, fought on the French side in the Napoleonic Wars, was captured by the Russians in 1812, and later joined the Russian army. In the Caucasus he commanded the Georgian grenadier regiment; in 1836 he was sent as Russian minister to Persia, replacing the murdered Griboedov.

56. **Salvator Rosa:** Italian Baroque painter (1615–1673), considered a "proto-Romantic" because of the dramatic lighting effects of his landscapes and portraits.

57. **Hakki Pasha:** Ismail Hakki Pasha (1798–1876) was a Turkish general and statesman, later briefly the governor of Arzrum.

58. **Colonel Anrep:** Roman Romanovich von Anrep (d. 1830), of a noble Swedish-Russian family, commanded an uhlan regiment in the Caucasus and was a close friend of Paskevich. A few years earlier, he and Pushkin had paid court to the same girl.

59. **Franks:** In Armenia Roman Catholics were referred to as "Franks," a custom that dated back to the time of the Crusades.

60. **the poet Yuzefovich:** Mikhail Vladimirovich Yuzefovich (1802–1889) was a cavalry captain and aide-de-camp to Raevsky. He left memoirs of his meetings with Pushkin during the campaign of 1829.

61. **Arnauts:** Turkish for Albanians.

62. **the battle of Poltava:** See note 11 to *The Moor of Peter the Great*. Pushkin gives the date according to the old (Julian) calendar, which was still used in Russia. By the Gregorian calendar it was July 8.

63. **Theodosius the Second:** Theodosius II (401–450) became emperor of the Eastern (Byzantine) Empire in 408, at the age of seven.

64. **Hajji-Baba . . . calf's ears . . . :** Pushkin is drawing on the three-volume novel *The Adventures of Hajji-Baba of Ispahan*, by the former diplomat James Justinian Morier (1780–1849), published in London in 1824, and in Russian translation in 1830. In the third volume, the Persian ambassador, whom Hajji-Baba serves as secretary, catches a courier who has stolen from him while passing through Arzrum. The ambassador orders the courier's ears cut off, against the local governor's protests, but the servants trick the ambassador, giving him two pieces of goat meat instead.

65. **Tournefort . . . the city:** Joseph Pitton de Tournefort (1656–1708), botanist and traveler, makes this observation in the eighteenth letter of his *Relation d'un voyage en Levant* ("An Account of a Journey to the Levant," 1717).

66. **the time of Godfrey:** Godfrey de Bouillon (1060–1100), directly descended from Charlemagne, lord of Bouillon and later Duke of Lower Lorraine (Lotharingia), took part in the first crusade in 1095, and in 1100 was made "king of Jerusalem." He died there in the same year. Godfrey became the subject of a number of medieval French *chansons de geste*, and Torquato Tasso (1544–1595) made him the hero of his epic poem *Jerusalem Delivered* (1581).

67. **composed by the janissary Amin-Oglu:** A fictitious personage; the verses are by Pushkin himself.

68. **Sukhorukov:** Vasily Dmitrievich Sukhorukov (1795–1841), officer in the Cossack guards regiment and military historian, was close to the Decembrists. After the uprising, the rich materials he had collected on the Don Cossack army were taken from him and never returned, and he was removed from his regiment and sent to serve in the Caucasus. There he gathered materials for a history of the campaign of 1829, but these, too, were confiscated in 1830. On his return to Petersburg, Pushkin tried unsuccessfully to recover them.

69. **Bey-bulat, the terror of the Caucasus:** In 1825 Bey-bulat Taymazov led the Caucasian mountaineers in a revolt against the Russians, but in 1829 he went over to the Russian side.

70. **Mr. Abramovich:** Pushkin gives only the initial A. The Russian editors of the 1975 edition followed here give the name Abramovich this first time, following the suggestion of the ethnographer Evgeny Gustavovich Veydenbaum in his *Travels in the Northern Caucasus* (1888), though others say that the cavalry captain Abramovich was not serving in the Caucasus at that time.

71. **Konovnitsyn:** Pyotr Petrovich Konovnitsyn (1802–1830) was the son of a distinguished general and count who fought in the Napoleonic Wars and ended as minister of war under Alexander I. The young Konovnitsyn joined the Decembrists, was broken to the ranks in 1826 and sent first to Semipalatinsk and then to the Caucasus. In 1828 he was promoted to ensign.

72. **Dorokhov:** Rufin Ivanovich Dorokhov (1801–1852) was broken to the ranks in 1820 for unruly behavior and dueling. From 1828 to 1833 he served in the Nizhegorodsky dragoons; in 1829 he was promoted to ensign. He was one of three models for Tolstoy's Fyodor Ivanovich Dolokhov in *War and Peace*. Pushkin addressed an epigram to him:

> You're lucky with charming little fools,
> In the service, at cards, and at feasts.
> You're St. Priest in caricatures,
> You're Neledinsky in verse;

You've been shot up in duels,
You've been cut up in war—
You may be a real, true hero,
But you're a thorough-going rake.

FRAGMENTS AND SKETCHES

The Guests Were Arriving at the Dacha (1828–1830)

1. **"One of our poets . . . beauty":** The poet Nikolai Ivanovich Gnedich (1784–1833) was most famous for his translation of the *Iliad*, which Pushkin greatly admired. The line is a slightly altered quotation from his idyll "The Fishermen" (1822).

2. **Hussein Pasha:** Hussein Dey (1765–1838), the last Ottoman ruler of Algeria.

3. **a last game of *écarté*:** A French card game for two players, in which each player can set aside (*écarter*) some of the cards dealt to him and draw others before starting to play.

4. **the English Embankment:** Then one of the most fashionable streets in Petersburg, along the left bank of the Neva. It was named for the British embassy and church located there. The emperor would have been Alexander I.

5. *Les Liaisons dangereuses* **. . . Jomini:** *Les Liaisons dangereuses* (1782), an epistolary novel by Pierre Choderlos de Laclos (1741–1803), portrays the decadence of the French aristocracy before the revolution. Antoine-Henri Jomini (1779–1869), a Swiss businessman and officer, joined the French army in 1805, but later went over to the Russian side and became a general and advisor to the emperors Alexander I and Nicholas I. His writings on military theory were widely used in European and American military academies.

6. **Rurik and Monomakh:** For Rurik, see note 7 to *The History of the Village of Goryukhino*. Vladimir II Monomakh (1053–1125) was grand prince of Kievan Rus from 1113 to 1125.

7. **Peter and Elizabeth:** Peter the Great (1672–1725) became tsar of Russia in 1682 and the first Russian emperor in 1721. His daughter, the empress Elizabeth (1709–1762), came to power in 1741.

8. **the duc de Montmorency . . . Clermont-Tonnerre:** Two of the most noble French families, the first going back to the tenth century, the second to the eleventh century. The lords of Montmorency bore the title of "first baron of Christendom" until 1327. The first duke was Anne de Montmorency (1493–1567), who became marshal and constable of France. The house of Clermont-Tonnerre furnished many important military leaders and statesmen.

9. **Karamzin . . . history:** See note 4 to *Roslavlev*.

A Novel in Letters (1829)

1. **Lamartine:** Alphonse de Lamartine (1790–1869), poet, writer, and statesman, was a major figure of French Romanticism. One of his finest poems is the elegy "Solitude," published in a collection in 1823.

2. **Krestovsky Island:** One of the islands in the mouth of the River Neva that make up St. Petersburg. The nobility used to have dachas there.

3. **Clarissa Harlowe:** The heroine of the epistolary novel *Clarissa, or the History of a Young Lady* (1748), by Samuel Richardson (see note 6 to "The Young Lady Peasant"). Pushkin found Richardson's work tedious, but it was very popular among young ladies.

4. **Lovelace . . . Adolphe:** Robert Lovelace is the villain of Richardson's *Clarissa*, who abducts and eventually rapes the heroine. The eponymous hero of the novel *Adolphe* (1816), by the Swiss-born writer and liberal activist Benjamin Constant (1767–1830), was a shy and introspective young man.

5. **the English Embankment:** See note 4 to "The Guests Were Arriving at the Dacha."

6. **Bellecourt . . . Charlotte:** Pushkin takes these as typical names in eighteenth-century French novels.

7. **Vyazemsky and Pushkin:** For Vyazemsky, see note 1 to "The Stationmaster." There are "provincial young ladies" in several of the *Tales of the Late Ivan Petrovich Belkin;* perhaps the most perfect example in Pushkin's work is Tatyana Larina, the heroine of his novel in verse, *Evgeny Onegin* (1825–1832).

8. **the *Herald of Europe*:** A biweekly journal published in Petersburg from 1802 to 1830. It began in a liberal spirit but turned more and more conservative, consistently attacking Pushkin's work, especially in the jeering personal critiques by Nikolai Ivanovich Nadezhdin (1804–1856) of the long poems *Poltava* and *Count Nulin*.

9. **Fornarina . . . *tableaux vivants*:** The *Portrait of a Young Woman* (1518–1520), by Raphael (1483–1520), known as *La Fornarina* ("The Baker Woman"), is said to be the portrait of the artist's Roman mistress, Margherita Luti, who appears in several of his paintings. The parlor game of *tableaux vivants* ("living pictures"), in which live people would simulate famous paintings, was popular in the nineteenth century.

10. **Minin . . . Pozharsky:** In 1818 a bronze sculpture was set up on Moscow's Red Square to commemorate Prince Dmitry Pozharsky and the merchant Kozma Minin (see note 8 to *Roslavlev*).

11. **collegiate assessor:** See note 43 to *Journey to Arzrum*.

12. **La Bruyère:** Jean de La Bruyère (1645–1696), moralist and philosopher, is known essentially for one book, *Les Caractères* (1688), a collection of portraits forming a chronicle of the French seventeenth century and its mores, written

with a sylistic sharpness and perfection that has served as a model ever since its publication, not least for Pushkin himself.

13. **Fonvizin . . . Prostakovs and Skotinins:** For Fonvizin, see note 1 to *The Tales of the Late Ivan Petrovich Belkin.* The names Prostakov and Skotinin, while perfectly normal in Russian, are suggestive of simple-mindedness and brutishness respectively.

14. **"And that's . . . patriots":** From act 2, scene 5 of Griboedov's *Woe from Wit* (see note 7 to "The Blizzard").

15. The first line refers to Pierre Terrail, the Chevalier Bayard (1475–1524), called by one of his fellow soldiers *le bon chevalier sans peur et sans reproche,* an embodiment of French chivalric ideals. The second line is from the device of Enguerrand III de Coucy (1182–1242) and his descendants. The full version reads *Je ne suis roy, ne prince, ne comte aussi, / Je suis le sire de Coucy.*

16. **Faublas . . . women:** *The Loves of the Chevalier de Faublas* (1787) was the first of a trilogy of novels about Faublas by Jean-Batiste Louvet de Couvrai (1760–1797), journalist, novelist, playwright, and revolutionary activist.

17. **hoarse-voiced guardsman of 1807:** According to Vyazemsky (see note 1 to "The Stationmaster"), the boastfulness and haughtiness of young Russian officers were combined with an affected huskiness of voice, a practice that began in 1807, the year of Napoleon's war with East Prussia, which ended with the treaty of Tilsit. Another explanation attributes the huskiness to the wearing of extremely tight-waisted uniforms.

18. **Adam Smith:** Scottish philosopher and economist (1723–1790). His book *The Wealth of Nations* (1776), setting forth the free market theory, was and remains a fundamental work in modern political economics.

Notes of a Young Man (1829–1830)

1. **the prodigal son:** See note 4 to "The Stationmaster."

My Fate Is Decided. I Am Getting Married . . . (1830)

1. **"My native land, adieu":** The words (in English) are an inexact quotation of an inserted lyric from canto 1, stanza 13, of *Childe Harold's Pilgrimage* (1812–1818), a long poem by Lord Byron: "Adieu, adieu! my native shore / Fades o'er the waters blue [. . .] / My Native Land—Good Night!"

2. **Mlle Sontag:** The soprano Henriette Sontag (1806–1854), born in Koblenz, Germany, made her début in 1821 and went on to become internationally famous.

A Romance at the Caucasian Waters (1831)

1. **Boston:** Already referred to in previous stories, Boston is a card game similar to whist, which became very popular in Europe during the later eighteenth century. It was probably named after the capital of the Massachusetts Bay Colony, birthplace of the American Revolution. At any rate, the game was not played by the British.

2. **Bukharans:** The Bukharans were inhabitants of the Muslim khanate of Bukhara, in the region of Uzbekistan, at that time a Russian protectorate.

3. **from Basmannaya to the Arbat:** At that time, Basmannaya Street and the Arbat were on opposite sides of Moscow.

A Russian Pelham (1834–1835)

1. **Pelham:** Edward Bulwer-Lytton (1803–1873), English writer and parliamentarian, published his best-selling novel *Pelham: or the Adventures of a Gentleman* in 1828.

2. **the late Count Sheremetev:** Count Nikolai Petrovich Sheremetev (1751–1809) was a member of an old and extremely wealthy noble family who were important patrons of the theater.

3. **the philistines:** A nickname given by German university students to the local townspeople.

We Were Spending the Evening at the Dacha . . . (1835)

1. **Mme de Staël:** See note 5 to *Roslavlev*.

2. **a Gambs armchair:** The Prussian furniture maker Heinrich Daniel Gambs (1769–1831) moved to Petersburg in 1795 and set up shop there.

3. **the Maid of Orleans . . . Mme Roland . . . :** *The Maid of Orleans*, referring to Joan of Arc, is the title of a satirical poem by Voltaire (see note 8 to *The Moor of Peter the Great*) published in 1762, and of a tragedy by Friedrich Schiller (1759–1805) first produced in 1801. Françoise d'Aubigné, Marquise de Maintenon (1635–1719), was a favorite and later the second wife of Louis XIV. Marie-Jeanne Phlippon Roland (1754–1793) and her husband were supporters of the French Revolution on the moderate Girondist side; purged by Robespierre during the Reign of Terror, she was imprisoned and died on the guillotine.

4. *Antony . . . La Physiologie du mariage:* The drama *Antony*, by Alexander Dumas (1802–1870), described by its author as "a scene of love, jealousy, and anger," was a great success when first produced in Paris in 1831. *La Physiologie du mariage*, by Honoré de Balzac (1799–1850), a rather daring essay for its time, was published in 1829.

5. **Aurelius Victor ... Cornelius Nepos ... Suetonius:** Sextus Aurelius Victor (ca. 320–ca. 390), was the author of the short historical work *De Caesaribus* ("On the Caesars"); several other works have been attributed to him, including *De Viris Illustribus* ("On Illustrious Men"). Most of the works of the Roman biographer Cornelius Nepos (ca. 110 BC–ca. 25 BC) have been lost, but he is referred to and quoted by a number of other Roman historians. Gaius Suetonius Tranquillus (ca. 69–ca. 122), Roman historian, was the author of *De Vita Caesarum*, best known in English as *The Twelve Caesars*.

6. **Tacitus ... Sallust:** Publius Cornelius Tacitus (ca. 56–ca. 117), Roman senator and historian, was the author of the *Annals* and the *Histories*, rather detailed accounts of the period of the emperors Tiberius, Claudius, and Nero. Gaius Sallustius Crispus (86–ca. 35 BC), the earliest Roman historian known by name, was of plebeian origin and a supporter of Julius Caesar during the civil war, for which he was made governor of the province of Africa Nova.

7. **the marquise George Sand:** Amantine-Lucile-Aurore Dupin (1804–1876), known by her literary pseudonym George Sand, was *baronne*, not *marquise*, Dudevant, but she was the author of *La Marquise* (1832), which Pushkin may have had in mind. Commenting on her "liberated" spirit, Turgenev said of her: "What a brave man she was, and what a good woman."

8. **does not desire the death of a sinner:** The words are familiar to Russians from several Orthodox prayers, particularly the prayer before confession.

A Story from Roman Life (1833–35)

1. **Titus Petronius:** Authorship of the Roman satirical novel *The Satyricon* is generally attributed to Gaius Petronius Arbiter (27–66), whose name may originally have been Titus Petronius Niger, as given in a fifteenth-century manuscript of the novel. The story of his death is recounted in book 16 of the *Annals* of Tacitus.

2. **Caesar ... Cumae ... Eumenides:** The Caesar in this case is Nero, under whom Petronius served as consul and *arbiter elegantiarum* ("judge of elegance"). Cumae was a town on the coast of the Campania north of Naples founded by Greek settlers in the eighth century BC, known especially for being the home of the Cumaean sibyl. In Greek mythology Eumenides was the name for the Furies (Erinyes) once they were placated; it means "kindly ones."

3. **Gray they've grown ... and lie forgot!:** Pushkin's loose translation of ode 44 (the numbering varies depending on the edition), by the Greek lyric poet Anacreon (ca. 582–ca. 485 BC).

4. **Proud steeds ... in their eyes:** Pushkin's version of Anacreon's ode 55 (again the numbering varies).

5. **Which of the gods ... a certain death:** Pushkin's loose version of ode 7 from

484 Note to Page 449

book 2 of the *Odes* of the Roman poet Horace (Quintus Horatius Flaccus, 65–8 BC). Horace was a great admirer of Anacreon. The term *quiritis*, referring to Roman citizens in their peacetime functions, was used by Caesar as a reproach to his soldiers; incidentally, it does not appear in Horace's ode.

6. **Sweet . . . country:** Line 13 from book 3, ode 2, by Horace.